The Fisherman Series

JEWEL E. ANN

THE FISHERMAN SERIES

BOOKS ONE & TWO

JEWEL E. ANN

FOREWORD

This special edition contains exclusive bonus content. The Fisherman Series was originally written and published from the heroine's point of view. It is her journey into womanhood, her journey to think for herself, her journey to evolve emotionally and spiritually. This is a story of love and loss, and freedom and redemption through the eyes of a passionate and vulnerable young woman.

I don't believe there is a one-size-fits-all when crafting a story. Life is experienced through many lenses, and it's often what we don't see that can have the greatest influence in our lives. As you will read, The Naked Fisherman has many "lessons" to teach Reese Capshaw. The best way to experience The Naked Fisherman is through the lens of the young woman who will forever be changed by her time with him.

Since its original publication, many readers have expressed great interest in the hero's point of view during pivotal moments in the story. I believe by the end of this story, you will know The Naked Fisherman. His actions are revealing and his words are honest—sometimes brutally honest.

However, I'm touched that so many readers have loved this story and read it more than once. For those of you who can't get enough and want to live in this world and with these characters a little longer, the bonus content at the end of each story is for you. Enjoy!

PLAYLIST

James TW — "Butterflies"
Holly Humberstone — "Livewire"
Holly Humberstone — "Please Don't Leave Just Yet"
Natalie Taylor — "Wrecked"
Drew Holcomb & The Neighbors — "Live Forever"
Judah & The Lion — "Only To Be With You"
(Unplugged)
Matt Maeson — "Put It on Me"
Matt Maeson — "Tribulation"
Matt Maeson — "Hallucinogenics"
John Legend — "Wild"
Josie Dunne — "Good Boys"
James Bay — "Wild Love"
ZAYN — "It's You"
HRVY — "Me Because of You"
The Driver Era — "Natural"

For Jenn, if only Fisher were Scottish ... this would be perfection.

THE NAKED FISHERMAN

CHAPTER ONE

THE DAY I met the naked fisherman, I was a wholesome eighteen-year-old girl, fresh out of high school with lots of opinions and zero big ideas. The perfect target. I had only heard about men like him through sermons and Bible studies on temptation.

However, as I spent the morning packing, I was unaware of his existence. I should have embraced the final few hours of my innocence instead of fretting over the thought of seeing my mom for the first time in over five years. It made me want to throw up my scrambled eggs and at least one piece of buttered toast. Six months earlier, she'd been released from a women's correctional facility in Nebraska. Apparently, she had a few too many marijuana plants growing in the storage room of her hair salon. My dad said he knew nothing about it, and the judge believed him.

My grandma snatched everything I tossed into my suitcase and refolded it. "You're an adult now, Therese. You don't have to live with her ... or us. You don't have to live with anyone. Are you sure you don't want to get an apartment with some friends? There are mission trips that can take you all around the world."

Three years earlier, my dad's heart had stopped working. A congenital defect he didn't know he had. No high blood pressure. No high cholesterol. Not a single sign before he just ... keeled over while sitting at his drawing board. We'd had pasta that night. I still couldn't look at pasta without tearing up.

He was a brilliant architect. My grandparents (his parents) got custody of me since my mom was in prison and her parents lived in a dinky but expensive apartment in Boston. They were Catholic liberals with a special detest for my father's parents—conservatives who took advantage of my mom's incarceration and my dad's death by enrolling me in a private Christian academy in Houston, Texas.

"She's my mom. I haven't seen her in five years. And it's only temporary until I decide what I want to do with my life." I gave my grandma a reassuring smile, but her frown told me she wasn't feeling the least bit reassured.

"You didn't invite her to your graduation. Why are you so curious now?"

Coughing before laughing, I shook my head. "Pa talked me out of inviting her, just like Dad would have done. And she's my *mom*, not a zoo animal I'm 'curious' about. If she's not what I remember, if she feels like a complete stranger and I feel no connection to her, then I'll come home."

"Therese, I worry that by not going to college right

away, you'll never go. And your father would have wanted you to get a degree."

I tossed a pair of sandals and flip-flops on top of the clothes she'd just refolded. "Statistically, people who take a gap year do better when they do go to college." A true statistic I played on repeat.

Lack of direction wasn't fun. At my graduation party, everyone asked where I was going to school ... what I planned on doing. I cringed and threw out my brilliant Gap Year Plan. It felt like code for "smart kid who happened to be an underachiever with little to no direction." Nobody actually said that to me, but I saw it on their faces. Then they listed all of the things I could do, as if I simply needed a good idea.

Grandma pressed her hands to my cheeks for a second before stroking my hair down my shoulders. My straight, dark brown hair and blue eyes were all my mom, but my grandma always said I looked like my dad. He had blond hair and hazel eyes. The only things I got from him were my full lips and obsession with crossword puzzles.

"I also worry your mom won't be the best influence." Grandma frowned as she continued to stroke my hair. There it was—her real fear.

"If she's on drugs or if she has taken up smoking three packs a day, I'll come home. Besides, I've already found a church to attend, and I'm sure I'll find good Christian friends who will keep me from falling under my mom's spell." I winked at Grandma. I was only half serious. There wasn't a rule book for reuniting with your mother after years of separation due to incarceration. Would she expect me to call her "Mom?" Would it feel natural to call her that? It felt natural at thirteen, the day I last saw her and cried fat tears while they removed her from the courtroom in handcuffs. Her tears matched mine as she mouthed, "I love you."

Dad hugged me and promised I'd see her soon.

Soon ...

That didn't happen.

"You can come back. Anytime. You know this, right?"

I nodded while zipping my suitcase. "Yep. That's why I've told you a million times that I'll come home if it doesn't work out. Besides, half of my stuff is still here. Of course I'm coming back. I just want to see what she's like now and see if I like Colorado."

Grandma's eyes glossed over with emotion. "Therese, I'm going to miss you so much. It's like I'm losing your dad all over again."

"God will watch over me."

"I know, honey." She kissed my forehead. "Let's have Pa load up your suitcase and drive you to the airport so you don't feel rushed getting to the gate. I still can't believe we're letting you fly by yourself."

I laughed a little. "I'm an adult now. I've got this." I wasn't sure eighteen felt like adulthood, but I put on a brave face because my friends were going on summer trips and preparing to head off to college. They were leaving the nest. I was moving to a different nest. The least I could do was fly by myself and pretend that I was a real adult for a few hours.

CHAPTER TWO

I WOULD HAVE BEEN LYING HAD I said I wasn't scared to death. My hands and my voice shook, fumbling my bags and ID while going through airport security. Everything freaked me out. Strange men looking at me. Women corralling their young kids while eyeing me like they wondered if they should report me to airport security—a young woman possibly being smuggled to some faraway place (like Colorado) to be sold as a sex slave. For five hours, I feigned confidence. When I exited the secured area of the Denver airport, it took me only a few seconds to spot my mom: brown almost black short hair, not quite touching her chin with bangs cut a little too short (just my opinion), and skinny as a rail. She sent me pictures after we made contact shortly after my eighteenth birthday, but she looked even thinner in person.

The mom I remembered from the courtroom had curves. She wasn't overweight, but she looked healthy and well nourished. Post-prison Mom looked like she ate to live and not one bite more. Her bones protruded from her cheeks, shoulders, and hips. Sunken blue eyes the color of a stormy sky at sunset eyed me with anticipation. And not as much as a single speck of makeup could be found on her face. The owner of a salon, she used to have long hair, nearly to her butt, always curled in princess-like ringlets.

Where did the hairdresser go? Makeup? Nail polish? Perfectly styled hair? I wondered if she remembered that person or if that person died over the five years I hadn't seen her. Over the five years she didn't get to see me.

"Reese!" She hooked her crossbody handbag over her shoulder and ran toward me.

Reese ... I hadn't been called that in years. I was Therese to my dad and my grandparents. I was Therese at the Christian academy and to my new Christian friends.

My body stiffened, panicked by the stranger ready to get up close and personal with me. Would she smell the same? Would her embrace feel the same?

"Hi," I croaked as she knocked the wind out of me and nearly tackled me to the ground.

"Oh my baby ..." She cried. Literally cried.

I had thought I would cry too, but there were no tears in sight. Nerves and sheer awkwardness gobbled them up before my eyes had a prayer of shedding even a single one.

Everything felt different.

Her embrace was not as comforting, probably too many bones and not enough fat.

She smelled woodsy, not the floral scent of her perfume I remembered.

I thanked God for reuniting us. My mind should have stopped there. That was all that mattered, but I couldn't stop thinking about all the ways she was a little *less* than I remembered. Did my thirteen-year-old self have her on a pedestal? Or was the eighteen-year-old version of me being unfairly judgmental?

Thou shalt not judge ...

That was always a hard one to obey.

"You've grown into the most beautiful young lady." She grabbed my shoulders and held me at arm's length, getting a good look at me.

"Thanks." I smiled.

"Well, let's get your luggage and head home. We have so much catching up to do before I leave town." She looped her arm around mine and led me toward the baggage claim.

"What? You're leaving?"

"It's just for a month. Six weeks tops. My new employer is sending me to L.A. to work at his salon there and get refreshed on my skills. I'll be working with people who do hair and makeup for celebrities. How awesome is that?"

"Um ... really awesome, I guess. So, I'll be living alone, in your house?"

"Yes and no." We stopped and waited for my luggage at the carousel. "And it's my landlord's house. Not mine. I just rent the basement. It has its own entrance at the back. He's the nicest guy. And adorable. We've become good friends. I've told him all about you. And he's also willing to give you a temporary job this summer while you figure out what you want to do."

"What kind of job?" I watched for my suitcase, sparing a quick side-glance for my mom.

"He owns a construction company. I'm not sure what you'd be doing, but I'm sure you couldn't ask for a better boss."

"Construction? Building houses? I'm not that great with a hammer." With a nervous laugh, I considered the bigger picture. My hammer abilities were the least of my concerns. My mom was leaving me with an *adorable* man. Adorable as in old and quirky?

She laughed. "I'm sure there's office stuff you can do."

I nodded several times, trying hard to formulate an image of adorable in my head. Kittens were adorable. "Okay. Yes, I can do office work. Thanks for asking him." *Mr. Adorable.*

She glanced over at me and smiled. "Of course. I want to do everything I can for you. Lots of lost time to make up for."

CHAPTER THREE

It took us forty-five minutes to get to her place. I'd never been to Colorado. Never seen the Rockies. I couldn't stop gawking at them in the distance. How had we lived in Nebraska for nearly fifteen years and never headed west? We'd made a million trips straight south to Texas and a few trips out east to visit my mom's parents. But never west.

"Home sweet home. I know it's not as nice as your grandparents' home in Houston, but I want you to feel like it's yours. We can decorate your room. Paint. Whatever you want. Fisher said as long as we don't tear down walls, the sky's the limit."

"Fisher?" I asked while climbing out of her Subaru Outback.

"Fisher Mann. My landlord."

"Interesting name." I chuckled while my mom retrieved my suitcase from the back of her car.

"It is." She grinned, nodding toward a cobblestone

path that wound around to the side of the sprawling ranch home with an unobstructed view of the mountains.

"There's a door to the house through the screened-in porch, but I usually go in through here because there's a locker area to put coats, shoes, purses, etcetera."

She unlocked the door, and I followed her into the basement. It was nice—way nicer than I expected, not basement feeling at all. A wall of west-facing windows gave it depth, not that it needed any illusion. The vast family room held a mammoth sectional, big screen TV, and a pool table.

"You've bought a lot of stuff."

"Pfft ..." She shook her head. "No. The family room came furnished. I purchased beds for the two bedrooms and bedding. Towels. Kitchen stuff. And by me, I mean my parents loaned me the money."

"I see." My other grandparents. I saw them three times while my mom was incarcerated. My father wasn't exactly accommodating.

"Let's see if Fisher is upstairs. I want you to meet him; then we can grab food and spend the rest of the evening catching up."

Catching up ... I found that odd. The catching up would be very one-sided. There was no way she had that much to catch me up on in regard to her life.

I followed her up the split staircase. She knocked on the door and waited a full two seconds before unlocking it and opening it. It was odd that there weren't locks on both sides like connected hotel rooms. As I followed her into a spacious kitchen with high ceilings, I glanced back and noticed there was a lock on his side. He just hadn't locked it.

"Fisher?" she called and waited a few seconds. "I'll check the garage. Sometimes he's working on a project or spit-shining his motorcycle."

I nodded, feeling nerves tighten in my stomach. Why? I wasn't sure, but two seconds later I quickly figured it out.

"Hey."

I turned toward the deep, male voice.

"Oh my gosh!" I made another quick turn, completing a full three-sixty in total. "I'm sorry."

"Why? Did you break in? Or are you Rory's daughter?"

I cleared my throat. "That ... um ... yeah ... Rory's daughter."

"Ah, Reese Capshaw. It's nice to finally meet you. Rory talks about you nonstop."

I nodded a half dozen times, refusing to turn back toward him and his nearly naked body. My initial glance caught lots of chest and water dripping down said chest and a loosely tied navy-blue towel hanging low on his waist. Oh ... yeah ... his hair was messy, wet, and light brown or maybe dark blond.

"Where's your mom?" He brushed past me. Like ... physically brushed past me. His wet arm bumped mine. And he didn't say "excuse me." Instead, he turned a few degrees just before reaching for the garage door handle. He eyed me from head to toe, a smirk reshaping his mouth into something I didn't trust. "You look just like your mom. Lucky girl."

In that moment, I knew Fisher Mann was bad news.

"There you are!" Mom started to open the door at the same moment Fisher turned the handle and pulled inward.

Was it the right time to tell my mom she couldn't go to Los Angeles because her landlord looked at me like his next meal? But more than that ... I couldn't believe she had no response to his nearly naked body on full display in front of her daughter.

"Sorry. I was in the shower," Fisher said while he gave his towel a slight adjustment *in the wrong direction!* He lowered it an inch.

Heat gathered in my cheeks. I had only seen men like him on television or with my friends when no one's parents were home. It felt forbidden then, and it didn't feel any less forbidden with my mom standing between us.

"So you met Reese. Isn't she beautiful? Even more stunning than her pictures. Don't you think?"

Dear God, please make this stop. Make HIM stop.

Stop being so ... everything.

My mom, too busy giving me her most adoring expression, looked on the verge of crying again, while Sin —with his disheveled hair, overexposed flesh, and hard muscles—wet his lips and nodded. "She's perfect, Rory. Almost angelic."

What was that supposed to mean? I contemplated his wording. Did he know I went to a Christian academy? Was he making a jab at my religion? My faith? My youth? My level of experience? Maybe it wasn't a biblical reference to an actual angel. What if he thought I was truly beautiful?

I quickly shook my head to derail that train of thought. Of course, I didn't want Fisher to find me attractive to any degree. He was older than me by more than a few years. He didn't look like a man of faith. Yes, I realized that was another judgment, but my mind did its own thing. Was he with my mom ... as in *with* her in the biblical sense?

"I told Reese you might have a job for her." She glanced back at the naked fisherman.

Ugh! Why did that have to go through my head? I would forever imagine him naked with a fishing pole in his hand ... maybe naked except for a pair of those fly-fishing boots reaching his mid-thigh region.

Stop!

"Sure. I can keep her busy with lots of odds and ends. Some days you could work in the office with my secretary, Hailey. Other days you might come with me to job sites. Drop off lunches. Grab supplies."

There was a long silence.

"Reese?" my mom said.

"Huh?" I hummed, slightly incoherently.

Fisher bent to the side like he was lowering his body to fit into the view of a camera lens. But there was no camera, just my gaze affixed to his abs and the teasing of dark hair peeking out from the top of his towel. The coveted happy trail. No not coveted. At least, not by me. Nope.

"Hello?" Fisher said, and that was when I realized

he'd caught me gawking at him, just inches from his ... uh ... lower pelvic area.

I needed the fire department to extinguish the embarrassment from my face. "S-sorry ..." I jerked my gaze away from him and folded my arms over my chest, staring down at my feet as I rocked back and forth on the balls of them several times. "A job. Yes. That would be great. Thanks."

"Everything okay?" my mom asked.

"Yeah. It's just been a long day of traveling. That's all." I shifted my focus to things around the kitchen. He kept it rather clean, unsure of what I expected from a guy who worked in construction. And he liked bananas and apples. He must have had two dozen bananas and an equal number of apples in a glass bowl by his toaster. Apples ... the fruit of temptation. How appropriate.

"We'll let you get dressed before your towel falls off, and you show Reese more than she wants to see. I haven't had the sex talk with her yet."

Let. Me. Die!

She really said that. To *him!* Prison had done things to my mom. I couldn't remember her being so forward, so blunt, so embarrassing.

"Oh my gosh ..." I covered my face with my hands. "Thanks for embarrassing me. I'm an adult now, ya know?"

I was an adult covering her flushed face. I was an adult who hadn't had sex because I wasn't married. I was an adult who fit in with my grandparents, my church family, and my friends from the Christian academy.

Apparently, I wasn't an adult in my mom's eyes, and something told me I wasn't an adult in Fisher's eyes. Or maybe I was. *That* was the most terrifying thought at that moment.

CHAPTER FOUR

"I'm sorry. I didn't mean to embarrass you." My mom laughed as we headed back downstairs. "I've been stressing out over how to treat you." She opened the fridge and plucked two sodas from the bottom shelf, handing one to me.

Orange soda. She used to give me that as a special treat. I wondered if she had those graham crackers shaped like bears as well since that used to be my favorite snack—when I was five years younger.

"I mean ... the last time I saw you, you weren't even old enough to drive a car. You hadn't gotten your period yet. And now you're a grown woman. I know it in my head, but my heart still remembers the little girl. I guess I want to get back time, but I can't."

"Thanks." I took the soda and sat on the U-shaped leather sectional. "I know. It's weird for me too. I guess we'll just have to pray about it, and God will help us through this."

Pausing the bottle at her lips, she shook her head.

"Boy ... they did a fine job of indoctrinating you. Didn't they?"

"What do you mean?"

"I mean the 'we'll just have to pray about it.' That's not what the average eighteen-year-old girl says. I've been a little isolated for a few years, but I know that much hasn't changed. You talk like a girl who's been reading the Bible more than romance novels. A girl who spends more time praying than watching Netflix."

"I have a love for Christ. Is that so wrong? We went to church before you went to prison."

She chuckled and took a sip of her orange soda. "We were Catholic."

"So? What's that matter?"

Again, she laughed. "Oh, it matters. But I don't want to talk religion with you. Your faith is between you and God. I want to know all the big moments you've experienced over the past five years. Your first boyfriend. Your first kiss. Your first heartbreak. I want you to tell me all about your friends. Did you keep in touch with your old friends? Or did you make new ones at your Christian school? Did your dad ever find another woman? Or did he die a lonely man?"

She had a lot of questions. I had only anticipated one or two of them. Maybe the boyfriend question and the one about my old friends from public school. Everything else left me a little speechless, especially the questions about Dad finding someone new after divorcing her.

"I've had a boyfriend. Two, actually."

"And ..." Her grin grew into something weird. A grin

19

like my friends used to give me after I'd gone out on a date.

It was hard to separate Rory from Mom. In fact, I hadn't used either name yet to her face because I wasn't sure what I should call her.

"It didn't last long either time."

"That's it?" She gave me a raised eyebrow. "That's the best you can do? What about your first kiss?"

I shrugged. "It was okay."

"You seem hesitant. Is it because I'm your mom? We used to talk about stuff all the time. You'd come home from school and tell me about your day." She sighed with a contented smile, like her five years in prison never happened. Like we should've been able to pick up where we left off.

I remembered watching a show about this plane that disappeared and then returned years later. Families assumed the plane went down, and there were no survivors. So when the plane returned home, things were different. Kids were older. Spouses remarried. But the people on the plane couldn't understand that because, for them, nothing had changed. My mom's time in prison was like her being on that plane.

"I wanted to visit you in prison." I changed the subject to what I had imagined we'd talk about.

Why Dad convinced me it was in my best interest to *not* visit her.

Why I didn't push harder to see her after he died.

How I felt the three times I did get to see her parents.

What it felt like being in prison.

How it changed her.

Literally anything but my dating life and details of my first kiss.

"I know." She frowned and dropped her chin. "I mean ... I didn't *know*, but I believed it in my heart. I knew someone had probably filled your head with reasons it was best to not visit me. And honestly, there were times that I was glad you didn't see me in that place. But..." she glanced up and forced a smile "...that was all then. This is now. If you don't want to relive any of that, if you don't want to share your 'firsts' with me, then we don't have to do that. We can start fresh. Well ..." Her eyes rolled dramatically, like I had done to my dad a million times. "We can start fresh when I get back from L.A. I leave in two days."

Two days.

I had two days before my mom, who was in many ways a stranger to me, left me with the naked fisherman.

———

THAT SOUND ... that echoing siren. I didn't have to think twice. I knew it was a tornado siren. Just my luck. My first night in Denver, first night with my mom in over five years, and the sirens went off.

"Reese, sweetie, come into the back room with us." Rory poked her head into my room and shined a flashlight on me.

I sat up in bed and rubbed my eyes. Taking two steps, I froze. "Oh!" My hands covered my boobs. They weren't out and about or anything crazy like that. I had on a thin white tank top, no bra. "Jeez, you ..."

The naked fisherman (okay, he had shorts on) eyed me and wore a smirk that wasn't all that comforting. "Yes, me. The basement is the safest place. Utility room. Let's go." He held up an actual flashlight, one of those long metal ones.

I guarded my eyes with one hand and snatched the blanket from the bed with my other hand.

"I can't remember the last time I heard the sirens go off, aside from testing it," Fisher said, shutting the door to the unfinished utility area.

"We should pray. I can do it."

My mom and Fisher stared blankly at me while we huddled in a small circle, sitting atop large plastic storage containers like the ones she used to store my old clothes and sentimental things from my childhood. I wondered what happened to those.

"Sure." Mom smiled. "Can't hurt. Do you want us to join hands?"

Eyeing the naked fisherman, I shook my head slowly. "We don't have to."

"What the heck. If we're asking God to spare our lives, holding hands might be the best way to show sincerity." He grabbed my mom's hand and then mine.

It felt small in his strong, calloused hand. Warm. Unfamiliar. And it jumbled my thoughts. It sent my mind into rewind, replaying him smirking at me, wearing nothing but a low hanging towel.

Abs.

Veiny arms.

Rivulets of water dotting his broad chest muscles.

"Is this a silent prayer?" Fisher asked, once again startling me back to reality. He squinted one eye at me like he'd just had both closed for the prayer. "Will you at least say the Amen part out loud?"

"Dear Lord ..." I jumped into prayer instead of acknowledging the awkward pause. "We pray that you watch over us and keep us safe from the storm. Amen."

"Amen," my mom and Fisher echoed.

"So we're good?" Fisher winked at me while releasing my hand. "Protected?"

I narrowed my eyes. "Are you being sarcastic?"

"It's the middle of the night, Reese. He's just tired, and it's probably coming across like he's a little punchy." My mom stuck up for him. That had to have meant they were together—a thing.

How did I feel about my mom being with a younger man? Well, that was a hard question to answer at the time because it had been so long since I'd not only seen my mom, but also since I'd seen my parents together.

"I'm not being punchy, Rory. I'm being a smart-ass. You can only take fifty percent of the things I say seriously, Reese. If you're going to work for me, you'll need to keep that in mind."

I twisted my lips and nodded slowly. "That's a bit vague. Kinda feels like you're setting me up to fail. Or did my grandparents call and ask you to ensure I fail so that I'll go crawling off to college?"

"Is ... everything okay, sweetie?"

Sweetie.

I'd wondered if my mom would call me that again. It used to be the only thing she called me. It made me feel loved and special. At eighteen, sitting next to the naked fisherman in his basement, it felt a little condescending—like everyone needed to remember that I was the youngest, least experienced one in the room. That sealed the deal. I wasn't going to call her "Mom."

"I'm good, Rory."

Her eyebrows slid toward the bridge of her nose as if I'd offended her in some way.

"Reese ... I don't think you are good. And I leave in less than forty-eight hours. I don't want to go if you're not okay here. I can do something else. I can tell my boss it's not good timing."

"Christ, Rory. She'll be fine. Stop coddling her." Fisher yawned and stretched his arms over his head. It made me feel like a twelve-year-old someone snuck into an R-rated movie. Was I old enough to see so much male skin in person? And why couldn't I stop thinking about what it would be like to have sex with him? That was the truth. And I wasn't happy that God could read my mind, but I also wasn't happy that my mind kept going there without my permission.

That Christian academy made it easy to keep my virginity, but nearly impossible to keep my sanity. A focused mind. A *clean* mind.

Dear Lord, please forgive me for my thoughts. Please fill my mind and spirit with your love and all things that bring you glory.

"Do you feel coddled, Reese?" Rory asked.

Confused?

Sinful?

Anxious?

Yes.

"No. I don't feel coddled."

She eyed Fisher with a frown. "See?"

"You've been reunited for all of ten seconds. Reese wouldn't tell you if she did feel coddled."

The sirens stopped.

"Thank god! I have to pee." My mom ran out of the back room.

Fisher stood and held out his hand. "We're alive. Looks like your prayer was answered."

I didn't take his hand or give any more attention to his statement because I felt certain that it fell into the fifty percent category that I needed to ignore.

He waited at the door for me to exit the back room. As I squeezed past him, I shot him a quick glance and inhaled deeply, proving that God didn't answer all my prayers.

"So ..." he rubbed his lips together.

I gulped a mouthful of saliva, unable to tear my gaze away from him.

"When do you want to do it?" His voice deepened.

My heart pounded to the point of feeling it in my throat. What if my mom had heard him? I wasn't having sex with him. And I lost all ability to speak those words because it was the boldest thing a man had ever said to me.

"Start working for me. When do you want to start working for me?" His voice was no longer low. And he slowed his words as if he were talking to a child or someone who didn't speak English well.

Embarrassed wasn't the right word to describe how I felt in that moment. More like ... mortified. And when

Fisher smiled, as if he'd been reading my mind the whole time, I wanted to do physical harm to him. Never had I felt so angry toward another human in my whole life. The most frustrating part? I wasn't sure why I was so angry with him. For not wearing a shirt? For having a sinful body? For winking and smiling? Maybe talking in a slightly deeper voice, which tripped my imagination, sending it tumbling into a dark, forbidden place.

"We can do it ... I mean ..." I pinched the bridge of my nose. "I can start working for you. Well ... your business ... whenever." *Gah!* I might as well of had "parochial-schooled virgin" tattooed on my forehead.

CHAPTER FIVE

THE NEXT DAY, my mom took me to lunch and gave me a quick tour of Denver, promising me we'd go to a Rockies game when she returned from Los Angeles. That night, I sat on her bed next to her suitcase while she packed.

"Is it weird?" I finally got the nerve to broach the subject. "Being with someone so much younger than you?" It wasn't the question I needed to ask her, but I hadn't worked up the nerve to ask her why she was growing pot in the storage room of her salon.

She folded a pair of black pants and added them to the growing pile in the suitcase. "You're my daughter." A hearty laugh followed her answer. "Or are you meaning that the women I was around in the correctional facility were all my age? Because they weren't. Crime comes in all ages, sizes, colors, and social statuses."

"No. I mean Fisher."

She shrugged. "He's my landlord. I think he's twelve years younger than me. So … twenty-eight. I suppose I'm a little envious that he's been so successful this early in his life. But it doesn't bother me to have a landlord younger than me."

My nose wrinkled. "Again, that's not what I'm talking about."

Her eyes narrowed, lips still curved into a grin. We had the same smile. My dad used to say it before she went to prison. Then he stopped comparing me to her at all. But she had tiny dimples like mine, and her smile was a little crooked like mine. Hair. Eyes. I was her mini me.

"Then what are you talking about?"

"Fisher is ... your boyfriend. Right? I mean ... I know he's your landlord too, but you seem to be close to him, more so than a landlord-tenant relationship."

Her lips parted, eyes unblinking for several seconds. "N-no ..." She coughed a laugh. "We're just friends. I can promise you that."

"Really?"

Another laugh. "Really."

"Does he have a girlfriend?" That question came out so quickly I didn't have a single second to stop it.

Adding more clothes to her suitcase, her eyebrows lifted a fraction. "No. Why? Are you into older men? Please say no."

"Of course not. I mean ... I'm not saying there's anything wrong with a year or two older, but not ten years older. I only asked because I noticed he didn't lock his side of the door at the top of the stairs. And I think if he had someone living with him or even visiting, he wouldn't want you going into his space unannounced. I'm not *at all* interested in him." I rolled my eyes.

My mom bit her lips and nodded slowly. "I see. Well,

I knocked, so that was my announcement, and he started it, so I know he's okay with me going upstairs."

"What do you mean he started it?"

"We're friends. *Just* friends. Sometimes we watch TV together down here. Sometimes we hang out and have a beer or two. I don't even know when it happened really, but he'd knock twice to come down here, and I'd have to go up the stairs to unlock the door. So eventually, I stopped locking it on my side, and he stopped locking it on his side. But, by all means, if it makes you more comfortable, you can lock it while I'm gone."

I traced my fingernail along the zipper to her suitcase. "It's no big deal. I might lock it if I remember." Oh ... I was locking it. That was a guarantee. However, there was no need for my mom to know just how little I trusted the naked fisherman.

"Well, I trust him. I wouldn't leave you in the same house with someone unless I trusted them with my life and yours. I'm a good judge of character. Fisher is one of the good ones. I mean..." she smirked "...don't get me wrong, I told him I'd remove his testicles if he for one minute looked at you inappropriately." She laughed.

I wasn't sure what she was laughing about because I felt certain he had already given me that look more than once.

So I wasn't so sure about his "good one" status, but I knew I was about to find out.

"Do you have a boyfriend?"

Keeping her gaze on the shirt in her hands, she smiled. A sad smile. "I don't have a boyfriend. I'm pretty sure I'm done with men."

"But you have so much life left to live. I've prayed for you. I've prayed that you would find happiness again. I've prayed that you would be able to stay clean too."

"Clean?" She glanced up.

"The marijuana."

After a few seconds of intense contemplation, she found her sad smile again. "Thanks for praying for me. I'm not sure God's ready to give me His grace yet, but I do appreciate you thinking I deserve it."

I let her finish packing without asking anymore questions, but I had a lot. There was so much Dad didn't tell me. Maybe he thought he was protecting me, but I didn't feel protected when he died, leaving me with so many unanswered questions.

"Fisher's taking me to the airport in the morning. We're leaving early ... four-thirty. You can come if you want to, but I understand if you want to sleep in." She zipped her suitcase and set it by her bedroom door next to her carry-on bag.

"I'll come."

That seemed to make her smile, a real one that showed both of her dimples. "Great. I've written down things for you. My number and the number for the salon where I'll be. Wi-Fi password. I wrote down Fisher's number too, in case he forgets to give it to you. You have your grandparents' contact information, and I'm leaving you the keys to my car and some money for gas and food."

"No." I shook my head. "You don't have to leave me money. I have money from Dad's ..." My nose wrinkled.

She blinked a few times before recognition ghosted along her face. "His life insurance."

"Yeah," I whispered.

We didn't talk anymore about my dad or the money that I had, the money that would be given to me in increments as I got older, including money assigned to my college fund that I wasn't sure I'd use.

We ate dinner. Watched TV. And turned in early for bed.

Four-thirty came too soon. I pulled my hair back into a ponytail and stretched on yoga pants and an oversized tee.

"Coffee?" Rory asked.

I shook my head and yawned. "I might go back to sleep when I get back here."

"Good idea. Let's go then. Fisher has already carried my suitcase up to his truck, and he's waiting on us."

"K" was all I managed on a second yawn as I followed her out the door and around to the front of the house, where a white truck with Mann Construction, Inc. on the side of it waited for us.

"Morning, ladies." Fisher smiled as I climbed into the back seat and my mom hopped into the front seat.

"Morning. I think Reese might be regretting her decision to ride with us to the airport." My mom laughed.

"I'm good," I said on yet another yawn.

Fisher and my mom chatted on the way to the airport while I grabbed a quick nap. When he pulled to a stop in the drop-off lane, I climbed out and stretched while he retrieved the suitcase from the bed of the truck.

"Take care of yourself, and take care of my baby girl," Mom said while giving Fisher a big hug. "And remember ... she's my *baby* girl. Nothing more."

What did that mean? Fisher winked at me over her shoulder. Really? What the heck was that all about?

I looked at him differently, knowing he wasn't my mom's boyfriend. I shouldn't have, but it made him even sexier. My gaze ate up everything about him—that strong jaw with a permanent five o'clock shadow that showed his maturity, not like the young men in caps and gowns at my graduation ceremony with molestaches.

Blue eyes with thick lashes.

Messy, dirty blond hair peeking out from under his baseball cap.

Defined arms.

Just six-plus solid feet of *strong man*.

Who ... wasn't my mom's boyfriend.

"Bye, sweetie. Call me. FaceTime. Text. Just ... let me know how you're doing or if you need anything." She hugged me.

Fisher glanced around while slipping his hands into the front pockets of his jeans as if he was giving us a little bubble of privacy.

All too quickly, she released me, slung her carry-on over her shoulder, and wheeled her suitcase toward the entrance with nothing but a quick glance back and a big smile.

"Breakfast?" Fisher asked while climbing into the truck.

I hopped into the passenger's seat and fastened my seat belt with shaky hands. It was officially just me and the naked fisherman. "It's five. Who eats breakfast at five?"

"Well, if you're working for me this summer, then *we*

do." Pulling away from the curb, he chuckled and shook his head.

I couldn't stop staring at him. The veins in his arms that continued to his large hands loosely gripping the steering wheel. His scent—all man, but like I imagined the mountains would smell. I was well in over my head with a river of inappropriate thoughts pulling me under.

"Thought you said we were going to breakfast?" I asked Fisher as he pulled his truck into the driveway.

"We are." He hopped out and walked into the garage.

Maybe he forgot something.

His wallet.

His phone.

I jumped as my door opened.

"This isn't a date. But good for you for insisting a guy open the door for you. I'll do it this one time, but my other employees can't see me doing this for you. So pull this lever toward you then push out on the door next time." Fisher smirked, really proud of himself for making me feel stupid.

I assumed we were leaving again. And I knew how to open a door.

Jerk.

"Thanks." I scowled at him while sliding out of his truck. "I thought we were going to breakfast."

"Jeez, we are. You must be starving since you can't stop asking me about it."

I followed him into his kitchen. "I'm not really that hungry. I'm just confused."

"Well, this is bread." He held up a loaf of bread. "And I put it in this little appliance that cooks it nice and brown to create something called toast." He dropped four slices into the toaster. "After that, the sky's the limit, baby. We can put almost anything we want on top of it. Think of it as the perfect vehicle to anywhere. I personally like going to peanut butter town with banana slices, but you can do butter, jelly, avocado, hummus, marshmallow cream ... really, the options are endless." After he set two white plates on the counter, he turned toward me and grinned.

"Why do you treat me like I'm eight instead of eighteen?" I crossed my arms over my chest and flipped out my hip.

"Because you wear this permanent deer-in-the-headlights look. I don't know if you're scared of me or just really confused. But since I don't think I'm a scary person, I have to assume you're confused. I don't know how they do things in Texas, so I'm just walking you through my routine."

"We have toasters in Texas. And for the record, I spent most of my life in Nebraska. It's a neighboring state to Colorado, in case you don't have good geography skills."

My reaction pleased him, or at least that was the look he chose to give me. Complete amusement.

I wasn't trying to amuse or please him.

"I'm not sure yoga pants are the best choice for work apparel. I suggest jeans for sure. Leather work boots for visiting job sites. And whatever shirt you want as long as you don't care if it gets dirty."

"I didn't know I was starting work today. And I don't have work boots. I have tennis shoes."

"Those will work." He grabbed the toast when it popped up and deposited two pieces onto each plate. "We'll get you work boots later. Maybe over our lunch break."

"Sounds ..." I started to say "sexy." Why? I didn't know. But I quickly replaced it with something less provocative. "Fashionable."

"Fashionable?" He glanced over his shoulder while spreading the peanut butter. "This isn't a job where you have to worry about being fashionable. Practical and safe for the win."

"I don't like peanut butter." I eyed his hand spreading it onto my toast too.

"Jesus, woman ... are you even human?" He scraped the peanut butter off the bread and returned it to the jar. "There's the fridge. Have at it. Put whatever you want on your toast."

It would still smell like peanut butter, but I opted to keep my mouth shut and just gut it down. He added his sliced bananas and took a seat on one of the painted metal barstools while I found a stick of butter and smeared lots of it over the residual peanut butter.

"I threw up a bunch of puppy chow ... you know, the corn or rice cereal with peanut butter, melted chocolate, and powdered sugar? And since then, I haven't been able to eat peanut butter."

"Thanks for sharing your peanut butter vomit story while I'm eating peanut butter."

I glanced over my shoulder while returning the butter to the fridge. "Oops. Sorry. Cinnamon?"

He nodded to the spice rack by the stove.

"Sugar?" I grabbed the cinnamon.

"Pantry."

"Where is your pantry?"

"The door to your right." He took a big bite of his toast and nodded to the cabinet door.

"Here?" I opened the door and a light turned on to a hidden pantry and walked inside. "This is cool."

"Second shelf on the right, clear to the back."

I plucked the bag of cane sugar from the shelf and exited the hidden pantry. "Did you build this house?"

"I did."

"Seriously?"

He chuckled. "If you didn't think I could *seriously* build this house, then why did you ask?"

I shrugged. "Just making conversation." I did my best to play it cool. When, in actuality, I was on a high.

Eighteen.

In a new state.

Mom out of town.

Living with a twenty-eight-year-old man who rented a large portion of space in my head. Dominating my thoughts—corrupting my thoughts. He even inter-rupted my prayer time. I quickly discovered that my on-and-off anger toward him was because he made me think and feel things that felt sinful. I wondered if I could have an innocent crush on him? He wasn't married. And if I didn't act on it, could it be a big deal? An actual sin?

"I built it three years ago. My dad is an electrician. My uncle is a plumber and a welder. I started working for a construction company when I was fourteen, over the summer. And I loved it. I knew I wanted to build houses. So my dad and uncle helped me get up and going. And things took off. I have more business than my crew and I can handle most days."

"So you have a crew?" I took a seat at the counter, leaving two chairs between us, and he smirked when he noticed that I was avoiding close proximity to him. "Does that mean you don't build the houses anymore?"

"I don't build as much, but I still do a lot of the trim carpentry in the custom homes we build."

I wasn't sure what that meant, but I didn't want to be the deer-in-the-headlights girl with him, so I nodded like I totally understood.

"You ever been married?" Why? Why did it happen again? Why couldn't I control my curiosity?

"No. You?"

I smiled over my bite of toast while wiping cinnamon and sugar from my lips. "Duh."

"Boyfriend?"

I did it. I started it. And he jumped on board, making me regret saying anything.

"No."

"Girlfriend?" he asked.

I whipped my head to the side, stopping mid-chew. "Um ... no."

He sipped his coffee and shrugged. "Don't look so

offended. You're eighteen. You're supposed to be woke enough to not be offended by the question like there's something wrong with being a lesbian."

"I ... I ..." Swallowing, I shook my head. "I didn't say there's anything wrong with being a lesbian. It's not their fault."

"Fault?" His jaw dropped. "Oh man, I'm embarrassed for you."

"What does that mean?" I set my toast down, no longer feeling hungry. Not that I was anyway because it was too dang early in the morning to eat.

"I'm pretty sure implying being a lesbian is a 'fault' would not score you points with a lot of people."

I felt so backed into a corner. I didn't know what to say. I knew all the things my grandparents had told me and all the things I was taught at the Christian academy. "You know what I mean," I said softly.

After a few seconds of eyeing me until I felt two inches tall, he nodded. "I do. I know what you mean. But not everyone would."

"You're gay," I said as it hit me. Everything so clear. Of course my mom wasn't with him. He was gay. That explained his reaction to what I said.

Without a shred of offense, he shook his head. "No. I'm not gay."

I frowned. "It's wrong." Rubbing my lips together, I shrugged. "I was taught that it's wrong."

He stared at the last bite of his toast for a few moments before popping it into his mouth and lifting a shoulder in a half shrug. "Well, good thing you're out of that place they called a school. Now you can fucking think for yourself."

Cringing at his use of the F-word, I felt insecure and completely exposed. I had no idea Fisher Mann would teach me *so* much during our time alone.

CHAPTER SIX

"What?" I looked down at my jeans, gray tee, and white tennis shoes as Fisher leaned against the back of his truck with one foot propped up behind him on the bumper, eyes taking way too much liberty with inspecting me.

"Approximately seventy percent of my young male crew will try to get into your pants. I'll do my best to keep them from humping your legs and licking your face, but I just want you to remember that they went to public school and lost their virginity before they could legally drive a car."

I hugged my arms to my waist. "And that makes it okay to act like animals?"

"No." He laughed, pushing off the truck. "They're not animals. Just guys being assholes because they haven't had a good woman to keep their dicks in check. Give them a day or two to get used to you before you go filing any sexual harassment complaints because they looked at you the wrong way or whistled a little too loudly. They're good workers. I need them more than I need you."

I should have been offended that he was suggesting I turn a forty-eight-hour blind eye to his crew's bad behavior—but I wasn't because I was too preoccupied with how he didn't need me. "If I'm nothing more than a burden, I don't have to work for you. I'm sure there are plenty of other people who would love to have me."

Fisher's crew? *Ha!*

He looked at me the wrong way, rarely keeping his gaze on mine. My boobs? Those he could have picked out in a lineup.

"Oh..." he forced his wandering gaze back to my face "...I'm sure there are lots of people who would love to have you. But for now, you're mine. So get in the truck."

Did I want to be his? *Pfft ... No.*

If God was keeping count of my lies, that one got a tally mark.

As soon as we pulled out of the driveway, he played music from a playlist on his phone. I hadn't heard the song. It was loud. Hard rock. Littered with swear words. And all about sex.

Conflict muddled my thoughts. I was an adult. I could hear bad words, even if I wasn't comfortable saying them. Technically, I could get married and have sex. So explicit music should not have felt so wrong. After all, it wasn't *my* playlist. But I felt uncomfortable because, like all sin, it tempted me. It tempted my mind. It made me think inappropriate things about my new boss.

"Too loud?" he asked, after the song ended.

I shook my head, a tight shake.

"Why are you so stiff?"

Blowing out a slow breath, I tried to relax my body and my mind. "Just ... just nervous about my first day." I pulled a pad of paper and pencil out of my backpack and opened it.

"Is that a crossword puzzle?" He turned down the music.

I nodded, adding boxes for my next word.

"Are you ... solving one or making your own?"

"I'm constructing my own."

"Why?" He laughed, but it was an odd laugh, a little forced.

"Because I enjoy doing it. My dad was an architect, and he also enjoyed crossword puzzles. Then he started making them just for fun. Eventually, he was submitting them to different places for publication." I wrote out the next clue.

Seven down: Clownish

Then I filled in the four letters: ZANY

"Doing it makes me feel like he's ... not as dead."

Fisher glanced over at me for a beat. "Not as dead. I like that. So ... what do you do with your puzzles?"

"Not a lot at the moment. However, when I was in school, I got extra credit from my English teachers for making them. The school had an online newsletter, and it included my puzzles. I don't know what I'll do with them now. Maybe I'll look for an online publication for them like my dad did. Maybe..." I grinned without taking my gaze off my paper "...they'll make it in *The New York Times*. That would get me some blogger buzz."

"People blog about crossword puzzles?"

Chuckling, I nodded several times. "Um ... there are bloggers for everything. There are plenty of programs to generate puzzles now, but this is authentic. I hope big publications always favor the diehard cruciverbalist."

"The diehard what?" He held his hand to his ear.

"Cruciverbalist. A person who is skilled at constructing or solving crossword puzzles."

"Damn. You're a nerd, Reese."

"No. I just do slightly unusual things to keep the memories of my parents alive."

"Parents? Your mom is still alive. You know this, right?"

"Yes. But I felt like I lost her five years ago."

"Did you do something that made you think of her like your dad and the crosswords?"

On a nervous laugh, I glanced up from my pad of paper and watched the traffic for a few seconds. "I ... do. Uh ..." More nervous laughter filled the air.

"What?"

"Just ... I collect stuff that she used to collect. Now that she's out of pris—" It occurred to me that Fisher might not know her past. Maybe he didn't do background checks on his tenants. I wasn't sure if Rory freely offered that information to people.

"I know she was in prison."

On a breath of relief, I nodded several times. "Okay. I mean, I figured she probably mentioned it. Background check. References. Surely she had to be accountable for the previous five years."

"I didn't ask. No background checks. She told me."

"Oh, okay."

After a few seconds, where I hoped he would forget what we were discussing, he cut his eyes to me for a few seconds. "So ... what did she and then you collect?"

As a young girl, my mom's hobby was cool. And I benefited from it. As an eighteen-year-old young woman with a slight crush on a guy ten years older than me, my mom's hobby that I took over no longer felt cool. In fact, embarrassed was the only word to describe it.

"She collected..." I needed to remind him that it wasn't really my hobby "...toys from Happy Meals."

"McDonald's Happy Meals?"

"Yeah. She felt certain that, eventually, they'd be worth a lot of money. So she bought Happy Meals. *Lots* of Happy Meals. Sometimes the same toy would be offered for a week or two, maybe even longer if it was really popular. When that happened, I scored a trip to McDonald's for a Happy Meal. She'd get two so I didn't feel cheated out of the toy. But when there were multiple interrelated items available at the same time, like collector cards or something like that, she'd buy *so* many Happy Meals just to get all of them. And since she was likely to get a lot of repeats before getting one of each ... whatever it was ... she'd buy more than we would ever consume, even taking a minivan full of my friends. So she'd take Happy Meals, minus the toys, and give them to homeless people. Well, I take that back. When the toys were repeats, she'd give them the toy too."

Fisher said nothing for a minute or two. The longest minute or two of my life. What must he have been thinking of Rory? Of me?

"And now *you* get Happy Meals for the toys?"

He was right. I had a nerd gene I didn't like to admit. But when he made that statement, even I couldn't deny I was a little zany.

"I don't, really. Not now, of course, because she's out of prison. There's no need for me to do it now. If she wants to continue, she can do it on her own."

The grin on his face swelled, and I wanted to crawl in a corner and die. "Did she ask you to do this while she was in prison?"

"Not exactly."

"Have you told her you did it?"

"Not yet. I really haven't had the chance to talk to her. I no sooner showed up and she left for California. I'll mention it when she comes home."

"But you're done? You won't be getting anymore Happy Meals. I mean ... isn't there an age limit for that?"

I rolled my eyes. "What are they going to do? Ask for the birth certificate of the child for whom you're buying the Happy Meal?"

Fisher shrugged. "They probably should. Wouldn't that be an interesting twist. Your mom going to prison for something that's now legal in most states, and you going to prison for Happy Meal fraud."

Covering my mouth, I giggled. He was being so ridiculous.

"Good thing you're done now."

I wasn't exactly done. There were Pokémon cards that month, and I still had three to get. Then I would be done. It felt weird ending with something as incomplete as Pokémon cards. "Yup." I popped my lips. "Good thing."

"I collected rocks."

Glancing at him as his attention remained affixed to the road, I ate up that grin of his—a mix between boyish and mischievous. "Like geodes and crystals? Precious stones?"

Pursing his lips upward a bit, he inched his head side to side. "No. Just rocks. Yard rocks. Playground rocks. Pebbles stuck in the soles of my shoes."

Biting back my smile, I nodded. "Sounds awesome. Do you still have your collection? Or do you still collect? I bet you find a lot of rocks in your line of work."

"I think my mom still has my shoeboxes full of rocks at home. I'll have to ask her. Why? Do you want to see it? I can show you my rocks, and you can show me your Happy Meal toys."

Again, he made me want to laugh, but I didn't trust myself to not be too transparent with my tiny crush on him. So I cleared my throat and swallowed back my amusement. "I didn't bring the collection with me. It's uh ..."

"A lot of shit? It has to be. I mean ... five years of collecting toys, you must have boxes and boxes of them? Or are they in a safe? Maybe safe deposit boxes for when they become collector items and you or your mom decide it's time to retire early?"

If he only knew ...

A few Christmas-tree sized Rubbermaid containers in my grandparents' basement.

"I don't know. You'll have to ask her. I just tried to continue her hobby while she was incarcerated. It's not like I got all of them. I was in school. I had other things going on. No time to keep militant track of Happy Meal toys."

I didn't miss a single one. If I were honest with him, I would have confessed just how much of my hard-earned money I spent *not* missing a single toy. And I even continued her tradition of giving out the Happy Meals to homeless people during times that required lots of purchases in a short amount of time. So really, I was a Good Samaritan. Feeding the homeless. WWJD? He would have handed out Happy Meals to everyone.

"I think that's cool. I mean, that you did that to feel connected to your mom. Just like the crosswords and your dad. Rory's a good person, even if she took the leap of faith and trusted me to keep an eye on you."

"Wait ..." My head jerked backward. "What do you mean by that? You make it sound like it was foolish of her. Which it might have been. I was a little surprised she trusted you. And for the record, I don't need anyone's eyes on me."

"You don't trust me?"

"No." I shifted my attention to the side window to hide my truth. Did I trust him? Not really. Did that give me a slight thrill? Unfortunately.

A hint of amusement lingered at his lips as he focused on the road. "That's fair. But I'm your boss during the day, so save your distrust for nights."

Oh my gosh ...

"That's ... a little creepy."

"Oh, Reese ... we're going to have so much fun." He turned up the music again. I glanced at his phone.

Matt Maeson, "Put It on Me."

The base vibrated my bones, and the lyrics rushed through my veins like ice water. A seductive and chilling song. It did nothing to make me trust the naked fisherman.

Rory must have felt desperate to find a friend—any friend—which made her susceptible to blind trust.

CHAPTER SEVEN

"Morning, Bossman." A wavy-haired blonde glanced up from a tiny desk nestled between a water cooler and a coffee machine.

"Morning. Hailey, this is Reese, Rory's daughter. If you have stuff for her to do here in the office, she'll hang with you today. Otherwise, I'll take her with me."

"Hi." I gave Hailey my best smile, silently begging for her to have some office work for me.

"Hey, Reese. Nice to meet you. I don't really have much today. But Monday you can help me enter bids in the computer and send them off."

Fisher grabbed a cup of coffee and sat at a desk opposite Hailey's. It was the smallest office I had ever seen.

"Or we could do it today," I suggested with a little too much enthusiasm.

"Sorry. I'm cutting out early for a doctor's appointment." She refocused on her computer.

I stood in the middle of the dinky room with my hands folded behind my back.

"Guess you're with me," Fisher said with a half grin, shooting me a quick glance before returning his attention to blueprints taking up his whole desk—sans a small corner where he set his coffee. "We need to get you some boots anyway."

"Yay ..." I said with zero enthusiasm.

"Atta girl, way to bring so much energy on a Friday."

Hailey snorted. "You're one to talk. I was surprised I got a full good morning from you today. Weren't you up extra early to take Rory to the airport?"

"Mmm ... yes, I was." He studied the plans, and I quickly learned I liked looking at him with or without clothes. He'd turned his baseball cap backward as if the bill somehow blocked his view or disrupted his thinking process.

"Fisher is not a morning person or a Monday person. He doesn't like his coffee cold or his water warm. He growls when he's mad at someone else and grumbles when he's mad at you."

"Hailey is full of shit. None of that is in the employee handbook."

"Because we don't have an employee handbook." She rolled her eyes.

"Not true. You just never took the time to read it." He reached in his pocket for his phone. "Fisher," he answered.

I made mental notes.

Growl = mad at someone else.

Grumble = mad at me.

"You're young." Hailey eyed me. "Sixteen? Seventeen?"

She wasn't exactly old either.

"Eighteen." I tipped my chin up and pushed out my chest. I was five-nine with a solid B-cup. "How old are you?"

"Twenty-eight, like Bossman."

I wouldn't have guessed that. Maybe twenty-three or twenty-four.

"I'll make sure the guys don't razz you too much. Except Jeremiah. He's twenty-one, really cute, and single," she said.

"Well, I'm not sure how long I'll be staying. My plans are just for the summer at this point."

With a conspiratorial grin, she winked. "Nothing wrong with hooking up just for the summer."

I wasn't hooking up. That would have required getting married, and I wasn't rushing into marriage just to have sex.

"Ready to head out to the first job site?" Fisher slipped his phone back into his pocket.

"The one they're roofing today?" Hailey asked.

"Yeah, that's one stop." Fisher turned his hat the right way again while nodding at me to head toward the door.

"Jeremiah is there. Make sure you introduce him to Reese. I said he'd be a good summer hookup."

"Reese isn't hooking up with Jeremiah this summer."

"Why?" Hailey asked as if I wasn't standing in the middle of their conversation about me and my sex life.

"Because Rory left me in charge of her." He disappeared out the door, and I shot out after him.

"Hey, you're not in charge of me. Maybe you're my

boss when I'm working, but Rory didn't leave you in charge of me. I'm an adult."

"You're eighteen." He hopped into the truck.

"Yeah ..." I fastened my seat belt. "Eighteen is a legal adult."

"Legal yes. But not in the practical sense."

I scowled at him, but he ignored me. When we got to the first site, I started to climb out of the truck.

"Stay put." He opened his door.

"Why?"

"Because it's a work site, and you don't have a hard hat yet."

I peered out the window at the crew roofing the house. "They're not wearing hard hats."

"They're on the roof. Nothing's going to fall onto them." He started to shut the door.

"Where's your hat?"

"I'm hardheaded. I'll be fine." The door shut before I had a chance for a rebuttal.

For three job inspections in a row, I waited in the truck and basically got paid to work on my crossword puzzles. Then we pulled into a supply and apparel store parking lot.

"Let's get you some boots and a hard hat." He jumped out of the truck and strode a good twenty feet before he turned around. After holding out his hands, he let them flop to his sides, returning to the truck and opening my door. "Did you already forget how to operate the little lever called the door handle?"

"No. I just wasn't sure if I was allowed to exit the

truck yet." I hopped out of the truck, and he shut and locked the door.

"I said we're getting you boots and a hard hat."

"Yes, Boss."

He glanced over at me, one eyebrow peaked. "Boss, huh?"

"That's what Hailey calls you. Bossman."

"I'm not sure she means it with any sort of respect."

"I'm not sure I'm saying it with any respect either."

He laughed and shook his head. "You're a spitfire, like your mom." Opening the door to the store, he waited for me to go inside.

I nodded for him to go first. "It's not a date."

"You're right. My mistake." He stepped inside and let go of the door.

It quickly started to close, and I grabbed the handle. My shoulder jerked in the direction of the door. It was a lot heavier than I anticipated. After I lugged it open and squeezed inside the store, I jogged to catch up to Fisher who was already halfway toward the back of the store.

"What's your shoe size?" he asked.

"Nine."

"Really?" He glanced back at me. "Big feet."

My nose wrinkled. "Nine isn't that big."

"For a woman it is."

"Pfft ..." I shook my head.

"Sit." He nodded toward a bench.

"I'm not a dog." I held my own to prove ... well ... that I wasn't a dog.

"You're right. A dog would be better behaved."

"Jerk." I plopped onto the bench while Fisher tracked down an employee.

A few minutes later, he returned with three boxes. "Take off your shoes."

I slipped out of my tennis shoes.

"Reese ..." He stared at my feet. "Where are your socks?"

"My shoes have wool inserts. They don't require socks."

He grumbled. That meant he was mad at me.

"Well, they don't." I shrugged.

Dropping the three boxes onto the bench next to me, he stomped his work boots in the direction of a rack of socks. After quickly picking a pair, he ripped the tag off them and handed them to me. "Put these socks on." His no-nonsense attitude prevented me from saying or doing anything but exactly what he asked me to do.

"Here." He retrieved a boot from the first box and loosened the laces before handing it to me.

I shoved my foot into it, but before I could tie it, Fisher hunched in front of me and tied the laces with fast and furious hands. "Walk."

Standing on command like a good dog, I walked, really hobbled because I only had on one boot. Stopping at a floor mirror, I inspected it.

"Well?" he said.

"They're ugly."

Another grumble. At least, I thought it was a grumble. Maybe it was a growl. "You know what else is ugly? Toes with nails poked through them or toes crushed by heavy objects. Let me reframe my question. How do they fit?"

"They? You mean it? Trying on one boot tells me nothing except that it's ugly ... and hard to walk in one boot."

"Great. Glad you like them. Here. Put on the other boot, and let's get you a hard hat."

I slipped on the other boot and tied it much slower than Fisher did. Then I followed him to another part of the store as he carried the boot box holding my tennis shoes and the tag to my socks.

"Let's see how this fits." He put a hard hat on my head.

"It's loose."

He removed it and tightened the inside strap.

"How about now?"

I nodded. "Better."

"Let's go."

"Did I do something wrong?" I asked, scurrying to catch up to him.

"Nope. We just have a busy afternoon."

"And I didn't wear socks."

"And you didn't wear socks," he echoed me, setting the box and the hard hat on the register counter.

"Are you going to fire me?"

The employee on the other side of the counter eyed us cautiously.

"Not until we get to the truck." He tapped his credit card to the machine and slipped it back in his wallet.

The employee's eyes widened, focusing mainly on me.

"Do I have to reimburse you for the boots and hat if you fire me?"

"Yes." He grabbed the box before she could put it in a bag, then shoved the hat on my head, a little crooked. "Let's go."

"That ... all of that back there ... it was part of the fifty percent that I should ignore. Right?"

"You're on the clock. Never ignore me when you're on the clock."

"So I can ignore you when I clock out?"

"You can do whatever you want to me when you clock out."

Gah!

There it was again. His words were so suggestive, leaving me with no choice but to let my mind think the most inappropriate things.

"What if I want to ..." I stopped. I had no clue where I was going with that. At least, not consciously.

He opened my door despite his rules about not opening it for me. "What if you want to what?"

"Nothing." I climbed into the seat and grabbed the box from him.

"I worry about you. What lies beneath the surface ..." He shook his head slowly.

Before I could act offended or actually be offended, he slammed my door shut.

———

My FIRST NIGHT ALONE, truly alone, was weird. I locked the door at the top of the stairs to keep the naked fisherman out of the basement. Yet, every time I heard a strange noise, all I wanted to do was run up the stairs and ask him to figure out where the noise came from. It didn't take long to understand what Fisher meant when he said I was only an adult in age. Hiding beneath my blankets, I felt like a ten-year-old hiding from the boogie man.

I didn't see Fisher at all on Saturday—then again, I never left the basement. On Sunday, I made my first big solo outing to a nearby church. They dressed a little more casual than what I was used to at my grandparents' church in Texas, but everyone was nice. I left with at least a dozen new contacts in my phone from members offering to help me get acclimated to the area in any way possible.

"What's the occasion?"

Getting out of my mom's Outback, I turned toward Fisher's voice. Seriously, did he ever wear a shirt at home? He was, in my mom's words, spit-shining his motorcycle in the driveway next to his truck.

Shorts that hung too low in front.

No shoes or socks.

Tan from head to toe. He was a mix of Theo James and Liam Hemsworth. Definitely Theo's smile when he wasn't grumbling.

"What do you mean?" I moseyed in his direction, sliding my purse strap onto my shoulder.

"The dress. Hair. Makeup." He shot me a quick glance before returning his attention to the motorcycle, working the chrome by the tires.

"Well, in all fairness, you've seen me after a long flight. With bedhead in the middle of the night. And thrown together early in the morning to take my mom to the airport."

"Let me rephrase. Where have you been?"

I stood next to his truck, keeping a good six feet between us. "Not that it's any of your business, because it's Sunday and I don't work for you today, but I went to church."

"Oh yeah? How'd that go?"

"Fine. I made a lot of friends."

"I can see that about you."

"Making friends?"

"Making friends at church."

"Ha. Ha. I can make friends outside of church too. But my boss won't let me out of his truck for more than two seconds, so I never get the chance to ..."

"To what?" He gave me another quick glance while wiping his arm along his forehead.

"To meet people like Jeremiah." I lifted a shoulder, casually hinting at my interest in Jeremiah whom I hadn't met yet.

"Like him? Or him?"

"Either."

"I don't think he attends church."

"Doesn't matter." Oh, it mattered a lot, but I hated the way Fisher made me feel like a prim and proper church girl.

"He swears," Fisher said.

"So?"

"So, I notice you cringe when I say fuck, shit, damn, crap, even dick. And dick's not a swear word, right? It's

58

more of a body part or synonym for asshole, which you don't like either."

"What's your point?"

"My point is, would you really enjoy being around Jeremiah if he used that language in all of his sentences?"

"It's not me saying it, so whatever."

"Really?" He stopped his polishing again to inspect me, to read me. "What if he wants to do more than hang out with you? Is that something you're down for?"

"I don't think the things I'm *down for* are any of your business."

"Maybe you should stick to your new church friends. I'd feel better about it and so would Rory."

"Well, I'm—"

"Yeah, yeah ... you're an adult. I've heard you mention it a time or two."

"Well, it's true. So that means I don't need your permission or Rory's permission to hang out with whomever I want to hang out with."

"How rebellious of you. Are you throwing your V-card to the wind and having a hot girl summer?"

"What makes you so sure I have my V-card?" I knew I was marching, with zero regard for self-preservation, straight into a snake pit.

He stood tall and draped the towel over his shoulder while scratching his jaw with his other hand, lips corkscrewed. "Just a wild guess."

"Because I went to a Christian school?"

"No." He chuckled. "That might actually make a better case for you not having your V-card. Repression and all that shit."

"Then what?"

"Just little things like the way you're so quick to get defensive, like now. Or the way you fidget when I make you uncomfortable with a topic like this. But really, it was the way you looked at me the day we met. Like you hadn't seen a guy without his shirt on. The way you're looking at me right now."

My gaze snapped from his chest to his face and embarrassment flamed up my neck to my cheeks. "You're a little too full of yourself. I've seen plenty of shirtless men."

"But have you seen any naked men?"

Dang it!

I walked right into that. Why did I stop and engage in conversation with him? I should have kept walking toward the basement. "I mean ..."

He grinned like he'd caught me. And my lack of ability to answer right away only added to his proof. "You wouldn't have had to technically see the guy's entire naked body to have sex with him, but I'd hope you would have insisted on it. The visual is half the fun."

The sun was no match for the heat in my face and really, everywhere along my body. Nobody had ever talked to me like Fisher talked to me. On one hand, he liked to treat me like a child, on the other hand, he spoke to me in a way that felt crude and borderline inappropriate.

But inappropriate for whom? His employee? Yes. The daughter of his tenant? Probably. An eighteen-year-old girl ... woman? Well, the *woman* in me wanted to say no, but the girl who did in fact still have her V-card cringed everywhere. That girl felt like a ten-year-old who just had a perv expose himself to her on the playground.

"I've seen a naked man."

Man. Yes, as in man oh man ... why couldn't I shut my stupid mouth and go bury my head beneath a pillow for the rest of the day? Or the rest of my life?

"Oh yeah?" He squinted against the sun. "That's good to know. It takes the pressure off me. I'm a clothing optional kind of guy. Rory has seen more than she bargained for. Of course, she was cool about it. Like mother like daughter, huh?"

Was I cool with seeing the naked fisherman? No. Could he not see my face? I was the complete opposite of cool. No 'like mother like daughter.' My mom had seen a naked man before. Maybe more than one. I never asked my parents about their relationships before they met each other. I never got the chance.

"I'm going to change my clothes and maybe head into the mountains. I've never been."

"Wait. What? You grew up in Nebraska and you've never been to the mountains?" he asked with the right amount of shock because it was shocking. A crime, really.

"No. Not the Rockies."

"That's insane. And you thinking your first trip into the mountains should be by yourself is just as insane. Let me change my clothes. I'll take you."

"I don't need a chaperone. Really. I have navigation on my phone. It's not snowing up there, is it?"

"Unlikely. But you'll encounter some steep grades. And people drive crazy fast on some of those winding roads because they're used to them. You're not used to them. Rory would kill me if I let you go alone."

"I'll let her know it was my decision."

"Your decision to get eaten by a bear or bitten by a rattlesnake. Great. Just what I need."

"What do you mean bears and rattlesnakes?"

"I mean the mammal that's brown or black and has sharp teeth and even sharper claws. And snakes are reptiles—"

"Fisher! I get it. I know what bears and snakes are. I just wasn't aware that they were a concern for a day trip to the mountains."

"Chill." He held up his hands in surrender. "I was only looking out for you. The problem with new adults, such as yourself, is that you abandon all common sense in the name of independence. You've been *all grown up* for two seconds. You've been here for less than two seconds. It's okay to ask for help or allow someone to go places with you when there's a chance you could get into a bad situation."

Widening my stance, I crossed my arms over my chest. "Are you going to spend the day lecturing me? Are you going to complain if I don't wear the right shoes or go without socks? Are you going to—"

"Fuck it, woman. No." He shook his head and sauntered into the garage. "I'm not going with you. It's my day off, and I shouldn't have to subject myself to your attitude. I regret mentioning any of it. Go conquer the world. I'm out of fucks to give."

I flinched with every "fuck," thankful he didn't see me because it would have confirmed his earlier accusations. Without another word, I escaped to the basement. He'd planted the seed, making me doubt my ability or even my sanity for going into the mountains alone. If I didn't go, it would've looked like I'd succumbed to his fear tactics. If I did go and anything bad happened, he would have to tell Rory, making me look like the stubborn, immature, fake adult he pegged me for.

"Gah! Stupid naked fisherman!" I ripped off my dress and pulled on a pair of shorts and a fitted red T-shirt. Then I found a pair of socks to wear with my tennis shoes.

Sunscreen.

Bug spray.

Water bottle.

Energy bar.

Cell phone.

What more could a girl need? I wasn't staying for a week, roughing it in the wilderness.

As I slung my backpack over my shoulder, my phone rang.

Rory.

"Hey." I headed out the door and closed and locked it behind me.

"Hey, sweetie. I just called Fisher to check in. He mentioned you taking a trip into the mountains today. It's not a good idea to go by yourself, given the fact you've never driven in the mountains."

"Thanks for your concern, but I'll be fine." I gazed out at the mountains. They didn't look so tough from where I stood.

"I'd feel better if Fisher went with you."

"Well, that makes one of us."

"Do you have a problem with Fisher?"

I closed my eyes and blew out a breath. "No. No problems with Fisher. It's just that he's my boss now, and maybe I don't want to be under his watchful eye on the weekend too. And really, do you think he wants to deal with me on his day off? No. I don't think so."

"He said he'd love to take you today."

Liar.

"He did, did he? Well, that's not what he said to me."

"Oh? What did he say to you?"

I couldn't tell her. It involved using the F-word twice, and I wasn't comfortable with saying it outside of my head.

"He basically said he didn't want to go because it's his day off. His day off from me."

"Wait until I get home. We'll go together."

"You want me to wait half the summer to go up into the mountains? That's not fair."

"Reese ..."

"I've got this. Really."

"I'm going to call Fisher back."

"No! I mean ... just let it go. Stop treating me like a child who needs a chaperone. I don't need someone watching me anymore. I didn't come here to have you or your *friend* watch me. I came here to be with you. Now you're gone, so I'm on my own. And that's fine. I get it. But don't think that Fisher is your replacement."

After a long pause, she cleared her throat. "Okay. You're right. Just ... be careful and text me when you get home, so I know you made it back safely."

"Fine." I huffed while ending the call.

College was starting to sound better and better, even if I had no clue what I would study if I got there. At least my life would have felt like mine. Mine to succeed. Mine to fail.

I marched past Fisher's driveway to Rory's Outback parked on the street. Without giving him a single glance, I tossed my backpack in the back seat and slipped into the driver's seat. Turning the key, nothing happened. I tried again. And again, nothing happened. Not a single sound.

"Are you kidding me? Dear Lord, please let this car start." I tried one more time.

Silence. Not one peep like the engine was making a single effort to turn on. I'd *just* driven it to church and back. God wasn't answering my prayer that day.

After reaching around and snatching my backpack from the back seat, I made the walk of shame past the driveway.

"Battery's dead. I've been telling Rory for weeks she needs a new one. I'll drop a new battery in it tomorrow after work."

I glanced over at Fisher using a squeegee to remove the water from his clean garage floor. "I can call someone."

"Or..." he shook his head and grinned "...you can call someone on your own."

I sulked toward the side of the house.

"I'm going for a ride on my motorcycle. Want to come along?"

"I'm sure my mom would think riding on the back of your motorcycle is a terrible idea."

"Probably." He hooked the squeegee on the wall and grabbed a towel to dry his hands. "That's why we won't tell her."

"Like you didn't tell her I was going into the mountains?"

He shrugged. "I didn't know it was a secret."

"I'm going to work on my crossword puzzles." I ducked my head and kept walking.

"I'm going to shower. I'll be leaving in fifteen minutes. If you're going, change into jeans."

"Have fun," I called back with virtually no sincerity.

CHAPTER EIGHT

AFTER DEPOSITING my bag onto my bed, I made myself a sandwich. Ten minutes later, with half of my sandwich gone, I eyed the time on my phone.

Fisher was leaving in less than five minutes. On his motorcycle. I'd never been on a motorcycle. They were dangerous and would have required me to hold on to his waist. It was a terrible idea. I had things to do. Puzzles to construct. Bible passages to study before Wednesday night, if I planned on attending the singles' group. That was where I would find a nice guy who didn't swear or make suggestive comments.

A guy who wore a shirt.

A guy closer to my age.

A guy who didn't care if I wore socks or not.

A guy who didn't ride a motorcycle.

After letting those sensible thoughts settle in my mind, I tossed the rest of my sandwich in the trash, changed into jeans, grabbed my backpack, and sprinted around the house just as Fisher started to pull out of the driveway.

"Wait!"

He stopped and slid up the visor to his helmet. I had no idea if one could truly have an orgasm just by looking at a guy. It seemed unlikely. A myth. But ... Fisher in jeans, black leather boots and jacket, and black gloves made me feel a little dizzy as something between my tummy and my chest tickled me in the most unfamiliar way. I imagined it was what it felt like to have a glass of wine or maybe get a little high. Not that I would ever find that out. I had a firm no drug policy for many reasons, but mainly because of my mom.

He said nothing, like I was supposed to read his mind, but really, I was asking him to read mine. That would have been embarrassing beyond my imagination.

"I'd like to go with you."

He made me squirm with his silence for a few seconds before killing the engine and removing his helmet. "Follow me."

In a matter of days, I'd become irritatingly infatuated with a man ten years older than me. I followed Fisher Mann into his garage, but I would have followed him off the edge of the mountain. That was the effect Devil in a Tool Belt had on me. I really hoped the whole once-saved-always-saved thing was true because there was a good chance I'd need that unconditional salvation.

"It's a woman's size." He tugged a helmet onto my head and fastened it under my chin.

"For all your women?" I tried to play coy, but my face

felt too heated to make anyone believe I could pull off coy or subtle at that point.

"Yes, for my harem." Turning toward a cabinet, he retrieved a riding jacket like his. "You have long arms, so this might be a little small on you. Something is better than nothing."

"Long arms? I don't have long arms." I threaded my arms through the jacket while he held it up for me. As he zipped the jacket, I tugged on the cuffs of the sleeves.

Fisher smirked. Yes, the sleeves were a little short.

"It's okay. Your legs are long too. And guys will overlook your octopus arms because you have legs for days."

"I'm not a giraffe."

"I didn't say that." He strutted to his bike, and I followed him ... to his bike ... off the side of the mountain.

He climbed onto his bike, and that feeling that stretched from the pit of my stomach to the center of my chest returned, only stronger as he helped me climb on behind him. When he reached around and grabbed my ass, pulling me closer to him, I almost died. It was the most forbidden feeling I had ever experienced. I realized how crazy that would seem to anyone else, but I was, in fact, the girl who spent the last three years of high school living with grandparents, attending a Christian academy.

"Rory can never know," I said.

"Hold on," Fisher replied.

I snaked my arms around his waist, trying not to actually press my hands to his stomach or my chest to his back.

"Hold on like your life depends on it ... because it does."

I tightened my grip, a lot. And two seconds later, he kicked the bike into gear, and we shot off down the street. It was unreal.

Me on the back of a motorcycle holding on to the sexiest man I had ever seen.

My heart in my throat.

The seeds of possibilities sprouting in my head.

It felt like an alternate universe where my mom hadn't gone to prison. My dad hadn't died. And I never left Nebraska and the public school with all my friends. I was daring, and flirting with mischief was my only purpose. Church was a ritual, an afterthought. And the God I worshipped wasn't anyone to fear. I was … normal.

Wild oats were mine to sow.

And my reality was whatever dream I dared to chase.

Fisher took me through town. I anticipated him heading back home, but he didn't. He drove me up the winding roads into the mountains—the steep inclines and the rollercoaster trips down hills at insane speeds. We passed cars, weaving from one lane to the next. Rory would have died had she seen her only child on the back of Fisher's motorcycle, flying through the increasingly steep terrain of the mountain highway.

"WOO HOO!" I let my lungs loose as we drove through the Eisenhower Tunnel.

Fisher's hand left the handlebar for a few seconds to press against my leg, giving it a soft squeeze. My arms tightened around him. We rode and rode. My butt went numb. Eventually, he pulled off at a scenic stop. My legs were numb too as I hobbled off the bike and unfastened my helmet.

"If you're enjoying the tour..." he took my helmet from me "...don't forget to leave a Yelp review."

I giggled. "Is this a side gig? And here I felt kind of special." I inched closer to the guardrail and a canyon filled with trees for miles. The view ... there were no words. "I bet this means nothing to you."

"The view?" he asked.

Of course the view. What did he think I meant? Tossing him a quick sideways glance, I nodded. "Yeah, the view."

"I think there are some things that are meant to provide a lifetime of awe. The mountains. The oceans. Rainbows. Shooting stars. First kisses."

Ten years. There were ten years between us. And he admitted that fifty percent of everything that left his mouth was not to be trusted. First kisses ... he was baiting me. I was surprised he didn't say unicorns.

"I have jaded memories," I said. "Not like my friends who vacationed every summer. Trips to Disney. Key West. The Grand Canyon. My big moments involved my parents fighting. My mom leaving our house in handcuffs. The day she was convicted. My dad didn't want me there, but I begged him. I told him I would never forgive him if he didn't let me go with him. She mouthed 'I love you,' as they took her away. I remember my dad telling me to let her go. He said she lost the privilege of being my mom because she chose the wrong path. He said she should have loved me more. And sometimes ... I believed him. Then he died. Another memory taking up so much space in my head. So this..." I nodded to the view "...it's a great picture to pin on top of the other pictures that don't take my breath away."

For several minutes, Fisher didn't reply. I'm sure it all sounded crazy to him. It sounded crazy to me, yet I couldn't roll my eyes and let it be someone else's pathetic life.

"You deserve to have your breath taken away ... every day."

Those. Those ten words. They wrapped around my heart like sticky peanut butter and jelly fingers.

Pure.

Innocent.

Unforgettable.

Perfect.

"Well..." I kept my gaze on the feathery green canvas "...mission accomplished."

"Want me to take a picture of you?" he asked, retrieving his phone from his pocket.

"Okay." I bit my lower lip to hide my true level of giddiness.

"Say, 'Sorry Rory.'"

I laughed. "Sorry Rory."

He studied the screen of his phone. "Perfect. I'll airdrop them to you when we get home."

"Want me to take your picture?"

He chuckled. "I'm good. I have at least a million already."

I tilted my head and wrinkled my nose. "Yeah, but not with me."

Something quite like a genuine smile bent his lips. "True." He stood next to me, one arm around my waist, pulling me close while he stretched out his other arm with the phone and took a selfie with me.

That was the one I wanted him to send me. It wasn't just the mountains; it was him, the motorcycle, the feeling (although foolish) that I was a woman enjoying the perfect Sunday afternoon with a man. The naked fisherman.

On our way back home, we stopped in Idaho Springs, an old mining town, for pizza at Beau Jo's. Not just any pizza. Nope. Thick wheat crust with loads of toppings. And we dipped our crust ends in honey. It blew my mind.

He blew my mind.

Fisher told me about his family. Two older sisters and a younger brother. His love for building things that started at an early age. And his all-star jock status in high school. All State everything. His coaches thought he would go on to college to do something—basketball, baseball, track. But he didn't love any of it as much as he loved his tool belt and the smell of fresh-cut lumber.

"Are you awake?" he asked, killing the engine inside his garage.

"Sort of," I mumbled as I almost fell on my butt getting off the back of his bike.

He grabbed my arm to steady me. "I got Rory's daughter back in one piece. Phew." He removed my helmet and unzipped my jacket.

"But she'll never know because we aren't telling her."

"She won't hear anything from me." He winked, removing his jacket.

"Thanks. I realize you probably weren't planning on a tagalong today."

"You can tag along anytime."

"Well ..." I nodded toward the garage door. "I'd better get to bed. My boss isn't a morning person or a Monday person, so I have to bring enough awesomeness for the both of us."

He smirked. "I'm sure your boss's reputation is unfair and exaggerated."

I shrugged. "Maybe. But just in case ... I'm off to bed. Goodnight." I headed toward the open garage door.

"Reese, you can go through the house. It's dark. No need to walk around the side of the house."

"You sure?"

Fisher held open the door to his house for me. "I'm sure. Just don't steal anything on your way through my kitchen."

With an eye roll, I stepped into his house and removed my shoes, carrying them through his kitchen. "Are you going to lock your basement door behind me?"

"Why? *Are* you going to rob me?"

"No." I giggled, opening the basement door.

"Are you going to sneak up in the middle of the night and do weird shit to me while I sleep?"

"What?" I coughed. "Um ... no. I just think if I rented out my basement, I'd lock my door."

"Noted. You have no self-control, and therefore I need to lock my door."

"I'm locking my side."

"I don't doubt that." He shoved his hands into his

back pockets and rested his shoulder against the threshold into the kitchen from the garage entrance.

Fisher and his overabundance of sexiness continued to give me all the feels. "Am I driving to the office in the morning or going with you?"

"The Outback's battery is dead."

I frowned. "That's right."

"We'll leave at six."

"Six." I gave him an unavoidable smile before shutting the door ... and locking it. As I tiptoed down the stairs, I listened for him to lock it on his side.

He never did.

CHAPTER NINE

MONDAY, I spent the day with Hailey sending out bids. Fisher put a new battery in the Outback then disappeared for the rest of the evening on his motorcycle. I didn't get an invite to join him.

Tuesday, I went with Hailey to pick up flooring for a kitchen. She drove a company pickup, and for some reason, I found that kind of cool. After that, we picked up lunch for the crew. Apparently, it was a perk Fisher offered his guys, not the norm in construction. I found that rather cool too.

Wednesday, I was back with Fisher and that thrilled me.

"Yesterday, Hailey introduced me to some of your crew. So you don't have to worry about introductions now. Except your dad and uncle. When will I meet them?"

"My dad is out of town until next week. My uncle just had knee surgery, so he's out for a while." Fisher lifted a brow and gave me a quick sidelong glance while we waited in the drive-thru to pick up our coffees on the way to the first job. "And it's a relief that I don't have to introduce you to anyone because that was high on my list of priorities today."

"Is that sarcasm?"

He pulled forward and grabbed our coffees. "Nope." He handed me both drinks and rolled up his window.

"Have you talked to Rory since Sunday?" I handed him his coffee.

"Nope." He sipped his drink and wrinkled his nose. "This one is not mine. It's sweet and disgusting." After depositing it in my cup holder, he reached over and snagged my coffee—his coffee—from me.

I frowned at the one in the drink holder. "Now you've tasted it."

"So? I'm not sick."

"Yeah, but you drank out of it."

He chuckled. "Have you never swapped a little saliva with anyone? I didn't spit anything back into the cup. It's the equivalent of a peck on the lips. I'm sure you've had a few tongues down your throat. What's the big deal?"

Sliding the drink from the holder, I brought it to my mouth and took a cautious sip.

Fisher shook his head at my hesitation. "Do I gross you out that much?"

Just the opposite. It felt intimate sharing a cup of coffee with him. I took another sip, trying to not think too hard about how I liked the idea of my mouth touching the same spot his lips had touched.

"It's fine." I stared out my window while sipping the coffee, brushing my lips over the lid a little too much.

"Reese?"

"Hmm?"

"You have kissed a guy before. Right?"

I scoffed. "Yes."

"An open-mouthed kiss? Tongue? Saliva swapping?" He was so crude. I loved it and hated it in equal parts.

"Duh."

"Duh is not an answer."

"Hailey invited me to her house for a party on Friday. Well, not this Friday ... next Friday." My attention remained steadfast out my window.

"You dodged my question."

"I think I'll go. It's a chance to make new friends if I don't have much luck tonight."

"What's tonight?"

"Singles' Bible study at the church."

"Sounds ... titillating."

"You could come with me."

Fisher laughed, a little too hard. "As tempting as the offer is, I have a date. Sorry."

A date.

Fisher had a date. That was okay. Of course he dated since he wasn't married, and he wasn't dating Rory. I bet he had sex too. That didn't feel quite as okay to me for utterly ridiculous reasons. It wasn't like Fisher Mann was mine no matter how incredibly sexy I found him, no matter how many thoughts he owned in my head. It wasn't like he was going to wait for me to figure my life out, marry me, and take my virginity on our wedding night.

Nope.

None of that was happening, so it was just great, awesome really, that Fisher had a date.

"A new date? Someone you've gone out with before?"

"Blind date. A friend of a friend."

I nodded slowly. "Where are you going?"

"Concert downtown."

"Sounds fun."

"I suppose."

"How old is she?"

He grinned before sipping his coffee. "I'm not sure. Why?"

"No reason."

"Well, if you decide to bring someone home from Bible study, I won't tell your mom. And the house is insulated really well, so don't ever worry about me hearing anything."

Oh my gosh ...

I bit my tongue so hard. What he implied was offensive and yes ... crude. As if I was going to pick up some guy at Bible study and bring him back to have sex. Clearly, Fisher had never attended church, which meant he probably wasn't saved. And I needed to remember that. I needed to remember all the reasons I shouldn't have obsessed over the naked fisherman.

"So I won't hear you either." I felt incredibly brave saying that to him. For a breath, I tried to feel like an equal. An adult who dated and had loud sex. But inside it really ... really bothered me to think of him having sex with someone else.

Or me, of course.

But mostly someone else.

"I'm not really a screamer. I may drop a few profanities if it's worthy of it."

Stop! Make him stop!

He enjoyed playing with me. I could tell from the smirk he wore like a favorite T-shirt. He ate my reactions up like a shark finding a wounded otter. Fisher knew I was way out of my comfort zone. And his favorite game seemed to be pushing me a few more inches with every remark. I refused to give him the verbal satisfaction, even if my feelings were on full display in the color of my face or the uncontrolled fidgeting of my hands.

"It won't matter. I'll probably be late anyway. Someone mentioned getting ice cream afterward." It sounded ridiculous the second I said it.

Biting his lips to mask more of his amusement, he nodded several times. "I can see that. Well, you have my number if things get too crazy and you need a ride home. Gut ache. Sugar jitters. Brain freeze. Whatever."

"Jerk." I couldn't help it. He brought out the worst in me, the crazy in me.

Fisher sniggered as he pulled to a stop at the first job site. The framers were already busy constructing the interior walls in the basement.

"Am I allowed out?" I asked.

Fisher grabbed my hard hat out of the back seat and plopped it on my head. "If you can stay out of trouble and not distract my crew with stories about wild ice cream socials."

Had I used swear words, I would have told him to fuck off, and it would have felt so liberating. But I remained silent because I knew those other words would feel foreign leaving my lips.

"Cat got your tongue?" Fisher grinned as I fumed.

I climbed out and mumbled to myself, "No. Jesus does."

WWJD?

Fisher walked around the perimeter looking at things. What? I had no clue. I assumed he knew what he was doing. I followed a few feet behind him.

"Plumber been here?" he asked one of the guys carrying a stack of two-by-fours on his shoulder and depositing it in the middle of the basement.

"Not yet," the guy said just as he adjusted his jeans and stood erect again.

Whoa ...

He was built like an ox. "Hi. I'm Jason."

"I'm—"

"What about Kevin? Has he been by yet?" Fisher totally cut me off. Rude.

"Not yet." Jason shook his head, scratching the back of his thick, tattooed neck.

I didn't think I was a big fan of tattoos, but Jason changed my mind.

"Christ ... are they fuckin' sleeping in this morning? I don't have time to wait around." Fisher pulled his phone from his pocket and walked a few feet away from me, answering it with a sharp "Fisher."

"Are you the sidekick this summer?" Jason asked, glancing up as he measured and marked a board.

"I guess. I think he offered me the job as a favor to my

mom. I feel like a shadow that's in his way. I think I prefer working with Hailey."

"Amen. She's awesome."

"Yeah." I slipped the tips of my fingers into my front pockets, glancing over my shoulder to see if Fisher was still on his phone. "Is he always in such a delightful mood?"

"Just in the mornings. He's not much of a morning person."

I laughed. "That's what Hailey said." I thought of our ride to the job site. He seemed fine with me.

"Let's go, Reese. It's going to be a long day." He made what I felt pretty sure was a growling sound which meant he was mad, but not at me or anyone in our proximity.

I cringed at Jason and he laughed, shaking his head.

"Well, it was nice meeting you."

"See ya around. Good luck with Mr. Sunshine."

"Thanks." I rolled my eyes and smiled. That smile quickly faded when I turned toward Fisher who was not smiling.

"Are you done rolling your eyes and talking about your boss?" Fisher asked me.

I had nothing to lose. I kinda knew he wasn't going to fire Rory's daughter. "For now." I shot him an extra toothy grin.

"No lunch for you," he murmured as he trekked toward his truck with me right behind him.

"I have a Cliff Bar in my bag. I came prepared for your less than stellar attitude. And AHHH!" I tripped. Stupid big boots. I hissed a sharp breath, sitting back on my knees as I brought my hand close to my chest with a dirty nail partially impaled into my palm. "Ouch! Oh my gosh! I'm fine." I hissed again. "I'm not fine. It hurts." Tears stung my eyes, but I refused to set them free in front of Fisher and his all-male framing crew.

"What did you do?" Fisher hunched down and reached for my arm.

"I tripped," I said with a bit of irritation lacing my words. What did he think happened?

"Let me see."

I shook my head and turned my torso, hiding my hand and the nail away from his line of sight. I didn't want him or anyone to touch it because it hurt too much.

"Don't. Touch. It." I felt my control slipping. I needed someone. A female. My grandma. I needed her to fix this. She was good at fixing and mending things.

"I just need to look at it. I won't touch it." Fisher grabbed my forearm and forced me to show him my hand. He frowned. "Well, looks like we'll be adding another stop to our morning."

That did it. That made my tears escape. "I'm sorry," I said with a trembling lower lip.

"Why? It was an accident. Shit happens. We'll get you fixed up. Okay?"

Sniffling. I nodded.

"Can you walk?" he asked. "Or do I need to carry you?"

He didn't want to open my door in front of anyone. I felt certain that carrying me was way out of the question as long as my legs weren't broken.

"I'm fine." I started to stand on the uneven pile of dirt and, just as quickly, my foot turned to the side, and I felt myself going down again, but not before Fisher grabbed my torso.

"I guess I'm carrying you." He lifted me up, cradling me in his arms like a needy two-year-old and carrying me to the truck. After he helped me into my seat, he grabbed my forearm again.

"Don't. Touch. It!"

He laughed. Laughed! "Just chill a sec. I'm going to get my first aid kit from the back and get some antibacterial wipes to clean the dirt off around it."

"Don't pull the nail out." I slowly released my bent arm so he could see my hand.

"I'm not going to pull the nail out. God ... you're a basket case." He disappeared to the back of the truck and returned with the wipes.

"Shouldn't you wear gloves so you don't get my blood on your hands?"

"You have my saliva inside of you. It's only fitting I get a little of your blood. Might as well let everything mingle today. Do you have an STD I need to know about?" Fisher squinted at me as his hands gently cleaned around the wound.

I frowned.

"It's a joke."

"Terrible timing." I jumped when his finger accidentally bumped the nail.

"Sorry." He cringed, giving me a sincere apologetic look. "Here, sit back. I'll get you fastened in." After he fastened the seat belt, he drove me to urgent care where we were ushered back surprisingly quick. They removed the nail. Cleaned the wound. Bandaged it. And gave me a tetanus shot because I couldn't remember the last time I'd had one.

"Do you need to go home?" Fisher asked when we got back into the truck.

"No." I felt stupid. I cried in front of him. How did I expect for him to think of me as a grown woman when I cried over a little puncture wound? I bet his date that night wasn't a crybaby like me.

"Sure?"

I nodded.

We finished off the day with me doing very little aside from waiting in the truck and holding sacks of food for the roofing crew at the final job where they were working late to finish before the rain.

After a quick stop at the office, we headed home around six.

"What time is your Bible study?" Fisher asked as we pulled into the driveway.

"Seven."

"Are you still going?" He opened his door and paused, eyeing me warily like for the first time he felt bad about my accident.

"Yes," I managed to say like all was good. But I was not going to Bible study. "After a nice soak in the tub, I'll be fine." I shut the door.

"Um ... have you not noticed that there's only a shower downstairs? A nice shower. A huge tiled shower with lots of shower heads, but still a shower."

I'd forgotten. "Shower." I gave him a forced smile. "That's what I meant." I took three more steps before he said my name.

"Reese, you're more than welcome to use my tub. It's a big soaker tub, and I rarely ever use it. I'll shower in my other bathroom."

"No. A shower is great. A shower is what I meant."

"Well, if you change your mind, the offer stands."

"Thanks," I called without looking back as I headed around to the side of the house. "I'm good. Have fun on your date."

CHAPTER TEN

I SHOWERED when I really wanted a bath.

I skipped Bible study because I just needed to sulk.

I stayed up way too late, making a gazillion trips to the top of the stairs to press my ear to the door, listening for any sign of Fisher.

By one in the morning, I gave up and went to bed, a little irritated that he either wasn't coming home at all or was out so late ... on a work night. People who were not morning people needed to get to bed earlier. My grand-parents went to bed at eight every night, and they were always a bucket full of smiles in the morning.

Thursday morning, I woke to a text from Fisher.

You're working in the office with Hailey today. Hopefully you can drive yourself. If not, call me.

What did that mean? Did he not come home the previous night? Was he out too late? Hung over? At *her* place? Naked in her bed?

NO!

I really needed to get control of my thoughts. I should have gone to Bible study instead of going out of my mind eavesdropping on Fisher when he wasn't home.

"Good morning. How's the hand?" Hailey asked as I set my backpack next to her desk. "You can sit at Boss-man's desk. I have a bunch of invoices for you to sort through today. Just set his shit in a pile on the floor."

"My hand is fine. Thanks." I gathered the papers and blueprints on his desk and set them on the floor in the corner. "Have you seen him this morning?" I asked.

"Not yet. I assumed you two would be riding together."

"He had a date last night." I poured myself a cup of coffee. "I don't think he came home."

"Oh ..." She lifted her eyebrows and grinned. "Go, Fisher, go."

No. Why did she say that? Maybe because she had sexual fantasies about other men, not her boss. I envied her. It's not like I wanted to pine for Fisher like a pathetic teenager.

Teenager.

Oh my gosh ... it wasn't until the word popped into my brain that I realized I had let the whole "adult" thing go to my head. Sure. Eighteen was legally adulthood, but I was eighteen which meant I was a still a teenager.

That seemed so wrong, to be a teenaged adult. Like an oxymoron.

Fisher got laid by a real woman. A non-teenaged adult woman. What was I thinking? And why couldn't I stop?

"Yay, Fisher," I said, lacking all enthusiasm just like the fake smile I tossed in Hailey's direction as I carried my coffee to Fisher's desk.

"I wonder if it was the orthodontist? Meghan or ... Keegan? I can't remember, but if it's Jason's friend from high school, then it's the orthodontist."

An orthodontist. How was I supposed to compete with that? Highly educated, self-sufficient, real adult orthodontist. Or ... teenaged adult who cried because she scraped her knees and got a little nail prick?

"Think you can hold things down for thirty minutes while I run a quick errand?"

My head snapped up at Hailey, and I nodded quickly. "Um ... sure."

"Cool. So here are the invoices. Just sort them by distributer then alphabetize them. They've all been scanned and saved on the computer, but Fisher likes hardcopy backups to everything."

"Got it."

"Can I get you anything while I'm out? A bagel? Better coffee?"

"I'm good. Thanks."

Twenty minutes into sorting invoices, the office door opened and *Bossman* sauntered inside carrying a to-go cup of coffee. "That's my desk."

"How was your date?" I kept sorting, refusing to look at him.

No need to see his messy hair, unfairly sexy body in dark jeans, boots, and a black tee with his construction logo on the back. I didn't care about his square jaw and sinful smile.

Nope.

I had stuff to sort.

"Fine. Where's Hailey? Where's my stuff?"

"On the floor." My hands kept sorting papers, but I stopped focusing on any sort of alphabetical order.

"Hailey or my stuff?"

I didn't want to grin, but I did. "Your stuff."

"And Hailey?" He squeezed behind me, pushing his desk chair (and me) forward an inch or so.

"Errands."

"What errands?" He hunched down and thumbed through the stack of papers I'd set on the floor.

"I didn't ask. How was the concert?" I was pretty proud of myself for slipping that in like it was no big deal.

"I said fine."

"No. You said your date was fine. I asked about the concert."

"It was fine too."

"You're such a guy." I rolled my eyes and sneaked a quick peek at him over my shoulder.

"Well, yes, last I checked, I was a guy." Pulling out a manila folder, he stood.

"Hailey thought your date was an orthodontist."

"She thought right."

I felt six inches tall sitting in his desk chair while discussing his date ... that date who had him *all* night.

"How was Bible study? Did you go out for ice cream?"

"It was fine." I covered my face with one hand and sighed. "It was ... well, I didn't go."

Fisher chuckled and rested his butt on the edge of his

desk, opening the folder. "Did you just try to lie? Are you incapable of lying?"

"No. Trust me. I can lie just fine. I just don't like to do it."

"Then why lie about last night. Why *try* to lie about it?"

"Because I don't want you to think that I didn't go because of my hand. I just didn't feel like it. That's all."

"Hey, you don't owe me an explanation."

I continued alphabetizing invoices while he remained leaning against the desk, close to me. So close I could smell his woodsy soap mixing with the coffee he set on the desk next to him. "So ... you must have been up early this morning. Since you uh ... texted me to drive myself. Were you meeting with the plumber?"

"No."

No? NO?

That was it. One word. No additional details. No explanation as to why he asked me to drive myself to work.

"You never sent me the photos from our trip into the mountains."

"Oh. Sorry." Without taking his attention away from the contents of the folder, he slipped his phone out of his pocket and unlocked it before handing it to me. "Go for it."

I had Fisher's phone. It felt oddly personal like I had his whole world in the palm of my hand.

Contacts.

Text messages.

Photos.

Apps—which could tell me a lot about a person.

I behaved despite my mind whirling with a million possibilities. Opening his photos app, I quickly found the ones he took of me and us because they were the most recent. My gaze flitted from his phone screen to him several times to see if he was paying any attention to me.

He wasn't.

I airdropped the photos to my phone, then I may have accidentally swiped up a few times to get a quick glimpse of other photos he'd taken. Most were from job sites.

"Did you get them?"

I jumped and fumbled his phone, trying to hand it back to him. "Yeah, thanks."

"Sure." He stood and tossed the folder back onto the pile on the floor. "Well, I'm out of here. I'll catch you later."

It killed me, as in physical pain clawing at my chest, to not say more to him.

Where was he?

Did he sleep with her?

If so, why?

Was it his MO to sleep with women on first dates?

Was he planning on seeing her—having sex with her—again?

So many crazy, irrational, and completely inappropriate questions chased each other in my head. But all I could do was smile like a sane person, like the adult teenager I was, even if a streak of insanity buzzed just beneath the surface.

OVER THE NEXT WEEK, Fisher tortured me by mowing the lawn without a shirt, eyeing me way too long in all the wrong places, and dropping slightly crude remarks at every chance. Then he'd buy me coffee and treat me like an equal for two seconds before the torture started all over again. I looked forward to every morning, even if all we did was banter and sling questionably appropriate comments at each other. (He was such a bad influence). And I liked the evenings when I'd take a walk only to return to him washing something in the driveway or watering plants—sans a shirt.

The wandering eyes.

The cocky smiles.

The slow wetting and rubbing of his lips together.

It felt like a game of cat and mouse, but I wasn't always sure who was the cat and who was the mouse.

The evenings I didn't like were the ones when he was gone ... the nights I assumed he was with the orthodontist. Every cell in my eighteen-year-old brain hyper-focused on my new crush in bed with another woman. Despite its extreme irrationality, it sucked.

And it sucked the most at my first party. Well, my first adult party at Hailey's house on Friday night. There must have been fifty people there, and she called it a small gathering. A lot of the guys from work showed up, some with wives, girlfriends, and even a few with boyfriends. That made me a little uneasy, and I hated that it made me uneasy. Fisher's words replayed in my head. *Now you can fucking think for yourself.*

That was hard for me. All my beliefs seemed to be interwoven with scripture, parental lectures, or sermons.

"Hey, you came." Jason playfully elbowed me before taking a swig of beer as we stood on the deck overlooking the backyard cluttered with people, yard games, kegs, and loud music.

"Hey, yeah. Good to see you again."

He wore cleaner jeans and a crisp white tee hugging his monstrous chest and arms covered in tattoos. "How's the hand?"

I laughed a little, holding up my hand with the tiny Band-aid. "Fine. Clumsy me."

"Drink?" He held his beer bottle toward me.

More shared germs? Did I want to swap saliva with Jason?

"Bossman!" Hailey hollered from the backyard.

I glanced over the railing to Fisher ... and his date. Hailey handed both of them red plastic cups of beer. Dr. Smile was a petite blonde with normal sized arms and legs—and of course perfect teeth. Mine were fairly perfect, but a few lower teeth had shifted after I stopped wearing my retainer. And she was at least a solid C-cup.

"Where did you get the bottled beer?" I asked Jason, feeling out of sorts with my emotions. I shouldn't have hopped on the back of Fisher's bike. That trip to the mountains messed with me.

"I brought my own beer. Don't care much for keg piss."

Staring at the amber bottle in his hand, I battled wrong and right in my head. Then I gave Fisher and his date another quick glance. She slid her hand around his waist.

"Maybe just a sip." I took the bottle from Jason's hand

and brought it to my lips taking a whiff. It smelled like beer. I had no idea if beers had different aromas like wine. Taking a hesitant sip, I let the slow mingling of carbonation and alcohol coat my mouth. It didn't burn like I'd imagined. Maybe that was just hard liquor. It didn't exactly taste great either.

"Let's head down," Jason said as he nodded toward the stairs.

I held the bottle out to him.

"Keep it. I'll get another from my cooler."

"I don't need it."

He chuckled, descending the stairs. "Nobody does, but it's a party, Reese."

My grip on the bottleneck tightened as I followed him down the stairs. Most of the other women were wearing nicer sun dresses or sexy shorts and cute sandals. I wore shorts that nearly hit my knees and a T-shirt that I was pretty sure was a unisex shirt with a big smiley face on it.

Minimal makeup.

No nail polish.

And my hair looked like I'd done nothing more than comb it and let it air dry after a shower ... because that's what I did.

Straight brown hair doing nothing special. No body. No highlights. No funky pink streaks. Could I have been more basic?

"Yo, Bossman," Jason said.

Fisher and his date turned around. He smiled at Jason, but his smile faded a fraction when he saw me standing a few feet back, clutching a beer bottle to my chest. "Having..." he eyed the bottle for a little too long before lifting his gaze to mine "...a good time?" That look, it was too parental.

Too challenging.

Too condescending.

Long-armed, tiny-boobed, fake-adult Reese.

Lifting the bottle to my lips, I nodded. "I believe I am."

Fisher shifted his focus from me to Jason. "Did you give her the beer?"

Jason shrugged. "Maybe."

Fisher nodded slowly. "She's eighteen, which means she's officially your responsibility."

No he didn't. He didn't just call me out like a child.

Jason turned and gave me a sad smile. "Sorry. I'm not in the mood to babysit tonight." He plucked the bottle of beer from my hand.

I was so embarrassed; I wanted to kill Fisher. Then I wanted to cry because it sucked being an adult, only not really a full adult. Jason disappeared, leaving me with an empty hand in front of Satan's awful son and his girlfriend.

"Reese, this is Teagan. Teagan, this is Reese. She and her mom rent out my basement."

I didn't rent squat. But it was *so* generous of him to make me look grown up in front of her after calling out my age and apparent need for a babysitter.

"Nice to meet you." She smiled instead of offering to shake my hand, probably because one of her hands held a beer and the other was still around Fisher's waist.

The ugly jealousy felt terrible. How did I get such an

extreme crush on a guy ten years older than me in a matter of weeks? It just added to all the other reasons I wasn't a mature adult yet. I felt certain Teagan didn't get stupid crushes on guys who were out of her league. Then again, she was a beautiful doctor with a great job, great hair, and great boobs. No guy was out of her league.

"Nice to meet you too."

Fisher took a swig of his beer, and I wanted to knock it out of his hand.

"Well, have fun. I'm going to grab something to eat." I wasn't hungry. It was code for "I'm leaving."

"You too," Teagan said. She sounded nice. She worked with a lot of kids, giving them great smiles. Of course she was nice. He deserved her.

I sulked my way through the crowd in the house, but not rushing anything to avoid looking like I was leaving. A few people were just outside the front door vaping— and probably smoking pot too—but they ignored me when I held my phone up to my ear, pretending to talk to someone.

When I got home, I opened a bag of cheese curls and ate half the bag. Then I downloaded some new music to my phone.

Matt Maeson.

After listening to several songs, I settled on "Tribulation." It was fitting in some ways. Tortured love.

Twenty minutes later, I knew every word.

Thirty minutes later, I ascended the stairs. And not surprisingly, he didn't lock his side of the door. I opened it slowly, even though I knew he wasn't home. I stole a banana and ate it. Then I opened the fridge door and frowned at all the peanut butter he had in the door. At least four jars. He must have been scared of a shortage. On the bottom shelf, there was beer. Lots of beer.

Biting my lips together for a few seconds while tapping my nails on the door, I contemplated borrowing ... *taking* just one beer.

One beer led to two beers, and I was buzzed. And it was good. I bobbed around his house holding my phone with music blaring while looking at photos of people I imagined were his family. Then I stumbled upon his bedroom.

"Oh, Fisher ..." I giggled, swaying a bit while I sauntered into his bedroom. "You make your bed like a good boy." I laughed some more and plopped onto my tummy, burying my nose in his pillow. "You smell sooo good." When I was convinced I'd sucked all of his scent from his pillow, I rolled to the side and right onto the floor. "Ouch ..."

More laughter.

More swaying as I lumbered to my feet and continued my self-guided tour, which led me to his bathroom. "There you are ... you big, beautiful tub."

I sighed. His bathroom was ginormous. And he had a wall of switches, at least twenty switches for all kinds of lighting around the sink, the shower, his wall of wardrobe cabinets, by my feet, even under the toilet.

"Too much." I pushed all the bottom buttons which turned off all the lights, leaving only natural moonlight coming from the big window by the tub and the two skylights. "That's better." I stripped, stepped into the soaker tub, and started the water, easing onto my butt with no grace. When the water reached an inch below my neck, I shut it off. "Where's my music?" I realized I'd left my phone on the bed or maybe on the floor, but the music had stopped anyway.

Closing my eyes, I enjoyed the silence ... and my buzz. The silence was interrupted with voices. I had enough sense to kind of care, but not enough sense to get out of the tub or say anything. Instead, I held still, really still ... and listened.

"It's beautiful, Fisher. You're incredibly talented. How long did it take you to build it?"

Teagan.

"About a year. I didn't rush anything, and I had some other jobs I was working on too." His voice got closer.

My senses ... my fight or flight? Yeah, they had the night off.

The lights turned on. All of them. There must have been a master switch. It was a little blinding at the moment. I squinted.

"Jesus ... what are you ..." Fisher turned his head like a real gentleman. No wonder Teagan liked him.

I liked him too.

"Oh! Reese!" Teagan jumped and turned as well. "Why is she in your tub?" she asked Fisher in a tone that made me think she wasn't too pleased.

"You said anytime ... I could use your tub anytime." I chuckled, cupping my hands together at the surface of the water and squirting it in different directions. "You didn't say I could drink your beer, so ... oops. I'll pay ya back." Another giggle.

"Fisher ..." Teagan's voice wasn't friendly like her

smile, like she worked with kids all day. It was really grumpy. Did he offer his tub to her too?

"I'll get out in a minute. When my head stops spinning."

The door shut, and I no longer saw them, but I heard the murmuring of their voices, and it wasn't good. A few moments later, the door opened again. It was Fisher, but he wasn't being as much of a gentleman. No hiding his eyes.

"Reese ..." he said in a slow and steady tone like I was that deer in the headlights he talked about.

"Fish-er ... I like that name. At first ... it was weird, like what were your parents thinking? But I like it now. A little too much. Ya know?"

"I *don't* know." He made his way to the tub, plucking my clothes from the floor one piece at a time. He sat on the edge of the tub with his back to me, holding my clothes in his hands as he drew in a deep breath and let it out slowly in a sound. My fuzzy head had trouble deciphering it. A grumble or a growl?

"Are you mad at me?"

Shaking his head, he pinched the bridge of his nose. "I don't know what I am."

"Is it the beer?"

He didn't respond.

"The bathtub? Were you just kidding about me using it whenever I wanted to?"

No response.

"I think I need a towel."

He nodded toward a tall stack of drawers by the sink on the opposite side of the bathroom. "Bottom drawer."

It might have been his proximity or the shock of him and Teagan showing up so early, but my buzz was quickly wearing off. "Aren't you going to get it for me?"

His lips twisted and he glanced over his shoulder at me. My hands moved to my breasts, and I crossed my legs as a big fat dose of reality began to register. The naked fisherman had seen *me* naked. Not briefly. He took his time, picking up my clothes while inching his way to the tub and my fully exposed body.

No bubbles.

No effort to cover myself.

Nothing.

"I'm not," he said.

"Why not?" My voice shook a bit. Sobriety stole the moment.

"Because I think you need to get it yourself."

"Are you going to leave now?"

"Nope." His gaze slid down my body.

My hands gripped my breasts harder as I squeezed my legs together tighter.

It was so wrong. *He* was so wrong.

Drawing my knees to my chest, I rocked forward and stood, lifting one leg out of the tub followed by the other, inches from Fisher. On a suffocating swallow, I closed my eyes and took a deep breath. He had an unobstructed view of my naked backside. I didn't have enough hands to cover everything.

"I thought you were a gentleman," I mumbled, making the walk of shame to the stack of drawers and hunching down instead of bending over to retrieve a towel.

"Why did you think that?"

Wrapping the towel around my body, I turned toward him. "Because you looked away when you first came into the bathroom."

"That was for Teagan. A gentleman doesn't stare at a naked woman in front of his date."

"So you're a gentleman for her, but not for me?"

He narrowed his eyes a second before returning a slow nod. "That's accurate."

Stupid fu—fudger.

"Because of my age?"

"Maybe."

"You're a real butt. Did you know that?"

"I know."

"So what's the point of all this?" I marched toward him and snatched my clothes from his hand.

"I need you to know that when you make poor decisions, men will take advantage of you."

"You said I could use your bathtub."

"Not drunk."

Hugging my clothes to my chest while keeping a firm grip on the towel, I frowned. "Well, if you're done teaching me ridiculous lessons, then I'm going to bed." Pivoting, I shuffled my feet to the bathroom door.

"I'm not done teaching."

I stopped, but I didn't look back at him.

"What now?"

"You need to bring your own towel. That one's mine. Leave it right where you're standing."

"You're a perv. How do you think Rory will react

when she finds out you were being so perverted with her daughter?"

"I don't know, but make sure you start the story with the part where you stole beer from my fridge."

Fucker!

It felt so good to scream it in my head; I just wished my body would have cooperated and screamed it to his face. He knew I'd never tell Rory about the night's events. So he took every opportunity to embarrass me.

"I'm filing a sexual harassment complaint against my boss on Monday."

"You do that." He was a steel beam, an immovable boulder. Always one step ahead of me.

CHAPTER ELEVEN

I SPENT Saturday in shameful regret, not venturing out once.

Sunday morning I bolted to the Outback to go to church and pray ... lots of prayers. And when I returned, God had answered at least one of my prayers: Fisher wasn't outside.

Monday morning, around five-thirty, my luck ran out.

Fisher: You're with me today. We'll leave in twenty minutes.

Someone might as well have said, "You've been found guilty. We're executing you in twenty minutes."

I wore my hair down to hide my face as much as possible. With not a second to spare, I dragged my feet up to the driveway and climbed into the truck, keeping my backpack between my legs on the floor instead of tossing it in the back where I might have accidentally made eye contact with Satan's son.

"Morning." I could feel his gloating expression. His amusement.

"Morning," I mumbled, keeping my head down.

"Listen, there's no need to drag your weekend to work with you on Monday. What happened, happened. No big deal. We move on."

My head snapped up, jaw open. "No big deal? You molested me with your eyes! I wouldn't call that no big deal."

Fisher's molesting eyes flared, a new kind of shock I hadn't seen on him before. I may have spent the whole weekend letting my emotions build into something a little ... explosive.

"You know what your problem is?"

My chin tipped up as my eyes narrowed. Yeah, I knew what my problem was ... *him*.

"You need to get laid. And so help me, if you even think of telling Rory I said that, I will tell her everything."

"I ..." My jaw flapped a few times. I couldn't believe he said it. If I would have had a hundred guesses as to what I imagined he thought my problem was, lack of sex would not have been on that list. "That ... you ..." My head wouldn't stop shaking side to side. "I do not need to get laid. You need to stop being so crude. Some people take sex seriously, not like a game to play with anyone willing to have it with them. It's supposed to be something beautiful between two people who love each other."

"You've clearly never had an orgasm."

"I have too." Once, by accident. And it irked me that he had a way of keeping me on the defensive. I wasn't proud of my accidental orgasm, but I felt the need to own it with him accusing me of needing one.

"Liar." He smirked.

"You can't call me a liar about this when you've known me for a few weeks. You don't know anything about me and my past."

"Did you give it to yourself or did someone else give it to you?"

"This ... this is a stupid topic and really inappropriate. You're my boss, driving me to work."

"I'll be your boss when we get there."

"Then let's go." I faced forward and folded my arms over my chest.

At the first job, he inspected the previous day's work and talked to a few of the workers. The second stop was a meeting with potential clients at an empty lot. I waited in the truck. We grabbed a fast-food lunch (unfortunately not Mickey D's) and headed to the final stop of the afternoon. It was a staircase he'd been working on for a client, but they weren't home.

"Did you buy these?" I asked, running my finger over the intricate details of a spindle.

"Nope. I made them." He slipped on his tool belt.

Although I kinda hated him from our morning conversation, I couldn't not appreciate how sexy he looked in a tool belt.

The scruff on his face a little longer.

His shirt nice and snug in the chest but loose over his tight abs.

"Are you serious?"

He glanced up, gathering the spindles in his arms to

haul them inside the house from the garage. "Why are you constantly doubting my skills?"

Because he was the most amazing man I had ever met, but I couldn't tell him that. I couldn't hand him the last drop of my dignity because I didn't trust him with it.

"I'm just used to seeing you walk around staring at other people's work or barking orders. I have yet to see you in action."

"Well, grab the rest of those spindles, and I'll show you some action."

I carried the spindles into the house.

I handed him tools.

I ran and grabbed stuff from his truck.

I got him ice water.

I answered his phone when people called for him.

I watched Fisher Mann feed my obsession with him to the point where I knew no other man would compare, which meant I'd die a single and barren virgin. Occasionally, he'd lift the front of his T-shirt to wipe the sweat from his face. And on more than one of those occasions, he caught me gawking at his abs while wetting my lips.

"I'm going to start deducting pay from your check if you keep stealing free peeks at my body."

I cleared my throat and glanced at his phone. "Hailey just texted you. She said Brad's crew is done. She wants to know if you're coming by the office before you go home."

"No."

I risked a glance up at him. "You want me to just say no?"

Sliding a pencil behind his ear, he lifted his gaze to

me from three steps down. "To Hailey, yes, I want you to say no."

"Who else would I say no to?"

He shrugged. "I'm hoping that's your last no of the day."

What did he mean by that?

I replied with a "no." Then I watched Fisher finish the railing. At some point I started nibbling at my fingernails; I wasn't a nail chewer.

"Grab the vac and clean the dust that didn't stay on the drop cloths."

"Um ... okay." I jumped to attention and did what he asked me to do while he loaded his tools in the trailer parked in their driveway.

"Are you done?" I handed him the vac.

"Almost. I'll finish up tomorrow afternoon." He closed the trailer and locked it.

"Think you can teach me something?" I asked with my hands in my pockets.

Fisher closed his tailgate and walked to my side of the truck, standing uncomfortably close to me. "Oh, Reese ... I think I can teach you a lot."

Choking on my words for several seconds, I coughed and shook my head. "A-about construction. Can you teach me how to cut and nail things?"

The grin that climbed up his face made me melt like M&Ms on a hundred-degree day. "We might wait on the cutting, but I think I can show you how I nail things."

Another gulp clogged my throat. "I'd ... um ... I'd like that."

"Oh..." his grin did the impossible and grew even bigger "...I have no doubt you'd like it."

Oh my gosh ...

I didn't think he was talking about construction. And I wondered if he understood that I *was* talking about it.

"Well..." I lifted my shoulders and shoved my hands even farther into my pockets "...time to call it a day?"

He eyed me with his signature predatory, ready-to-pounce-on-its-prey look for several seconds. "Definitely."

WHEN WE PULLED into the driveway after a ride home with no conversation, only music—his sexually explicit music—I jumped out before he got the truck into *Park*.

"Goodnight. See you tomorrow." I ran—sprinted—to the back of the house and fumbled the key with shaky hands. Rocks crushed under big boots—Fisher following me.

"Open!" I begged the key and my hands to work together.

Just as he turned the corner, it opened.

"Are you running from me?"

"Nope." I slid inside and shut the door behind me, locked it too. On a sigh of relief, I turned and made a straight line to my bedroom.

Click.

The door unlocked and opened. Of course he had a key. It was his house. The door clicked again when he shut it behind him.

"Whatcha need?" I asked with the last little bit of

breath left in my lungs. His proximity made breathing so hard. It made my heart work even harder. It made my thoughts cross lines that should not have been crossed.

"Why are you running from me?" He was right at my back.

I forced myself to turn toward him, and it took superhero strength. He stepped toward me.

I stepped back.

We did this dance until a wall stopped my retreat.

He pressed his hands to the wall above my head, and my heart rate spiked a thousand percent. The air exchange in my lungs sounded like that of someone finishing a marathon.

Was I reading him wrong?

It wouldn't have been the first time I got it wrong and felt like a fool. But that moment felt different.

The look in his eyes wasn't the same.

The part of his lips.

The increased intensity of his own chest rising and falling.

"You can't have my virginity," I whispered.

It took him a few more breaths to respond. And when he did, it blew my mind.

"What can I have?" he whispered back.

In that most unexpected moment, my foolish, adult teenaged heart cracked open and made room for Fisher Mann. And I immediately wondered how long it took to fall in love.

Years?

Weeks?

Seconds?

Did common sense and timelines rule emotions?

"What do you want?" My words were weak when I wanted—more than anything—to sound brave.

Something so very tiny shifted along his face, like he was smiling without actually smiling. His right hand slid off the wall and cupped my jaw, his thumb teasing my bottom lip that trembled like the rest of me.

"A-are you g-going to kiss me?"

His lips pulled into a hint of amusement. "I was thinking about it." Fisher's patience killed me, completely slayed me. It was as if he had to solve the world's problems in his head before he kissed me.

But I didn't want to be a problem of the world. I wanted to be the girl—the woman—he kissed on a Monday night for no good reason. Not everything in life needed an explanation. Couldn't we steal a few seconds, a kiss, without accountability?

"Will you be done thinking about it anytime soo—"

Fisher kissed me.

It wasn't hard or rushed. It didn't make me feel inexperienced. And it didn't feel wrong.

After a few seconds, he pulled back an inch, maybe two. I sucked in a quick breath, and he kissed me again. It was just like the first kiss.

Perfect.

And just like the first one, he pulled back, but this time he smiled. My own smile came to life too, big and embarrassing.

Every imaginable "what-if" dominated my thoughts. What were we doing? Did those two kisses mean the world to me and nothing to him?

Seventy-two hours earlier, he'd been upstairs showing Teagan the house he built. And she loved it. She didn't question his abilities with a "seriously" because she was too mature for that.

What was he doing kissing *me*?

"I'm going to shower and grab dinner. I'll see you in the morning. Five-forty-five?"

I nodded, still wearing that impossibly huge smile.

He disappeared from my bedroom, his footsteps fading as he climbed the stairs.

CHAPTER TWELVE

I DIDN'T SLEEP that night. I tried, but I couldn't sleep after that kiss. Well, those two kisses. It took too long to figure out why he did it. And I never came up with a good explanation.

My trek around the house to the garage was the longest walk of my life. I couldn't breathe. It was eerily similar to how I felt the previous night. Would he be different with me? Regretful? Act like it never happened? Kiss me again?

I crossed my fingers for the third kiss. Which was why I brushed twice, flossed, and rinsed with mouthwash for a full minute. Just as I rounded the corner to an empty driveway, my phone chimed.

Fisher: You're with Hailey today. Had to go out of town to pick up some things.

Not even a "good morning." No XO. And not a single

emoji. Did he not know how to use emojis? It was the most emotionless, lackluster text ever. It wasn't the text you sent someone you'd kissed.

I typed my reply a dozen times and erased all of them. My drafts contained words like "good morning" and emojis. Hearts and kisses. Maybe it was a dream. Maybe it was another cruel lesson.

Reese: OK

As heartbroken as I was to be just as emotionless, I felt a sense of pride and maybe even a sense of maturity for keeping it professional. When I got to the office with my burning tongue (a minute of swishing mouthwash was *a lot*), Hailey greeted me with her usual bubbly smile and a stack of things to sort through. I got the feeling nothing had been sorted until Fisher hired me.

"Is it the weekend yet? Why did Monday feel like the longest day ever? It should be Thursday not Tuesday."

"Mondays aren't always bad." I shrugged, depositing my backpack on the floor and grabbing coffee.

"Are you ..." She tilted her head. "Blushing?"

"No." I dipped my chin and dove into the messy piles of papers.

"You are. Did you have a hot date last night? A *Monday* date?"

"No." I laughed like it was ridiculous. "No date."

"Okay then. I noticed you left the party early. But so did Bossman and his new girlfriend. She was all over him. I imagine he had quite the Friday night. Was he in a good mood yesterday morning?"

"Um ..." I tried to sound as aloof as possible. "Yeah, he seemed fine."

"Did he mention her? Is it serious? This time of year, I only get to see him for a few seconds a day, at the most. He's always on the go and constantly running thirty minutes behind."

"He didn't mention her. I don't think it's serious, but I'm not really sure."

"Why do you think it's not serious? Did he say something?"

"No. Just a feeling. I'm not sure. Maybe guys don't say much even if they do have serious feelings about someone. Like ... they probably don't send gushing texts or use a bunch of emojis."

"Ha! Not my ex. He sent me the dirtiest texts all the time with a string of eggplant and peach emojis. I bet Bossman sends her dirty texts. I can see him having a dirty side."

Hailey wasn't helping my emotional situation one bit. *Was* he sending Teagan texts? Were they still together? Did he play me? The more I thought about it, I felt so played by him. He and Teagan were having a good laugh over my foolishness.

I spent the better part of my day silently fuming while sorting and alphabetizing invoices and receipts. Even the lunch Hailey brought me was left half-uneaten because I couldn't stomach it *and* the very real possibility that I was a pawn.

"I'm taking off," I said after placing the last sorted pile into the file box.

"Okay. Have a good night. Will I see you tomorrow?"

"Who knows. I never seem to know myself until the last possible minute."

"Sounds about right." Hailey laughed as I pushed through the door.

On the way home, I stopped at the grocery store and grabbed a few essentials. Then I made the short drive home, parking across the street just as Fisher pulled into the driveway on his motorcycle with a woman on the back.

Unbelievable.

My heart deflated as a cynical voice in my head laughed at me. I grabbed my two bags of groceries from the back and marched past the driveway to the path leading down the hill, not giving a single glance in the direction of Fisher and the dark blonde as they removed their helmets.

"Reese?" he called.

I walked faster.

"Reese?" His voice and the rest of his terrible self followed me.

I unlocked the door and picked up the bags, continuing into the basement like I didn't hear him or see him. Then I told myself not to cry. I even prayed for my tears to stay in check. Crying after one kiss (well, two) was something an eighteen-year-old virgin would do. And even if that was me, I wasn't offering that version to Fisher. Not anymore. He couldn't be trusted with my heart. I wouldn't have trusted him to hold my kite string on a breezy day.

"Why do you make me chase you?"

I hoisted the bags onto the counter and released a slow breath while plastering on a fake smile as I turned toward him. "The question is ... why are you always chasing me? I'm just the *girl* living in your basement. The employee you see several times a week. Seems silly that you're even giving me the time of day right now when you have some blonde waiting for you to ... I don't know ..." Shrugging, I tapped my chin. "Kiss her. Or do more than that."

Resting one hand on his hip and his other hand rubbing the back of his neck, he eyed me with no regret. "Are you done?"

My frown deepened. "Yes."

"I'm not going to kiss the blonde because she's my sister, so that would be weird. Occasionally, she likes to ride with me. That's her red Honda you parked next to."

After processing his explanation, I shrugged. "What about Teagan?"

"What about her?" He unzipped his jacket.

"Are you still with her?"

A slow grin made its way up his face as he shook his head. "I'm not sure I was ever 'with' her, but she's not okay being 'with' me since you were in my bathtub."

Was I a consolation prize? Since the beautiful doctor didn't want to be with him, he got the naked girl in his bathtub? Was I even that? I felt certain he'd had sex with her, yet he didn't think they were together? What could a simple kiss possibly have meant to him?

"Sorry. I shouldn't have taken a bath in your tub." Pivoting, I unloaded my groceries.

"I disagree. I gave you permission. I'm still giving you permission. Do you want to take a bath? Right now?"

Couldn't he let me be mad for a few seconds? No.

Releasing an unavoidable laugh, I shook my head while closing the fridge. "I don't want or need a bath right now. And where's your sister?"

"She had to leave." He slipped off his jacket and tossed it on the sectional.

I folded the paper bags, eyeing his moves as he made his way to me. A wall of shields lifted around my heart as an inner voice chanted, *No. No. No.*

"Did you get a lot of work done today?" He gripped my waist, and my hands flew to his shoulders because I wasn't sure what he was doing. Then he lifted me onto the counter and stepped into the space between my spread legs.

Just like the previous night, everything in my body kicked into overdrive. "I ..." Swallowing hard, I gave him a nervous smile. "I sorted and filed today."

"That's good." He brushed my hair away from my shoulders and dipped his face into my neck.

I stiffened feeling the warmth of his breath spread along my skin. My hands slid from his shoulders to his hair, searching for control. If I didn't want him to kiss my neck, I could have yanked him away.

But I did.

I wanted to be kissed where I'd never been kissed before. Boys had kissed me, but I'd never *made out* with anyone. No kisses on my neck. No hickeys.

Two things happened at the exact same time, and I

didn't know where to give my attention because they both set me ablaze and out of my mind. Fisher's hands shifted from my hips to my legs, his thumbs pressing on my inner thighs *really* close to my crotch as his lips pressed to my neck for only a second before he licked ... *he licked* a path to my ear.

A sharp, audible gasp left my parted lips just as he sucked my earlobe into his mouth and released it a second later by dragging his teeth along it. *All* the weird things happened at once.

Heat in my cheeks worked its way down to *everywhere.*

Pressure built between my legs.

I swear it felt like I'd peed a little, but I knew better.

Heaviness in my breasts.

Even my nipples felt different—sensitive as they pressed against the fabric of my bra.

Copious amounts of saliva required constant swallowing to keep from drooling. I was afraid to be touched anymore yet *needed* to be touched. It was so foreign and impossible to articulate even to myself.

My grip on his hair tightened which made him chuckle, kissing along my jaw. I didn't find anything funny. I was crawling out of my skin in the most wicked way.

"F-Fisher ..." I closed my eyes because everything he did made the room spin.

When his mouth covered mine, he didn't kiss me slowly like the first time. He kissed me like I'd always imagined a *man* kissing a *woman.*

This time he teased my lips with his tongue, tasting me like he'd tasted my neck and my ear. Then he kissed me hard again, and the foreign invasion of his tongue sliding deep into my mouth ... well ... I liked it.

So much.

Too much.

It felt sinful, but I didn't want him to stop.

For a few seconds, I wasn't sure what I was supposed to do with my tongue, but he showed me. Teased it. Teased me. And of all the lessons Fisher had tried to teach me up until that point, kissing was my favorite.

I was a good student. An eager student.

Then my phone rang, and I jumped, tearing myself away from him. I fished it out of my purse, a few inches away from where I sat on the counter. "Rory," I said on a labored breath while I stared at the screen.

As I swiped the screen and brought it to my ear, Fisher stepped back, rubbing his well-kissed lips together while ...

Oh my gosh!

He adjusted himself, and it gave me a moment's pause, a little shock. I wasn't experienced, but I also wasn't stupid. I knew he was adjusting his *erection*, but for some reason I still felt a little shocked that kissing *me* did that to him.

Seeing my shock, he rolled his eyes and murmured, "Don't look so surprised."

I swallowed and cleared my throat, a tiny smile (a little triumphant) stole my lips as I found my voice. "Hey!"

"Hi. You sound happy. A good day?" Rory asked.

"Yeah, it was ... fine."

Fisher grabbed his jacket from the sectional and walked up the stairs. No look back. No kisses blown in my direction. I realized it was his way of giving me some privacy, but it was like the text ... I wanted the emoji, the wink.

Something!

"I have some good news," Rory said, bringing me out of my Fisher bubble.

"Yeah? What's that?"

"Things are going well here. And I'll be home early. Next week."

"That's ... great."

Rory laughed. "Don't sound so enthused. I thought you'd be excited. I felt bad leaving right after we reunited after so long. Once I get home, we'll have all the time we want to do whatever you want. And I have so much to tell you. So many things have been left unsaid for too long."

I wasn't sure what that really meant.

"Have you met any friends at church yet? Or work? Hailey is sweet, isn't she?"

"Yeah, I like her a lot."

"Any boys at church that have caught your attention?"

"Uh ... no." My face wrinkled. "And let's call them guys not boys. I'm not dating twelve-year-olds."

"Sorry. Guys. Young men. And there's no need to rush into anything. You are so young. Love can be incredibly messy and confusing. Find *you* first."

"I'm not lost."

"Reese, you know what I mean."

"I actually like working for Fisher."

"Well, sure. But there's not a lot of room for advancement unless you're going to actually learn to build stuff."

"He's going to teach me some things."

"Oh, he is? Like ... he's going to teach you things about construction?"

"I think so. I asked him if he would."

There was a pause before she replied with a "Huh ... okay. He's a talented guy. I'm sure he's the best one to teach you things."

I couldn't have agreed more.

"Hope you're being smart around his crew. He's employed a lot of single guys who I'm sure will find you quite appealing, but they need to remember you're eighteen."

"Which means I'm an adult."

She sighs. "Yes, but guys with five to ten years on you are not in your best interest right now unless you meet them at church. Alcohol. Sex. Drugs. I just don't want you getting in over your head before you reach twenty. I'd love for you to find a group of friends close to your age."

"You don't need to worry about me."

"I know. I'm not. I'm sure Fisher is keeping a close eye on you whether you like it or not."

"Yes, he's ... all over me." I bit my lips together to hide my grin.

"I knew it. I had a feeling he'd be a big brother to you."

That comparison nauseated me a bit.

"Anyhoo, I'll let you go. Let's talk again this weekend

when we have more time. Maybe video chat so I can see your beautiful face."

"Sounds good."

"Bye, sweetie."

"Bye." I slid my phone onto the counter and stared at the staircase leading to *him*.

I wasn't sure if my mom's call was bad timing on her part or good timing on God's part. And what happened next? Was I supposed to go upstairs to continue what we started? Ending where? In his bed, sans my virginity?

Why did he have to be twenty-eight and my mom's friend/landlord? Why did he have to be twenty-eight with way more life and sexual experience than me?

I grabbed a pre-made salad from the fridge and ate it with a handful of wheat crackers. Then I changed into jogging shorts, tennis shoes, and a tank top. I assumed Fisher was eating dinner or taking a shower, but as I trekked around to the front of the house, I was proven wrong.

Shorts. No shirt (of course). Bare feet.

He used a hose and spray nozzle to water some plants and flowers by his front door. Shirtless Fisher was not a good idea for me. My body still hadn't recovered from his hands on my legs, his thumbs dangerously close to the top of my inner thighs.

"Going for a jog?" he asked.

"Walk." I didn't stop. Stopping was a bad idea.

"Want company?"

Bad idea.

"Okay." I turned with a little too much bounce to my

step, too much enthusiasm in my voice, and way too big of a grin on my face.

Rory was coming home in one week. And I didn't know what that would mean for Fisher and me. I wasn't in his head. I could guess that Rory wouldn't like the idea of me having a physical relationship with a man ten years older than me. And if I was being honest with myself, I wasn't sure how I felt about it either.

Him ... I knew how I felt about him, but I couldn't turn off all common sense, ignore the logistics of our situation. What I wanted and what made sense were not the same things.

"Let me put on some shoes." He shut off the hose and disappeared into the house via the front door.

When he returned with only shoes, still no shirt, I had a mild panic attack. When he grabbed my hand and grinned, it escalated to a moderate panic attack.

"So Rory's coming home in a week," he said as we strolled down the street, my fingers laced with his.

Every new touch brought a new sensation. Holding hands wasn't kissing, yet it felt equally as intimate. I'd held his hand before, during the storm prayer, but this was different. That was an awkward clasp; this was *more*.

"Were you eavesdropping?"

He chuckled. "No. She called me after she called you."

"Oh. Well ... what did you say?"

"I said you'd be excited to see her." He glanced down at me for a second.

"No." I kept my gaze in front of us. "What did you say about us?"

"I told her you have a fantastic mouth and a silky tongue that tastes like heaven, legs that bring me to my knees, and a truckload of attitude."

"Oh my gosh ..." I stopped and turned toward him, yanking my hand away from his.

He narrowed his eyes. "What? I didn't tell her about the bathtub incident or that you stole beer from me."

"Fisher!"

His brow relaxed as that stupid smirk appeared. "Stop being so gullible."

"Ugh! Jerk!" I hammered my fists into his chest.

He grabbed my wrists and held me to him, held my hands to his chest. "I'm not saying a word to her."

I stared at his chest as my fists relaxed, as my palms pressed to his firm muscles and tan skin. Another new and intimate feeling. "I ... I don't think ..." My gaze inched its way up to meet his. "I don't want her to know about ..."

Rolling his lips together, he nodded several times. "Yeah. I don't either. She wouldn't be very happy with me."

Grunting a laugh, I glanced to the side, "Then what's the point of this?"

"I don't know." His honesty bled through his words. It was a brief moment when I didn't feel that Fisher was a decade older, a decade more mature, a decade more experienced.

Maybe connecting with someone didn't have boundaries or timelines. I liked the idea of him feeling as drawn to me as I felt to him. It made me feel like we were equals in this, whatever *this* was.

"So we just ..." I wasn't sure if the thoughts in my mind reflected my true emotions or if I needed to say them to ease his burden. "We just stop when she gets home. Like it never happened."

Twisting his lips, he studied me for a few moments before returning a single slow nod. "Like it never happened."

CHAPTER THIRTEEN

Our "It Never Happened" agreement put a damper on the rest of the evening. We walked. He kissed me goodnight, but it wasn't like the kiss in the kitchen. And that was it.

Friday morning I got a text from Fisher as I was buttering a piece of toast, freshly showered with wet hair, but dressed sans shoes and socks.

Fisher: I'm leaving early for a meeting. You can work in the office if Hailey has stuff for you or you can have the day off.

Immediate let down.

I dropped the butter knife and sprinted to the front of the house without any shoes on just as Fisher started his truck. "Stop!" I smacked my hand on his window.

He jerked his head to the side and started to roll down his window, but I opened his door instead.

"Didn't you get my text?" He squinted.

"Yeah, but didn't you get the memo that Rory's

JEWEL E. ANN

coming home soon?" I stepped up, forcing him to wrap his arm around my waist to keep me from falling out of the truck as I planted my face an inch from his.

He grinned. "Your hair is still wet."

"So?" I whispered, my gaze sliding along his face from his eyes to his full lips so close to mine. "Are you going to kiss me?"

Wetting those full lips, he lifted his right shoulder into a half shrug. "I was thinking about it."

My foolish grin showed all my teeth. "Don't think."

Fisher lifted his other hand and cupped my face, ghosting his thumb along my cheek. "I never do when I'm with you."

A soft breeze blew my wet hair into my face and his, but it didn't stop him from kissing me.

"Now, if you don't get out of my truck," he said releasing my lips, "I'm going to want more."

I giggled, kissing along his cheek as his hand moved from my waist to my butt.

"Like that book *If You Give a Mouse a Cookie*, have you read it?"

I nodded, relishing the feel of his scruffy face against my lips. "Fisher," I whispered at his ear, feeling brave enough to tease his earlobe like he had teased mine with his teeth, "are you saying you want my cookie?"

He laughed, threading fingers through my wet hair and bringing my lips back to his. "Your cookie."

Kiss.

"Your muffins."

Kiss.

I giggled against his mouth.

"I'm going to want the whole fucking bakery."

Kiss.

I wanted his crude and dirty mouth. The kisses … I wanted *all* of his kisses. His laughter. And the way he looked at me like I was the bane of his existence in the most beautiful way.

"Well…" I stepped down, rubbing my lips together to relish the taste of toothpaste, coffee, and the naked fisherman "…you have work. And the bakery is closed."

"Killjoy." He adjusted himself. Again, it made my grin double. "Are you going to work?"

Twisting my lips, I slipped my hands into my pockets. "I figured I would. I haven't called Hailey yet."

"Take the day off."

I frowned. "And do what?"

"Take a bath in my tub."

I giggled. "I just showered."

"Roll around in my bed naked."

Another giggle.

Our banter felt a little wrong—the way *we* felt a little wrong. And that wrong felt perfectly right in that moment. I knew the upside down version of my world wouldn't last long, so I didn't try to fix it. I just let it be whatever it was meant to be.

A little wrong. A little right.

Just … us.

"Bye." I took one step back, then another.

Fisher shook his head, but his smile made the bigger statement as he shut his door and put his truck into drive. I pressed my fingers to my lips and kissed them, blowing it to him. He winked and drove out of the driveway.

"Oh, naked fisherman ... this is going to hurt." I crossed my hands over my chest to comfort my heart. Who was I kidding? I knew I was already too invested in him. And even if I also knew I would have to let us end when Rory returned, it still hurt. Even if Fisher didn't share the same emotions, I knew he would always be my first love—that really good kind of love where my brain had no say. The kind with no logical explanation. The kind that took a special place in my heart as *first*.

God willing, I would go on to love another. Have a family. And die in the arms of my husband. But ... *first* would always be Fisher Mann.

HAILEY WASN'T FEELING WELL, so I went to work. I delivered lunch to the roofers.

"Thanks. You must be Reese." A guy with black hair and a major suntan smiled at me; it made his teeth stark white.

"Yes." I handed him the sacks of food and slipped my hands into the back pockets of my jeans.

He inspected the sacks and smiled a little. I ignored his smirk, his unspoken observation. "I'm Jeremiah. Hailey was telling me about you." He peeled his eyes from the big sacks filled with little sacks.

Jeremiah was hot. That wasn't really up for debate. I could see why Hailey thought I'd like him.

"Funny, she might have mentioned you to me as well." I tried to control my grin.

"I missed her party. I heard you were there ... alone."

"Yeah, I was."

He glanced over my shoulder. "I'd better get to eating my lunch. Bossman's here."

I twisted my body and squinted at the white truck and *Bossman* climbing out. Aviators on. He sipped something red from the straw of a big plastic cup from a convenience store.

"Boss," Jeremiah said.

"Jeremiah," Fisher said in a fairly neutral tone.

"Can I get your number from Hailey later?" Jeremiah asked me as if Fisher wasn't hearing every word. "We could hangout this weekend if you don't have plans. My parents have a place near Breckenridge."

Fisher stepped right next to me. My attention shifted between the two men. I anticipated Fisher saying something, but he didn't. Instead, he sipped his drink like a ten-year-old who just got his favorite beverage and couldn't stop nursing it.

"I ... uh ... have plans already. But thanks." I pressed my lips together so Fisher didn't think I was flirting with Jeremiah.

"Maybe another time?"

I didn't know how to reply, so I nodded just before Jeremiah took off with the bags of food for the crew.

"What are your plans?" Fisher asked, taking a two second break from his straw.

"What are you doing here?"

"Working." He shrugged, taking a longer break from his drink. "What are you doing here?"

"Delivering lunch."

"Did you bring me lunch?"

I shook my head. "I can get you lunch. What do you want?"

"You."

On a nervous laugh, I glanced around to see if anyone heard him. "I don't think I know what that means."

"I think you do." He brushed past me to the crew sitting along the side of the house in the shade, eating their lunch.

I didn't move, mostly because I wasn't sure if he wanted me to head back to the office or get him lunch ... me ... which ... yeah, I had an idea of what that might have entailed. But it wasn't on the menu. However, just thinking about it, made me feel an unfamiliar need, a foreign feeling between my legs, and the recently new wet feeling that wasn't a bladder issue.

It had to be better than men getting untimely erections. After all, I could hide it. Still, I *felt* like everyone who looked at me somehow knew.

As Fisher chatted with his crew, inspected their lunches while shaking his head, I thought long and hard about the definition of sex and temptation. I tried to make a case for sex being only intercourse. That left a lot of options.

"Let's go." Fisher strutted toward me, sipping his red drink.

"What is that?" My nose scrunched.

"Fruit punch and iced tea." He held it out for me.

I eyed the guys eating their lunches, making sure they weren't watching us before I took a sip.

"Don't do that." Fisher grimaced, taking his drink and crossing the street toward his truck.

"Do what?" I followed him since I was parked behind him.

"Lick your lips like that."

I chuckled. "I didn't lick them *like* anything. Why?"

"Because I've been dealing with a fucking hard-on since you climbed into my truck this morning."

Fisher ... so uncensored.

He had no idea—or maybe he did—how much it thrilled me to know that I could slowly unravel him in that way. It made me feel powerful, yet incredibly weak at the same time because I had no clue what to do with my accidental sorcery.

"Do you need a formal apology?"

Fisher opened the door to his truck then rubbed the pads of his fingers over his mouth like he was trying to wipe off his smile before I saw it.

"Say it." Everything I didn't want to hear or see three weeks earlier had become my obsession, my new education, my real-world path to enlightenment. Fisher thought something, but he didn't want to say it. He didn't think I could handle it.

"Nothing."

I took the four long strides to get from my driver's door to his. With my hands on my hips, feeling way more confident than I should have been, I tipped my chin up. "Say. It."

"It's not for your ears." He eyed me, pushing back with as much confidence—probably more.

"That's code for it's inappropriate. Since when has that stopped you before?"

On a small, controlled chuckle, he shook his head and

focused on something over my shoulder, avoiding eye contact with me. "You offered an apology. I was going to say apologies were just lip service. Then I thought ..." He dragged his teeth over his lower lip and met my gaze.

"You thought?"

"I thought lip service wouldn't be the worst thing for my problem."

It took me a few seconds ... then I got it. My eyes widened, brows sliding up my forehead.

Fisher was a little *extra* that day.

If someone wouldn't have coined the term oral sex, oral *sex*, I would have been able to make a better case for it. Why couldn't it have just been oral or something else like ... tonguing? I needed a line, a line I wouldn't cross. And I was okay with moving the line a smidge if I could rationalize something. I couldn't go there ... not yet.

Oh the hypocrisy ...

"Nothing that ends in the word sex. I just can't."

His eyebrows jumped, one slightly higher than the other. Fisher's expressions were so sexy. How did I expect to not perform any act ending in the word "sex" when the man before me was the definition of sex?

"So ... everything else is on the table?"

What was I missing? I knew it would come back to bite me in the backside. Still, I nodded while chewing on the corner of my bottom lip and wringing my hands together.

"Meet you at home." He turned and climbed into his truck.

"Wait ... you're done for the day? It's only one?"

"I am now." He shut his door and started his truck.

CHAPTER FOURTEEN

REGRET MULTIPLIED the closer I got to home.

Home ...

Was that my home? Was my grandparents' house my home? Did I truly have a home? I wasn't sure I'd ever felt so emotionally and physically displaced in my life. Saying I was at a crossroad was an understatement. "Finding myself" was not right either.

Fisher was getting his mail as I slowed to a stop. How could he so casually get his mail and thumb through it? I barely made it home without wrecking Rory's car because my hands were shaking so much. I climbed out and heaved my bag onto my shoulder, taking cautious steps toward the house.

Fisher kept his head bowed at his mail. "I can hear your teeth chattering. Are you cold?"

I clenched my jaw to stop the chattering. "No."

"Having second thoughts about your offer?"

That felt like a direct challenge to my age, my maturity, and my sexual experience. Did he want me to back out? Was this another lesson?

"No." I infused as much confidence as I could muster, which was very little.

"You know ..." He continued into his garage, and I followed, leaving a good ten feet between us. "When you've had sex, things aren't so awkward and scary. I'm not implying you should abandon your morals." He held open the door for me, and I removed my boots and set my bag next to them. "I'm just saying it becomes a little more thrilling and less scary. You know what to expect. You know the end game and why you should want to experience it."

"I take it..." I padded my feet into his kitchen and slowly walked around the island, dragging my fingertips along the countertop "...you've had a lot of sex?"

He tossed one piece of mail onto the counter and discarded the rest in the pullout recycling bin. "I'm twenty-eight and single. Yes. I've had a lot of sex."

His words formed a tight knot in my stomach. It wasn't that I didn't expect that to be his truth; I just didn't expect him to be so forthcoming about it.

"How old were you when you first had it?"

"Sixteen."

I nodded, staring at my fingers tracing the lines in the granite instead of him eyeing me from the opposite side.

"What..." he laughed a little "...do you see happening? Do you think I'm going to tie you to my bed and do weird things to you?"

My gaze shot up to meet his, and I didn't blink once. "That hadn't occurred to me."

"Then what occurred to you on that long drive home?"

I shrugged. "I don't know."

"Liar."

"Stop calling me a liar. You can't read my mind."

"Do you touch yourself?"

"Jeez ..." My head bowed to hide my embarrassment.

"I'll take that as a no." He walked to the basement door and opened it. "Go touch yourself. I'm going to take a shower and touch myself. Then we'll have dinner and see how the evening progresses."

Oh ... my ... gosh ...

He was serious. I didn't know what was most unsettling: the idea of him giving me a homework assignment to masturbate or him confessing his own intentions.

I laughed, a little too loudly. "I'm ... I'm not going to ..."

"Touch yourself? Why the hell not?"

Swallowing hard, I shook my head. I felt like the world's biggest prude. And that shouldn't have bothered me. I had my faith. I *did* have morals. And if I gave in and handed him my virginity, what would I have to give my husband on our wedding night. Those were the words I'd heard from my grandma and people at church so many times. Except my grandma took it one step further with a cringe-worthy analogy.

"Therese, if you don't have that to give your husband, it's like borrowing a used sanitary napkin from a friend. You don't want to be a used sanitary napkin, do you?"

So there it was ... not having my virginity on my wedding night was not only disrespectful to my husband

and to God, it was gross and had the potential to spread disease. And I bought it. Not only did I buy it, I repeated it to my friends to help remind them of the importance of staying virgins.

Making the virgin walk of shame, I sulked toward the stairs, stopping and glancing up at Fisher.

"Have fun." He gave me a tight smile.

I blinked several times. "I can't do this."

"Why not?"

My head shook in frustration. "B-because I don't want to make myself feel good; I want *you* to make me feel good! I want to feel like I felt last night, like I felt this morning."

He pinched the bridge of his nose and closed his eyes. "Fiiine ..." When he opened his eyes, he blew out a long breath. "But *I* need a shower before that happens again."

"Why?"

"Jesus, Reese ... because. Okay? Because. Can it just be okay with you?"

"No!" I covered my mouth after I yelled my answer.

He growled and grumbled. Things were worse than I thought. Fisher was mad at me and the rest of the world, but mainly me.

"I want to be the reason you ... well ... you know."

"Done." He gave me a slight nudge, forcing me down the first stair. "I will think of you the whole time. Happy now?"

I deflated. "You don't deserve my dreams, naked fisherman." Turning, I descended the stairs and headed straight to my bedroom, where I wasn't going to touch myself regardless of what Fisher did in the shower.

Plopping onto my bed face-first, I turned my head toward the window and stared at the mountains, thinking I should just go ... just take a drive alone.

"Happy Meals? Really, Reese. You got Happy Meals for my crew today?"

"They didn't complain."

"Not to you. I hope you got the toys you needed, the toys you're no longer collecting."

I didn't respond.

"So ..." his voice got closer to me. "Naked fisherman?"

"Shut up." I didn't turn toward him, even though I knew he was next to my bed.

"Tell me about your dreams."

I sighed. "Sorry. They're mine. Get your own."

The other side of my bed dipped. I turned my head toward Fisher next to me on his back, hands folded on his chest as he stared at the ceiling.

"Take your shirt and pants off," he said.

"What?"

He closed his eyes. "Just ... take them off. Nothing more, just your shirt and pants."

I didn't move.

"Do you trust me?"

"Not really."

He grinned a tiny grin, but he didn't open his eyes. "Well, try ... just this once."

Sitting up slowly, I removed my shirt, eyeing him to see if he was peeking.

He wasn't.

I had to stand to shimmy out of my jeans, leaving

them on the floor next to my shirt—leaving me in a white bra and panties.

Fisher's eyes fluttered open, and I held my breath, holding back the urge to cover myself. "You're truly beautiful."

My skin turned pink all over. "Thank you," I whispered, fighting the insecurity to ask him if he thought I was as beautiful as Teagan or the million other women he'd been with while I was just a young girl.

"Come here."

After a few seconds of hesitation, I crawled onto the bed close to him.

"Straddle my legs."

Biting my quivering lower lip, I straddled his jean-clad legs. The level of intimacy made it nearly impossible to breathe.

"Higher."

I scooted higher.

He sat up, shrugging off his shirt, and I jumped as his hands found my hips, his fingers grazing my butt. Our noses nearly touched.

"I'm going to kiss you. And touch you." His voice was just a whisper, a warm breath over my lips. "And you're going to do whatever you need to do to feel ... *good*. And if you get scared, I want you to close your eyes and know that I've got you. You're not too young or too anything. You are you. And I just think that you're ... beautiful."

"Fisher ..." I leaned forward and pressed my lips to his.

We kissed, unhurried, almost lazily.

My hands navigated his chest and back, every

muscle, every bend in the terrain of his body. Fisher feathered his calloused hands over my bare skin, sending goose bumps spreading across it.

Our kiss deepened, a soft moan breaking the silence. It took me a few seconds to realize it was me, not him. Fisher's fingers slid up my inner thighs. I stiffened, eyes wide. He blinked a few times and slowly kissed me again. When I closed my eyes, I let go ... finding trust in the man who "had me." His fingers teased the leg of my panties. My right hand found his hair as my left hand clawed his back.

I was so scared. A good scared. The kind of scared I felt climbing a steep hill on a rollercoaster. As he flicked his tongue against mine, a single finger inched beneath the crotch of my panties.

I fisted his hair as my breath hiked.

"Beautiful ..." he whispered against my mouth, along my jaw, and down my neck. Over and over.

Beautiful ... Beautiful ... Beautiful ...

Fisher. The first man other than my father to call me beautiful.

That finger? It moved a fraction of an inch, and I jerked. His finger, his entire body, stilled except for his lips at my ear, his breath whispering, "Make it feel good ..."

Fear shook me. My faith. My fragile beliefs. I held my breath for few seconds like I did at the top of that rollercoaster hill. Then I kissed him. He didn't kiss me.

I. Kissed. Him.

My pelvis moved just enough to rub my clit against

the pad of his idle finger. I rocked it a little more until it touched me lower, where I was wet between my legs.

And not once did he move.

I kissed along his jaw and neck, feeling safe, feeling the slow building of my confidence as a woman.

My hips rocked a little harder until I realized what I was feeling ... what I was rubbing ... wasn't so much his finger. It was his erection hard against me. The denim scratched my inner thighs, but I didn't care.

"Fisher ... m-move ..."

"Move what?" he asked with so much control I thought I might die of my own impatience.

"E-everything. Just ... move."

His strong hands claimed my hips again, only this time, they gripped me a little harder, and he moved me over him.

He did it for me, and it felt so addictive I couldn't formulate a coherent thought.

He did it for him, and his breaths grew more labored, his kisses more desperate.

I wanted nothing more than to know what it would feel like for him to be inside of me. "Fisher ... I ... I think I want you to take off your jeans."

He reclined back onto my pillow and grinned as I leaned forward, resting my hands on his chest, my hair falling around my face and his.

"You don't ... not yet." His eyelids grew heavy as his pelvis lifted from the bed.

Giving more.

Taking more.

Proving just how *extra* he was that day.

We weren't having sex. But *we were* ... having sex.

It was wrong. But it was right.

My head spun in dizzying circles as up became down and down became up, and nothing made sense, nor did I really want it to make sense.

And when it happened, that all-consuming, mind-numbing sensation, I gasped and hissed a "Yesss."

Vulnerable.

Out of control.

Fear crept into my conscience. I didn't want him to know how scared I felt, like a teenager trying to be an adult.

Fisher held my hips still as he pumped his up several more times and released a drawn-out expletive that I never said aloud but found it fitting, and even a little sexy, coming from him. Collapsing against his chest, I buried my face into his neck, a little winded and a lot ... happy. As frustrated as Fisher made me, I felt blissful with him.

Was I a terrible person?

Did I disappoint God?

Probably "yes" on both accounts.

Fisher left one hand on my ass and lifted his other hand to the back of my head, stroking my hair several times. "Nine across. Six letters. The first one is 'S' and the fourth one is 'W.' Hint: It's something I still need."

I laughed, nodding without lifting my head from his neck. "Are you trying to speak my language? It's kinda sexy." Lifting my head, I kissed his jaw. "Yes. You can *shower* now."

THINGS I NEVER TOLD FISHER ...

After he left me to take his shower, I sat in the corner of my own shower and cried. It was more than I could handle.

My faith.

My thoughts.

My beliefs.

My desires.

My emotions.

They all took different paths. I felt pulled in so many directions, each feeling equally right and equally wrong for many different reasons. As strong as I felt my faith was, there wasn't a day that passed when I didn't question it. Question Him. His existence. His role in our lives. And our interpretation of His words.

What happened with Fisher didn't feel wrong. We weren't hurting anyone. We weren't harming anything. We were two souls enjoying our physical bodies. Why did it have to be a form of immorality?

The rest ... the guilt ... the lecture I could recite on my own? It felt awful. Was that the point of life? To walk a line of righteousness and feel guilty and sinful for occasionally stepping off the line? Why give us freedom of choice if there was only one right choice?

After drying my hair and applying a little makeup, I slipped on a tank top and a pair of shorts before climbing the stairs. Did I need to knock?

I knocked.

"It's not locked."

I grinned, slowly opening the door.

Wearing only a pair of shorts hanging low on his

perfect hips, wet hair, lean, cut body casually resting against the kitchen island with one ankle crossed over the other, Fisher glanced up from his phone. "Hey."

"Hey." I closed the door and fidgeted with the hem of my tank top.

"My parents invited us to dinner."

"Us?" I narrowed my eyes. "You told them about us?"

With a slight shake of his head and a tiny grin, he set his phone on the counter and crossed his arms over his bare chest. "Is that a problem?"

"I ... well ..." I felt everything inside of me tremble. Age didn't matter, but it *did* matter.

"They know you're Rory's daughter. They know you work for me. And they know we were going to grill tonight since neither one of us has plans."

I didn't know we were grilling. "They don't know about ..." I pressed my lips together. What was I supposed to say? That we had sex? We didn't. That I got off on him? That. I *did* do.

"No. I left that part out, but if you feel obligated to tell them, that's your prerogative."

"No." I inched my head side to side. "I don't feel a particular need to tell them or anyone."

"Are you ashamed of me?" He cocked his head to the side.

I padded my bare feet to him and collapsed into his naked chest, pressing my face directly over his heart and inhaling his clean scent. "I don't know what I am." I kissed along his pec muscles as he snaked his arms around my waist.

"So we go as friends. My sisters will be there. Nieces and nephews. No big deal."

My head jerked up. "Your whole family?"

"Not everyone, but most of them. Why?"

"No reason."

"Think you can keep your hands off me for one night?"

"Depends ... will you wear a shirt?"

"Yes." He grinned.

"Then I'll be fine." Taking a step back, I slipped my hands into the front pockets of my shorts.

"Is this solely about my body?" He narrowed one eye.

"Of course. Your personality is just okay, and as a boss, you're kind of grumpy." I put on my best mask and tried to act mature. Cool. Controlled. On the inside, I hadn't stopped reeling from what took place on my bed.

Was Fisher too experienced and mature to let his thoughts linger on something as trivial as what we did?

"I'm ignoring your bullshit. Just like this is the only day that I'm going to let your Happy Meal catering slide."

"I did it to finish off the collection for my mom. I'm done. And if you're upset that I spent your money on them, then I'll pay you back. Are you happy now?"

Wearing a smirk, he cocked his head to the side. "I don't believe you're done. I don't believe it's for Rory anymore. You've allowed this to become your hobby, your addiction. It's cute. Really. But I can't have you stealing toys from some of the Happy Meals. It's going to cause fights with my crew if everyone doesn't get a toy."

"Kiss my backside, Fisher." I narrowed my eyes.

"Your *ass*? You want me to kiss your ass?"

Rolling my eyes, I shook my head.

"Turn around."

Releasing a nervous laugh, I eased back a step. "It was a joke because you were giving me a hard time over the Happy Meals."

"Yes." He crooked a finger at me. "But now I want to kiss your ass."

"Stop it." I giggled through my nerves.

"Come here. I'm not going to chase you this time."

Gathering up my bravery like collecting the contents of a spilled purse in the grocery store aisle, I turned and bent over, resting my hands on my knees. If he wanted to kiss my backside, then I would let him. No big deal. Nothing to be nervous about.

"Oh, Reese ..." He drew out my name while kneeling behind me.

I wasn't sure why he needed to kneel behind me.

Bend down and kiss it. Whatever. Just do it and be done.

But my thoughts were simpler than his.

"You're a walking wet dream."

"What are you doing!" I jumped.

"Kissing your ass," he said in his calm voice while curling his fingers into the waistband of my jogging shorts and slowly pulling them down to expose my *bare* backside.

I grabbed one of his arms to stop him.

"I'm not kissing your shorts."

Fisher ignored my hand gripping his forearm as he exposed one side of my butt. With my other hand, I gripped the front of my waistband and held on for life so he couldn't completely remove my shorts *and* panties.

He kissed my bare butt slowly at first. Then, he kissed it harder with a lot more suction.

"Fisher ..." I squeezed my glutes. "You're going to leave a mark."

"Mmm ..." He licked the spot that he kissed so hard. "No mark."

As I started to relax, he gave a quick tug and pulled down the other side, totally exposing my entire backside. And before I could protest, he kissed that side and ...

"Ouch!"

He. Bit. Me.

He bit my ass, and I knew there was no way it wasn't going to leave a mark, his freaking dental records on my *ass*!

Lapping his tongue over the area several times, he chuckled. "Now I've left a mark."

It wasn't funny.

Then he kissed it.

"Why did you do that?" I said, a little breathless and completely stunned.

"Because..." his hands pressed to the front of my thighs as he kissed my backside everywhere "...I wanted to."

Beneath the shock, I felt turned on. It felt good. And that confused me. Sex was black and white for me. This was murky and confusing. It wasn't sex, but it was sexual. It was intimate. And I knew it would have to stop soon because Rory was coming home.

My hands relaxed and the front of my shorts and

panties immediately dropped a couple of inches from the tension at the back. Fisher stilled his motions when he realized what I did. I don't know why I did it or what I expected to happen next. I just ... I liked him touching me even when it felt a little wrong.

So I stood there, waiting for him to deliver more kisses, waiting for his hands to move from the front of my thighs to ... That was just it. I really didn't know what I expected or wanted from him. I guess I wanted him to teach me something.

Something new.

Something intimate.

Something a little forbidden.

With my heartbeat tripping over itself, looking for a normal rhythm, I started to turn toward him. He gripped my legs tighter and rested his forehead on my lower back.

"Don't." He sighed. "Just ..." He blew out another harsh breath, and I felt his forehead rolling side to side against my back. "Fuck ... we ... can't." He pulled up my panties and shorts. "Rory's coming home soon." He stood behind me and kissed the top of my head. "I'm going to get dressed. Go put on jeans. We should head to my parents' house now."

CHAPTER FIFTEEN

"My hair is going to be a mess." I tugged off my helmet after he pulled into his parents' gravel drive in Coal Creek Canyon. They lived in an A-frame house shrouded in pine trees with not a neighbor in sight.

He took my helmet and my jacket as I ran my fingers through my hair. After a few seconds, I glanced up at Fisher smiling at me with a hint of something in his eyes.

"What?"

He shook his head. "You're killing me."

"Why?" I continued to comb out my hair.

"Because I want to do very naughty things to you right now, but little kids are staring out the window at us, so I have to keep my hands to myself. And it's really fucking hard."

I paused my hands.

"Stop blushing," he said. "They can see you."

I talked through gritted teeth and a fake smile. "I can't exactly control it when you say things like that to me. Why? Why did you say it?"

He glanced at the window and the peering eyes for a second before turning toward me. "Because for forty-five minutes, you've been wrapped around me, and I now know what your face looks like when you come, so it's all I thought about."

It thrilled me to know it wasn't just me. That he wasn't as cool and collected as I thought. Fisher was far from unaffected by me.

Where was the switch? In one week, we were going to have to turn off the switch to *us*.

"Thank you," I whispered, glancing down at my feet.

He laughed. "For what?"

"For being strong for me."

"What are you talking about?"

I glanced up, giving the window crowd the quickest of glances. Aching to take the two steps between us and wrap my arms around him. "I wouldn't have stopped you, had you asked me. And then in the kitchen ... I wanted ... more." I shrugged one shoulder while pressing my lips together to hide my guilty grin.

Recognition flitted across his face. His smile died, turning into something more somber. "Don't thank me. It wasn't easy. And I can't promise to always be that strong."

Clearing my throat, I changed the topic. "We should go inside before your family suspects there's something going on between us."

"We don't have to worry about that. There's no way they'd suspect that." He turned and headed toward the house.

"Wow. That's a bit harsh." I jogged to catch up to him.

"TGIF!" A woman, I assumed his mom, opened the door. I was never part of a family that got that excited over Friday. I may have been a little envious in that moment.

"Hey, Mom. This is Reese. Reese, this is my mom, Laurie."

"Hi, Reese. So glad you decided to join us. Come on in. There's food and drinks out back."

"Thank you so much." I followed Laurie and Fisher through an open great room. Three young kids hopped down from the sofa where they'd been spying on us. We passed the kitchen to a sunporch and door to a covered deck where everyone else congregated.

I wanted Fisher to take my hand or put his arm around me. I felt naked in front of these strangers without some physical connection, a grounding of sorts.

"Hey!" The greeting from everyone on the deck was just as exuberant as Laurie's.

"Hey." Fisher turned, waiting for me to stop hiding behind him. "Everyone, this is Reese, Rory's daughter. Rory is my tenant, for anyone who hasn't met her. Reese is also working for me this summer. Reese, this is the crew. Pat, Shayla, Teena, Arnie ... blah blah blah ... let them introduce themselves. And don't ask me to remember the names of the rug rats running around here."

"Oh stop." Laurie shook her head. "He knows everyone's name. Grab a drink, Hun, there's a cooler with pop and water and another cooler with beer and wine. We have burgers and brats on the grill."

"Thanks." I smiled at Laurie and looked around for Fisher. He was already down the stairs, playing a bean bag game with the kids.

Sink or swim for me.

"Beer? Wine?" The woman I believe he nodded to as Shayla, held open a cooler for me.

Did I look older, or did they not care?

"Actually, I'll just have some water for now."

"No problem." She opened the other cooler and handed me a bottle of water. "So ... I'm Shayla. Sorry Fisher is so clueless when it comes to manners. I'm his big sister. And Teena ... chasing the girl in just a diaper down there is his other big sister. Our dad, Pat, is manning the grill."

"I sure am," Pat said while lifting the lid.

"My husband Darren couldn't make it, but Ryan..." she ruffled a blond guy's hair as he sipped his beer "...is here, and he's Teena's husband."

"Don't forget your other brother," Laurie said as she collapsed into a padded chair that rocked and swiveled.

"Oh, yes ..." Shayla rolled her eyes. "Arnie is the baby of the family. He's the one with dark hair and ridiculous blond tips and ... a crazy number of tattoos on his arms and legs."

"I can hear you," Arnie called from the opposite side of the bean bag game as Fisher.

I giggled at his response. "The baby, huh? How old is he?"

"Twenty-two, but he doesn't act a day over five."

"Still hearing you," he yelled, tossing a bean bag with one hand while holding a beer in his other hand.

"So, are you in college?" Laurie asked.

"No. I'm not ruling it out someday, but for now I'm just working and getting reacquainted with my mom."

"Oh? Have you been separated from her? Divorce?"

I nodded. "Yes. Divorce. And my dad died three years ago. And ..." I drew in a deep breath. "My mom sorta just got out of prison."

"Oh ... wow. That's good. Or bad." Laurie cringed. "Good that's she's out. Bad that she went. Just ... ignore me." She pressed the heel of her hand to her forehead.

"It's fine. I've had to learn to just own it as part of my life. It's still awkward, but maybe now that she's out, I can eventually stop feeling the need to mention it."

"Champions!" One of the young boys yelled, high-fiving Fisher.

Arnie climbed the stairs, shaking his head. "Cheaters. They're all cheaters."

Arnie was basically a slightly smaller version of Fisher, but with tattoos, wilder hair, and a piercing through his nose. Fisher would have looked better in tattoos because he had more defined muscles, but Arnie had a boyish grin and his own level of sexy, bad-boy appeal.

"My brother's been holding out on me," Arnie said while easing into the chair next to me.

"Stop it." Shayla rolled her eyes. "I'm fairly certain Fisher didn't bring Reese here for you to hit on her."

"What?" He smirked. "I'm not hitting on you, Reese."

I laughed a little.

"Unless you want me to hit on you, then I'm totally hitting on you."

"Arnie ..." Laurie eyed him with a motherly warning.

"Kidding." He winked at me (just like Fisher) before taking a long pull of his beer.

"Are you in the construction business too?" I asked.

Arnie shook his head while rubbing his wet lips together. "No. I'm in a band."

"A band?" I couldn't hide my surprise. "Seriously?"

"Fisher never mentioned his brother is a famous rock star?" Arnie acted offended.

"You're not famous." Shayla had to give her verbal jab.

"Fisher and that hot doctor came to a concert last week. That's how proud he is of me."

Teagan. He took Teagan to see his brother perform. Yet he hadn't mentioned anything to me about it being his brother's band.

"Food's ready," Pat called.

Arnie stood. "Ladies first."

I couldn't hide my smile as he held out his hand to me. So I took it and stood.

"I perform again tomorrow night. You should come. I know the lead singer." He gave me the most confident grin. "Front row seating."

"Rory's not going to be okay with you hitting on her daughter."

I glanced back, not noticing that Fisher had gotten in the food line behind us.

"Rory loves me. She'll be thrilled to know that I'm

inviting her daughter to one of my concerts. I'll text her just to make sure." Arnie pulled his phone out of his pocket.

"Put your phone away, dickhead." Fisher playfully grabbed the back of Arnie's neck and squeezed it.

Arnie wriggled out of his hold. "You and that doctor should come and bring Reese with you. We can grab food and drinks after. A double date with my big bro."

"Now that actually sounds like a good idea." Teena butted in on the conversation while wrangling her toddler on the way up the deck stairs.

I didn't look at anyone, just my feet because they couldn't tell how uncomfortable I was caught in the middle.

"Teagan and I aren't dating anymore."

"Dude, that was short-lived. She was effin' amazing. What did you do?"

"What makes you think *I* did anything?"

"Just a hunch." Arnie continued to prod Fisher.

"Angie's in town for the summer. You have to call her, Fisher." Shayla took a seat with her plate of food as I smiled at Pat when he handed me a plate and nodded to the choices of meat next to a dozen different salads and bags of chips.

"Angie's here?" Arnie and Laurie said at the same time.

"Fisher, call that woman, right now. You know I've imagined you two getting married ever since you were six years old." Laurie accidentally stomped all over my heart.

"Angie's in town. It's a sign, Bro." Arnie filled his plate behind me. "Bring Angie and Reese tomorrow night. Don't even try to make up some excuse. It's *Angie.* You're totally in, right Reese?"

Feeling zero hunger by then, I returned a tight smile to Arnie and nodded slowly. What else was I supposed to do?

"It's official ... almost." Arnie set his plate on the railing and plucked Fisher's phone from his pocket.

"What the f—" Fisher held his tongue with the kids around. Then, he stomped down the deck stairs after Arnie.

"Ha! I knew it. Same predictable code and ..." He ran from Fisher. "You still have her number!" A few seconds later, Arnie slowed and held out one hand, signaling Fisher to stop as he used his other hand to hold the phone to his ear.

I couldn't hear him, but I could see him talking while Fisher rested one hand on his hip and hung his head.

"It's on!" Arnie tossed Fisher's phone to him and strutted back toward the house.

If I read Fisher's lips correctly, he called Arnie a "stupid fucker."

"You'll love Angie," Shayla said as I sat next to her. "The love of Fisher's life since grade school. He's been too stupid to just marry her, so she's now living in California. She comes back here a lot because her mom is disabled and her dad passed away several years ago."

Just great ...

Eighteen-year-old me, with no real-life goals, had known Fisher for just over three weeks, and I was supposed to compete with "the love of his life?"

"Why did she move to California?" I asked despite my better judgment.

"Aside from Fisher not proposing?" Teena sat in the chair across from me after Ryan took the squirming toddler. "She's a biologist. Wicked smart."

I had to give Fisher credit; he knew how to attract smart, successful women—until me. Well, I was smart, but how much success could I have claimed at eighteen, even if I had enrolled in college courses?

"Take my seat, Fisher. I have to check on Isaac." Shayla vacated her spot.

Fisher sat next to me with his plate of food and a beer. I force-fed myself, chewing slowly, swallowing hard, and keeping my head down. That day, being eighteen sucked. I hadn't grown out of my foolish heart. It wasn't enough for me. Fisher's attraction to me wasn't enough. I wanted his heart to be mine and only mine. But maybe that wasn't how his brain or his heart functioned.

"Fisher, did you bid on that job in Aurora?" Pat asked as he removed his apron and sat down to eat.

Their conversation lasted for a long time. Enough time for me to eat as much as I could and not look like I was tossing half of my food in the trash. When I did take my plate into the kitchen, I also looked for a bathroom— an escape.

"Oh, hey ... I was looking for the restroom," I said to Shayla when she startled me as I turned the corner from the kitchen to the small hallway.

"Isaac is using the restroom. He could be awhile." She grimaced. "There's one downstairs."

"Okay. Thanks." I pivoted and headed downstairs.

Nobody was in the basement filled with furniture, a big TV like the one in Fisher's basement, a ping-pong table, a wood burning stove, and many collages of photos on the wall. I inspected the photos, smiling at young Fisher and his family that I envied so much.

"I wondered where you went. I was afraid you forgot there are bears and rattlesnakes."

I glanced back at Fisher. "I was looking for the bathroom, but I got sidetracked with all of your family photos."

He nodded, looking at me, not the photos. "About tomorrow night—"

"It's fine, Fisher." That lie made my chest hurt, but it wasn't a pain I could show him. "Your family clearly adores Angie. And you must too. And Arnie seems really excited about the four of us going out." I shrugged. "I have no other plans, so ... why not?"

"It's not a date."

Turning back toward the photos, I dug deep for a little more confidence. "It's fine if it is. Rory comes home next week. You said it yourself. Your parents would never believe you were ... interested in me. And now I know why."

"You don't."

"No? Well, it doesn't matter."

"No. It doesn't." He took ahold of my wrist and pulled me into a dark bedroom, closing the door behind us and flipping on the light.

I waited for Fisher to say whatever it was he needed to say. He didn't say anything for many seconds, maybe a minute or more. It was just silence and the anguish on his face. Finally, he scrubbed his hands over his face and blew out a long breath.

"We don't have to wait any longer," I filled the silence with whatever I thought might make him a little less stressed because he seemed *so* stressed out. "It can be over now. Maybe it's stupid to act like one more week matters. Maybe I shouldn't have been in your bathtub that night. Maybe hiding from everyone is more trouble than it's worth. And now this Angie person is back, and that would suck for you to miss out on an opportunity because we decided to do..." I shrugged "...*whatever* for one more week."

He narrowed his eyes. "You want it to end? Now?"

"Yes."

Gah! Stupid, untimely tears rushed to my eyes.

"Liar."

Clenching my jaw to lock down all emotions on the verge of breaking the dam, I shook my head.

He cocked his head to the side and pressed his hand to my face, brushing his thumb across my cheek to the corner of my eye, giving it just enough pressure to release one tear and then another. "Let's go," he whispered.

"Where?" I sucked in a shaky breath as my strength wavered.

"Home. Rory comes home soon. And I don't want to share you with anyone else tonight."

"F-Fisher ..." I sniffled. "You can't have my heart."

He smiled and nodded several times while bending down to kiss the corner of my mouth. "I know ... I'll add it to the list."

Kiss.

"What list?"

He opened the door and shut off the light. "The parts of Reese Capshaw that I can't have."

I opened my mouth to respond, but I had nothing. Not one thing.

"We're taking off," Fisher announced as we stepped onto the deck.

"Already? I made pie and there's ice cream." Laurie looked a little surprised.

"Reese has a tummy ache. Maybe one of the salads sat in the sun too long."

What the heck!

I had to have looked just as surprised ... and mortified.

"Oh dear! I'm so sorry." Laurie pressed her hand to her chest.

A string of "that's too bads" and "feel betters" followed from everyone else.

"Take an antacid..." Arnie made a drinking motion with his hand "...and you'll be good for tomorrow night."

Fisher ignored him, and I ... well, I ignored everyone because I still hadn't fully processed what just happened.

"Well, thanks. Goodnight," Fisher said, resting his hand on my back in the platonic region to guide me to the front door.

As soon as he closed the door behind us, I spun around. "Are you kidding me? Did you really just tell your whole family that I have a *tummy ache*? What am I? Five?"

He shrugged, shouldering past mc to the driveway. "Kids were around. I couldn't say you had the shits."

"Fisher! Why did you do that?"

"Because we needed an excuse to leave." He handed me my helmet.

"Why didn't you tell them *you* have a tummy ache? Why embarrass me like that?"

He fastened his helmet and grinned. "I haven't had so much as a sniffle for years. I'm kind of a freak of nature like that. They never would have believed it had I said it was me."

"Well ... well ... maybe I haven't been sick in years. Did you even think about that? Maybe I'm a freak of nature."

"Oh." He chuckled while throwing his leg over the seat. "I have no doubt that you're a special kind of freak of nature. Get on."

I was the one grumbling by that point as I climbed onto the back of his bike.

By the time we got home, I was still fuming.

"I'm going to bed ... I have a *tummy ache*." I tossed my helmet on the ground along with the riding jacket and marched my way to the basement door. After kicking my shoes off, I ran up the stairs and locked the door at the top. We were done.

CHAPTER SIXTEEN

Fisher: I'm sorry.

Fisher: Are you going to stay mad at me forever?

Fisher: I'll call my family and tell them it was a lie. That I just wanted to be alone with you.

I ROLLED my eyes at the last text. He wasn't going to tell his Angie-loving family that he wanted to be alone with me.

My phone rang. I didn't want to answer it, knowing it was him. But when I spared a quick glance at the screen, I realized it wasn't him. It was Christina, my only friend from public school who kept in touch with me.

"Heyyy!"

"Hey, Reese! What's up with you? It's been forever."

"I know. It has. Where are you? Last I heard you'd moved to South Carolina."

"We did, but my sister's getting married in a week, so I'm staying with her to help her survive the chaos."

"Amelia's getting married? Wow!"

"Yes. And she's getting married in Colorado Springs. And I heard you're in Denver. I'm in Denver for the weekend. We *have* to get together."

"Yeah, I'd love that. I have no plans ... well ..." I thought about Arnie's concert.

"If you're going to say you have plans with a guy, that's cool. My boyfriend's with me. We should all go out."

"It's ... um ... actually, I was invited to a concert tomorrow night. Local band. I know the lead singer. His brother is my landlord and my boss."

"Oh ... that sounds perfect. Where? When?"

"I'm not sure yet. Can I text you the info in the morning?"

"Absolutely. Gah! I can't wait to see you!"

"Me too. I'm so glad you called. We'll talk in the morning."

"Sounds great. Bye."

I pressed *End* and groaned because I didn't have Arnie's number. I didn't know the time or location of the concert. After a quick internet search for "Arnie Mann band in Denver," I found everything I needed and quickly texted Christina before going to bed early and praying the naked fisherman stayed out of my dreams.

The next morning, I dressed and headed out for a walk. Fisher's truck was gone. It didn't surprise me. Hailey told me it wasn't unusual for him to work on Saturdays.

After my walk and breakfast, I grabbed my crossword puzzle sketch pad and sat on the screened-in porch. After an hour or so, the roar of an approaching lawnmower grew louder. I looked up to shirtless Fisher mowing the lawn. He didn't see me at first. And I liked that. Even if I wasn't sure I liked him anymore, I liked things about him.

His body.

The concentrated look on his scruffy face when he was focused on a task, especially if it involved tools.

In the middle of me contemplating the things I did like about him, Fisher glanced up and our gazes met. He paused for a moment then continued mowing.

Weed eating.

And he finished the afternoon by pulling weeds on his hands and knees in the landscaping. I slipped inside and filled a tall glass with ice water and took it out to him.

"You should hydrate. You're pretty sweaty." I stood beside him and held out the glass.

Fisher lifted onto his knees and sat back on his heels, sweat and dirt covering his naked chest and back. "Thank you." He pulled off his work gloves and took the glass from me. In one breath, he guzzled the whole thing and sighed while handing it back to me.

"I ... uh ... I forgive you. I just wasn't ready to say it last night when you messaged me."

He wiped his arm over his forehead. "I figured."

"My friend called me last night. She's in Denver for the weekend with her boyfriend. Her sister's getting married in Colorado Springs next weekend. Anyway ... she wanted to get together, so I suggested Arnie's concert. Do you think he can get us two extra seats?"

"I didn't figure you'd want to go."

"I didn't. But I want to see my friend, and she's really excited about it, so ..."

Squinting against the sun, he nodded. "I'm sure Arnie can make it happen."

"Are you taking ... a date?"

Fisher glanced away and shook his head while offering a little chuckle. "You mean, am I taking Angie?"

I nodded, tapping my fingernails on the glass and doing my weird rolling back and forth on my heels thing.

"Arnie invited her. It's virtually impossible for me to *not* take her at this point."

I lifted my shoulders. "It's fine. I was just asking. Should I uh ... drive? Or are we all going together?"

"She messaged me last night. She'll pick us up at six. I said I needed to verify that you were going, but now that you are ... I'll let her know."

"You're not driving?"

He shook his head. "I have a work truck and a motor-cycle. You've seen all the shit in my truck, and I don't think all of us can fit on my motorcycle."

"Yeah. Of course. Well ..." I took a few steps backward. "I'll be ready at six."

As soon as I stepped into the house, I rifled through my clothes and found nothing ... nothing to wear on a date. Or double date ... triple date? I didn't know. But I knew Christina would be dressed in something trendy and on point. I hadn't met Angie, but I had to anticipate someone from California bringing her own brand of style.

"You suck," I berated myself ... my wardrobe. In the next beat, I was out the door with my purse and car keys.

Buzzing past Fisher, I hopped into the Outback and sped down the street in mad search of something to wear.

Just under two hours later, I returned with a new outfit, shoes, and a smaller handbag.

With under an hour to get ready, I shaved everything ... and I hadn't shaved everything ever. Then I slathered lotion on all my shaved areas, dried my hair, curled it, and applied makeup the way my mom used to apply makeup.

Smoky eyes.

A bit of pink high on my cheekbones.

And red lips.

I made a final inspection in the mirror as I stuffed the essentials into my new clutch. My dad had to be turning over in his grave. And God? I could only imagine.

White shorts that barely ... just barely covered my backside making my legs look even longer. A floral, sleeveless spaghetti strap top. And nineties inspired plat-form shoes with straps around my ankles.

After a quick glance at my watch, I made my way up front. There was no car in the driveway aside from Fish-er's truck, so I stood under his covered porch and waited, clutching my purse in both hands.

"She's running a few minutes late. You can wait inside."

I turned toward Fisher's voice.

Well, dang ...

He was freshly showered with dark jeans that looked fairly new, gray leather sneakers with thick white soles, and a faded gray tee that molded to his chest and shoul-ders. His biceps looked twice as big, and the veins in his arms did weird things to me. Veins weren't supposed to be sexy.

"O-okay ..." I gulped.

He eyed my legs for a long moment before meeting my gaze as I walked toward the door. "I have a feeling someone will get beat up or arrested tonight."

"Why would you say that?" I stopped just inside his front door.

"Because you're eighteen going on thirty."

"Don't talk like a parent, Fisher."

He shut the door and leaned against it, crossing his sexy arms over his even sexier chest. "Fine. Every guy that sees you is going to get a hard-on. And I promised Rory I'd keep an eye on you."

"I'm sure Angie doesn't want you keeping an eye on me."

He narrowed his eyes at my chest, ignoring my Angie comment. "For fuck's sake ... are you wearing a bra?"

I glanced down. "No. I can't wear one with this top."

"Then go change tops and put on a bra."

"Again ... too much parental talk. I don't need you to dress me."

"And I don't need my horny brother seeing your nipples."

Glancing down again, I shook my head. "It's a dark shirt. You can't see them."

"I can see their outline ... I can see they are erect."

I slowly ran the pads of my fingers over them to push my nipples in so he couldn't see them anymore.

"Just ... fucking stop ..." He pinched the bridge of his nose.

"I pushed them in."

"Jesus ... you're a walking wet dream. Just stop touching yourself." He adjusted himself in his jeans.

And just like that, my nipples popped out again. It took him all of two seconds to notice.

"I'm going to kill Rory for leaving you with me." He took a step forward and grabbed the back of my hair, clenching it in his hand and forcing my head to the side as he sucked and licked my neck.

"F-Fisher ..." I clawed his biceps to steady myself. He wasn't kissing my red lips and smearing my lipstick. I gave him a little credit for that, but he still seemed to be teetering on the verge of control as his other hand slid up the front of my shirt.

I gasped when his rough hand palmed my bare breast. He groaned, his thumb circling my nipple.

"Oh my God—gosh ..." I stumbled over using the Lord's name in vain.

His hand moved to my other breast, giving it the same torturous treatment.

"We ... should ..." I couldn't catch my breath to complete a sentence. I thought we should stop, but my words never got that far.

He whipped me around so my back hit the door, releasing my hair before lifting me up, guiding my legs around his waist with one hand while shoving my shirt up to my neck with his other hand.

"Ah! Oh ... oh ... god!" I lost all ability to censor my words when he covered my breast with his mouth, sucking and biting it relentlessly.

Then ... the doorbell rang.

I froze. Fisher rested his forehead between my bared breasts, breathing a little harder than usual. His hands dropped to my legs, but he didn't unpin me from the door.

"Fuck ..."

The doorbell rang again.

He eased me to my feet, my shirt dropping back into place. I gazed up at him in shock. *What just happened?*

"Just a sec," he said loud enough for Angie (I assumed) to hear him and stop ringing the doorbell. He seemed ... frustrated?

"I-I'm ... going to go put on a bra and a different shirt," I said softly. I needed to change into dry panties as well, but I didn't think he needed to know that.

Fisher said nothing, but he bit his lips together and nodded slowly. He also didn't give me much space, so I had to awkwardly squeeze past him, retrieve my clutch from the floor, and run to the basement door.

After I put on a bra and a boring tank top, I ran back up the stairs then paused. I wondered if it would seem weird ... me exiting on the main floor? So I made a big production to go around the side of the house.

A woman with curly jet-black hair to her shoulders and a well-defined body turned toward me and smiled. She wasn't as tall as me, but she had *more* in all the other departments. If I won the battle a few minutes earlier, I was sure to lose the war with Angie back in town.

"Angie, this is Reese Capshaw. Reese, this is Angie Flynn."

"So nice to meet you. Cute top." She nodded to my Life is Good top with a huge sunflower on the front of it.

Cute. I was cute.

She was killing it in a red dress and heels.

Trying to not completely deflate, I rummaged through my emotions for a friendly expression and nailed it to my face. "Thanks. Nice to meet you too. Fisher's family had so many amazing things to say about you."

Fisher eyed me from a few feet behind her, eyes a little squinted as if he wasn't happy with me for saying that.

Angie twisted her body to look at him. "Aw ... your family is the best. They really feel like my family after all these years."

Fisher lifted his eyebrows, lips curled into a reluctant smile as he gave her a nod.

"Well, let's go. You can drive, babe." She tossed Fisher her keys. "I don't know where we're going."

Babe ...

I slithered into the back seat behind Fisher's seat as Angie climbed into the passenger's seat of the white, compact SUV.

"Are you in college, Reese?" Angie asked before we pulled out of the driveway.

Yay ... this line of questioning.

"Nope. Just working for Fisher this summer." I didn't have the energy to make myself sound any more promising like, "I'm taking a gap year," which insinuated I'd be starting college, only a year later.

Angie won. Rory would be home in less than a week. There was no need to try.

"Fisher is the most talented human I have ever met. He's always been good at everything. Such a natural. But what's it like to work for him?" She reached over and squeezed his leg, his upper thigh.

I glanced up in the rearview mirror and caught his gaze on me. Totally unreadable.

"Fisher's an okay boss." I glanced out my window.

Angie laughed, moving her hand from his leg to the nape of his neck. "I can see that about you. I bet it's your intensity. Such a perfectionist, huh, Fish?"

He didn't respond. I felt sure he had some expression to give her, but I didn't want to see it.

Babe ... Fish ...

Lucky for me, Angie shifted the conversation to her mom and that gobbled up the rest of the drive to the venue—where I couldn't get out of the SUV quick enough. Lucky for me, Christina and her boyfriend were waiting at the door. I ran to her, anything to get away from the fated love birds.

"Eek! Reese!" She gave me a huge hug.

"It's so good to see you. I've missed you so freaking much." I released her and glanced at the handsome guy with the richest dark brown skin and black hair I had ever seen.

"Reese, this is Jamison. Jamison this is my BFF since ... gah ... forever. She left me for church school, and I've never forgiven her." Christina winked.

I wondered if she had told Jamison about the fate of my parents and *why* I was forced to leave her for "church school."

Sensing someone right at my back, I turned. "Oh ..." I gave Fisher a tiny smile, but there was no way I was looking at Angie. "Hey, this is my friend Christina and her boyfriend Jamison. Guys, this is my boss, Fisher and ..." *What? His girlfriend?* "Angie."

"Nice to meet you," they all seemed to chime at once.

"So ... where's your rock star boyfriend?" Christina nudged me.

"Fish, you didn't tell me Arnie and Reese were a thing," Angie wrapped her arm around Fisher's arm and gave him a pouty face.

I wanted to vomit.

"He just met her yesterday and invited her and us to his show. I'm not sure that qualifies as 'together.'" He brushed past us to the box office and claimed our tickets.

"But you can and should tell everyone he's your boyfriend." My BFF winked at me while taking Jamison's hand and following Fisher and Angie into the venue.

It wasn't a big venue, more of a dive bar with a stage. I was surprised tickets were required at all. But there was a table right by the stage reserved for us.

Christina didn't even take a seat; she sat on Jamison's lap while Angie pulled her chair so close to Fisher's chair she might as well have perched onto his lap. I sat off to the side, by myself.

"Can I get everyone drinks?" the waitress asked.

Angie ordered a martini. Fisher got a beer. Jamison ordered beer too and had to show an ID. Then Christina ordered a glass of wine and sure enough ... she had an ID too.

"And for you?" the waitress looked at me.

"Water. Thanks."

"I can go to the bar in a sec and get you something," Christina whispered in my ear. "I can't believe you don't have a fake ID."

"I'm good." I gave her a tight smile. "Really."

Fisher eyed me every two seconds, and I knew this because my gaze kept drifting to him as well.

Shortly after our drinks were served, the band came onto the stage while the bar erupted into loud clapping, hooting, and even a few screamers behind us.

"Whoa ... you are *so* getting some of that tonight," Christina said loud enough for Fisher and everyone else to hear. "He's hot, Reese."

Jamison poked her in the side and gave her an eye roll. Angie laughed. I shifted my gaze to Arnie, and Christina was right ... he was hot under the lights. Tattoos. That wild, blond tipped hair. And a guitar hugging his body.

My phone vibrated, and I pulled it from my handbag.

Fisher: You are NOT getting any of that tonight.

When I glanced up, his head was still bowed to his phone.

Reese: Sure thing, BABE! (eye roll emoji)

He lifted his face from his phone and frowned at me. I turned my attention to the stage.

After the final song, Arnie took off his shirt and tossed it to *me*. I grinned as the women in the venue went crazy, including Christina, despite her boyfriend right next to her. Arnie nodded for us to make our way backstage.

Christina and Jamison headed through the gated off

area along with Angie while Fisher stayed back as if he was simply letting everyone else go first.

Except me.

He slid his finger though the belt loop at the back of my shorts to stop me. Then he leaned down and whispered in my ear, "Tell Arnie to do his own fucking laundry."

I barked a laugh and shook my head, glancing back at him. He grinned and gave me a quick wink, making me want to turn around and throw my arms around him. I wanted to pretend it was just us at the concert, and we were going out with Arnie and some other woman Arnie had invited along with my friends.

That wasn't the reality.

He let go of my belt loop, and we squeezed through the opening between two security guards, where Arnie and the rest of our group waited for us.

"You were amazing. I can't believe Fisher hasn't been bragging about you." From the corner of my eye, I could see Fisher frown as I gushed to Arnie.

I could also see Angie's arm slide around Fisher's waist the way Teagan had once laid claim to him. Would it ever be me doing that? I wondered.

"Thanks, gorgeous." Arnie took my hand and pulled me toward an exit. "Let's grab some food. I'm starving." He seemed high. It had to be a real adrenaline rush playing to a roomful of screaming fans.

"Don't you need your shirt?"

"Nah. That's for you. I have another one in my vehicle."

Making a quick glance backward, I made sure

everyone else was following us. Yep. The two couples arm-in-arm. Three happy faces and a grumpy naked fisherman.

I rode with Arnie in his Escalade with the others behind us. He didn't make me the least bit uncomfortable, which surprised me. We talked about his band and where he'd played, along with his future gigs across the U.S. opening for some bigger bands.

We ended up at a fancy European restaurant, and I felt so underdressed. I would not have, had I left on my nipples top. Even Arnie slipped on a nicer button-down over his white tee.

"Have you been here?" he asked, again taking my hand and leading me toward the entrance as everyone else pulled into parking spaces.

"I have not."

"You'll love it. The food is phenomenal. And the atmosphere is even better. Big crystal chandeliers. Checkered floors. It's a little dark." He gave my hand a squeeze. "And a little sexy."

"Sounds ... cool," I squeaked the words because my level of comfort started to decline. Even if I wasn't *with* the guy I wanted to be with, I was glad that Arnie and I weren't alone.

"I don't know if we can afford this," Christina joked as we gathered just inside the door. But I didn't think it was entirely a lie.

"I know the owner. And it's on me. No worries." Arnie puffed out his chest and grinned.

I didn't have to look at Fisher to know his eyes were rolling around in his head at his brother's need to flaunt.

As soon as we were seated, Christina stood. "Ladies' room?" She eyed me.

I nodded.

Out of courtesy, we gave Angie a quick questioning glance, but she didn't even look our way. She was too busy drooling over *my guy*!

As soon as we slipped into the posh ladies' room, Christina grabbed my shoulders. "Oh my god. Arnie is so into you. Seriously, what if he makes it really big? You could tour with him. Live the life of a rock star's girlfriend."

"I don't see us being that serious." I laughed it off.

"Well, everyone sees the way he's looking at you, so there's no doubt about what he wants to do with you." She turned and fixed her hair in the frame-lit mirror.

I didn't say anything, but I must have had a slight grimace on my face because she glanced up at my reflection and narrowed her eyes. "I know you went to that church school, but ... you've had sex, right?"

"Well ..." I rubbed my lips together, thinking of the right answer.

"Oh my god. *Well* is not a yes. It's a no." She whipped around. "Reese! You're a virgin?"

If I didn't have a true grimace before, I definitely did after she yelled that. I surveyed the room, praying we were the only ones in there, and it appeared that we were.

"I'm waiting until I'm married. It's no big deal."

"No. If it were no big deal, you'd be all over that rock star out there. I have a boyfriend, but Arnie makes me want to not have one ... for just one night."

"When..." I bit the end of my thumbnail "...when did you have sex for the first time?"

"A week before my seventeenth birthday. Tate Hoover. Remember him?"

"You had sex with Tate Hoover? The kid who rarely talked and played trombone?"

"Yes." She shrugged. "He was nice. And had strong lips from all the trombone playing. Also, his rhythm was perfection."

I covered my mouth and snorted. "Oh my gosh."

Christina smirked. "So ... you haven't had sex. What have you done? I know you've kissed a guy. Maybe two, yeah?"

I nodded slowly. "And uh ... recently I had a date, a couple of dates with someone. *Not* Arnie. And we did some stuff."

She lifted a perfectly drawn eyebrow. "Elaborate on *stuff.*"

My cheeks felt warm just thinking about it. "We kissed ... a lot. And I ... well ..."

"Oh my god, just spill. Did he go down on you?"

I shook my head.

"Did you give him head?"

Another head shake.

"Did he finger you?"

My lips twisted.

She grinned. "So he's had his hand in your panties?"

I nodded. I liked the yes and no questions best.

"Have you seen his cock?"

Biting my lower lip, I shook my head.

"Touched it?"

Head shake.

"Hand up your shirt?"

Nod.

"Mouth on your breasts?"

Nod.

"Has he made you orgasm?"

Nod.

"Oh ... then you're close. You're basically going through all the motions. Just do it. I don't really think you get extra points from God for being a virgin."

I rolled my eyes. "I disagree."

"You've been brainwashed for three years. Of course you disagree."

"I haven't been brainwashed."

She shot me a look, a look like she didn't believe me or couldn't believe I really believed it either.

"How's your mom? I heard that's why you're in Denver."

"I don't know. I've spent less than three days with her. She's out in California doing some training. She comes back at the end of the week."

"So you've been living alone?"

"Well, sort of. She rents the basement of Fisher's house. So I'm in the basement alone, but he lives on the main floor."

"Living with your sexy boss, huh? Rough life. Too bad he has a girlfriend. And he's a little old for you."

I took the chance to mess with my hair in the mirror. "You think ten years older is too old? I mean ... I'm just asking because I know people who are married who have ten or more years between them."

"Yeah. I suppose. I couldn't imagine dating someone ten years older than me right now. Jamison is four years older, and sometimes I feel like we have to find things in common because he's just at a different place in his life. Ten years would be even crazier. Speaking of Jamison, we'd better get back out there. You didn't actually have to pee, right?"

"I'm good."

"Everything fine?" Jamison asked Christina as we sat back down at the table.

"Totally. Sorry we took so long. I had to cool Reese down. Her date tonight has her overheating."

Oh no. No. No. NO! Why did she say that?

Arnie lit up, more than a little pleased to hear that. Angie nudged Fisher and grinned like she needed to urge him to be excited to hear that. But Fisher's stony expression didn't give that same happy vibe.

And what was I supposed to say? No. I wasn't attracted to Arnie? That would have been a slap in the face to the guy who got us front row seats and was paying for dinner at an expensive restaurant.

So ... with a shy grin, I sat down and didn't confirm nor deny it.

The alcohol flowed nonstop over the next two hours. The food was ridiculously good. And the company wasn't bad. Aside from my glass of ice water, I felt like a real adult on a date with the wrong guy.

With every sip of wine, Angie got more handsy with Fisher, and that made me remain idle when Arnie rested his arm on the back of my chair, squeezed my leg playfully, and whispered things in my ear. Some things I couldn't understand because he'd had too much to drink, but other short phrases included things like "you look so hot tonight" or "I can't stop staring at you."

Those little things seemed to feed Fisher's need to drink more too. By the time Arnie lazily signed for the meal, Jamison and I were the only sober ones at the table. I was glad he was being responsible for my friend.

"I'll order a ride," Fisher mumbled as he pulled his phone out of his pocket.

"Good idea, babe." Angie hugged his arm and rested her head on his shoulder.

"I can drive." I shrugged.

"Yesss ..." Arnie stood and held out his hand. "You can drive them home." He nodded to Fisher and Angie. "Then you can drive me. And I'll get you home in the morning." He smiled like it was a genius idea.

"Fuck no ..." Fisher spoke up, and I froze. Where was he going with his objection? Would he vomit the truth in his inebriated condition? "I told Rory I'd watch her. I can't watch her at your house."

"Babe." Angie pinched his cheeks. "I don't think you can watch anyone ..." She giggled. "Except me."

I grabbed Arnie's key fob from his hand. "Let's go. We'll figure it out."

Just outside of the restaurant, Christina hugged me. "Bye, my bestest friend ever. I hope you get some yum yum tonight." She giggled.

"Bye." I shook my head as Jamison rolled his eyes at her drunkenness.

I was able to just click "Home" on Arnie's navigation since no one was with it enough to give me his address. It took fifteen minutes to get there. I hopped out to make sure he made it to his door okay.

"Stay." He put his hands into prayer position. "Please."

"I have to take them home. But I had fun. Thank you so much."

"Fine." He sighed. "Goodnight, hot girl."

Just as I started to laugh, he grabbed my face and kissed me. It was hard, but rather still. Not a lot of movement.

"Goddamn ... you taste good." He opened his door and stumbled inside.

As soon as the door shut, I wiped my mouth and descended the walk to his Escalade. When I climbed into the driver's seat, I could feel Fisher's gaze on me from the back seat with Angie draped across his lap sleeping.

"What's Angie's address?"

"Just go home," Fisher said.

"It's no problem. I can take—"

"She's staying with me tonight, and we'll get her vehicle tomorrow. Just go."

I think I would have preferred an actual kick to my gut than to hear his anger. Maybe it was the alcohol. Maybe it wasn't. Either way, I couldn't talk past the lump in my throat all the way home.

"Let's go. Can you walk?" Fisher asked Angie.

"Carry me, babe," she said in a sleepy voice.

As I shut the driver's door, he lifted her from the back seat and kicked the door shut, wobbling a bit as if being reminded that he, too, had plenty to drink.

"Ninety-three-eleven is my garage code," Fisher said.

I typed it in and led the way to open the door to the house, wondering who this woman really was in his life. How did she come and go like they were still together?

Touching him.

Calling him "babe."

Batting her eyelashes.

I didn't get it.

"Can you find your feet?" he asked her as he eased her from his arms.

Angie wobbled a bit on her heels before stepping out of them and wobbling a bit more as she made her way down the short hallway to his bedroom. "Don't make me wait," she said, unzipping her dress and letting it fall to the floor a few feet from his door.

I lost sight of her as she reached to unhook her bra.

Fisher rubbed his temples, closing his eyes. "Thanks for driving."

A naked woman awaited him in his bedroom just hours after he sucked my breasts while pinning me to his front door, and "Thanks for driving" was his response?

"I'm going to church in the morning, so someone else will have to get Arnie's vehicle back to him." My emotions teetered on the edge of a complete breakdown. I knew Fisher would deal with Arnie and his vehicle, but I felt the need to act as unaffected as possible by what he was likely getting ready to do with his childhood sweetheart. And talking about the Escalade was better than screaming at him because that's what I really wanted to do.

"Of course." He moseyed to the kitchen sink to get a glass of water, taking it down just as quickly as he did earlier that day when I brought him water while he was mowing the lawn.

I opened my mouth to say goodnight, but I couldn't do it. I didn't want him to have a *good night*. So I opened the basement door and just as quickly closed it behind me before the tears released.

Just as I reached the bottom of the stairs, the door opened. My fingers made swift moves to wipe my cheeks.

One step.

Two steps.

"What do you need?" I asked.

Three steps.

Four steps.

"There's a naked woman in your bedroom. Better not keep her waiting." I turned on the light in the family room and slipped off my sandals, keeping my back to him as I used the back of the sectional to steady myself while balancing on one foot and then the other.

"If it's not you, then I don't give a fuck who's naked in my bed." He slid his hand around my waist and pulled my back to his chest.

Gripping his arm with my hands, I drew in a slow breath.

Angie was upstairs.

"You're drunk," I whispered.

He chuckled, burying his nose in my hair. "I'm over the legal limit; I'm not drunk. There's a difference."

"Well, *babe* ..." I peeled his arms away from me and put a few feet between us. "Why are you not married to that woman upstairs? Your family adores her. I mean *adores* her. And she obviously thinks the two of you are in some never-ending relationship. Why is that? Are you? Is she your endgame, but for now you're screwing around with other women until you're ready to commit? Because you guys are not broken up. She doesn't just show up out of nowhere and fall back into *your bed*."

Twisting his lips, he cocked his head a fraction. I made him think. Really think.

"You have the best tits. Not too small, but not too big. And I could suck on your nipples all day. They are nothing short of perfect."

Never mind. I didn't make him think at all. I ignored my blush. He brought it out of me with a look, and when he talked dirty to me, it took over my whole body.

"You're drunk." I crossed my arms over my chest.

"No." He grinned holding up two fingers then three. Then back to two. "Scouts honor. In the morning, I will still find your tits to be the best thing I've seen or tasted in a very long time. If they were on Yelp, I'd leave a five-star review of them."

"Stop." I bit my lips to keep from grinning.

"I will not stop. I haven't even started talking about your legs." He took two steps toward me, and I retreated to keep the distance.

"Angie is beautiful. I'm not blind. I'm sure her ... *breasts* are Yelp worthy, and her legs are incredibly toned, along with her arms. Her silky hair and skin. And she's successful. Age appropriate. And she's naked in your bed. So you might have to explain to me why you're down here with me."

Fisher deflated, a long breath releasing from his nose as his shoulders dropped an inch. "She wants a husband

and a houseful of babies. A dog. Two cats. And a minivan."

"And you don't?"

"Not yet."

"So ..." I glanced up at the ceiling and laughed, but it didn't really feel funny. "You *are* looking for someone to mess around with until you decide you're ready for wife material. That's awesome, Fisher. Rory comes home in a few days. What's the point? I'm not having sex with you. And why are you so anti-family? You're twenty-eight. Do you know how many men have a family by the time they're your age?"

"No." He prowled toward me again, this time without stopping. "And neither do you. So what's *your* point? You're eighteen. The whole point of your life should be to live in the fucking moment without caring if everything you do makes complete sense."

"Stop." I shook my head, running out of space to escape him as my butt rammed into the pool table.

"I don't want to stop. Do you? Do you really want to stop?"

"I don't know," I whispered. I didn't love the taste of beer, but I thought I'd like it if I tasted it in his mouth. So I kissed him, and he kissed me back. I was right ... beer tasted best on Fisher's tongue. Every well-sorted moral thought in my head jumbled, like the wind catching a neatly stacked pile of papers and scattering them everywhere.

No page numbers.

No sense of meaning.

Just a big, unimaginable mess.

That was what Fisher Mann did to me. He messed with my thoughts.

And that was why I didn't protest when he removed my shirt ... and my bra.

I didn't protest when he unbuttoned my shorts and dropped to his knees in front of me to slide them down my legs, along with my panties. My eyes glossed over with an unfamiliar feeling, like everything he did entered my bloodstream—a drug that robbed any sense of control or objection my brain might have otherwise formulated.

Lifting one leg and then the other, he freed them from my shorts.

"Fisher ..." Everything inside of me felt heavy and slow. My dry mouth panted slowly.

Was he going to put his mouth between my legs?

Was I going to stop him if he did?

All these things I didn't know for sure. Part of me wanted him to stop because I wasn't sure I had the will power to do it myself. But a bigger part of me indulged the curiosity that seemed to have the greatest power over my decisions in that moment.

What were his plans for us? Sex? Oral sex?

He kissed my hipbone and moved a little lower ... and a little lower yet. My heart thundered so loudly in my chest, sending blood whooshing past my ears with such force, I could barely hear him when he did speak.

"Do you want me to kiss you here?" He brushed his lips lightly over *that* part of me.

"I ... I ... don't know." Harsh breaths rushed past my lips as I rested my hands on the side of the pool table to steady myself.

"No?" He left a tiny kiss *there*, before navigating up my body, resting his hands on the pool table next to mine while he flicked his tongue over my nipple before standing straight and shrugging off his shirt. "We'll go until you tell me to stop?"

My lazy gaze worked its way up his body to meet his gaze, and after a few seconds, I nodded. I didn't really know my limit that night. Sex didn't feel right, but stopping felt a little wrong and even a little impossible. All I could do was let him continue and hope that I'd find my limit, that stopping point.

Fisher grabbed my face and kissed me, our tongues mingling as my nipples brushed his chest. And I needed more. My fingers teased his abs just above the waist of his jeans, and he moaned into the kiss. Then my brave and completely inexperienced fingers moved lower, tracing the outline of his erection, and his hips thrust forward into my touch as he moaned a little louder ... kissed me a little harder ... and lifted me onto the edge of the pool table.

It was wrong. I thought. I maybe even knew. But I didn't want to take responsibility ... not yet. The feeling ... the drug he became ... was too strong.

After rocking his hips into me a couple of times, he moved his mouth to my neck, sucking and biting as he unbuttoned his jeans. Things started to feel ... real. Very, very real.

My heart managed to beat even faster. Anticipation soared in my head, making me dizzier.

Stop.

Don't stop.

Gah!

I was so conflicted—those scattered pieces of paper all over the floor without anyone to pick them up and sort them to make sense again.

Fisher's hand tangled in my hair as his mouth returned to mine and his erection, covered only by his underwear, wedged between my legs.

The friction.

The wet feeling.

The heat.

I wasn't ready for sex, or maybe I was. I just didn't know. And as much as I knew, I really knew we needed to stop, I wasn't ready to tell him to stop. It wasn't sex, right? We weren't having actual sex. As much as I wanted more to happen, without actually having sex, I didn't know how to articulate it because I wasn't exactly sure what *more* meant. I only knew I wanted to at least feel him against me, really against me.

My hand rested on his hip, my fingers teasing his underwear's waistband. Sliding one finger beneath it, I slowly inched my way to the front. Just before touching him *there,* putting just enough pressure on the waistband to expose the head of his ... *cock? Penis? No ... Dick?*

Fisher stopped kissing me, and with quick breaths escaping past his parted lips, he glanced down at my finger still curled around the waistband. It was my first glimpse at a man's ... head. That head.

"I need to get a condom," he whispered.

I shook my head slowly. We weren't having sex. I felt fairly certain of that. I just wanted ... well ... I wasn't sure. I wanted to see him and feel him, but not actually have sex. "I want ..." I swallowed hard. "I just want to feel you."

"God ... feel me, Reese." He grabbed my hand and slipped it down the front of his underwear, closing his eyes as his tongue swiped along his lower lip. He released my hand.

It took me a few seconds to move my hand, to gently wrap it around him. He was warm and hard, yet smooth and long. I slid my hand up slowly.

"Fuuuck ..." He dropped his chin and opened his eyes again, watching me touch him, his abs tightening even more than seconds earlier.

My gaze flitted between my hand and his gaze, like I wasn't fully aware that I was the one giving him that pleasure. Me. Not Teagan. Not the woman upstairs in his bed.

Me.

I felt like a queen. A goddess.

The head was even smoother ... and wet ... and a little sticky.

"Reese ..." He closed his eyes, squeezing them shut as if in some sort of agony. "Let me get a condom."

"No. I ... I just want to feel you."

"Fuck ..." His mouth landed on my neck and shoulder again, his hand grabbing my breast with a little bit of desperation. "You *are* feeling me, and it's killing me."

"No. I want to feel you ..." I pushed down a fraction on his erection, forcing his underwear down a little more and positioning him extremely close to the center of my spread legs. "Here. I want to feel you here, but ... just ... on the outside."

"Reese ..." He rested his forehead on my shoulder and dropped his hand to the edge of the pool table again as we both focused on my hand bringing him so incredibly close to me. Taking the tiniest of steps closer, the head of it touched me there.

"Stop." My breath hitched.

The warmth and silkiness felt out of this world.

After hearing him gulp a loud swallow, I rubbed it against me. It felt so good. Everything about him felt good ... maybe even right, from his lips at my shoulder to his right hand on my knee, gently pushing it out to spread my legs a little wider.

With micro movements, he dipped his hips forward a fraction of an inch, hitting my clit, then back. Forward again. Back again.

It wasn't sex.

It wasn't sex.

It wasn't sex.

That chant played on an endless loop in my head.

"God ..." I closed my eyes and said a quick apology prayer for using the Lord's name in vain, but I somehow ignored the obvious apology for sitting naked on the edge of Fisher's pool table while we rubbed his cock along my ... area.

His movements sped up a bit, becoming ragged like his breathing.

"Fisher!" I gasped, digging my fingernails into his shoulders as he stilled.

He stilled because the head of it went in the wrong

direction. It went in ... a fraction. Fisher was inside of me, literally a quarter of an inch, at the very most. But still ... he was there. And he could have moved. He could have jumped back. But he didn't.

I could have moved. I could have scooted back that quarter of an inch. I could have pushed him away. But I didn't.

"I'm so—" He started to apologize. I thought. I wasn't sure. Things were a little foggy at that point.

"No. Don't ... move." I think I meant to say "don't apologize," but I didn't. I had bigger issues than that. I didn't want him to move toward me at all. But ... I also didn't want him to step back. I liked him there. Too much. And if he would have moved forward and pushed farther inside of me, I know I would have let him, but the regret might have been too much. Yet the thought of him stepping away felt nearly as excruciating.

"Reeeese ... I can't fucking stay here." His breaths were little staccatos along my cheek as he dragged his lips from my ear to my mouth and bit my lower lip kinda hard.

Because I couldn't make up my stupid mind, and he was running out of patience, I grabbed *it* and moved it up to my clit again. That time I didn't let go. I made sure every time his pelvis rocked forward, it didn't go inside of me.

But I wanted it to go there. And that was a part of my brain I couldn't control. I couldn't pray away those thoughts. I wanted to have sex with Fisher Mann nearly as much as my lungs wanted oxygen.

"Lean back." He pressed a hand between my breasts.

I couldn't lean back without letting go of him. And if I let go of him, *things* were sure to happen.

Fisher saw the concern on my face and shook his head. "I'm not taking your virginity ... tonight." He smirked.

I didn't trust him. Then again, I didn't trust myself. So I moved forward with another bad decision. I had a whole stack of them that night, and I leaned back onto my forearms. Fisher rested his hands on my knees and spread my legs wider.

"If you let me put my mouth on you..." his gaze landed between my legs "...I could make you scream."

Biting my lip, I shook my head at least a half dozen times.

Oral *sex*.

Nope. It had sex in the name. So I had to pass.

As if God were applauding me at that point for showing restraint.

Fisher leaned forward, rubbing me in the perfect spot with his erection, again and again, as his mouth found my breasts. As the pressure built, I shifted my hips, but not on purpose.

"Fuck!" He stilled again. And again, he was inside of me, a little. A little more actually, but only maybe a half inch this time. "You can't move like that." He breathed heavily.

I wanted it.

In that moment, I made the decision to ... go to Hell maybe. But I wasn't going there a virgin. I was going there with the naked fisherman inside of me.

"Fisher ..." I rested my heels firmly on the edge of the pool table and lifted my hips a tiny bit.

"Fuck. Fuck. Fuck! Stop!" He grabbed my hips and pushed them back down to the pool table. "I don't have on a condom."

"Then get one."

He closed his eye and shook his head. "They're upstairs."

With Angie.

"Fisher ..." I tried to lift my hips again.

Again, he shook his head and held me down while pulling the head of his erection out of me. Then he used one hand to give me an orgasm while using his other hand to give himself one—the result of it landing on my stomach. That part was sort of weird for me.

"Damnation is in your future, little girl." He pulled up his underwear and jeans before sauntering to the kitchen to grab some paper towels.

"Then you're going with me."

He shook his head. "Only after Rory murders me."

CHAPTER SEVENTEEN

I STILL HAD eighty percent of my virginity. It took some complicated math to come up with that. It also meant I still had an eighty percent chance of going to Heaven— one hundred if I followed the once-saved-always-saved philosophy. That was probably the best way to go at that point.

My guilt held on with more permanence than what I'd hoped, but my remorse declined a bit since the dry humping in my bed incident. That brought me to tears afterward. The pool table? No tears. I think I was in shock that I wanted to go all the way. *Fisher* stopped me. The crude, naked fisherman. I never imagined that. He said we'd go until I said stop. I never said stop. If anything, I had my own little cheering section in my head chanting, "Go! Go! Go!"

Creeping along the side of the house, I made my escape the next morning. A little Sunday morning gospel to cleanse my soul.

Tiptoeing along the side of Fisher's truck, I hid from sight in case he was watering his plants.

"Off to confess your sins?"

I jumped and glanced at the garage with both doors wide open and Fisher bent over his weight bench working his triceps.

No shirt, of course.

"Um ..." I cleared my throat, eyeing Arnie's Escalade. Did it mean Angie was still there too? "Yes. I'm going to church." I tightened my grip on the clutch purse I'd used the previous night and took slow steps into the garage.

"You look nice." He eyed me in my simple white romper and silver Birkenstocks.

"Thanks. Is..." my gaze signaled to the door to the house "...Angie gone?"

"Nope," he replied with a strained voice as he continued his workout. "In the shower."

"Oh. Did you ... sleep on the sofa or in a spare room?"

"No. It's my bed. Why should I have done that?"

Swallowing hard, I clenched my teeth and shrugged with stiff shoulders. My entire body tensed with anger. "No reason." I managed to eke out the words. "Later." I pivoted, holding my breath—holding *everything* that tried to pry open my lips to be set free.

"You want to know if I had sex with her, huh?"

My feet stopped in place, but I couldn't turn around. "No."

"No? Really? Well, we did. Full penetration. There's really nothing better than being buried balls deep in a woman. No holding back. No fragile hymens. No guilt. Just raw fucking."

Tears stung my eyes before I had a chance to flinch at his vulgarity, and I forced my feet to make speedy, gigantic strides out of the garage.

"Not so quick." I heard the *thunk* of weights hitting the rubber mat, and in the next breath he grabbed my arm and whipped me around to face him. "It's a joke." He shook his head and grinned as his other hand blotted the wet corners of my eyes.

"It's a terrible joke," I whispered past the lump in my throat.

"Probably. But Rory comes home in a few days." He blew out a long breath. "And *you* said it would stop then. You said you didn't want her to know. So if we're a few days from ending whatever this is ... then you need to get ahold of yourself."

That confirmation? The one that said his feelings toward me were *way* different than mine were toward him? It sucked.

Jerking my hand away, I finished wiping my eyes before a new round of emotion made its way to the stage. "I *have* ahold of myself. I'm just not emotionally dead like you are. Not because I'm eighteen. It's because I'm a good person with real emotions, and that will never change. So excuse me if the idea of you screwing someone immediately after consuming me like some tasteless appetizer is a little disheartening, but it's only because I don't offer myself up to just anyone like you obviously do."

Fisher's head jerked backward. "First..." he held up a finger in my face "...you didn't really let me taste you, so the tasteless reference is unfair. And second..." he held up another finger "...if you're insinuating Angie is *just anyone*, then you need to check your facts again."

My face scrunched into my most menacing expression, which probably only made me look constipated. "You are ... you're ..." My hands balled into tight fists.

He smirked.

Gah!

I hated him for smirking at me when there was nothing funny about anything we were discussing.

"For a cruciv—cruciferous whatever that made-up word was you called yourself, you sure lack in vocabulary when the pressure's on."

My hate grew. First his smirk, then his stupid fumbling of the word cruciverbalist. I didn't want to smile. It wasn't okay for him to steal my anger with his intentional or unintentional humor. Yet there I stood, with my hands still fisted and an unavoidable grin climbing up my face.

"You're so stupid. Never again do you get to reference my age since you just called me a botany term denoting cabbage family plants. *Not* the same thing as cruciverbalist—one who constructs or is good at solving crossword puzzles." I added an eye roll for good measure.

"Broccoli. Cabbage. Cauliflower. I know. I'm not as stupid as you think I am. Again, you just don't get my humor."

"I'm going to church." I turned on my heel and continued toward the Outback.

"Say hi to the virgins for me."

"Jerk," I mumbled—but not without grinning because Fisher Mann was so ... *extra.*

"WELCOME BACK. It's good to see you again." A somewhat familiar face greeted me as I took a chair in the Sunday school classroom. "It's Brendon."

I nodded. "Yeah. I remember." I didn't really. "Thanks. We missed you at the singles' Bible study on Wednesday night."

"I wasn't feeling well. Headache." The hardest part about having a church family was the accountability which led to truths they didn't want to hear or lies they happily swallowed while God knew. He always knew. Like earlier that morning during the sermon, I wasn't thinking about the words echoing through the sanctuary. My mind replayed the previous night. With my Bible open on my lap and people all around me responding to the day's gospel with "Amens," I squeezed my thighs together and thought about Fisher between my legs while silently saying my own kind of Amens.

"Well, I hope you're feeling better now." Brendon sat next to me.

"Much better. Thanks."

"Would you like to have lunch with me today?"

Brendon wasn't terrible looking. He had a great smile, and he was taller than me which was always a bonus. But ... there was Fisher.

And ... there was Rory coming home in a matter of days.

"Just lunch." Brendon chuckled as if he could read my mind. "I don't have that many friends."

"Okay. Lunch would be great. I could use a friend

too." If Fisher had Angie in his bed ... in whatever capacity ... I could have lunch with a male friend.

After class, we raced to the parking lot to beat the crowd and congestion of vehicles trying to maneuver out of the tight spaces.

"Shoot. I'm trapped." Brendon frowned at his car blocked in a parallel parking spot at the west end of the lot. He barely had two inches in the front or the back to maneuver. "Guess I'm waiting for the crowd after all."

"Leave it. I'll drive and drop you off after lunch."

"You sure?"

I nodded.

He followed me to my car and gave me an extended glance over the top of it as I unlocked the doors. "How old are you?"

"Eighteen." I unlocked the car and slid into the driver's seat as he got in on the other side.

"Really? Wow. I thought you were older."

"How old are you?"

"Twenty-four."

I wouldn't have guessed that. Maybe twenty. "You look young for twenty-four." I smiled, giving him a quick sideways glance as I backed out of the parking space.

"Good thing this isn't a date. I'd feel a little weird with you being eighteen."

"I'm an adult," I said my new and thoroughly recycled mantra.

We settled on a Mediterranean restaurant and a large booth near the open kitchen.

"We're just a few blocks from my house. I've passed this place many times on my walks."

"You live in this neighborhood?" He narrowed one eye. "With your parents? It's just ... a really nice neighborhood. I couldn't afford to live here by myself or even with a houseful of roommates."

I sipped my water then shook my head. "I live with my mom. And she rents the basement of a house. So I can't afford to live here and neither could she if it weren't a basement rental situation."

"I see. Makes sense. So what are you doing this summer? Getting ready for college?"

"I'm taking a gap year." There it was. My go-to. "But this summer, I'm working for a construction company doing random things in the office or delivering lunch to the crew."

"Sounds..." he smirked "...fun."

"It's interesting. Fun? Probably not."

"Do you like your boss?"

"What?" My head snapped up from the menu. "Why would you ask me that?"

"Uh ..." His eyes rolled quickly to one side and then the other. "Just making conversation."

I relaxed my defensive posture. "Sorry. Yeah. He's nice. He's actually my mom's landlord. It's his house. He lives on the main level. And he was kind enough to offer me a summer job."

"That's a cool situation."

I nodded. It was cool. And sexy. And my newest obsession.

"So ... what do you do?" I asked. "I assume since you're twenty-four, you must be out of college, if you went."

"I went." He nodded while studying his menu. "I just graduated from law school, actually."

"Can you be a lawyer at twenty-four?"

He laughed. "If you graduated high school a year early. Yes. You can."

"Wow. Brainy."

Brendon set his menu down and shook his head. I was pretty sure that was a blush on his face. "Good memory. That's all."

"Photographic?"

He shrugged. "Maybe. I've never been officially tested. I can read quite quickly too. My dad died when I was in fifth grade. And my mom spent all of her time working to put me and my sisters through school, so we didn't spend a whole lot of time figuring me out. And we didn't have a lot of money, so I spent more time reading than watching the single television we had in the house. No cellphone until I earned money to buy my own and pay for a plan. No computer outside of the ones we used in school. No video games. Pretty boring, huh?"

I felt an instant connection to Brendon in that moment. "Well, my dad died too. Three years ago. Then I moved to Texas to live with my grandparents until I graduated. I didn't have a phone either until I bought my own ... which my grandparents didn't let me do until I was eighteen. So I've literally had a cell phone for less than a year. Now who's boring?"

"Really?" Brendon smiled as if my confession, albeit a little sad and pathetic, made him feel some joy.

"However, we did have a computer in the house. I had one from the school that we could bring home. So it's not like I didn't have internet access even if it was monitored for appropriate content." My nose wrinkled.

"No internet porn for you."

That made my face heat a bit. Just the word porn did that. "No." I returned a nervous laugh. But I had seen porn. Once ... okay twice. My friend Kat lived with her dad, and her dad worked nights so he was always sleeping during the day. Kat thought it was fun to check out her dad's browser history on the computer; he wasn't only paying bills and ordering socks from Amazon while Kat and her younger brother were at the Christian academy. Worth noting too ... he taught the teen's Sunday school class at church.

"Have you taken the bar exam?"

"Nope. I've taken a job with a law firm here in Denver, and they're adamant about helping me study for it. But honestly ..." He winked. It wasn't a Fisher wink, but it was still adorable in its own way. "I've got this."

Confidence.

Man ... what I wouldn't give to have had even half of his confidence. And direction. That was it more than anything. A sense of direction imparted a certain level of confidence. I didn't know if gap-year kids had as much confidence.

We ordered food and chatted for over an hour. Brendon's mom lived just outside of Chicago. And his two younger sisters still lived there too.

"Enough about me. Tell me about your mom? Why were you living with your grandparents after your dad died?"

"My mom had some ... *issues* after the divorce. So my

dad had custody of me. Then my grandparents stepped in after he died because my mom was still not able to take care of me."

Why did I lie? I didn't know. Out of all the people I should have been honest with, Brendon was at the top. He was a Christian, which meant he would not have judged me. (Yes, I realized that thought held zero actual truth.) He wasn't trying to date me, so I had no need to impress him. And I'd been upfront about my mom's situation with so many other people before him. I don't even remember making the conscious decision to lie to him. My mouth started moving, and it took a bit for my brain to process the automated lie.

"So how is it now ... with your mom? Are things weird?"

"Well, that's hard to answer. I no sooner arrived and she left for L.A. to do some salon training. She'll be home in a few days."

"You must be excited about that?"

Was I excited? Rory home equaled things ending with Fisher.

"Sure." I smiled, but it barely bent my lips.

After he bought my lunch, in which I argued because it wasn't a date, we climbed back into the car and started to pull out of the parallel parking spot and into traffic.

"Show me where you live."

"Why?" I laughed through some uncontrolled nerves. My goal that day was to avoid going home for as long as possible.

Brendon shrugged. "Sunday afternoon drive. It's a

great neighborhood. And when you mentioned you lived close by, it piqued my curiosity."

Scraping my teeth along my bottom lip a few times, I nodded slowly. "Okay. We can do a drive-by."

It took less than three minutes to get to the house. I slowed down, but not much. "That's it, right there."

"Wow ... wait ... slow down. The view from the back has to be spectacular."

"Yeah, it's fine."

"Reese." He laughed. "Seriously, are you not going to stop? Can I see the back of the house?"

"Not a good idea." I slowed down a little more. Arnie's Escalade was gone and the garage doors were shut.

"Why? Because you don't really live here?"

"What?" I stopped the car. "Of course I live here. You think I'm lying?"

He smirked. "There's only one way to find out."

"Gah. Fine!" I pulled along the side of the street and hopped out. "Let's go in back."

Brendon followed me around to the back of the house.

"Happy now?"

Slipping his hands into his pockets, he nodded. His blue eyes bright and the gel in his hair reflecting the sunlight. "Not unless we go inside."

"Are you serious?"

"Are *you* serious?" He shot back at me.

I couldn't hide my smile, so I rolled my eyes and led him to the door. "See?" I said as the key fit the lock and I opened the door.

"Yeah, I see. You weren't lying." He followed me into the basement. "This is huge. And really nice. When you said you were living in a basement, I think it conjures images of dinky spaces with no light, cobwebs, and a growling furnace. This is by far nicer than any place I've ever lived." He milled around the space, running his fingers along the edge of the pool table. "You play?"

I had used the pool table, just not for pool.

"A little."

"Then let's play." He grabbed two sticks and handed one to me.

Midway through our game, the door upstairs opened and footsteps followed. Brendon shot me a narrowed-eyed glance. Of course, he had to be thinking ... who would be coming down the stairs? Surely, I locked the door. Right?

Wrong.

You didn't lock the door when you secretly hoped your landlord would sneak down with a condom so you didn't have to stay stuck at an eighty-percent virgin status.

"Hey," Fisher said coming to an abrupt halt at the bottom of the stairs.

"Hey," I said. "What's up?" I pretended that his uninvited trip downstairs was no big deal.

Was he coming downstairs to take the rest of my virginity? I thought a million things along that line.

"I'm Fisher." He ignored me and made his way to the pool table with his hand held out for Brendon.

"Brendon." My non-date friend shook Fisher's hand. "You have an amazing house."

"Thanks." Fisher shot me a quick glance.

I bit my lips together for a second before realizing we were suspended in silence. "Fisher built this house. He's really amazing."

"It's great, man. Really incredible." Brendon rested the end of his pool stick on the floor and leaned into it casually.

"Thanks," Fisher said once again while shooting me another glance, this time with his head slightly canted and an unusual look in his eyes. "I think that's the first time you've complimented me on my skills."

My eyebrows shot up my forehead. "Oh? I don't know about that. Did you ..." I dropped my pool stick on the ground with my fidgety hands, and it made an embarrassing *clank*. "Uh ..." I quickly retrieved it. "Did you ..." I totally forgot what I was going to say or ask.

"Did I ...?"

"Uh ... need something?"

The smile that swelled on Fisher's face was almost too much to handle without wearing more absorbent panties. "Yeah, I needed something, but it can wait until you don't have company."

Brendon's cool expression morphed into something a little more uncomfortable like he sensed a third-wheel feeling.

"Was it about work?" I made an effort to normalize the situation.

"No," Fisher said slowly, as slowly as he shook his head, as slowly as he made me weak in the knees.

"Did you hear from my mom?"

"No ..." He dragged out another long, torturous no.

"Oh ... I know. Duh. I was going to show you where water's getting into the back room."

Fisher lifted a single brow. I ignored him, handing Brendon my pool stick. "Be right back." I marched to the back room with Fisher right behind me. As soon as he shut the door, I turned.

"Who's your friend? Your introduction skills are not up to par. I know his name is Brendon and he likes my house. Care to elaborate now?"

"No. Why did you come downstairs?" I took one step then another toward him, my hands itching to touch him, my eyes disappointed that he was wearing a T-shirt. "Did you bring a condom?"

A half grin formed on his sexy, scruffy face. "No. Give your innocence to Brendon. I'm not in the business of pissing off my friends. And if I were you, I'd look for a new church. The sermon has already worn off. You're looking for sin just hours after crossing the threshold of the church's doors."

"Who's your *friend*?" I fisted his shirt, telling my unwise heart to ignore his comment about giving myself to Brendon or his rambling about finding a new church.

"Rory." He kept his hands to himself and eyed me with caution.

"Rory is your tenant."

"And my friend."

"So you thought she'd be good with you only inserting the tip?" I could barely say those words without burning up.

"You're a temptress. A typical church girl playing the innocent role. You should be truly ashamed."

"Fisher?"

He waited a second to respond, but when his gaze fell to my lips, I knew I had him. "What?"

"Are you going to kiss me?"

"I was thinking about it."

"Don't think."

Wetting his lips as his grin hit full capacity, he said, "I never do when I'm with you." Then he slid his hand to the back of my neck and kissed me. The knuckles of his other hand brushed my cheek. His touch so gentle—too gentle. It felt different. And maybe it was just my foolish heart hoping for more, but it didn't feel like a purely physical moment.

"Send your friend home," he murmured over my lips. "I want you all to myself."

"I can't. I have to drive him." I pulled back, releasing his shirt as he released my neck.

"Did you pick him up at church?"

"His car was pinned in, and we wanted to go to lunch before the crowd flooded the parking lot."

"A date?"

I started to respond but stopped just as quickly. "Why? Do you have a problem with me dating him?"

Say yes, Fisher. Just please say yes.

He twisted his lips, like his silence twisted my heart. "No."

Fisher ... why?

"Well, it wasn't a date." I shoved his chest, forcing him to move out of my way. "But thanks for reminding me how little this means to you."

"Reese ..."

I opened the door, tipped my chin up, and plastered a smile on my face. "Sorry. Problem solved. Now ... where were we? Was it my turn?"

"Yes." Brendon handed me my pool stick as I ignored Fisher's exit from the utility room.

"Nice meeting you, Brendon. You two have fun."

I clenched my jaw, trying to hide my slight wince at his words while keeping my back to him.

"Thanks. Nice meeting you too."

It was really nice that they got along so well. Brendon didn't want to date me because I was too young for him. And Fisher didn't want my virginity because he wasn't in that business anymore. I felt a little rejected.

After Brendon won three games in a row, I drove him back to the church.

"Thanks for lunch. Again, I would have paid for mine."

He opened his door. "It was my pleasure." Pausing for a second he narrowed his eyes and lifted his gaze to mine. "What if..." he pressed his lips together, again pausing for a second "...our age difference didn't really matter? What if we did this again, but we called it a date?"

"A date?" I echoed in a soft tone just before taking a hard swallow. "I ... well ... maybe we can discuss it next weekend after church."

"Discuss it?" He laughed a little. "Wow, you really take dating seriously. Since we both have cell phones now, how about we exchange numbers and discuss it this week before church next Sunday?"

I thought about Fisher. Then, I thought about Rory

before nodding. With his number and several social media follows, he grinned and closed the door. At any other time in my life, I would have been thrilled to have met Brendon. He was closer to my age. Employed. And he attended church. I also felt certain that he wasn't a crude talker.

On the way home, I gave myself a pep talk. It involved ignoring Fisher until Monday morning. Eating dinner alone. And going to bed early with a book or my current crossword puzzle.

So much for pep talks ...

The second I climbed out of Rory's car, I marched straight to his front door and rang the doorbell. A few seconds later, he opened the door, eyeing me from head to toe before stepping back and silently inviting me into his domain.

"So ... you won't take my virginity." It felt weird having that conversation because he'd said something so eerily similar to me. "What will you take from me?"

With a contemplative expression that seemed to border on the painful side, he whispered, "Let's start with your clothes."

I wondered ... I wondered *so hard* when he made the decision to draw a line. He knew as well as I did that Rory wouldn't be okay with anything we had done together. It wasn't just me pushing lines and bending rules to serve my own needs and desires; Fisher did it too.

I just didn't know why. He could have had Angie or Teagan or a million other women meeting his sexual needs.

Why me?

Why seek something you know you won't conquer ... out of choice?

So many thoughts stirred in my head, but they didn't stop my hands from sliding my shoulders and arms out of my romper, letting it drop to the floor.

That confused and painful expression remained affixed to Fisher's face until he met my gaze. Then it vanished, leaving the Fisher I knew all too well.

Cocky.

Confident.

Unapologetically crude.

"Shoes."

I slipped out of my shoes.

"Bra."

Reaching both hands behind me, I unhooked my bra and let it slide down my chest and arms. He focused on my bare breasts, on my erect nipples.

After the bra landed on the floor at my feet with my romper, I reached for my panties.

"No." He inched his head side to side. "Leave them on. Turn that way. And walk slowly to my bedroom."

There I was, following Fisher off the side of the mountain. Did he know I would do anything for him? Did he know what that meant?

Turning, I feigned confidence and made the slow walk down the hallway to his bedroom.

"Stop."

I stopped because he told me to stop.

"Turn around."

I turned around, centered at the threshold to his bedroom.

Fisher took his time making his way to me, slowly peeling off his shirt, leaving him in bare feet and exercise shorts. When he reached the doorway, he pressed his hands to the wood frame. "Put your hands below mine."

Eyeing his hands for a few seconds, I pressed my hands to the frame. "W-why?"

"Because." He kneeled in front of me. "Your knees will want to give out soon." Sliding his hands to the back of my legs, he moved my hips toward his face, stopping with his mouth just above the waist of my panties. "Can I kiss you here?"

I couldn't speak. Swallowing and breathing heavily became a full-time job. Fisher pressed his mouth to my skin and glanced up at me.

I nodded.

He kissed lower. "Here?"

I nodded, gripping the wood with anticipation. My knees were already weak.

His lips descended another inch or more. *There.* He was right there. A whooshing sound—a thumping that matched my ever-escalating heartbeat—made it hard to hear anything else.

"Here?"

I barely heard him, but I still nodded.

Fisher pressed a soft kiss over my panties. Then his grip on my legs tightened, and he kissed me a little harder, sucking some of the thin cotton into his mouth. Biting it. And tugging it. Exposing part of my flesh.

Again, he kissed me hard. Sucked. Bit. Tugged.

My panties were no longer covering much. I fought the gullible thoughts tripping over themselves in my head. Thoughts of love and happily ever after's. Some men showered women with poems and flowers. Maybe oral sex was Fisher's way of expressing his love. Sadly, my panties between his teeth wasn't exactly something I could photograph and share with my friends on social media.

#relationshipgoals

#myfirsttime

#LazySunday

#LickIt

We weren't going public with our relationship anyway because it was ending soon.

"I'm going to fucking devour you," he said just before his mouth covered my bare flesh.

Just before his tongue parted me.

Just before he hummed.

I was ...

Terrified to have his mouth there.

Elated because it felt so good. Too good. Sinfully good.

Confused because it wasn't sex, but it was sex.

Surely, the look he gave me fell under Rory's testicle removal threat. Did he think about that? Even once?

All the blood in my body made its way to the exact spot his mouth was on me. And it made it impossible to think or breathe. And yes, it made it really hard to keep from falling to the floor beneath my shaky knees.

"Fisher ..." I found a tiny voice to speak one word as my body teetered to the side, my whole forearm resting on the frame as my other hand claimed a large handful of his hair and my knees bowed inward.

It was *wrong!* I knew it. I just didn't have the mental or emotional capacity to stop it. A prime example of why giving in to temptation was a bad idea. There were points of no return, and I had breezed past mine the second he opened his front door.

Fisher was unrelenting and hungry. He seemed famished. Then he seemed ... impatient, ripping my panties down my legs. I released his hair and reached for them, as if they were my last line of defense, even if they weren't covering anything whatsoever at that point. Did keeping one item of clothing on make it less wrong?

Oops ... I didn't even remove my panties. He accidentally tripped and his mouth just landed there.

Fisher's hands guided my legs to spread wider before he resumed his *oral* navigation and, in general, driving me to the edge of passing out or using really bad words.

"This is so wrong ..." I mumbled.

In the next breath, he was gone. Well, his mouth was gone.

Fisher stood and chuckled, resting his hands on my hips to guide me backward to his bed while he kissed my neck. "Do you want to stop?"

The back of my knees hit the bed, and I plunked onto my butt.

"We can stop right now."

Resting back on my elbows, I shook my head. "I just don't want it to be wrong."

"Well ..." He twisted his lips. "Sorry. I can make it good, but I can't make it right in your head."

"I want ..." I bit my lip and searched for the right words. "I want it like last night."

He squinted one eye. "No fucking way."

Swallowing, I frowned. "I want to ..."

Feel like we're having sex, even if you won't actually have it with me!

"I want it like last night or ... more," I said with defeat to my voice. At that point, I was already dirty. Would finishing the job before taking a spiritual shower really have made that much of a difference?

"Despite you being naked on my bed, despite you incessantly wetting your lips while staring at my erection ..."

Busted!

I cut my gaze straight to his, grinning with admission that he caught me gawking at his tented shorts.

"I'm not taking your virginity. I had a little talk with myself about it, and we—me and my moderately well-honed conscience—decided to pass on the offer. I don't feel worthy of it."

"Worthy of it?" I coughed a laugh. "You mean to tell me you've never taken someone's virginity?"

"I didn't say that." He grabbed my leg, forcing me onto my back while he brought my foot to his mouth and kissed the pad of my big toe.

"Why? You can't say that and not have an explanation. Why was it okay then?"

"Because it wasn't some crowned jewel. It wasn't a prized possession. There was no hesitation. No chanting 'this is so wrong.'"

I frowned.

"I can't give it back, Reese. If or *when* you have second thoughts or regret, I can't give it back to you."

"So you'd rather borrow someone's used sanitary napkin?"

Dropping my foot to the bed, he ran a hand through his hair. "Um ... what?"

I sat up and crisscrossed my legs, covering my breasts in my cupped hands. "My grandma used to say that not having your virginity to give your husband was like borrowing someone's used sanitary napkin on your wedding night."

Fisher blinked slowly for several silent seconds. "I ... I don't even know how to respond to that. Were you ... raised in a cult? What the fuck? Who says that?"

I winced, feeling a little defensive. It wasn't that I believed my grandma, but I didn't like him insinuating that she was crazy or some cult member.

"Listen ..." He sighed and took a seat next to me on the bed with his legs dangling off the end. "I haven't walked in your shoes. So I don't know what's been planted into your brain. I liked what just happened in the doorway. It's that simple for me. I liked it. I'd like to do it again. And I don't want to feel guilty for being a consenting *adult* with you. My opinion should mean nothing to you. So while I'd like to tell you to spend more time touching yourself than worrying about going to Hell, it's not my place."

After letting his words resonate for a moment, I released my breasts and stood on my knees, swinging one leg over his lap. "Fisher ..." I laced my fingers together behind his neck while positioning myself so his cock (covered by his briefs and shorts) was pressed between my legs again, much like the previous night.

"What are you doing?" he whispered, eyeing my mouth while his hands gripped my hips.

"I like how you feel between my legs, naked fisherman."

"Fuuuck ..." He closed his eyes for a brief moment, gripping my hips tighter while pushing me down a fraction—pushing into me a fraction.

Cock.

Briefs.

Shorts.

"Yes ..." I closed my eyes.

"Don't say that," he said with a strained voice and lines of tension along his forehead.

Thrust.

Thrust.

Thrust.

He prodded me like he, too, knew that point of no return was a mile behind us in a foggy rearview mirror.

My hands ghosted down his back. His hands gripped my butt.

Thrust.

Thrust.

Thrust.

I spread my legs wider, allowing him to push into me a fraction more.

Thrust.

Thrust.

Thrust.

Each move a little harder.

Each breath a little more ragged, just like his next words.

"I." *Thrust.*

"Want." *Thrust.*

"Inside of you." *Thrust. Thrust. Thrust.*

"So fucking bad."

I did too. And while I knew it would be different, that it would be painful the first time, I still wanted it. I wanted it with Fisher. Instead, we were dry humping harder than two people had probably ever dry humped. I swore his cock, briefs, and shorts were halfway in by that point—like a clothes condom—and soaking wet from me ... and maybe a little from him too.

"Fisher!" I seethed when he ducked his head and bit my nipple and tugged it like he was trying to rip it off.

Thrust.

Thrust.

Thrust.

"No." He released my nipple and grabbed my hand when I reached between us, sliding my hand down the front of his shorts and briefs. "Not a good idea."

I kissed his neck. "I promise I won't. I just want to feel you."

He groaned or grumbled, clearly warring with the decision to stop me or trust me to not cross the next line.

Releasing me, he rested that hand on the bed behind him, chin dipped, watching me slide down the front of his shorts and briefs.

"Make it feel good," he whispered while a grin stole his lips.

My teeth scraped along my bottom lip as I gathered up as much confidence as I could find. My hand wrapped around the top half of his cock while I rubbed myself along the bottom part. It was so much better than the scratchy fabric.

That day, the naked fisherman taught me how to make it feel good for me and for him at the same time while keeping that eighty percent of my virginity.

I knew it was wrong. I just started to care a little less about its wrongness.

While Fisher showered, I ran downstairs to get my computer. I had several important searches to do.

Is oral sex as morally wrong as intercourse?

What does the Bible say about masturbation?

Can a woman get pregnant if a man ejaculates between her legs without penetration?

That last search sent me into a frenzy. I peed.

Prayed.

Jumped into the shower and put the handheld head between my legs to rid myself of any residual semen.

Prayed again.

Checked my phone for my monthly cycle app to see if I was anywhere near ovulation.

Prayed again.

Dressed.

Sprinted up the stairs.

"YOU CAN GET PREGNANT WITHOUT PENETRATION!"

Fisher closed the refrigerator door, popping the top of a beer and taking a swig, eyeing me intently the whole time. "I'm a guy. I can't get pregnant."

"Ugh! Shut up! I'm talking about me."

Totally relaxed, he perched himself atop one of the barstools. "I came on my own fucking stomach, not anywhere on you. Sperm might be fast swimmers, but I don't think they jump from one person to another."

"Fisher! I rubbed against you. My..." I motioned between my legs "...I rubbed against you. And it ... *you* ... might have dripped. What if all of it didn't go onto your stomach? What if a drop or two mixed with my ... you know? And you can have SEVEN HUNDRED AND FIFTY THOUSAND sperm in one drop of semen. Did you know that? Because I didn't."

Still, he didn't seem the least bit phased by my concern. "I think the odds are greatly in your favor of *not* getting pregnant. That would be quite the story." He chuckled before taking another swig of beer.

"No." I shook my head a half dozen times. "That would not be quite the story."

"Are you ovulating?" He stole some of my fire.

No. According to my app, I wasn't ovulating. But ... abstinence was the only certainty. And while we abstained from intercourse—well, full, bare penetration—we didn't abstain from possibly mixing bodily fluids.

It was like he read my mind ... my next train of thought.

"I would have thought you might have been more concerned about STDs than a rogue drop of semen. I know I'm safe with Virgin Therese, but you know I've been with other women. Yet you never asked me. Kinda stupid on your part, don't you think?"

I deflated. I had been stupid. Young and so very stupid.

"I haven't had unprotected sex ... except what just happened with you, since I was last tested. You're safe.

So at least if you're pregnant, you'll have one less thing to worry about," he said.

"Not helpful."

Fisher grinned. "It's a little helpful."

"I'm not ovulating."

"Well, that's a relief. I was really worried about it."

"That can't happen again."

He set down his beer and held up his hands in surrender. "I'm pretty sure you knocked on my door. And I guarantee you I wasn't going to get you pregnant with my face between your legs."

My jaw flapped a few times, but nothing came out.

"Maybe you should think about getting on birth control."

"What?" My head jerked backward. "I'm not having sex."

"Reese." His smile vanished because he was being twenty-eight and I was being ... younger. A lot younger.

Stupid.

Naive.

Childish.

I wasn't stupid. I was scared and disappointed in myself. It was easier to act shocked and offended by his comment than to admit my part in what we did.

"It just ..." I admitted my wrongdoing with the change—the defeat—in my tone instead of saying the actual words. "It can't happen again."

With a quick half shrug, he reached for his bottle of beer. "Agreed."

"What if ..." I cleared my throat. "Hypothetically, what if I were pregnant?"

"No." He grunted. "No. We are not doing this. If you come back to me in a few weeks with a positive test, we'll have this conversation. But I'm not having it now."

"Why?"

"Because I'm not."

"I think it's irresponsible to not at least have a plan."

"Me too. If I had a vagina, and I wanted to play peek-aboo with the head of a guy's dick, I'd plan ahead and be on *birth control*."

Wow.

That hurt.

Fisher wasn't just cold about it; he was cruel. Aloof, like he didn't care about me.

"I'll see you in the morning, unless I'm driving to the office and we're not together."

We're not together.

It was funny how I managed to say exactly what was on my mind, just in a different context.

"We're together."

That hurt too because I knew he meant it completely in the work sense. He let Angie go. He let Teagan go. Why did I think I would be any different?

"Goodnight."

CHAPTER EIGHTEEN

I CALLED Christina while making a sandwich, even though I wasn't hungry because the previous twenty-four hours with Fisher had been unbelievable.

"Miss me already?" she answered.

"I need to talk. In person. Where are you?"

"Thirty minutes outside of Colorado Springs."

"Ugh!" I viciously cut through my sandwich.

"What is it? Just tell me."

"Do you have me on speaker?"

"No, why?"

"Because I'm out of control, and I ... I don't want anyone else to know. But I need advice because I'm losing my mind."

She chuckled. "Okay. Take a breath. Tell me what's going on. Does it have to do with Arnie or the other guy?"

Arnie.

I'd forgotten about Arnie and the made-up other guy, who wasn't actually made-up at all.

"The other guy. He doesn't want to have sex with me

224

because I'm a virgin, so we've been doing everything *but* having actual sex ... intercourse ... you know what I mean. Anyway—"

"Whoa ... wait. Back that shit up. He doesn't want to have—"

"SHH! Don't say it out loud. I don't want Jamison to know I'm having issues in that department."

"Okay, fine. So he doesn't want to try your ... cooking. That's insane. Why not?"

"Because he's worried that my *cooking* is too important to me. So he wants someone else to try my cooking first because he said he's not in the business of trying my cooking."

"Maybe he's never tried a woman's cooking ... like her first official dinner, and he's nervous about it."

"No." I took a bite of my sandwich and chewed it a few seconds. "He's tried other women's *first dinners* because it apparently didn't matter to them."

"Well, does your cooking matter to you?"

"No. Yes. Gah! I don't know. I mean ... can't it somewhat matter to me yet still be okay for him to try it before anyone else does? I'm not asking him to ... open a restaurant for me."

Christina laughed. "I love this conversation. So you go out to eat a lot, and you both enjoy that and mutually want to eat out, but he just won't try your cooking?"

"Right. But, Christina ... I'm not on the pill. And we've been doing things that are risky, but again, not penetration. And I casually asked him what he would do if I ended up pregnant, and he changed. Like his whole demeanor changed. He refused to discuss it with me unless I find out that I am pregnant ... which I highly doubt I am."

"Uh ... Reese, why would you even think that if you ... if he didn't try your cooking?"

"Because he ... you know. And I ... you know. And what if there was a mixing of ... ingredients ..."

"A mixing where?"

"Just ... never mind. It doesn't matter. I'm not near my ovulation time."

"Kudos to you for knowing that."

"I use an app."

"Oh. That's smart. So what do you need from me? I'm obviously no help. Sorry, bae."

"Well, I guess I want to know what you think I should do? He obviously is just in it for the physical part. And I want to have sex with him ... but he won't, despite his total disconnect to the emotional part."

"And you're sure you want him to?"

"Yes. No. I don't know. I know that I wouldn't say no, even if I'd be filled with regret."

"Call Arnie. He'll take it. Probably won't even care if it's more than a one and done. Then you can ... *cook* for anyone without this being an issue."

I didn't want to *cook* for anyone but Fisher.

"Thanks." I sighed. "I'll figure it out."

"Okay. Call me if you need anything, even if I'm not much help."

"Will do."

"Good morning." Fisher walked out of the garage with a mug of coffee in his hand just as I rounded the corner to his truck.

Dang! He looked hot that morning.

Jeans.

Tee.

Work boots.

Wet hair.

Scruffy face.

The same as other days, but different too.

Just ... hotter.

"Morning." I couldn't maintain eye contact with him. Looking at him without thinking about him naked presented itself as the world's most impossible task. Truth? There was a reason I'd thought of him as the "naked fisherman" since the day we met.

"Coffee's still hot inside if you want a cup to go." He opened his door as I opened my side.

"I'm good. Thanks."

As we pulled out of the driveway, he shot me a brief glance. "How was your weekend?"

I tried and failed to hide my grin. As if he didn't know ...

"Fine. How was yours?"

"Not too bad. Mowed the lawn. Went to my brother's concert. Did a few loads of laundry. Oh ... and I got a damn good hand job last night."

My head whipped in his direction. "I didn't give you a hand job."

He sipped his coffee while focusing on the road.

"Your hand *did the job*. That's pretty much the definition of a hand job."

My words fell flat before finding an actual voice to go with them. I didn't give him a hand job. I held his cock while I pleasured myself. I held it to prevent it from going inside of me. I wasn't ...

Or was I?

I cleared my throat. "What am I doing today?"

"What's your *job* today? Hmm ... let me think on that. What do you want your job to be today?"

On a nervous laugh, I shrugged. "You're the boss."

"Oh, my choice? I like that."

"I think we should stick to construction stuff."

"As opposed to?" He spared me another lightning-fast side glance.

"I think you should teach me something today."

"Fine. After we make our morning stops, we'll grab lunch and go to my workshop."

"You have a workshop?"

Driving with one hand casually draped over the top of the steering wheel and his other hand holding his coffee, he smiled. "Of course. I was there until just before midnight last night working on wardrobe drawers."

After we ... did what we did, he left. And I had a breakdown on the phone with Christina. Once again, my actions showed my age. Fisher didn't have time to call a friend and overanalyze what had happened between him and the girl from the basement (it wasn't a glamorous label, but it wasn't inaccurate either) because he was a *real* adult with a job and responsibilities. He didn't have his virginity to babysit 24-7. Sex was—not a life-changing choice that required copious amounts of prayer, guilt, overthinking, and dramatization.

We made the morning's stops. I followed him like a good puppy. He asked Hailey to deliver lunches so we could head to his shop after grabbing lunch for ourselves.

"Is this a joke?" I asked as he pulled into the McDonald's drive-thru.

"Lunch. Not a joke." He rolled down his window. "Do you want the Hamburger Happy Meal or the Chicken McNuggets Happy Meal?"

I narrowed my eyes at him.

"I'm doing the hamburger because I'm not overly trusting of chicken nuggets."

I didn't trust *him*. So ... I softly murmured, "Hamburger."

"Drink? I'm splurging on a chocolate milk."

"Juice," I said in the same cautious tone.

He ordered our Happy Meals and pulled to the window.

"Use the change to pay for as many orders as you can behind me." He handed the guy a hundred-dollar bill.

Fisher was a pay it forward (or in that case backward) kind of guy. Why? Why did he have to be so ... *extra*?

"That's kind of you," the guy at the window said, handing Fisher the bags.

As we pulled onto the main road, Fisher tapped the bags. "Aren't you going to see if the toys are something you don't have?"

I shook my head.

"Why?"

"Because it's no longer my hobby. Rory can get them if she wants them."

"You got all the current ones when you picked up Happy Meals for my crew, didn't you?"

Rubbing my lips together and keeping my gaze locked on the dash, I returned a single nod.

Fisher chuckled.

Ten minutes later, we pulled into the driveway.

"I thought we were going to your shop."

"We are." He grabbed the bags and hopped out of the truck.

I wasted no time following him. In his garage, he grabbed the side of a gray cabinet and pulled on it.

"What the heck?"

He grinned as a light turned on to a stairway leading downstairs, below his garage.

I slowly made my way down the stairs as he closed the cabinet or door behind us. At the bottom, there was a huge space, a second garage, but this one was filled with piles of wood, partially finished cabinets, saws, and walls of hanging tools.

"We're in the basement."

He nodded, wiping his hand across a small high-top table in the corner that had two tall barstools.

"But how do you get here from the basement?"

"Hidden passage, of course. Sit." He nodded to the other barstool and set the Happy Meal bags on the table.

I didn't sit. Not yet. I milled around the shop, feathering my fingers over pieces of wood and cabinets sanded to perfection.

"Is there anything you can't do?" I made my way to

the table, and he pulled his burger, fries, and sliced apples out of the sack.

He grinned, but he didn't meet my gaze. "You."

I climbed onto the stool, eyeing him, begging for him to look at me, to give me more than that one-word answer.

He didn't.

We ate in silence for at least five minutes. In that time, he ate every bite of his lunch, and I ate two bites of my burger and maybe three fries because I was too distracted by him.

His secret shop.

His insane talent.

And that comment.

Me. He didn't think he could do me.

"Do you want to cut, sand, or nail?" He wadded up his wrappers and shoved them back into the bag.

"Nail," I said without flinching.

He rubbed his hand over his mouth as if he could wipe the tiny grin from his lips, but the knowing glint in his eyes couldn't be missed. "Let's sand. No sharp blades and no nails. We've made one urgent care trip since Rory left town. Let's not have to make another."

I used a french fry to trace my lips slowly.

Fisher snatched it from my hand and ate it. "Knock that shit off. You're on the clock."

"Okay, Boss." I hopped off the stool and followed him to the opposite side of his workshop.

"These are nearly finished, but if you feel a few of the areas, you'll notice they could use just a light sanding." He rubbed his hand across the front of a drawer then took my hand and moved it where his had been. "Feel that?"

I nodded. "Light." He handed me the sandpaper. "Very lightly. Just until it's smooth."

I sanded it. Felt it. Sanded it more. "Like this?"

Fisher feathered the pads of his fingers over it. "Perfect."

My spine grew two inches with his compliment.

We spent the afternoon in his workshop. I didn't graduate past sanding with the finest sandpaper, but that was okay. Just watching Fisher do his thing was a gift. He wore his safety glasses as he cut the pieces of wood, his gaze so focused on the task. He had no idea that his most intent expression involved him wetting and rubbing his lips together. It was nearly too much.

"Time to call it a day." He tore off his safety glasses and glanced at his watch.

"This was fun. Thanks for letting me see you in your element." I brushed my hands together, removing a light dusting of residue from sanding.

"Anytime."

"Don't say it unless you mean it." I smirked. "The last time you said 'anytime,' I took you seriously and ended up in your tub when you brought your date home."

His lips twisted as he returned a slow nod. "Mmm ... yes. You did."

"Well ..." I jabbed my thumb over my shoulder. "I'm going to take a shower."

Fisher kept nodding slowly, his backside leaned against one of the workbenches, his hands slightly tucked into his front pockets.

Basically ... irresistible.

"Rory comes home this week," he said.

"Yeah," I whispered.

"I'm sorry if I did anything that made you feel—"

"No!" I didn't mean to cut him off so quickly. It was a knee-jerk reaction. "You ... you haven't done anything wrong. You didn't make me feel anything but ... good."

Make it feel good.

"And..." I couldn't help my grin "...a little crazy."

He stared at his feet. "So we're ... good? Friends. What happened, happened and we move on. No big deal?"

The biggest deal of my eighteen years—well, the good kind of big deal. It was hard to top Rory going to prison and my dad dying for life-changing, catastrophic events.

"Friends," I said just above a whisper. "No big deal ... we're ... good." Someone needed to use some sandpaper on my heart because it felt rough and splintered.

———

THE NEXT MORNING, I woke up to a text from Fisher.

You're with Hailey today, drive your mom's car.

He'd sent the text an hour before my alarm went off.

Hailey had me enter bids into the computer and deliver lunches. Then she had me file—my least favorite job.

"Can I ask you something personal?" I asked her.

"Sure," she said slowly without a glance up from her computer screen.

"Did you like sex the first time you had it?"

Her fingers stilled, and her gaze lifted to meet mine. "Did you just have sex for the first time?"

"No."

"Have you had sex?"

"Not really."

Hailey laughed. "Oh my god, 'not really' is not an answer." Her smile faded when she realized I wasn't finding anything that amusing. "Sorry. My first time ... god ... I don't remember much. Isn't that pathetic? I don't recall it being great. But I didn't have the most considerate man—boy actually—exerting any effort to make it great. He didn't know it was my first time until it was over."

"Was he mad?"

"Mad? What do you mean?"

"That it was your first time and you didn't tell him?"

"No." She chuckled. "Why?"

I shrugged and shook my head.

"You know you can tell me anything. Right? If you have guy problems, I'm your girl. I've had every guy problem imaginable. Cheaters. Married men. Assholes. Narcissists. Stalkers."

My eyebrows peaked as I stopped filing. "Seriously?"

"Oh yes. You name it. I've probably experienced it or have a friend who did."

"Have you been with older men?"

"Yes. Well ... how old? I don't date grandpas, even if they are rich."

"I don't know ... five ... ten years older?"

"Sure. You like an older man?"

"Maybe."

The office door opened and Fisher stepped inside, again sipping one of his big red drinks from a straw. "Hey," he said to Hailey or me. Maybe both of us. "How's it going today?"

"We're about to clock out, Bossman. After I get done giving Reese some dating advice."

I ducked my head and focused hard on the papers in front of me. Why did she say that?

"Oh yeah? What advice is that?" He slid behind me and opened the desk drawer to my right, dropping a set of keys into it.

His proximity raised the temperature in the room a good ten degrees.

"I'm not sure yet; you walked in and interrupted us."

"Sorry." He chuckled. "Do you want me to leave?"

"No. Just do your thing and ignore us. As you were saying, Reese ..."

I shook my head as Fisher lifted some of the papers around me like he was searching for something on his desk. "It's not a big deal. We can talk later."

"Don't let me stop you. Maybe I can be of help. I'm a guy. So I know a lot about them." Fisher found a folder and turned, resting his butt on the edge of the desk.

I felt his gaze on me, but there was no way I could look at him.

"Yeah, ask Bossman. He's a walking example of failed relationships." Hailey giggled.

"Then he's definitely not the one I need to ask," I murmured.

"Reese was asking me about dating older men. You've

dated plenty of women younger than you. What's your take on it?" Hailey asked Fisher.

I didn't want in on the conversation. I didn't even want to be in the same state as they talked about me or my dating life.

"I think Reese needs to find herself a nice Christian who can make her feel good about herself and her decisions."

"No." Hailey drummed her fingernails on the desk. "That's a terrible idea. You're eighteen. You have to *live*. Don't settle for safe and boring."

"I think Rory would love for Reese to settle for that," Fisher added.

"No. Just ... no. Reese, listen to me. You won't regret the bad decisions you make now. You'll only regret the missed opportunities to make mistakes and *live*. You don't need a good guy to give you a home and needy kids. You need a string of bad guys to give you experience. You'll never know what you do want in life until you experience everything you don't want in life."

"Said no mother ever." Fisher shook his head.

"Mothers are hardwired to protect their offspring. If you want advice on canning or ironing, ask your mom. If you want advice on being a woman ... a free-spirited woman ... then don't ever ask your mom. Well ..." Hailey tapped her chin with her finger. "Come to think of it, you could probably ask Rory. She's cooler than most moms."

I glance up at her. "Why do you say that?"

"Just because."

Fisher cleared his throat. "Clock out, Hailey. Have a good night."

"Are you dismissing me? I feel dismissed. Are you shooing me out of here so you can give Reese some lame advice on dating because Rory's made you feel protective of her?"

"Yes. Leave so I can give her some lame advice." Fisher closed the folder and tossed it onto the desk next to my piles of papers.

"Don't listen to him, Reese. Call me later." Hailey hiked her purse onto her shoulder.

I nodded, giving her a tight grin.

After the door closed behind her, Fisher used his leg to swivel the desk chair so I was facing him. "Who are you dating?"

"No one." I gave him two full seconds of my gaze before averting it to the side.

"So why are you talking to Hailey about it?"

"None of your business."

"Am I the guy?"

"There is no guy."

"Yet, you're talking to Hailey about a guy."

"Oh my gosh!" I skittered to my feet to wheel the chair backward a good six feet, hitting the front of Hailey's desk. "I wasn't asking her about dating. I was asking her about sex. There. Are you happy?"

"Why not ask me about it?"

With an incredulous laugh, I shook my head. "Sorry. What was I thinking? I'm sure you're experienced with how it feels to have a penis in your vagina. Does it hurt the first time?"

Fisher excelled at masking his reactions to things, but I had him. I didn't miss his Adam's apple bobbing with a hard swallow. He didn't see that question coming. A month earlier, he didn't see *me* coming.

"I'm not talking—"

"Full. Of. Yourself!" I cut him off, shooting straight up from the chair and planting my fists onto my hips. "You are so full of yourself. What makes you think I'm talking about you? We're over. Remember? And you didn't want my virginity. It was too inconvenient for you. So stop assuming you're some bright star that I orbit."

He narrowed his eyes. "What are you so angry about?"

HIM!

Life.

My dad dying.

My mom missing out on my high school years.

Church school.

The cloak of guilt I wore because of church.

God.

Yeah, I was angry at God too because I didn't understand what kind of god would give me so many emotions, desires, and uncontrolled feelings, then tell me I had to suppress them until I was married.

What if I didn't want to get married yet? Did "good" Christians get married just to remove the sin from sex?

There wasn't anything Fisher could say to make me feel less agitated. His silence showed his maturity and understanding of that, yet it also infuriated me. I wanted him to at least *try* to make a case for himself.

"Why me? And I don't mean it like I have no sense of self-esteem. It's not that. I'm not ugly. I'm not stupid. I'm fun. I have a decent list of quality traits. But you're not ugly either. Or stupid. And you can be fun. But you're also ten years older than me. With *so* many options. I just don't get it. Was I a game? A toy? Were you bored? I know I've asked you this before, but I just don't get it. Why engage with an eighteen-year-old who has no solid direction in her life yet, can't drink legally, and who's a virgin. I just don't get it."

He let my words settle, dissipate, and vanish, replaced with silence. "What did you like about the mountains?"

I shrugged. "What didn't I like? The air. The tranquility. The vastness. Just ... I don't know. When we stopped at that overlook, I just liked how I felt. There. In the moment. It's hard to describe."

"Because you can't."

"Maybe." I tried to think of the right words, but they fell short.

"Well, neither can I."

"It ..." I shook my head. "It still doesn't make sense."

"To whom? How you feel about ... everything—people, places, things, events, good times, tragedies, the past, the future—it only has to make sense to you. In this life, we don't owe anyone anything. No explanation. Feelings are the most personal part of who we are. You're not accountable for your feelings any more than you're accountable for the amount of oxygen you consume. Think for yourself. And don't ever let anyone tell you how to feel."

I frowned. "I think you tried to make me feel bad when I told you I was taught that homosexuality was wrong."

"Well, if you think I was trying to tell you how to feel, then fuck me. But I don't believe our thoughts are always in-line with our feelings. And sometimes we think what we believe we're supposed to think, despite our feelings. When your feelings align with your thoughts, then you're thinking for your fucking self. So if you feel it's wrong to love someone who is of the same sex, then don't let anybody tell you your *feelings* are wrong. But show the rest of the world the same courtesy, and don't tell anyone else how they should feel."

I nodded a few times. He was right. Professor Fisher teaching more life lessons. I didn't know how to distinguish between my feelings and my thoughts. How much of me was authentic and how much of me was manufactured through sermons and lectures?

"How do you feel about me, Fisher?"

With a neutral expression, he lifted his shoulder into a slow-motion shrug. "It's none of your business."

And just that magically, I wasn't angry. Not at Fisher, or my parents, or God. All that seemed to matter was Fisher Mann *did* have feelings for me. My business or not. He felt things for me.

"I'm leaving." I stood and grabbed my backpack.

He nodded twice. "I'm watching you leave."

When I reached the door, I turned my head, restraining my grin for a few seconds. "But is it as good as watching me come?"

Fisher smiled like blowing up a balloon, one centimeter at a time. "Speechless."

CHAPTER NINETEEN

"HEY! Oh my gosh. I wasn't expecting you today." I knew something was up when the basement door wasn't locked.

Rory glanced up from the kitchen counter where her hands furiously chopped vegetables. "Surprise. I got an earlier flight. And since I wanted it to be a true surprise, I grabbed an Uber home. I didn't even tell Fisher I was coming home today ... until about five minutes ago. I just texted him. I'm making dinner for the three of us."

The three of us.

Lovely.

"He said you had just left the office. So ... sit." She nodded toward the barstool. "Tell me everything. I want to know everything you've been up to while I've been in California." With a knife in one hand she used her other arm to give me a side hug and kiss on my head.

She didn't want to know what I'd been up to.

"Just working." I climbed onto the stool and rested my crossed arms on the counter. "I work in the office with

Hailey some days and other days I go to job sites with Fisher. Church on Sundays. Evening walks. Crossword puzzles."

"Crossword puzzles? You like them?"

I nodded.

"Your dad did too."

"I know. That's why I construct them."

Her eyes widened. "You're constructing them?"

Another nod.

"Oh, Reese ... your dad would be so proud."

"I think so too. It makes me feel close to him."

"Well, you'll have to let me see them. I used to try to solve your dad's, but I was terrible at it."

"How was California?"

"Amazing. More than amazing! I feel all energized with fun new skills and techniques to use on clients. I go back to work tomorrow. I was thinking we need to get you a car."

"Yeah, I was thinking that too. Fisher gives me a ride some days, but other days, like today, I drive into the office by myself."

"I can ask my parents—your grandparents—for some help to get you a car."

"I can afford a car."

Rory gave me a fake smile of recognition. "Of course. Your dad left you money."

"Yeah. I was going to look for one right away, but then you left, and I had your car to drive, so there wasn't the urgency. I should go look for one tomorrow. I'll ask Fisher for—"

"Ask Fisher for what?" Fisher said, coming down the stairs.

"Hey, there's my handsome guy." Rory dropped her knife, wiped her hands, and hugged Fisher.

I wondered why she wasn't interested in him. Clearly, she liked him. Maybe the age thing bothered her more than it bothered me.

Fisher sat right next to me. He could have chosen a different stool or even scooted that stool over a few inches, but he didn't. "What do you need to ask me?" He rested his arms on the counter and nudged my elbow. It was so ... weird.

Dare I say it was *brotherly?*

"I need to buy a car."

"And you need to borrow money? How much do you need?"

I shook my head. "No. I have money. I need time off tomorrow to go get a car."

"You taking her?" He glanced up at Rory.

"Not tomorrow. I have to work. I can see about getting off early on Saturday and taking her."

"Why does anyone have to take me? I'll get an Uber and drive my new car home."

Fisher's eyebrows slid up an inch.

"She has money from her dad. She's going to pay cash for it."

He nodded slowly. "What car are you getting?"

"I don't know."

"I'll go with you," he said.

"I don't need you to go with me."

"Oh ..." Rory wiped her hands again and picked up

her phone. "I have to get this it's ... a friend. I'll be right back."

I squinted at her odd behavior while she hustled to her bedroom and shut the door.

"I realize this is going to piss you off, but it's just life right now. If you take me with you, you'll get a better deal on a car because there will be a *male adult* negotiating for you."

"That's—"

"Sexist? Not fair? Ridiculous? Yes. Yes, it is. But it doesn't make it less true."

"You have work."

He grabbed my stool and turned me to face him, my knees tucked between his spread legs. "I know the boss. I can get the morning off." He rested his hands on my legs.

I made a quick glance at the closed bedroom door.

"She'll be in there for a while."

I turned back toward Fisher. "How do you know?"

"Because she's talking to Rose."

"Who's Rose?"

"Her friend."

"Were they in prison together?"

Fisher inched his head side to side.

"Oh. Do they work together?"

"Rose is a teacher. She teaches middle school art."

I nodded, twisting my lips. "She's probably a client."

"Yeah, Rory does her hair."

"Once a social butterfly, always a social butterfly. I'm more introverted like my dad." When I allowed myself to look at Fisher for more than two seconds, I realized he was looking at me. It was that more than friends look.

"I wonder how long it will take before I no longer want to kiss you."

Again, I checked her bedroom door while pressing my lips together. "Y-you want to kiss me?"

He grinned while squeezing my legs. "Desperately."

I don't know why I thought Fisher had everything on a switch, including his emotions or his attraction to me, but I did. I thought it. I relied on it.

"We're done. Right?" I punctuated the *right* with serious doubt like I really needed him to answer me because I wasn't sure where any of this was coming from.

"I think that was the agreement."

That wasn't an answer. He threw it back on me. I was the one who first said things would have to end when Rory came home. I said I didn't want her to know about us, but he agreed.

He. Agreed!

"Yeah. It was the *mutual* agreement." I rested my hands on his hands to slide them off my legs, but when my skin touched his, it wasn't that easy.

"How's that leak in the back room?" he asked.

"I don't know. Should we check?"

Fisher grinned and slid off his stool. I followed him to the back room.

Door closed.

His hands in my hair.

My hands up the back of his shirt, fingers digging into his skin.

Our mouths colliding.

Tongues exploring.

My hum mixed with his hum, vibrating our lips.

We didn't have an official last kiss, so who could blame us for needing to officially end things ... with a mind-numbing kiss.

"Reese? Fisher?"

We jumped apart, breathless and a little disheveled.

"Where'd you guys go?"

Fisher ran a hand through his hair, even though it wasn't *his* hair that got manhandled and tangled.

I wiped my mouth and combed my fingers through my hair as he grinned and shot me a quick wink before opening the door.

Fisher and his winks.

"Back here. Reese thought she'd been hearing some dripping noise in the back room, but I think it's just condensation from the furnace."

"Oh. Yeah, probably." Rory lifted the cutting board full of cut veggies and dumped it into a wok.

"Who's Rose?" I asked. "Fisher said you have a friend who's an art teacher. How did you meet her?" I hopped back onto the chair as he walked behind me to join my mom in the kitchen, but not before letting his fingers tease the skin on my lower back where my shirt had slid up just above the waistband of my jeans.

I jerked, but Rory didn't seem to notice.

"Rose. Um ..." Rory shot Fisher a funny look. Did she see him touch me? "I've actually known her for many years. She was a client of mine when I owned my salon in Nebraska."

"Wow. Really? That's cool. And now she lives here too and is seeing you again?"

Pressing her lips together, she nodded. "Mmm-hmm."

"Nice."

"Very nice." Fisher stole a sliced carrot from the wok, and Rory smacked his hand.

"How have the two of you been getting along?" she asked.

I cut my gaze straight to Fisher, but he didn't give a single glance in my direction. No. He was too cool to act guilty in the slightest way.

"Fine. She's a bit of a handful at work. We've made a trip to urgent care for a nail in her hand as a result of her clumsiness, and she got it in her head that Happy Meals were a good idea for my crew, but other than that ... it's been pretty uneventful."

It took me a minute to unpack his insane summary of our time together.

"You went to urgent care? Why didn't you tell me?"

I shrugged. "It was no big deal. No stitches."

Rory blinked several times and nodded. Then, she smiled. "Happy Meals?"

I rolled my eyes. "It's no big deal."

"It's a gigantic deal." Fisher ruffled my hair.

Ruffled my hair!

Like I was five. What the heck?

"Your daughter carried on your collection while you were in prison. How sweet is that?" He climbed onto the stool next to me.

I ignored him.

"Really? Oh, Reese ..." Tears filled her eyes.

"It's no big deal. And I'm sure I missed plenty of

items. It's like making a few crossword puzzles after Dad died."

"A few?" Fisher opened his big, dumb mouth. "More like an entire book full of them."

With a tight smile, I shot him an evil glare.

Rory added a bunch of seasonings to the wok filled with veggies and chicken. "You are the sweetest girl."

I didn't respond with more than a small grin.

"Have you met anyone at church? Any nice boys?"

Fisher rested his elbow on the counter and his head in his hand, staring at the side of my face like he was waiting anxiously for my response—taking his "extraness" to a whole new level.

"I did, actually. His name is Brendon. He's twenty-four, and he just graduated from law school. We had lunch and played pool here. We're planning on doing something again this Sunday." I narrowed my eyes and shot Fisher another glare—a "take that, you obnoxious jerk!"

He focused solely on my lips while wetting his.

Why did he always one-up me?

"Sweetheart, I'm so happy for you. Sounds like quite the catch. A lawyer."

"He *is* quite the catch." I kicked Fisher in the shin because he was mocking me with his overtly enthusiastic gestures while I talked to Rory.

"He's not the best pool player," Fisher said, pinching the hell out of my leg just above my knee.

I had to bite my lower lip to keep from yelping. "You never saw him play," I said through gritted teeth.

"I saw him holding the pool stick. Total amateur."

All I could think was … "Who are you?"

Really, Fisher was so *so* much extra. Was he jealous? Or was he just trying to pester me, poke the bear? Treat me like a child?

"I knew it." Rory shook her head while stirring dinner. "I knew you two would end up acting like brother and sister."

My stomach turned.

Fisher? He seemed amused.

Gross.

"Let's eat out on the screened-in porch." She spooned stir fry onto three plates and slid two toward us. "Grab whatever you want to drink. Fisher, if you want beer, you'll have to get your own. I didn't get any before I left since Reese won't drink it …" She walked by me and bopped my nose. "Because she's not twenty-one, and I know she's not a drinker."

She stepped out onto the screened-in porch, and I followed her with Fisher right behind me.

"You sure have her fooled. You drink and give a killer hand job. But we'll keep that between us."

I whipped around, nearly sending my dinner flying off my plate. "I didn't give you a hand job," I whispered.

"Oh, Reese … you're just adorable. Really."

I narrowed my eyes and growled, taking a page from his playbook.

Fisher glanced over my shoulder, probably seeing if Rory was watching us. "If you growl at me, I'll bite your ass again …" His gaze cut to me. "And you'll like it."

"I will *not* like it." I turned back around.

Fisher's face landed right next to my ear. "You will if I tie you up first."

My back came to attention as I choked on a little saliva.

What the heck? Tie me up? Who does that?

"What are you two talking about?" Rory eyed us suspiciously as we stepped out onto the porch.

"Just sibling stuff." Fisher grinned while taking a seat.

I chose the chair in the opposite corner of the porch as Fisher sat on the sectional.

"Rose wants to go to a jazz club Friday. Why don't you come, Fisher? She's bringing another friend. A single friend who happens to be an interior designer. Rose thinks she's a good match for you. What do you say?"

"I like jazz," I said.

Rory frowned. "Oh, sorry, sweetheart. You have to be twenty-one to get into the club."

I focused on my plate of food, stirring it with my fork, waiting for it to cool down ... waiting for *me* to cool down.

"Sounds fun. Count me in."

My head snapped up, shooting my gaze right to Fisher. He chewed slowly, giving me a challenging look.

For the rest of dinner, I stay quiet, letting Fisher and Rory catch up.

"I'm going to my room to read before I go to bed. Thanks for dinner." I headed toward the door.

"Okay. Sweet dreams, love," Rory said.

"Don't let the bed bugs *bite*." Fisher leaned back on the sectional, stretching both arms across the back.

I wanted to kill him. He excelled at bringing out the worst in me. Why did I find him the least bit attractive?

CHAPTER TWENTY

THE NEXT MORNING, Rory had coffee and breakfast made for me by the time I dressed, pulled my hair into a ponytail, and brushed my teeth.

"You're up early," I said.

"I'm a morning person. I didn't used to be, but that changed."

In prison.

I nodded. "Thanks." I took a few sips of coffee and grabbed one of the muffins she made. "Gotta go. I'm sure he's already waiting for me." Slinging my backpack over my shoulder, I smiled.

"Have a good day. I'll be home from work around four. If you want, we can grab dinner."

"We'll see. We're supposed to look for a car for me today. So who knows how my day will go?"

"Okay. Bye, sweetheart."

"Bye."

Sure enough, Fisher was in the truck by the time I made it to the driveway.

"Morning." He grinned when I opened the door.

I stared at my muffin as I tried to maneuver my bag into the back without squishing the muffin.

"Here." Fisher leaned over and took the muffin to hold it for me.

I thought about saying "thanks," but then I remembered I was mad at him for his behavior the previous night.

Tossing my bag in the back, I climbed into the seat and fastened my seat belt.

"Hey!" My mouth fell open as I gasped.

Fisher had eaten half of my muffin.

"You jerk! That was my muffin!" I grabbed his wrist with one hand while trying to pry the rest of the muffin from his grip with my other hand. By the time he softened his grip, the muffin looked like a squished ball of dough.

"Oops ..." he stared at the ball in his hand.

"You dumb fucker!" The second that left my mouth, an audible *whoosh* of air filled my lungs a split second before my cupped hand covered my mouth.

Fisher's eyes doubled in size as he eased his head to the side like a dog.

I turned away and crossed my arms over my chest. "Just drive."

Fisher hopped out of the truck. I didn't care where he was going. I officially didn't care about him at all. A few minutes later, he returned with another muffin.

"Are we good now?"

I stared at the muffin in his hand. "What did you tell

Rory?" I took the muffin and held it because I was no longer hungry.

Fisher put the truck into *Drive* and pulled out of the driveway. "I told her I took a bite of your muffin. You had a hissy fit and called me a dumb fucker."

"You what?" I whipped my head back toward him.

"Don't worry. She didn't believe me. You have her fooled. You have everyone fooled. Except me. I know you. And you are not the innocent little Christian you pretend to be."

"Well, you're not the nice guy everyone thinks you are."

Fisher shot me a sour expression. "Oh, I'm absolutely the nice guy everyone thinks I am. I've been looking out for your immature ass for weeks."

I scoffed. "You've been *looking* at my butt for weeks, not looking out for it."

"You must think you have a great ass. What if you're the only one?"

I started to scoff again, but I caught myself. Nope. I wasn't going to let him drag me down to his level of cruelty. Once again, he proved how much of a terrible influence he was on me.

My inclination to do what was right.

And my desire to be a kind person.

Fisher granted me some silence, but only for ten minutes. Then he pulled into a car dealership.

"How much are you planning on spending?"

Ugh ...

I'd planned on giving him the silent treatment for the

better part of the day, but he had to make car shopping our first stop of the day.

"I don't know. I should probably check with my grandparents. They'll have to release the money to my account."

"Well, it would have been smart of you to do that before suggesting we go car shopping."

I frowned. "I thought it would be smart to know what car I wanted before going to them. They're going to ask me about the car and how much money I need."

"Okey dokey." He pulled into an empty parking space and hopped out of the truck.

I climbed out just as he rounded the front of the truck and held open the door before shutting it behind me and locking it.

He turned, sauntering toward the lot of cars. I leaned my back against the truck door, resting one foot on the running board. A few seconds later, he glanced a foot behind him only to realize I wasn't there. Then his gaze lifted to me.

Turning, he visibly blew out a long breath.

Yes, Fisher ... I don't always wear socks, and I reserve the right to be upset with you even if you are taking me car shopping.

I maintained my emotionless expression, giving nothing away, yet demanding everything.

His booted feet planted right in front of me as he rested one hand on a hip and tipped his chin toward his chest.

Another sigh.

"Apologize," I said.

Ever so slowly, he lifted his gaze to me, a tiny grin quirking one side of his mouth. "For?"

"Exactly. I'm glad we agree that you have *so* much to apologize for."

"The muffin?"

I nodded.

"I got you a new one."

"But you didn't apologize."

"Actions speak louder than words. I. Got. You. A. New. One."

"And last night? Your obnoxiousness? You agreeing to go on a date like ... ten minutes after sticking your tongue down my throat? Making unnecessary jabs at Brendon, whom you've met once, for two seconds. What about that?"

Twisting his lips to the side, he narrowed his eyes. "Do you want a verbal apology? Or do you want a physical one?"

I wasn't sure where he was going with that offering? A physical one?

"I'm not giving you both. So ... choose carefully."

"Define physical."

"It's something I do, instead of something I say."

"What would you do?"

"I'm not telling you. Just choose."

It was so ridiculous. Why couldn't he simply say sorry and go on with the day? And why couldn't I just choose the verbal apology? Why was I so curious about his physical gesture?

"Am I a toy to you?"

Fisher's gaze slid down my body and inched its way back up to my face. That answered my question.

"Are you asking if I enjoy playing with you?"

"Are you going to sleep with your Friday night date?"

"And by sleep, you mean?"

"Fisher ..."

"Are you going to sleep with your Sunday afternoon date?" He lifted one eyebrow.

"You know that answer."

Fisher nodded slowly. "I do. But is it because of Jesus or because you gave me a hand job?"

"Are you going to sleep with your date because you have no moral code or because my hand job wasn't good enough?"

Satisfaction lit up his entire face. "So you *do* admit it was a hand job."

"Fisher ..."

"Let's find you a car so we can get to work." He turned ninety degrees and retraced his original path toward the lot of cars.

I followed with my heart dragging behind me, getting bruised and scraped by the harsh road that was Fisher Mann.

"Hey, looking for anything specific?" the salesman asked.

"Something reliable with good gas mileage," Fisher spoke for me.

"Something fast," I said with a serious face.

The salesman gave me a dismissive "hehe" laugh.

"I have a Honda Accord over here. One owner. Sixty-five thousand miles. Good gas mileage. Reliable."

"I'm thinking about an SUV because I'll be making a lot of trips into the mountains."

Again, the salesman gave me a look like I wasn't the one purchasing the vehicle. "Subaru Outback?"

"Sounds good. Let's see it," Fisher said.

I shook my head. "My mom has one. I don't want the same car."

"It's a good car. You can take it into the mountains." Fisher tried to make a case for the Outback.

"I see you have a Porsche Cayenne at the front of the lot."

Both men looked at me like I was crazy.

"Um ... we do. It has close to forty-thousand miles on it, and it's fifty-five thousand, but we could probably get you into it for a little less."

"She's not looking for a fifty-thousand-dollar vehicle," Fisher said, walking down the row with the boring Outbacks and Accords.

"*She* is looking for whatever *she* wants." I crossed my arms over my chest and followed him.

"We'll test drive this one," Fisher nodded toward a Subaru.

"I don't want an Outback."

"It's a Forester." He peered inside the window before reading the specifics on the sticker.

"I'll grab the keys," the salesman said.

"I needed a ride, not a parent. A ride, not a bully. What is your deal? This is my purchase. My decision."

He took a break from the sticker to look at me. "Should we call Rory?"

"No." I tipped up my chin.

"Then we're test driving the Forester."

"Fine. But I'm not buying it."

He eyed the salesman getting closer behind me. "We're not buying anything today, just test driving."

"*We're* not buying anything ever. *I'm* buying it."

"I'll just need to see your driver's license, miss."

I turned and huffed as I dug it out of my wallet.

"You can head north. It's a nice three-mile loop."

I took the key without acknowledging his suggestion or Fisher's satisfied smile.

I wasn't buying it.

And I wasn't coming back with Fisher when I did decide to buy a car. Maybe Brendon would come with me. I felt fairly certain an attorney could negotiate a car deal for me just as if not better than Fisher.

"Left," Fisher said as I pulled to a stop at the lot entrance.

"Shut up."

I didn't give him my full attention, but I also didn't miss his smirk, how much he enjoyed me in my most unruly state.

We drove a mile up the road.

"It's a nice vehicle."

I ignored him.

Another mile.

"You could fit four friends and some camping gear in the back. If you have four friends."

I swerved across three lanes of traffic to an exit.

"Jesus Christ!" He grabbed the dash. "What in the hell are you doing? Trying to get us killed?"

I pulled into the empty parking lot of an elementary

school. "Would you just shut up?" I punched the button to my seat belt and climbed out of the vehicle, marching with no purpose other than to get away from him.

Landing at the playground, I planted my butt on a swing, gripped the chains, and hung my head to take a timeout ... a few long breaths to regain my composure.

Fisher's work boots made it into my line of sight, but I wasn't ready to look at him or talk to him or ... acknowledge his existence on the planet.

As I said a silent prayer for him to not say anything, God answered it.

Fisher walked behind me and grabbed the chains close to the seat, pulling me backward and giving me a gentle push forward.

He did it again and again, until I was so high I felt like the younger version of myself taking a deep breath and staring at the blue sky, imagining what it would be like to touch it.

After ... I didn't know. Five minutes? Ten minutes? He stopped pushing me and waited for me to come to a complete stop without forcing it with my feet or anything else. It was hard to explain how that moment touched me. It was stupid, really, but I had never felt so much patience given to me from another human as I felt as Fisher waited for me to come to a complete stop.

Feet dangling in virtual stillness.

The mulch crunched beneath his boots as he appeared in front of me again. Kneeling in the dirty mulch, he slid his arms around my waist and rested his head on my lap.

My poor teenaged adult heart. It didn't care if Fisher was

good for me. It didn't care about anything other than the way he made me feel in that moment. I released the chain with my right hand and threaded my fingers through his hair.

"I'm trying so hard..." I whispered, my voice shaky in my chest and wobbly as the words fell from my lips "... trying *so* hard not to fall in love with you."

A few breaths later, he whispered back, "I know."

I didn't know what that meant. He knew I was falling in love with him? Or he, too, was trying to keep from loving me?

It didn't matter, not at that moment. All that mattered was he knew *me*.

Fisher released my waist and sat back on his heels, resting his hands on the top of my work boots dangling in front of him. "What do you want?" He gave me his eyes and a world of sincerity in them.

It shook me.

Maybe because I had never experienced real love in the romantic sense.

Maybe because I was scared.

Maybe because I didn't really know what I wanted.

"The Porsche Cayenne," I said, giving him the tiniest of smiles because I knew what he meant, but I wasn't emotionally ready to answer that question.

Him.

I wanted him, but I had no idea what that really looked like. Me, an eighteen-year-old teenaged adult with no real direction, and him, a twenty-eight-year-old adult with his own house, his own business, and many people relying on him.

We couldn't have been at more different places in our lives, yet ... we somehow found each other. And there was something there.

Something undeniable.

Something real.

Something I wasn't ready for, but I sure didn't want to let it go.

With a painful flash of amusement, he returned the hint of a grin and nodded while standing and holding out his hand to me. "Can you afford the Cayenne?"

I nodded.

"Then get the Cayenne."

Resting my hand in his, I hopped off the swing. He interlaced our fingers and led me back to the Forester. We returned the keys and got in his truck to go to work.

Fifty grand. That's what I needed to ask my grandparents to give me because I wanted the Cayenne because it was sexy and fun—just like the naked fisherman.

He dropped me off at the office. And later that day, he asked Hailey to give me a ride home since he had to play catch up from taking me car shopping.

"Good timing," Rory said, getting out of her Outback right as I climbed out of Hailey's truck. "Hey, Hailey. Long time no see. How are you?"

"Good, Rory," Hailey said with her window down. "How was California?"

"Good, but I'm sure glad to be back here. Thanks for giving Reese a ride home."

"No problem. Talk to you later." She rolled up her

window and backed out of the driveway as I gave her a wave.

"Where's Fisher?" Rory asked as we walked around to the back of the house.

"Still working. He took me car shopping this morning, so I think that put him a little behind today."

"Oh, that's right. Did you find anything?"

I shrugged. "I suppose. I just need to talk to Grandma and Grandpa since they have to approve all large purchases and transfer the money to my account."

She opened the door. "So what did you find? I love my Outback. Did you look at Subarus?"

"Um ... yeah, we actually test drove a Forester."

"Nice. Was it in your price range?"

"Yeah, but I saw another small SUV that I liked too. We didn't test drive it today, but I might another day."

"That's good. You don't want to make a rash decision. It's your first big purchase."

"I know." I unlaced my boots, slipped them off, and tossed my backpack onto my bed. "I'm going to grab a quick shower."

"Okay. I'll start dinner," Rory called.

CHAPTER TWENTY-ONE

I DIDN'T SEE Fisher again until Friday afternoon. He was buried in work, so Rory took me to the office in the morning and Hailey dropped me off after work.

Fisher texted me later that day.

I'll give you a ride home. See you in twenty.

"Fisher's picking me up," I said to Hailey as I sat at Fisher's desk, going through receipts submitted by subcontractors.

"Then, I am out of here. Tell Bossman I had to run to the post office before it closed."

Eyeing her, I grinned. "You don't have to run to the post office, do you?"

She winked. "I have a date. And I'd love a pedicure."

"Have fun."

"Oh, I will. Bye." She floated out the door with a big grin.

Hailey deserved to grin. She had a date. Fisher had a

date. Rory didn't have a date, but she had a friend to hang out with on a Friday night. I had my tumultuous thoughts and crossword puzzles to build.

Just as I finished paper-clipping the last of the receipts, Fisher came through the door. His beard was a little scruffier than usual. His jeans a little dirtier. And he wore a baseball cap that looked pretty used and soiled as well.

"Hey," he said, flipping through the pile of notes for him from Hailey on the corner of his desk.

"Hey." I piled everything neatly in the bottom drawer of the filing cabinet then stood and hiked my bag onto my shoulder. "I was surprised you messaged me. Hailey could have given me a ride home."

"I had to knock off early anyway. Rory wants to leave by six."

Eyes wide, I bit my tongue and nodded several times.

"What are you doing tonight?" He filled a coffee mug with water from the cooler.

Missing you. Soothing my aching heart. Hating Rory for inviting you.

"I'm not sure yet. I'm sure I'll find something age appropriate to do."

Fisher finished gulping the water and set the mug on his desk. "I remember being your age and feeling like I wasn't old enough to do anything fun."

"I have plenty of fun things to do." I walked to the door.

"I'm going for Rory. It would seem very odd to her if I didn't go. Before you moved here, I went out to clubs with them a lot."

"Well, you're going. I don't need to hear your reasoning." I sulked to his truck and climbed into the passenger's seat.

On the way home, I didn't say anything. What could I say? Fisher didn't speak either, but he took every chance to give me a quick glance like I was going to give away something in my demeanor or meet his gaze and talk. I had nothing to say about his big date night.

"Whose car is that?" I asked when we pulled into the driveway. But I quickly figured it out.

"Rose's," Fisher said.

On his porch, sat three women. Rory and who I assumed was Rose and Fisher's date. They were all in dresses. All laughing. And all sipping wine like non-teenaged adults.

"Well, I hope there's a DD tonight." I pulled hard on the door handle and hopped out of the truck before he put it in *Park,* slamming it shut with a little extra attitude.

"Sweetie, come meet my friends," Rory called.

I didn't want to meet her friends. Well, I didn't mind meeting Rose, but the interior designer could have sucked my proverbial cock. As soon as those words floated through my mind, I made the decision that I would spend the night in prayer and scripture because I didn't want to be the person thinking someone could suck my proverbial cock. Yet ... that was my situation, and I hated it.

"Hi." I plastered on a fake smile.

"Reese, this is Rose and Rose's friend, Tiffany."

"So nice to see you again," Rose said. "We actually met when you were much younger. Your mom had you at the salon in Nebraska one day when I came in for my appointment. But ... you had a long summer's worth of freckles on your face and pigtails. You've grown into a beautiful young woman."

Fisher stood just inches behind me; I could feel his nearness as Rose made sure we all were reminded of my age. Pigtails and freckles.

Fantastic.

"Thanks." I forced my manners instead of acting like a disgruntled, pouty child who didn't get to go out with the adults on a Friday night.

"Fisher, this is Tiffany. Tiff, this is Fisher." Rose made the introduction, and I stepped aside so I wasn't blocking them from their big introduction.

"Hi, nice to meet you." Fisher nodded and smiled. "I didn't expect everyone to be here so early. I need to grab a quick shower."

"Take your time," Rory said. "We have more wine." She laughed and so did Rose and Tiffany.

Me? Not so much.

As soon as Fisher disappeared into the house, Tiffany's jaw hit the ground. "Oh. My. God ..." She fanned herself. "You weren't kidding. He's just ... smokin'. I should have waxed everything, not just my legs."

The ladies giggled.

Again, I didn't share in their amusement. I definitely wasn't going to laugh about Tiffany's bold assumption that Fisher would see some unshaved part of her body.

Gah ... I hope he doesn't.

Feeling sufficiently nauseous, I excused myself. "I'm

going to head downstairs and grab a shower too. Have a fun time."

"I hope you have plans, sweetie. I feel bad leaving you if you don't, but you're just not old enough to get into the club."

Rose and Tiffany gave me sad expressions.

My fake smile jumped to the rescue. "Yeah, I might meet up with some friends from church."

"Okay. Be safe. I'll see you tomorrow. If we're going to be too late, I might just crash at Rose's house. So I don't want you to worry if you don't see me until morning."

Rory crashing with Rose.

Tiffany offering her unshaved parts to Fisher.

Just wonderful. I could not have been more excited for the real adults.

"Sounds good. Goodnight."

I lugged my bag around the house to the basement. As soon as I removed my boots, I ran up the stairs and pressed my ear to the door. When I didn't hear anything, I opened it slowly and peeked into the kitchen. When I didn't see anyone, I slid around the corner and padded down the hallway to the closed master bedroom door. Pressing my ear to it, I listened for Fisher, but I heard nothing. Again, I slowly opened the door. The lights were on in his bathroom, so I stepped inside his bedroom and quietly closed the door behind me.

My bare feet made a silent trek to his bathroom, where I peeked around a third door.

"You don't know how to knock, do you?" Fisher looked at me in his mirror as he stood in front of his sink, ruffling his wet hair, wearing nothing but a bath towel around his waist.

"They're drunk. I hope you're driving." I peeled my gaze away from his reflection and moseyed into his walk-in closet.

"I'm sure I am." He appeared in the doorway to his closet as I browsed around at his hanging clothes, mostly button-down shirts. He must have kept his work shirts in one of the drawers by my feet.

"Tiffany's pretty excited. She thinks you're 'smokin'' and she regrets not waxing *everything*."

"Is that so?"

I turned toward Fisher; his shoulder leaned against the door frame and his arms crossed over his bare chest. Of course, Tiffany was planning on *all* things with Fisher. How could any sane, single woman not think like that?

"Yes. That's so."

"Is that why you're in my room? In my closet? To tell me about Tiffany's grooming habits?"

I nibbled the inside of my cheek while running my hand down one of his long-sleeved button-downs. "Pretty much."

"Well, thanks for the heads-up. I'll keep that in mind tonight."

I made my way to him, but he didn't move to let me leave. He uncrossed his arms and took a step closer, so there were no more steps for either one of us to take.

My right hand lifted, feathering along his abs. They tightened even more under my touch.

The tips of my fingers met the top of his towel,

pausing there as I lifted my gaze to his. His full lips parted, and the look in his eyes was pure sin.

"Don't have sex with her tonight." I couldn't keep my eyes from averting to the side and then to my feet. I had no right to ask him for that favor. After all, it wasn't like I was offering him anything.

"There's a lot we can do without having sex. You know this."

I wasn't sure what ached more, my fractured heart or my nauseous stomach. My brave fingers tugged at his towel. It fell to the floor. Fisher didn't flinch.

I had no clue what my plan was ... I officially had the naked fisherman in front of me.

Completely naked.

Cock erect.

Eyes hooded.

Tongue slowly swiping his lower lip when I forced my gaze from his cock to his face.

"What now?" He smirked.

I had *no* clue, but my jealous mind drifted to partially waxed Tiffany. She wanted my naked fisherman.

"She can't have you." I tried to infuse confidence into my words, but I think it fell a little short of the mark.

"No?" He canted his head to the side.

"No."

"What makes you so sure?"

I lowered to my knees, *way* out of my comfort zone. Way out of my own league of intimacy. And definitely scared out of my mind. I just ... I wanted to be an adult with Fisher. I wanted to be a *woman* with him. And I didn't want some hairless hussy meeting his needs.

"Reese ..." His voice held reservation. It was the first sign since I came into his room that he was dealing with his own emotions, his own expectations or maybe lack thereof.

My hands ghosted up his legs and gently took ahold of him.

"I don't expect this from you," he whispered.

From you ...

He expected it from other women? Like Tiffany? Teagan? Angie?

As if dealing with God wasn't enough, I felt so much conflict because I had no clue what I was doing. Fisher became his own godlike man in my life. And I wanted to please him, nearly as much as God, who was surely frowning at my behavior ... at what I was about to do out of wedlock.

Before Fisher could talk me out of it, I wrapped my lips around the head.

He closed his eyes.

I continued doing things to him with my mouth that seemed to please him, despite my cluelessness, keeping my eyes on his face the whole time like a guide. That was how I knew what he liked.

What made him breathe heavier.

What made his teeth dig into his lower lip.

What made his hands grip the side of the doorway, knuckles white.

What made him rock his hips ever so slightly.

Dropping one hand, he gently threaded his fingers into my hair. His muscles tightened, even the ones in his face.

At the last second, he took a step back. Gripping his cock in his hand, he dropped to his knees and kissed me, keeping one hand in my hair while his other hand did something ...

I wasn't sure what until his tongue drove deep into my mouth and a loud moan vibrated from his chest and throat, his body making a few short jerking motions.

Then he relaxed, releasing my mouth. I glanced down.

Whoa ... okay ...

He finished ... the ...uh ... *job* on his bath towel.

"Fisher?" Rory called as three knocks tapped his bedroom door. "Are you coming?"

He grinned at me. It was so big and beautiful as he answered her. "Yes, I'm definitely coming."

My cheeks caught fire.

"Give me five more minutes, Rory."

I skittered to my feet and turned my back toward him, breathing heavily and wondering if she heard anything, if she knew I wasn't downstairs.

"I have five minutes," Fisher said just above a whisper as he pressed his naked body to my back and snaked a hand around my waist. His fingers dipped an inch into the front of my jeans.

"You should get dressed," I said in a nervous tone, stepping out of his hold and circling to get out of his closet while tugging on my shirt to fan the heat away from my skin.

He chuckled. "What should I wear?"

I ignored him as I splashed water on my face and pressed a hand towel to it, trying to slow my breathing, trying to not think about my mom and her friends in the other room.

Tiffany ... he was still going on a date with her. I bet she would do more than what I did to him, and she'd probably do it with way more confidence and experience. Fisher stood a few feet from me when I pulled the towel away from my face. He looked painfully sexy in his dark jeans, light blue button-down with the sleeves rolled up, and stark white sneakers.

He looked painfully sexy for someone else.

I was ready to puke.

"Why the face?"

I shook my head.

"Don't shake your head." He glanced at his watch. "I have three minutes left. What can I do to ease your anxiety?"

Don't go.

"I'm not anxious."

Lies ... lies ... lies ...

"Then are we going out there together? Are we letting everyone know that you like to watch me shower and dress?"

I needed a second round of cold water on my face. "I didn't watch you shower."

He smirked. "But you'd like it, wouldn't you?"

"You're a jerk."

Holding that smug expression for a beat, he nodded once. "Probably." Again, he glanced at his watch. "Two minutes. Are you sure there's nothing I can do?"

I rolled my eyes. "What are you going to do in two minutes?"

"Anything you want."

My voice didn't exist. It must have required more than eighteen years to find my voice. To unapologetically ask for what I wanted without fearing embarrassment or rejection.

I wanted him to not go.

I wanted him to stay with me.

I wanted him to touch me and *make it feel good*.

But I wanted him to do it without me having to ask.

"Time's up." He turned, making his way to the bedroom door with confident strides.

I balled my hands and clenched my teeth, fighting for one word, the smallest semblance of a voice.

Nothing.

He shut his door behind him and voices sounded from the other room. I squeezed my eyes shut and pressed my hands to my face, grumbling at myself for a few seconds before heading straight to the door and plastering my ear against it.

"Tiffany was the interior designer of the house you built in Golden last month," Rose said.

"Oh really?" Fisher seemed a little too enthused.

"I was. It's a beautiful home, Fisher. It's my dream to have you build something for me someday."

I rolled my eyes at Tiffany's gushing reply.

"In fact, I'd take this house right here," she continued.

Really? Could she have been any more obvious and needy? It was just ... gross.

"I'd love to see what you did with the house in Golden," Fisher said.

"Oh ... absolutely. I'll call the Jensens. They'd be

totally cool with me showing it to you." She laughed. "But I'm sure they know you quite well. I suppose you could call them too. Maybe we can make a date of it sometime."

No. No. NO!

Peeling my ear from the door, I pressed both palms to it and sank into a squat, my forehead gently pressed to it as I closed my eyes and prayed for God to erase the past month from it.

Take me back to Texas.

And never let me think of Fisher Mann again.

CHAPTER TWENTY-TWO

It was one night. I should have stuffed my face and gone to sleep in a food coma. Instead, I skipped dinner and went for a run. Then I did an hour of yoga.

Shower.

Crossword puzzles.

Bible.

Prayer.

More prayer.

Ear to the upstairs door, listening for any sign of Fisher.

More prayer.

I went all in, asking for forgiveness for my thoughts and for putting Fisher's penis in my mouth. Did God get a lot of penis prayers? It seemed unlikely. Maybe guys with STDs praying for a quick recovery and promising to return to celibacy.

I didn't promise celibacy because technically, I was still celibate. Or so I told myself.

A little before one in the morning, I took my restless self to the screened-in porch, wearing a tee and white panties. Blanket in hand.

Reaching for the light switch, I accidentally hit another switch and strings of globe lights illuminated the porch. I didn't know they were there. How did I miss them?

It was ... enchanting.

I grinned. My first grin since Fisher left me for Tiffany and jazz music. Curling up in the corner of the patio sectional, I took a deep breath of the chilly night's air and closed my eyes. That was all it took for my mind to settle and sleep to find me.

At some point, my eyes fluttered open, a weird feeling that someone was there.

Fisher ...

He stood next to me, watching me sleep.

"What time is it?" I squinted my eyes.

"Two."

"Where's Rory?" I rubbed one eye.

"She stayed at Rose's place to sober up."

I nodded and yawned.

"Why are you sleeping out here?" he asked.

"Because I couldn't sleep inside."

"Why?" He toed off his shoes.

"I ..." I lifted a shoulder, feeling embarrassed about my terrible thoughts. "I don't know."

He sat at the end of the sofa, stretching his legs out, swallowing the entire length. "Come here," he whispered.

I gave his request a moment's pause before crawling toward him with my blanket. Settling my body between his legs and over his chest, I nuzzled my face into his neck.

He still smelled like pine and soap. And not *her*.

I so desperately wanted to ask him if he did anything with her. Held her hand. Kissed her. Promised her another date. But I didn't because I was enveloped in his arms in the middle of the night beneath the glow of several dozen globe lights, and it was pretty perfect.

A few minutes later, Fisher sat up partway, taking me with him, guiding my legs to straddle his midsection. He held the most contemplative expression on his face. I wanted to solve it like one of my puzzles, looking for clues in his eyes, the part of his lips, or his hand brushing the hair away from my face before caressing his knuckles down my neck.

I closed my eyes, reveling in the moment, in the way he made me feel like I was flying. Free of everything that kept me from finding myself, my voice, my place in the world.

When I opened my eyes, he feathered his other hand along my cheek, his thumb tracing my bottom lip. The night air was no comparison to the way Fisher's touch elicited an endless emergence of goose bumps along my skin.

"What are you doing?" I whispered.

His gaze followed the trail of his hand along my skin for another breath or two before he gave me those intense eyes of his. "I'm apologizing."

From earlier that week ...

The car dealership. The park. His extreme *extra*.

Sorry meant nothing if that kind of touch was his way of apologizing. My soul felt it.

"Fisher?" I whispered.

He seemed mesmerized with my lips—his thumb ghosting along them, eyes drifting from mine to his thumb.

"Are you going to kiss me?"

The hint of a grin moved his mouth. "I was thinking about it."

My hand curled around his wrist, pulling his hand from my mouth as I leaned in a few inches and grinned while my lips brushed along his. "You think too much."

We kissed.

We let our hands explore each other's bodies.

We made out ... the first time I actually made out with a guy.

No sex.

No orgasms.

Just lots of kissing and touching.

Eventually, our hands stilled, our bodies entwined, and our lips eased apart as we fell asleep.

In the morning, I woke first, lifting my head from his chest. One of his hands rested on top of mine pressed to his chest next to my head. His other hand ... it was resting on my butt ... on the inside of my panties. I wasn't sure when it laid claim to that spot, but I kinda liked it.

That was a lie.

I kinda loved it.

If I was going to Hell, I wanted to go there with Fisher's hands all over me, his lips on mine, and his dirty words in my ear.

"Good morning, Ed." Rory's voice sent me into major panic mode as she greeted the neighbor on her way around to the basement. To us!

"Oh my gosh!" I whisper yelled. "Get up!" I tugged on Fisher's arm.

He squinted, not entirely awake.

"Rory's coming! GET UP!" Had I whispered any louder, she would have heard me.

Fisher stumbled getting up. I pushed him with all my strength toward the door.

"Go! Hurry!"

"Christ, woman ... I'm going already." He walked like a drunk man with his shirt unbuttoned and hanging off one shoulder and his hair matted in back.

As soon as he made it to the stairs, I rushed back to the porch.

"Look who's up early," Rory said in a cheery voice as I grabbed the blanket and kicked Fisher's sneakers under the sofa.

"Yeah, I uh ... slept out here last night. When I discovered the lights, I couldn't resist."

She opened the door to the porch instead of going in through the main door. "Oh, yeah. I should have told you. I guess I figured you'd see them and look for the switch."

I wrapped the blanket around my shoulders. "So ... did you have fun?" I sat back down on the sofa while she took a seat in the rocker.

"We had a great time. When you're older, we'll have to go to all the clubs. There are some really great ones around here. If ..." Her nose wrinkled. She sometimes forgot that I spent the previous three years with my grandparents in a very conservative home and school. "If you're comfortable with it or you want to." Her pained expression softened into the mom I once knew, the face of unconditional love.

The face of absolute comfort. She was my safe place. I was never a daddy's girl, despite my interest in his job and his hobby. I idolized my mom, and I didn't think she ever really knew.

"I want you to be whoever you need to be to feel comfortable in your own skin. I want you to never feel the need to fit in or follow others if it's not who *you* are. Okay?"

Right there. That was my *mom*.

Pressing my lips together, I nodded slowly. And I almost, *almost* told her that my path had crossed with Fisher's path.

Collided.

Crashed.

And I wasn't sure I'd ever find my own way again because I loved him. More than that ... despite my battered and prodded ego ... I liked who I was with him, even if it made no sense. Even if I'd never tell him that.

Did love have to make sense?

"So the club was fun?"

She nodded. "Yes. One of our favorites was playing."

"And Tiffany and Fisher ... did they hit it off?"

"Yeah, I think so. They have a lot in common. They

chatted it up during the breaks and at the bar we went to after the jazz club. She's definitely interested in him, but I haven't had the chance to talk to him yet. I'd like to see him find someone. I know he has the eternal heart of a bachelor, but Fisher deserves more."

I wanted to be that more.

CHAPTER TWENTY-THREE

I DIDN'T SEE Fisher the rest of Saturday because Rory took me shopping, then we had lunch. We ended the day at her salon where she gave me a haircut, even though it was her day off, and we both got manicures and pedicures.

It was a good day, one that started with me in Fisher's arms and his hand on my butt.

Sunday morning, I showered and slipped on a striped romper and my Birkenstocks for church.

"Coffee?" Rory asked from her corner of the sofa, robe on, hair pulled into a low ponytail.

"I'm good. They have coffee and a buffet of baked goods at church. You know, you could go with me."

"Mmm ..." She wrinkled her nose. "I'm not sure I'm church material anymore."

I giggled, slipping a few items into my smaller purse. "I don't think there's such a thing as church material. All are welcomed in the Lord's house."

"When I think of the Lord's house, I think of Heaven,

not a lackluster building with a gymnasium, fitness center, coffee and donuts. Really ... they used to build churches—cathedrals—to make you feel like God himself resided in the building, his spirit woven around the intricate wooden carvings, flying buttresses, and stunning stained glass works of art. Sorry ... I don't think the Lord's house has a basketball hoop ... and I love basketball."

"Fair." I laughed. "I'll see you later. I'm not sure when. I told Brendon we could go out for lunch again after church."

A date. I basically committed myself to another date. But if Fisher could go out and enjoy his time with half-waxed Tiffany, then I could break bread with Brendon after Sunday service.

"You need my keys?" Rory asked as I opened the door.

I forgot to mention that Brendon was also my ride to church since I didn't have a car yet, and I didn't want to take Rory's car with her back in town.

"Brendon's picking me up."

Rory's smile doubled. "That's ... good. Yeah?" She latched onto that like a dog on a rabbit.

"A ride? I suppose it is. I'm still working out some things with Grandma and Grandpa on the money for my car."

It was a flat "no" when I called them last week. They said "yes" to the Accord or the Forester.

"You know what I mean." Rory shook her head.

"Byeee ..." I closed the door and headed up front.

The two men in my world, if I could call them that, arrived at the same time. Brendon pulled into the driveway just as shirtless Fisher finished his morning jog. One of them nearly gave me an orgasm.

"Brandon," Fisher said as my church date rolled down his window.

"Hi, it's uh ... Brendon," *Brendon* corrected him.

Fisher knew his name, and the grin he gave me when his back was to Brendon's window said as much.

"Reese." Fisher stripped me with one look. I think he also took the rest of my virginity with that same look.

I needed to check on the specifics of getting re-baptized.

Clearing my throat and forcing my gaze to stay on his face instead of his sweat covered chest, I smiled, "Morning, Fisher."

"You going to confession?" he asked.

"It's a Christian church. We don't have confession."

"Mmm ..." He winked before heading into the garage. "A shame."

Brendon smiled as I climbed into his car. "You look nice."

"Thanks, you do too."

He laughed like my reciprocating the compliment wasn't necessary.

"Thanks for picking me up. I'm having trouble deciding on a car."

"Oh?" Brendon backed out of Fisher's driveway.

"Yeah, well ... it's that my grandparents don't want to give me the money for the car I want, even though it's my money."

"What car do you want?"

I stared out the window to my right and shrugged like it was no big deal. "It's a used Porsche Cayenne."

"A Porsche?" Brendon choked on his words.

"I want something sporty that can go into the mountains."

"Reese, I think you can find something a little more practical. After all, you're eighteen. Don't blow through your money before you get a chance to make some decisions on your future like going to college. Maybe you'll want a down payment on a house. Maybe you could invest some of the money."

Why did he have to sound so sensible—so parental —too?

During the church service, Brendon shared his Bible with me since I forgot mine. At least I got points for forgetting it because it was by my bed because I'd been reading it—all the parts on sins of the flesh.

In Sunday school, we played games, more like twenty questions to test our morals. I did quite well, just because I'd sinned didn't mean I wasn't aware of my sins. Some of the other people in class were legitimately clueless. That meant they were ripe for accepting their opportunity at salvation.

"You choose the lunch spot today," Brendon said as we made our mad dash to the parking lot again to beat the after-church crowd. This time he parked where he couldn't get trapped.

"It's hot today. Let's do something light like a big salad."

"So ... ice cream for lunch?" Brendon shot me a

conspiratorial grin over the top of his car just before I lowered into the seat.

"I knew I liked you." I returned the same grin.

We stopped at an ice cream shop for sundaes and spent over two hours there talking about ... everything. It was easy and refreshing.

"I talked with my boss ... well, bosses at the law firm. After I take the bar, I'm going to go on a mission trip for six months. I told them I understood if they can't hold my position, but they were really great. They said I'd have a job waiting when I returned."

"Wow ..." I sipped my second glass of water as Brendon fiddled with his spoon and empty sundae bowl. "A mission trip. Where to?"

"Thailand."

"That's ..." I shook my head. "Great?" I laughed at my own response. "Brave? I don't know."

"Exciting with a dash of scary." Brendon grinned. "I've done small trips to places in Central America, just through my church. But this one is through a bigger organization. It's a bucket list thing for me. I want to feel like my life is useful beyond settling disputes among people wealthy enough to hire an attorney from a big law firm. I just ..." He focused on his spoon for a few seconds. "I just want to stay grounded in my purpose. I want to always feel like I'm taking opportunities to really serve and do God's work. You know?"

I did. And I didn't.

Truth?

I envied Brendon's direction in life. He was focused and driven. He wasn't lost in his journey or stalled along the side of the road like me. I felt certain he didn't stay awake at night worrying if the object of his affection was holding hands with someone else or kissing them.

My priorities were shameful.

"You know ..." he continued. "It might be something for you to consider too. If you're not going to college right away, and you don't really know what direction you want to go, it might be a good way to get a direction. Focus. Perspective. And if it doesn't give you any of that, you'll still have done something great. Made a difference."

Brendon would be a good attorney. He had mad skills at making a good case for things.

"Well..." I frowned "...now I feel like a loser."

He laughed and shook his head. "No. Don't feel like that. Not at all. You're eighteen. You have your whole life to work, volunteer, make a difference. There's nothing wrong with just being young and a little lost."

"Pfft ..." I rolled my eyes. "Says the guy who, I'm sure, was going on mission trips at my age."

With a sheepish grin, he shrugged. "Only because I legit had no life beyond that. Now who's the loser?"

I sighed. "I just don't know what to do."

"Just ... think about it. I'm not saying you have to go to Thailand with me, but I'm not saying it would be a bad thing either." Brendon relinquished a very endearing and maybe even convincing smile.

"I guess I'd feel silly getting an expensive car if I were planning on leaving for six months."

"Practicality wins." He winked.

As handsome and flirty as Brendon was, I didn't care

for his winks. Only one man could wink at me and make my insides turn to gooey mush.

"Well, I'll take you home. How would you feel about going out some night this week?"

"Um ..."

He held up his hands. "No pressure."

"No. I ... it ... well, you have my number. I guess text me."

Brendon lit up with satisfaction, a glow of victory. "I'll do that."

He drove me home and pulled in the driveway. Fisher and my mom were on the front porch drinking iced tea ... or maybe beer. I couldn't tell for sure.

"We have an audience," Brendon said.

"Yeah. We do."

"I guess that means I'll have to wait to kiss you another time."

Gulp ...

On a nervous laugh, I nodded. "I guess so. Well, thanks for the ice cream. It was fun." I opened the door.

"Wait! I messed up when I picked you up. I'm not going to screw this up in front of your mom." Brendon jumped out and ran around the car to open my door.

"Oh." Another nervous laugh. "Thanks." I climbed out of his car.

"Reese, introduce me," Rory called.

Brendon took my hand.

He took my hand!

And we walked to the front porch. A kiss was more than he wanted to do in front of an audience, but he thought hand-holding was okay?

I died a million deaths.

After warning Fisher about Tiffany, after losing hours of sleep from thoughts of kissing or *hand-holding*, my hand was latched to Brendon's right in front of Fisher.

"Hi, you must be Rory. I'm Brendon. So nice to meet you." Brendon released my hand to shake Rory's hand.

Fisher slowly sipped his drink, his eyes saying everything as he focused on my hand that had just been attached to Brendon's.

"The pleasure is all mine," Rory gushed. "Reese told me so much about you."

I did?

I mentioned him and maybe a few things about him, but I didn't go on and on about him. Too late. Brendon glanced at me, a huge smile on his face. I returned more of a tight grin. What could I say?

"Well, I think Reese is pretty great. We have so much in common. And it's easy to talk for hours."

Rory eyed me. Either she was ready to plan my wedding or she wanted to date Brendon herself. I feared it was the former.

"I'm going to take off. Nice to meet you, Rory. And good to see you again, Fisher."

Fisher returned a slow nod, no smile.

Brendon grabbed my hand again and gave it a quick squeeze, but something crossed his face, like he was contemplating something. Before I could stop it, he leaned in (IN FRONT OF THEM) and kissed my cheek.

I felt like an adulterer.

"Aw ..." Rory rested her hand on Fisher's arm like, *"Look at your sister. She's found a nice boy."*

"Bye," I whispered past the painful lump in my throat. After Brendon pulled out of the driveway, I forced my gaze back to Rory and Fisher.

"He seems perfect, Reese." Rory beamed.

"He's nice." I couldn't hold my gaze to Fisher's, so I stared at my feet, kicking at a few landscaping rocks that were on the paving stones.

"Well, I'm going to run to the store and grab some groceries for the week. Do you want to come with me?"

"Um ... would it be okay if I didn't go? I feel like I've been gone all day."

"No problem. Anything special you want me to get for you?"

"Whatever you get is fine." I risked a glance at Fisher.

He had the most unreadable expression.

"Okay. Thanks for the tea, Fisher."

"Yup," Fisher said in a monotone voice.

I waited for her to go into the house to presumably put her glass in his kitchen and get her purse. Sitting in her chair, I waited for him to say something.

He didn't.

A few minutes later, Rory came back out the front door with her purse over her shoulder. "Text me if you think of anything you do want me to get for you."

"Okay," I murmured.

We watched her get into her Outback and drive down the street.

"I'm sorry. I didn't know he was going to—"

"For god's sake, Reese." He stood, making his way to

the front door. "Don't do this. Don't apologize for finding an age-appropriate guy."

I jumped to my feet and followed him. "I didn't find *an age-appropriate guy*. We're just friends."

"Didn't look like that." He put his empty glass in the dishwasher.

"Well, he's mistaken. And I'll let him know that when I see him again."

Fisher turned, eyes narrowed, hands sliding into his back pockets. "Rory likes him."

I shrugged one shoulder. "Then she can date him."

He grunted. "I don't think he's her type."

"Well, he's not my type."

"No?"

I shook my head.

"He should be."

"Are you ..." I sauntered toward him. "Are you jealous?"

"I'm not fucking jealous of Bible Boy." He glanced down at me, hands still planted in his back pockets.

I frowned. "Be nice."

"What if I don't want to be nice?"

"Then tie me up and bite my ass, but don't take it out on Brendon."

It thrilled me that Fisher didn't want to smile, but he couldn't help it. "Did you just say ass?"

"It's a donkey."

"So you want me to tie you up then bite your donkey?"

"I thought *you* wanted to tie me up?" I wasn't sure how to back my way out of the donkey comment.

"I'm open to the idea."

Gah!

What did that mean? I would have handed over my entire inheritance for the chance to read Fisher Mann's mind.

I tipped my chin up. "Maybe I am too."

I wasn't. Not at all.

First ... I had some claustrophobia issues.

Second ... I didn't trust him with my body if I couldn't control my limbs.

And third ... back to the claustrophobia issues. That was a big one for me.

But I sure liked acting brave with Fisher. It was the most exhilarating feeling. Some people bungee jumped or jumped out of planes with parachutes on their backs. My adrenaline rush came from my cat and mouse game with Fisher.

"I have some work to do in my woodshop." He removed his hands from his pockets and brushed past me to the back door.

"Will you teach me something?"

Stopping, he glanced over his shoulder. "If you can listen without distracting me."

"How would I distract you?"

He nodded to my outfit. "Go change your clothes. I don't want to see your bare legs. And you need a thicker bra. I can't teach you shit when your nipples are popped out like that. And wear your work boots."

Biting my lips to hide my grin. I nodded. "Yes, sir."

CHAPTER TWENTY-FOUR

Fisher taught me how to measure and cut. Glue and screw. Properly use a hammer and level.

An hour later, Rory found us. "There you are. I was looking for you."

I turned away from Fisher's workbench, my safety glasses a little foggy. "He's teaching me things, so I'll be more useful."

Fisher stayed focused on piecing together the drawer he'd just made. "I don't know about useful, but a smidge less useless."

Rory laughed. "Well, I was thinking about inviting Rose over to grill out. Fisher, do you have plans? Tiffany might come too."

"No plans," Fisher mumbled, ultra-focused on the joint he just glued.

I wanted to knee him in the balls. No plans? Another date?

"Reese, do you prefer chicken or steak? Or I have tofu. Rose doesn't eat meat."

As my gaze bored a hole in his temple, I murmured, "Doesn't matter."

"Okay. Does an hour give you enough time to finish up?"

Fisher didn't give her a verbal answer, just a tiny nod.

"Cool. I'll let you know when they're here."

After Rory's feet *tapped tapped tapped* their way to the top of the stairs and the door clicked shut behind her, I rammed the toe of my work boot into Fisher's shin.

"Ouch! The fuck?" He reached down and rubbed his shin.

"Another date with Tiffany? Are you kidding me?"

He seemed too aggravated over his shin and me interrupting his work to spare the slightest glint of regret. "What did you expect me to say?"

"I expected you to say you had plans."

"But I don't. And you're going to be here too. What's the big deal?"

"The big deal is she likes you. A lot!"

"Like Brendon likes you *a lot*?" He shot me a scowl.

"I'm not inviting him to dinner." I parked my fists on my hips.

"Well, maybe you should. Sounds like Rory has lots of food, and the more the merrier. Right?"

"Now you're being a jerk. Such a jerk."

Standing erect, he pulled off his glasses and tossed them onto the workbench. "Oh really. *I'm* being the jerk? What about you?"

"You should have lied." That was my answer. Church schooled, Bible study, virgin me advocating lying. It was a new low.

"I won't kiss her cheek or hold her hand. Are we good now?"

My ego was in overdrive. We weren't good. Well, he was probably good. Twenty-eight-year-olds had a little more maturity and self-control. Achieving good status was probably easier for him.

Teenaged adults, such as myself, struggled with letting the little stuff go and just being ... good.

"I'm *not* good."

"No?" He cocked his head to the side.

I think I knew I was in trouble, but I wasn't sure how trouble would play out.

"Then let's make you good." He grabbed my shoulders and pushed me backward.

I stumbled, but he kept me standing. Squatting in front of me, he untied my work books.

"W-what are you d-doing?" I couldn't hide my nerves.

Fisher didn't answer. His quick hands discarded my boots to the side.

"Fisher ... what are ..." My words caught in my throat. I'd poked the bear a little too hard. Actually, I had kicked him in the shin.

He didn't look at me. He was too busy focusing on my jeans.

Unbuttoning them.

Unzipping them.

Peeling them down my legs.

"Fisher ...we can't ... not here ..." I gave him a weak protest.

What if Rory came back? The door wasn't locked.

My jeans landed next to my boots as he tossed them aside. Still, he hadn't made a single glance upward to see my sheer panic.

As his fingers curled inside the waist of my panties, I grabbed one of his hands. "Fisher, we can't ..."

He stopped, completely still. Eyes homing in on my hand clawing at his hand. Then his lips twisted as he squinted. His head swiveled, surveying one side of the room and then the other.

Leaving me half naked and panicky, he stood and took several steps to a stack of drawers. After opening several of them, he retrieved something and shoved it into his back pocket, and something else from another drawer. Then he turned.

"No ..." I shook my head when I saw the zip ties in his hand. "No ... I can't. I'm claustrophobic. My heart will stop. No ..."

He ignored me while grabbing a couple of dirty rags.

"Fisher ... no!" I tried to pull my hand out of his grip.

"Shh ..." He shook his head slowly, still not looking at me while he wrapped a rag around one wrist and then a zip tie.

"Uh-uh ..." My head jerked side to side. "No. I said no ..."

"Shh ..." He repeated the process with my other wrist.

With unnatural ease, he lifted me onto the barstool and used two more ties to restrain my hands to my sides by looping them around the legs of the stool.

"Fisher!" I jerked my arms, but they didn't move.

He finally looked at me, holding a stiff finger to his lips for several seconds before kissing me.

I yelped into his mouth, and he swallowed it again and again. His hands peeled my panties past my butt to my knees. He lifted his boot and stepped on them, shoving them the rest of the way off my legs as his kiss grew hungrier. His hands gripped my knees and spread them wide before his fingers teased me.

Made me jump.

Made me moan.

Made me crazy.

He pulled his mouth away from mine. "Tell me no, and I'll release you," he whispered over my lips.

His fingers were making me delirious, drunk, incapable of forming a coherent thought.

"Fish ... Fisher ..." My heavy eyelids closed for a second.

He was relentless.

I was ... I didn't even know. But I wasn't thinking about my hands being restrained. There wasn't enough blood in my head to acknowledge my claustrophobia. It had all pooled around the sensitive bundle of nerves between my legs.

He dropped to his knees and ...

Oh my ... fuck ... fuck ... FUCKITY FUUUCK!

Ten seconds ... not even, I orgasmed so quickly, and I did it with one of Fisher's hands on my knee, keeping my legs wide open and his other hand over my mouth, muffling my unholy chain of uncensored words.

Fisher's hand fell from my mouth as he sat back on

his heels like he did that day at the park and rested both hands on his thighs.

His gaze affixed to the very spot his mouth had been just seconds earlier. I couldn't imagine what it must have looked like.

I eased my legs together, and he lifted his gaze slowly up my body to meet my eyes. And they were filled with tears.

"Are you *good* now?"

I blinked and the tears fell down my face. "A-are you m-mine?" My lower lip quivered.

Fisher owned me. Maybe it was stupid and childish … maybe it made me a weak woman, but Fisher Mann owned me. And the thing that scared me more than absolutely anything in the world was that he wasn't mine.

He reached into his back pocket and pulled out a pair of wire cutters. After clipping the ties and tossing the rags aside, he bent down and snagged my panties off the floor, sliding them back up my legs and lifting me off the stool to finish pulling them over my butt. Next, he put my jeans back on.

Tug.

Zip.

Button.

Finishing with my boots, he tied them with expert precision like he did the day he bought them for me.

There I stood, limp, my heart lodged in my throat, and an unattended stream of tears on my cheeks. Fisher stood again and met my gaze. He slid my foggy safety glasses onto my head, then his thumbs took care of my tears.

"You know the answer to that." Ducking his head, he kissed me.

Not hard.

Not demanding.

Not like he did when he tied me to the chair.

He kissed me like ... I was his and ... *he was mine.*

"Go get ready for dinner. I have to clean up." His knuckles caressed my cheek. It was my favorite gesture.

So tender.

So endearing.

It made me feel unequivocally special.

I nodded before turning my head so his palm brushed my lips, and I kissed it. "Fisher ..." I grinned.

"Yeah?"

My hand ghosted over his, guiding it so my lips met his wrist. I closed my eyes for a second, feeling his pulse—that heartbeat that I wanted to claim as mine. I wanted it to beat for me.

"I'm *good*," I whispered.

CHAPTER TWENTY-FIVE

I took a quick shower and put on my nicest sheer blouse and fitted jeans. Then, I plugged in my curling iron and applied a little makeup.

"You about done?" Rory poked her head into my bathroom.

"Yeah." I glossed my lips.

"It's casual. You don't have to get all dolled up."

I shrugged. "Yesterday, it was fun having my hair curled. And with my day job, I rarely get to look *dolled up*. So ... why not?"

I smiled at her reflection in my bathroom mirror.

"You're absolutely right." She took my big comb and ran it through my hair. "It took me awhile, after I was released, to feel like I wanted to make the effort. But sometimes we do. Even if it's just for family and close friends." She grabbed the curling iron and nodded for me to sit on the toilet seat. "Even if it's just for ourselves."

I closed my eyes and hummed as she curled my hair. I loved it. I had always loved it.

"I should have told you to invite Brendon."

My eyes opened. "I'm not sure my feelings for him are the same as his are for me. I think he's great. And we do fall into the easiest conversations, but I don't know if there's more. At least for me. So I just don't want you to get your hopes up."

"Oh, sweetie, I think you're just not seeing it. Oftentimes, the greatest friendships turn into beautiful love stories. So I'm not saying he's your forever, but I want you to always keep your heart open to let love grow. Not everything in life starts with sparks and flies to the sky in a wave of butterflies."

"Were you and Dad friends first?"

"No." She laughed. "Those were sparks."

"Clearly, those sparks worked for you two."

She nodded slowly, hesitantly. "Until it didn't."

Because you went to prison.

I opened my mouth to ask her why. Why was she growing marijuana? Why did she risk everything for drugs?

But I knew Rose and Tiffany were on the screened-in porch waiting for us. And Fisher was upstairs taking a shower.

It wasn't the right time.

"There." She unplugged the curling iron. "You have the most beautiful hair." She loosely ran her fingers through my dark curls to relax them just a bit, giving my hair a beach wave look.

I grinned. "I have your hair."

"Only better." She kissed my cheek. "Let's go eat. Would you mind running upstairs and knocking on

Fisher's door? Tell him everyone is here and dinner is ready."

"Sure." I held my enthusiasm inside. Go get Fisher?

Yes, please.

As Rory carried a tray of drinks to the porch, I ran upstairs and opened the door. No Fisher in the kitchen. So I listened for him as I made my way to his bedroom. Just as I reached for the handle, he opened it.

A whoosh of his clean scent nearly made my knees give out on me, not to mention his killer smile.

Jeans. Tee. Wet hair.

He glanced over my shoulder as if to see if anyone else was upstairs with me.

"Dinner is ready. And your date is here."

"Where is here?" He gave me a quick once-over that I *felt*.

"Downstairs on the porch."

Pursing his lips, face so serious, he nodded several times. "Well, get your sexy ass in here." He grabbed my arm and yanked me into his bedroom.

"Fisher!" I yelled a little louder than intended. I wasn't expecting him to do that.

Or shut the door behind us.

Or toss me onto his bed.

Or dive onto the bed after me.

I flinched. "Eek!" I curled my body, not completely trusting him to not squash me.

Like a cat, he landed on all fours, straddling my body. His grinning face hovering over mine.

"Hi, beautiful."

Oh, naked fisherman ... how does it feel to carry my heart in your pocket? Its fate solely dependent on you?

"Handsome." I matched his grin a second before he kissed me.

One leg at a time, he wedged himself between my legs and rested over me on his elbows. Our kiss so slow, almost lazy. Maybe it was the comfort in knowing it wasn't our first, and it wouldn't be our last.

"You smell edible." He kissed my neck while inhaling deeply.

"They're waiting on us," I said with little to no true concern in my voice. I liked the naked fisherman universe too much to care about the mortals on planet Earth or the screened-in porch.

He took liberty with the deep exposed V of my shirt that I left unbuttoned to the top of my cleavage. Then he took more, unbuttoning the next two buttons.

"Fisher," I whispered on a weak breath. His touch never failed to jolt my pulse out of rhythm, never failed to rob my brain of blood and sensible thoughts.

"What is it?" he whispered, a breath before sliding my bra down just enough to expose my nipple.

On a hitched breath, my back arched into his touch as he sucked it slowly, teasing it with his tongue and teeth.

"W-we ..." I tried so hard to be the mature one, but it was a monumental struggle. "We ... have to go to ... dinner."

"Yeah?" he said between kisses, working his way to my other breast.

"Yes ..." I hissed when he trapped my nipple between his teeth and tugged it.

"Cock blocker." He lifted his head and adjusted my bra back into place before buttoning those two buttons.

I giggled. "You can't call me that. I want ..." I bit my lips together before anymore words tumbled from my lips.

"You want what?" He grinned, dipping his face to my neck again. Biting and sucking it. "My cock?"

My fingers played in his hair as my drunk eyes drifted shut again. "Yes," I whispered.

"Well, what are we going to do about that?" He continued his assault on my neck, and I felt certain my neck and face would be red from his scratchy face.

"Fisher ..." I didn't recognize that voice, but it was mine. It was me wrapping my legs around his waist, begging him for ... well, his cock.

He chuckled, coming onto his arms to get off the bed, to get off of me.

My legs locked around his waist and my arms did the same around his neck.

Again, he laughed, standing with me wrapped around him. "I think you said dinner's ready."

"Fisher," I whispered just before kissing his neck the way he had been kissing mine just seconds earlier. "I ..."

Kiss.

"Want ..."

Kiss. Bite. Long lick up to his ear.

"You."

He pushed my back against the door and grabbed my face, kissing the life out of me. I felt it heaving in my breasts and radiating all the way down to the spot his erection hit between my legs.

"Fuck ..." He pulled away breathless as his forehead hit the door just behind my shoulder. "You are *killing* me."

I grinned, teasing the nape of his neck with my fingers. Killing Fisher wasn't my intention, but I didn't exactly *not* like it either. My confidence feasted on his words.

"When is dinner?" He lifted his head. "Because I already know this erection is going to last more than four hours. I might need a trip to urgent care." He reached for my legs, forcing me to unlock them so he could set me on my feet. "Now, go tell them I'm on my way. In four hours." He sauntered to his bathroom.

"Are you going to ..."

He glanced back at me as I wrinkled my nose and bit my lip. "Rub one off? Yes. Fuck yes. It's the only way I'll make it to dinner."

"Do you want me to—"

"Nope. I've got it." He shut the bathroom door and locked it.

I covered my mouth and squealed into my cupped hands. So much dopamine in my veins. Fisher was the most glorious addiction. And I wanted him. All of him. And I knew what that meant, but I didn't care. I wanted to have sex with Fisher. Lots of naked fisherman sex. And after that? I didn't know. I just knew we'd figure it out a day at a time.

CHAPTER TWENTY-SIX

I RAN from the bottom of the stairs to my bathroom.

"Fisher ..." I frowned at my reflection in the mirror. He totally destroyed my hair. And my face, neck, and chest had a severe case of whisker burn. So I splashed lots of water on my face and reapplied my makeup. Then, I buttoned my blouse to the top and tied a lightweight scarf around my neck.

"Sorry. Fisher was still in the shower, so I had to wait for him to get out so I could tell him dinner was ready." The lies came way too easily.

"Cute scarf," Rose said.

I touched my scarf, making sure it was coving my neck. "Thanks."

"Your mom said you work for Fisher, is that correct?" Tiffany asked as I took a seat on the sectional, the spot where I slept with Fisher. Tiffany sat at the opposite end.

"Yes, for now." I persuaded my lips to curl into a smile for Fisher's date.

"What's it like working for him? He's such a perfectionist. I bet it's intense." Tiffany sipped her sangria that Rory made.

"Yes, what's it like?" Fisher appeared in the doorway, giving me a serious expression as he sat on the sofa, not too close to me, but definitely closer to me than Tiffany.

"It's like working for a man child." I gave him a toothy smile.

Rory and Rose laughed, rocking in the only two rockers on the porch. Tiffany seemed uneasy. Her gaze ping-ponged between me and Fisher.

"Brave girl." She cringed. "I'd never talk to my boss like that."

Fisher leaned forward and grabbed a glass of sangria from the tray. "I'll fire her on Monday."

"Oh, Fisher. Do you want to go with me to the Jensen's this week? I messaged them, and they're out of town this week, but they gave me their door code and said we can stop by anytime."

Fisher sipped his sangria before rubbing his lips together and nodding. "Let me check my schedule and see how my week goes."

"Absolutely. I'm really flexible."

"And by flexible, she means she does yoga." Rose threw Tiffany under the bus.

Rory laughed. Fisher smirked with slight amusement. Tiffany turned as red as the sangria. And I grinned past my clenched teeth.

"I know you won't, but I'm fine with you having a glass of sangria if you'd like to try it, Reese." Rory nodded to the last glass on the tray.

"My mom wasn't near as cool as your mom, Reese," Rose said. "It's the best sangria. Try it."

"Don't push her." Rory shot Rose a look. "She's accustomed to a more conservative lifestyle, and we need to respect that." Rory worked overtime trying to convince everyone, including me, that I wouldn't or maybe shouldn't try the sangria.

"I'll try it." I shrugged.

Fisher leaned forward again and handed me the last glass.

"Thanks," I murmured, giving him a quick glance.

"Nice scarf," he said so only I could hear him.

My eyes narrowed a fraction as I sipped my drink.

"Well?" Rory waited for my response to the sangria.

"It's really good."

"Easy, lightweight," Fisher said, eliciting laughter.

I lifted my foot onto the sofa and kicked the side of his leg.

He grabbed my ankle and held it, nearly making me spill my drink as I tried to break free from his grip.

"Now ... now ... *kids.*" Rory rolled her eyes. "I wasn't the least bit surprised to find these two acting like siblings when I got home from California. We have guests. I don't need you two wrestling around on the floor."

Fisher released my ankle, but his touch lingered on my skin. I liked his hands on me. So very much.

Tiffany watched us, a slight catty expression pinned to her face.

"I shut off the grill, but everything is ready. Steak. Chicken. Tofu. And in the foil, there's veggies and pota-toes. Want to grab the food off the grill, Fisher?"

"Sure thing." He stood, setting his glass onto the tray.

"Grab the cookie sheet on the counter and set everything on it. Reese can help you."

I didn't waste a second before standing and heading into the house behind Fisher.

"Tiffany keeps scowling at me. Do you think she suspects something? I don't think she likes me," I said as Fisher grabbed the cookie sheet and the grill tongs.

"I've sucked your tits and you came in my mouth today. She probably senses that I'm still craving more of you."

When I didn't respond, because my jaw dropped open, out of commission for a few seconds, Fisher turned toward me and smirked.

"Don't." He shook his head. "You're not allowed to act offended anymore. Tits is not a bad word. I gave you the PG version. Really, you should thank me."

"W-what ..." I loosened my scarf. "What's the adult version?" I glanced over my shoulder to make sure we were still alone and out of earshot. "Oral sex?" I whispered.

Fisher rolled his lips together to hide his amusement, but it hid nothing. He was laughing at me. My age. My innocence ... or what was left of it.

"What?" I narrowed my eyes.

"Could you be any more clinical?"

"Could you be any more crude?"

"Yes." He took a step toward me, also eyeing the gathering on the porch behind me. "I could have said I jerked off thinking about biting your nipples and eating you out earlier in the day."

I did *not* like the phrase "eating you out." It made me shudder. I wasn't an apple. Although, I probably felt like the forbidden fruit to Fisher.

"Did you learn to be so crude? Or is it genetic?"

He shrugged. "It's the Y chromosome."

"No." I crossed my arms over my chest and shook my head. "I know plenty of men who are not crude and filthy like you."

"You *think* you do. Like ... Bible Boy. You think his chivalrous hand-holding and sweet peck on the cheek is who he is. It's not. It's who he's been trained to be. But I promise you, after he got home this afternoon, he rubbed one off thinking about you in the most unholy ways. He's thought about your cunt and your tits *so* many times." Fisher brushed past me.

"Don't say the C word."

"Too late. I already did." He opened the storm door and shot the ladies his sexy grin before heading out to the grill.

I followed, adjusting my scarf that covered my whisker burn and my embarrassment. I probably had half the Bible committed to memory, yet I managed to fall in love with the son of Satan.

As Fisher opened the lid to the grill, I sidled up next to him. "Have you ever been to church?"

"Yes. I went to a Presbyterian church every Sunday until my parents could no longer physically pick me up and force me to go."

"Do you believe in God?"

He set the meat and tofu kabobs onto the cookie sheet. "Why? Are you on a mission to save me?"

Selfishly, no. I was on a mission to save myself. But I wasn't ready to give up my newest addiction, so I thought God would reward me for making Fisher a little less ... *extra.*

Unfortunately, my religion didn't believe the way to salvation was through good deeds.

Bummer.

"Because ... I'm getting mixed signals. I think you want me to have sex with you, but you also want to do what Jesus would do. Which means I need to marry you to have sex with you, and I'm not marrying you just to have sex with you." He peered down at me with raised brows and a tilted head as if to make sure I understood him.

I did not.

Fisher was the king of statements that could be interpreted in more than one way. He wasn't going to marry me and therefore we weren't having sex? Or he wasn't going to marry me *just* for sex, but it was possible he would marry me for sex *and* other reasons?

"You want to know the funny part ... even if it's not that funny?"

He closed the lid to the grill. "I'm intrigued now. What's the not-so-funny part?"

"The only thing that stands between virgin me and non-virgin me is you having a condom on you at the right time."

"No." He shook his head. "It's not my lack of preparedness, it's just bad sex. *Deflowering* isn't all it's cracked up to be. And unless you're trying to be biblical about it, it's not a gift. It's a curse. You are not going to enjoy that moment when some guy's dick rams into (pun intended) *virgin* territory. You'll wince, nearly cry, then fail epically at faking an orgasm. No." He shook his head. "I'm not having any part of that."

I blinked slowly several times. Shocked. Speechless. "Uh ... has this happened to you?"

He rolled his eyes and took the tray from me. "Yes. Yes, it has."

Again, I skittered on his heels, desperate for more information. How many virgins had he deflowered? When did he retire from his deflowering job? Did the naked fisherman have virgin phobia? But the most pressing question was ... why was I so eager to give him my virginity? Sex wasn't special to him. He wasn't going to declare his love for me to the world after bad, de-virgining sex.

No rings.

No proposals in the sky.

No "Here Comes the Bride."

"This is super informal. Just grab your food. There's more sangria in the pitcher." Rory turned on music. Jazz. Then she flipped on the globe lights.

I didn't want the globe lights on with Tiffany there. Those were lights for me and Fisher.

"Oh my gosh ... I love the lights!" Tiffany's eyes widened for a second before she sat with her plate of food on the sofa *right* next to Fisher. She might as well have sat onto his lap.

My monkey brain spun in circles like an out of control tilt a whirl. She wasn't a virgin. No "bad sex" with her. No deflowering dilemma.

Fisher leaned over and tapped my plate with his fork, startling me from my self-destructive trance.

"You're not eating. Are you good?"

Tiffany watched with minimal concern as Fisher's question seemed benign to everyone else.

Are you *good*?

I let my gaze remain locked to his for a few seconds. I thought of how I felt when he zip-tied me to the stool, when he said those words "you know the answer to that."

Tiffany thought she was on another date. She flirted with him. She sat right next to him. And I couldn't blame her one bit for finding him irresistible. But ... he was mine.

"I'm good." I smiled.

He rewarded me with a wink. And anyone else could have seen it, and maybe someone did. But he didn't care, and I loved him for it.

After dinner, Rory made a comment about her menstrual cycle.

Rose and Tiffany laughed, eyeing Fisher.

He shook his head and sipped another glass of sangria.

"This is important stuff, Fisher." Rory grinned. "Your wife will thank me someday for enlightening you on the matter."

"She'll thank you for me knowing when it's time to leave the room." He stood. "Like now. I'll just tidy up the kitchen. Have fun with your discussion." He grabbed the empty plates and left the overabundance of estrogen on the porch.

I spent the next twenty minutes listening to Rory and

Rose discuss perimenopause. Tiffany was too young to add much to the conversation, but she still laughed and pretended to know.

My ability to pretend ran out five minutes after Fisher left. I could no longer see him in the kitchen. The dishes were clean, but I didn't see him leave.

"Anyone else need anything? I'm going to use the bathroom and get some water," I interrupted.

They shook their heads, mumbling, "We're good, thanks."

It was a quarter to nine on a Sunday night. Didn't they have jobs in the morning?

After I peed, I decided to sneak upstairs to see if Fisher was there, but I didn't make it past the doorway to my bedroom.

"What are you doing?" I asked Fisher, who was sitting on the floor at the end of the bed.

Taking a few more steps in the room and shutting the door behind me, I saw exactly what he was doing.

Solving my crossword puzzles.

I would have been upset had he not been using a pencil.

"Do you like crossword puzzles?" I asked, plopping onto the bed, on my belly with my head next to his. I rested my chin on his shoulder and watched him focus on one of my hardest puzzles.

"I like them better than talking about menstrual cycles."

I giggled. He turned his head just enough to grin at me and press a short kiss to my lips. Then he returned his attention to the puzzle.

"You're not going to get fourteen across."

"Gulping in haste," he whispered the clue.

I smirked, knowing he'd never ever get it.

Five letters.

Second letter was E.

Last letter was Z.

"Move on to the next one." I bit his earlobe and tugged it. "You're going to break your brain trying to figure it out."

"Zip it," he said, and it made me giggle more.

I kissed along his neck, and he cocked his head to the side, giving me better access.

"Xertz," he said, filling in the missing letters.

I jerked my head straight. "How did you get that? You cheated. You used your phone."

Fisher tossed the puzzle and pencil aside before reaching back and grabbing me, pulling me onto the floor.

"Fish—"

"Shh ..." He covered my mouth with his hand while kissing my neck.

I quieted. His hand slid away from my mouth and his lips replaced it. He rolled us so that I was on top of him, my hair in his face, his hands on my butt, my hands on either side of his head.

"Fisher ..." I deposited kisses all over his face. "If I'm yours..." my lips brushed the shell of his ear "...then you have to take the bad with the good."

Bad sex.

I wanted him to take the bad sex that would come with our first time.

"What if ..." He threaded his fingers through my hair,

pulling it away from our faces. "What if you're not supposed to be mine?"

Before I could present my most heartbroken frown, a fist tapped my door twice, and then it opened.

There was no time to stand. There was barely time to blink.

"Reese, do you have—" Rose stilled. Eyes wide. Lips parted into a huge O. "I ... I'm sorry." She backed out of the room and shut the door.

"Rose ..." I flew to my feet and out of my bedroom.

Grabbing Rose's arm before she got more than two steps toward the porch, I pulled her into my bathroom and shut the door.

Closing my eyes for a brief second, I blew out a slow breath. When I opened them, Rose eyed me with concern.

She didn't see us kissing. Our clothes were on. And for a split second I considered pretending that we were wrestling like siblings. But Rose wasn't stupid.

"If you tell my mom ..." I had no clue what came after those words. I didn't actually know how Rory would react, but with a certain level of certainty, I knew it wouldn't be good.

"She'll send you back to Texas and kill Fisher," Rose said without hesitation.

I nodded. That worked. Honestly, Rose knew Rory better than I did. I trusted her prediction.

"Reese, he's *ten* years older than you. You know that, right?"

Another nod while biting my lips together.

"What has he done? Have you ..."

I shook my head at least a half dozen times. "We haven't done ... *that.*" It bothered me that Rose jumped immediately to Fisher, as if he had taken advantage of me. Like a predator or child molester.

"It's a terrible idea."

"I know," I whispered, even though I *didn't* know anything for certain when it came to Fisher Mann. "Please ... *please* don't say anything to Rory. Let me tell her when I'm ready."

"Uh ..." She chuckled. "I don't think she ever needs to know. If you're not having sex ..." She narrowed her eyes as if she was clarifying again that we hadn't had sex. "Then it's nothing more than wasted infatuation. Boredom. And it will and should end soon. Right?"

My answer didn't come out right away because I didn't know the answer.

"Reese, listen, honey ... Fisher is a wonderful man. And he's your *boss.* Rory and I adore him. And for the right person at the right time, he will be quite the catch. But ... and I mean this in the kindest way possible, Fisher is a man whore."

My eyes narrowed.

"He's not ready to settle down. He enjoys dating. He enjoys casual sex. And that's great for women who are in the same place in their lives. Like Tiffany. She's not ready to settle down tomorrow. She's looking for casual and fun. Fisher is a great fit for her right now. But I honestly have no idea what he has to offer you beyond a job. If you're not sexually active, then you need to be smart. You need to remind Fisher that he's your boss, your mom's friend, and that's it. Anything else makes him a guy who is way too mature for you and focused on only one thing ... trying to get into your pants. And your heart will get broken because I know enough about you to know that you are not that girl looking for anything less than the fairytale. Fisher is not anyone's Prince Charming right now. Okay?"

Her words paralyzed me. I couldn't speak. I couldn't piece together a string of thoughts that made sense. A man whore? That seemed extreme. And he didn't want into my pants. Or did he? Was it the game? Was I his toy?

"If you want me to talk to him—"

"No!" I shook my head. "Please, just let me handle it. Don't tell Rory or anyone for that matter. I'll ... handle it."

CHAPTER TWENTY-SEVEN

FISHER WAS GONE, upstairs I assumed, by the time Rose and I exited the bathroom. Rose suggested she and Tiffany leave. I didn't know what she was going to say to Tiffany, but I felt confident that it might be a "Fisher is a man whore you deserve better" speech.

"Night, sweetheart." Rory poked her head into my bedroom a little before ten as I reorganized my puzzles after Fisher rifled through them, solving the hardest ones.

After Rory's bedroom door clicked shut, I texted Fisher.

Reese: Hi. Rose isn't going to tell Rory or anyone.
Fisher: We leave at six in the morning.

I deflated at his cold response.

Reese: Are you mad?

I waited over fifteen minutes for a response.

Nothing.

So I decided to sleep on it. Things would be better in the morning.

Or so I thought.

When I reached the driveway the next morning, Fisher was already waiting, and it wasn't six yet.

"Morning," I smiled, hopping into the truck and tossing my bag in the back.

"Morning." He gave me a forced smile for less than a second and put the truck into drive.

I gave him time. Five minutes. Ten minutes.

He said nothing and played music with the volume turned way up.

"What's your car situation?" He broke the silence.

"Car situation?"

"Did you talk to your grandparents?"

"Yeah." I turned my attention to the brake lights in front of us as we pulled to a stop at the light.

"And?"

"And they're not going to give me the money for the Porsche, which is stupid because it's *my* freaking money."

"So you get the Forester?"

I shrugged with a single shoulder and sighed. "I suppose so."

"Great. Get the money in your account and we'll go get it tomorrow if it's still there. Or you can go with Rory or Brendon. I really don't care."

He really didn't care. Just what I wanted to hear. Rose was right. Fisher would crush my heart. As we waited for the light to change, my heart took off. Running away.

Away from the naked fisherman.

I wasn't sure what propelled me to make my next move. I don't remember my brain making some grand decision. It was instinct. Impulse. Survival.

Snagging my backpack from the back and unlatching my seat belt, I jumped out of the truck.

"Reese!"

Weaving through three lanes of stopped traffic, I sprinted through the steep dip of the ditch, my boots splashing in a small pool of standing water.

Down a less busy street.

Across a park.

Through someone's backyard.

Down another residential street.

Stopping at a bus stop.

Bending over, I rested my hands on my knees and fought to catch my breath for a few seconds before collapsing onto the bench behind me.

My phone vibrated in the side pocket of my bag. I ignored it.

How did I get there? Less than twenty-four hours earlier, I was on Fisher's bed. We were laughing.

Touching.

Kissing.

Existing only for each other.

He made me feel hopeful.

My phone kept vibrating, so I pulled it out of the pocket to shut it off.

It was Fisher.

And there were a string of texts from him too.

Where are you?

Answer your phone.

I'm sorry.

Please pick up your phone.

Don't make me call Rory.

Or the police.

I was eighteen. He wasn't going to call the police. And I didn't believe he would call Rory either. Not yet.

When the bus stopped, I got on. And I spent the next three hours taking various bus routes around Denver.

Earbuds in.

Music playing.

My mind sorting through everything.

I just needed time.

After my dad died, family rushed to console me. Feed me. Fix me. So I ran away for twelve hours because I needed time. I took the bus that day too. A bus ride didn't solve every problem, but it was cathartic. The passing miles. The passengers coming and going. Time to imagine that my life wasn't any worse than anybody else's life.

After grabbing a sandwich, I found the bus stop closest to the office and walked the rest of the way.

"Hey!" Hailey jumped out of her chair. "Where have you been? Fisher said you bolted this morning. He told me not to tell anyone, but I've been so worried." She hugged me as I stood limp in her arms.

"Sorry. I didn't mean to make anyone worry."

Except Fisher.

I wanted to make him worry. I wanted him to feel a little bit of my pain. My frustration.

"Where have you been?" She released me.

I set my backpack by Fisher's desk. "I just needed time to think about stuff."

"Reese ..." She handed me a glass of water. I had a fair amount of sweat pooling along my forehead and running down my back from walking in the heat with my backpack.

"Can we not talk about it?" I gave her my best pleading glance.

With worry lining her face, she nibbled the inside of her cheek and nodded slowly. "Okay. But if you do want to talk, you can talk to me about absolutely anything. Okay?"

Plopping into Fisher's chair, I nodded.

Hailey gave me a few easy things to do before grabbing her purse. "Your ride is here. I'm taking off early. Remember, I'm always here."

I was impressed that it took a full hour for Fisher to arrive.

"Thanks," I murmured as Fisher opened the door and Hailey squeezed past him, shooting him a cringing expression.

"You're fired."

My gaze lifted to Fisher. I wasn't surprised, yet ... I was.

"The tile shop where I get most of my tile, they're looking to hire someone to answer the phone. I got you an interview. It's just a formality. They will offer you the job. I'm going to tell Rory I found you a new job because

I didn't want you on the job sites where you could get hurt. And Hailey doesn't really need your help most days."

I swallowed the lump of emotion in my throat. "Is this about yesterday? Or this morning?" I managed to say in a shaky voice.

"Yes," he replied flatly, just as flat as the expression on his face.

"Rose promised not to tell Rory," I said.

"She lied. Rose will absolutely tell Rory unless we end it."

I had all these what-ifs lining the tip of my tongue.

What if *we* told Rory first?

What if we were more careful?

What if the world ended?

What happened to living in the moment? Living your best life? Loving the one you're with? That was all I did. Rory left me, and I fell in love with Fisher because he was the one I was with. It was really Rory's fault.

"Rory's taking the morning off tomorrow to help you get a car. The interview with the tile shop is the following morning. You'll be able to drive there on your own."

"Are you mad at me?" I whispered.

He returned a tiny wince before pinching the bridge of his nose and blowing out a breath. "No. I'm mad at myself."

The only thing more painful than rejection was regret. Fisher brought his A game. One brutal punch after the next.

A stupid, selfish, errant tear made its way to my cheek, and I looked away quickly to wipe it.

"Fuck ..." he mumbled. "This is what I wanted to avoid. Rory is my friend. Rose is my friend. I didn't want to be the villain. The guy who broke Rory's daughter's heart."

I stood and grabbed my backpack, refusing to look at him as I shouldered past him to the door. "You're such an arrogant asshole."

Yeah, I said it. No regrets.

"And you're the most beautiful and infuriating woman I have ever met."

I stopped at the door like it was a wall that appeared out of nowhere. All the friends of that rebel tear showed up to ruin my carefully constructed facade, busting open the flood gates.

"And in a different time ... a different place in our lives, I'd tell Rory and the rest of the world to go fuck themselves. I'd prove them all wrong. *We'd* prove the naysayers wrong. But ... I don't think they're wrong. Not now."

Sniffling and ignoring the unstoppable tears, I turned. "I'm beautiful ..." I nodded slowly. "A pretty face. Long legs. Perky *tits*. And I sucked your cock. No college education. No fantastic job. Nothing ... but I'm beautiful. Young. Innocent. And maybe the perfect amount of naive. It makes sense now." I laughed through my tears. A crazy laugh. The edge of my sanity laugh. "Stupid, stupid me. I thought we were this magical thing that couldn't be described. We didn't make sense because magic, fate, and serendipity don't have to make sense. I actually *liked* that we didn't make sense, yet my universe seemed perfect when it was just us. I guess the eight-letter word for that is illusion. You played me. You liked the chase. The game. And what better chase than the virgin wearing a cross around her neck?"

Fisher shook his head slowly. "You don't know what you're talking about."

"Because I'm eighteen?"

"Because you're scared."

"Of what?"

"Failure. Eighteen-letter word. Starts with a K."

I wasn't following him. So I said nothing. I did nothing but blink my tear-ladened eyelashes.

"Kakorrhaphiophobia. An abnormal fear of failure. That's why you're here and not chasing a dream. Not in college. Not making any plans in your life. Your dad died. Your mom went to prison. And you've been left with a Bible that prepares you for death and makes you feel ashamed of anything you do in this life to truly *live*."

He opened the door, and I waited for more, but he didn't give me more. We climbed into his truck and headed home, or so I assumed. We didn't make it home. We pulled into his parents' driveway instead.

"Let's go." He hopped out.

I didn't.

Fisher came to my side and opened my door. I assumed my recent firing allowed him to open my door.

"They're out of town. Let's go."

I eased out of the truck and followed him into the house. He opened a door to a storage and utility room, scanning a wall of boxes and plastic containers. When he found what he was looking for, he pulled a box from the shelf and brought it out to the family room.

"Sit." He nodded to the sofa.

I eased my butt down to it, watching him kneel on the floor and open the box. I couldn't see what was inside. He paused, staring at its contents.

"I told you I played sports. And I loved construction. But my real talent came in the form of spelling bees." He pulled out a stack of plaques, certificates, and trophies. "I took first place at a national competition." His face held a bit of harnessed pride as he set everything at my feet. "I liked words. Dissecting them. Studying their origin. A full year of Latin. My mom used to say I'd never find a woman who really appreciated my word-loving soul. And she was so disappointed in me when I let that love of words die, when I found my new favorite words like..." he smirked "...well, most of them were and still are four-letter words. Sometimes simplicity is best. So gone were the days of winklepicker shoes and ulotrichous women. I gravitated toward fuck, fucker, and fucking. It helped me fit in."

His gaze seemed to be focused on the past or maybe whatever was still in the box. "Who would have ever imagined that a girl ... a young woman ten years younger than me would breeze into my life. Beautiful? Yes. Quirky? Absolutely. Innocent? Painfully so. But also a cruciverbalist." Shaking his head, gazing in the box, and irony curling his lips, he pulled out tablets and note-books, tossing them at my feet with the spelling bee awards.

I bent down and picked one up. Inside, it was filled with hand drawn crossword puzzles.

"Cruciferous ..." I whispered, easing my head side to

side. He pretended to not know what a cruciverbalist was. Fisher did play me, just not in the way I thought.

"An eighteen-year-old cruciverbalist. Really, what were the chances?"

"Why didn't you tell me?" I glanced up at him.

He ran a hand through his hair and exhaled. "I don't know. I think I was in shock. And maybe a little awe was involved. A suffocating dose of confusion. A little anger at the timing, at your age. At the fact that you're Rory's daughter."

I thumbed through more pages of his notebook. "Do you love me, Fisher?" My gaze remained on the notebook, my voice steady, almost passive as if I was asking him about the weather or his day.

"Reese, it doesn't matter."

My head inched side to side. "You mean it doesn't change anything. And maybe you're right. But ..." I lifted my gaze. "It *matters*."

He climbed to his feet and drifted to the windows overlooking the backyard. Hands in the front pockets of his jeans. "I think I loved you before I met you. But we don't always get what we want. I let go of my crossword puzzles and word obsession because it didn't fit into my life any longer. The thing is ... I don't know where you fit into my life. And I know, I *know* you don't like your age to matter, but it does. I won't be the reason you don't take chances in life. Don't make marriage and sex your life's goals. If Rory found out, she'd want to know why. Why I would get involved with an eighteen-year-old girl? And I don't think cruciverbalist would work. Maybe if our ten-year-age gap was more like twenty-five and thirty-five, I could make a case for word geeks and kismet."

He turned to face me, every ounce of his vulnerability on full display. No walls. No lies. Just the hard truth. "Loving you is my favorite thing to do. It's automatic and effortless. And you're right, that matters. But ..."

"It changes nothing," I whispered, setting the notebook on the sofa and pressing my hands to my legs as I stood. Gazing up at the ceiling, I took a deep breath, closed my eyes and blew it out in one big whoosh. "Naked fisherman, you are incorrigible. Moody. Bold. Unpredictable. Brash ... and a million other things that are bad for me. Yet it felt like you were the first person in my life who just ... fit. The version of myself I dreaded ... the version I blamed on your bad behavior, I came to love it. It started to feel like my true skin. It felt good to smile without something in my brain telling me I should smile. You gave my days this vibrant color, and I don't know what I will see when you're not..." I drew in a shaky breath as emotions stung my eyes "...when you're not mine."

His arms slid around my waist, his chest to my back, his face bowed to my shoulder. And I shook as emotion took my body like an earthquake. Unsettling emotions needed to be released. Grief suffocated my lungs. Reality tore at my heart.

Fisher turned me in his arms and pressed my cheek to his chest. He soothed me with soft kisses to the top of my head and gentle strokes from his other hand down my back.

I was so tired of the unfairness in my life. The unanswered prayers. The testing of my faith.

My dad died, and it made no sense. And I didn't want anyone, not even God himself, trying to convince me otherwise.

Rory's decisions made no sense to me either. It was like one day she was my mom, my world, and the next day she was this stranger being sentenced to five years.

Did I have an unnatural fear of failure? Yes. Success felt like a myth. Happiness ... an unreachable destination.

And love ... well, it was something blurry and always changing forms in my life. I chased love.

Love for my father.

Love for God.

Love for Rory.

But it always felt just out of reach. Until Fisher. With him, I touched love. I held it in my hands, like reaching the end of a rainbow or lassoing the moon.

CHAPTER TWENTY-EIGHT

I GOT the Forester and the tile shop job. And I missed Fisher. Sometimes I saw him mowing the lawn or working in the garage when I got back from my evening walks or jogs. Sometimes I saw him at the tile shop picking up something.

We mastered courteous.

We perfected our sibling relationship around Rory.

But mostly, I spent my time praying for the crater in my heart to heal and ... missing him.

It would have been easier had I stayed angry at him, had I not known everything, had I not felt his love.

"I'm going to Texas this weekend," I announced to Rory, Rose, and Fisher as we ate pizza and cake on a Wednesday night to celebrate Rory's birthday.

"Oh?" Rory eyed me suspiciously from her favorite rocking chair on the porch.

"It was a last-minute decision. It's Grandma's and Grandpa's fiftieth wedding anniversary, and their church is having a party for them. They invited me. Paid for my airfare. And they'll pick me up at the airport Friday evening when I land. Just a quick getaway. I'll be home Sunday night because I have to work Monday."

"Well, tell them happy anniversary from me." Rory wrinkled her nose. "Not that they'll care. I'm not exactly the favorite daughter-in-law anymore."

"Do you need a ride to the airport?" Fisher asked. It was a rare moment of us sharing direct conversation instead of keeping our focus on Rory or Rose like usual.

"No. I'm leaving my vehicle at the airport since I'll be getting in late Sunday. I didn't want anyone to worry about picking me up." After talking to my plate because I still couldn't look him in the eye, I did the impossible—I lifted my gaze to his for a split second.

"Okay." The hint of a smile touched his lips. It was the Fisher smile I had come to love.

"How's your new job going?" Rose asked.

"It's fine. A little monotonous, but the people I work with are nice."

Rose's gaze slid to Fisher. He glanced away from all of us.

"I'm not implying my last job was bad or the people weren't nice." I should have kept my mouth shut.

Fisher grunted a laugh, gazing out in the distance.

"It's a safer job," Rory added.

Fisher fired me because he didn't want to be around me after breaking up with me. It might not have been an actual breakup. We weren't together in the traditional sense. Still, the breakup, real or not, was thick and suffocating in the air between us.

"It is ..." I nodded slowly.

"Have you talked to Brendon lately?" Nice subject change from Rory. Not that I wanted to talk about Brendon in front of Fisher.

"I see him at church. And I saw him last Wednesday night at Bible study."

"No dates?"

I shook my head. "He's been busy studying, and I've been ..." With a half-smile, I lifted a shoulder. "Not thinking much about dating."

Rose continued to eye Fisher and me. If she couldn't see the distance between us, the emotional distance between us, then she was blind.

"Well, remember what I said. It's a good thing to cultivate the friendship first."

No whirlwind love affairs.

Nothing forbidden.

No passion.

Was that the life I wanted?

I stole a quick glance at Fisher and his slumped shoulders, quiet demeanor, and faraway gaze. It didn't matter what I wanted.

I was eighteen with stuff to do like ... figure out *what* to do.

"How about you, Fisher?" Rory swiped a glob of frosting from her piece of cake and sucked it off her finger. "Rose said things fizzled out with Tiffany. Any other prospects? Or are you still content with one-night stands and a solid grip on your bachelorhood?"

Was he having one-night stands? After investing so much time in Virgin Therese, he deserved to have a normal sexual encounter that involved ... sex.

"I'm going to get some more ice cream." I grabbed my plate and headed into the house.

"Get it together," I whispered to myself as I set my plate on the counter and rested my hands on the edge, my head hanging low.

"I thought I could use some more ice cream too."

My head lifted as Rose shut the door behind her.

Clearing my throat, I smiled. "Yeah. Of course." Turning, I opened the freezer.

"I think we both know you don't want more ice cream. And neither do I."

I closed the freezer door and leaned against it. "If you're concerned that Fisher and I—"

"You've stopped ... whatever you were doing." She climbed onto a barstool. "I can see that. He's been quite the bore lately. I've been making up excuses for him because Rory sees it too. You've actually done a better job of hiding it. Good for you."

Good for me?

I laughed. "Well, it doesn't feel good."

"I know." She gave me a sad smile.

"Do you? Do you know what it's like to have feelings for someone and them have feelings for you, but you can't be together because the timing in life sucks? It just ..." I rolled my lips between my teeth and shook my head. "Sucks."

"I fell in love once. And the timing was all wrong. But love doesn't care. Your heart doesn't understand. And the scariest part is you want to believe that someday it will work, but you don't *know*. You just don't know. Will patience be rewarded? Will God answer your prayers with the answers you want? You tell yourself that if it's meant to be ... it will be." She pushed a long breath out of her nose and offered a weak smile. "And sometimes the answer is yes. But sometimes the answer is no. So the most you can do is find love and life in every day. The one thing I can promise you is that life rarely goes in the direction we think it will. And that's not always a bad thing. Sometimes it's the most amazing surprise."

My gaze affixed to Fisher on the porch. *He* was the most amazing surprise.

"I want to have this conversation with my mom. There have been so many moments over the past five years that I've thought, 'I need my mom.' And now she's here, but I can't talk to her. And I hate it because he didn't take advantage of me. It wasn't like that. And I know what you said about him being a man whore, but that wasn't who he was with me."

Rose gave me a look like she didn't entirely believe me. Or maybe she believed that *I* believed what I said, but it was just my foolish heart, my naive eighteen-year-old brain blinded by my first real crush.

"Well, I'm glad that's not who he was with you. That at least shows he had a little respect for Rory, but it's not enough for her to overlook the obvious. He's twenty-eight and you're eighteen. He should have known better. He should have had self-control."

I shook my head. "It wasn't all him. Despite what everyone seems to think, I do have the ability to make grown-up decisions. Maybe I'm the one who pursued him."

Rose lifted two sharp-peaked eyebrows. "Did you?"

With frustration filling my head and rekindling my anger, I shook my head. "I ... I don't know. It just ... happened."

"I know it's not the same, but I'm here if you want to talk more."

"It's ... fine. I'm good." I was the opposite of good. Still, I couldn't believe how quickly things flipped. One minute he was tearing at my clothes and biting my nipples, and the next ... we were in his parents' basement as he revealed to me why we were *perfect* for each other.

One minute my mom was braiding my hair—the next she was being hauled off in handcuffs.

One minute my dad was eating pasta with me at our favorite restaurant—the next he was dead.

I really didn't trust *life*.

CHAPTER TWENTY-NINE

"Do you have everything packed?" Rory seemed concerned about my big two-night trip to Texas. "If they ask how things are going here, what are you going to say?"

I rolled my carry-on suitcase out of the bedroom. "Are you chewing your nails?"

Rory jerked her hand away from her mouth. "No."

"Why do you seem so panicked?"

She sighed, blowing her hair out of her face. "It's just that I know they think I'm a complete failure, and I don't want them thinking I'm a bad influence because I've tried to do things right. Ya know? I mean, I let you have a little sangria, but I've tried to make sure you have everything you need. And Fisher has been so great at helping watch out for you too. I just want them to know that."

"Why?" I narrowed my eyes. It made no sense. They couldn't take me away from her.

Pressing her fingers over her closed eyes, she grumbled. "Ugh ... it's just that they used to like me. I went out of my way to impress them. And I don't care what they think of me, but I know they have influence over you, probably way more than I do. And I don't want them to persuade you to move back to Texas because..." she pushed out her lower lip "...I'm selfish. I want you with me for as long as you're willing to stay. It's not that I think I can make up for the years I was gone, but I want the chance to be your mom again. Really be your mom."

I held out my arms and hugged her. "I'm going to tell them that it's been great. You bake and cook. You're appropriately overprotective. You don't go to church with me, but they don't need to know that."

"I love you, Reese. I love you more than anything or anyone in this world. I always have and I always will."

I released her and grabbed my bag in one hand and my suitcase in my other hand. "I love you too." It was the first time I had said that to her in over five years. It felt right. It felt true.

"Oh ... let me run up and get Fisher. He'll carry your suitcase to the car so you don't have to lug it up by yourself."

"I've got it."

"He'll get it. I don't want you tripping or anything." She ran up the stairs.

"I've got it. Really." I started to open the door to carry it up to my car.

"Fisher can you give Reese a hand with her suitcase?" *Gah! Why?*

I barely got it out the door before Rory returned with Fisher.

Fisher in his exercise shorts and no shirt. Tennis shoes untied like he'd just slipped them on his bare feet.

If he wasn't going to marry me and put ten babies in my womb, then the shirtless thing was nothing more than a big F-you to me.

"I said I can do it. She's coddling me. Again." I rolled my eyes to lighten the mood and give my eyes something to do besides gawk at his unnaturally flawless body.

"Well, I'm here now. I'll carry it." He took the suitcase from me and headed up the side of the house.

"Bye, sweetie. Text me as soon as you land." Rory gave me one last hug.

"I will. See you Sunday." I closed the door and jogged to catch up to Fisher. "Sorry. Really, I had it."

Fisher loaded it into the back of my Forester. "It's no big deal." He closed the back.

"Well, thanks."

"Enjoy your trip."

I nodded, feeling the heat of his body. I always felt him without ever touching him. My body seemed to naturally gravitate toward him like it knew where it belonged before my brain figured it out.

We couldn't work together. We couldn't ride in the same vehicle. We could barely be in the same room without a clawing need ripping me apart from the inside. That must have been what withdrawal felt like.

"Reese?"

I turned after opening my door.

"I'm sorry."

It was a terrible apology. I didn't want his words. Fisher showed me. That was what he did. He showed me when he was sorry. It meant more. No ... it meant everything. But that ... that sad uttering of apology from his lips felt empty, like he was drained but he'd managed to gather a few drops of apology as if it would quench my thirst. My unquenchable thirst for him.

"I should have known better. It was selfish of me." He added yet another layer of pain to my already throbbing wounds.

Regret.

It was always the regret that hurt the most.

"Well, I'm not sorry. Not for any of it. You know it's..." I shook my head "...ironic. Adults, *real* adults, like to lecture young adults like me. They like to paint this picture of hopes and dreams, endless possibilities, and constantly remind us that we can *do* anything, *be* anything. But that's a lie. Because all I wanted was to live a day at a time and figure things out one moment at a time. That's all I wanted to *do*. And all I wanted to *be* was yours." After a quick shrug, I rolled my eyes toward the sky to ward off the tears. "I don't want your apologies or your help because they don't get me you."

He said nothing. Not a word. Not a single muscle in his body moved. Defeat personified.

"I'm going to fall in love. And some guy will be lucky to have me. He'll love me for me. And he won't care where I've been or where I'm going. He'll just feel so *fucking* lucky to be the one who kisses me goodnight and wakes up in the morning with me in his arms. He won't be burdened by my virginity or aggravated that I don't wear socks with my sneakers. He will be a better man for having found me, and I will be a better woman for having found him. I know they say love is patient, but it's not. Love is the brightest star in the sky. It doesn't have an off switch or a timer. It doesn't wear a watch or look at a calendar. It's why we're here. It's the only true reason for our existence."

Fisher was good at taking punches. He didn't duck or even wince. He swallowed every word and let it settle somewhere deep inside of his mind, his heart, maybe his soul. And if he felt unsteady or even a pang of discomfort, I never knew.

"I have to go."

He smiled ever so slightly. "Have a safe trip."

I returned a single nod and climbed into my car. Then, I made it a full three blocks before I cried all the tears.

It was him. He was the someday guy.

The kiss goodnight. It was him.

Waking in the morning in *his* arms.

It felt like I would forever carry a Fisher-shaped mold around with me, trying to shove other men into a place they would never fit.

The wrong key.

The wrong piece to a puzzle.

I was destined to settle and that sucked.

CHAPTER THIRTY

THE WORST PART about late flights? When they were canceled for mechanical issues, it meant a night in the airport or, in my case, a trip home only to wake up five hours later and drive back to the airport for an early flight.

I didn't even bother pulling my suitcase out of the back of my Forester. Not for five hours. Rose's car was parked in the driveway, and as I made my way around the side of the house, the glow of the globe lights illuminated the walkway for me. They were probably having a party since I was supposed to be out of town for the weekend. I prepared myself for some new girl Rose found to fix up with Fisher.

It didn't matter. I knew I would give them a quick flight update and go straight to bed.

No obsessing over the real adults having fun without me.

No stressing over a new girl (a new *woman*) for Fisher.

To my surprise and relief, there wasn't a party on the screened-in porch, just a couple of empty plates and wine glasses. I toed off my shoes just inside of the door and set my bag on my bed. I knew Rory wasn't asleep because she wouldn't have left the lights on.

I knocked several quick times on her bedroom door before opening it. "My flight got canceled so—"

She wasn't in her bedroom, but the lights were on.

They were upstairs with Fisher. I wasn't sure I wanted or needed to go upstairs. I'd had enough Fisher time for the night. As I started to shut her bedroom door, I heard a noise. It was coming from her bathroom, so I made my way through her bedroom to her bathroom. The door was cracked open, so I eased it open, hearing the water running in the shower.

It took me too long to make sense of what I was seeing in that moment—too much time letting the vision make a permeant stain on my memory. I knew I would never be able to forget. It would play in my mind on an endless loop for ... maybe the rest of my life.

It just *didn't* make sense.

Rory was in the shower, her back against the far wall, her eyes closed, mouth open. One hand pressed to the wall to steady herself. Her other hand was tangled in *Rose's* hair. *Rose* was on her knees with one of Rory's legs hooked over her shoulder. *Rose* was ... well, she was fingering *my mom* while simultaneously giving her oral sex.

I blinked again and again. I couldn't stop blinking. I couldn't move. Despite the crushing feeling of complete devastation, my world turning upside down ...

I. Couldn't. Turn. Away.

Had it been literally anyone else, I would have turned and ran, feeling horrified for the predictable reason like, it's embarrassing to accidentally walk in on two people having sex.

Then it happened. Those eyes ... the ones that shot me a final glance before leaving the courtroom ... they opened and landed on me.

Contrite and apologetic.

Like cells dividing at a rapid pace, forming something from nothing, ten thousand pieces of a puzzle putting themselves together ... I saw it.

All of it.

It wasn't a coincidence that Rose was in Colorado. They'd been friends for years.

Friends.

That was why my dad was so quick to divorce Rory after she went to prison. So many things I never fully understood. They all started to come together.

"Reese!" Rory called just as I tore my gaze away from the nightmare in the shower and ran out of the house. As soon as I reached the driveway, Fisher pulled in on his motorcycle.

"Did you know?" I yelled.

He drove past me, parking his motorcycle in the garage.

I charged after him. "Did you know?" My hands balled at my sides.

Fisher pulled off his helmet. "What are you doing here?" He climbed off his bike and carried his helmet to the cabinet.

"Did. You. KNOW?"

"Jesus, Reese." He turned, unzipping his jacket. "What the hell is going on?"

"Did you know that my mom is a *lesbian?* Gay. Homosexual. Are you understanding me now?" I shook my head over and over again, running my hands through my hair.

It wasn't real. It wasn't true.

I didn't deserve that, not after *everything* I'd been through. What was God doing? He wasn't supposed to give me more than I could handle. That was way more than I could handle.

Fisher slowed his movements, easing his arms out of his jacket and returning it to the cabinet next to his helmet. Fisher wasn't tense like me. He wasn't stunned, frozen in place.

No bugged-out eyes.

No jaw dropping to the ground.

Not a single sign that I was presenting him with new information.

"Did I know your mom and Rose are together? Yes."

My anger kept my tears at bay, but just barely.

"How could you?"

"How could I what?" He rested his hands on his hips, staring me down like *I* had done something wrong.

"Not tell me!"

"Rory's personal life is not mine to share."

"Rory's *personal life?* Are you kidding me? She's my mom!"

"Your point?"

"I walked in on them. In the shower. My mom and

her *girlfriend.* The friend who just happened to be in Colorado after having been a 'client' of hers in Nebraska. She cheated on my dad. That's why he divorced her."

"Is that why you're losing your mind? Because you think your mom cheated on your dad? Or are you upset because Rory is a 'lesbian, homosexual, gay?' Because I'm not sure why you're freaking the fuck out about this."

"You should have told me."

"And what would you have done? How would you have reacted? Like this? I hate to be the one to state the obvious, but your dad died, and that's terrible. Your mom went to prison ... also terrible. But that's in the past. If you want to be a grown ass adult, then start acting like one."

"I'm so tired of the age card." I shoved his chest. "Just because you don't understand my feelings doesn't make it my fault—a product of my age. *Nobody* likes being lied to."

"Nobody lied."

"Omission of the truth is deceptive ... a lie."

"So have we been lying to Rory about us?"

"There is *no* us."

Fisher nodded slowly. His control angered me even more. I needed to be angry. I needed to yell at someone.

"We might choose who we're with, but we don't choose who we love."

"Are you making excuses for her?"

He shook his head, scratching the nape of his neck. "What if I'm making *excuses* for us? Would that be okay with you? Would it be okay because we're not gay?"

My jaw clenched as I swallowed hard. "That's not it."

"You continue to tell yourself that."

I kept shaking my head. It wasn't about Rory's sexuality. It wasn't. Was it?

"Then why are you one blink away from falling apart? Because you're ashamed of her sins?" He held up air quotes. "Or because you need it to be wrong? If you let it be okay, you'll have to question everything that those people put into your head. You'll have to look within to find *your* truth. And then what will you be? Lost? Isn't that the point? Bring the lost to God and they will be found?"

"She cheated on my dad." I blinked, falling apart like he knew I would do.

"She fell in love."

I shook my head. "She was supposed to love him."

"Well, life never goes like it's supposed to. So what are you going to do about it?"

"Reese," Rory said my name.

I kept my back to her, my head bowed so I didn't have to look at her or Fisher. "I'm moving back to Texas. There is nothing for me here."

"Reese, let me explain."

"Explain?" I scoffed, walking toward the corner of the garage where I didn't have to face anyone. I wasn't sure I could ever look at her again. "No explanation needed. Everything I just saw, and will never be able to erase from my mind, was self-explanatory. The reason Dad divorced you. The reason he didn't want me to see you. It's so very clear now."

"You only know half of it. His half, not mine."

Resting my hands on my hips, I stared up at the ceiling, the shelving above the garage door. "I don't want your half. I don't want anything from you ever again. The lesson was mine to learn, and I learned it. Dad was right. You're incredibly selfish, and you don't care about anyone but yourself."

"Reese."

I heard the emotion in her shaky voice, but I wasn't going to look at her no matter how emotional she got, no matter how hurt she felt.

"Don't talk to your mom like that."

That demanded my attention. Fisher's way-out-of-line comment.

I whipped around to face him. "You ... *you* out of all people don't get to tell me how to talk to her. If she knew the things you've said to me ..." I shook my head, eyes narrowed, daring him to say one more word. "If she only knew ..."

Fisher didn't back down. It wasn't his personality.

"What is she talking about?" Rory asked while Fisher and I stared down.

I was on the verge of blowing up everyone's world, including my own. Rory would be mad at Fisher and Rose. Rose would be mad at me. Fisher would be angry with ... well, I wasn't sure. But since I was livid with *all* of them. I didn't care.

"I'm out. You two figure your shit out. I'm done." Fisher escaped into the house. Still ... I couldn't look at Rory because all I'd see was the face she made when Rose was doing those things to her in the shower.

"How long have you known that you're gay?"

"I think my whole life."

I grunted, shaking my head. "Yet you married Dad and had me. Why?"

"Because it's a sin. Against God's will. That's what I thought at the time. That's what you're thinking. That's what you've been brainwashed into thinking."

"Let me rephrase." I forced myself to look at her with her wet hair, baggy sweats, and fitted tee. "When did you stop caring? Stop caring that it's a sin? Stopped caring about Dad? Stopped caring about our family?"

"Those are unfair questions."

"Oh?" I canted my head. "What are fair questions?"

"Ask me when I decided to honor who I am? Ask me when I decided I could love myself *and* love you?"

After a few silent seconds, I rubbed my lips together and shrugged a shoulder. "Well? What are your answers to those questions?"

She hugged her arms to herself and stared at her bare feet. "I met Rose when you were ten. She literally walked in off the street to see if I had time to trim her bangs. I was booked solid that day. I didn't have time to pee. But I couldn't say no because I knew ... with one look I knew ... she was the piece of me that I'd hidden and suppressed my whole life.

"So I cut her bangs. And she came back the following week for a full cut. Then she scheduled a highlight. Then she just showed up one day with a plate of cookies. That led to lunch. Then meeting at the same coffee shop every morning for coffee. A movie here. A concert there. We became friends. She was married and so was I. And I remember the day I was going to say something to her, confront the elephant in the room. I'd worked it out in my head a million times. Maybe I didn't know what it would mean for my family or her marriage, but I knew even if it didn't change any of that, it would change me on a cellular level. I knew it would be the most honest moment of my life."

I didn't care. I told myself I didn't care. She lied to Dad. She lied to me. It felt unforgivable, yet I found myself asking her, "What happened?"

Rory glanced up at me. "Well, she had something to say to me that day too. And from the pain in her expression, I thought it was the something I wanted to tell her. The 'I love you, but I don't think we can be together, but I just need to tell you.' I knew ... I just knew that's what I saw in her eyes. But it wasn't, not that day. No. She needed to tell me she had stage three colon cancer, and her husband was leaving her because he didn't have the strength to watch her die. She needed someone to take her to treatments and doctor appointments."

I don't care. I don't care.

"And you did?"

She nodded. "I did. Then I drove her here, to Colorado, right after they legalized marijuana. It helped her a lot." Rory's lips turned into a sad smile as she averted her gaze. "It helped me a lot. It made dealing with my reality a little less stressful, dealing with the possibility of losing Rose a little less painful. Then one day Rose decided to grow her own, in the very illegal state of Nebraska, but she didn't have a great place to do it. So I suggested we use the back room of my salon. No one besides me ever went back there. For years all that had been back there were some old chairs, cracked sinks, and expired products. A few tables and grow lamps and we were growing our own marijuana. No more tiring trips to Colorado. No more paying for something we grew on our own for pennies."

She chuckled, running a hand through her wet hair. "It was stupid. Most things people do in the name of love *are* stupid. I never thought about getting caught. I was too busy worrying about Rose. Besides ... who would ever think to look in the back of my salon? I was a mom with a child and husband. We went to church every weekend, never cheated on our taxes. I hadn't ever received as much as a parking ticket in my life."

"Dad said it was a break-in."

Rory nodded. "Yes, in the middle of the night, someone broke into my salon. The security alarms went off and whoever broke in didn't stick around. But the cops came and that's how my world shattered. I lost your dad. My freedom. Five years with you. And according to her doctors, it was unlikely Rose would make it to see me get out of prison. But she did. She made a full recovery."

"And Dad? How did he find out about the two of you?"

"We talked before the trial. He didn't understand why I would grow marijuana for a friend, a friend I'd met through my salon. Why would I risk so much? And he kept digging and digging until I cracked. I told him I did it because I was in love with Rose."

"You loved her more than you loved me."

Rory shook her head over and over. "No. I have never nor will I ever love anyone the way I love you."

"Yet, you chose to do something that took you away from me."

Her head continued to shake as she squeezed her eyes shut. "I ... I wasn't for one minute thinking I would get caught. I wasn't thinking that someone would break into my shop and therefore bring the police right to me."

"Well it happened. So do you regret it?"

Rory hesitated. That was my answer.

"I'll sleep at the airport." I stomped past her.

"Wait! No! Just ..." She grabbed my arm, her hand sliding down to my wrist as she inched her body to hunch in front of me, head hanging low. "Yes ..." Her voice broke.

I didn't want to cry for her. She didn't deserve my tears. Rory destroyed our family. She destroyed *us*.

"Yes ..." She sobbed. "I regret the st-stupidity and r-recklessness. I regret risking s-so much when *you* were ... *are* my w-world. I'm so *very* sorry."

Her honesty and apology meant something, but I wasn't sure what. I needed time to think. After believing one thing for five years, I wasn't able to erase my thoughts and feelings to embrace her version of the story. Not yet.

"I'll be back Sunday, but I don't know if I'll stay here. I just ... don't know." I pulled away as she continued to sob.

I ARRIVED in Houston by noon on Saturday. My grandparents took me to lunch. I put on a brave face and gushed about how much fun I'd been having in Colorado. An interesting mix of truths and lies.

On the way back to their house after we left the restaurant, I got a text from Fisher.

If you're not dead, text Rory and tell her you made it safely to Houston. Don't be a total asshole about it.

I read the text three times to verify what I was seeing on my screen. Fisher was calling me an asshole, or at least a partial one since he insinuated not texting Rory would make me a "total asshole."

Like the impure and sinful thoughts that often made their way into my head, but were never allowed to leave my head, I typed my knee-jerk response knowing I would never actually send it. Sending it would be equivalent to saying it, and I would never say this to anyone, not even Fisher.

Reese: Go fuck yourself!

I smiled at the screen, allowing myself to enjoy my bravery for just a few seconds before deleting it and responding with a WWJD attitude.

"Stay in your lane!" Grandpa honked the horn as he quickly swerved, moving my thumb just enough to send the text.

It sent.

"Oh my gosh," I whispered.

"You okay, honey?" Grandma looked over her shoulder at me.

On a thick swallow, I nodded slowly, but I wasn't okay. I was horrified.

My phone vibrated with a new text from Fisher.

I'll let her know you're not dead.

I was in a quandary. Reply? Tell him it was a mistake? Autocorrect? Would my autocorrect default to go fuck yourself?

I didn't text him back.

Instead, I focused on my grandparents, got ready for the party, fielded a million questions at the party about my summer in Colorado, and made it to bed just after ten.

The next morning, we attended church service and fellowship dinner. More questions. More fake smiles and half-truths.

On the way to the airport that afternoon, I picked my grandma's brain.

"I work with someone who is gay. She's so nice and so is her girlfriend. Do you think that's wrong?"

"Of course it's wrong, Therese. The Bible says unnatural desire is an abomination punishable by eternal fire. You know this."

I nodded once while twisting my lips.

"You should pray for her."

"Yeah," I whispered. "Do you think it's worse than any other sexual immorality?"

"It's not my job to judge that, but I know your friend will not be welcomed in Heaven if she doesn't stop her actions and accept Christ as her savior."

"Well ..." I bit my thumbnail. "Saying that sounds like you are in fact judging her."

"No. I'm simply stating what the Bible says. I tell you, I don't envy your generation. This LGB etcetera etcetera stuff has gotten way out of hand. I don't understand why everyone feels the need to stand out."

"I'm uh ... I'm not sure it's about standing out. What if it's just about fitting in? What if they just want to be themselves without being seen as different or inferior or less worthy? I'm just ... thinking aloud."

"I'm worried your friend is brainwashing you. Honestly, I worried that your time in Colorado would be difficult on you. I really hope you're not skipping church. I hope you're spending time in God's word every day."

Looking out the window, I murmured, "Yeah, I am."

After landing in Denver, I took my time getting my car and making my way home. To my disappointment, Fisher and Rory were on his front porch, drinking beer and it was nearly dark.

Rory gave me a reserved smile as I wheeled my carry-on suitcase up the driveway. "Hey, how was your trip?"

"It was just overnight, barely a trip, but it was fine."

"Did they have a nice anniversary party?"

I nodded.

Things were so awkward. After leaving Rory in tears, with the uncertainty as to whether or not I'd ever forgive her, and sending Fisher a F-you text, I wasn't sure what to say.

"I'm going to go unpack and do a load of laundry."

"Need help?" Rory asked.

"I'm good."

"Have you had dinner?"

I shook my head. "I'm not hungry."

"Rose and I are going for pizza. We'd love for you to come too."

My head continued to shake. "I'm not hungry. Enjoy your pizza," I said, my voice void of all emotion as I turned and started to head toward the basement. After a few steps, I turned back toward Rory. "I don't know how God feels about you and Rose." I shrugged. "I just know that I've felt lost for the past five years. The lie didn't protect me. And my reaction the other night wasn't really to Rose ... or you and Rose. I know this because I've had time to sort through my feelings. It wasn't Dad. It wasn't even your arrest that destroyed our family; the fact that you tried to live the wrong life ... that's what destroyed us. And it might take me awhile to come to terms with everything, but I can imagine it must have been painful to find the right person at the worst possible time." I kept my attention laser focused on Rory. Had I given Fisher the quickest of glances, I would have lost it.

Rory returned a smile. It was a little sad and a little relieved. "Thank you." Tears shined in her eyes.

***

AFTER I UNPACKED and tossed in a load of laundry, I grabbed one of Rory's beers from the fridge and took a seat on the porch, music flowing from my phone and my gaze on the sun setting behind the mountains.

"I fucked myself."

I didn't want to grin as Fisher stood at the door to the

porch, but I couldn't help it. I took a swig of the beer to hide my grin.

"I'm pretty good." He stepped onto the porch and sat in the rocker where Rory usually sat.

"I don't doubt that." I rubbed my lips together. "But what do I know? I'm just an asshole."

Fisher eyed the beer in my hand, but he didn't say anything about it. "Rory grilled me on what I said to you while she was gone. Thanks for that."

I nodded. "You're welcome." After a long pause of silence, I caved. "What did you tell her?"

"I told her I used a lot of swear words around you."

"And she believed you?"

He lifted a shoulder. "I don't know. I guess so."

I took another big swig of beer, praying for a little buzz to soothe my nerves.

"What are you going to do, Reese? Move back to Texas because your mom is going to Hell?"

"I don't know, Fisher. Would that make me a *total asshole*?"

"Probably."

I rolled my eyes and refocused on the view. "Well, you would know what it's like to be a total asshole."

"Why? Because I wouldn't fuck you?"

"Well, from what I hear, I'm the only single female in a twenty-mile radius you haven't put your dick into. That makes me a unicorn. Maybe that makes me the *one* woman you can't have."

He stood and took two steps in my direction, snagging the bottle of beer from my hand and drinking the rest of it in one shot. "If I wanted you, I could have you, and we both know it."

"No." I shook my head. "You can't have me. Not now. Not ever. I don't want you anymore."

"You do." He handed the empty bottle back to me.

"I don't!" I stood, chin up, shoulders back, teeth clenched.

With a smug expression, he eyed me like he used to do, but I didn't fall for it. "It's almost too easy."

"What's too—"

He kissed me. Hard. Harder than he had ever kissed me. And I fought him, but I lost because I *did* want him to kiss me. It's *all* I wanted. But it didn't mean I was going to give myself to him. No matter how much I wanted his kiss, it didn't change what had happened between us.

My hand dropping the empty bottle to the floor so my fingers could dive into his hair didn't change anything either.

His hands grabbed my ass and lifted me off my feet. Fisher kissed me and carried me up the stairs like a drunk man on a mission.

Through the door.

Down the hallway.

Onto his bed.

His demanding mouth made it impossible to protest, not that I had one ready to go, not yet. We'd been there before, done that. It wasn't sex. I was still in control.

He discarded my shirt. I still had control.

When he ripped down the cups to my bra and did things to my breasts that made me moan and claw at his back, I *still* had control. I could play his game.

Fisher sat up, kneeling between my spread legs, eyes hooded, lips parted as he unbuttoned my jeans and peeled them from my legs.

I ... I had control.

He kissed his way down one leg, pressing his lips to the inside of my thigh as his finger slipped beneath the crotch of my panties, circling my clit once before sliding lower. Keeping his mouth on my leg, that finger pushed inside of me.

I sucked in a breath. It was a finger, larger than a tampon but not his dick.

In. Out. In. Out.

Agonizingly slow, my vision began to blur. Fisher removed his finger and slid off my panties. After tossing them aside, he unbuttoned his jeans and pulled down the zipper.

"I'm ..." I breathed embarrassingly heavy. "I'm not having sex with you." Despite my slightly compromised position and lack of blood going to my brain, I felt proud of my will power. The days of being Fisher's toy ... his favorite game ... were over. I was the master, the powerful queen who would take down the king.

Checkmate.

"No?" He leaned forward and slid his hands behind me, unhooking my bra. As he slid it off my arms, he smirked. "We'll see."

"Ah!" I jerked when he bit my nipple, when that finger slid inside of me again, when he added a second finger partway, making me feel so filled. Was he going to take my virginity with his fingers?

His mouth latched onto mine. My hips and legs

braced, not moving an inch because Fisher's fingers edged me out of my comfort zone.

What if he pushed them inside of me the whole way? Would it hurt? Would I bleed?

And then ... they were gone. He stood at the end of the bed and removed his jeans, challenging me. I saw it in his eyes.

"I won't do it. You don't deserve it. You had your chance." My bravery tank nearly hit empty.

"We'll see." He crawled onto the bed and his tongue went to work. Swiping between my legs. Flicking my nipples. Making a trail up my neck, and finally landing in my mouth, making slow strokes as his pelvis settled between my legs. That dangerous thin layer of cotton the only thing separating his dick from my entrance.

Thrust.

Thrust.

Thrust.

I reminded myself that we had done this before. We'd been in that position. And we didn't have sex.

Thrust.

Thrust.

Thrust.

My hips lifted from the bed to meet him. That was when he pulled back. That was when he rolled onto his back, taking me with him so I sat on top of him, my legs straddling him right *there.*

With one look, he dared me to quit. *And* he dared me to keep going.

"No sex," I nearly choked on the words.

Fisher jackknifed to sitting, his face a breath away

from mine. "We'll see." He kissed me, tangling one hand in my hair while his other hand guided my hand beneath the waistband of his briefs.

So warm.

So hard.

I stroked him as he teased his tongue against mine.

I stroked him as he fingered me again, but just that agonizing partway.

Slow. Too slow.

The more I stroked him, the more I wanted *more*. Not just more. I wanted all of him.

He broke our kiss and stretched his torso to the side, opening the drawer to his nightstand and pulling out a condom.

That was when things got real.

Using his teeth, he tore it open, tossed the wrapper to the side, and pushed down the front of his briefs to roll it on.

He grabbed my face and kissed me a little softer than just seconds earlier. Dragging his lips across my face, dotting it with kisses, he whispered in my ear, "Your husband can thank me."

Those words stopped my heart. The warm blood in my veins ran cold, sending an icy jolt along my spine.

Fisher lifted my hips and positioned me over him, pushing into me an inch, maybe not even.

Tears filled my eyes as I stilled, not letting him move my hips any farther. And I saw it in his eyes.

The pain.

The love.

The conflict.

More than anything, I saw all the reasons I fell for Fisher Mann. He knew we weren't at the right place to make *us* work, but he was willing to give me the one thing I thought I wanted. He wanted to give me all he had to give, even though he knew it wouldn't be enough.

My hands pressed to his face as tears covered my cheeks, the saltiness pooling at my lips. "Thank you, Fisher."

I eased off his lap.

He said nothing. There wasn't anything to say.

After I dressed, I lifted my teary gaze to him. "I'm volunteering to go on a mission trip to Thailand for six months. And then ..." I lifted one shoulder, drawing in a shaky breath that elicited more tears. "I don't know, but I'll figure it out. I'll figure *me* out." Turning, I took several steps and turned, giving him a sad smile. "There's more to life than crossword puzzles, right?"

His jaw stiffened as he swallowed hard and nodded, his eyes a little red. "I hope so."

To be continued ...

BOOK ONE BONUS CONTENT
SELECT CHAPTERS FROM FISHER'S POINT OF VIEW

FISHER
CHAPTER THREE

"Fisher?" Rory called.

I finished drying off, tied my towel around my waist, and headed toward the kitchen. Ten bucks said she couldn't get her car started. The battery needed to be replaced.

The woman near the back door wasn't Rory, but she had the same dark brown hair, just longer.

"Hey," I said.

She turned. Big blue eyes, just like Rory's, widened quickly. "Oh my gosh!" She whipped around, giving me her back. "I'm sorry."

"Why? Did you break in? Or are you Rory's daughter?" I knew the answer. She was the spitting image of her mother.

She cleared her throat. "That ... um ... yeah ... Rory's daughter."

"Ah, Reese Capshaw. It's nice to finally meet you. Rory talks about you nonstop." I stepped closer, and she angled her body again to keep me at her back.

She nodded over and over again.

"Where's your mom?" I brushed past her, touching her arm with mine like poking a little bird just to watch it jump. Her nerves were palpable. It was almost laughable. She may have looked like Rory, but she was a bundle of nerves compared to Rory's calm confidence. I glanced back at her just before opening the door to the garage. She didn't blink, and her hands were tightly woven together at her waist. She had legs for days, and I couldn't help but grin at the thought of Rory reading my mind. Reese was a girl in a woman's body. I'd be good. Well, good enough. "You look like your mom. Lucky girl."

Just as her lips parted, the door opened.

"There you are!" Rory said.

"Sorry. I was in the shower." I adjusted my towel, lowering it a smidge to see what Reese would do. To see if she blinked. I hadn't seen her blink yet.

"So you met Reese. Isn't she beautiful? Even more stunning than her pictures. Don't you think?"

Fucking Rory.

When she said her daughter was coming for the summer, I imagined ... Well, I'm not sure what I imagined, but I agreed. Her pictures were deceiving; I thought they were from years ago.

Rory is my friend. I will behave. Rory is my friend. I will behave.

I had a new mantra. Wetting my lips, because I couldn't look at those legs, that silky hair, and those perfect little tits without running my tongue across my lips. "She's perfect, Rory. Almost angelic." I nodded.

Reese narrowed her eyes at me like something in her

pretty little head didn't make sense. Her eyes started to relax as she let her gaze wander down my body. She was one hundred percent imagining what was behind my towel. Fuck ... I really, really needed to behave, but it was too easy. Too tempting. Too much fun.

"I told Reese you might have a job for her." Rory eyed me just as Reese grimaced like something bit her in the ass.

"Sure. I can keep her busy with lots of odds and ends. Some days you could work in the office with my secretary Hailey. Other days you might come with me to job sites. Drop off lunches. Grab supplies."

Reese didn't respond. I thought she was secretly hoping my towel would fall from my body. I could barely keep a straight face. It wasn't funny. I needed to treat her like a child. She was Rory's child. Not a toy for me.

"Reese?" Rory said.

"Huh?" She hummed before wetting her lips.

I bent to the side to put my face into her line of sight. "Hello?"

She ripped her gaze away from my abs and folded her arms over her chest and those peekaboo nipples while staring at her feet and rocking back and forth on them several times. "A job. That would be great. Thanks."

"Everything okay?" Rory asked.

"Yeah. It's been a long day of traveling. That's all." She glanced around my kitchen.

"We'll let you get dressed before your towel falls off, and you show Reese more than she wants to see. I haven't had the sex talk with her yet."

"Oh my gosh ..." Reese's face turned bright red as her

hands covered it. "Thanks for embarrassing me." She dropped her hands but refused to look at me. "I'm an adult now, ya know."

I was a little conflicted. Did I want to think of Rory's daughter as an adult?

FISHER
CHAPTER ELEVEN

I'D BEEN GIVEN a one way ticket to Hell, and her name was Reese Capshaw.

I suspected it the day I dropped Rory off at the airport. But seeing her daughter naked in my bathtub pretty much confirmed it.

I didn't see her the rest of the weekend, and that was probably for the best because I saw all I needed to see.

Around five-thirty Monday morning, I texted her.

Fisher: You're with me today. We'll leave in twenty minutes.

At the last possible second, she opened the door to my truck and climbed inside, stuffing her backpack between her feet but not looking at me. Not one single glance.

"Morning," I said.

"Morning," she mumbled, keeping her head down.

"Listen, there's no need to drag your weekend to

work with you on Monday. What happened, happened. No big deal," I said with a shrug.

Her head snapped up, jaw unhinged, blue eyes unblinking. "No big deal? You molested me with your eyes! I wouldn't call that no big deal."

What the fuck?

Eyeing her quickly, as if I didn't hear her correctly, I shook my head and blew out a slow breath. "You know what your problem is?"

She tipped her chin up but said nothing.

"You need to get laid. And so help me, if you even think of telling Rory I said that, I will tell her everything."

"I ..." Her mouth moved more but nothing came out. "That ... you ..." Her head repeatedly moved side to side. "I do not need to get laid. You need to stop being so crude. Some people take sex seriously, not like a game to play with anyone willing to have it with them. It's supposed to be something beautiful between two people who love each other."

"You've clearly never had an orgasm." She was going to die a virgin, but I didn't go that far. It was best she figure that out on her own.

"I have too."

No fucking way. "Liar." I smirked.

"You can't call me a liar about this when you've known me for a few weeks. You don't know anything about me and my past."

"Did you give it to yourself or did someone else give it to you?" I can't help myself. She teed it up every single time. It was just too easy.

"This ... this is a stupid topic and really inappropriate. You're my boss, driving me to work."

"I'm your boss when we get there."

"Then let's go." She faced forward and ignored me the rest of the way.

I managed to focus on work the remainder of the day, despite those big blue eyes watching my every move, despite her either not wearing a bra or wearing one so thin it really made no sense to even wear it. I made a mental note to give Rory a hint to go buy her daughter better bras. Our last job was a staircase I'd been working on for a client who was out of town that week.

"Did you buy these?" Reese asked, running her finger over the spindle curves.

"Nope. I made them." I put on my tool belt.

"Are you serious?"

I glanced up, collecting the spindles to haul into the house. "Why are you constantly doubting my skills?"

"I'm just used to seeing you walk around staring at other people's work or barking orders. I have yet to see you in action."

"Well, grab the rest of those spindles, and I'll show you some action." Just saying the words made my dick hard. It had been hard since the bathtub incident, and no amount of jerking off made a difference.

While I worked on the staircase, Reese proved to be a good helper, handing me things, running to get things, answering my phone. When I wiped the sweat from my brow, she enjoyed gazing at my abs while wetting her lips. And because I was a glutton for punishment, I kept doing it because I had my own fantasies about those lips she kept licking.

"I'm going to start deducting pay from your check if you keep stealing free peeks at my body." The only thing more satisfying than staring at her mouth was eliciting a deep crimson blush along her face and down her neck.

She cleared her throat and stared at my phone in her hand. "Hailey just texted you. She said Brad's crew is done She wants to know if you're coming by the office before you go home?"

"No," I said.

She glanced up at me. "You want me to just say no?"

Tucking a pencil behind my ear, I nodded. "To Hailey, yes, I want you to say no."

Reese's innocence fed something inside of me. Those deer-in-the-headlights looks. I had no intention of ever taking her innocence, at least not all of it, but I enjoyed toying with it, testing it, testing her.

"Who else would I say no to?"

I shrugged. "I'm hoping that's your last no of the day."

After several slow blinks, she glanced at my phone and typed a reply.

When I finished for the day, I had her vac the area around the drop cloths.

"Are you done?" she asked, handing me the vac after things were clean.

"Almost. I'll finish up tomorrow afternoon." I closed my trailer and locked it.

"Think you can teach me something?" She slid her

hands into her pockets as my mind wandered into dangerous territory.

I walked to the passenger's door, letting very little space exist between us. My gaze affixed to her lips for several seconds before meeting her eyes. "Oh, Reese ... I think I can teach you a lot."

She swallowed hard. "A-about construction? Can you teach me how to cut and nail things?"

I was *painfully* hard by that point. And my grin swelled to the point of pain as well. "We might wait on the cutting, but I think I can show you how I nail things."

Again she swallowed hard. "I'd ... um ... I'd like that."

"Oh ... I have no doubt you'd like it."

I could feel the heat radiating from her pink cheeks.

"Well..." she lifted her shoulder and pushed her hands farther into her pockets "...time to call it a day?"

Digging my teeth into my lower lip, I nodded slowly. "Definitely."

ON THE WAY HOME, I played all of my favorite music, which happened to be the songs that made Reese fidget and blush. Again, I knew Hell was my final destination.

Before I got the truck into *Park,* she flew out with a quick, "Goodnight. See you tomorrow."

I parked and followed her around the side of the house, where I heard her begging the door to open.

"Are you running from me?" I asked.

"Nope." She jumped inside the house and locked the door.

I chuckled to myself, retrieving my key. Was it wrong to invade her space? Absolutely? Did I care? Not so much.

Click.

I unlocked the door and stepped inside

"Whatcha need? she asked with a shaky voice, tossing her shoes into her bedroom.

"Why are you running from me?" I stood right behind her.

She turned slowly and drew in a long breath.

I took another step. She took another one backward. We did this until her back bumped the wall. I pressed my hands to it just above her head, caging her like a scared animal. I could hear her quick breaths, but as I parted my lips, I realized my breathing had accelerated as well.

"You can't have my virginity," she whispered.

Game over. That should have been it. The end. Turn around and walk away.

It wasn't over. It was just beginning, and I couldn't have stopped it had I wanted to because I needed to know ... I needed to know how her lips tasted. If God existed, they needed to taste like fruit picked too soon. Sour. Young. Immature. An aftertaste that would make me walk away and do the right thing.

"What can I have?" I whispered back.

She stared at my mouth so long I nearly died. I knew if I pressed my body a little closer to hers that I'd feel her chest rub against mine, feel those hard nipples I fucking dreamed of biting and licking.

Cupping her jaw, my thumb grazed her trembling

lower lip. I should have walked away. She was in over her head because I was pushing her under the water.

But then she whispered, "A-are you g-going to kiss me?"

I couldn't help but grin. "I was thinking about it."

Rory would kill me. Unless ... it was just a kiss. Maybe a bad kiss. I made myself think it would be a bad kiss. My morbidly curious mind would be settled, and I'd send her to church to find a better man.

"Will you be done thinking about it anytime soo—"

I kissed her, and fuck me if she didn't taste like the ripest fruit on the tree, picked at the perfect time. Sweet. Juicy. And addictive. Releasing her lips, I pulled back just enough to gauge her reaction. She sucked in a slow breath, which made her chest brush against mine, and so I kissed her again. I had to tell myself to take it slow. Control myself.

Forcing myself to pull back again, I grinned, but so did she.

"I'm going to shower and grab dinner." A cold shower. "I'll see you in the morning. Five-forty-five?"

She nodded, grinning like I just gave her the secret to life. Before she tempted me to do something that would cause Rory to remove my testicles, I ascended the stairs and headed straight to the shower.

FISHER
CHAPTER SIXTEEN

IN MY DEFENSE ... I didn't get sick. I was a freak of nature that way. My family never would have believed we were leaving because I was sick. However, it was a dick move to tell them that Reese had gastrointestinal issues. I just said the first thing that came to mind because I wanted out ... I wanted to be alone with her.

Fisher: I'm sorry.
Fisher: Are you going to stay mad at me forever?
Fisher: I'll call my family and tell them it was a lie. That I just wanted to be alone with you.

Reese didn't respond to my texts. I didn't see her until I mowed the lawn the following day. When I glanced up, she was staring at me with an unreadable expression. I kept mowing. Ran the weed eater. And pulled weeds in the landscaping.

"You should hydrate. You're pretty sweaty." She stood beside me, holding a glass of water.

I lifted onto my knees and sat back on my heels, sweat and dirt covering my torso. "Thank you." I pulled off my work gloves and took the glass of water, guzzling it down all at once before handing the glass back to her.

"I ... uh ... I forgive you. I just wasn't ready to say it last night when you messaged me."

Wiping my forehead with my arm, I said, "I figured."

"My friend called me last night. She's in Denver for the weekend with her boyfriend. Her sister's getting married in Colorado Springs next weekend. Anyway ... she wanted to get together, so I suggested Arnie's concert. Do you think he can get us two extra seats?"

"I didn't figure you'd want to go." I didn't want to go. The last thing I needed was a night out with my ex while my brother tried to get into Reese's pants. And I knew that was rich coming from me, but Rory asked me to look out for her daughter, so I felt like I was in charge of who did and didn't get into her pants.

"I didn't. But I want to see my friend and she's really excited about it, so ..."

Glancing up at her, I squinted against the sun and nodded. "I'm sure Arnie can make it happen."

"Are you taking a ... date?"

I shook my head and chuckled, glancing out at the yard. "You mean, am I taking Angie?"

Reese rocked back and forth on her heels like she always did when she was nervous.

"Arnie invited her. It's virtually impossible for me to *not* take her at this point."

She shrugged. "It's fine. I was just asking. Should I uh ... drive? Or are we all going together?"

"She messaged me last night. She'll pick us up at six. I said I needed to verify that you were going, but now that you are ... I'll let her know."

"You're not driving?"

I shook my head. "I have a work truck and a motorcycle. You've seen all the shit in my truck, and I don't think all of us can fit on my motorcycle."

"Yeah. Of course. Well ..." She took a few steps backward. "I'll be ready at six." She disappeared into the house, only to zoom past me a bit later to hop into Rory's Outback and speed off.

Hours later, Angie texted me to let me know she was running a few minutes late. Reese, however, was on time. Standing on my front porch, staring at the street. I opened the door. "She's running a few minutes late. You can wait inside."

She turned and I swallowed back my knee-jerk reaction to cancel the whole night. What the fuck was she doing to me? Those legs. That hair. Makeup that made her look ten years older.

"O-okay ..." she swallowed and stepped inside the house.

"I have a feeling someone will get beat up or arrested tonight," I said.

"Why would you say that?"

"Because you're eighteen going on thirty."

"Don't talk like a parent, Fisher."

I shut the door and leaned against it, crossing my arms over my chest. Parent? I wasn't looking at her like a parent. Far from it. "Fine," I said. "Every guy that sees you is going to get a hard-on. And I promised Rory I'd keep an eye on you." Rory was my altruistic excuse. Let's be honest ... she would have removed my testicles had she known what I had done to her daughter, not to mention all the things I still wanted to do.

"I'm sure Angie doesn't want you keeping an eye on me."

Nipples. Those goddamn nipples of hers. "For fuck's sake ... are you wearing a bra?"

She glanced down at herself. "No. I can't wear one with this top."

"Then go change tops and put on a bra." I was angry that she obviously didn't glance in the mirror before heading out the door. I was angry that Angie was going to be arriving any minute. And I was angry because my dick was hard as fuck.

"Again ... too much parental talk. I don't need you to dress me."

"And I don't need my horny brother seeing your nipples."

Again, she glanced down at herself.

Oh for Christ's sake ...

"It's a dark shirt. You can't see them."

"I can see their outline ... I can see they are erect." As was I. So. Fucking. Erect.

Reese ran the pads of her finger over them.

"Just ... fucking stop ..." I pinched the bridge of my nose.

"I pushed them in."

"Jesus ... you're a walking wet dream. Just stop touching yourself."

She watched me adjust myself.

Her nipples popped right back out.

Fuck my life.

"I'm going to kill Rory for leaving you with me." I took a long stride, grabbed the back of her hair, guided her head to the side, and sucked the skin along her neck so hard I thought it might leave a mark. But I couldn't kiss her red glossed lips without making a mess of her and me.

"F-Fisher ..." She grabbed my biceps, knees wobbling.

My hand shot straight up her shirt and cupped her bare breast as my thumb brushed her taut nipple, eliciting a groan from my own chest.

"Oh my God—gosh ..." she stuttered.

I gave her other breast equal attention as she continued to fumble her words. "We ... should ..."

I turned her so her back pressed to the door, lifting her up and guiding her legs around my waist with one hand while shoving her shirt up with my other hand. I wanted every inch of her body.

"Ah! Oh ... oh ... god!"

Then ... the doorbell rang.

Reese stiffened. I rested my forehead between her breasts, my breaths chasing each other. It was hard to explain my growing obsession with her. Reducing the mind-fuck of emotions that I had into something as simplistic as solving clues to form words and phrases on a grid of white and black-shaded squares seemed ridiculous. But ... that's what did it for me. That was the spark that couldn't be extinguished.

Reese wasn't merely a pretty face attached to a hot body—although she had both—she was my own little puzzle to solve.

"Fuck ..." I mumbled knowing Angie was on the other side of the door. I eased Reese back onto her feet as she gazed up at me with confusion on her face. More like total shock. "Just a sec," I said with an edge of frustration.

"I-I'm ... going to go put on a bra and a different shirt," she said just above a whisper.

Biting my lips together, I nodded. Reese squeezed past me and scurried to the basement as I adjusted myself before opening the door.

"Hey, handsome." Angie stepped inside and lifted onto her toes to give me a kiss.

I turned, offering her my cheek instead of my lips—lips that still tasted like Reese. Angie thought we could always pick up where we left off, no matter how long it had been, no matter how many other people we'd been with during our time apart. And sometimes, that was fine.

Convenient.

Mutually beneficial.

No big deal.

I couldn't properly terrorize Rory's Bible-preaching daughter with Angie in town and my family rooting for the great reunion—the great *union*.

"Hey. You look nice." I managed a smile and a compliment as I nodded for her to head out to the driveway with me.

"Nice?" She gave me a sly grin. "This red dress used to get a better reaction from you than *nice*."

That was before I decided to engage in a little cat and mouse with Reese Capshaw ... who saved the day by trekking around the corner of the house just in time so I didn't have to answer Angie.

"Angie, this is Reese Capshaw. Reese, this is Angie Flynn."

"So nice to meet you. Cute top." Angie nodded to Reese's Life is Good top.

Reese deflated. I could almost hear her mind battling the urge to make a case for her adult woman status, violently rejecting anyone calling her shirt cute. It was cute. And appropriate. And I knew it wouldn't stop Arnie from being inappropriate with her, but it took my temperature down a few degrees.

"Thanks," Reese said with a pathetically fake smile that nearly made me snort. "Nice to meet you too." She hated Angie. Maybe her gospel-filled mind wouldn't let her say the word "hate," but I was sure that was what she felt. Maybe if she had managed to greet Angie without balling her fists, it wouldn't have been so obvious.

"Fisher's family had so many amazing things to say about you."

Shut up, Reese. Just shut the fuck up.

The last thing I needed was Angie getting her hopes up, like *I* was the one saying so many amazing things about her. I wasn't.

Too late.

Angie turned toward me with that look in her eyes. "Aw ... your family is the best. They really feel like my family after all these years."

With a stiff smile, I gave her a hesitant nod.

"Well, let's go. You can drive, babe." Angie tossed me her keys. "I don't know where we're going."

Reese fought the urge to wrinkle her nose; her

expression quickly taking on the look of someone who was just given a sour candy.

Yes, I sucked her tits just minutes earlier.

Yes, another woman called me "babe."

It was life in all its complicated forms. Reese needed to learn to deal with it.

"Are you in college, Reese?" Angie asked before I put the car into *Reverse*.

"Nope. Just working for Fisher this summer. I'm taking a gap year."

Angie rested her hand on my upper thigh, giving it a squeeze. "Fisher is the most talented human I have ever met. He's always been good at everything. Such a natural. But what's it like to work for him?" Angie's gushing compliments used to do it for me. Her stroking my ego used to feel about as good as her stroking my dick. Those days were over.

All of her compliments felt like she was trying too hard.

Trying to save something that was dead.

Trying to light a fire in the rain.

I just ... didn't feel it any longer. Things had happened that changed us, and I couldn't ignore it even if she tried to pretend we were good—pretend that we were the same two young kids who fell in love.

We weren't.

"Fisher's an okay boss." Reese glanced out the window, not giving me her attention in the rearview mirror. *That* did it for me.

The more Reese jabbed, the more I wanted her. I didn't want her submissive; I wanted her angry and conflicted. I wanted to feel like a sin to her. *That* stroked my ego. And it almost felt as good as her stroking my dick, which she had yet to do ... but the night was young.

Angie teased the nape of my neck and laughed. "I can see that about you. I bet it's your intensity. Such a perfectionist, huh, Fish?"

Perfectionist? No.

Sadist might have been a more accurate term.

"Oh, Fisher, you need to visit my mom. She's asked about you."

I didn't want to talk about Angie's mom, but Reese's stiff posture seemed to relax with the change of subject, so I engaged in conversation with Angie about her mom the rest of the way to the venue.

Barely getting the vehicle in *Park,* I glanced over my shoulder only to see Reese halfway out the door. She ran toward the entrance.

"She's adorable, Fish," Angie said, playfully nudging my arm as we followed Reese's trail.

Adorable? Did she want to adopt her? I didn't want to adopt her. I had much different plans for her that weren't "adorable."

Reese's friends glanced over her shoulder at me, so Reese turned, giving me a tiny and very fake smile. "Hey, this is my friend Christina and her boyfriend Jamison. Guys, this is my boss, Fisher and ..."

There it was, that unavoidable bitter expression again. "Angie," she managed to say.

"Nice to meet you," everyone said almost in unison.

"So ... where's your rock star boyfriend?" Christina nudged Reese.

"Fish, you didn't tell me Arnie and Reese were a thing." Angie wrapped her arm around my arm and offered me a pouty look.

I hated that pouty look. I hadn't always hated it, but like most things in broken relationships, what was once endearing became unnerving—nearly unbearable.

"He just met her yesterday and invited her and us to his show. I'm not sure that qualifies as 'together.'" I shouldered past everyone to pick up the tickets at the box office.

We filed into the dark bar and found a table Arnie reserved for us right by the stage. Reese's friends cozied up in the same chair while Angie moved her chair so close to mine it was like one big seat. I risked a glance up at Reese and caught her deathly scowl.

We ordered drinks, and Reese got a water. I gave her a disapproving stare when her friend offered to buy her an alcoholic beverage. She needed to keep a clear mind around Arnie.

"I'm good. Really." She gave Christina a stiff smile.

When the band came onto the stage, the crowd erupted into applause, a few high-pitched screams, and whistles.

"Whoa ... you are *so* getting some of that tonight," Christina yelled into Reese's ear, but everyone heard it.

With Angie adequately distracted, I messaged Reese.

Fisher: You are NOT getting any of that tonight.
Reese: Sure thing, BABE! (Eye roll emoji)

I lifted my head and eyed her, but she shifted her

attention to the stage. Reese was pissed off about Angie. It wasn't my fault, and she damn well knew it. She was at my parents' house when it all went down.

After the final song, Arnie peeled off his sweaty, stinky shirt and tossed it to Reese. I knew his game, and it wasn't happening. Not with her. He wasn't the one in charge of looking out for her. I was. Admittedly, I was doing a terrible job, but that was between me and Rory. God ... I hoped I could keep my head on straight and not take the cat and mouse game too far.

Arnie nodded for us to head backstage. I gestured for Reese's friends to go first. As Reese started to follow them, I hooked my finger through the belt loop at the back of her shorts. Then I ducked my head and whispered in her ear, "Tell Arnie to do his own fucking laundry."

The most spectacular sound vibrated from her chest, up past her lips, as she shook her head, laughing. As much as I enjoyed making her cringe and blush, I loved her smile and her spontaneous laughter so much more. She sucked at pretending, and I could tell that bothered her, but I craved every raw inch of honesty that bled from her—that I could bleed from her.

Releasing her belt loop, we shouldered our way toward security, where Arnie and her friends waited for us.

"You were amazing! I can't believe Fisher hasn't been bragging about you."

I tried not to scowl or show any reaction, but fuck ... it stung seeing her so enamored with my brother's talent. Angie, sensing my disapproval, wrapped her arm around my waist, a subtle attempt to claim something that was no longer hers.

"Thanks, gorgeous." Arnie grabbed Reese's hand, pulling her toward the exit.

She's not mine. She's not mine. She's not mine.

But I wanted her beyond any sort of reason.

We followed Arnie and Reese to the restaurant. Just inside the door, Christina expressed her concern over being able to afford such a fancy restaurant.

"I know the owner. And it's on me. No worries," Arnie said with a cocky grin.

I was proud of my brother. Really. And on any other day, I was his biggest fan, but not when he was making a play for the woman whose tits had been in my mouth just hours earlier.

No sooner did we get seated at the table, Christina beckoned Reese to the ladies' room with her, and Angie wasted no time scooting her chair too close to mine. Again.

"Everything fine?" Jamison asked Christina when the ladies returned after a long visit to the ladies' room.

"Totally. Sorry we took so long. I had to cool Reese down. Her date tonight has her overheating."

Fuck my life. Why does Rory hate me?

Angie gave me a nudge and grinned like we were witnessing a marriage. Reese eased into her chair, sporting a tiny grin as she glanced in my direction. I was all out of grins to share.

As the night progressed, so did my need to numb the anxiety plucking at my very last nerve while I watched Arnie whisper in Reese's ear, touch her, smile at her ...

There really wasn't enough alcohol in the restaurant to alleviate the ache. Just because she wasn't mine, didn't mean she was his.

"I'll order a ride," I said, pulling my phone out of my pocket as my head spun with the wrong kind of intoxication.

"Good idea, babe." Angie hung on my arm with her head on my shoulder.

"I can drive," Reese said, clearing her throat.

"Yes!" Arnie stood, offering his hand. "You can drive them home." He gestured to me and Angie. "Then you can drive me home. And I'll get you home in the morning."

"Fuck no," I said so quickly everyone paused, eyeing me. "I told Rory I'd watch her. I can't watch her at your house."

"Babe." Angie pinched my fucking cheeks like a mother would do to a child. "I don't think you can watch anyone except me."

At one time, I loved Angie. It was real. And I might have let myself believe it would be forever. But all of those feelings fizzled into friendship and nothing more, but she didn't get the memo, and neither did my family.

"Let's go. We'll figure it out," Reese said, grabbing Arnie's key fob from his hand.

The vehicle remained eerily quiet on the way to Arnie's place, where Reese helped him to his door.

He looked like he was begging her for something with his hands pressed together at his chest.

Where he fucking. Kissed. Her.

"What's Angie's address?" Reese asked me when she climbed back into the driver's seat.

"Just go home," I said.

"It's no problem. I can take—"

"She's staying with me tonight, and we'll get her vehicle tomorrow. Just go." I wasn't leaving drunk Angie alone. Friends didn't do that. And if that pissed off Reese, which it clearly did, that was too bad. I wasn't exactly in the best mood either.

"Let's go. Can you walk?" I asked Angie when we arrived home.

"Carry me, babe," she mumbled.

Lifting her from the back seat and kicking the door shut, I gave Reese the garage code. "Ninety-three-eleven."

Inside the house, I slowly released Angie. "Can you find your feet?"

She found them, but just barely, as she swayed back and forth down the hallway, stepping out of her heels and her dress while Reese stood behind me.

"Thanks for driving," I rubbed my eyes and turned.

"I'm going to church in the morning, so someone else will have to get Arnie's vehicle back to him."

"Of course." I headed to the kitchen for a drink of water, feeling parched. By the time I set the glass on the counter, Reese was gone, so I followed her. I had to follow her. "What do you *need*?" I asked, taking the final steps to the basement.

"There's a naked woman in your bedroom. Better not keep her waiting," Reese turned on the light and removed her sandals with her back to me.

"If it's not you, then I don't give a fuck who's naked in my bed." My hand snaked around her narrow waist, and I pulled her back into my chest.

"You're drunk," she whispered on a shaky breath as I buried my nose into her hair.

"I'm over the legal limit; I'm not drunk. There's a difference."

"Well, *babe* ..." She shoved my arms away and took a few steps away from me. "Why are you not married to that woman upstairs? Your family adores her. I mean *adores* her. And she obviously thinks the two of you are in some never-ending relationship. Why is that? Are you? Is she your endgame, but for now you're screwing around with other women until you're ready to commit? Because you guys are not broken up. She doesn't just show up out of nowhere and fall back into *your bed*."

I gave her a few seconds, out of curtesy. She had it all wrong, but I wasn't in the mood to set things straight. I had more pressing things that required my attention. "You have the best tits. Not too small, but not too big. And I could suck on your nipples all day. They are nothing short of perfect."

"You're drunk." She crossed her arms over her chest like a flimsy shield. It did great things to said tits.

"No." I held up two then three fingers. Back to two. I had no clue. I hadn't been a Scout, but she didn't know that. "Scout's honor. In the morning, I will still find your tits to be the best thing I've seen or tasted in a very long time. If they were on Yelp, I'd leave a five-star review of them."

"Stop." She tried to hide her grin.

"I will not stop. I haven't even started talking about your legs." I crept my way toward her, and she retreated.

Cat and mouse.

"Angie is beautiful. I'm not blind. I'm sure her ... *breasts* are Yelp worthy, and her legs are incredibly toned, along with her arms. Her silky hair and skin. And she's successful. Age appropriate. And she's naked in your bed. So you might have to explain to me why you're down here with me."

Angie. Angie. Angie.

I couldn't help but wonder if I would ever escape her, or if we were meant to live miserably together forever just because everyone else expected it—because it seemed to make some sort of sense to everyone else except me.

Sighing, I narrowed my eyes. "She wants a husband and a houseful of babies. A dog. Two cats. And a minivan."

"And you don't?"

"Not yet."

"So ..." Reese gazed up at the ceiling and laughed. "You *are* looking for someone to mess around with until you decide you're ready for wife material. That's awesome, Fisher. Rory comes home in a few days. What's the point? I'm not having sex with you. And why are you so anti-family? You're twenty-eight. Do you know how many men have a family by the time they're your age?"

"No." I continued closing in on her. "And neither do you. So what's *your* point? You're eighteen. The whole point of your life should be to live in the fucking moment without caring if everything you do makes complete sense."

"Stop." She shook her head as the pool table behind her stopped her from getting away from me.

"I don't want to stop. Do you? Do you really want to stop?"

"I don't know," she whispered.

We hit the very edge of her comfort zone. As much as I physically wanted her because she was a fucking cruciverbalist unicorn, I couldn't push her too far. But then ... she kissed me.

Hard.

Passionately.

Tongue-down-my-throat kind of kiss.

So I kissed her back. I was a decent guy, but far from a saint. Then *more* just happened.

She wasn't Rory's daughter ...

She wasn't eighteen ...

She wasn't my employee ... as I unbuttoned her shorts and lowered to my knees, sliding them down her long legs —along with her panties. Her lips parted as her stare weighed heavily on me like she was drunk, yet completely sober.

"Fisher ..." God. Seriously. My name falling from those full lips did things to me, things so much stronger than any drug.

Was that my excuse? She drugged me with her voice? With my own fucking name? Did I need an excuse? We were consenting adults. Why the hell did anything else have to matter?

I kissed along the slight curve of her hips, working my way down. "Do you want me to kiss you here?" My mouth hovered a fraction of an inch from where I felt certain no man had ever been before me.

"I ... I ... don't know," she stuttered between labored breaths while gripping the edge of the pool table.

"No?" I couldn't help my slight grin as I pressed my lips to the exact spot without affirmative permission.

Her breath hitched, muscles in her legs clenching as I rested my hands next to hers and tasted her fanfucking-tastic tits before shrugging off my shirt. "We'll go until you tell me to stop?" I said—I asked because I did need *her* consent even if I didn't need Rory's or Angie's or my family's ... or God's for that matter.

Her gaze made a slow ascent up my body before she wet her lips and nodded.

That was all I needed. Grabbing her face, I kissed her again like she had kissed me. A deep moan worked its way up the back of my throat when her hard nipples teased my chest. Another moan escaped when her fingers ghosted along my abs down to the waist of my jeans until her shaky fingers found my dick. I couldn't help it; my hips jerked into her touch as she teased me. Control had never felt so goddamn torturous.

I lifted her onto the edge of the pool table and wedged myself between her spread legs, rocking my greedy hips into her—once, twice. A tiny whimper left her lips as I sucked the warm skin along her neck while unbuttoning my jeans. My hand claimed a fistful of her hair, but it did little to calm my surging *need* to be inside of her, to consume her in every way possible. The only thing that felt wrong at the moment was the cotton of my briefs preventing me from fucking the life out of her as I wedged myself as far as possible between her legs ... as I felt her warm and wet against me.

Control was scarce, virtually extinct, when her fingers teased the waistband of my briefs. I lost a good five years off my life when her finger slid beneath it, exposing the head of my cock. I tore my mouth from hers, both of us breathing heavily as we stared at her hand nudging my briefs down another inch.

"I need a condom," I managed to whisper with very little control.

Reese's head moved side to side slowly. "I want ... I just want to feel you."

"God ... feel me, Reese." I barely recognized my own desperate voice. No woman had ever unraveled me so slowly. I questioned if I'd die before we finished whatever we were or weren't about to do.

I guided her hand down the front of my briefs. For the record, *nothing* felt better than a woman's warm, delicate hand wrapped around my cock for the first time. "Fuuuck ..." I fought to keep from losing it all right there as my abs tightened, and I watched her hand slowly—fucking painfully—explore my dick like it was her first time. I *was* her first time, and that made it infinitely worse in a good but excruciatingly painful way.

"Reese ..." I pinched my eyes shut. "Let me get a condom."

"No. I ... I just want to feel you."

"Fuck ..." I kissed her neck and palmed her breast, probably a little too hard, while tweaking her nipple. So much pent up energy and no place to release it.

I was. DYING!

"You *are* feeling me, and it's killing me," I said without trying to actually sound like a badly wounded animal. I would have settled for anything at the moment. I would have dropped back down to my knees, buried my face between her spread legs, and rubbed one off had I known the path of torment she had planned for me.

"No. I want to feel you ..." She forced my briefs down until I was free, until she could position my erection in the direction of her spread legs. "Here. I want to feel you here, but ... just ... on the outside."

Fuck my life.

And fuck Rory.

And while we're at it, fuck all religions that teach abstinence, thus creating a sexually frustrated society filled with suicidal virgins.

Okay, she wasn't technically suicidal, but pressing the head of my dick between her legs was like pointing a gun to her head but instructing me not to shoot while my finger rested heavily on the trigger.

"Reese ..." I dropped my forehead to her shoulder and released her breast, bracing my hand next to hers again on the edge of the pool table so I didn't accidentally fuck her. It could have happened, my knees were weak and sheer gravity could have pushed me all the way inside of her.

As I took a tiny step closer, she gasped, "Stop ..."

I was there ... between her legs. Everything was so warm, wet, and intoxicating—like a few more shots of tequila got dumped into my bloodstream—as she gipped me tighter, rubbing the head of my dick against her clit and a little lower.

My lips pressed to her shoulder again as I resisted the urge to dig my teeth into her flesh, but I couldn't resist the urge to rest my hand on her knee to spread her legs a little wider, to press into her a fraction of an inch more. My hips rocked slowly, teetering on that edge.

It wasn't sex, but goddamn … it was better than sex in some ways. Torture. The really fucking good kind.

"God …" she moaned, closing her eyes as I rocked into her over and over, just enough to stroke her clit. It was torture to stay in control.

"Fisher!" she gasped, fingernails digging into my shoulders.

I stopped. Completely froze. It slipped. The head was inside of her—just the tip.

"I'm so—" I tried to retreat.

"No. Don't … move." She panted, her breath hot over my lips.

"Reese … I can't fucking stay here." I bit her lower lip a little harder than I should have and growled. It was her indecisiveness that crushed every last ounce of my control. If she wanted to stop, that I could have done. But it was the way she seemed hell-bent on living for eternity with just the head of my cock inside of her that obliterated my control.

"Lean back." I pressed my hand between her breasts and guided her back onto the pool table.

She silently fought me on it.

"I'm not taking your virginity … tonight." I grinned.

She relinquished control and leaned back. Pressing my hands to her knees, I spread her legs wide.

"If you let me put my mouth on you…" my gaze

affixed to her spread legs—it was hard to tear it away "...I could make you scream."

After a few breaths, she pressed her lips together and inched her head side to side.

Kill me. Just kill me!

I was an inch inside of her, but no oral sex?

Swallowing my reaction, my disappointment, my mouth found her breasts, and I used my erection to get her off. It wasn't completely selfless. But then she shifted her hips.

"Fuck!" I made myself stop, but it wasn't easy. Again, I was inside of her a fraction. "You can't move like that," I pleaded through a heavy pant.

"Fisher ..." Her heels dug into the edge of the pool table, and she lifted her hips again.

"Fuck. Fuck. Fuck! Stop!" I grabbed her hips, pushing them back down to the pool table. "I don't have a condom."

"Then get one."

God. I hoped she didn't ever tease another guy like she was teasing me. It took herculean control to keep from going all the way and dealing with the consequences later.

"They're upstairs," I said with clipped words while closing my eyes and shaking my head.

"Fisher ..." Again she tried to lift her hips.

Again, I held her down while pulling out of her.

Before she could protest again, I pressed my thumb to her clit, making slow circles while using my other hand to get myself off. She covered my hand with hers like she wanted me to show her how to do it. As I sped up, her hips jerked off the table over and over. Just seconds after she arched her back and closed her eyes while releasing a long moan, I came on her stomach, breaths labored, body a little achy from resisting it for so long.

"Damnation is in your future, little girl." I pulled up my underwear and jeans . Then I grabbed paper towels to clean her up.

"Then you're going with me," she murmured.

I shook my head. "Only after Rory murders me."

Why was I so conflicted? Reese said it a million times —she was an adult. An adult with her V-card. I didn't force her to do anything. She wanted it too. She told me to get the condom. I could have gone upstairs to get the condom. Angie probably would not have heard me.

I could have whispered a bunch of sweet things over Reese's lips to convince her to let me take her virginity, promising to pull out, using words that made her feel special and loved.

I did no such thing. She wanted to get off and so did I. So that was what we did, and we did it while keeping that V-card mostly intact. Honestly, I wanted to have sex with her, but I had no desire to be her first.

Who am I kidding? I'm going to Hell.

Rose knew.

It was only a matter of time before Rory knew. We were friends. The three of us, but I wasn't delusional. I knew Rose was too loyal to Rory to keep something like that from her.

The next morning, Reese hopped into my truck with a marginally confined smile. "Morning."

"Morning," I said, attempting to act unaffected about our fate as I pulled out of the driveway and turned up the music, hoping she'd get the hint that I wasn't in the mood to talk.

Eventually, I broke the silence. "What's your car situation?"

"Car situation?"

"Did you talk to your grandparents?"

"Yeah," she murmured as we pulled to a stop at the light.

"And?"

"And they're not going to give me the money for the Porsche, which is stupid because it's *my* freaking money."

"So you get the Forester?"

She sighed with a half shrug. "I suppose so."

"Great. Get the money in your account and we'll go get it tomorrow if it's still there. Or you can go with Rory or Brendon. I don't really care."

I cared.

I cared too much. But my caring wasn't what Reese needed at eighteen with no direction. Rory losing her shit wasn't what either one of us needed.

After the longest pause, she grabbed her backpack from the backseat. I thought she was retrieving her sketch pad of puzzles, but then she unfastened her seat belt and bolted out of the truck before I knew what was happening.

"Reese!"

The light changed and people started to honk their horns.

"Fuck ..." I sped through the light and took the first right to try and cut her off, but I lost her. I called her phone over and over, but she didn't answer.

I sent off a string of texts.

Where are you?

Answer your phone.

I'm sorry.

Please pick up your phone.

Don't make me call Rory.

Or the police.

When she didn't respond, I didn't call the police or Rory. Instead, I silently went out of my mind, driving around looking for her before ending up at the office.

"Have you seen or heard from Reese?" I asked Hailey.

Her brow wrinkled. "No. Why?"

"Because she ran off like a fucking child, and I don't know where she's at." I grabbed a water from the cooler and chugged it.

"Did you call Rory?"

"No. And I don't want you to either. She'll show up. I just ..."

"Why did she run off?"

Resting my hand on my hip, I dropped my chin and sighed. "Just ... stupid stuff. Call me if she shows up." I tossed the bottle into the trash and headed out to look for her again.

Eventually, I got a text from Hailey. **She's here**. It took me an hour to get through traffic. As I opened the door to the office, Hailey squeezed past me and whispered, "Go easy on her."

After the door shut behind me, I said, "You're fired."

From my desk chair, Reese's wide-eyed gaze lifted to mine.

"The tile shop where I get most of my tile, they're looking to hire someone to answer the phone. I got you an interview. It's just a formality. They will offer you the job. I'm going to tell Rory I found you a new job because I don't need you on the job sites where you could get hurt. And Hailey doesn't really need your help most days."

She deflated before my eyes. I kept my reaction neutral. I liked her ... a whole fucking lot. I liked her too much to be an enabler. She needed to really grow up.

"Is this about yesterday? Or this morning?" she asked in a shaky voice.

"Yes."

"Rose promised not to tell Rory," she said.

"She lied. Rose will absolutely tell Rory unless we end it." Whether she liked it or not, I knew her mom and Rose better than she did. "Rory's taking the morning off tomorrow to help you get a car. The interview with the tile shop is the following morning. You'll be able to drive there on your own."

"Are you mad at me?" she whispered.

Pinching the bridge of my nose, I shook my head. "No. I'm mad at myself."

Her eyes filled with tears. When one escaped, she quickly wiped it and turned away from me.

"Fuck ... this is what I wanted to avoid. Rory is my friend. Rose is my friend. I didn't want to be the villain. The guy who broke Rory's daughter's heart."

Or mine. I felt it too. I felt it in my chest, and it hurt because I allowed myself to feel things for Reese that were more than the cat and mouse game, more than a physical attraction, more than a casual fascination.

Reese stood and plucked her backpack from the floor, keeping her gaze on anything but me as she brushed past me to the door. "You're such an arrogant asshole."

She wasn't wrong. And she wasn't entirely right either.

"And you're the most beautiful and infuriating

woman I have ever met," I said. "And in a different time ... a different place in our lives, I'd tell Rory and the rest of the world to go fuck themselves. I'd prove them all wrong. *We'd* prove the naysayers wrong. But ... I don't think they're wrong. Not now."

"I'm beautiful ..." She nodded while turning toward me. "A pretty face. Long legs. Perky *tits*. And I sucked your cock. No college education. No fantastic job. Nothing ... but I'm beautiful. Young. Innocent. And maybe the perfect amount of naive. It makes sense now." She laughed maniacally. "Stupid, stupid me. I thought we were this magical thing that couldn't be described. We didn't make sense because magic, fate, and serendipity don't have to make sense. I actually *liked* that we didn't make sense, yet my universe seemed perfect when it was just us. I guess the eight-letter word for that is illusion. You played me. You liked the chase. The game. And what better chase than the virgin wearing a cross around her neck?"

I shook my head. "You don't know what you're talking about." She had no clue. Not. One.

"Because I'm eighteen?"

"Because you're scared."

"Of what?" She narrowed her eyes.

"Failure. Eighteen-letter word. Starts with K," I said. She blinked several times.

"Kakorrhaphiophobia. An abnormal fear of failure. That's why you're here and not chasing a dream. Not in college. Not making plans in your life. Your dad died. Your mom went to prison. And you've been left with a Bible that prepares you for death and makes you feel ashamed of anything you do in this life to truly *live*." I opened the door and she waited for several more seconds before heading to my truck.

As soon as I started it, I knew we weren't going home. Not yet. We needed to make a trip to my parents' house first.

"Let's go," I said, hopping out of the truck after a silent drive to their house. I opened her door. She took a few more seconds of hesitation before climbing out of it. "They're out of town. Let's go."

Leading her to the basement, I retrieved a box from the utility room and carried it to the family room while Reese watched in mere silence. "Sit." I gestured to the sofa.

As she sat, I kneeled by the box and opened it.

"I told you I played sports. And I loved construction. But my real talent came in the form of spelling bees." I pulled out a stack of plaques, certificates, and trophies.

She eyed them.

"I took first place at a national competition. I liked words. Dissecting them. Studying their origin. A full year of Latin. My mom used to say I'd never find a woman who really appreciated my word-loving soul. And she was so disappointed in me when I let my love of words die, when I found my new favorite words like..." I grinned "...well, most of them were and still are four-letter words. Sometimes simplicity is best. So gone were the days of winklepicker shoes and ulotrichous women. I gravitated toward fuck, fucker, and fucking. It helped me fit in."

I could still see my mom rolling her eyes and frowning at my new language. "Who would have ever imagined that a girl ... a young woman ten years younger than me would breeze into my life. Beautiful? Yes. Quirky? Absolutely. Innocent? Painfully so. But also a cruciverbalist." My head inched side to side as I reached for the notebooks and tablets in the box that I hadn't touched in years. Tossing them on the floor with my awards, I lifted my gaze to hers, but all she did was stare at the pile of notebooks.

Bending down slowly, she retrieved one and opened it to the pages of hand drawn crossword puzzles. "Cruciverbalist ..." she whispered.

Where had she been my whole life? And why did she have to come to me in the most forbidden form? My brain didn't understand and neither did my heart. It was so *fucking* unfair. I cleared my throat. "An eighteen-year-old cruciverbalist. Really, what were the chances?"

It wasn't that we shared a unique hobby. It was the mentality of loving words, of studying them, of dreaming of them. Something so rare that finding someone who loved them as much as I did felt like finding the one person who could see my soul. And I couldn't have her. Not really. Not in the way two people were meant to fall in love.

"Why didn't you tell me?" She glanced up at me.

Running a hand through my hair, I sighed. "I don't know. I think I was in shock. And maybe a little awe was involved. A suffocating dose of confusion. A little anger at the timing, at your age. At the fact that you're Rory's daughter."

Reese flipped through more pages of the notebook. It

felt intimate, her seeing—touching—something that I hid from the rest of the world.

Without looking at me, she said five words I never wanted her to say ... to ask. "Do you love me, Fisher?"

"Reese, it doesn't matter."

She slowly shook her head. "You mean it doesn't change anything. And maybe you're right. But ..." She lifted her gaze to mine. "It *matters*."

Lumbering to my feet, I took a few steps to stare out the window, sliding my hands in my pockets. "I think I loved you before I met you. But we don't always get what we want. I let go of my crossword puzzles and word obsession because it didn't fit into my life any longer. The thing is ... I don't know where you fit into my life. And I know, I *know* you don't like your age to matter, but it does. I won't be the reason you don't take chances in life. Don't make marriage and sex your life's goals. If Rory found out, she'd want to know why. Why I would get involved with an eighteen-year-old girl? And I don't think cruciverbalist would work. Maybe if our ten-year-age gap was more like twenty-five and thirty-five, I could make a case for word geeks and kismet."

I turned to face her, to show her how much sincerity my words held. "Loving you is my favorite thing to do. It's automatic and effortless. And you're right, that matters. But ..."

"It changes nothing," she whispered, setting the notebook on the sofa before glancing up at the ceiling. "Naked fisherman, you are incorrigible. Moody. Bold. Unpredictable. Brash ... and a million other things that are bad for me. Yet it felt like you were the first person in my life who just ... fit. The version of myself I dreaded ... the version I blamed on your bad behavior, I came to love it. It started to feel like my true skin. It felt good to smile without something in my brain telling me I should smile. You gave my days this vibrant color, and I don't know what I will see when you're not..." she pulled in a shaky breath, and it strangled that thing beating in my chest "... when you're not mine."

I slid my arms around her waist as she shook with sobs. Her not being mine seemed like a cruel fate. Turning her in my arms, I pressed her cheek to my chest, hoping my heart could whisper the emotions I was too weak to say.

I love you.

I love you now.

I'll love you when you're not mine.

I'll love you forever.

FISHER
CHAPTER TWENTY-NINE

I KNEW she was leaving for Texas. I needed her to leave. My head needed the space to think again.

"Fisher, can you give Reese a hand with her suitcase?" Rory called upstairs as I drank a tall glass of water after my workout in the garage.

I was hoping to avoid an official goodbye. No such luck.

"I said I can do it. She's coddling me again," Reese protested after I jogged down the stairs.

"Well, I'm here now. I'll carry it." I took the suitcase and headed up front and loaded it into the back of her Forester.

"Sorry. Really, I had it."

I shrugged before closing the hatch back. "It's no big deal."

"Well, thanks."

"Enjoy your trip."

She remained silent, her gaze avoiding mine.

"Reese?"

She paused opening the door.

"I'm sorry," I said. "I should have known better. It was selfish of me."

After a hard swallow, she shook her head. "Well, I'm not sorry. Not for any of it. You know, it's ironic. Adults, *real* adults, like to lecture young adults like me. They like to paint this picture of hopes and dreams, endless possibilities, and constantly remind us that we can *do* anything, *be* anything. But that's a lie. Because all I wanted was to live a day at a time and figure things out one moment at a time. That's all I wanted to *do*. And all I wanted to *be* was yours." She shrugged, glancing up at the sky. "I don't want your apologies or your help because they don't get me you."

I already was hers. I just would never *ever* say the words because she deserved more than the infatuation of new love.

"I'm going to fall in love," she continued, and I listened. I let her poke tiny holes in my heart with her honesty and her innocence. "And some guy will be lucky to have me. He'll love me for me. And he won't care where I've been or where I'm going. He'll just feel so *fucking* lucky to be the one who kisses me goodnight and wakes up in the morning with me in his arms. He won't be burdened by my virginity or aggravated that I don't wear socks with my sneakers. He will be a better man for having found me, and I will be a better woman for having found him. I know they say love is patient, but it's not. Love is the brightest star in the sky. It doesn't have a switch or timer. It doesn't wear a watch or look at a calendar. It's why we're here. It's the only true reason for our existence."

In that moment, I knew she'd be okay, even if I wasn't. I knew she'd find her way in the world. I knew she'd experience many hard lessons along her way, and I knew she'd only let them make her stronger. And I envied the man who would have that version of her, but I also felt really fucking proud of myself for not standing in her way.

"I have to go."

I smiled. "Have a safe trip."

I had ten years on her. Ten more years of development. Ten more years of my brain perfecting the ability to reason. So why did I feel like my heart just drove off in a Subaru Forester?

FISHER
CHAPTER THIRTY

A<small>FTER A LONG RIDE</small> on my motorcycle, I returned home to Reese in my driveway, hands balled, jaw clenched. She was supposed to be on a plane.

She yelled something as I parked in the garage and removed my helmet.

"What are you doing here?" I asked, returning my helmet to the cabinet.

"Did. You. KNOW?"

I hadn't seen her so angry, and that said a lot because I had been her greatest source of anger quite a few times.

"Jesus, Reese." I turned toward her, unzipping my jacket. "What the hell is going on?"

"Did you know that my mom is a *lesbian*? Gay. Homosexual. Are you understanding me now?" She shook her head and clawed at her hair.

It wasn't the woman I knew. It was her Bible. A poisoned congregation of judgmental people telling her what was right and wrong. It didn't anger me as much as it ripped at my heart. She was broken, and I couldn't fix her. No one could fix her. Only time could peel away at the layers of false ideas, the years of brain washing. I wasn't an expert on God, but I couldn't imagine him not loving every single one of his "children." That was how I was raised.

"Did I know your mom and Rose are together? Yes."

"How could you?" she seethed.

Oh, Reese, what the hell did they do to you?

"How could I what?" I planted my hands on my hips, eyeing her carefully.

"Not tell me!"

"Rory's personal life is not mine to share."

"Rory's *personal life?* Are you kidding me? She's my mom!"

"Your point?"

"I walked in on them. In the shower. My mom and her *girlfriend.* The friend who just happened to be in Colorado after having been a 'client' of hers in Nebraska. She cheated on my dad. That's why he divorced her."

Reality could be a bitch. Reese needed to deal with that bitch. That was what adults did. They swallowed the fucking truth and learned to deal with it.

"Is that why you're losing your mind? Because you think your mom cheated on your dad? Or are you upset because Rory is a 'lesbian, homosexual, gay?' Because I'm not sure why you're freaking the fuck out about this."

"You should have told me."

"And what would you have done? How would you have reacted? Like this? I hate to be the one to state the obvious, but your dad died, and that's terrible. Your mom went to prison ... also terrible. But that's in the past. If you want to be a grown-ass adult, then start acting like one."

"I'm so tired of the age card." She shoved my chest. I wanted to grab her and hug all the ugly from her. I wanted to cleanse her of the lies. The pain. The anger.

"Just because you don't understand my feelings doesn't make it my fault—a product of my age. *Nobody* likes being lied to."

"Nobody lied."

"Omission of the truth is deceptive ... a lie."

Her youth bled through her words. It wasn't her fault. She had so many seeds planted in that head of hers.

"So have we been lying to Rory about us?"

"There is *no* us." Her anger grew, jaw clenched.

I nodded slowly. "We might choose who we're with, but we don't choose who we love."

"Are you making excuses for her?"

"What if I'm making excuses for us? Would that be okay with you? Would it be okay because we're not gay?"

She clenched her jaw. "That's not it."

"You continue to tell yourself that."

She shook her head nonstop, drowning in denial.

"Then why are you one blink away from falling apart? Because you're ashamed of her sins?" I air quoted. "Or because you need it to be wrong? If you let it be okay, you'll have to question everything that those people put into your head. You'll have to look within to find *your* truth. And then what will you be? Lost? Isn't that the point? Bring the lost to God and they will be found?"

"She cheated on my dad." With one blink, she did

what I knew she needed to do ... she fell apart. A flood of tears raced down her face.

I wanted to throttle every person who distorted her view of love, who twisted something beautiful into something so ugly. "She fell in love."

Her lower lip trembled. "She was supposed to love him."

"Well, life never goes like it's supposed to. So what are you going to do about it?"

"Reese," Rory appeared around the corner of the garage.

"I'm moving back to Texas. There is nothing for me here." Reese couldn't even look at Rory.

"Reese, let me explain."

"Explain?" She retreated to the corner of the garage, but she couldn't escape the truth. Not anymore. "No explanation needed. Everything I just saw, and will never be able to erase from my mind, was self-explanatory. The reason Dad divorced you. The reason he didn't want me to see you. It's so very clear now."

"You only know half of it. His half, not mine."

"I don't want your half. I don't want anything from you ever again. The lesson was mine to learn, and I learned it. Dad was right. You're incredibly selfish, and you don't care about anyone but yourself."

"Reese ..." Rory's eyes filled with tears.

"Don't talk to your mom like that." I couldn't stay quiet any longer. Rory was my friend.

Reese whipped around, her gaze sharp and unforgiving as she eyed me. "You ... *you* out of all people don't get to tell me how to talk to her. If she knew the things you've said to me ..." She shook her head and narrowed her eyes even more. "If she only knew ..."

"What is she talking about?" Rory asked.

Reese wouldn't tell her. That much I knew. She had too much pride. And confessing to Rory would have been too much of an admission of her "sins."

"I'm out. You two figure your shit out. I'm done." I left them in the garage as I headed inside for a beer or ten.

WITH NO WORD FROM REESE, I finally texted her on Saturday.

If you're not dead, text Rory and tell her you made it safely to Houston. Don't be a total asshole.

The kid gloves were off. Everything I fed to Reese from that point forward would be real adult shit. That was what she wanted ... that was what I was going to give her.

Reese: Go fuck yourself!

I laughed out loud. Her reply made me proud for some strange reason. She was in Texas with her conservative grandparents and texting me to go fuck myself.

Late Sunday afternoon, Rory and I waited on the porch for Reese to arrive. Her idea, not mine.

"Think she'll ever forgive me?" Rory asked as we drank our beer.

"I don't think there's anything to forgive. I think she'll accept you in her own time. She's ... better than the crap that's been preached to her for so long." I shrugged. "She's too stubborn to see the truth that's right in front of her."

"What's the truth?" Rory rolled her head toward me.

I kept my gaze on the driveway. "She's better than you and your ex-husband combined. She's just too scared to walk on her own without the crutch of her past."

"Amen, brother."

We both laughed just as Reese pulled up along the side of the street. As she rolled her suitcase toward the porch, Rory perked up. "Hey, how was your trip?"

"It was just overnight, barely a trip, but it was fine."

"Did they have a nice anniversary party?" Rory continued her attempts to engage Reese in conversation, like their relationship didn't implode before she left just over twenty-four hours earlier.

Reese nodded. "I'm going to go unpack and do a load of laundry."

"Need help?" Rory asked.

"I'm good."

"Have you had dinner?"

Reese shook her head. "I'm not hungry."

"Rose and I are going for pizza. We'd love for you to come too."

Reese's head continued to shake. Her lips turned into a pouty frown. "I'm not hungry. Enjoy your pizza." She headed toward the basement. After a few steps, she turned, giving Rory a tiny smile. "I don't know how God feels about you and Rose. I just know that I've felt lost for the past five years. The lie didn't protect me. And my reaction the other night wasn't really to Rose ... or you and Rose. I know this because I've had time to sort through my feelings. It wasn't Dad. It wasn't even your arrest that destroyed our family; the fact that you tried to live the wrong life ... that's what destroyed us. And it might take me awhile to come to terms with everything, but I can imagine it must have been painful to find the right person at the worst possible time."

I wanted her to look at me because I knew she wasn't just talking about Rory and Rose, but she didn't look at me.

"Thank you," Rose whispered.

When Reese disappeared around the corner of the house, I set my beer down and stood, pulling Rory to her feet and hugging her as she wept with relief.

"Told you," I said.

Rory left.

I sat upstairs letting words, thoughts, and emotions war in my head. Then I headed downstairs, stopping at the door to the porch. Reese watched the sunset with a beer in her hand, music on her phone, and her feet tucked beneath her.

My cruciverbalist.

"I fucked myself," I said.

She pursed her lips, but she couldn't completely hide her grin as she took a swig of her beer.

"I'm pretty good." I sat in the rocker next to her.

"I don't doubt that." She rubbed her lips together. "But what do I know? I'm just an asshole."

"Rory grilled me on what I said to you while she was gone. Thanks for that."

Reese nodded. "You're welcome."

I waited ... she had to ask.

"What did you tell her?"

"I told her I used a lot of swear words around you."

"And she believed you?"

I shrugged. "I don't know. I guess so."

She drank more beer. It felt like she was doing it for a reason that didn't involve a buzz. I felt like she was giving someone the middle finger with that bottle of beer.

Rory?

Me?

God?

"What are you going to do, Reese? Move back to Texas because your mom is going to Hell?"

"I don't know, Fisher. Would that make me a *total asshole*?"

I inwardly laughed at how much my asshole comment bothered her. "Probably," I said.

She rolled her eyes. "Well, you would know what it's like to be a total asshole."

"Why? Because I wouldn't fuck you?"

"Well, from what I hear, I'm the only single female in a twenty-mile radius you haven't put your dick into. That makes me a unicorn. Maybe that makes me the *one* woman you can't have."

She had it all wrong. It made her the one I gave a shit about. It made her special, but not in the way her crazy brain thought. I stood and plucked the bottle of beer from her hand, taking the rest down in one shot. "If I wanted you, I could have you, and we both know it."

No more cat and mouse. I gave her the facts.

"No." She shook her head. "You can't have me. Not now. Not ever. I don't want you anymore."

"You do." I handed her the empty bottle.

"I don't!" She bolted from her seat, chin up, determination etched into her face.

I had to fight the laughter that tickled my chest. "It's almost too easy."

"What's too—"

I kissed her so hard she didn't have a chance to protest worth a shit. The bottle dropped to the floor. Her fingers claimed two fists full of hair. I grabbed her ass, lifting her up to me and carrying her straight up the stairs without letting go of her mouth. God ... that mouth of hers ...

As soon as I set her on the bed, I tore off her shirt.

She kept a defiant expression on her face, despite her greedy hands reaching for me as I ripped down the front of her bra, sucking and biting her tits.

"Fish ... er ..."

Kneeling between her legs, I peeled off her jeans. She eyed me with something so distinctly different than anything I had seen from her before that moment. I was done letting her be the indecisive teenager grappling with her sexuality and where it fit with her god. We weren't in high school, hiding from parents. We were adults doing very adult things. I no longer gave a fuck about her stupid V-card.

I just ... wanted her. And I knew she wanted me. So I was going to take everything. And she was going to hate herself ... and me. I didn't fit on her pedestal. I was too human. I was too fucking flawed.

Kissing my way up her leg, I paused along her inner thighs and slipped my finger beneath the crotch of her panties, circling her clit.

She moaned, hips jerking.

My finger slid lower. My tongue teased the skin along her leg, and I pushed my finger inside of her. She gasped. Pulling it out, I repeated it over and over again.

Yes, Reese ... I'm going to fuck you like this. I'm going to take what you've been begging me to take. And you're going to hate me because you're still too tethered by the guilt of it all.

Removing my finger, I slid off her panties, ignoring the conflicted expression on her beautiful face. Then I unbuttoned my jeans.

"I'm ..." She breathed heavily. "I'm not having sex with you." The lies came so easily by that point. They weren't even her words. They were regurgitated sermons filling the space that belonged to her real conscience, her true self.

"No?" I snaked my hands behind her, unhooking her bra. "We'll see."

She didn't protest.

"Ah!" She jumped when I bit her nipple, when I slid not one but two fingers inside of her.

Pumping them.

Prepping her.

Kissing her.

She whimpered when I released her, standing to remove my jeans. After a quick swallow like she needed to swallow the part of her that was losing control, she whispered, "I won't do it. You don't deserve it. You had your chance."

"We'll see." I crawled onto the bed, working my way back up her legs, my tongue making a slow, deep swipe between those sexy legs.

She jumped, back arching from the bed, hands flying to my hair.

Her perfectly curved hips, her breasts and hard nipples, the delicate skin along her neck ... I took it all.

We kissed as I settled between her legs, once again, in the familiar spot separated by nothing but my briefs.

I rocked into her over and over. She lifted her hips, searching for the very thing she said she wouldn't do. I wasn't her savior. If she didn't want it, she was going to have to be a grown woman and stop it.

Rolling onto my back, I took her with me. I gave her the upper hand, every opportunity to stop it.

"No sex," she said in a fractured voice.

I was breaking her. And maybe that was wrong, but she needed to learn so many lessons in life, and that moment was one of them. Even if she regretted it, I knew she would be a better woman—a better lover—because I didn't try to make *it* (that damn V-card) feel special; I just ... loved her. All of her.

I sat up, face to face with her. "We'll see." I kissed her, and she denied me nothing. She just kept giving more and more as I grabbed her hair with one hand and guided her hand beneath my briefs with my other hand.

She stroked me.

I fingered her slowly, making her squirm with need for more.

Breaking our kiss, I reached for the nightstand drawer and retrieved a condom, using my teeth to open it as Reese gazed at me with wide eyes and parted lips, body stiff. I pushed down the front of my briefs and rolled on the condom.

Then I kissed her, but gentler, slower. She had the chance to stop it.

She didn't. And I wasn't going to save her.

Ghosting my lips across her face, to her ear, I whispered, "Your husband can thank me."

Again, her whole body turned rigid against mine, but she said nothing. Did nothing.

I lifted her hips and positioned her over my cock. I knew I'd go slow ... but I also knew I'd go all the way and ignore every last pang of regret that she had managed to make me feel over the previous months.

Then ... she resisted my hands pulling on her hips, preventing me for taking it any further. Her blue eyes turned into enormous pools of tears that spilled over and down her face.

I knew I'd love her for saying yes, and I knew I'd love her even more for saying no. For finding her voice. For taking that first step toward finding her place in the world —even if it wasn't with me.

Reese pressed her hands to my face. "Thank you, Fisher." She climbed off my lap.

I didn't stop her.

She dressed.

I didn't stop her.

"I'm volunteering to go on a mission trip to Thailand for six months. And then ..." She shrugged while taking a shaky breath. "I don't know, but I'll figure it out. I'll figure *me* out." She turned. After a couple steps, she glanced over her shoulder, offering a sad smile. "There's more to life than crossword puzzles, right?"

I could barely breathe past the lump in my throat, let alone speak. Letting her go felt infinitely harder than holding on to her. Clenching my jaw to keep my emotions from changing her mind, I nodded and my eyes burned with my own tears. "I hope so."

Once again ... and maybe for the last time ... my heart left my body with an eighteen-year-old cruciverbalist.

THE LOST FISHERMAN

CHAPTER ONE

Six months in Thailand turned into twelve months in Thailand with Brendon. Rory was right. Friendships had a way of turning into more.

Playful nudges.

Teasing.

Flirty glances.

Hand-holding.

Stolen kisses.

All the little things checked off the boxes. If the boxes were checked, it had to be love. Right?

A stop in Tokyo and another in Los Angeles was all that stood between me and my mom—between me and the naked fisherman.

Brendon spent the month prior to our trip home hinting about marriage.

Did I see myself having a destination wedding or a church wedding?

How many kids did I want?

Would I choose to live in the city or in the mountains?

A dog and two cats? Or no cats and two dogs?

Brendon still had his job waiting for him at the law firm in Denver. He would make good money with room for advancement, maybe even make partner one day.

I had the chance to do ... nothing. Well, not true. There would be kids to raise, dogs to walk, and cakes to bake.

Fisher made good money. If I was destined for the life of a wife and stay-at-home mom, why did I leave him? I thought about Fisher more in the days leading up to our departure than I had done for the previous twelve months.

Brendon convinced me to prolong our trip by a few days so we could spend a few nights in Tokyo.

"Reese, slow down," he mumbled over my mouth—my anxious mouth—as we took the elevator to the hotel room.

I had this clawing feeling that Brendon's reason for the extra days in Tokyo had everything to do with a marriage proposal.

Proposal.

Wedding.

Sex.

That was his plan.

I had other plans. For some reason, I didn't want to lose my virginity, or what was left of it, on my wedding night. What if I married Brendon and the sex wasn't good? What if I spent every second comparing him to Fisher?

I had to know.

"Whoa ... seriously, what's up with you?" Brendon pulled my hand away from his crotch just as the elevator doors opened.

"I don't want to wait. I know ... I know it's wrong, but I don't want to wait."

He narrowed his eyes. "Reese, I think you're just experiencing some mixed feelings over going home after being away for a year. Go take a shower, drink some water, and sleep on it. Okay?" He stopped at the door to my room.

His answer to sex was shower, hydrate, and sleep on it? Would every man I met reject me? Would I ever have sex?

"Okay." I nodded. "You're right. Night."

That night, I showered, thought about Fisher, and I touched myself.

The next morning, we were first in line to go to the observation tower of the Tokyo Skytree. With Mt. Fuji visible in the distance on the clear day, Brendon got on one knee and proposed to me with his grandmother's diamond ring.

Onlookers smiled and gasped, all eyes on us. No ... all eyes on *me*.

"You're the woman of my dreams, Therese Capshaw, and I think I knew it from the day we met. Do me the honor of being my wife."

My brain was paralyzed. But in the moment, all I could do to make everyone stop staring at me, including Brendon, was nod.

"Yes!" He slipped the ring on my finger and stood, pulling me in for a big hug and a kiss on the cheek.

I was engaged, and I got a kiss on the cheek.

On the way back to our hotel, I pulled on his arm, tugging him into a drugstore.

"What are you doing?" He laughed.

I led him up one aisle and down the next, stopping at the condoms.

He narrowed his eyes. "Reese ..."

"It doesn't mean we have to; it just means ... we're prepared."

"Prepared to sin?"

"Prepared to not have to explain why we need to rush our wedding if we do happen to sin."

Brendon shook his head, and I knew he wasn't comfortable with it, but I wasn't comfortable marrying him and not having sex with him first. And that should have been the only sign I needed.

But I was still that teenaged adult with *so* much to learn, and my favorite teacher happened to be half a world away and retired from teaching me any more than tough love and the oh-so-important "sink or swim."

With a miserable grimace and his teeth digging into his lip, Brendon nodded.

That nod led to anticipation.

Anticipation led to the allure of the forbidden.

He might not have initiated it on his own, but when we found ourselves in his hotel room after dinner that night, things quickly moved in the direction of that box of condoms.

"I love you so much," Brendon chanted over and over

between kisses and amid discarding our clothes. Maybe he thought God wouldn't be so critical of our decision if he kept reminding me (and God) how much he loved me. It wasn't merely a physical need—and hopefully not an immoral act; we were in love and committed to each other.

And by "we" I meant Brendon more than me.

I just wanted to know what it felt like to have sex with him. And I loved him; it just didn't feel like it did with Fisher. Maybe it wasn't supposed to feel like it did with Fisher.

"I'm so nervous my hands won't stop shaking," Brendon said as he fumbled the condom.

After he rolled it on, I closed my eyes—another sign things weren't great with Brendon. He touched me, and I imagined it was Fisher.

He started to push into me, and I replayed moments with Fisher. But Brendon didn't touch me like Fisher had touched me. He didn't really touch me at all, just his cock suited up between my legs and his lips nervously hovering over my lips.

Did he not notice my breasts? Maybe he wasn't a breast man.

Did he not want to kiss me between my legs? Locate my clit? Run his tongue along the length of my neck before biting my earlobe?

It was all so different.

I winced when he pushed all the way into me. It didn't feel great, maybe because he wasn't doing anything to make it feel at least a little less than awful and painful.

For the next five minutes, maybe not even, he jabbed

me with an erratic rhythm. He missed my clit every time while his heavy breaths washed over my face—grunting and occasionally pressing a limp, sloppy kiss to my mouth.

"Oh my ..." Brendon squeezed his eyes shut and stilled for a few seconds before a full-body shiver shook him. He opened his eyes and grinned. "That was..." he blew out a breath "...amazing. I love you *so* very much."

When he rolled off me, I slowly sat up with my back to him and tears in my eyes. I gave him my virginity, and I didn't regret it, not on my part. Brendon deserved it because it meant something to him. I think it meant more to him than it meant to me.

The tears?

Guilt?

Not because I'd sinned.

Because I tempted him. He sinned for me. He did it because he loved me. He did it because it seemed a little less wrong since I agreed to marry him.

Tears ... I couldn't stop the tears because I knew I couldn't marry him.

And I couldn't go home to Rory ... to Fisher.

It was time to do something for myself. It was time to fall in love with endless possibilities. Time to walk alone. Time to grow up.

Time to *"fucking think for yourself."*

CHAPTER TWO

Four years later ...

"Oh my BABY GIRL!" Rory threw her hands in the air and charged me like she did at the airport in Denver after getting out of prison.

I was a teenaged adult then. Deer in the headlights. And no clue where my journey even began, let alone where it might take me.

It took me to Fisher, then it took me to Thailand, then it took me to Ann Arbor, Michigan. In Thailand, I volunteered to help a woman named Alesha. She was fifty-three. A midwife. Much like working for Fisher, I was grunt labor. No experience needed. And much like Fisher, Alesha taught me a lot. I watched (sometimes helped) her deliver thirty-three babies during my year in Thailand. But I knew after the very first delivery, that she had the best job in the world.

After breaking Brendon's heart that night in Tokyo, I

changed my travel plans. Instead of going back to Colorado, I returned to Houston. My grandparents helped me make financial arrangements for college.

Nursing school at the University of Michigan.

A new place where I didn't know a soul. The perfect place to follow *my* dream.

"Your dad would be so proud." Rory hugged me the day I received my bachelor's degree.

I loved her for acknowledging Dad. He really would have been proud of me.

My mom's parents were overjoyed for me too. My dad's parents plastered on their fake smiles, watching Rory and Rose congratulate me. They were not okay with my mom and her lesbian partner. I loved my mom, and I loved Rose too. During my four years in Ann Arbor, they averaged three visits a year. I never made it to Denver, but they didn't mind coming to me.

The sour looks on my dad's parents' faces didn't bother me. They were old. Set in their ways. And their opinions no longer shaped mine.

I thought for myself. I found a way to love God without fear or guilt—the most liberating feeling ever.

Sex? Yes ... I'd had a handful of boyfriends during my four years in Michigan. And they were *all* better lovers than Brendon. To be fair ... it was his first time too.

Alcohol? I wasn't a binge drinker, but I enjoyed a fun night out with friends.

Friends ... I had so many friends from nursing school. They felt more like sisters and brothers to me.

I even got a tattoo ... but no one, aside from my lovers,

had seen it. Fisher wasn't the only one who deserved a harem.

"Lunch?" Rory asked.

"Sounds perfect!" I hugged my grandparents just before we headed toward the parking lot. Mom and Rose rode with me while my grandparents drove their rental cars.

"So when do you start your new job?" Rose asked.

I laughed. "First I have to pass my NCLEX exam. Then I'll find a job."

"Then you'll be able to start your master's degree next fall, correct?"

I nodded. "That's the plan."

"We're moving out of the basement. Getting our own place. There will be plenty of room for you if you decide to come back to Denver," Mom said.

"Moving out of Fisher's basement?" I shot her a quick side-glance. It felt weird saying his name. I'd thought about him a lot, but I hadn't actually said his name.

"Did you ever get to meet Angie?" Rory asked.

I swallowed hard and nodded. "Um, I think so. His childhood sweetheart?"

"Yes. Well, she moved back to Denver last year for good because her mom wasn't doing well. In fact, she recently passed. She and Fisher just got engaged."

It didn't matter. I said this to myself over and over again. My brain got it, but the translation got messed up somewhere between my brain and my heart, causing unnecessary pain.

Five years ... it had been five years since I'd seen or talked to Fisher. I thought I made a nice clean break. So why did the edges of that hole in my heart feel so jagged, like they hadn't healed? Like they would never heal.

"So it's time to move out. Angie is nice, but I think they want the house to themselves to start a family," Rory said.

I nodded slowly. "Yeah," I whispered past the lump in my throat.

At the restaurant, Rose grabbed my hand after I got out of the car. She gave it a quick squeeze and offered me a soft smile, an "are you okay" smile.

All those years ... and she never told my mom about Fisher and me. It was another reason I loved Rose. Another reason why I knew my mom fell in love with her.

Channeling the happiness from the morning's events, from my special day, I squeezed her hand in return and smiled.

Rose winked and released my hand, leaving Rory none the wiser.

Fisher and I ended in the best possible way. I felt his love, and I always believed he felt mine. It just wasn't our time.

Life took over.

I didn't wait for him.

He didn't wait for me.

And that was okay. That was life.

With the news of his engagement, it solidified what I had always feared. There would *never* be a time for us.

"Oh ..." Rory turned around just before we entered the restaurant. "Speaking of Fisher, he sent a card." She dug through her bag and pulled out an envelope.

"Thanks." I took it and slipped it into my bag. I couldn't read it until I was alone. Even if it was nothing more than a generic graduation card with his signature, I needed privacy to deal with anything Fisher Mann.

IT TOOK me three days to open his card. My family went home. And my two roommates (fellow nursing school graduates) were gone for the day.

As I slowly unsealed it by wedging my finger into the corner, I took a deep breath. It was, in fact, a generic card, but there was more than just his signature. He'd left me a long note taking up the entire left side of the card.

Reese,

Can I say how proud of you I am without it sounding condescending? Without you thinking it's an age reference? I am. More than that, I'm happy for you. Rory said you plan to be a midwife and deliver babies. I knew you'd change the world, touch lives ... like you touched mine.

I'm sure Rory's told you that I'm getting married. It feels like the smart choice at this point in my life. My family is thrilled, and I'm good, in case you do care, which you might not. Go be the amazing woman I knew you would be. Find your place, your people, the life you deserve.

Congratulations,

The Naked Fisherman

I laughed through my tears. So many tears. He signed it The Naked Fisherman. It made me happy and incredibly heartbroken at the same time. Was he waiting for me? Did he, one day, decide to stop waiting and please his family by proposing to Angie? Good ... he was good.

CHAPTER THREE

I PASSED MY NCLEX.

I got my own apartment.

And I had an interview scheduled with a pediatric office.

Life continued to give me sunny days despite the Fisher Mann engagement news.

The morning of my interview, Rory called me.

"I haven't had the interview yet," I said as I made my way to my car. "I'm on my way there now."

"Reese," her voice hit my ear with a chilling gravity.

It stopped me in my tracks. "What is it?"

"Fisher was in an accident on his motorcycle. He's in surgery now. We don't know the extent of his injuries yet. I just thought I'd let you know in case you wanted to say a prayer for him."

"W-what?" I covered my mouth with my hand as tears instantly filled my eyes.

"I'll let you know when he's out of surgery ... if he comes out of surgery."

If...

"Okay?" she asked.

I nodded and pushed a tiny "okay" past the boulder in my throat.

After Rory ended the call, my phone and keys fell to the ground, cracking my screen. Sobs racked my body, one wave after another.

All I could see was his face. Those eyes. That wink. The smile he gave me just before he said something that made me blush.

"Are you going to kiss me?"

"I'm thinking about it."

"A-are you m-mine?"

"You know the answer to that."

"I'm trying so hard to not fall in love with you."

"I know."

I was okay ... maybe not good ... but I was okay not having Fisher in my life, but I wasn't okay with him no longer being *in* this life. If that happened, I would never be good again.

Picking up my phone, I managed to bring up the number to the office where I had the interview. Canceled it and booked a flight to Denver.

When I arrived, I called Rory.

"No news yet. He's still in surgery. Did your interview go okay?"

"I'm here in Denver, at the airport."

"What?"

"What hospital is he at?"

"Reese, there's nothing you can do. I was planning on

calling you as soon as he got out of surgery and we knew more."

"Mom!" It was a rare time of me calling her Mom instead of Rory. "What. Hospital?"

"I'll come get you," she said in a calmer tone before ending the call.

Forty-five minutes later, Rose climbed out of the passenger's seat when they pulled up to the curb. "We're all praying for him," she whispered when she hugged me.

I blinked back the emotions burning my eyes and nodded in lieu of actual words.

When we arrived at the hospital, Fisher's family and other familiar faces from work crowded the waiting room.

His parents and siblings.

Hailey.

Angie.

We shared a few sober "hellos" before I tucked myself in the far corner of the room with Rory and Rose. And then we waited. When the doctor came out, his parents and Angie gathered in a circle around him. A collective sigh of relief could be felt. It was good news. He made it through surgery.

When we determined only family would be allowed to see him later that night, I went home with Rose and Rory to their new house.

"You didn't move that far." I found a small grin when they pulled into the driveway of the home that was maybe three blocks from Fisher's house.

"This was a foreclosure. We basically stole it. Works great. We find ourselves taking a walk several nights a week and still ending up at Fisher's house, drinking beer and wine on his front porch or the back screened-in porch." Rory shrugged, shutting off the car. "What can I say, he's family. Only ..." She frowned. "Not enough to get to see him tonight."

Rose squeezed my mom's leg. "We'll see him tomorrow."

Rory nodded.

We ordered dinner, but none of us were that hungry. Instead, we shared funny Fisher stories as if he was dead and we were reminiscing about his life.

"Oh..." Rory drained the rest of her wine "...how'd your interview go?"

I shook my head while pouring another glass of wine for myself. Finally, I was able to join the real adults in the room. "I canceled it. Told them it was a family emergency."

"I was a little surprised when you called from the airport," Rory said. "I know you two worked together for a while, and I joked about you acting like siblings, but when was the last time the two of you even spoke?"

Rose gave me a nervous glance. I considered just telling Rory about Fisher and me. I was nearly twenty-four—what would she have been able to say or do at that point? I'd moved on. He'd moved on.

For whatever reason, with him in the hospital and engaged, I opted to wait. Maybe until a better time. Maybe never. Did it matter any longer?

"I don't know ... it was weird. I mean ... it's been years since we've spoken, but when you told me, it hit me hard. I'm not sure why. And I didn't even think; I just canceled my interview and got the first flight to

Denver. Maybe it's because I know how close *you* are to him."

"I'm sure he'll be thrilled to see you, even if the circumstances are crappy."

I nodded slowly. Would he be *thrilled* to see me?

THE NEXT MORNING, we made our way to the hospital after Rory talked to Arnie. He said Fisher was a little fuzzy in the head, but otherwise okay. The accident was just that, an accident in the rain. A large truck couldn't stop and ran into Fisher.

When we reached the waiting room, Angie was in tears as Fisher's sisters consoled her.

Did he take a sudden turn?

It wasn't impossible. I'd seen my fair share of patients come out of surgery, seem stable and fine, only to flatline hours later.

Arnie broke away from the pack of women. "Long time no see. How have you been?" He gave me a hug.

"Good." I lied. "Are you famous yet?"

He released me and chuckled. "Almost."

"What's going on?" I nodded to Angie and his sisters.

Arnie frowned. "Oh, my brother's acting a little drunk that's all. I'm sure it's the pain meds. The doctors aren't too concerned yet."

"What do you mean he's acting a little drunk?" I asked.

"Memory issues. He doesn't seem to know everyone. Well, he knows me. Our sisters. Our parents. But nobody from work thus far. In fact, he doesn't remember building homes. And..." he scrunched his nose and whispered "... he doesn't recognize Angie at the moment."

"Oh no." Rory's eyes widened as her jaw fell open.

"Come on, might as well see if he remembers his favorite drinking buddies." Arnie smirked at Rory and Rose.

I followed the three of them to Fisher's room.

"More visitors. Pretend like you recognize them." Arnie teased Fisher as we filed into his room.

I stood behind Rory and Rose as they paused at the foot of his bed. I could only see bits and pieces of him.

His bandaged face.

His casted arm.

"Rory and Rose," he said in a rather weak voice.

It didn't matter how weak his voice was; it still did things to my crazy heart.

"Ding. Ding. Ding." Arnie gave Fisher a slow clap. "Two for two, Bro."

"No more motorcycle for you," Rose said as she moved to one side of his bed while Rory inched closer on the other side of the bed, leaving me in clear sight.

He knew them, so he would know me. I was quite certain of it. I gave him a small smile.

He smiled back. "Hi."

"Hi."

"Please tell me we haven't met. I fear I've already made too many people feel insignificant today," Fisher said.

Rory and Rose exchanged a look.

"How has your brain misfired so badly that the

hottest women in your life are just ... poof ... gone?" Arnie shook his head at Fisher.

Fisher narrowed his gaze, as if doing so increased his chance of recognizing me, as if it were his eyes' fault and not his brain's fault.

"This is Reese, my daughter," Rory said. "But you haven't seen her in years, so don't stress. She lived with me in your basement for a few months. And she worked with you for less than ... what?" She glanced at me. "A few months?"

I nodded. It was all I could do. Of course Angie was crying. When the man you love (loved) didn't recognize you, it wasn't a great feeling.

"She just graduated from nursing school in Michigan. She's going to get her master's starting next year. Midwifery. She's going to deliver babies."

Fisher returned a slight nod. "Congratulations."

I cleared the thick emotion from my throat. I think only Rose sensed my true level of emotions. "Thanks," I managed to say. "I'm really happy to see that you're okay."

"Yeah. That's what they tell me. I don't remember the accident either."

"The doctors think his memory loss is probably temporary," Arnie said.

I knew it could be temporary. Or it could last a long time. Or it could be permanent. The brain was hard to predict.

"I hope so." Fisher stared out the window for a few seconds. "That um ... woman was really upset. My fiancée?"

Oh my gosh ...

That woman. He reduced Angie to "that woman." I was never an Angie fan, but I also wasn't a monster. I felt her pain. He didn't ask me to marry him, but I felt total devastation at his lack of recognition. I could only imagine how Angie must have felt.

"Well..." I returned a nervous laugh, feeling Rose's gaze on me "...I'm sure it must be heartbreaking to be a stranger to the one you love most."

Fisher's brow tightened into lines of wrinkles. "I'm sure you're right."

"We'll let you get some rest." Rory leaned down and kissed the side of his head. I wanted to be that close to him.

Feel the warmth of his skin, the brush of his lips, the intensity of his eyes as he looked at me with wonder and anticipation.

The irony? Had I "given" him my virginity, he wouldn't have remembered. I don't regret it being Brendon, even if I hurt him. Had it been Fisher, I wouldn't have been able to walk away. I would have treated losing my virginity like donating a kidney.

More Fisher Mann lessons ...

It wasn't about firsts. *Every* moment mattered. Every touch. Every word. It was selfish to think of our lives as nothing more than an endless series of giving and taking. It implied we were, more or less, just moving from one moment to the next with no meaning. I knew ... deep down I *knew* it was never about my virginity. Not with Fisher. It was always about my heart.

Looking at Fisher in that bed and being unrecognizable to him was a clear reminder that I, nor anyone else, shouldn't rely on another human to be a measure of self-worth and success.

"Ready?" Rory asked me.

I nodded slowly.

CHAPTER FOUR

"I've missed this ... you know ... time with you two," I said on a long sigh as the three of us took a hike in the mountains several days after seeing Fisher in the hospital.

"We never took our trip up here," Rory said, reaching for her water bottle in the side pocket of her backpack as we stopped at a clearing. "I promised to bring you here. Remember when you were adamant about coming up here by yourself?"

I nodded. "Can I be honest now?" I smirked.

She rolled her eyes. "You drove up here anyway?"

Shaking my head, I chuckled. "No. Fisher brought me ... on his motorcycle."

"Oh, Reese." Rory shook her head. "I didn't need to know that, especially since his accident."

"I said you wouldn't be happy about it, but he said we didn't have to tell you. He really was a terrible influence. I can't believe you left me with him."

Rose rubbed her lips together, enjoying the way I was telling Rory so much, yet nothing at all.

"Well, as soon as he gets out of the hospital, I'll have a word with him."

Rose laughed. "You're going to talk to him about taking your daughter on his motorcycle when he doesn't remember her? Good plan. Make sure I'm with you when this conversation takes place. I want to listen."

I laughed too. It wasn't funny, but it was.

"What do you think will happen if he doesn't regain all his memory?" Rory slipped her water bottle back into her backpack. "Do you think he will fall back in love with Angie?"

Rose shrugged. "If it happens, it will be incredibly romantic. What is there? Over seven billion people in the world? And he falls in love with the same person twice? Sadly, I fear it won't happen like that. I mean, I can see him being the nice guy who marries her anyway because everyone adores her, and he'll trust the people he does remember."

"He's known her forever," Rory said. "I think he'll remember her. She owns too much of his heart."

"Unless ..." My big mouth opened without me realizing it. Then it was too late.

"Unless what?" Rory asked.

Abort!

"Unless it's not about time. I mean, you said you knew there was a connection between you and Rose from the day you met. Sure, Fisher's known Angie for years, but why did it take him so long to decide to marry her? It wasn't like you and Rose. Nobody was standing in their way. Just the opposite. Everyone wanted it. Except Fisher. I'm just saying ... the length of their history isn't necessarily an indicator for the likelihood that he'll fall back in love with her. What if he wasn't truly in love with her? What if she was just the obvious choice for lack of a better one?"

Rory blinked slowly. "Okay, everyone make a note that Reese is never allowed to talk to Angie."

"I'm not saying she isn't nice." We started walking again. "Or a good catch. But there must be more. That's all I'm saying."

Rose nudged my arm. "We know ... you're *just saying*."

I smirked. Yes, despite my life experiences and emotional revelations—a lot prompted by Fisher—I still liked the idea that he fell in love with me in a matter of weeks, despite it making no sense to anyone else. And since he couldn't dispute it, because he had no recollection of me or us, I felt perfectly fine with letting that version of our story live in my head forever.

"I LOVE HAVING YOU HERE. Are you thinking of moving back to Denver? There are jobs here. You can get your master's here," Rory questioned me as we drove back to Denver.

"Let her be," Rose scolded my mom.

"I'm not pressuring you. I'm simply asking the question and stating a few facts."

"She's not staying." Rose rolled her eyes at Rory.

"It's not a terrible idea," I murmured from the back seat.

"What?" Rose twisted her body to give me a wide-eyed expression.

"See? I know my girl. She's always been *my* girl."

I didn't break Rory's heart by disputing that. I *was* her girl, and maybe part of me always would be, but my intentions for considering a move back to Denver had little to do with her.

And from the look on Rose's face, she knew it. And she wasn't happy about it.

I didn't care.

I wasn't the eighteen-year-old girl she found on the floor with Fisher. A lot had happened. And while I had no expectations of him ever remembering me, I just ... I wanted to be near him. I needed to know that he would be okay, even if that meant standing by while he fell in love with Angie again, while he married her, while he started a family with her.

My faith hadn't completely died. I did have faith that things would work out, whatever that meant.

CHAPTER FIVE

"Hey, girl!" Hailey pushed her desk chair back as I opened the office door.

"Hey, yourself." I hugged her.

"Congratulations, Nurse Capshaw."

I laughed, releasing her. "Thank you. I'm not done. But I'm excited to spend the next year working instead of being in school. Then I'll finish up my master's."

"We didn't get a chance to talk at the hospital. But ... a midwife, right?" She sat on the edge of her desk.

"Yes. I worked with a midwife in Thailand. I didn't make an instant decision that I wanted to be a midwife, but I looked forward to every day with her. I got butterflies whenever she announced that someone was in labor. And I couldn't sleep for hours after a birth. The adrenaline. The sheer amazement. And it never got old. I witnessed nearly thirty births, and they were all a little different. They were all special in their own way. So ..." I didn't have to grin. I realized I'd been grinning since the second she said the word midwife.

"That is awesome. I'm thrilled for you. Maybe you should move back here and deliver my babies when I have them. Hopefully sooner versus later." She held out her hand.

"Oh my gosh! You're engaged?"

"Married." She shook her head. "Hawaii wedding. Less than ten people were there. His name is Seth and he's a mechanical engineer. Met him online. We're actually coming up on our one-year anniversary."

"No way! I can't believe my mom didn't tell me. Congratulations."

"Thanks. So ... did you make it in the room to see Fisher? I hear he might go home in a few days. What's it been? Three weeks now?"

I nodded. "Yeah. I heard he's going home soon. And I did see him once."

Her nose wrinkled. "Did he recognize you?"

My head inched side to side. "But at least I'm not his fiancée."

"Oh my god! Right? I feel so bad for Angie. Like ... what if he never gets back those lost memories? And will he be able to work? He doesn't remember anyone from work except his dad and uncle. Does he remember his skills?"

I shrugged. "Hard to say. He might not. Or he might get all his memories back tomorrow. But what does Angie do? Wait for them to come back? Or settle into the possibility that he won't remember her, and she needs to see if they can fall in love again?"

"Not Fisher." Hailey shook her head. "I'm not saying the accident hasn't possibly changed other things about him, but I can see him just doing it. Like ... his family telling him how much he loved Angie. How they had gone through so much over the years to finally be together. And how he was all in, ready for that life. I see him nodding and just ... marrying her. Figuring the rest out later."

"That would be..." I wrinkled my nose "...interesting. It would feel like an arranged marriage on his part. The whole 'Trust us, you're perfect for each other.' I couldn't do it. I was engaged to the wrong guy for a day, and I couldn't go through with it."

"Wait, you were ..."

I put my finger to my lips. "And Rory doesn't know. Nobody knows. I don't know if he told anyone. Since I broke it off, I highly doubt he told anyone."

"A day?" She laughed. "What happened?"

He wasn't Fisher Mann.

"It was impulsive. On his part and mine. And I still hadn't made a clear decision on the direction of my future, so I couldn't say yes to marriage and a family. Not yet."

"Smart girl."

"How are things here? Who's in charge now that Fisher's recovering?"

"Me of course." She winked. "His dad and uncle have been covering things. He has great guys working for him. There's not a lot to worry about. Houses are still getting built."

"That's good."

"So when do you go home? You've been here for weeks, right?"

"I don't have a job at the moment, so there's been no rush to get back home. It's been nice spending time with my mom and Rose. But I'll probably head back to Michigan soon."

After Fisher goes home.

"Sure you don't want to stick around here?" She tilted her head and gave me a goofy smile.

"Actually, I'm not ruling it out, if I can find a good job. And I'd need to look into the master's program. But ..." I shrugged.

"Do it!" She giggled. "I'm a little biased, but DO IT!"

I laughed. "I'll see what happens in the next month with job prospects. Rory and Rose are already on top of looking for things around here. When I get back to Michigan, I'll see where things stand with a few openings that were available before I came here."

Before I skipped out on an interview because my heart was more mature but still just as foolish as ever when it came to the naked fisherman.

"Well, don't be a stranger. Five years is too long." She winked.

"Agreed." I hugged her again. "Good to see you."

UNDER THE GUISE of job searching, I stayed just long enough for Fisher to get released from the hospital. Rory didn't complain at all. Rose didn't either, but I knew she was on to me.

"I called Angie and told her we'd drop dinner off but not stay long. I don't want her to worry about food or have the burden be on his family." Rory packed containers of food into bags. It was more than one meal's worth.

"Good idea," Rose said from the kitchen table, working on lesson plans.

"Peanut butter cookies." Rory shook a container filled with cookies. "Fisher loves peanut butter. I bet that makes your stomach turn, huh, sweetie?"

Fisher didn't make my stomach turn. He still made it do things, but only good things. But peanut butter was not back on my food list yet.

"I've tried it several times during school, but nope ... still can't do it." I glanced up from my phone. "Ready?"

She nodded.

"Don't hate me, but I'm staying here. I'll stop by this weekend to see him. I'm just behind with my lesson plans." Rose frowned.

"He'll understand." Rory kissed Rose's head. "Love you. See you in a bit."

"Love you too," she muttered.

All the terrible things I was told about homosexuality. All the terrible, *judgmental* things that went through my head. And there I was watching my mom and Rose so in love. How could so many awful things be said and done in the name of God? It wasn't His fault. It was a flaw with humanity's need for control.

"Maybe being home will spark something with his memory," Rory said as we drove to his house.

"Maybe. Is Angie living with him?"

"Yes, she has been since her mom passed. I bet

tonight will be weird for them. Getting in bed with a stranger."

I nodded slowly, preferring not to think about Angie and Fisher in bed. The last time I recalled her being in his bed, he was in the basement with me, and we were on the pool table doing very naughty things. Maybe the pool table was what they needed to show him.

Don't be that person ...

My conscience berated me and rightfully so.

When we pulled into the driveway next to Fisher's work truck, I grabbed one of the bags from Rory, just to have something to do with my hands to hide my shakiness, my nerves.

"He got a new work truck?"

"Yeah, I think it was about two years ago," Rory said, ringing the doorbell.

"Hi. Come in. This is so generous of you." Angie took the bags from us as soon as we stepped inside.

Fisher was in a leather recliner, TV on, blanket over his legs.

"Hey, handsome. Welcome home." Rory took the liberty of being one of the people he knew, and she kissed him on the head and patted his good hand. His other arm was still in a cast.

Fisher lit up like a child at daycare when a parent picked them up. Familiarity. "Hi. It's good to be home." He eyed me.

I smiled. "I saw Hailey the other day. She assured me things were fine. You need to just recover."

"Hailey?"

"Hailey runs your office. Reese worked for you

briefly. Remember? I told you that in the hospital. Reese stopped by to see Hailey."

"Sorry." He rubbed his forehead. "A lot happened in the hospital."

"It's fine. How are you feeling?" I asked.

"Pretty good. Can't sleep well yet, but I'm tired a lot. I don't like how the pain meds make me feel, but everyone seems to think I should still take them. I think they just want me to shut up and sleep while they pray my memory fully returns."

Just as he said that, Angie appeared from the kitchen, and just as quickly, she returned to the kitchen. Rory gave me a look. "I'm going to see if Angie has any questions about the food we brought."

I nodded.

"You can have a seat." Fisher lifted his chin, signaling to the sofa.

"Thanks." I eased my butt onto the edge, gripping my knees to keep my hands steady. Everything was so weird, so awkward.

"What do you do?" He caught nothing Rory said to him at the hospital.

"I just graduated from nursing school."

His lips twisted. "Did Rory tell me that? Is that something I should have known?"

"I think she mentioned it, but it's fine. You sent me a graduation card." With a goofy, tight smile, I shrugged. "So ... thanks."

He chuckled. That was the Fisher I remembered. That soft chuckle accompanied by a slight head shake. "You're welcome. Did I put money in the card?"

"No money."

"Hmm ..." He frowned. "Kinda cheap of me. Sorry about that."

Okay, maybe he wasn't the same Fisher. It was really hard to tell at that point.

It was my turn to laugh. "It's fine. I don't think college graduations are like high school graduations."

"Maybe. Did I write something nice in the card?"

I found his genuine interest entertaining. As heartbreaking as his accident was, as his memory loss was, I couldn't deny the new Fisher brought a smile to my face. "Yes, I believe you wrote something nice in the card."

"Was it lame like, 'The future is yours,' or 'Much success?'"

On another laugh, I shook my head. "No. If I recall correctly, you were way more original than that."

"It's funny. I'm trying to remember if I ever recall Rory talking about having a daughter."

"Well, if you don't remember me, then it's unlikely you'd remember her talking about me."

He stared at the television, but I sensed he wasn't focused on the show. "Did you like working for me?"

Biting my lips together, I gave that careful thought. That wasn't an easy question.

"You're hesitating. Is that a no?"

"You were focused and driven. I was young and, honestly, a little clueless in my life at the time. You hired me as a favor to my mom, but I'm certain you had some days that you questioned why you made that offer."

"Oh? Why do you say that?"

Before I could answer, Rory and Angie returned. Angie's eyes were red. She'd clearly been crying.

"Everything okay?" Fisher asked, concern etched into his face. "Did I mess up again?"

Oh, Fisher ...

It was hard to fully put myself in his shoes, but I tried. I tried to imagine a complete stranger coming up to me and telling me they were my fiancé. We were in love. And I simply didn't remember. How does one navigate that? Would I have been able to play the part? Pretend to be in love?

It wasn't that I didn't see it from her side—clearly, he didn't remember me either—but I kind of saw it from his side a little more. Probably because I wanted to see it more from his side.

"You didn't do anything, babe. It's just been an emotional few weeks. You're home now. Life will start to feel normal again, and I'll get past my silly emotions." Angie kneeled on the floor next to Fisher's chair and held his good hand, giving it a kiss and pressing it to her cheek.

Fisher visibly stiffened, and when Angie glanced up at him, he forced a smile. The smile one would have given to a stranger.

She had no choice but to put her heart out in the open on a platter for him to cut into tiny pieces with his unintentionally insensitive comments. However, I kept my heart a little more guarded.

We ended.

I moved on.

He moved on.

End of story.

That was my brain's version of the story. Another reason I kept my heart guarded was to keep it from fighting with my brain. It didn't feel like I had moved on. It didn't like to think of Fisher moving on. And it definitely didn't like to think our story had ended.

"We'll give you two some privacy. I'm so glad you're home," Rory said.

Before she could take a single step toward the door, Fisher spoke up. "You should stay for dinner. I know you sent way too much food for two people."

"Oh ..." Rory shook her head, giving Angie a questioning expression on a quick glance. "No. Rose is home. And I made the food for you two. You don't have to eat it all in one night. We'll drop by another night. Maybe we'll bring pizza and beer."

"Yeah, babe. You need to rest anyway." Angie continued to pet his hand and arm. He didn't want to be alone with her.

"What's so funny?" Rory asked.

"What?" I narrowed my eyes.

"You're smiling. What's so funny?"

"Nothing. Sorry. I didn't mean to smile. I'll rein that in."

Fisher snorted a laugh. "Yep. She's your daughter, Rory."

With no success, Rory attempted to hide her grin from me. "Let's go, *Daughter*. Don't you have a job to find or crosswords to construct?"

"Crossword puzzles?" Fisher did that head tilt that I'd always adored. My little puppy dog. More like a wolf back then.

"Yes." I smiled, wondering if that would jog his memory. "A cruciverbalist. Ever heard of that?"

I knew Rory missed it, and Angie did too, but I didn't. I saw that tiny twitch at the corner of his mouth just before he shook his head once. "I ... I'm not sure."

"Fisher's not a crossword puzzle guy. But he did win a spelling bee. Right, babe? I think your mom told me that once." Angie tried to demonstrate her expertise.

It *thrilled* me to know that he shared that secret with me and not her. And his memory might have cherry-picked things from his brain, but not the crossword puzzles because I saw it, the twitch, even his eyes changed a tiny bit into something along the lines of curiosity or satisfaction.

"A cruciverbalist is a person who enjoys crossword puzzles or constructs them," I said.

Fisher ...

That look. Was it the look he gave me the very first time I told him about my pastime? Was *that* the look I missed? Was that the moment he knew I was more than just an eighteen-year-old girl with freakishly long arms and unlikely to wear socks with my tennis shoes?

I wasn't trying to take him away from Angie. I was only trying to find *my* naked fisherman.

My naked fisherman *did* enjoy crossword puzzles.

My naked fisherman wouldn't marry someone just because his family thought it was the right thing to do.

My naked fisherman ... well, I didn't know if he still existed.

But I sure wanted to find out.

"No offense, but it sounds like a nerdy hobby."

"Fisher, that's not nice." Angie, bless her ignorant heart, came to my rescue.

"Reese's dad used to construct puzzles." Rory played the middle ground. Very matter-of-fact. She wasn't trying to make anyone feel bad.

Fisher nodded several times. "Your ex-husband died. Right?"

Wow.

Fisher remembered that, but not me.

"Yes. Shortly before Reese turned fifteen."

"Well, I'm on a roll today. Another asshole remark from me. Maybe I should just take my meds and go to sleep."

"It's fine," I said. "I'm sure someday I'll find my nerdy, cruciverbalist soul mate. And he will find my affinity for clues and words to be endearing. Maybe even sexy." I winked.

A wink.

For my naked fisherman.

Then it happened again. The corner of his mouth twitched.

Yes, Fisher. You're my cruciverbalist soul mate, you stubborn ass with a broken brain.

"I'm sure he's out there. Good luck." Fisher kept his gaze on me.

"He's probably in hiding. Not all cruciverbalists are brave enough to admit their passion to the world."

"Mmm ..." he hummed while giving me an easy nod.

I had his attention.

Not his memory.

Not his engagement ring.

Not his bed.

Shaky ground at best, but I took it.

"Well, goodnight, you two," Rory said as I followed her to the door.

"Thanks again," Angie replied.

"Yes. Thanks," Fisher added.

CHAPTER SIX

DEAR LOST FISHERMAN,

I just got home after spending weeks in Denver making sure you'd be okay. You don't remember me. That's fine. Maybe it's best if you don't.

After five years, the world's shortest engagement, college, a tattoo, and some serious sinning, I thought I was over you. I found my passion and followed it. I gave my virginity to a worthy man who might have cherished it more than I did. And I found my fucking voice.

Then I saw you. And it was ...

Nine across: Eleven letters. Hint: A calamity.

Catastrophe.

I found it therapeutic to write down my thoughts and feelings. It was the easiest way to let go of them. It had been years, not since my father died, that I felt the need to journal my thoughts. But losing Fisher brought out *everything*.

Anxiety.

Unsettled emotions.

Destructive hope.

Loss of direction.

I gave myself some time. Some time to sort out my feelings before taking a job anywhere. I let my resurrected naked fisherman emotions sort themselves out.

Rory kept me updated on Fisher during my break for perspective. It didn't help my perspective.

Rory: Fisher's doing better. A little stir crazy.

Rory: Fisher can't sleep. Terrible anxiety.

Rory: Fisher tried to go back to work today. Angie is not happy.

Rory: Feeling so bad for Angie. It's going to be a long road for her and Fisher.

Most of my replies were short like, "Sorry to hear that," or "That's too bad."

Two weeks later, Rory called me.

"Hi."

"I found you a job," she said.

I laughed. "What makes you think I'm still looking for a job?"

"Because it's two in the afternoon on a Thursday and you answered your phone on the first ring. And if you had a job, you would have told me by now."

"Speaking of jobs, don't you still have one?"

"My next client canceled at the last minute. Anyway, speaking of clients and jobs ... this morning I had a new client. Know what she does?"

"As a matter of fact, I don't," I said.

"She's a midwife. She works in a clinic with three other midwives. They practice midwifery and all kinds of women's healthcare. I'm actually going to start seeing her. She tests for hormone imbalances and stuff like that. I could use a good balancing. I told her about you, and she said she'd love to talk to you about possibly working with her, assisting in the clinic and during labors because she just lost her nurse whose husband got transferred to another state for his job. I told her I'd call you right away. I also gave her your contact information, so expect a call. She's really excited that you assisted a midwife in Thailand for nearly a year."

"She's in Denver?"

"Well ... yes. Of course."

"How do you know I'm for sure still thinking about moving back to Denver?"

My relationship with Fisher was much better when there was a good twelve hundred miles between us. Going back to Denver would magnify everything again.

"Because you love Rose and me and you miss us. And did you hear me say *midwife*?"

It was a great opportunity.

"I'll talk with her. No promises. How's ... Rose?"

"She's fine. I guess a few of her students are driving her crazier than normal. She's thinking it might be time to look for a new position, something in high school."

"That's probably smart. How's ..." I worked my way

to my real question. Not that I didn't care about Rose. "Fisher?"

"Oh, Fisher ... I don't know. I mean. He's upset that he's still in a cast. Upset that he can't sleep. Upset that he can't remember the people who work for him or anything else about his job. But if I'm reading between the lines correctly, he's upset that he can't remember the woman living with him. And I feel *so* incredibly bad for Angie. She's considering taking a new job in pharmaceutical sales because it involves traveling, and she thinks it might be good for her and Fisher to have some separation. She's hoping absence makes the heart grow fonder, but I gotta be honest with you, I'm not sure he'll miss her. And it's not *her*. It's him. He's hating life at the moment. Drinking more. Smiling less. Rose and I feel like enablers more than friends when we stop by to see him. It's like he's dying for an excuse to drink. And he knows Angie won't drink with us because she's too busy researching memory loss and a million ways to bring it back. It's all very awkward."

"Is he seeing a therapist?"

"No." Rory laughed. "Angie is, but Fisher won't. Not yet. He doesn't feel comfortable talking to a stranger about a bunch of other strangers. His words."

"Sounds about right. Well, everyone needs to let him find his own way through this. If he doesn't want help, you can't force it on him. And maybe Angie's right. Giving him space might help. Stress doesn't help the healing process, and his brain needs to heal."

"Yeah, Rose and I told her to take the job, but Fisher's family isn't so sure. They think her job should be getting

Fisher to fall in love with her again. But unrequited love is very hard on the heart."

I nodded to myself. "Yes. It is."

"Call me after you talk to Holly. That's the midwife. Holly Dillon."

"I will. And thanks. It does sound like the perfect opportunity, even if I'm not looking forward to moving again."

"I know. Talk soon, sweetie."

THE PHONE INTERVIEW with Holly went well. Perfect, in fact. Breaking my year lease wasn't the ideal way to manage my money, but I took the loss, rented a small U-Haul trailer to pull behind my car, and drove to Denver over the course of three days and two nights.

What I didn't expect to find was Rory, Rose, *and* Fisher sitting on Rory's and Rose's front porch when I arrived around dinnertime. My nerves did stupid things along with my heart and the butterflies in my tummy. He didn't remember me. Why did I act like a naked student on the first day of school?

"She's home!" Rory set her wine aside and ran toward me.

"Hi." I hugged her when she did her attempted tackle move on me.

"How was the drive?"

I sighed, blowing my hair out of my face. "Long."

"Hungry?"

"Starving," I said.

"Let's eat first then we'll unload your stuff. I made chili and cornbread muffins."

"Sounds amazing." I followed her toward the porch.

"Hey, girlie girl." Rose stood and hugged me. "So good to see you."

"You too."

"I'm just going to pop the muffins back in the oven for a bit to warm up." Rory opened the front door.

"I'll get the table set." Rose followed her.

The door shut, then it was just us.

"Hi." I smiled. It was difficult to approximate the proper size of a smile to give Fisher. Nothing too exuberant. Nothing too pitiful like I felt bad that he was in a cast and suffering from anxiety ... maybe even on the verge of alcoholism as his favorite coping mechanism.

"Welcome home. And congratulations on your new job."

"Thanks. I hear you're recovering well."

He grunted a laugh before taking a pull of his beer. "Who told you that?"

"Rory."

"I'm recovering. Well? Not so sure about that."

"Where's Angie?"

"My fiancée?"

On a nervous laugh, I nodded. "Um ... yeah."

He shrugged. "Not sure. I said something to piss her off *again*. So she left. She'll return. She always does."

"Well..." I leaned against the corner pillar of the porch "...you sound like a bundle of joy. I can't imagine why she'd leave your cheeriness."

That brought a tiny grin to his face, and he slowly

shook his head before scratching the back of his neck. "She's fine. Really. A beautiful *stranger*. I was clearly a lucky man."

"Was? You survived a pretty intense accident on your motorcycle. I'd say you're still lucky. And you still have a fiancée. What's the problem? Are you having erectile dysfunction issues? It's not uncommon after accidents."

He choked on his beer and wiped his mouth with the back of his hand. "What the fuck? No. Why would you ask me that?"

I took his beer and helped myself to a long swig. A little mixing of saliva.

He raised a single eyebrow.

Yeah, Fisher ... I'm not the deer-in-the-headlights girl you don't remember. I swap saliva. Drink beer. And have sex. Sometimes I even touch myself because it feels "good."

"I'm a nurse. It's strictly a medical question. It can be hard on relationships when accidents impair sexual function. And sometimes it's not a physical disability as much as it's an emotional issue."

"My dick works just fine."

"Maybe you should do something that takes your mind off your situation."

"What's my situation?" He grabbed the beer bottle back from me and frowned when he noticed it was empty.

"Your arm is still in a cast. I'm sure your family is still coddling you. And you're living with a stranger who wants you to get fitted for a tux so she can take your name and have your babies."

His lips twisted. After a few seconds, he nodded several times. "That's not entirely inaccurate. So what distraction do you suggest?"

"I could give you some of my crossword puzzles to work on."

There it was again. That look. The one I missed as a nervous eighteen-year-old girl with an insane crush on the naked fisherman. The one I *didn't* miss when we took dinner to his house after he came home from the hospital and I told him about my hobby.

"Why do you keep mentioning puzzles? I'm not sure I even like crossword puzzles."

"No?" I did his signature head cock. "Huh ... I thought I felt a vibe. Must not have."

"A crossword puzzle vibe?"

"Something like that." My lips pressed together to conceal my grin.

"Dinner's ready," Rory said as she opened the door.

Fisher's gaze stayed glued to me, just where I liked it. Where it belonged.

"Need help standing?" I pushed off the pillar and held out my hand.

Shaking his head, he leaned forward and stood on his own while mumbling, "I don't need help getting anything up."

"Believing you can is half the battle," I murmured back to him as I headed into the house.

It was just a whisper, but I felt pretty certain he said, "Smart ass," as he followed me into the house.

"Let's get your stuff unloaded," Rose suggested right after dinner.

"I don't have a lot. I sold the big pieces because I knew you wouldn't have room for them, and I didn't want to store them." I headed out to the driveway.

"Fisher, do you want a ride home?" Rory asked as she set the dinner dishes by the sink.

"It's three blocks. I think I can manage. Besides, I should help unload Reese's things from the trailer."

"No." I turned just as I stepped outside. "Your arm is in a cast."

"So?"

"So we've got it."

"I have one good arm." He stepped outside, forcing me to take a step backward.

"Save it. We've got this. You know my arms are freakishly long." I said it, and I couldn't unsay it. For a second, I let myself forget that Fisher didn't remember me or anything about me.

"They are?"

I nodded slowly before turning and making quick strides to the trailer. "That's what some jerk told me once." Opening the trailer, I grabbed one box while Rose took another box.

Fisher grabbed a box too and wedged it between his arm and chest, following us into the house, into my bedroom.

Rose set her box down and headed back outside. I set my box on the bed and started to brush past Fisher as he set his box next to mine.

"Was I the *some jerk*?"

I stopped in the doorway with my back to him. After a few seconds to figure out an honest answer, I glanced over my shoulder. "You were my favorite jerk." I shot him an exaggerated smile, using fake humor to hide the depths of my emotions. "But yes ... you made fun of my long arms." Without waiting for his response, I strode outside again.

Rory joined us, and the four of us had everything unloaded in less than ten minutes.

"Thank you, Fisher." Rory thanked him before I got the chance to do it. "You sure you don't want a ride?"

"No ride. Thanks for dinner."

"Night, Fish," Rose called from the kitchen as she started washing dishes.

"I'm going to lock the trailer and my car," I said to Rory as I followed Fisher out the door.

"Okay."

We said nothing while strolling down the driveway. I veered off to the left to lock the trailer.

Fisher stopped, sliding his good hand into his back jeans pocket. "I don't really think I'm going to care for them, but if you want to drop off some puzzles ... just..." he shrugged "...whenever. I'll give them a try. No rush. It's really ... no big deal."

I locked the trailer and leaned my back against it, crossing my arms over my chest. "Okay. I'll drop some off tomorrow."

"There's no rush." He tried so hard to be nonchalant with me.

"Okay." I nodded several times. "So ... I'll drop them off tomorrow."

He fought his grin, but it won.

I won.

"I guess tomorrow is fine."

I didn't know who Angie got when they were together. I didn't know the anxiety ridden Fisher my mom had told me about.

My Fisher was still in his skin. Too cool for his own good.

A streak of crudeness.

And a little *extra*.

"I was uh..." he tipped his chin to his chest "...looking through pictures on my phone. And I came across some of you and one of us. We were in the mountains. Your hair was longer. But other than that, you looked the same. Do you remember that?" Fisher forced his gaze up to meet mine. Confusion ate into his face along his brow and at the corners of his eyes.

I smiled. "Yes. My memory is fine."

"And ... what were we doing? Was Rory there too? She wasn't in any of the pictures."

"No. It was just us. Rory was in California for work. I had never been in the mountains, and I really wanted to go. But both you and Rory had a little fit over me driving there by myself. So you took me. On your motorcycle. We stopped at that lookout point and snapped a few pictures. Then we ate pizza at Beau Jo's pizza on our way home. It ..."

My grin swelled. "It was a good day. A great day, really. My first time in the Rockies. My first time on the back of a motorcycle. My first time dipping thick wheat pizza crust in honey."

He nodded slowly. "So we did stuff outside of work?"

"Sometimes. We went on a double ... well ... triple date once. Arnie invited me to one of his concerts. You and Angie were there, and my friend and her boyfriend joined us as well. I was underage; therefore, I was the DD that night."

"Huh ..." He inched his head side to side. "It's so weird. Like Angie showing me a million photos and videos from our time together, and nothing is familiar. I don't remember the trip to the mountains or the concert."

On an easy smile, I stood straight and uncrossed my arms. "Well, I remember for the both of us."

"You don't appear bothered that I don't remember. Angie seems on the edge of going nuclear after we've spent hours trying to jog my memory with the photos and videos."

I nodded slowly. "I think love—the good kind—holds an equal mix of wonder and familiarity. That feeling like you know someone, yet you also know parts of them are still a mystery that you can't wait to slowly discover. If there's no wonder, I think the love *can* die. If there's no familiarity, I think the love already feels dead. If I were the one marrying you, I would be bothered more than I am. But you chose her."

Oh ... my ... sweet ... lord ...

That was not the right choice of words. And as much as I hoped and prayed Fisher would let my word choice slip by without a second thought, it didn't happen.

"I chose her?"

FUCK!

Yes, I adopted that word into my vocabulary, like a

favorite tool in a toolbox that I used only on a need-to basis.

"Gosh..." I twisted my lips and rolled my eyes dramatically "...that sounded really weird, didn't it?" For good measure, I threw in an awkward laugh. "I'm so freaking tired from long days of driving. I meant *proposed.*" I shook my head. "Yeah, that's what I meant. You *proposed* to her. Just her. Not like you had a choice between her and someone else. At least ... not that I know of. And definitely not me, of course, because until your accident, I hadn't seen you in five years. Gah ..." I covered my face with my hands. "Please just tell me to shut up."

He smirked just like the Fisher I knew five years earlier. Like the Fisher who *didn't* choose me. The Fisher who was finally willing to take my virginity with the understanding that *my husband* (not him) would thank him someday.

"I find your rambling too entertaining to tell you to shut up."

"Go home and find your fiancée entertaining."

Something between a grunt and laugh left this chest. "I'll do my best."

"Night, Fisher. Thanks for your help."

He turned and headed down the sidewalk. "Anytime."

CHAPTER SEVEN

I PLAYED it cool the next day for a full three hours after waking before I walked the crossword puzzles over to Fisher's house. Rory and Rose were at work, and I didn't start my job until the following week, so no one was keeping tabs on me.

I knocked on the door several times.

No answer.

I rang the doorbell.

No answer.

As I gave up and started to retreat down the sidewalk, Fisher opened the door.

Just my luck ...

He was wet and holding a towel around his waist. The past replayed itself. I liked the idea of a redo with Fisher.

"I'm running late, babe!" Angie appeared in the doorway in a pantsuit and her handbag dangling from one arm. She lifted onto her toes and kissed him on the lips. He kissed her back.

It wasn't a long kiss, but it wasn't one sided either.

"Morning, Reese. Can't stay and chat. Byeee!" She waved to me with her left hand, big diamond, and manicured nails, just before hopping into her car.

I mumbled a barely audible "hi" and turned my attention to the resurrected naked fisherman. As I made my way to the front porch, he watched Angie back out of the driveway before shifting his attention to me.

"Good morning."

My gaze struggled to stay on his face.

"Not pretty, huh?" he said.

I shook my head as if I hadn't been staring at his road rash that was healing fairly well. "You're alive. I think the prettiness of your skin should be an afterthought."

He retreated into the house, leaving the door open— which I took as an invitation to go inside.

"Angie seemed in a good mood. You must have done something right for once."

He continued down the hallway toward his (their) bedroom. "Apparently she just needed to get laid. Had I known, I could have obliged her sooner." He shut the door behind him.

That was a pretty hard hit. It took a good pep talk to get my emotions in check before he reemerged from the bedroom.

He proposed to her.

She said yes.

Even if he didn't remember her, it didn't mean they couldn't have sex. Sex didn't have to involve emotions. Men paid for sex with prostitutes—not that Angie was a prostitute or Fisher was the kind of guy who would pay for sex. I needed a way to wrap my brain around it before the disappointment sent me spiraling out of control.

I took a seat at the island in the kitchen. A few minutes later, he came into the room in jeans and a white tee. Hair still wet. "My dick works, Nurse Capshaw. In case you're still concerned." He poured himself a cup of coffee and dropped two slices of bread into the toaster.

My breakfast was a mini vomit in my mouth that I swallowed back down. "Still so crude."

"Crude?" He turned and leaned his butt against the counter, sipping his coffee. "Was I crude to you?"

Did he want the truth?

"Had my mom not been living in your basement, I'm pretty sure I could have won a sexual harassment lawsuit against you and your crudeness." I might have been feeling a bit feral and defensive after confirmation that he screwed Angie the previous night.

How dare he have sex with his fiancée. (Internal eye roll at myself).

"Are you..." he squinted at me "...serious? I was inappropriate with you?"

Wow! It seemed to really bother him.

I gave my answer some thought. Of course, my knee-jerk response would have been, "You zip-tied me to a stool and *ate me out.*" That response gave away too much information. I wasn't actively trying to break up his engagement. Not consciously, anyway.

"You had a gift for making me blush. That's all."

He kept his mouth hidden behind his coffee mug. Was he grinning?

"Do tell. What kinds of things did I do to make you blush?"

"I ..." I laughed. "I'm not going to tell you. I'm sure most of it was because I was young. I'd spent the previous three years in a Christian academy, and Rory was gone, so I think you were bored. Embarrassing me became your favorite pastime."

After another sip of his coffee, he set his mug on the counter. "Well, I'm sorry." He seemed serious.

The long moment of silence conveyed a level of genuineness. Then a case of untimely giggles hit me. I just ... started laughing, and I couldn't stop.

Even with my hand cupped at my mouth, my laughter continued. "I'm ... I'm sorry. I just don't believe you."

"What don't you believe?"

"That ..." I took a deep breath to control my laughter. "That you're sorry. You told me your dick still works."

"Only because yesterday you asked me if it worked."

"As a nurse. I asked you in a professional way."

"But you're not *my* nurse, so it made you look like my friend's daughter simply asking about my dick." He retrieved the butter from the fridge.

"No peanut butter? You can't possibly be out of peanut butter."

He shrugged. "Yeah, I don't know what's up with that. Everyone tells me I love peanut butter. Rory made peanut butter cookies. I mean, it's all right, but I don't feel a big love for it."

"I hate it."

"Really? That's interesting. I don't know what I hate.

Or I don't remember what I hate. It's weird how some things are clear and other things just don't exist. Not like I don't remember them well, it's that they are not there at all."

I nodded. "The brain is a mysterious place. For everything we do know about it, there seems to be so much we still don't know and may never fully understand. Don't stress over it."

"I'm not, but I feel the stress from everyone around me."

I didn't know what to say. So I said nothing more about it for a minute or so before changing the subject. "I brought you some crossword puzzles." I set the folder on the counter.

"Oh ..." He glanced over his shoulder. "Are we done talking about my memory and my dick?" That smirk ...

Different guy, yet same guy. Just missing a few memories.

"I hope so. Do you need help spreading that on your toast?"

"Do I look like I do?" He had butter on his cast and his toast kept slipping off his plate onto the counter as he tried to spread it.

"No. You don't. You look like you have everything under control."

He hugged the tub of butter to his chest with his casted arm and used his good hand to press the lid back onto it. After he returned it to the fridge, I noticed a glob of smeared butter on his shirt. Rolling my lips between my teeth, I kept silent.

"You not working today?" He looked down, frowning at his shirt.

"I start my new job on Monday. Are you not working today? Because you clearly could do about anything. That cast isn't holding you back one bit." I snorted.

Fisher glanced up, eyes narrowed. "Are you picking on a disabled person? How Christian of you."

"Sorry. What can I do for you today? Rake the leaves in your yard? Shave your scruffy face?"

"My face?" He paused his chewing. "Angie said I needed to shave or at least trim my beard. She offered to do it, but I said I could do it myself."

"Of course you did." I smirked. "If you were left-handed, you'd be fine. But you're not left-handed."

"You know my handedness?"

"Yes, but if there was any question, that butter fiasco I just witnessed confirmed it."

"Smart ass." He ate his toast.

I watched him eat it. And we shared familiar glances. Well, familiar to me.

"I'll let you trim my beard. But you can't tell anyone."

"Okay. Why is that?"

"Because I want Angie to think I did it on my own."

"You do realize ... this is the woman you asked to marry you. The whole 'in sickness and in health' thing. Right?"

He shook his head. "I didn't propose. She did."

"Uh ... you remember that?"

"She told me. She's told me everything. I officially have all the memories of our life thus far; they just aren't mine. They're hers, which makes it about as real to me as someone reading me a fictional book."

"And she proposed?"

"Yes."

"How do you feel about that?"

He shrugged. "I don't know. I asked her if she knew why I hadn't proposed."

"What did she say?"

"She said I needed a nudge."

"Interesting." That shocked me. Rory didn't tell me Angie was the one who proposed. "Well ... are you done? If I'm going to secretly trim your beard, I should do it now. I have some errands to run."

"Okay. We can do it now." He set his plate in the sink and nodded toward the hallway.

I followed him to the master bathroom where he shrugged off his shirt with his good arm and tossed the shirt on the floor.

"Have you trimmed a beard before?" he asked, pulling the trimmer from its base and turning it on like he was testing the battery.

"Yes. I've trimmed lots of things." I plucked the trimmer from his hand. "Sit." I nodded to the vanity bench that wasn't there when Fisher lived alone.

He sat down, draping a towel over his lap to catch the hair. I focused on his face. Not his scars. And definitely not his abs or happy trail. Nope. I was a total professional. Except for my thoughts. They played in my head like a day at an amusement park.

I've been in that tub naked.

I know what your penis looks like because I gave you a blowjob in that doorway to your closet.

"What's so funny?" he asked.

"What?" I turned on the trimmer.

"You were grinning."

I really needed to practice a straight face while fantasizing about the naked fisherman.

"Sorry. I won't smile again." I started near his sideburns.

"Don't apologize. It's a great smile."

I felt his gaze on my face, but I kept my focus on the trimmers so I didn't do anything stupid like nick his ear or kiss him.

"Did you leave a boyfriend behind in Michigan?"

He made it hard to control my breathing in his close proximity, and asking me personal questions didn't help the situation. "I left several boyfriends behind in Michigan, but I left them long before I decided to move back here."

"Do you like Colorado better than Michigan? Or did you want to be closer to family?"

I wanted to be closer to you.

"A little bit of both. I think I knew that if I didn't move back here, your beard would never get trimmed."

"Ha ha ..."

I stole a tiny glance into his eyes before resuming the beard trim. "I do love it here. And I missed my mom. We no sooner reunited after five years of separation while in prison, and she left for California. Not long after she returned, I went to Thailand. Then Michigan."

"It's crazy that I remember Rory but I don't remember her going to California."

"Well..." I used my finger to tip his chin up "...if you remembered her going to California, then you would remember me."

"True. What did you do in Thailand?"

I missed you. Developed feelings for another man. Gave away my virginity. Found my calling in life. And missed you some more.

"Mission trip. Originally, it was just going to be for six months. But the friend who convinced me to go, he wanted to stay for another six months. Best decision ever. I assisted a midwife. And that's where I fell in love with midwifery. So I went back to Texas after Thailand, just long enough to have my grandparents help me get my tuition paid."

"So you owe this guy, your friend, a big thanks for convincing you to go to Thailand."

"I suppose I do."

And Fisher. I owed him a thank-you for helping me see just how terrible the timing was for *us*.

"That's pretty cool," Fisher said. "I like when fate does its thing. Had a friend of my dad's not given me a summer job with his construction company, I probably would have gone to college just to play sports. Who knows how that would have ended?" Fisher shrugged a shoulder. "Angie said she wanted me to play baseball in college. She thinks I would have gone pro." He chuckled. "Apparently, I've known her since we were six. Our moms had our wedding planned before we left elementary school."

"So ... you remember that you love construction, but you don't remember owning a construction company? And you remember your family, but you don't remember the girl you met when you were six? The woman who you proposed ... well, said 'yes' to?"

"Maybe it's a sign."

"A sign?" I tilted my head.

"Maybe it's a sign we need more time."

"Oof ... I hope you haven't said that to her." I turned off the trimmer, removed the guard, and blew on the blades before returning the guard to its place and setting it on the counter.

Fisher ran his hand over his closely trimmed beard. "What if I don't remember her? What if I don't ..." He rubbed his lips together, his gaze averted to the floor.

"What if you don't what?" I took the towel from his lap and shook the whiskers into the trash.

"What if I don't fall in love with her again?"

I coughed a laugh. "Um ... you had sex with her last night." I couldn't look at him. I wasn't eighteen, but I also wasn't immune to the bathroom we were in or talking about sex with the naked fisherman.

He jerked his head back as if my statement made no sense. "Sex isn't love."

"It might be to your *fiancée*."

"She wanted it. And you suggested my dick might not be working properly, so I did it. Now she's happy. And Nurse Capshaw is satisfied too."

I shook my head and cleared my throat while tossing the towel in the hamper. "Please don't have sex with ... *anyone* to satisfy me. I'm just an old employee, your friend's daughter who you can't remember. And ..." I held up my arm to look at my watch, being very dramatic about it so he would drop the topic. "I need to run errands now."

"Where are you going?" He followed me out of the bathroom.

"I just said I'm running errands."

"Yeah, I'm not deaf. I meant, what errands?"

"Target and the uniform store to get some new scrubs."

"You should invite me."

As I reached his front door, I turned. "You think so?"

He shrugged, looking so handsome it made me want to cry. Stupid life timing. What I wouldn't have given for him to have stepped closer, to have made me melt with one look.

Are you going to kiss me?

I'm thinking about it.

"Give me thirty minutes to get home and make my list. Then I'll pick you up."

A slow grin worked its way up his face, warming my skin and forcing my heart to do some silly beat skipping.

CHAPTER EIGHT

"NEVER THOUGHT I'd see this day," I said as Fisher climbed into my vehicle.

"What day is that?" He fastened his seat belt.

"The day you jumped at a chance to go to Target and a uniform store because you're so bored."

"I'm not bored. In fact, I finished one of the crossword puzzles while waiting for you."

Tossing him a quick glance, my eyes narrowed. "You didn't. They weren't easy puzzles."

"Maybe not to you." He stared out his window and shrugged.

He left me speechless for a few blocks.

"I need gas." I pulled into a gas station. After filling the tank, I ran inside to get something.

Fisher eyed me and the drink in my hand when I returned.

"For you." I handed him the plastic cup filled with red liquid.

"What is this?"

"Iced tea and fruit punch." I handed him a straw too. "Your favorite."

He ripped open the straw and poked it into the lid. "It is? How do I not remember things I like and dislike? Do I have food allergies? Will shellfish kill me? I mean ... I don't know." He took a sip. "But what I do know is this is really good. I clearly knew my shit."

I grinned, putting the car into *Drive*. "Easy partner. Your head's getting too big."

He took another long sip. "What else should I know about you?"

"Me?"

"Yeah. I know everything about that Angie girl because she's told me everything. She's AB blood type. Allergic to walnuts. Scared of spiders. And she cries easily."

I laughed. "Well, hmm ... I'm O-positive. No allergies. You already know I don't like peanut butter. Spiders are okay. I like my coffee extra sweet. And I don't watch a lot of TV."

"I watch a lot of TV. It's a distraction from the stranger living with me."

"The *stranger* you had sex with last night."

"Yes, to prove that my dick worked and to get her to stop being so weird."

I giggled. "Weird? What do you mean by weird?"

"She's constantly watching me. It's creepy. And she's too ... cheery. Not like you."

"Whoa ... not like me?"

"No. You're selectively happy. Which is normal in my mind. Like you are who you are. You could hate puppies and rainbows and not give a shit what anyone thinks about it."

"I ..." I shook my head. Was that how he saw me? "I do not hate puppies. But rainbows are a little overrated."

His shoulders shook on a light chuckle as he sucked on the straw.

"I do like learning new things, and you taught me how to sand wood. Nothing too hard, but I asked you to teach me things, and you did. I still like hands-on things."

"I taught you things? Sanding?"

I nodded.

"In my workshop?"

Another nod.

"Huh ..." He seemed perplexed.

"Is that surprising?"

"I think so."

"Why?"

"Because I've been told by more than one person that I like to do my own thing. I hire people who already know what they're doing. I'm not much of a teacher. I don't have enough patience."

"Mmm ..." I nodded. "They might be right. And I said you taught me. I didn't say you were patient with me. I'm sure you indulged me just to be nice to Rory."

Fisher hummed. "Maybe," he murmured.

We pulled into Target. "Are you staying in the car? I only have a few things to grab." Tampons. I needed tampons. And deodorant.

"No. I have my own list of things to get." He climbed out of the vehicle.

After we walked into the store, he grabbed a shopping cart while I plucked a basket from the stack.

"You can just put your stuff in my cart."

"Or you can get the stuff on your list and I can get the stuff on my list, and we can meet back here when we're done."

"What's the rush? I don't have to work. You don't have to work. We might as well walk the aisles and let the end displays tell us what we didn't know we needed," said the guy who dragged me in and out of an apparel store in record time when I needed boots and a hard hat.

Surrendering to the fact that I'd be making a second trip that day to get my tampons, I slid my basket back into the stack and followed Fisher's lead.

"So what are you getting?" I asked.

"What are *you* getting? Show me your list and I'll show you mine."

I rolled my eyes, despite my grin and complete feeling of bliss. "My list is in my head."

"Mine too."

I giggled as we strolled through the electronics aisles. "Then how are you going to 'show' me your list?"

"I assumed you could read my mind. You know ... since you guessed my favorite drink."

"I didn't guess." I playfully nudged his good arm as we crossed over into the cards and party stuff.

"Did you get lots of birthday parties when you were a kid?" He grabbed a big party hat from a tall stack and set it on my head.

I kept walking down the aisle with the hat on my head. "I got lots of parties since I was an only child, until

Rory went to prison. Mostly Disney princess parties. What about you?" I snagged a funny pair of glasses that had a big nose and mustache attached to them. Then I slipped it onto Fisher's face.

"Oh yes. My parents have always celebrated everything. And I have a huge family, so even things that weren't a big deal seemed like one because fifty gazillion people were there, and that was literally 'close family.' You were at the hospital. Tell me the waiting room wasn't filled to capacity with my family."

I laughed as we continued to stroll, garnering funny looks from other shoppers since I still had on the hat and he wore the glasses. "Point made."

"Do you use an alarm clock?" Fisher picked up a retro looking alarm clock, the kind with an actual bell.

"I use my phone. Does anyone use an alarm clock?"

He pointed to the clock in his hands. "Someone does."

"Fake plants or real plants?" I buried my nose in a fake bouquet of decorative flowers.

"Real."

"Agreed." I nodded.

"Halloween. Best holiday ever or most annoying holiday ever?" Fisher asked when we crossed a main aisle to the seasonal displays. Lots of Halloween stuff.

"I'm inclined to say best."

He wrinkled his nose at my answer.

I turned to face him, holding onto the cart while walking backward. "And before you unfairly judge me, you have to know that after Rory went to prison, I didn't get to go to parties because my grandparents said

Halloween was Satan's holiday, so my dad caved to their nonsense and didn't let me go. Then he died and I didn't have a prayer of ever going to anything fun like a costume party. So imagine my excitement when my roommates wanted to have a Halloween party my first year of nursing school."

He grinned, matching mine. "Let me guess, you dressed up as a naughty nurse."

"Pfft ..." I shook my head.

I totally dressed up as a naughty nurse. I also had sex with Batman that night. Good sex. Two beers, lowered inhibitions, and false confidence sex.

Naughty nurse ended up dating Batman for eight weeks.

Fisher eyed me through his funny glasses. "Then what was your costume?"

"Um ..." I glanced around as if I'd see something and use it.

"You were a naughty nurse."

"I wasn't!" I giggled.

"Liar."

I turned forward again, still giggling. He knew. And I could no longer hide it.

We spent an hour in Target. There was a lot one could learn about a person by spending an hour with them in Target, such as neither one of us cared that people were looking at us in our hat and glasses.

Fisher was a huge Star Wars fan.

I owned over thirty Barbies by the time I was ten.

We both loved big mirrors.

Fisher had never played pickle ball.

And I was a sucker for bookends in the shape of animals. Specifically elephants.

"Your list ... what did you need?" he asked as we approached the pharmacy area.

I sighed, no longer feeling like I wanted to hide my list and come back later. "I need deodorant and tampons. What do you need?" I quickly countered before he had a chance to react to the tampons.

"Mouthwash and condoms."

Gulp ...

He steered the cart toward the tampons first.

Figures.

"Applicator? No applicator? Regular? Super? These are made with organic cotton in case your vagina is eco-conscious."

And there it came ... that blush only Fisher could bring out of me so quickly. I snagged the box I needed and tossed it into the cart.

"So your vagina *is* eco-conscious." He grinned. "Noted."

Oh my gosh ... what exactly is he "noting" and why?

We grabbed my deodorant and his mouthwash, making our final stop in the condom aisle.

"I'm a little surprised Angie isn't on the pill." I fidgeted with the hem of my T-shirt. Old habits never died.

"Apparently, she went off the pill in preparation for getting pregnant."

I nodded. "So you're going to have kids right away. That's exciting."

He tossed a box of condoms in the cart. "I'm not sure

if it's exciting, hence the condoms. I'm a little hesitant to make a child with someone if I'm not sold on the idea of marrying them yet."

I followed a few steps behind him.

"So you're just going to hump her and dump her."

He stopped so quickly I ran into his back.

"Oof ... why'd you stop?"

Facing me, he squinted and twisted his lips. "You don't think I should have sex with her if I'm not certain I want to marry her?"

With a tight smile, I lifted a shoulder. "I don't have a strong opinion on it. But I imagine she does. Maybe you should make sure you're on the same page. The intimacy might lead her to believe all is good between the two of you. That's all. It's the male brain versus the female brain."

Fisher waited until I felt a little squirmy before he responded with a sharp nod. "Good tip." Turning, he headed toward the checkout lane.

CHAPTER NINE

"It's like getting to wear pajamas to work," Fisher said, checking out the racks of scrubs.

"It sure is. And I can wear comfy shoes instead of work boots."

He glanced up at me, his hand resting on a pile of scrub tops. "Are you making a jab at me? Did I tell you to wear work boots? I should have. It's a safety issue."

"Yes." I picked out a top. "You took me to buy boots and a hard hat, but I wasn't wearing socks and that chapped you."

"Well, who doesn't wear socks to work?"

"Lifeguards," I said casually, moving a few steps to a different round rack. "I bet strippers don't wear socks either."

He tipped his head, pretending to be really interested in a pair of smiley faced scrubs. Then he chuckled. "They might wear fishnet stockings."

"Do you think you would have been okay with me wearing fishnet stockings with my work boots?"

Clearing his throat, he glanced around the store. "I'm dealing with some memory loss, so I can't say for sure where my head might have been in that moment." His lips twisted as his gaze landed on me. A tiny grin teased his lips. "I might have been okay with it."

"Well, that's shocking." I took my scrubs to the checkout counter and paid for them while Fisher waited by the door.

"Time to return you before your curfew."

"Curfew. Pfft." He rolled his eyes. "I was thinking lunch."

"You're milking this outing."

"I'm in a cast. Going crazy. Help a guy out."

"Help a guy out ..." I mumbled as we headed to the car.

I helped the guy out, as if my eternally foolish heart had a choice. We found a soup and sandwich cafe with whimsical decor and a quaint little booth in the back surrounded by snake ferns and hanging Pothos.

"Tell me all about Thailand," Fisher said after we ordered our food and drinks.

"How much time do you have?" I chuckled.

Leaning back, he stretched his good arm along the back of the booth. "I'm yours for the rest of the day."

Oh, Fisher ... you're no longer mine.

We spent the next hour and a half eating and talking all things Thailand. While it was my story to tell, Fisher asked lots of questions and seemed genuinely engaged and curious.

We laughed.

I got a little teary eyed telling him about a still birth that tore out my heart.

But for the most part, I shared my stories with enthusiasm, using my hands and making crazy expressions. He seemed to eat it up. Every word.

We ordered a slice of chocolate pie to share. Sharing our germs. Saliva swapping.

I didn't go into much detail about Brendon. Not our romance. Not our engagement. I never even said his name. Fisher was none the wiser. And not once did I think about the eighteen-year-old girl he didn't remember. I was too busy enjoying the moment—the moment he got to know the woman I'd become.

"Thanks for letting me tag along," Fisher said when I dropped him off at his house a little before three in the afternoon.

"Thanks for lunch. You didn't have to pay."

He ducked his head back into my car and grinned. "I invited myself. It was the least I could do." He winked.

THAT. That was almost too much. Tears came out of nowhere, sending me fumbling for my sunglasses.

"Well ..." I fumbled my words like my fingers fumbled my glasses. "Have a good rest of your day."

"I'll have a good enough day." He shut the door.

I made it out of his driveway and about ten feet down the street before my tears escaped on a heavy blink. Why did he have to wink at me?

Why did he have to be so fun and goofy in Target?

Why did he have to be so interested in my trip to Thailand, so interested in *me*?

CHAPTER TEN

SUNDAY MORNING BROUGHT an unexpected guest to our house. I had just returned from my morning jog. Three long faces at the kitchen table greeted me.

Rory. Rose. And Angie.

"Hey," I said with caution.

"How was your run?" Rory asked.

"Fine," I replied slowly, filling a glass with water. "Is ... everything okay?"

"Fisher suggested Angie move out and they date again." Just Rose giving me the quick explanation made Angie cry. Again, I assumed.

"Oh." That was the best I had, but I dug deeper for more. "Well, I'm sure that's hard to hear. But he's not saying he doesn't want you. And it's impossible for any of us to put ourselves in Fisher's shoes. But I'd imagine he's feeling overwhelmed."

"And how do you think I'm feeling?" Angie cried.

Rory frowned at me like it was my fault.

"I imagine you're feeling scared. Grateful that you

didn't lose him in that accident, yet you *did* lose him in many ways. It's like the family of someone with Alzheimer's. You realize that all the pictures and souvenirs from life mean nothing without the actual memories. You're a stranger to the person you love most in the world. And falling in love with someone is like offering a part of yourself to them. If Fisher doesn't recognize you, it's like you're missing a part of yourself. And you're questioning who you are or who you will be if you never get that piece back. But honestly, I'd imagine your biggest fear right now is that Fisher won't fall in love with you again." I pressed my lips together for a few seconds. I might have gone too far. "At least, that's how I would feel if I were in your shoes."

Angie blinked a new round of tears as her face wrinkled. "Y-yes ... that's exactly h-how I f-feel."

Rose hugged her. "He'll come around. You're a beautiful, kind, talented woman. He'd be a fool to not fall in love with you again."

"W-what am I supposed to do..." she sniffled and wiped her face "...about the wedding? Do we cancel? We've put money down on a venue. A florist. I've bought a d-dress."

Rory looked to me, her silent plea for help. Just because I read her mind regarding her emotions didn't mean I had great advice for her wedding plans.

With wide eyes, I shrugged and turned my attention to the rest of the water in my glass, gulping it down. "I'm going to grab a shower. I hope it all works out how it should."

Sadly, I thought it should work out differently than

she did.

MY FIRST DAY with Holly could not have been better. She was the midwife I wanted to be. Patient. Calm. Caring. Encouraging. The clinic was an old house with the rooms converted into 'exam' rooms, if you could call them that. They were decorated with a Zen theme. Nothing cold and sterile about them.

The midwives scheduled two hours with every person to give them the chance to ask questions and express concerns or fears about ... anything. One of Holly's clients was three months pregnant and stressed over what car to get for their growing family. Holly grabbed her computer and helped search for good options for safety, gas milage, best value, etc.

Who did that at a routine prenatal visit?

That was what I loved about Holly and the other midwives at the clinic. Nothing they did felt routine at all. Every client had their own birth plan, no two exactly alike.

Different needs.

Different inherent risks.

Different concerns.

She respected their decisions without judgment.

"How was your day?" Rory asked when I arrived home a little after six in the evening.

As if she couldn't tell from the grin on my face and the exaggerated bounce in my step. We spent the next hour eating dinner and discussing my first day.

"Enough about me, how was your day?"

"Interesting," Rory said.

"Understatement." Rose rolled her eyes as I grabbed her empty plate from the table.

"Do tell." I carried our dishes to the sink.

"Hailey called me on my way to work. Apparently, Angie unloaded on her too. Hailey asked me to talk to Fisher. *Then* Fisher's sister called me. Again, asking *me* to talk to Fisher. Then it hit me ... I must be his only friend. Why does everyone think that I can fix this? That he will listen to me? And I don't even know what I'm supposed to tell him because I *know* what it's like to not be in love with the person everyone thinks you should love."

My dad.

"Sorry, Reese," she whispered as Rose kissed the top of her head.

I leaned against the counter and crossed my arms over my chest. "Dad died ten years ago. I think you can officially retire from feeling guilty for not loving him the way you love Rose. Okay?"

She nodded slowly. "Thank you."

"As for Fisher, I think you can talk with him, but I'd listen more than preach to him. Think of what you wanted from people around you when you knew you were going to disappoint everyone for having feelings that only you could understand."

Rory gave me a look for a few seconds. I couldn't quite decode it.

"You sure have grown up. I'm so proud of you."

I wasn't sure how grown-up I felt. Experienced in

love and heartbreak? Yes. So much more than Rory realized.

"Thank you." I couldn't help my grin or the warmth in my heart. Nothing compared to feeling a mother's love. That year in Thailand with the midwife made me appreciate Rory so much more. "I'm going to read for a while and then try to get to bed early. Holly has two clients due in the next two weeks, so I'm on call. It's usually a rotating call, but two of the other midwives are out. One is on vacation. The other one has a child going in for heart surgery. So this could be a crazy and exhausting two weeks, but I'm so excited!"

"We're excited for you. Goodnight," Rose and Mom said to me.

The next morning, I headed out for my run. Waiting at the stoplight stood a familiar figure with a casted arm.

"You're up early." I slowed to a stop at the crosswalk.

Fisher grinned so big. "Good morning." And just like the Fisher I remembered, he took a few extra seconds to slide his gaze along the full length of my body.

My long-sleeved running shirt.

My jogging shorts.

Pink running shoes.

Shoulder-length hair pulled into a short ponytail.

I was so close to calling him out on it, the way I might have done five years earlier, but I didn't want to make him uncomfortable, given his present relationship status. Also, I feared he might stop looking at me that way if I said something.

"How was your first day?" he asked as we got the light to cross the street.

"Amazing, even though no babies were born. I'm on call. Should be two babies coming into the world in the next two weeks."

He chuckled, giving me a quick side-glance when we made it across the street. "Too bad you're not excited about it."

I laughed. Yeah, I *felt* completely lit up when talking about it. I could only imagine what he saw when he looked at me and my impossibly huge grin.

I nodded to the right, knowing he needed to go left.

Fisher looked down at our feet for a few seconds with his own grin solidly affixed to his face. He nudged the toe of my shoe with the toe of his shoe. "Well ..." His gaze slowly lifted to mine. Fisher wasn't ten years older than me. He was a twelve-year-old boy with his first crush on a girl. And I ... was that girl. And that was a side to Fisher Mann I didn't get to see five years earlier.

I never got to see anything but his confident side.

"I've solved all your puzzles, despite the difficultly of filling in the boxes with my left hand."

My nose wrinkled. I never thought about that.

"So I might need a few more to get me by until next week."

"What's next week?"

"I'm going back to work, whether anyone thinks I'm ready or not."

"I've seen you shop at Target. You're ready."

Fisher nodded while laughing a little. "Exactly."

"I'll drop off some puzzles after I get home from work later today."

"Perfect."

"Okay."

We clogged up the sidewalk, people passing us on both sides, as we stood in the middle of it facing each other in our little bubble.

My smile faded. "Rory is going to talk to you about Angie. I don't know what she's going to say, but everyone has been asking her to talk to you, to convince you to rethink things with Angie." My words flew out a mile a minute. In some ways, it didn't feel like my place to say anything to anyone, yet I couldn't *not* say something. "But I think you need to do what's right for you. It's not Rory or your family marrying her. It's you. And..." a pang of guilt tightened my stomach "...Angie is a good person. That doesn't mean we fall in love with someone just because they're a good person. I'm just saying, even if she's scared of it, she deserves honesty. And..." I shrugged "...my opinion should mean nothing to you, so take this with a grain of salt, less than a grain of salt. I think taking a step back and seeing if you can fall in love with her again is a good idea."

Fisher's brow wrinkled as he nodded slowly. "Thanks," he murmured.

I found my tiny grin again and gave it to him. "Bye, Fisher." I took a step backward, shaking my head as his gaze made a second trip up and down my body.

Oh, Fisher ...

We were in trouble, and I think he knew it as well. "Have a good day," I said.

"I'll have a good enough day."

Wink.

Gah! That wink.

CHAPTER ELEVEN

Dear Lost Fisherman,

I'm falling in love with you, again. But this time, you're earning it, even if it's not your intention. It's not that I ever fell completely out of love with you. Timing ... it really is everything in life. And I still struggle with all the things I was taught to believe. Are our lives predestined? Where does free will play a part? Are destiny and fate real? Or is it merely what we call events in life after we're willing to acknowledge them, even if we refuse to accept them? I just ... don't know.

In the meantime, keep the smiles and winks coming my way.

Ten across: Seven letters. Clue: Awakening.

Rebirth.

"Hey, Rose. Where's Rory?" I asked as I set my bag by the entry and slipped off my shoes after work.

Rose glanced back at me from the stove. "She's having dinner with Fisher. The talk."

I raised my brows. "Sounds intense."

"She's in an awkward position."

I nodded. Seeing her stirring pasta, I grabbed a jar of sauce and emptied it into a pot. "She should have told his family and even Angie that it's not her place to tell Fisher what to think or do."

"Is that your unbiased opinion?" Rose shot me a look.

I smirked. "It's been five years. I've had other boyfriends. Angie asked Fisher to marry her. Why would you think my opinion by this point would be biased?"

"Maybe because you were so easily able to articulate everything that Angie's feeling. Like you have or *are* in her shoes. Like you're in love with a man who doesn't remember you."

Keeping my chin down, gaze on the sauce as I stirred it, I shrugged. "Want to know what I think would be incredibly romantic?"

"I don't know, do I?"

I released a quick laugh. "Probably not, but I'm going to tell you anyway since you've managed to keep my and Fisher's secret all these years."

"Lucky me. Then do tell. What would be incredibly romantic?"

"A true second-chance romance. Falling in love with the same person twice. Each time, feeling brand new. No memories of the first time. Just ... something about that person that makes you fall in love with them. Every. Single. Time.

"That chilling kind of love that maybe does last more than one lifetime. The truest definition of soul mates. If I were Angie, I wouldn't want to marry Fisher unless he did, in fact, truly fall in love with me again.

"Nothing forced. No timeline. No expectations. Just the butterflies in the stomach and insane giddiness of new love. If Angie loved him the way she claims to love him, she'd see that he's not the same Fisher. She'd see the subtle changes in his personality. And she'd feel this indescribable excitement at the chance to get to know the new Fisher and fall in love with him all over again."

Rose turned off the burner and rested her hand on my wrist to stop me from stirring the pasta sauce.

I looked over at her, the lines of concern along her face and the intensity—the concern—in her eyes. "Oh, Reese, you're going to get hurt."

On a nervous laugh, I shook my head and continued stirring as her hand dropped to her side. "I don't know what you're talking about."

"You didn't see them. Before his accident, you didn't see them. They were in love. You can't be that person, the one who tries to steal another woman's man."

"Like you stole my mom?"

She deflated.

I shut off my burner and set the spoon on the small plate as I blew out a long breath. "Rose, I love you. I love you with my mom. And I think things turned out exactly how they were supposed to turn out *because* you didn't give up on her. You never thought you were taking something—someone—who wasn't yours because you knew, you just *knew* she was, in fact, meant to be with you. What if I know? What if he's meant to be with me?"

She gave me a sad smile. "What if he's not?"

I swallowed hard. I wasn't delusional, just hopeful. "Then he's not."

"And you'll stay out of the way?"

"If he falls in love with her, if he decides to go through with the wedding, then I will stay out of the way."

"I'm worried you're going to play unfairly." Rose frowned.

Coughing on a laugh, I shook my head. "It's not a game, Rose. It's real life. I don't even know how I could play unfairly. I'm not the one living with him. I'm not the one sleeping in his bed. I haven't told him that we were more than friends, more than employee/employer *because* I want him to fall in love with me, not a bunch of memories of an eighteen-year-old girl." There. I said the quiet part aloud. I wanted Fisher Mann to fall in love with me ... again.

Angie gave him her whole damn body, a million photos, a million memories and stories of life since they were kids. I was a huge underdog. All I gave him was cruciverbalist. So if that trumped everything Angie gave him, then I thought everyone needed to back the hell off and let the two geeky word peeps have our happily ever after.

If ...

I knew it was a big *if*. An unlikely *if*. Maybe even an impossible *if*.

But here was the thing (it was an important thing), if a fifty-micrometer sperm could join with a point-one millimeter egg and result in an entire human being, then two cruciverbalists could fall in love … twice.

"It might be time to tell Rory."

I shook my head. "There's nothing to tell. The past is the past. And here in the present, there's still nothing to tell. But if anything changes and becomes *something* to tell, I will tell Rory."

"You promise?"

"Promise. Now, let's eat. I have to take some crossword puzzles over to Fisher tonight, after Rory gets home, of course."

"Reese …" Rose shook her head and rolled her eyes.

I grinned and shrugged. "Hey, he asked me to bring him more puzzles. No big deal."

"Angie packed a bag and has decided to stay with a friend. I think you visiting her fiancé will feel like a big deal."

"Well, then we won't tell her because they're puzzles, not nude photos of me. I'm saving the nude photos for closer to Christmas."

"Reese!" She playfully punched my arm as I giggled.

<hr />

"How'd it go?" Rose asked the second Rory walked through the door.

I glanced up from my book, one of many books on birth Holly gave me to read.

"Dinner was great. Just me and my friend Fisher,

enjoying pizza and beer. I talked. He listened. And he didn't seem the least bit surprised by anything I said. I'm sure he's been anticipating it since everyone else has talked with him already." She set her purse on the counter and plopped onto the sofa next to Rose, giving her a quick peck on the lips. "He wasn't angry. I think he's trying to put himself in Angie's shoes. I really do. But it doesn't change his feelings. And right now, she's a stranger. He thinks he enjoys spending time with her, but he also wants time to himself. I think she's still too much of a stranger to him to have her *there* so much. He wants space and time. He doesn't want to feel like he's the groom in an arranged marriage. Fisher wants to fall in love with his wife before he marries her." Rory shrugged. "And I can't blame him. He's having dinner—a date— with Angie this Friday night. So he's trying. He wants to date her. I say ... let them date. Let things happen naturally."

I nodded slowly with a tight grin. Rose gave me a quick evil glare in return. When Rory glanced at her phone, head down, I stuck my tongue out at Rose. She had to bite her lips together to keep from laughing.

"Well, if Fisher's home, I'm going to run these cross-word puzzles over to him before I crash for the night. He asked for more. Isn't that crazy?" I closed my book and stood.

"That is crazy. But I love that you have someone working on your puzzles." Rory smiled.

"I do." I smiled back, ignoring distrusting Rose. "See ya after a bit."

Since it was getting late, I drove to Fisher's house

instead of walking there. I may have also added a little makeup in the car and a dab of perfume to make up for the rest of my casual attire, jeans and a hoodie. I wouldn't have gotten away with anything dressier, not with Rose silently rooting for Team Angie.

"It's late. I assumed you weren't coming," Fisher said when he opened the front door. I stole a silent moment to take him in—always sexy in jeans and a tee. That messy, dark blond hair. The beard I trimmed for him.

"Rose told me you were having dinner with my mom, so I waited until she got home. If it's too late, I'll just give you these..." I handed him the pile of puzzles "...and head home."

"Too late for what? My roommate moved out. I'm officially free."

I frowned, following him into the house. "I heard Angie's staying with a friend while you *date* her. Big Friday night plans?"

He gestured to the sofa, and I sat in the middle while he took a seat in his recliner. "I don't know. What should we do? Dinner and movie? Just dinner? Do I bring her back here? Or is that too weird since I asked her to move out?"

"You don't remember the woman you're engaged to. I think worrying about weird at this point is an afterthought. Do whatever feels right."

Fisher ran his hands through his hair. "Ugh ... I don't know what feels right because I don't know how I'm supposed to feel about her."

"It's not about what you're *supposed to* feel about her. Ask yourself how you honestly *do* feel about her. Let that be your starting point. I think you've already done that to some degree. I'm sure it wasn't your family's idea for her to move out and the two of you date. That was you. Go with that voice."

"It's hard to go with that voice because I do have this other voice in my head, the one that tries to put myself in her shoes. I'm sure I would be really messed-up if I loved someone and they didn't remember me. I don't think I could just walk away without a fight."

Pulling my feet up and crisscrossing them, I formulated my response. He had no idea I was trying to see if I fit into his equation. "I couldn't ..." I smiled softly. "I couldn't walk away without a fight."

"You're so young." His lips turned into a pleasant smile. "How old are you?"

I chuckled. "What you mean is, how *young* am I? I'll be twenty-four soon."

"So you're twenty-three."

My eyes rolled upward. "Yes. I'm twenty-three."

"And have you ever been in love?"

Oh, Fisher ...

My mind immediately jumped back five years to the day on the playground.

"I'm trying so hard..." I whispered, my voice shaky in my chest and wobbly as the words fell from my lips "... trying so hard not to fall in love with you."

A few breaths later, he whispered back, "I know."

"Yes."

"Tell me about him. What happened?"

I laughed and cleared my throat, cleared the pain from the memories. *My* memories. Fisher didn't have memories of us. "Bad timing. I was young. And I was trying to figure out some things in my life. He had things in his life figured out quite well. So ..." I pulled in a shaky breath and shrugged. "It was just ... bad timing."

"Did he love you back?" Fisher wasn't the same man. The old Fisher wouldn't have asked me those questions.

"I think so." I couldn't look at him, so I fiddled with the hem to my shirt and kept my gaze on my lap.

"Do you know where he is now? Have you thought about finding him?"

More pain escaped my chest, disguised as laughter while I pinched the bridge of my nose. "Yes, I've thought about finding him."

"And?"

My head inched side to side as I continued to pinch the bridge of my nose. "And I'm not sure he's ready to be found by me."

"Why would you say that?"

My gaze lifted slowly to his. "Because he's found someone else." My lips fell into a frown as I lifted one shoulder like it was no big deal.

"Married?"

I shook my head. "No."

"Then he's fair game."

Barking a laugh, I glanced up at the ceiling again, gathering my hair in one hand and slowly releasing it as I made eye contact with him. "Fisher, you certainly have a liberal view of dating. You're not married to Angie, but you're dating her. So would you be okay with another guy making moves on her?"

Fisher shrugged, lips twisted. "If another guy made

moves on her and she responded to his moves, then I think I'd have my answer about us."

"What happened to fighting for what you want?"

"I think fighting for something when you have an actual chance is different than fighting for second place."

"Stick to building houses, Fisher. I don't think you have a future in couples counseling."

"No?" He grinned. "I'm just saying, if you're still interested in the guy, knock on his door and say, 'Remember me?' Then at least you'll know."

"And what if he doesn't remember me?"

"Then he never loved you."

I swallowed hard and nodded. "Well ..." I scratched my chin. "That's harsh and a little heartbreaking."

"Life is harsh and heartbreaking."

I giggled. "Who are you? Because this is not the Fisher Mann I knew. Did your head injury awaken some deep philosophical part of your brain?"

"No." He stood and stretched his good arm above his head and his casted arm about half the way. His shirt lifted a few inches, revealing his abs.

My gaze stuck like sticky spider fingers, and when I tore it away, after he dropped his arms back to his side, Fisher was looking at me. I felt the deer-in-the-headlights look on my face. His expression was more unexpected. Not the cocky one I remembered. It was more of a curious expression like he was in disbelief that I had been staring at his exposed skin.

That familiar blush crawled up my neck.

"I should go," I whispered, scrambling to my feet and brushing my hair away from my face.

"Thanks for the puzzles." His grin held so much satisfaction, his eyes filled with that familiar look he'd given me so many times before.

"You're welcome."

My phone vibrated and I pulled it from the pocket of my hoodie. "Oh my gosh ... oh my gosh! It's time."

"Time for what exactly?"

I glanced up from the screen, eyes wide, smile even wider. "Holly's client is in labor! I have to go. I'm ... I'm going to help deliver a baby. Eek!" I jumped up and down hysterically, and before I realized what was happening, I had my arms thrown around Fisher's neck, my body still doing its spastic jumping motion.

He rested his good hand on my back and chuckled.

"This is happening!" My hands went from his neck to his face, framing it, and I kissed him. It was quick, but ... *ugh!* It was on. The. Mouth. My excitement completely erased reality just long enough for my brain to fart.

Jumping away from him, my eyes widened even more as I covered my mouth with my hand. "I ... oh ... shit ... I'm so sorry. I ... oh ... shit. Fisher, I'm ..." I shook my head repeatedly.

When the shock dissipated from his face, he grinned. "It's fine."

I tucked my phone back into my pocket and turned toward the door. "I have to go. I'm so embarrassed. It was nice knowing ya." Flying out the door, I hopped into my car and bolted. I couldn't get miles between us fast enough.

CHAPTER TWELVE

I HELPED DELIVER a seven-pound twelve-ounce baby boy after twelve hours of labor. A water birth.

Then two days later, I did the follow up visit with the family to check on the baby and mom. She was glowing.

I focused on work and reading through the books Holly gave me, basically anything to keep from thinking about kissing Fisher. The weekend came and went. Rory and Rose hung out with Fisher on Saturday night, probably to get the scoop on his Friday night date with Angie. They invited me, but I declined, opting to just keep reading, just keep avoiding Fisher for approximately forever.

On Wednesday of the following week, I helped deliver a baby girl. Six pounds, eleven ounces. And perfect.

I loved every aspect of Holly's job. Wellness visits. Prenatal visits. Postnatal visits. Happy families. Tiny babies. Women feeling alive again after working with Holly to get their hormones balanced—to get their lives balanced again. Very rewarding work.

Holly and I had Thursday off to recoup from a long night of waiting for that sweet girl to make her way into the world. I was so tired and grateful for the time to get some sleep. After hours of not moving an inch in my bed, Rory woke me up.

"Are you having dinner with us?" She ran her hand through my hair.

I blinked my heavy eyelids open. "Um …" I rolled onto my back and stretched. "Yeah. I think so. What time is it?"

"Six."

"Yeah, I'd better get up so I can sleep later." I sat up and rubbed my eyes.

"No rush, sleepy head. Dinner won't be ready for another thirty minutes if you need a shower or whatever."

I nodded. "Yeah, I need a shower, at least to wake up."

"Okay." She kissed my head and left my room.

I padded to the bathroom and stripped into my bra and panties. There were no clean towels on the shelf, which meant Rory probably hadn't taken them out of the dryer.

I opened the door and crossed the hallway to the laundry room. Sure enough, clean towels were in the dryer. As I crossed the hallway again, I made a casual glance to the side, seeing something move. Someone move …

Fisher stood maybe three feet from me.

Me in my bra and panties.

Me holding the bath towel in my hand instead of covering my body.

He didn't hide his wandering gaze, not one bit. And I didn't hide any part of my body. After a hard swallow, he met my gaze. "I'll use Rory's bathroom."

"K," I whispered, wanting some tiny part of his lost memory to return upon seeing so much of my bared flesh. With no rush, I moseyed into the bathroom and shut the door.

Then I showered and touched myself while replaying Fisher's slow inspection of me. My hand pressed to the side of the shower, eyes pinched shut, jaw slack as I came, feeling weak in the knees.

Feeling empty.

Feeling impatient.

Feeling confused.

With wet hair, jeans, and a long-sleeved tee, I made my way to the kitchen. "Smells good." I smiled at Rory while taking a seat next to Fisher, the only seat left to take.

Rose passed me the dish filled with chicken and roasted veggies. "New baby?" she asked.

"Yes." I spooned food onto my plate. "A girl. Ivy Elizabeth. Tons of black hair. Ten fingers. Ten toes. And a strong, beautiful cry. When it was finally time, she pushed three times. It was a water birth. Fourth child." I laughed. "I'm not sure why we were there. The mom did everything. She knew when to push. When to rest. How to breathe. She grabbed the baby all by herself. Ivy cried. The mom put her right to the breast. It was ... beautiful." I realized I had tears in my eyes, and I quickly blotted the corners.

"Oh ... that sounds amazing, sweetie," Rory said, clearly not missing my emotions.

I refused to look at Fisher. What did he think of my sappy side?

"So ... how was everyone else's day?" I asked.

"Crazy, as usual." Rose laughed.

"How was your day, Fisher?" Rory asked him.

He wiped his mouth. "Fine. I've been playing catch-up this week, driving around to see where we stand on all the jobs. It's weird. So hard to describe. I don't remember the projects, but I know what to do. I have these skills that my brain does remember. And all I need are the plans and an update on where each project stands, and I magically know what to do. So then I met with new clients over lunch. And I spent a few hours this afternoon in my workshop. Who knew I had unfinished projects? I don't remember starting them, but again ... I know what needs to be done. When I get this fucking cast off, it will be easier to do things. I need to grow an extra hand to help hold things when I glue and clamp pieces together."

"When are you seeing Angie again?" Rory asked.

"Saturday. It's my dad's birthday, so they're having a get-together, and of course, she was invited."

I couldn't read him. Was he fine with that?

"Things going okay?" Rose asked while I kept my focus on my plate.

"I suppose. I'm trying, but sometimes I feel like she doesn't think I'm trying hard enough. She texts or calls me every day. And I think on the days I don't suggest we go somewhere or do something, that she's disappointed. Sometimes I don't answer her call because I don't know what to say. So then she texts me. And since I don't really *know* her yet, I can't possibly read her."

"Before Rose and I moved in together, we called or texted each other every day. I think it's normal for two people who are in love to talk every day. So you can't blame her for that." Rory did the best job of playing the middle ground. Trying to be the facilitator, the peacemaker.

Fisher nodded slowly. "Yeah, I suppose you're right."

Unless you don't love her. Do you love her?

"What do you need help with? In your shop? Because I'm up now. I won't be sleeping anytime soon. After dinner, I could help hold stuff for you."

"Just a corner shelving unit. And that would be great." He gave me a sideways glance.

I eased my head to the right just enough to give him a tiny smile, still unable to hold his gaze for more than two seconds. "No problem," I mumbled.

And just like that, we ended the Angie subject, and the mood lightened.

After dinner, I walked with Fisher to his house.

"Thanks for saving me," he said, playfully nudging my arm with his like I had done to him in Target.

Everything between us felt effortless and natural.

"Saving you?" I looked both ways before we crossed the street.

"All Rory talks about is Angie. I miss my beer drinking friend who used to tell me stories about her time in prison or her dreams of owning her own salon again."

"Rory has told you stories from prison? She hasn't told me any."

"I'm sure they're not stories she cares to share with her daughter."

I frowned.

"Speaking of stories, I love watching you come to life talking about your job."

My face filled with heat. "You mean when I lose my mind and kiss my mom's friend."

"You know..." he bumped the side of his body against mine again "...I don't have to just be Rory's friend. I can be your friend. The friend you kissed because you were so excited. I thought you might wet your pants." He opened his garage door.

"I wasn't going to wet my pants." I scoffed, following him down the stairs to his workshop. "But I did lose my mind. I was just so excited. So I don't want you to think I kissed you for any other reason than you just happened to be the only one in the room when I got drunk on an adrenaline and dopamine cocktail. I literally would have kissed anyone in that moment."

He eyed me over his shoulder, squinting as he flipped on the rest of the shop lights. "I'm not feeling quite as special at the moment. Why did you have to take that away from me?"

I laughed because it was funny, right? He wasn't serious. I didn't know how to handle him being serious about kissing me. Not yet.

As much as I wanted to steal back the naked fisherman, I didn't want to hurt Angie. But what if he didn't love her? If you loved someone, you wanted to hear their voice. Every text felt like a digital kiss. A wink of acknowledgment. That "hey, it's just me letting you know I think the world of you."

"Sorry," I said jokingly. "I'm sure you're really disappointed I didn't set out to intentionally kiss my *engaged* friend." And I added my signature eye roll to fully sell my innocent intentions.

Fisher seemed to let it all slide with nothing more than a grin. "I'm going to glue these two pieces, then you're going to hold them together while I clamp them. Okay?"

"Okay."

He glued. I held. He clamped.

We did this with a half dozen parts to the shelf.

"Perfect." He finished propping up the last two clamped pieces.

I ate up that look on his face, that look of satisfaction. I'd forgotten how much I missed watching Fisher do what he did best. Well, one of the things he did best.

"I am," he said, running his hand over the smooth board, his back to me.

"You are what?"

"I'm ... disappointed that you didn't intentionally set out to kiss your friend when you were overcome with excitement. And ..." He slowly shook his head. "I'm not proud of my feelings. Still, they're unintentional which makes them feel so very real. So here I am ... waiting for my memory to return so I can not only remember Angie but remember why I agreed to marry her. And maybe that's tomorrow. Maybe tomorrow I get my memory back, and it will make the feelings I'm having right this minute seem inconsequential. Nothing but the wandering mind of a crazy man." He turned, wearing a sad face.

"But what if my memory never returns? What if I spend months going on dates with Angie, dates where I'm not really thinking about her because I'm really wondering what Nurse Capshaw is doing. Is she working on crossword puzzles for me? Is she shopping at Target without me? Is she running in her sexy running shorts? Or is she delivering someone's baby and grinning from ear to ear? Is she so excited that she needs someone to kiss? And if I'm on a date with Angie, how can *I* be the one Nurse Capshaw kisses? And why is my thirty-three-year-old brain thinking about a woman ten years younger than me? Is it the accident? *Did* I permanently damage something? And after all these thoughts, my brain circles back around to the possibility that I might remember everything tomorrow. It's quite the quandary."

Yes. So many quandaries. I was in *quite the quandary* myself.

"Well ..." I inhaled and released it slowly. "I don't know how to respond other than to say that this Nurse Capshaw is a very lucky nurse. If she knew your feelings, I'm certain she would be flattered. And maybe a little sad too. Sad that you're feeling so tortured by your thoughts and the uncertainty of what tomorrow or a thousand tomorrows after that will bring. And I wish I had the answer for you. But I don't."

With several easy nods, he seemed to process my words. I was so ready to go knock on his door and say, "Hey, remember me?" But I knew he didn't.

"I finished your crossword puzzles. Do you want to see them?"

"You mean, do I want to check your work?"

"No. My work is correct. I mean, do you want to see them. I'm bragging, not looking for confirmation that I did them correctly."

I giggled. "So much confidence for someone who wasn't even sure he liked crossword puzzles."

"I still didn't say I liked them." He passed me and headed up the stairs. "I was just painfully bored."

Sure, Fisher ...

I followed him into the house.

"Beer? Wine? Water?"

"Wine would be great. I'm not on call for the next seventy-two hours."

"Wine it is." He pulled a bottle of wine from his wine rack, a corkscrew, and two glasses. "Let's go downstairs."

"Is that where your crossword puzzles are at?"

"Yes. I've framed them and hung them on the walls."

I laughed. "Sounds about right."

The puzzles weren't on the wall, but he flipped on my favorite globe lights and led me to the screened-in porch. So many memories.

The folders of puzzles were on the table along with several pens.

"Have a seat." He nodded to the chair where Rory used to sit.

I took a seat on the sectional, instead, in the exact spot we slept that night over five years earlier.

"You took my spot." He frowned, handing me my glass before trying to uncork the wine.

"Fucking cast," he grumbled, fumbling with the corkscrew in his left hand.

"Let me." I took the bottle from him.

He kept his frown pinned to his face; it only made me grin bigger as I easily uncorked it.

"And this isn't your seat." I poured myself a generous glass before handing him the bottle. "It's where I used to sit. And I know you don't remember that, but I do. So sit somewhere else."

He turned and started to sit on my lap.

"Fisher!" I held up my glass so it didn't spill.

On a hearty laugh, he adjusted his aim and sat right next to me. It was a little weird since it was a big sectional and there were two chairs as well.

"There they are. Read 'em and weep." He nodded to the puzzles.

"I don't need to read them. I have no doubt that you finished them. And I'm not a weeper." I sipped my wine.

"My cast comes off Monday."

"That's exciting. And nobody signed it. Not even Rory. Fisher, you need better friends."

"I'll second that. Here..." he leaned over me, putting way too much of his body heat and woodsy scent right under my nose "...you sign it." He handed me an extra fine-tipped Sharpie. That's how confident he was in solving the puzzles I gave him.

"You're getting it off Monday."

"So."

I shook my head, set my wine glass aside, and removed the cap to the Sharpie. Then I pulled his casted arm into my lap, bringing him close to me again. So close his breath brushed my forehead.

My heart screamed for me to do something more, but my brain unsheathed its own sword of common sense.

He was still engaged. I thought. Actually, I didn't know.

I lifted my head just enough that our mouths were sharing the same oxygen. Fisher's gaze fell to my lips for a breath, my lips that parted slightly. Then he met my gaze again.

"Are you going to kiss me?" he said.

He. Said. It!

It flipped my world on its head. Opposite world. A new kind of déjà vu.

I dipped my chin and pressed the tip of the Sharpie to his cast, making slow strokes, thinking extra hard to make each letter because I was writing it upside down so that he could easily read it when I was finished.

I'm thinking about it.

Keeping my chin tipped to my chest, I capped the Sharpie as he read his cast.

"And what exactly are you thinking?" he asked.

"I'm thinking about Angie. And I'm thinking about tomorrow," I whispered, tracing my finger along the letters on his cast. "If neither existed, I'd kiss you. Because ..." I released a long breath. "I *really* want to kiss you. Which means I should go home." On a nervous laugh, I stood and set the Sharpie back onto the table.

Fisher's good hand encircled my wrist. "Don't go. We still have wine to drink. And you haven't given stars or smiley faces to my completed crossword puzzles. And there's pool. Do you like to play pool? Or we could—"

In the middle of his desperate ramblings, his valiant effort to keep me from leaving, it hit me. No one had ever tried so hard to just ... be with me. And it felt amazing.

Pulling my arm from his grip, I turned and pressed my hands to his face, kissing him slowly while crawling on the sofa and straddling his lap, standing on my knees so it put me a little higher than him, so I felt in control.

Control of the kiss.

Control of the moment.

Maybe even the crazy illusion that I had control over what he did to my heart.

If he remembered Angie, that meant he'd remember me. He'd remember us. And I wanted that to be enough, but I didn't know what made him say yes when Angie proposed to him. If it was love, then I needed to keep my heart on a tight leash while we did ... whatever we were about to do.

When I ended our kiss, I smiled over his lips and he smiled back. "You can have all the stars, Fisher. And the smiley faces too. But I'm going to kick your ass at pool, and I won't feel sorry for you when you *weep* like a baby."

"We'll see."

We'll see ...

Oh the memories those two words brought back to me.

"But for now. Kiss me again." He lifted his head to capture my lips, but I pulled away. "No. That's it. That's all you get today. If you still want me to kiss you tomorrow, then I'll kiss you tomorrow. One day at a time, Lost Fisherman." I climbed off his lap and headed to the door.

"Lost Fisherman?" He stood.

"Yes. You are my lost fisherman. Waiting to be found."

"Who's going to find me?" He followed me into the house. "You?"

I grabbed two pool sticks. "No. I already found you." I handed him a stick.

"Then who?"

I racked up the balls.

"Angie?" he asked, eyeing me carefully.

"You, Fisher."

"What if I don't get my memories back? Does that mean I'll forever be lost?"

I grinned, shaking my head before taking the first shot. "I hope not. That would be tragic. You'll know when you're not lost."

He chuckled. "That makes no sense."

"When you're not lost, it will make perfect sense. That's how you'll know you're no longer the lost fisherman."

He continued to eye me with confusion, maybe even a little distrust, as we took turns making the balls disappear into the pockets.

After we each won a game, I nodded toward the stairs. "I do have to go now."

"I'll walk you home."

"No. Don't be silly. It's not that far. I'll be fine."

"Probably, but I'm still walking you home." He turned off the porch lights and followed me up the stairs.

When we stepped out the front door, he moved to my right side. I gave him a funny look. Then he took my hand. He had to move so his good hand could hold mine. We walked without any rush, taking twice as much time as necessary.

"I want you to date Angie. And do whatever you need to do to figure things out and to feel sure about the decisions you make. I don't want you to be impulsive or scared. Don't make a decision about your life unless you're certain it's the right one. Because these aren't small decisions, Fisher. And I know you can't even imagine what that feels like right now ... to make a decision and feel confident and certain about it because you're living with the fear of the unknown."

We stopped just before reaching the driveway. "I'm sorry." I released his hand and covered my face with both hands. "I'm rambling. I just don't want you to feel like I expect anything from you right now." I dropped my hands. "Okay?"

After a few seconds, his brow tightened and he nodded. "Okay. But I'm going to kiss you goodnight because I'm really confident and certain that it's what I want to do right now ... it's *all* I want to do right now."

"I said tomorrow."

He held up his good arm and tapped the screen of his watch.

12:14 a.m.

I twisted my lips as if I was contemplating it. "Sorry. No goodnight kiss for you."

His good hand slid around my neck, his fingers teasing my nape. "Why?" he whispered.

Biting my lips to keep him from stealing anything, I shrugged. "Because it's officially morning, not night."

Fisher grinned a second before kissing me.

Patient.

Soft.

Teasing.

Perfect.

When he released my lips, he whispered, "Good morning."

CHAPTER THIRTEEN

IF IT WAS FINALLY our time, why was it so hard to be with Fisher? Did our time have to include him losing his memories of me? Did it have to include a fiancée?

It definitely didn't have to include an invitation to his dad's birthday party. A party at his parents' house. A party with Angie on the invitation list. Yet ... it did.

"I don't think I'm going." I sulked into the living room, wearing old sweats, my hair in need of a comb.

"Are you not feeling well?" Rory asked.

Rose pressed her hand to my forehead. "No fever. You can go."

"That's not an accurate way to take someone's temperature." I frowned.

"She doesn't have to go." Rory finished wrapping Pat's gift from us.

I stuck my tongue out at Rose. She grinned and shook her head. I knew she only wanted me to go so I'd see Fisher and Angie in their element, surrounded by his family. A huge Team Angie party. But Rose didn't know about the two—scratch that—three kisses. The underdog was making progress. And I was doing it without telling Fisher about our past. I wasn't only playing fairly; I was playing with one hand *zip-tied* behind my back.

"I think Laurie is going to get Fisher to commit to sticking with the wedding date. June third." Rose gave me a tight grin, baiting me.

"Oh, I wasn't sure it was even still an option. So they're dating, but officially still engaged?" Rory asked.

I shared her surprised sentiment. "I'll shower." I grinned at Rose. "Give me twenty minutes."

She glanced at her watch. "Fifteen."

I got ready in thirteen minutes and a few seconds, saving my makeup for the car ride.

When we pulled into their big driveway, there must have been ten other cars there. It was more than family. I wasn't sure how that would play out for me. Would they all be friends who knew Angie? Probably.

One of the grandkids let us into the house filled with people. It was a cooler fall day in the foothills, so it forced the festivities inside.

"Welcome!" Laurie greeted us. "So glad you made it. There's a table for cards and gifts over there. Don't forget to sign the guest book. And help yourself to food in the dining room. Games and more seating downstairs. I don't know where Pat disappeared to, but you'll find him somewhere."

I followed Rose and Rory like a shadow to the gift table. To the kitchen. In line for food in the dining room.

"Hey!" Angie appeared in tight black pants and a

white sweater. Her curly black hair was softened into big curls. Perfect nails and makeup.

"Hi, hon." Rory hugged her. "You good?"

She nodded. "I really am. Things are going well. I think this party is exactly what I need, what *we* need." She glanced around. "Where'd Fisher go? He's probably in the garage trying to cut off his cast. He's been so unruly about it lately. It comes off Monday."

Angie nodded to my shoes. "Cute shoes, Reese. You always look so adorable."

I grinned without showing any teeth. Adorable. Exactly what I was going for.

Angie tootled away, the glowing bride-to-be. It had been forty-eight hours since I'd seen Fisher. Did something happen? Did he get his memory back?

We filled our plates with food and cake. We found Pat and wished him happy birthday, and I broke away from my mom and Rose, sneaking downstairs with the kids. All the kids.

And ... Arnie and Fisher. They were playing ping-pong with the kids as well as video games on the big TV.

Fisher missed the ball when he looked up at me.

"Champion!" Arnie declared, tossing his paddle aside and throwing his arms in the air.

I cringed, a silent apology for being a distraction and costing him the game.

Arnie looked over his shoulder at me. "Reese! Just in time. You're my next competitor."

"Me?" I laughed.

He snagged Fisher's paddle and handed it to me.

"Scat." He shooed Fisher away. "You lost. Go play with the kids."

Fisher shook his head, grin huge and eyes on me. I tried not to stare too long, afraid everyone would see right through me.

After I beat Arnie three times in a row, he tucked his tail between his legs and headed upstairs for more cake.

Fisher handed one of his nephews his controller and made his way toward me as I hung back behind the sofa a few feet, watching the games on the big screen TV.

"Hi." He grinned.

I rubbed my lips together, fighting to keep from showing him how thrilled I was to see him. "Hi."

"You killed Arnie. He'll never recover."

I laughed. "He'll manage."

"I wasn't sure you'd come." He stood right next to me and touched his hand to mine on purpose in a way that no one would notice, especially since we were surrounded by a bunch of distracted kids. "But I honestly had no idea who they invited. My mom called it a small, cozy gathering." He chuckled.

I laughed. "She might have missed the mark if that's the case."

"There you are." Angie peeked around the corner.

Fisher took a step to the side so our hands no longer touched. "What's up?"

She wrapped her arms around him, giving him a hug while kissing his neck. "Come upstairs with the adults. Everyone keeps asking about our wedding, and I don't know what to say. What do you want me to say?"

Without a word, I slowly drifted away, up the stairs

and back in the shadows of Rory and Rose. A few minutes later, Arnie stood on a chair in the middle of the great room and whistled with his thumb and middle finger up to his mouth. It was a loud and impressive whistle that silenced the room.

"Rock star always has to be the center of attention," Shayla yelled, eliciting a wave of laughter from the room.

Arnie grinned, owning the truth. "Not today. It's our dad's big day. The man who showed us what it means to work from sun up to sun down. What it means to put family first. Patrick Mann is my hero."

Emotion filled the room when Arnie got a little choked up. "He's *my* rock star."

A collective "Aw ..." filled the space.

"And just recently," Arnie continued, "he once again showed us what a real man does. When my brother fell off his little bike and got a boo boo on his head ..."

Tears quickly turned into laughter. Arnie was a true artist. A true performer.

"Our dad was the voice of reason and the voice of hope. He knew, no matter the outcome, our family would get through this. He stepped up and filled Fisher's shoes at work. He spent many nights at the hospital, right next to Fisher's bed. He worried about us, our mom, Angie ... just everyone more than himself. And as a side note, it is worth mentioning that we are *all* glad that Fisher came out with his life and at least part of his brain intact. And while he struggles to remember a few things like the girl he has loved since he was just a little boy racing to the potty before wetting his pants ..."

More laughter.

I told myself not to look, but I couldn't help it, I had to do it. Lifting onto my toes, I glanced at Fisher and Angie standing at the top of the stairs. She looked up at him so adoringly.

"We know it's only a matter of time. Angie's the girl schmucks like me write sappy love songs for. The love you've shared for nearly three decades is once in a lifetime. And you lived, Fisher ... so don't screw this up. Marry the girl and count yourself one lucky bastard every single day."

"Marry the girl!" Shayla lifted her glass.

Then Teena followed. Then another person. And another person. And it just went on and on like a herd of wild horses trampling relentlessly over my heart.

Then the clinking of silverware tapping glasses took over. "Kiss. Kiss. Kiss."

Angie lifted onto her toes and slid her hands around Fisher's neck. And he relinquished the last few inches and kissed her.

I turned away, in the wrong direction. Rose wasn't looking at them like Rory was; she was looking at me. Not gloating. As much as I knew Rose didn't understand Fisher and me, I knew she loved me. She grabbed my hand and squeezed it. That "you'll be okay" squeeze. I couldn't blame Fisher. I thought of all the things I did to please my dad, to please my grandparents, to please God. There were so many times in life we did what was expected of us. A soldier putting their country before self. That room was Fisher's country.

I couldn't even hate Angie. Nope. She was kind. And she fell in love with Fisher when he was just a young boy.

It seemed like the perfect example of fate and destiny. She'd lost her parents. She didn't have siblings. Fisher and his family were her family.

Maybe … I thought just maybe … it really wasn't our time. And that meant it would never be our time.

After Rose released my hand, I took slow steps in the direction of the front door, making sure no one was watching me, and I slipped outside into the crisp air. I hugged my arms to myself and walked toward the end of the drive to grab my jacket from Rory's car, but she'd locked it.

"Ugh! Rory … no one's going to steal your car," I grumbled to myself. I gave the idea of going back inside a full three seconds of consideration before I headed down the gravel road, hoping my toes in my "cute" green suede boots wouldn't freeze right off. I picked up my pace, trying to warm the rest of my body—it was at least twenty degrees colder than in Denver that day.

Crunch. Crunch. Crunch.

I glanced behind me. "Don't. Just leave me alone." I started to jog.

"Slow down. I'm not a fan of jogging in a cast."

"Then go back to your family, Fisher."

"Slow … the … fuck … down …" He caught up to me and grabbed my arm.

I yanked it out of his grip, not because I was mad at him. I was just … mad at life. Mad at the timing thus far in my life.

"It's cold." He shrugged off his jacket and wrapped it around me.

"I'm fine."

"Your teeth are chattering." He chuckled.

I threaded my arms through the sleeves while he zipped it. Maybe my arms were freakishly long, but his jacket was still an ocean on me.

"I'm mad too."

I glanced up at him, but I didn't say a word. He read my mind.

"I'm mad because the people who have known me the longest and should know me best don't seem to know me at all right now." He blew out a breath, a white cloud in the cold air. "And maybe it's not their fault. Maybe I'm not the same. So I feel like it's this cluster-fuck situation and no one is to blame. Yet no one knows how to navigate the way out."

My gaze dropped to our feet.

"I don't care if I remember these missing pieces or not. I really don't. I just wish someone could tell me for sure. Yes, Fisher, you're going to get your memory back in six weeks. Or no, Fisher, this is it. You will never remember. Because I can't fall in love with photographs. I can't fall in love with someone else's memories. I just ..." He shook his head. "Can't."

"What do you need, Fisher?" I lifted my gaze and looked into his lost eyes.

"Time. And space."

I nodded. "You followed me," I whispered.

"See, that's the problem. The people I need time and space from just refuse to give it to me. And the one person I need *more* time with and much less space from is the one who keeps running or driving away from me."

"I was running to keep warm. And the day I drove away, I had to help deliver a baby."

Fisher grinned while easing his head side to side. "That's your story?"

I shrugged. "It's the truth."

"My family thought I did a great job trimming my beard."

"As they should have. I did an impeccable job. But it's getting scruffy again."

"I'll make you dinner tonight if you come over and trim my beard."

"You get your cast off in two days."

"But I like it when you do it."

"Well, that's just lazy, Fisher."

"I'll let you help me finish the bookshelf in my shop."

"What time is dinner?"

He grinned and it was glorious. It was for me. All me. Fisher wanted to spend *time* with me. Fisher wanted as little *space* between us as possible. I let myself believe it wasn't about Angie, like Rory's relationship with Rose wasn't about my dad or even about me.

"Six."

"Fine." I acted like it was such a sacrifice.

A car drove past us, and Fisher waved to them as I turned my head so maybe they'd think I was Angie.

"Come prepared. I'm going to kiss you until your lips go numb."

I pressed said lips together to keep from grinning.

"I might even make a play for second base. Dress accordingly."

I snorted, no longer able to contain it. "Who are you?"

"According to you, I'm the lost fisherman. Just trying to find myself."

"And you think you'll find yourself on the way to second base with me?"

He glanced over my shoulder into the distance, head bobbing a little bit. "Maybe not on my way to second base. Third base ..." His lips twisted. "That's a much higher possibility. I think a home run would make me not give a shit if I found myself or anyone else for that matter."

"It's funny because you're talking, and I see your lips moving, but I'm still thinking about you teaching me how to build that shelving unit. Do you think I'll get to use more than just sandpaper? Like a hammer, a saw, or a screwdriver?"

Fisher eyed me, a tiny grin bending his full lips. "You're getting a little excited. Am I about to get kissed? Or fondled? Pinned to a pine tree so you can have your way with me?"

"What about that tool that drills the little holes for the shelf pins?" I ignored his questions. "Could you teach me how to use that?"

The more I ignored him, the more amused he seemed to get. And I loved it.

"A shelf pin jig?"

"Sure. Call it what you want. I just want to know if you're going to teach me how to use it?"

"I'm not calling it what I want. I'm calling it what it

is." He shook his head. "I can't believe I ever agreed to teach you anything. I think you're lying about that."

"I'm not lying. And you're going to let me use the jig thingy if I'm going to let you explore second base."

Fisher eased his head to the side, that puppy dog head cock. Lips corkscrewed. Eyes narrowed. "Shelf pin jig it is. Six o'clock. Now we have to get back. Separately."

I shrugged off his jacket. "Here. You need to return as you left."

"You need to get back before you freeze to death. How am I supposed to do *things* to you later if you're frozen to death?"

I laughed. "Your biggest concern about me dying is what that means for you getting to second base? Do you need me to grant you a special ten-second rule?"

"I'm listening." He tipped his chin up while glancing down at me.

"I die. You get ten seconds to fondle me before it will be considered perverse."

Fisher's eyebrows crawled up his head. "You're one sick chick."

"Is that a yes or a no?"

"It's a solid yes, but I just want it on record that it was your idea."

"Noted."

"Seriously, your lips are blue. Go. Run. I'll wait a few minutes before heading that way, and I'll go in through the lower door."

"Six." I grinned a second before turning and jogging toward the drive.

"Reese?"

I turned.

Fisher grinned before shaking his head and wiping his mouth to hide his grin. "Nothing. Just ... go."

I giggled all the way back to the driveway. My teeth hurt and my lips were frozen to my gums. A small group of people exited the house, and I used that opportunity to sneak back inside without drawing any attention to myself.

"Want to see Angie's wedding dress?" Teena whispered in my ear as I snuck a handful of chips.

I turned, eyes wide, wondering if she meant to whisper that in *my* ear. Of course she did. I was Fisher's best friend's daughter. A family friend. Fisher's ex-employee. Why wouldn't I want to see his fiancée's wedding gown?

"Um ..." I shoved a few chips into my mouth to buy time and feed my anxiety.

"She's in my parents' bedroom. We're not telling Fisher. It might freak him out. But it's stunning. You have to see it."

"Okay," I mumbled, barely audible over the chips. I might have even spit a few pieces into the air on my reply. And I didn't have that much of a choice anyway as Teena grabbed my arm and dragged me down the hallway and into the master bedroom filled with a handful of women, including Rory and Rose.

Angie stood in the corner, facing a full-length mirror, wearing a strapless white gown. Simple. Elegant. A perfect choice for her. She looked like a princess.

As she smiled, a tear trailed down her cheek, and she

quickly wiped it away. "Sorry." She sniffled. "I just always imagined my mom being here to see me in my wedding dress." Another sniffle. "And I imagined my dad walking me down the aisle."

Well fuck ... (necessary use of the F-word)

She made my eyes burn with emotion, along with everyone else in the room. I wasn't a total monster. She fell in love with Fisher when they were six. Six!

Rose shot me a tight grin. A "are you really going to try to take *Fisher* away from her too" look. I wasn't trying to take Fisher away from her.

I. Really. Wasn't.

Sure, I kissed him, but it was a complete lapse in all coherent thought. I would have kissed anyone standing in front of me when I got the text. Had Angie been there, I would have kissed her.

Really.

As for the kisses that followed that first kiss, they were mutual. Some might have even said they were Fisher's idea.

"My girl." Laurie hugged Angie. "We are your family. Always. You've felt like one of my own girls since as long as I can remember. And Fisher has loved you since his stubborn little heart knew what it meant to fall in love. And he's going to remember you. And he's going to feel like a fool for hesitating for one single second."

Oh boy ...

By that point, I had to wear a fake smile, not blink, and definitely not look at Rose. I had to lock up my most irrational feelings. The ones where my heart felt heavy because Laurie wasn't hugging me. Laurie wasn't saying how I was family. Laurie wasn't reminding me that I owned Fisher's heart.

To be fair, she had no idea that *I* was the one who Fisher invited to dinner. I was the one who took Fisher to Target. And I was the one (not that I was proud of it) who very inadvertently encouraged him to have sex with Angie. Basically, I was a superhero, and like all superheroes, nobody knew my true identity. I remained in the shadows being a do-gooder without an ounce of recognition.

So selfless.

CHAPTER FOURTEEN

"Where are you headed?" Rory stopped me as I failed in my attempt to sneak out of the house.

"I'm uh ... going to Fisher's to help him finish his shelving unit. Then I suppose we might order pizza or something. Just depends on how long it takes us to finish it."

"Sounds fun. I need to finish a couple loads of laundry. Then Rose and I will order pizza, our treat, and head over. I found a new beer I think Fisher should try. Will Angie be there too? She prefers something a little sweeter like a Riesling or a Moscato. I can pick up a bottle for her too."

There went our night, and there was nothing I could do about it. The smirk on Rose's face confirmed it as she thumbed through a pile of papers from school.

"Sounds great. Give us a couple hours."

"If we get there early, we're good with waiting for you two to finish," Rose said.

"Absolutely." Rory nodded. "Tell Fisher there's no rush."

"Mkay." I nodded, sulking out the door to my car. I would have walked, but the duo of Terrible Ideas and her sidekick Even Worse Ideas butted in on our night. I wasn't putting it past them to call Angie just to make sure she'd be there too.

"Hey. Good timing." Fisher opened the front door and grinned.

"No. Nothing about us is good timing." Too bad he didn't know just how much truth I packed into that statement.

"Uh oh ... what happened?" He stepped aside.

"Rory saw me leaving and asked what I was doing. And the next thing I knew, she was inviting herself and Rose over for pizza and beer. Maybe Angie too. I'm not sure." I frowned.

"And you're upset why?" He shut the door and leaned against it, his good hand in his front pocket.

With a long gaze, I remained silent. Was he really going to make me say it?

"I mean, for me it sucks," he started. "I've been thinking about second base all afternoon. But for you wanting to learn how to use the shelf pin jig, I don't know how additional company will affect that. Are you worried that everyone else will want to learn how to use it as well, and you don't want to share the experience with them?"

I'm afraid that Angie is the love of your life and you're just too confused to see it. I'm afraid our time is limited and I'm only postponing the inevitable heartbreak.

"I'm reneging. If I die, you will not get ten seconds to fondle me."

"That's a little harsh. You're acting like it's my fault you did such a terrible job of sneaking out of the house. So now we're down to only two options."

I crossed my arms over my chest. "What two options?"

"Either you don't die, or I fondle you now."

Stupid Fisher. There he went again, making me laugh. Indulging me in ridiculous behavior and even more ridiculous conversation. Did he talk about fondling dead bodies with Angie? I couldn't see that. She seemed a little too sophisticated for that. I thought ninety-nine percent of the world's adult population was likely too sophisticated to talk about fondling dead bodies. And the other one percent was probably in prison or on a Most Wanted list.

"What if I don't die *and* you fondle me now? Why does it have to be a choice?"

Fisher grinned. "See, that's why we work. Two great minds." Pushing off the door, he took three steps, slid his good hand behind my neck, and kissed me.

I giggled into his kiss. The kiss lasted longer than I expected, his casted hand idle at his side and his good hand on my neck. Fisher was killing it at first base. It was everything, but not nearly enough. Not when I knew what it felt like to have Fisher sliding into home plate but falling a few inches short.

My hands rested on his T-shirt clad chest for several seconds before heading south.

"Oh ..." He pulled back, a single brow lifted as he

glanced down at my fingers making a move on the button to his jeans. "Second base is everything above the waist."

Above the waist. Was he kidding? That left chest and abs for me. Not that Fisher didn't have a great chest and abs, but men had nothing forbidden above their waist. Second base was clearly defined by a man.

Or ... and this thought was the most disturbing ... Fisher Mann was *never* going to have sex with me.

Not. Ever.

We were destined to be professional flirters who dabbled in foreplay, an occasional dry hump. The players who never reached home plate.

"I don't trust Rory and Rose. They could show up any minute. Let's get to work on that shelving unit and showing me how to use that jiggy thing." I brushed past him and around the corner to the garage door.

"Whoa ... whoa ... whoa ..." He followed me. "Are you mad? Did you think *that* back there was me rejecting you?"

My feet made fast work taking me down the stairs. I so badly wanted to turn around, ball my hands, and tell him how I'd secretly felt rejected by him for more than *five years!* But that day, I saw Angie in a wedding gown that she picked out to marry the boy she fell in love with before she could ever imagine her life as a biologist, her life as a woman, her life as an orphan. My problems seemed petty at best. I needed to settle into the fact that Fisher would not be all mine for a while, maybe ever. That meant I had to decide what my heart could handle. Did it have the strength and patience to go the distance for the slim chance that it would be me? That *I* would be the person he loved with or without the memories of us or of Angie.

"I'm only going to feel rejected if you don't show me jiggy action."

"I'm not buying it. Here. I was stupid. I wanted to wait until my cast came off before I suggested more, but I'm clearly the world's biggest idiot."

When I turned to assure him he wasn't the world's biggest idiot because I had already taken that title years earlier, I stumbled on my words and nothing came out.

He stood at the bottom of the stairs with his shirt off and his jeans pushed down to his ankles over his work boots. Just black briefs and a killer grin. "Forgive me?"

After my eyes got their fill, after my tongue made a half dozen swipes along my lower lip, I nodded. "Put your clothes on."

"Are you sure?" He waddled toward me, taking tiny steps restricted by his jeans at his ankles. Fisher was the sexiest duck I had ever seen.

"Stop." I giggled. "Just ... put your clothes on."

"Now *I* feel rejected."

"Then we're even." I laughed.

"I knew it!" He pointed a finger at my face. "So you did feel rejected."

My smile faded and I curled my hair behind my ears. "No." I shook my head slowly before hunching in front of him and pulling his jeans up his legs.

Fisher's breaths kicked up a notch, maybe in anticipation of what I was doing, maybe from my proximity to his erection pressed against the black cotton.

I watched my hands, as did he, while I buttoned and

zipped his jeans. "Today I saw Angie in her wedding gown. Spoiler alert: she looked stunning. And emotional. She looked like the girl who had dreamed of one boy and only one boy her whole life." My fingers traced the scars along his abs and chest; they tightened even more under my touch.

"I'm not saying that you should marry her. And anything short of wearing that dress for you will cut her deeply. So I'm also not saying that I think my walking away will change how you feel about her or how she will feel if you don't marry her. But I need perspective, Fisher." I lifted my gaze to his.

Concern lined his beautiful face.

"I'm not in this to destroy a woman's dreams," I said. "I'm not in this for a quick lay. It's not a game, even if every moment with you feels exciting and filled with so much life. So thank you." I found a small and easy smile for him.

"For what?"

"For stopping me. For rejecting me. It's easy to lose perspective when I'm with you."

"No." He shook his head. "Again, I didn't reject you. And you are never allowed to thank me for stopping us from getting naked. Just ... no. I won't allow it."

"Put your shirt on. We have work to do." I took a step backward.

He snagged his shirt from the floor and pulled it over his head, threading his arms through it slowly. I turned and ran my hand over the wood pieces we glued two nights earlier.

"I'm sorry," he whispered, pressing his chest to my

back and kissing the top of my head. "I'm sure seeing Angie in her wedding gown was not easy for you. I wish I knew with certainty how this story will end." He bent lower and kissed my neck as his good hand slid around my waist. "I know how I want it to end right now. But I'm so fucking scared of the plot twist because there are just too many chapters left. And I no longer trust life and its plot twists."

If only we could've just packed a couple of bags and left with one-way tickets to someplace far away and never returned. But we weren't running from Rory and Rose or even Angie and his family. We were running away from his lost memories.

I turned in his arms and snaked mine around his neck. "Let's not read any further." I grinned. "Let's go back to the beginning and reread—relive—our favorite chapters, like this one."

"This one?" He narrowed his eyes a fraction.

I pulled him to me, lifting onto my toes as my lips brushed back and forth over his. "Yeah," I whispered before giving his mouth a slow kiss. My right hand reached for his left hand, and I guided it under the hem of my shirt.

Up.

Up.

Up.

"This is the chapter where the lost fisherman makes it to second base."

Fisher grinned before I kissed him again. His hand cupped my breast, and his thumb slid under the fabric and grazed my nipple.

We knew it wouldn't go past that. So we took our time kissing, like sipping coffee on a lazy Sunday morning.

The naked fisherman wouldn't have had that much self-control, neither would have that scatterbrained, hormonal eighteen-year-old girl. We knew and patience were our only options, our only hope.

I didn't know how long it would last, how long *we* would last, but I loved the new version of us. Fisher didn't take my virginity because he wasn't sure he deserved it, and he wasn't sure I was truly ready to give it to him.

Five years later, we were in the same situation, but this time it wasn't my virginity. It was my heart. And like five years earlier, I trusted Fisher explicitly to take what he felt he deserved and leave anything he might hurt.

"Fisher ..." I whispered in his ear as he kissed along my cheek.

"Hmm?"

"Teach me."

"Teach you what?" His knuckles ghosted along my other cheek.

"Everything."

CHAPTER FIFTEEN

Fisher showed me how to use the jiggy thing. He showed me how to get things prepped to stain the pieces which we would do at a later time. He even took me through all his tools, giving me a brief explanation of what they did and examples of when he used them. He did have patience, maybe only with me, but that was all that mattered.

Fisher wanted to be with *me*.

"Hello?" Rory called down the stairs just as we were sweeping the floor.

Fisher squatted to hold the dustpan as I swept the small pile into it. "Down here."

Tap.

Tap.

Tap.

Rory made her way down the stairs. "Pizza's here."

"Okay. We're done." Fisher stood and dumped the sawdust into the trash.

"Maybe you should have been a trim carpenter

instead of a midwife." Rory eyed me as I dusted off my jeans.

"Fisher's pretty amazing at what he does, but he hasn't pushed an entire human being out of his vagina. So I'll stick to my new job."

"Aaannnd ... we're done down here." Fisher flipped off the lights, leaving only the light on above the stairway.

Rory laughed and headed back up the stairs with Fisher and me right behind her.

"Hey, babe." To no one's surprise, Angie was in the kitchen, setting out plates and napkins.

I really needed a game plan. One that involved telling my mother that she was *ruining* my life. It was a speech I didn't get the chance to give her before she went to prison. Rory had no idea, so was it fair to blame her? I wondered if she'd have felt bad had I told her. Or would she have been way too upset with Fisher and me to care about her role in keeping Angie's hopes and dreams alive?

"Hey." Fisher had no problem switching roles, maybe because Rose reserved her distrusting scowls for me.

I pulled his pants up, Rose. I pulled them up! Zipped. Buttoned. That was all me.

Angie hugged Fisher and gave him a quick peck on the lips. I'd signed up for *The Bachelor*. Oh the joys of sharing one guy.

"Reese, you're setting the bar pretty high for our future kids." Angie poured herself a glass of wine while Fisher opened a bottle of beer and took a long swig.

"Oh?" I said with caution as I poured a glass of red wine for myself. Just what I wanted to do, talk about their future kids.

"Your mom said you love working in Fisher's shop downstairs. I don't go down there. It's too dusty. But I'm sure he dreams of teaching our kids his skills someday. If they show no interest, he'll wonder why he didn't get a child like you."

I choked on my wine, and Rose came to the rescue, slapping my back a little too hard while Rory jumped into the conversation. "Reese has always been curious and hands-on with things. Even as a little girl, she wanted to do everything she saw her dad and me doing."

"Oh ..." Angie's nose wrinkled. "That sounded weird. I'm sorry." She slapped her palm to her forehead. "I wasn't implying you're a child. That ... just ..." She set her wine down and buried her face in Fisher's chest.

He held his good arm, the one holding the beer, out to the side so as not to spill it on impact.

"It's been a long day." She chuckled, rolling her forehead against his chest as his casted arm rested gently on her back.

Every thirty seconds I had to remind myself that Angie's mind remembered everything about Fisher Mann since he was six years old. She felt comfortable in his presence and in his embrace. Not just as a lover, but as a friend of nearly thirty years.

"It's fine. I knew what you meant."

Nope. I had no idea what she meant. It was the craziest comparison. But I wasn't in the business of making people feel bad or uncomfortable. If Angie and I wouldn't have been competing for the same bachelor, we might have been better friends. I related to her being an only child and losing a parent. For the three years between my dad dying and Rory getting out of prison, I felt like an orphan. Angie loved a good glass of wine and pretty dresses. So did I. And she loved Fisher Mann ... and so did I.

I didn't hate her.

In many ways, I was her.

"I turned on the porch heater. Let's go out there." Rory handed Rose her beer and grabbed the two pizza boxes.

Fisher and Angie snagged the plates and napkins while I carried my wine out with two hands like a good little girl.

Fisher's main level porch was a three-season porch with nice furniture and lots of plants. Rory deposited the pizzas on the irregular shaped wood coffee table before taking a seat next to Rose on a love seat while Fisher sat on the opposing love seat with Angie right next to him, her back partially molded to his chest like she was his stuffed animal to cuddle.

That left the light gray bean-bag-like chair for me. Its back and arms were more structured than a bean bag, which made it the most comfortable chair in the house. That seemed fair since I drew the fifth-wheel spot for the night.

"Well, someone has a birthday in two weeks." Rory sipped her beer and eyed me.

I returned a tight-lipped grin and focused on not spilling my red wine on Fisher's light gray chair.

"If you're not on call, we should go camping."

"Sounds cold." After taking a slow sip of my wine, I shot her a toothy grin.

"Campfire. Warm sleeping bags. Wool mittens. We'll be fine. We never went camping when you were younger. Your dad wasn't a camper. But Rose and I bought camping gear several years ago. And we think it would be fun to go as a group."

"A group?" I discouraged my curious mind from steering my gaze toward Fisher as I hoped her group reference was to a group of people from her work or some camping group they joined. If that was even a thing.

"Us. Your village." Rory circled her head, signaling to the room. "What do you two say? Are you in for camping on Reese's birthday?" she asked Fisher and Angie.

"Sounds fun. I haven't been camping in years. I think Fish has plenty of gear from all the camping he's done with his family. Right, babe?"

Fish. Babe.

I had no nicknames for Fisher. At least none that I could use in front of anyone else. Just like I couldn't kiss him or hold his hand in front of anyone else. Five years changed everything ... and nothing. We were both in a better place, but the timing was still wrong. I wanted to close my eyes and nod my head like a genie and skip ahead a year so I would know.

I would know if he fell in love and married Angie. If his memory returned. If my heart survived all the *ifs*.

Fisher nodded. "I have a lot of camping gear between the basement and what's at my parents' house."

Happy birthday to me, I thought, while putting on a brave face. For my special day, I would get to freeze my butt off in a tent, probably by myself, while the lovers snuggled in for the night in their tents after a romantic evening by the campfire.

"Say yes, sweetie. Take a chance. I think you'll love camping. You said you love the mountains. What could be better than spending the weekend there with good friends and family?"

Jabbing my eyeballs out with an ice pick. Removing my fingernails with pliers. Eating cockroaches. Wiping my butt with sandpaper. So many things would be better than Rory's group camping idea.

I wasn't on call that weekend, but I considered lying. With my luck, Rory would have seen Holly at the salon. Poof! Outed!

"Sounds amazing." I shoved nearly half a piece of pizza into my mouth. It was time to eat my frustrations. "Oh!"

It happened. *Of course* it happened.

I spilled my wine all over me and his amazing chair.

"Shit. Er ... shoot. I'm ... I'm so very sorry."

And embarrassed. I couldn't look at anyone, least of all Fisher, as I scrambled to get out of the chair and blot the red wine with a wad of napkins.

"It was an accident. No worries, Reese. We'll take care of it if you want to go get yourself cleaned up." Angie jumped to the rescue as everyone else tossed their napkins onto the pile to save the chair from as much wine soaking through to the filling as possible.

I pulled the wet fabric of my T-shirt away from my skin as I ducked my head and sped my way to the guest bathroom, shutting the door behind me before staring at myself in the mirror. After a good two minutes of internally scolding myself for being so clumsy in my flustered state following the camping topic, I took off my shirt and ran the stained part under water.

Two soft knocks tapped the door.

"I'm good. Just give me a minute."

The door opened because I hadn't lock it—because who opens a closed bathroom door uninvited?

Snatching the hand towel from the counter, I held it to my chest as Fisher peered through the crack he made with the door.

"What?" I tipped up my chin, fighting the urge to have a mini-emotional breakdown.

If he looked too long into my eyes, he would have seen me teetering on the edge of losing it.

"Shirt for you." Opening the door just enough to squeeze his hand through, he handed me a T-shirt.

"It will be huge on you, but it might also cover the stain on your pants."

I nodded slowly as my gaze dropped to the T-shirt in my hand. "I'm really sorry about your chair. I'll pay for any damage or a new chair." Turning my back to the door, I dropped the hand towel and slipped on his shirt.

"Angie is drinking too much wine tonight. I can't let her drive home. So she'll stay here."

I turned. "I wasn't talking about Angie's level of sobriety. I was talking about your chair."

"Well, I don't give a fuck about the chair."

After clenching my teeth for a few seconds, I fired back. "Well I don't give one if she stays here or not. I'm not stupid. I know you're having sex with her. You told me, *and* I was with you when you purchased condoms."

There was no other way to describe that moment other than to say, I had super fucking (necessary use of the word) hero bravery to say those words to him without my heart exploding through my chest and shattering onto the floor. The thought of him having sex with Angie ... it was unbearable. My chest felt physical pain that worked its way up my throat, twisting into a tight knot that made every word a struggle to get out of my mouth.

Burning eyes.

Racing heart.

Nauseous stomach.

But the bravest of faces.

Because ... *because* I loved Fisher, and even if my chances of happiness with him were less than one percent, he was worth it.

Fisher deflated a little like I had disappointed him. I wasn't trying to disappoint him or anyone for that matter. That was why I agreed to go camping. That was why I kept my feelings about Angie and him locked up tightly.

"It was a box of twelve. The box is unopened. All twelve are there now. All twelve will be there in the morning."

My gaze remained averted out of self-preservation, and I shrugged. "Whatever." I wadded my dirty shirt in my hand and opened the door, brushing past him. As soon as I noticed Angie, Rose, and Rory still hard at work on the stained chair, using some bottle of special cleaner, I turned back around. My hands landed on Fisher's chest, catching him off guard as I pushed him down the hallway to his bedroom.

I didn't turn on the light or shut his door. I guided

him through the room, to his bathroom, stopping in his closet. A slow dance lit only by some moonlight filtering through the window shades and skylights.

Dropping the wet shirt to the floor, I crumpled his shirt in my fists and pulled him to me, pressing my lips to his—giving him all my unspoken emotions in that one slow kiss.

His good hand tangled in my hair, deepening the kiss, and I softly moaned. I loved our bubble, but I hated the fate of it, like the fate of every bubble. Eventually, all bubbles popped.

Pulling back, I released his mouth but kept my hold on his neck so he kept his lips close to mine as I whispered, "I'm in. I'm in as long as you want me to be in your life. Even on the days it hurts like hell. I'm in."

He rested his forehead on mine and blew out a slow breath. "Can I tell you something truly terrible?"

I grinned, lifting my chin and brushing my lips against his as I giggled. "Tell me."

Fisher dragged his mouth along my cheek, depositing small kisses on his way to my ear. "The only memories of my past I want to get back ... are the ones of you."

There was no way out of *whatever* it was that all of us were in together. And I knew it wasn't *if* things fell apart in the most tragic fashion ... it was when.

Rory would be hurt, angry, and disappointed in me and Fisher and Rose too.

And either Angie or I would be left alone. Fisherman-less. Undeniably heartbroken. And even if other feelings like resentment or anger played a part, the only thing that would last forever would be the Fisher-sized vacancy in someone's chest.

I should have had the advantage of knowing that he had a choice to make. And it should have prepared me. But there was no way to prepare for losing *the one* you loved more than any other.

As he started to release his hold on me, I tightened my grip on him. "Ten more seconds," I whispered, nestling my face into his neck and taking a deep inhale.

Fisher counted down from ten.

"Ten."

Kiss on my head.

"Nine."

Another kiss.

All the way to one.

When he released me, when we released each other, I had all I needed to make it another day, another round. Another mile in the marathon.

CHAPTER SIXTEEN

THAT FIRST CRY.

There really was nothing that signified life more than a baby's first cry. It was like she announced her place in the world. As equal and deserving as anyone else.

Life would be hard.

Life would be beautiful.

And she would have to fight to find the courage to keep that voice, not be silenced by guilt or circumstance. She would have to make difficult choices—sometimes choosing her own happiness over someone else's happiness.

Who did we die for?

Who did we live for?

Was there a right answer?

"Oh ... my ... gosh ..." I breathed the words in astonishment.

"You're witnessing a rare moment." Holly glanced over at me and smiled as she delivered a baby en caul—in an intact amniotic sac.

A peaceful little girl with one hand on her head and the other hand at her mouth. A firsthand glimpse at what a baby looked like in the womb. She was outside of her mother, but not really born yet.

"It's my first." Holly got teary eyed as we observed the phenomenon with the stunned parents, doula, and birth photographer.

"Is she okay?" the dad asked, his voice a little shaky.

"She's perfect," Holly whispered, running her finger along the thin sack, touching the baby's foot.

"What do you do?" the mom asked.

Holly shrugged. "I can remove the sac now or we can let her be for a few more minutes if you want to take in the moment a little longer."

After delivering hundreds of babies, Holly still treated each birth like she, too, was experiencing a miracle in her own life. I felt that as well.

The photographer took a slew of photos of the rare moment. One in eighty-thousand births. I knew I might never witness it again.

When Holly and the mom released the baby from its sac, I laughed, but it was more of a sob as tears fell in relentless streams down my face.

"I SAW A BABY BORN EN CAUL!" I ran into the house at eight on a Thursday night. I didn't know if anyone was home. I hadn't talked to Rory or Rose in over eighteen hours. And I hadn't seen Fisher since Saturday night at his house—the wine incident. "Hello?" I ran down the hallway.

Nobody.

I ran downstairs.

Nobody.

I checked the garage.

Rose's car was gone.

Too much adrenaline ran through my veins. I had to tell someone, so I ran over to Fisher's house in the dark. When I got there, more air deflated from my lungs. I wanted to cry because all I needed was a person. Anyone at that point to share my day. But Angie's car was in the driveway. Despite my complete lack of peppiness by that point, I gave myself a pep talk.

If I would have been his clear choice, we would have already been together. No secrets. No guilt. But he hadn't made his choice because on one side there was me, on the other side was Angie and his entire family. It wasn't that his family didn't like me, but there was no way they were going to shrug and kiss Angie goodbye then turn to me with open arms.

No way.

One of the many reasons I loved Fisher was *because* he had such a close-knit family, something that unraveled in my own life when I needed it the most.

"She's out of town."

I turned, standing at the end of his driveway as Fisher walked toward me in his jogging shorts and a hoodie.

He pulled out his earbuds. "She asked me to take her car to get the oil changed if I had time." He shrugged. "Seemed like the nice thing to do."

Yet another reason to love Fisher Mann.

"One in eighty thousand babies is born en caul. That means it comes out of its mother's body still in the amniotic fluid sac. It's the most amazing sight. I ..." I shook my head. "I can't even describe it. But I saw it. I. Saw. It!"

He grinned, a gleam visible in his eyes under the street light. "Do you need to kiss somebody?"

My smile nearly cracked my face in half as I shook my head. "Not somebody. I need to kiss *you*."

"Then what are you waiting for?"

I giggled, threw myself into his arms, and kissed him with my hands pressed to his scruffy face. He grabbed my butt with both hands. That was when I released his lips and turned to look at his arm.

"You got your cast off. How does it feel?"

"Better on your ass." He grabbed my butt again and pulled me back to him. "Are you coming inside? Or did you just come over here to stare at my house?"

I rolled my eyes. "Nobody was home at my house. And I had to tell someone, so I ran over here."

"So I *am* just somebody?"

Grabbing the neck of his hoodie, I tilted my head back. "I share you, so *you* have to share me and my enthusiasm. If you must know, I was looking for my mom and Rose first because occasionally I value self-preservation. And I was reminded of that when I got here and saw Angie's car."

"Come trim my beard before I get into the shower."

"Your cast is off."

He grinned slowly, taking my hands away from the neck of his hoodie and pressing them to his face and the beard he wanted me to trim. "Come trim my beard before I get into the shower." Fisher's signature expression always seemed to be mischievous, but only with me. I never saw it quite the same way when he looked at other people.

Not his friends, Rory and Rose.

Not his sort-of fiancée.

Not his family.

Just me.

"I have to get home soon. I'm still on call for the next few days."

"Come trim my beard before I get in the shower."

I laughed at my lost fisherman stuck on repeat. A one-track mind and the most convincing smile.

"Remember what I said about self-preservation?"

Turning his head, he kissed my palm. "I would never hurt you."

Oh, Fisher ... I'm already hurting in ways you can't even imagine because you don't remember.

"What do you want for your birthday?"

I laughed, pulling my hands away from his face. "To not go camping with you and your fiancée. I realize you can't say you're sick because you're never sick, but you could make up some excuse."

"How do you know that I'm never sick?"

"Because you told me."

He frowned. "I don't remember that."

"I know you don't. Trust me ... I know."

Taking my hand, he pulled me toward his front door.

"I'm going home." I made a weak attempt at pulling away from him.

"Eventually," he said.

"Fisher ..."

"Nurse Capshaw, queen of the veiled birth."

As the door closed behind me and he started to release my hand, I squeezed my grip on him and yanked him to stop. "Veiled birth?"

"It's another term for en caul."

I nodded once. "I'm aware. But how do you know that?"

He shrugged. "Probably a crossword puzzle or something."

"I haven't put that in my puzzles."

Fisher shrugged a second time and tried to turn away from me.

Again, I tugged his arm. "Fisher Mann ... you like crossword puzzles. You liked them before I made them for you."

He eyed me for a few seconds with the most contemplative expression. "Are you genuinely asking me or are you testing me?"

"What do you mean?"

"I know so much about Angie that there are some days I don't feel like I've lost memories of her. I start to wonder if the events in my head are my memories or things I've been told because I've been told *everything*. The only test I have with her is my feelings. I don't remember how I felt about her. But with you it's different."

"Different how?" I released his hand, feeling the shift. Now I was the one being interrogated, not him.

"I feel like you've given me bits and pieces, on a need-to-know basis. My story with Angie makes sense in my head. Childhood friends. On and off again relationship when we got older. Me doing my thing. Her doing her thing. Our families keeping us connected. She comes back to town for her mom. We rekindle our romance. Even if I don't *feel* it now, it makes sense to me."

"Well, that's good." I gave him a tight grin as I fiddled with the hem of my shirt.

"From everything my family has told me about who I was, I don't think I would have taken a part-time employee to my workshop. I wouldn't have showed her how to sand anything. Yet that's your story."

"You thought a lot of Rory. I'm sure it was a favor to her. And I was relentless. You probably just did it to shut me up."

With his brow drawn tight, almost cemented in place, he inched his head side to side. "Why were you so certain I'd like crossword puzzles?"

Another half shrug. "I wasn't. Why are you being so weird? Have you remembered something? Memories can return slowly, and they can cause confusion as you try to piece them together and make sense of them."

"Do you know an attorney named Brendon?"

I swallowed hard. "What? Why?" It barely made its way past the constriction of my throat.

"Because I saw him yesterday."

"Where?"

"At my therapist's office."

"You have a therapist?"

Fisher nodded like it wasn't a big deal.

"Since when?" I asked.

"Since yesterday."

"Why?"

"We're not talking about me."

"We are. Why?"

"Because I was in an accident. I'm missing part of my memory, and I have a fiancée and maybe a girlfriend." He shook his head like talking about it bothered him. "And it's not my point anyway."

"What's your point?"

And did you tell your therapist about me?

"Brendon recognized me. He must be a patient at the same office. He was leaving when I arrived. He said hi. Of course, I had to apologize for not knowing him and give my quick spiel about my accident."

Brendon was in therapy. I cringed a little, wondering if I was the reason? Gosh ... I hoped not.

"How is he?"

"Why do you ask?"

"No reason. I mean ... I haven't seen him in years. We used to go to the same church, not too far from here."

"So you were church friends?"

I nodded, completely gambling on the hope that in such a short encounter, Brendon didn't back up the dump truck and unload onto Fisher.

"Just church friends?" He knew something.

"Brendon was the one who convinced me to go to Thailand. He's actually the friend who went with me."

"He's the one, isn't he?"

"Yes, I just said he's the one who went with me to—"

"No." Fisher shook his head. "That's not what I'm talking about. He's the one you loved. The one we talked about. You said he's with someone else, but not married. I told you to go knock on his door."

It was such a game. Playing one card at a time, neither one of us knew what was in the other one's hand. I so badly wanted to lay down my hand and show him every card.

It's you, Fisher! Everything is you.

My heartstrings were so tangled in Fisher, I could barely breathe. Every move seemed to create a new knot. When we got too close. When we were too far apart.

"Why do you think it's him?"

"That's not an answer."

"It's not him."

"Fuck ..." He rubbed his temples with his thumb and middle finger. "I didn't see that answer coming."

"Why?" A twinge of frustration gripped my words, making them tight and clipped.

He chuckled. "Well, because he casually mentioned having not seen you since you agreed to *marry him* and broke off the engagement all within twenty-four hours."

Well fuck. (Mandatory use of the F-word)

"I told him you were back in Denver. He said to tell you hi. So ..." Another chuckle. "You were going to marry Brendon for two seconds, and he's not the guy you were talking about? This other guy must be quite something if he's the one you think about when you think of being in love instead of the guy you said yes to marrying."

On a slow deflate, I whispered, "He is."

"Is he the reason you broke up with Brendon?"

My eyes narrowed at the floor while I thought about my answer. The truth. "No. I ... I only said yes to

Brendon because he asked me in front of a group of people, and I didn't want to embarrass him. The reason I didn't marry him was because I still hadn't done anything for myself. And I wasn't ready for Wife and Mother to be my new titles and full-time profession, which was funny because I had been watching all these babies come into the world. And I was longing for a husband like the men holding their wives' hands. The love. The family. I wanted it, just not yet. And I didn't want it with Brendon. And that truly sucked because he was ... I'm sure still *is* an amazing, kind, smart, and loving man. Just not the one for me."

"What if I can't live up to him? Will I be the next Brendon?"

Oh my lost fisherman ...

"No. You won't be the next Brendon because he got a parting gift, I suppose."

"What was that?"

"My virginity."

Fisher's head jerked backward. "You loved someone else, but Brendon from *church* took your virginity?"

"*Took* might be a strong word. I gave it to him. Persuaded him to take it." I curled my hair behind my ears and risked a glance up at Fisher.

"Why didn't you give it to the guy you loved?"

Such a fantastic question, Fisher. Thanks for asking.

"He didn't want it."

His eyes widened and his jaw dropped. "What?"

"He knew the timing wasn't right for us. And he knew, at the time, that I had mixed emotions about my V-card. After Rory going to prison, my dad dying, and attending a Christian academy while living with my ultra-conservative grandparents ... Jesus, God, and every chapter of the Bible haunted me."

"But you wanted to have sex with him?"

The hint of a smile twitched my lips. "Yes."

"I rescind what I told you about him. Don't go knock on his door. He doesn't deserve you. If he didn't have the balls to man the fuck up when you chose him, then he didn't deserve it or you. He choked, and that's pretty pathetic."

I laughed. "Yeah, well ... I didn't look at it like that. So let's not stone him for his decision. Besides, you have some things in common with him."

He crossed his arms over his chest. "Such as?"

"You weren't going to let me go past second base."

"Fuck. Stop. Just ... no." He shook his head. "We are never talking about that again. It was a joke. I would have hit the damn home run and you know it."

I brushed past him, moseying down the hallway toward his bathroom. "Sure. Sure. That's what *he* said."

"He's an idiot."

I giggled. "Sometimes."

Fisher peeled off his shirt and tossed it into the hamper. Then he sat on the vanity bench. I draped the towel over his legs and grabbed the trimmers. He spread his legs wide, unlike the previous time, and pulled me between them with his hands on the back of my thighs.

I laughed as the towel on his lap fell onto the floor. He didn't care. I turned on the trimmers, and he buried his face in my chest.

"I've missed you," he mumbled.

"It's only been five days." I ran my free hand through his hair.

"And nights." He lifted his head. "Nights too. Don't forget nights."

"Because we've spent so many nights together?" I made my first swipe with the trimmers.

"You're with me every night. In my dreams. You're naked, except for my tool belt. You're always wearing my tool belt."

I laughed. "Sounds interesting. Am I building something?"

He frowned. "No. You're always just teasing me."

"Funny. In my dreams, you're always a baby with an adult head, sucking a pacifier."

"Not funny." He tightened his grip on the back of my legs.

I jumped, holding the trimmer away from his face. "Careful." I continued to trim his beard. "And it's actually quite funny."

He said nothing more while I finished, but I felt his eyes on me the whole time.

"Perfect. As usual." I set the trimmers on the counter. "Well, my trim is perfect, considering what I had to work with."

Fisher remained a little subdued, not as quick to jab back. In fact, he didn't take the bait at all.

"I'll grab the vac hose to sweep up the mess."

"Leave it." He pulled me closer to him again.

I smiled, running my palms along his face. "So handsome."

He closed his eyes and took an audible breath, releasing it like it carried some pretty heavy stuff with it.

"Did you tell your therapist about me? I know it's none of my business, but—"

"Yes." He opened his eyes.

I nodded slowly, pressing my lips together.

"I told her I'm engaged to a woman I've known nearly my whole life. But I'm in love with a woman I've known for a breath, maybe two."

Drawing in another one of those breaths of time, a shaky one, I blew it out with a whisper, "You love me?"

He shrugged. Of course he shrugged. It was Fisher. "I'm assuming that's what this annoying feeling is."

"Annoying feeling?" I narrowed my eyes.

"The increased heart rate I get just from thinking about you. Oh ... and that. The *constant* thinking about you. The stupid smile that I can't seem to wipe off my face because I'm thinking about you *all the damn time.*"

He seemed so annoyed. It made me grin, but I fought it by biting my lower lip.

"The dreams. The driving by your house just to see if your car is there. Lack of focus on anything or anyone but you. It's ..." He shook his head. "It's bad." His gaze met mine. "What about you? Do you have any feelings toward me? Or do you just want into my pants? Be honest ... am I the girl in this relationship?"

"Fisher ..." I whispered. His humor didn't completely mask his nerves. How did two people fall in love so quickly? Then how did they do it twice? Just as quickly, just as passionately? And with terrible timing *again?* I pressed my lips to his.

We kissed.

Fisher loved me. *Me* ...

So we continued to kiss because that's what people who loved each other did.

He unbuttoned my jeans and eased down the zipper. Then he kissed my exposed skin just above my panties.

My fingers laced through his thick hair. "I love you, my lost fisherman."

He stilled for a second before his gaze lifted to mine. Those blue eyes. That heartbreakingly lost look in his eyes.

"This is so messy." I gave him a cautious smile.

"That's how we know it's real." He slowly stood, taking my shirt with him.

I lifted my arms, willingly surrendering.

He dropped my shirt onto the floor and kissed me again, easing my bra straps down my shoulders as I reached around and unhooked it.

Maybe our future was uncertain, at best. But not his touch. I knew ... I just *knew* he didn't touch her like he touched me.

The slide of his warm tongue.

The brush of his thumb over my nipple.

And the hum, almost a tiny growl, like he was a little angry that everything had to be so damn complicated.

That slow kiss took us all the way to the bed. I wasn't the nervous girl anymore. And knowing he wasn't getting my virginity didn't make it feel any less special.

I wasn't a used sanitary napkin.

I was the woman who put myself first, who loved

myself first. I was the girl who left the love of her life to *find* a life.

There were mistakes.

Lessons to learn.

Tears to cry.

Intimate moments with other people.

Risks to take.

And I did it all.

I did it not because I thought it would lead me back to Fisher; I did it for me. The only gift I cared to give my future husband was the most confident version of myself. A full heart and a humbled soul.

As I leaned back on the bed, Fisher pulled my jeans down my legs. "Not even death will take this memory away from me." He grinned.

As his mouth made its way up my body, he stopped briefly to tease the sensitive flesh between my legs while sliding off my panties.

"Fisher ..." I closed my heavy eyelids, and my hands fisted the bedding, my hips lifting from the mattress looking for absolutely anything he would give me. When I opened them, he was discarding his jogging shorts and briefs.

That grin ... so sexy.

The slow prowl, bringing every inch of that body to me. I'd never felt so alive. My legs spread wider. My fingers feathered his chest, his abs, and the hard muscles along his back.

Settling between my legs, teasing me like he did to the eighteen-year-old virgin, he kissed my breasts, my neck, my ... everything. Fisher had always been the patient one with me. And that night was no exception. He guided me onto my stomach and kissed along my back and the curve of my butt like an artist admiring every detail of a fine work of art or ... a lost fisherman exploring Target with the woman he was destined to fall for every single time.

I liked that analogy best.

And that smile ... the grin I felt every so often when he kissed my body.

Fisher was happy.

Happy with me.

"What ... do we have here?" He angled my butt toward the window and the sliver of streetlight coming through it.

Oh ... I forgot about that.

"A tattoo? You have a tattoo?"

I craned my neck to look over my shoulder as he held me firmly in place, closely inspecting my butt cheek.

"Callipygian," he said slowly.

"I was drunk, hence the hidden tattoo on my butt. It means—"

"It means you have a shapely ass. Alcohol makes you confident and a little vain." He chuckled before biting it.

"Ouch!" I wriggled out of his grip and rolled onto my back. "How do you know that word?"

He guided my knees apart. "Because I have the same word tattooed on my ass."

I giggled. "You do not."

He dipped his head between my legs.

"Stop teasing me," I pled my case with my hands claiming his hair as he tried to set up camp down there.

"Don't hurry me."

I smiled as his mouth made a lazy exploration up to my lips, making several stops along the way. He didn't understand my rush because in his mind, he'd been waiting weeks for this. I'd been waiting years.

He seemed pretty proud of himself when he made a production of getting a condom from the *unopened* box.

"Wipe that grin off your face." I rolled on top of him and pinned his arms next to his head.

Our mirrored smiles faded as I lowered my head and kissed him. He guided my hips over his erection.

I sat up just enough to let him push into me the whole way. Drunk on the feeling, I couldn't move. I just wanted to stay in that exact position forever. I'd imagined that feeling so many times, and despite the other men I'd been with, there was no comparing them or anything I'd done with them to Fisher being inside of me.

Him sitting up and kissing me.

Him rolling us again and again.

Arms and legs tangling together with the sheets woven every which way.

The look in his eyes when he moved inside of me—so intense. His strong hands all over my body, laced with my fingers, and tangled in my hair as he kissed me.

The whispered promise of never forgetting that moment—so heartbreaking.

The focused expression and taut muscles in his jaw and face when he made sure I came before he did, but only by a few seconds. So many emotions flooded me in that moment.

I had *never* felt so vulnerable in my life, a permeating

579

fear that I just gave him something so much greater than my virginity.

After long minutes of stillness with him collapsed on top of me and still inside of me, he rolled to the side. "My therapist is going to be really pissed off with me."

I shifted toward him, finding my new favorite place— my naked body molded to his. My face in the crook of his neck, his in my hair, and his hand on my butt. "Why?" I asked.

"Because she told me to take a step back, to not get distracted by the physical part of my relationships."

"I'd get a second opinion. Because in my humble opinion, we should do this again ... maybe even a lot."

Fisher chuckled. "I second that opinion." Kissing my head, he moved to sitting on the edge of the bed. "I'm going to take a shower. You should join me."

I sat up, hugging his back and teasing his earlobe with my teeth. "I'm going home. You distracted me with sex, but I wasn't done telling the world about the birth I witnessed."

He turned his head to look at me. "Are you saying the birth was more memorable than the sex?"

I hopped out of bed and dressed quickly. "I'm saying it's my constitutional right to not answer your question."

"You can't plead the Fifth on this." He grabbed his shorts and sauntered into the bathroom.

I slowed my hands as I hooked my bra, taking a few seconds to watch his callipygian figure. "Did you hear me say that birth was one in *eighty thousand?*"

Seconds later, he appeared around the corner in

sweatpants and a tee, leaning against the wall, hands crossed over his chest.

"Tonight, you were one in a billion ... times infinity. But if I didn't live up to one in eighty thousand, then I think we're done here." Fisher didn't even smile. He simply bowed his head.

"Tonight, *you were one in a billion ... times infinity.*"

If Fisher didn't pick me, fall eternally in love with me, if he got his memory back and it brought with it an unmatchable love for Angie, I knew I would be the one in therapy for the rest of my life.

"You're right." I squeezed past him, ignoring his pouty face, and grabbed my shirt from the bathroom floor. I shook the hair off it and pulled it over my head. "Angie has been giving you everything. She wants you to remember how you felt about her. And if I were wearing a diamond ring you gave to me, I'd probably be doing the same thing. Retelling our story to you a thousand times in a thousand different ways. But for me, it doesn't matter if you loved me then, it only matters if you love me now."

He turned.

"Just ..." I whispered. "Love me today."

I saw it in his eyes. And I thought he would say it, say something like "I'll love you every day," or "I'll love you always." And what woman in her right mind wouldn't have wanted a man to say that to her?

Me.

So either I was the exception or I wasn't in my right mind.

Fisher got lost. I got lost. And nobody could help me

find my way. It was something I had to do myself. In my own way. In my own time.

I couldn't ask for more from Fisher than I was willing to give myself. If that meant he had to risk losing me to find himself, then I would accept that.

"I love you today," he said.

That was his reply. The perfect reply.

I nodded toward him. "Thought you were going to shower."

"After I drive you home."

I grinned, taking two steps to him then taking his hand and pulling him toward the front door. "You're one, Fisher."

"One in what?"

I opened the door, and he closed it behind us.

"Not *in* anything. Not one in eighty thousand. Not one in a billion times infinity. You're just one. *The one.*"

CHAPTER SEVENTEEN

"Where have you been? I messaged you and tried calling you," Rory asked before I got both feet in the house.

I missed that message, which wasn't good since I was on call. Retrieving my phone from my pocket, I checked for messages or missed calls other than Rory's.

She glanced over my shoulder as I started to shut the door while slipping my phone back into my pocket. "You were with Fisher?"

"Um ..." I locked the door. "Yeah. I was looking for you and Rose when I got home because I've had the Best. Day. Ever! And I was dying to share it. So I ran to Fisher's house on pure adrenaline, thinking you might be there. But you weren't. He was. So I told him all about my day. And he gave me a ride home." I toed off my shoes.

"It's eleven, sweetie. What time did you get home? And why didn't you just call me? Rose and I went out with friends. I didn't know when you were going to be home."

"It's fine." I headed into the kitchen for a glass of water, feeling a little parched after my unexpected workout with Fisher. "Hey, Rose." I smiled as she sat in her robe at the kitchen table with her laptop in front of her.

"What time did you go to Fisher's?" Rose asked, looking at me over her reading glasses. They made her look sixty instead of forty-eight. And I loved the way they made sure I knew the time, like I was fifteen and past curfew.

"What?" I narrowed my eyes just before gulping down the water.

"What's your great story? It must be a long one since you're just now getting back from Fisher's." Rory seemed concerned about the length of time I spent at Fisher's too.

"Well, it's late. So you're just getting the abbreviated version of the story because I'm tired." And I didn't want to play Twenty Questions about my time at Fisher's house.

"Holly delivered a baby, an en caul baby. That means the baby was born in an intact amniotic sac. It's a one in eighty thousand occurrence. It was the coolest thing I have ever seen. I mean ... the baby was basically still in the womb, calm and content. And we just watched it, in total awe for close to five minutes."

"That's incredible." Rory shook her head. "I didn't know that was even possible."

I yawned. It had been a long time since I'd slept. "Rare, but possible. And that's my news. Sorry, I acted way more excited about it earlier, but now I'm dead tired."

"So you just told Fisher and then he brought you home?" Rose ... she was such a little devil.

"No. We talked about some other things. He's seeing a therapist, but don't say anything in case I'm not supposed to share that information. He saw Brendon the other day, so he mentioned that because Brendon recognized him. Then we talked about other random stuff, and I trimmed his beard."

"You trimmed his beard?" Rory laughed, locking the door to the deck.

"Yes. Another secret you have to keep. I did it once before too, but he wanted everyone else to think he'd done it so he didn't look incapable of doing it. You know how he can be."

"Yeah, but he got his cast off. Why did he need you to do it again?" Rose's eyebrows peaked with too much curiosity.

I shrugged. "I don't know. He asked. I had nothing else to do, so I did it. You know, some guys get their beards trimmed professionally. Maybe it's easier for him to let someone else do it. Maybe the cast is off but his arm has lost some muscle and it needs to build up strength again. Maybe he was just using me because he's too lazy to do it himself."

"That was nice of you, sweetie." Rory kissed my head and shuffled down the hallway. "I'm going to bed, ladies. Shut off the lights."

Rose slowly closed her computer.

"Night." I tried to make the same quick escape that Rory made.

"Reese," Rose said.

No escape for me.

"Yes?" I turned slowly, already deflated from the speech she hadn't yet given me but knew it was coming.

"Is there *something* to tell?"

I promised I would tell Rory if the day came that there was something to tell.

"Not yet."

Her head tilted to the side. "Are you sure?"

After several seconds, I nodded slowly, but I couldn't hide what she saw on my face—worry and fear.

"Night." I sulked to my bedroom and shut the door. As I sat on the end of my bed, my door opened slowly. Rose squeezed through the partially opened door and softly closed it behind her.

I blinked and the tears escaped. "I love him," I whispered as Rose kneeled in front of me, resting her hands on my legs.

"Does he love you?"

I nodded.

"Are you sure?"

"Yes."

Rose didn't ask me how I knew; she simply gave me several slow nods, tiny crevices of concern etched into her forehead.

"Do you think he loves Angie?"

I wiped my face and sniffled. "I don't know. I think he cares about her. But he doesn't love her like he loves me."

"And if he gets his memory back, will he love her the way he loves you?"

A billion ... times infinity.

"No," I whispered like it wasn't my brain answering her. It was my soul whispering its truth.

That seemed to bring out an additional dose of worry. Rose looked at me like I was in love with a movie star. An infatuation that had gone too far. "How can you say that?" she whispered.

"Because what we have is effortless. It just ... happens. What we have doesn't care if it's right or wrong. It doesn't care about timing. It doesn't care about age. And it doesn't need memories to live or survive. Fisher doesn't have to remember that he loves me. It's simply that he does, whether he makes a conscious choice to do it or not. I think he loved Angie because he'd convinced himself it made sense. And if his memory comes back, I think he's going to realize that, and then he's going to realize it no longer makes sense."

Rose shook her head, gaze pointed at the floor, at my feet.

"I know you're Team Angie. It's fine. She's great. If I wasn't heart and soul in love with Fisher, I'd be Team Angie too," I said with a little defeat to my voice.

"Oh, hon ... I'm Team Reese. Always." She lifted her gaze. "I love you like my own daughter, which is precisely why I'm so protective of you. And it's nothing against Fisher. I love Fisher too. But I saw him with Angie. It wasn't one sided. He loved her. It wasn't pity love. It wasn't a second-choice love. And I know what that looks like because I was married to the wrong person for too many years. So as much as I want to feel as confident as you do that this will all work its way out in your favor ... I'm not as sure."

After a long pause, I nodded. "It's okay. I don't know if it's going to work out in my favor either, but I know this ... if he gets his memory back and chooses her, I will understand. And it won't change my love for him. And when he waits for her at the altar, he will find me in the crowd of people, and we will share a look." I wiped a few more tears from my eyes. "That look that says we know he loves me more." I shifted my gaze to Rose. "The way you knew my mom loved you more than my dad."

With a sad smile pulling at her lips, she nodded several times.

CHAPTER EIGHTEEN

I took my en-caul-birth-and-sex-with-Fisher high and rode it for days. It didn't matter that Angie came home and dominated Fisher's time that weekend. I knew he wasn't having sex with her.

The following week, I stayed busy with work, reading books for work, morning jogs, and crossword puzzles. Rory and Rose went over to Fisher's one night to have dinner with him and Angie. I was invited, but I declined. My heart needed more time to prepare for that awkward moment—seeing him again with Angie after what we did together.

That moment came all too quickly. My birthday weekend. Camping. Party of five. A fifth wheel on my own birthday.

Not cool.

"Rory's running late," Rose announced when I got home from work Friday afternoon. "She had a client who had a fender bender but apparently 'needed' her hair highlighted before leaving town tomorrow. So I'm going to wait for her. And you'll ride with Fisher and Angie to get everything set up before it gets dark." Rose moved food from the fridge to a cooler, shooting me a wrinkled nose smile. "Sorry."

"Or we can leave in the morning."

Rose shook her head. "Nope. Your mom wants you to wake up in the mountains on your birthday. Pancakes on the camping griddle. And a hike before lunch."

"I'm telling her about Fisher. I'm just telling her. And she can figure out how to deal with it. I'm tired of her unintentionally sabotaging my love life and now ruining my birthday by inviting my boyfriend's fiancée for a weekend camping trip."

Rose chuckled, shaking her head. "Just stop for a second and think about how insane that sounds. Your *boyfriend's fiancée.*"

I frowned.

"Go get ready. Fisher and Angie will be here to get you in less than an hour."

Dragging my feet, I made my way to my bedroom to change my clothes and finish packing a few things including a warm jacket, boots, gloves, and a hat. There was a slight chance of snow in the mountains for my pre-Halloween birthday.

After zipping my bag and grabbing a jacket, I took a few deep breaths and let them out slowly just as there were two quick knocks on the front door.

"Hello?"

Fisher's voice.

I should have been happy to hear his voice, but it just meant I had to put on a fake smile. I had to be the odd woman out, sitting in the back of his truck for several hours while Angie fiddled with his hair, talked about their wedding, and in general made me sick to my stomach.

"She should be ready. Reese?" Rose called.

On another deep breath, I pulled back my shoulders and played the part of the happy birthday girl as I trekked to the front door.

It was a chillier day in Denver, and it was the first time I had seen Fisher in a beanie. I wanted to cry. He looked so sexy. Sexy for her, not me.

"Hey." He grinned too big, said *hey* with too much enthusiasm.

I managed to return two raised eyebrows and a closed-lipped smile.

"Let me take your bag. I'll meet you in the truck. No rush."

I relinquished my bag.

"Hopefully, we'll only be an hour or two behind. Did you get our gear that I set by the garage?" Rose asked.

"I did," Fisher said just before shutting the door.

"No pouting. It's not the worst thing ever." Rose handed me a thermos. "Hot chocolate for the road."

"Thanks." I took it.

"See you in a few hours?"

"Yup." I went out the front door.

Fisher's truck was backed into the driveway. I wasn't going to sit behind Fisher and have Angie glancing at me every two seconds, so I walked around to the passenger side so my view would be of Fisher.

I opened the back door. "Um ..." I glanced up front to

the empty seat. "I thought you picked Angie up already." I climbed into the back.

"Get your ass up here." He glanced at me and grinned.

I narrowed my eyes.

"Happy birthday."

"It's not my birthday until tomorrow."

"Yes, but I'm giving you your present now."

"My present is riding in the front seat? I'm not ten. And Angie riding in back is just weird."

"But Angie's not going, so it's only weird if you ride in back."

"What?" My eyes widened.

"She's not going. Just get up front before Rose comes out here because she doesn't understand why I'm still parked in the driveway."

I hopped in the front seat, and Fisher wasted no time pulling out of the driveway.

"Is she okay?" I didn't want to accidentally smile or squeal with joy if something was wrong with Angie. I wasn't a catty bitch by nature.

"She's fine. Just a little headache."

"She stayed home for just a little headache?"

He shrugged. "I suggested she stay home."

"Why?"

With a contemplative expression, he kept his gaze forward. "Because I love you today. And I think there's a high probability that I will love you tomorrow—on your birthday. Loving you means making your birthday as special as possible."

"Pull over."

"What?" He shot me a quick glance. "You feeling okay?"

"Pull over now."

He veered off the road just before we reached the interstate.

I unbuckled and crawled over the console.

"Whoa ... what are you—"

With one leg still on the console and my other leg pressed between his legs so my knee was on the seat, I grabbed his face and kissed him.

It took him a second—two at the most—to get past the shock of my sudden need to kiss him, hug him, *love* him. One of his hands found my waist and his other hand palmed my backside.

"I love you." I moved my eager mouth from his lips to his cheeks, showering him with kisses. "I love you so much."

"Yeah?" He chuckled. "I picked the right present for your birthday?"

"Yes."

Kiss.

"Yes."

Kiss.

Fisher laughed a little more. I couldn't stop kissing him. It had been over a week since I'd seen him. And he exceeded my expectations in every way possible. I pulled off his beanie.

"Hey, that's my hat."

I slowly ran my hands through his hair and brought our noses together, closing my eyes for a brief second as I exhaled. "I just ... need to feel you everywhere I can," I whispered. "It's how I know you're mine. It's how I know it's *real*."

Fisher brought his chin up so our lips pressed together again, kissing like he kissed me the night in his bathroom. Then he pulled back, hands sliding up my back, gaze sweeping across my face. "If we waste too much time here, we won't get to the campsite in time to set up and do ... *things* before Rory and Rose get there."

I grinned, slipping his beanie back onto his head. "Things? What kind of things do you plan on doing to me?" A jolt of excitement shot through my veins.

"All the things."

I swallowed hard. "Well, why didn't you start with that?" I pushed him away, as if he were the one who forced me onto his lap, and I scrambled to get fastened into my seat. "Go. Don't wait for me. Go! Go! Go!"

He laughed, shaking his head while pulling back into traffic. I synced my phone with his truck so I could control the music. John Legend's "Wild."

I knew Fisher hadn't heard it because he wore a slight scowl on his face when the song started. But as the lyrics flowed through his speakers, his scowl turned into something resembling ... *lust.*

Next, I played Josie Dunne's "Good Boys."

Fisher shot me a smirk. Who were we kidding? He wasn't a good boy even if he didn't remember all the crude things he said to me. I remembered.

James Bay's "Wild Love."

ZAYN's "It's You."

HRVY's "Me Because of You."

Song after song.

I sang them all. All the lyrics. Serenading my lost fisherman.

By the time we pulled into the campsite, I was only a few verses into "Natural" by The Driver Era.

Fisher jumped out much faster than I did. He pulled the tents out of the back of his truck. "Do you know how to put up a tent?"

"I think so."

"Great. Get moving." He tossed one of the tents at my feet.

I laughed. "Okay."

He finished putting up the two bigger tents by the time I had the smaller tent assembled.

With my hands on my hips, I stared at the small tent and frowned. "This is mine, isn't it? Big tents for the couples. And birthday girl gets the smaller tent with nothing but a sleeping bag to keep me warm at a night."

Fisher didn't seem interested in my pity party for one. He unloaded a cooler, sleeping bags, his backpack and mine.

And I just stared at the small tent. Was he going to keep Angie warm? Probably. Why wouldn't he have?

"What the fuck are you doing?" He stepped in front of me, blocking the view of my tent and bending down so his face was level with mine.

"Just thinking about how things could have gone," I said in a monotone voice.

"*That's* what I figured. When are you going to start trusting me?"

I lifted a shoulder. "I don't know. I trust you ... just not your memory."

"Well, that makes two of us." He grabbed my hand and pulled me toward one of the bigger tents, squatting down to untie my shoes for me before unzipping the door. "But I remember what you felt like and what you tasted like. That's all the memory I need. So get your ass in the tent."

Still feeling too pouty for a nearly twenty-four-year-old, I stepped into the tent and moved to the middle of it where I could stand up. He already had two open sleeping bags and extra blankets and pillows spread over a big pad. Why was I so bothered by a small tent? Why was I so bothered by "what if" should Angie have come too? It was stupid. A big what-if that did not matter at all. I guess we all had triggers. Who knew a tent would be mine?

I jumped when Fisher's hands landed on my hips, but he wasn't standing behind me; he was kneeling, his lips finding their way under my fleece jacket and my shirt to the skin along my lower back.

Tiny kisses.

Hands sliding to the button of my jeans.

Unbutton ... unzip ...

I closed my eyes, trying to shake off the negativity. Fisher peeled my jeans down my legs.

So ... very ... slowly.

As his hands took charge of my jeans, his teeth took care of my panties. And that did it ...

Fisher removing my panties with his teeth was the most erotic thing ever.

Really. *Ever!*

Angie? Angie who?

Little tent? What little tent?

I let Fisher undress me and do *all the things*. He kissed me in places only he could kiss me and make it feel sexy, make me feel beautiful and desired. When he touched me, it didn't feel like my body. It felt like an extension of him, and I just got to experience him giving me a thorough tour of it.

Every touch was a silent whisper, all the things he said to me by *showing me*.

This is how I make you moan.

This is how I steal your breath.

This is how I make you beg.

This is where you make me feel like a god.

Because I don't remember you, but I know you.

I. Know. You.

Nestled between two open sleeping bags, we made love, we made noise .... and we made new memories.

CHAPTER NINETEEN

"What did you say to make Angie stay?" I asked while piecing myself back together. There was no time left for cuddling. Rory and Rose would be there soon.

"I said that my therapist wanted to make sure I was setting aside time to think, time to be alone, but not just at work. Since she had a headache, I suggested this weekend be that time." He zipped his jeans, still on his back so that I could have the tallest part of the tent.

Yeah ... he loved me.

"I said you, Rory, and Rose would probably do some things without me. Or maybe not want to take the same hikes I take, so I'd have time to be alone with my thoughts. And she agreed." He sat up and pulled on his thermal waffle shirt and his beanie.

"And you did it for me?"

Staring at me in silence for several seconds, he nodded. "Yes. For you." Then a tiny smirk hijacked his serious expression. "I mean ... I might have done it a little bit for me too."

"Yeah?" I trapped my lower lip between my teeth.

"Don't give me that look." He shook his head and crawled toward the door to the tent. "It will lead to *things*, and we are out of time. They'll be here soon. And I need to get a fire made."

I giggled, following him out of the tent with my pillow, backpack, and a sleeping bag and extra blanket. After tossing everything into the smaller tent, I helped Fisher make a fire and set up the camping chairs around it. Shortly after we started roasting hot dogs, Rory and Rose arrived.

"I texted Angie to make sure you had everything and that we didn't need to stop on our way out of town, and she said she wasn't coming. Why didn't you tell us?" Rory asked Fisher.

I kept my gaze on the fire and the hot dog at the end of my stick.

"Spaced it, I guess. After I took Reese's stuff to the car and loaded the equipment, I didn't go back inside."

"Angie said she had a headache. I told her to take something for it and come with us. But she said no. I asked why, and she said to ask you?" Rory had Fisher in the hot seat.

I glanced up at Rose as she walked past me to put their bags in their tent.

Yes, Rose. We planned this. And while you were driving through the winding mountain roads, I was having the best sex EVER!

I wasn't sure if she got all that from my tiny smirk, but I knew she wasn't stupid. And I don't think she was mad either. Her silence said as much. Before our little heart-to-heart, she was the first to call me out on everything.

I mean ... even with my hat on, I must have had a terrible case of sex hair that stuck out in all directions beneath my hat. Fisher put me in every position imaginable, often grabbing my hair until I submitted by bending, spreading, or opening at his command. My cheeks filled with heat just thinking about it.

In return, Rose lifted a single brow and shook her head. She knew I was thinking about *things* that would have made Rory shudder, shattering her naive little world, at least when it came to me.

"It was kind of my therapist's suggestion," Fisher said to Rory.

"What does that mean?" Rory took a seat as Fisher handed her a stick and the package of hot dogs.

"It means, while I sort out my situation and consider all possibilities ... meaning the possibility of getting my memory back as well as the possibility of not getting my memory back ... it's important for me to have time to clear my head without the influence of outside opinions."

"So we're not allowed to give you our two cents this weekend?" Rory grinned, putting her hot dog over the fire.

"Correct. No Angie talk. No accident talk. No wedding talk. We can talk about you or Rose or the birthday girl." Fisher gave a resolute nod, clearly proud of his little speech.

"Okay. Let's talk about the birthday girl." Rory grinned at me from across the fire. "One of the other ladies who works at the salon has a brother that I think would be a perfect match for you."

My gaze shifted to Fisher for a split second, but he kept his attention on the fire, jaw a little tighter than usual.

Rose sat next to my mom, shooting me a tiny grin. Yeah, I needed to find a way to tell Rory everything.

"What makes him a perfect match for me?"

"He's a third-year resident in pediatrics." Rory's smile could have crossed the Grand Canyon. Really, she thought she hit the jackpot for me.

I chuckled. "That makes him perfect for me?"

"He loves traveling, reading, *puzzles*, animals, all sports, and he's a Christian. Oh ... did I mention he is incredibly hot? During his undergrad years, he did body-building competitions. He's not like over-the-top bulky with massive, hard veins popping out of his skin everywhere. Just extremely fit."

But would he peel my panties off with his teeth while kneeling behind me?

"I'm sure he's great, but he's also a resident which means he lives at the hospital. And I'm starting my master's next year which means I won't have a lot of free time either."

"Reese, stop waiting to find love. The timing will never be perfect. You can't pass up opportunities. When the right person comes along, you should grab him. Nothing would make me happier than you finding love. Like I found with Rose." She reached over and squeezed Rose's leg. "Like Angie and Fisher. I want the people who mean the most to me to have the best life has to offer."

"What if she just wants to work and finish school?" Fisher said. "What if she wants to live freely like I did at her age? What if she doesn't want one man? What if she wants a different guy every night because ..." He shrugged. "Why the fuck not? Why rush into anything?"

I wasn't sure who was in more shock, me or Rory. On the one hand, he was kind of sticking up for me. On the other hand, *did* he believe the things he said to her? Did Fisher think I was still too young? Was that our fate? Our reality?

When I was seventy, was he still going to play the age card?

"Reese, you might have a little arthritis, but wait until you're eighty and you can't get out of bed in the morning without a handful of pain meds consumed with a stiff drink."

Rose did a commendable job of taking Rory's hot dog from her and getting it on a bun with ketchup and mustard, acting like it wasn't the most uncomfortable conversation.

"Is that what you want, Reese? Just ... random hookups? Have you completely left your religious morals behind?"

"Well ..." I wasn't sure how to answer that. How to make the whole conversation end or shift the focus to someone besides me. "Maybe there's something between marriage and sleeping with three guys a week. Maybe I can just focus on my job and let my love life happen organically without being fixed up right now." I took a big bite of my hot dog. "But thanks," I mumbled over the food in my mouth.

Rory was just looking out for her daughter. And a few months earlier, I would have been really excited about Dr. Awesome.

After another hour of fire, beer, and marshmallows, Rory and Rose escaped into the woods to do their business.

As soon as I felt confident they were out of earshot, I kicked Fisher's leg.

"What was that for?" Fisher narrowed his eyes at me.

"You think I should be with a different guy every night?"

"I think I hate asking you to wait for me to get my life straightened out."

That wasn't the answer I wanted. "I'm going to catch up with them." With a flashlight in hand, I stomped my way into the woods.

"Reese ..."

I didn't respond.

By the time we returned to the campsite, Fisher had extinguished the fire and returned the chairs to the back of his truck.

"Fisher? You ready for bed?" Rory called.

"Yup," he called from inside his tent. "I went potty and brushed my teeth. Thanks, Mom."

Rory laughed. "Okay. Night."

I started to unzip the door to my tent.

"Night, sweetie. See you in the morning, birthday girl." Rory hugged me and so did Rose.

"Night." Turning on the lantern light for my tent, I

paused on my knees just before zipping my door shut. My sleeping bag was laid out along with an extra blanket and my pillow at the top with a note on it.

I'll ask anyway … wait for me.

Taking the note, I hugged it to my chest, then I changed into my thermal leggings and matching long-sleeved shirt before crawling into my sleeping bag and shutting off the light.

It took me forever to get to sleep, probably because Rory and Rose were up so late playing mancala. Then a little after two in the morning, I woke from the cold, tossing and turning, unable to get warm. After letting my teeth chatter for nearly another half hour, I wrapped the blanket around me, shoved my feet into my shoes, and tiptoed to Fisher's tent.

He didn't move when I unzipped his tent nor when I zipped it shut. Peaceful Fisher nestled into his sleeping bag, curled onto his side … happy birthday to me, I thought.

Until …

The most jarring sound blared out.

I nearly wet my pants.

Fisher shot up. "What are you doing?"

"Oh my god … Fisher?" Rory called.

I dove out of his tent, but not before Rory and Rose were out of their tent with flashlights shining on both Fisher's tent (and me) and his truck with its alarm blaring.

It stopped when Fisher stepped out of his tent, holding the key fob.

"Jesus, was it a bear?" Rose asked.

"Reese, what on earth were you doing in Fisher's

tent?" Rory didn't seem to care about the possibility of a bear setting off Fisher's truck alarm.

I tightened my grip on my blanket, still shivering, even more so since my body was in shock from the alarm sounding. "I ... I was f-freezing. And ..." I needed to think fast, but it was hard because I was so cold and feeling terrible for waking everyone, and it was technically my birthday, and yeah ... I started to cry.

"She just poked her head into my tent to ask for my truck keys because she was cold and wanted to sleep in the truck, but when she crawled next to me to wake me up, she hit the key fob and set off the alarm." Fisher for the save.

Rory eyed me, shining the stupid flashlight in my eyes. "Sweetie, your lips are blue. Oh my goodness."

I sniffled and quickly wiped my eyes, feeling so stupid and terrible for everything as Rory hugged me.

"Get in our tent. We'll keep you warm."

Shooting Fisher a quick glance, I followed them to their tent.

CHAPTER TWENTY

My attempts to get warm next to Fisher failed miserably. However, his attempt to come up with a good excuse for me being in his tent was a total success. Rory didn't think twice about it.

Then I, the lucky birthday girl, got to wake up nestled between Rose and Rory instead of nestled into the naked chest of Fisher. Twenty-four was already an unforgettable birthday.

"I have to pee," I whispered, peeling myself out of the middle.

"Okay. Happy birthday, sweetie," Rory mumbled. It was still early. "I'll go with you." She sounded half awake at best.

"I'm good. Really."

"Sure?"

"Yep."

"I'll get up and start breakfast soon."

"No rush. I'm not hungry yet." I escaped their tent with Rose still sleeping and Rory likely on the verge of going back to sleep.

After I got dressed, Fisher greeted me at the opening of my tent with a thermos of coffee, handing it to me.

"Th—" I started to thank him, but he held a finger to his lips.

Then he smiled while ducking his head to my ear. "Happy birthday."

With my free hand, I gripped his fleece jacket. He dragged his mouth along my cheek to my lips and kissed me, using his hands to hold my face.

I wasn't sure if the absence of Angie was my gift or the sex in his tent the previous night ... or the coffee? The kiss? Or was it the huge grin he gave me after the kiss as he nodded to the right and took my hand?

Fisher was the gift.

He took the thermos from my hand and set it by the tent before taking my hand again and pulling me toward the woods.

"Where are we going? I have to pee," I whispered.

"On a hike. We'll find you a rock to pee on."

I laughed as he led us out of earshot from Rory and Rose. "Why a rock?"

"It's the more eco-friendly place to pee. It dries. Nothing is harmed. And I know you're an eco-friendly girl." He glanced back and smirked.

The organic cotton tampons.

"What about Rory and Rose?" I asked.

"I don't know what tampons they use."

Rolling eyes, I shook my head. "I mean, what happens when they wake up and we're gone?"

"I'm going with alien abduction. Rose is a real conspiracy theorist. And I know she believes in aliens."

"She does?"

"Fuck. I don't know. I'm just making shit up to entertain you. Are you entertained?" He shot me a sideways glance as I caught up to him.

I didn't want to grin, but I did. He squeezed my hand as we made our way up the incline. I wondered if he had meaningless banter like that with Angie. And by meaningless, I meant it was everything. It meant we made each other laugh. It meant he enjoyed being with me as much as I enjoyed being with him.

And I wanted it to mean that we were meant to be together—that we *would* be together.

"I'm always entertained by you. And ... I still need to pee. We're passing a lot of good rocks."

"Sorry." He released my hand and pointed to a rock just off the trail. "That one should work."

I glanced in both directions. There didn't seem to be anyone close by us. "Okay." I maneuvered my way to the rock and turned toward the trail, hands starting to unbutton my jeans and pull down my zipper. "What are you doing?"

He stood on the trail, arms crossed over his chest. "What do you mean?"

"I mean, why are you standing there, staring at me?"

"I'm keeping a watch out for you."

"But you're staring at me. I'm not going to pee with you staring at me."

"I've seen you naked."

"And I've seen you naked, but I don't want to watch you pee."

"I didn't say I *wanted* to watch you. I said I'm keeping a watch out for you."

"Turn around."

"Just hurry up."

"I can't hurry up! I have to remove my boots and my jeans."

"Why are you removing your boots?"

"Because I have to remove my boots to take off my jeans."

"Why are you taking off your jeans?"

"Because I don't have a penis!"

And then ... a middle-aged gentleman made his way down the trail, hearing me loud and clear, a tiny grin pinned to his face as he glanced over at me with my jeans unbuttoned and unzipped.

"Morning." Fisher smiled and gave the guy a little chin nod.

I dropped my face in my hands. "Kill me now," I whispered.

"I'll turn around." He chuckled.

There was most likely an art to squat-peeing without removing one's jeans, but I wasn't trained well in that technique. I knew my attempt would have led to my jeans being doused in urine. So yeah, I removed everything below my waist before angling myself to pee on the rock.

"Someone's coming. Hurry up."

"What?"

"I said someone's—"

"I heard you." I cut my pee off midstream.

"Then why did you say *what?*"

"I meant it like WHAT!"

"Like what the fuck?"

I rolled my eyes and scrambled for my panties, but they were caught in my jeans because one of the legs to my jeans was inside out.

"What are you doing?" He turned around, and I didn't have time to care.

"My jeans are messed-up!" I stabbed my arm in the inside-out leg.

Beanie.

Thermal shirt and fleece jacket.

And socks. That was it. All I had on.

I glanced to the right. The couple coming up the hill were getting closer.

"Fisher!"

That stupid smirk slid onto his face as he took his time trekking toward me. I wadded my jeans in front of me to cover as much as possible as Fisher stood in front of me, facing the trail and angling his body to keep me as hidden as possible when the couple passed us.

"Morning." He shared another friendly greeting as I pressed my face into his back to hide from ... life at the moment.

"Gah! I should have gone farther off this stupid trail. How embarrassing!" I fought with my jeans to free my panties. Then I dressed as fast as I could. When I glanced up while buttoning my jeans, Fisher had his lips trapped between his teeth while he adjusted himself. "Are you ... turned on?" I asked in disbelief, feeling a little irritated that he had the nerve to find my unfortunate situation sexy.

He lifted one shoulder. "I'm not ... *not* turned on."

"Screw the foliage or eco-friendly etiquette. I should have just peed in the brush." I stomped my way up the hill, keeping a good six feet ahead of him.

"Are you mad at me?" he asked.

"No."

"Sounds like you're mad at me. Is it because I have a penis and you don't? Because I didn't ask for a penis. It just came with my body."

"Stop it," I tried to say with a completely serious tone, but it was difficult.

"Stop what?" He took a few long strides to catch up to me.

"Stop talking."

"Why?"

"Because you're trying to make me laugh, and I don't want to laugh. I want to be mad."

"It's your birthday. You can't be mad on your birthday."

I stopped and faced him, hands balled at my sides. "I can be mad on my birthday because I froze my ass—my butt off last night! And when I tried to warm up, your stupid truck's alarm went off. And then I spent the rest of the night sleeping between my mom and Rose. And they both snore. And ..." I started to run out of steam.

"Were you going to ask me to warm you up?"

"No. I wasn't going to ask you. I was just going to wedge my cold body next to yours in your sleeping bag."

"Naked?" His eyebrows lifted.

"I ... I don't know." I shook my head, feeling irritated that he asked me that. And feeling irritated that he wouldn't stop grinning.

"That would have been the only way to really warm you up. Both of us naked. You're a nurse. You should know that."

I started to speak, but I had no great reply to his gibberish.

His head cocked to the side. "You were ... you were going to get into my sleeping bag naked. You were going to get warm and then try to get some. Am I right? A little early birthday delight."

It hurt the muscles in my lips too much to not smile. I had to grin. I had to giggle.

Fisher refused to let me be anything but happy. And wasn't that the whole purpose in life? To find one's happy place and stay there as long as possible? He was mine.

Bliss.

Smiles.

Giggles.

"There she is." His already ginormous grin managed to swell a little more. He tugged my beanie down a fraction of an inch, a playful, teasing gesture.

"Can I ask you something?" My smile faded a little.

"Of course."

"What do you fear most? Is it your memory returning and you suddenly knowing what you felt for her and why you felt it? Is it disappointing your family if you don't marry her? Is it making the wrong decision?"

He tucked his hands into my back pockets and kissed

my forehead. "It's losing you while I attempt to do the right thing."

"What is the right thing?"

"That's..." he shook his head slowly as creases formed along his brow "...just it. I'm not sure. I feel like a nearly thirty-year friendship deserves something ... even if it's just a little more time. And while I don't remember loving Angie, I'm not immune to her feelings now. I'm not immune to my family's feelings either. And they still have this great hope that I will get my memory back. And this huge part of me, the part that loves you, doesn't care to remember the past. But this other part feels like I can't end this planned future without remembering my past."

"And what if you never remember? I mean ... I'm here. I'm here for you. And my heart is firm on this ... I'm in it for as long as I'm *in* it. But my brain will eventually try to override my heart in an effort for self-preservation. You haven't canceled your wedding. If you don't remember by then ... then what? You marry her?"

"No. I don't marry her. I ... I ..."

He didn't know. How could he?

"I postpone it."

"You postpone it?" My jaw dropped. "You postpone something you want to happen, just at a later date."

"What do you want me to say? What would *you* want me to do if you were in Angie's shoes?"

"I'd want you to love me. Love me now. Love me without any yesterdays. And if you couldn't love me like that, then I'd want you to let me go."

He nodded slowly. "Then I'll let her go."

I couldn't believe he said it. He said it without hesitation. He said it with such absolution it made my heart pause for a second.

So why ... why did my paused heart hurt so much in that moment? Was I asking too much? It hadn't been that long since his accident. We fell in love so quickly. And maybe that did mean everything. But did I say what I said because it was really how I would have felt in Angie's shoes? Or was it easy to say that because I already had his love?

Why did it have to be so hard? So messy?

Closing my eyes, I shook my head. "Give it ... give it more time." I opened my eyes. "But draw a line. Like two months, six months, a year, whatever. Just draw a line so when we get there, we know it's over. Whatever *over* means at that time. Then let yourself *live*. Because you are alive with or without the past."

"January first."

"January first," I repeated. Just over two months away.

"If it doesn't come back by then, I move forward without trying to look back anymore. I let her go. I let my family know I can't marry someone I don't love."

"I can do January first." I nodded several times. After five years and a handful of months without Fisher, I could survive two more months if it meant we would be together. "So ... I'll just keep my distance while you do your part to remember things and keep your family happy for as long as possible."

His eyes narrowed. "Keep your distance? It's going to be hard for you to keep your distance with my dick inside of you at every possible chance."

There's my crude naked fisherman. I've missed you.

I started walking again, my face revisiting its eighteen-year-old version of itself—flushed cheeks and neck. "And when do you think your next possible chance might be?"

"Can't say." He took my hand again.

"Why not?"

"Because it's your birthday. And birthdays are for surprises."

"So you're going to surprise me with your dick?" I giggled.

"You'll never see it coming."

"Well, I won't if it's inside of me."

He laughed.

I laughed.

And we spent the next hour hiking the trail that circled back around to the campsite. A few yards before the clearing, he stopped and pushed me off the trail, my back hitting a tree trunk.

He kissed me with a hunger that I felt in my bones. And as quickly as he pulled me off the trail and attacked my mouth, he ended the kiss and returned without me.

He nodded toward the clearing up ahead. "Coming?"

I peeled my back off the tree and fixed my beanie and straightened my jacket. "What was that?"

"What was what?" Fisher tucked his hands innocently in the pockets of his jacket.

"See ... told you they didn't get eaten by a bear," Rose said to Rory as we made it back to the tents.

Rory rolled her eyes. "I didn't think that."

"You said it." Rose eyed Rory flipping pancakes on the grill.

"Well, I was just kidding ... sort of. Why didn't you wake us up to go with you?" Rory asked.

"I thought I'd take the kiddo for a walk while you two had a little alone time." Fisher gave them a suggestive grin. "Since she crashed your night with the truck alarm, blue lips, and chattering teeth."

Rory and Rose laughed, but then they shared a look that said they *did* take advantage of their alone time. Which ... made me think of the time I saw them in the shower. Yeah, that image was eternally burned into my brain.

"Take the kiddo for a walk?" I scowled at Fisher. "You make me sound like a five-year-old ... or a dog."

"If the leash fits." He grabbed a bottle of orange juice out of the cooler.

I nudged the back of his knee, making his leg bend unexpectedly, throwing him a little off balance as he shut the cooler.

"Watch it." He gave me a narrowed-eyed expression.

"Watch what, old man?"

"Listen to you two ... it's just like old times. Fisher, you and Reese used to fight and banter all the time, just like two siblings," Rory said, handing me a plate of pancakes.

I took a seat in one of the camping chairs, and Rose poured syrup onto my stack of pancakes, pressing her lips together for a second before murmuring, "Siblings my ass," so only I could hear her.

I winked at her, one of those cocky Fisher-style winks.

"No mancala for you two tonight," I said to my mom and Rose. "You're too loud. Too competitive."

"Sorry." Rory cringed. "Did we keep you up?"

I held up my thumb and forefinger an inch apart. "A wee bit."

"Mancala? I love that game," Fisher said. "We should play it tonight."

"It's only a two-person game," Rory said, handing Fisher his plate of pancakes.

"Well, you two played it last night, so I'll play it with the birthday girl tonight." Fisher took a bite of his pancakes and grinned at me. "Do you want to play with me tonight, Reese?"

My chewing slowed. He said that. Yes, he sure did. Rory paid no attention to his comment. But Rose choked on a bite of her pancake.

"You okay, babe?" Rory asked her.

Rose patted her chest several times and nodded. "F-fine."

After swallowing my bite, I smirked at Rose while answering Fisher. "That sounds fun. I'd love to play with you tonight."

Rose's face looked like a ripe red apple, and there was nothing she could do to stop us. And Fisher had no idea she knew. He thought our innuendos were solely between the two of us.

"I'm not going to go easy on you. I'm pretty competitive. I like to be on top at the end."

Again, Rose coughed and Rory handed her a bottled

water. "Drink. And chew your food better." Rory shifted her attention to Fisher. "Don't get too cocky and underestimate Reese. She has a competitive streak too. I can see her winning ... being on top instead of you. So no pouting tomorrow."

By that point, Rose had her head bowed, fingers pinching the bridge of her nose. I felt certain she was silently chanting, "Make them stop!"

But all that mattered to me was Fisher and I were going to play.

CHAPTER TWENTY-ONE

BEFORE I LEFT Texas to reunite with Rory, I knew three things.

One: I wasn't ever going to drink or do drugs.

Two: No sex before marriage.

Three: I would think about God first in all my decisions.

At twenty-four, I knew nothing.

After another group hike, lunch, and taking a million pictures, we started a fire for dinner, and then we drank too much. The conversation took a turn because of me. Someone should have cut me off earlier.

"Have you ever told Fisher how he loved Angie?" I asked, picking at the label to my beer bottle. I didn't even like beer that much—that was how much I'd had to drink.

"What?" Rory said.

"I mean ... everyone says how much he loved her. Maybe if someone told him why they thought that ... like ... what specifically did he do to make you think he loved her? Then he might remember."

I had no idea alcohol could spark a self-destructive case of jealousy. Yet there I was ... intoxicated and jealous.

Rory glanced over at Rose. "He sent her flowers."

Rose nodded. "They were cuddly ..." She laughed, buzzed like the rest of us. "Is cuddly a word?" Rose laughed more.

"He took her to lunch a lot," Rory added.

"Sometimes you took her for rides on your motorcycle." Rose shifted her attention to Fisher.

I glanced over at him.

He nursed his beer, gaze on the fire as if he wasn't hearing any of the conversation.

"The four of us spent so many nights in the screened-in porch just talking about life. Fisher said he wanted two kids. Angie wanted four. They compromised on three." Rory grinned at Fisher.

Still ... he showed no response other than to narrow his eyes a bit as if he was trying to make sense of what they were saying about him.

Did it still feel like someone else's life? A biography that wasn't his?

"And after Angie's mom died, Fisher just ... did everything. He helped take care of her mom's property. He practically planned the funeral. Moved Angie into his house. Cooked for her for ... weeks while she grieved her mom. I wish you could remember, Fisher. I really do." Rory frowned.

Fisher stood. "I'm going to bed." He didn't look at me or anyone as he tossed his bottle into a bin in the back of his truck before wandering into the woods to pee.

Rose shook her head. "I don't think we jogged his memory. I think he's miserable."

Rory stood and stretched. "Miserable? That's a strong word."

"It's not. It's the right word, trust me." Rose started to collapse the chairs.

I helped her load them into the truck.

"You two still going to play mancala?" Rory handed me the game. "It's late." She laughed. "And we've all had too much to drink. But whatever ..." She hugged me. "Happy birthday, sweetie."

"Thanks," I murmured.

"It's been a good day. Love you, birthday girl." Rose hugged me and kissed my cheek. Then she whispered in my ear, "He's not in a good mood. Let him be tonight."

I didn't say anything. I just gave a single nod to let her know I heard her.

After they found a spot to pee and retired to their tent, I planted my ass on the ground by the fire. When Fisher returned, he sat next to me, both of us with our knees bent and our arms resting on them.

"If it's January ..." I whispered. "Then we wait for January. I can't ..." I shook my head slowly. "Do this ..."

I couldn't sneak around with another woman's fiancé any longer. If the alcohol imparted a sense of jealousy, then sobering up imparted a sense of regret.

"I know," he whispered back. "I'm going to fix this."

"Fix this?" I had trouble keeping my voice lowered. "How are you going to do that?"

"Do you trust me?"

I grunted a laugh. How many times had he questioned my trust in him? And where had it gotten me?

"I told you. I trust you. I just don't trust your—"

"Yeah, yeah ... my memory. Fuck my memory." He stood. "Come on." He held out his hand.

I took it. "I can't do anything with you." My inflamed conscience showed up to be the party pooper at my birthday party.

"We can play mancala."

My head canted as I eyed him.

"For real. Mancala." He tugged my hand.

We sat across from each other in his tent and played mancala for almost two hours, and it was fun. Everything with Fisher was fun and happy. He was bliss. And I couldn't imagine my life without bliss.

"I'm going to ..." I motioned toward the tent door. "Go to bed now."

"You'll be cold."

"I know."

"You could sleep with me." He set the game aside.

"I said I'm not—"

"Sleep. Just sleep."

"What about Rory and—"

"I'll kick you out before they wake in the morning."

I shook my head. "I don't think it's a good idea."

"Can't control yourself?"

"Full. Of. Yourself."

His grin faded, gaze averting to the space between us. Confusion replaced all amusement. "Full of yourself," he whispered before lifting his gaze to meet mine. "You've said that before. At my office. You ..." He shook his head. "You were mad at me. Do you remember?"

It took me a few seconds to realize what was happening. "Do *you* remember that?"

"Yes. No. I don't know. It's like déjà vu. You said that and it was too familiar, like we've played this out before, but not here."

I wasn't entirely sure when I said that to him. It was over five years earlier. Those were words I could have used on multiple occasions.

"I don't know. What else did I say?"

Fisher continued to shake his head. "I ... I don't know. But if it's a memory ..."

I nodded. "Then you might be getting your memory back or at least your brain is trying to make some connections again."

"Maybe." He nodded slowly, confusion still veiling his face.

Was it time to tell him about us? He had fallen in love with me, without those memories, without me telling him about us.

He reclined onto his pillow. "So weird ... I see you with your hands on your hips. You're angry. Do you remember being angry with me?"

I chuckled. "Sorry. I was mad at you on lots of occasions. You're not narrowing it down much."

"Maybe it's the beer." He sighed, closing his eyes.

"Maybe." I shut off the lantern light and curled up next to him, covering us with the top of his sleeping bag and a fleece blanket.

"You're staying?" he mumbled. So much exhaustion in his voice.

"I'm staying." I hugged his body and kissed his neck.

CHAPTER TWENTY-TWO

THE NIGHT in the tent was the beginning of what felt like the end, even if I wasn't sure what the end really meant for me. For us.

I immersed myself in work and read absolutely everything Holly gave me to read.

Halloween.

Early November snow.

And no Fisher.

Was I avoiding him? Yes.

Did he know why? Yes.

However, it was nearly impossible to avoid him until January, as I found out three weeks after my birthday. On my way home from a birth around noon on a Saturday, I stopped for gas. As I waited for it to get filled up, Fisher's work truck pulled in the opposite side of the pump.

My heart crashed against my chest. *He's here!* And my conscience said to chill out. Stay calm. No big deal.

A crazy big grin stretched across his face as he

climbed out of his truck in jeans, work boots, and a dirty hoodie. "Hey."

My heart won. I matched his grin, maybe even upped it a notch. "Hey."

"On your way to work or heading home?" he asked, leaning against the beam next to the pump.

"Home. See the bags under my eyes?"

"Did you help bring a tiny human into the world last night?"

"Seven this morning. Little boy. Grant. Eight pounds exactly. How about you? Working today?"

"Just finished installing shelves in a pantry."

I returned the nozzle to the pump and took my receipt. "Well, I'm going home to crash for a few hours."

"Reese ..." He studied me for a few seconds. "We're not strangers. And I've been biding my time for three weeks. Sorting these memories as they come back. But I miss you. And I'm not going to let you get in your car and just leave with a friendly smile and tiny wave."

"What memories?" Rory and Rose hadn't said anything.

"Come here."

I shook my head. "What memories?"

"Come. Here." He wet his lips.

I tried not to look at his lips, but they were right there, full and recently touched by his tongue. I took a few steps closer.

He pushed off the beam and slid his hand through my hair. "I love you today."

"Fisher ..."

He kissed me. And I couldn't stop him because I

didn't want to stop him. His proximity fed my soul. His lips awakened my heart with possibilities.

Then it ended.

It was just a kiss. We had control.

Until he kissed me again.

Harder. Longer.

His hands slid to my butt, and he moaned, gripping me hard. "Fuck ..." He pulled his mouth away from mine and buried his face in my neck. "Follow me to my house. Please just ..." His desperation fueled my need.

I was so tired, and it weakened my resolve because there was nothing I wanted more than to go home with Fisher. Let him make me feel *good*. And fall asleep in his arms.

As another car pulled in behind my car, I broke away from Fisher's hold and cleared my throat. "What memories? You said your memories came back."

He sighed, adjusting himself. "I remembered Angie. Well, one memory of her. Of us."

"What memory?"

"A party at her parents' house. Her twenty-first birthday."

"What triggered that?"

He glanced over my shoulder, off into the distance. "I'm not sure."

"Where were you when you remembered it?"

His lips twisted as he continued to stare off into ... the past? "She came over last week for dinner. And we were talking about her cousin's wedding. And she said her cousin just found out she's pregnant."

I nodded slowly. "Was her cousin at Angie's birthday party?"

"No."

"Hmm. That's weird. But it's a memory. That's good right?"

Fisher seemed anything but feeling *good* about his recent recalled memory. "I'll let you get home to sleep."

He went from insatiable to listless in a matter of minutes.

"Are you okay?"

He returned a single nod, more of a tiny drop of his chin. Then he stared at me for a long moment before a sad smile tugged at his lips. "I miss you."

"I miss you too."

"Bye."

That was it. A sad goodbye.

That sad goodbye ate at me as I drove home. Instead of pulling into the driveway, I kept going and made my way to Fisher's house, arriving just as he pulled into his driveway.

I walked across the street as he hopped out of his truck. "What aren't you telling me about your memories?"

"What do you mean?" He didn't stop to address me face-to-face. He kept walking into his garage.

I stopped right behind him as he bent over to unlace his work boots. Then I followed him into his house.

"You know what I mean. When you told me about the party memory, you looked frightened or maybe in complete shock. Why? Did that memory of her bring back feelings for her?"

He grabbed a beer from the fridge and opened it. After a long swig, he blew out a slow breath. "At her party, Angie pulled me aside and told me she was pregnant."

Did *not* see that coming. Neither did my delicate heart.

"I couldn't remember what happened after that. Angie said she miscarried two weeks later. Then ... I could. That's all she had to say, and I remembered what happened."

"What happened?" I whispered past the lump in my throat.

"We were supposed to meet for dinner after I finished working. But she showed up at the apartment I was living in at the time, and she was in tears. She'd miscarried. But ..." He glanced up at me. "I had a ring. I was going to propose to her that night."

"But you didn't."

He shook his head and took another pull of beer.

"Why?"

"Because I didn't want to get married. Not yet. I was doing it because it seemed like the right thing to do."

"So she never knew?"

"I don't think so."

"Did you tell her? When your memory came back, did you tell her about the ring?"

"No," he whispered.

Then it hit me. What he said to me five years earlier when I freaked out at the possibility of being pregnant.

"*What if ...*" I cleared my throat. "*Hypothetically, what if I were pregnant.*"

"No." He grunted. "No. We are not doing this. If you come back to me in a few weeks with a positive test, we'll have this conversation. But I'm not having it now."

"Why?"

"Because I'm not."

"I think it's irresponsible to not at least have a plan."

Fisher was hard and standoffish. That was why. The last thing he wanted was another pregnancy scare when he wasn't ready to be a father or get married.

But things changed ...

Rory and Reese said as much when they said Angie and Fisher had discussed kids. Three kids.

"It's interesting that Angie told you everything about your past together, but not this."

His head eased side to side. "I think it was too tragic for her. She got pretty emotional when I told her about my memory."

After a long moment, I crossed the kitchen and wrapped my arms around him, resting my cheek against his chest so I could hear his heart. I never thought about Fisher's memories coming back in tiny pieces. And I didn't think about those tiny pieces cutting so deeply.

"I invited her over for dinner that night to tell her we needed to cancel the wedding."

My gaze shot up to his as I released him. "What? Are you ... are you serious?"

He frowned. "Then the memory came back. Then she started crying. And I couldn't add more to her that night. So it turned into a total disaster because she had me backed into a corner. And while her eyes were still puffy, she asked me to go to her cousin's wedding with her."

I took another step backward.

"And she started crying again thinking about how her mom wouldn't be there. So I told her I'd go with her."

"Okay ..." I drew out the word with caution. "So you go to a wedding with her. No big deal."

"It's in Costa Rica."

Not okay. That was *not* okay.

"We'll be gone for four days. It will be fine. Maybe it will be a good chance for me to really talk with her, express my feelings or lack thereof for her."

It sounded logical coming from him. He presented it like it really wasn't a big deal. But it felt like my bachelor was taking another woman to the fantasy suite instead of me. And they were just going to "talk."

"Tell me you're okay with this."

I backed up another few steps and shook my head. "I'm just really tired. I don't have the mental or emotional capacity to feel anything right now."

"Reese ..." He set his beer bottle on the counter and followed me to the back door.

"I'm going to crash. I'm over twenty-four hours with no sleep."

"Then crash here."

"It's not a good idea." I shoved my feet into my shoes and opened the door.

Fisher pressed his hand above my head to the door and shut it on me. "It's the *best* idea I've ever had."

I turned and shoved his chest.

He lifted an eyebrow and smirked. "You can shove

me as much as you want, but it still doesn't change what I want."

I coughed a laugh. "What you want? What *you* want? What about what I—"

In a blink he was all over me.

Lips.

Tongue.

Hands.

A fisherman tornado.

My jacket ... his hoodie ... gone.

Three steps toward the hallway ... shirts discarded.

Several more steps ... the tie to my scrubs yanked undone while I made haste with the button and zipper to his jeans.

Several feet from the bedroom door, he pushed my back to the wall and kissed down my neck while shoving the straps of my bra down my arms, exposing my breasts.

"Fisher ..." My fingers dove into his hair as he licked, sucked, and bit my nipples.

"Hello. Hello. Hello ..."

Rory.

We froze, but there was no time to run or hide. No time to gather the trail of clothes from the door to our exact spot, which happened to be in plain sight of Rory and her unnaturally wide-eyed expression, hand cupped over her mouth.

I closed my eyes and cringed.

Fisher stood tall and buttoned and zipped his jeans before taking my shoulders and guiding me toward the bedroom and shutting me inside.

I fixed my bra and pressed my ear to the door, but it was hard to hear past my rapid breathing.

"Rory ... ever heard of knocking?"

"What in GOD'S NAME is going on?"

I flinched. I couldn't remember a time in my entire life when I heard my mom's voice sound that angry.

"I love her."

Dead. Fisher just slayed me. Lassoed my heart. And locked it up in his castle where it will take an army or an act of God to steal it from him.

"That is not an answer! *That* is my daughter. What the fuck are you doing with my daughter? She is *ten* years younger than you ... and YOU ARE ENGAGED!"

There was an uncomfortable silence for a few seconds.

Then Fisher spoke. Calm. Controlled. Matter-of-fact.

"I love her."

Tears burned my eyes, and I couldn't take it any longer. I opened the door.

"Stay in the bedroom, Reese," Fisher said with his back to me as Rory stared me down.

My hero. Protecting me. *Loving me ...*

Tying my scrub pants, I slowly shuffled my feet down the hallway.

Rory's jaw clenched, readying for whatever she might have thought I was about to say.

Plead my case?

Apologize?

Beg for forgiveness?

None of the above. I came out of the bedroom for one reason and one reason only. Turning to face Fisher, I blinked and the tears fell in heavy streams as I lifted onto my toes, pressed my palms to his face, and whispered, "I love you, my lost fisherman," before kissing him.

Soft and slow.

No regard for Rory and her audible gasp.

When the kiss ended, he smiled and wiped my cheeks, looking at me so adoringly like Rory wasn't there. Like we were in our bubble.

Then I turned and gathered my shirt and jacket, slipping them on as I made my way to the garage door where I shoved my feet back into my shoes. "Let's go home, Mom."

Mom.

I rarely, if ever, called her that, but that day I was leaving Fisher's house with a full heart, going home to tell my mom everything.

It was one thing to hear someone tell you they love you. It was something entirely different, infinitely more special to hear them say the words to someone else like it was a three-word explanation for their existence.

I love her.

I was the luckiest *her* in the world.

CHAPTER TWENTY-THREE

I MADE it home a few minutes before Rory. She might have stayed to give Fisher a few more pieces of her mind.

"Hey, you look exhausted," Rose said as she glanced up from her computer at the kitchen table. Then she narrowed her eyes. "Have you been crying?"

I nodded, setting my bag on the floor by the hallway. "Rory will be here any minute. I need to talk with her alone. Can you work at a cafe or the library for a while?"

Rose kept her concerned expression for a few seconds before nodding. "Is it time?"

Feeling another round of tears, I simply nodded. "Past time," I managed to eke out.

"She knows."

I nodded.

Rose stood and closed her computer. "Oh boy ... it's going to be a rough weekend." She slipped her computer in her messenger bag and hiked it onto her shoulder just as Rory entered the house.

They made eye contact. And it was like Rose coffered her part with one look.

Rory slowly shook her head and grimaced. "Un-fuck-ing-believable."

Rose stopped before going out the back door. "Remember forbidden love?" She leaned over to kiss Rory's cheek, but Rory pulled away.

She wouldn't make eye contact with Rose, let alone acknowledge her comment. Rose nodded several times in acceptance as she bowed her head and headed out the door, gently closing it behind her.

"What have you done?" Rory whispered.

"I moved to Colorado to reunite with my mother after she got out of prison. Then she left me for a month. She left me alone in a new state, in a house with a stranger, and with complete trust in said stranger to watch out for me. And I did what you asked me to do. I trusted him. And then I fell in love with him."

Rory slowly lifted her gaze, a map of confusion distorting her pretty face. "W-when ..." It was like I'd knocked the air out of her lungs for a second time. "When did this start? Did this start *then*? Has this been going on for *years*?" She started to get worked up again.

"We haven't been together for *years*. So, no. It hasn't been going on for years. It wasn't the right time for us then. So I left. I pursued my dreams. And I let him go. I never imagined coming back here to him this way. Him not remembering me, not remembering us. And I never imagined the side note to the tragedy would be him having a fiancée who he also doesn't remember."

"Jesus ... Reese ... were you ... were the two of you ..."

I shook my head. "Don't. Don't ask that. The answer isn't so black and white. And the truth that you don't want to hear is that whatever we did, we did as two consenting adults. He didn't take advantage of me."

She wiped her eyes before her tears fell. "Did he h-hurt you?"

I gave her a sad smile. "No. Well, just my heart. He hurt my heart, but only because I was too young and stupid to guard it a little better."

"When did you tell him?" She made her way to the kitchen table and eased into a chair as I remained propped up against the wall by the fridge.

"Tell him what?"

"Well, he didn't remember you. So when did you tell him about the two of you? About *whatever* went on between the two of you five years ago."

On a tiny head shake, I murmured, "I haven't told him."

Rory squinted. "You haven't told him anything?"

I shrugged. "I told him that I lived with you in his basement for a while. I told him I worked for him. I told him we were friends. When you were in California, we went to one of Arnie's concerts. I met up with a friend from school and her boyfriend. Fisher went and took Angie because she was in town and his family insisted he take her to the concert. A triple date of sorts."

"Who was your date?"

"Arnie."

"Were you and Arnie also—"

"No." I chuckled. "It was a front because Fisher and I

couldn't tell anyone because we knew nobody would understand or approve, least of all you."

Rory started to say something, then she clamped her mouth shut. She knew I was right. She threatened something along the lines of castration if Fisher so much as looked at me the wrong way.

"And Rose?"

"She was in the wrong place at the wrong time, depending on how you look at it. She walked in and saw Fisher and I *close*. Maybe kissing. I honestly don't remember. She gave me a huge lecture and told me to end it. And we agreed it would be best not to tell you … especially if there was no longer anything to tell. Unfortunately, she's been caught in the middle yet again. And for that, I truly am sorry. I don't want what's happened between Fisher and me to affect your relationship."

Rory ran her hands through her hair and blew out a long breath. "Reese … Fisher fell back in love with Angie during those five years you were gone. And they got engaged. Yes, he had an accident and has temporarily lost his memories of her, but that doesn't mean he won't get them back. And when he remembers her, I don't know what it will mean for you."

It was like she hadn't just heard Fisher profess his love for me.

I love her.

He didn't say, "I love her too," like he loved Angie and me equally. No, he loved me.

But he was going to Costa Rica with Angie.

"He does remember her. He remembers her twenty-first birthday party. He remembers her telling him she was pregnant."

Rory's head jerked backward.

"And he remembers buying a ring to propose to her two weeks later. But she miscarried the baby. And he didn't propose because he didn't really want to marry her."

And he didn't want to have a baby with me and marry me five years ago either.

My mind did a spectacular job of building my hopes up ... Fisher Mann, King of my Heart. Then it just as quickly tossed a grenade of doubt on everything.

Poof! Gone.

And once again, I was left in a rubble of confusion.

"He told you that?"

I nodded.

"And Angie knows he remembered that?"

Another nod.

"That must have dug up some painful memories for her as well."

Yes, Angie had been dealt a few bad hands in her life. She lost a baby and lost her parents. Her fiancé was in an accident and couldn't remember her. Did that have to mean that she deserved Fisher more than I did?

"And the night he remembered that, Angie was having dinner with him, and he was going to tell her that the wedding's off."

Rory frowned. "He didn't ..."

I rolled my eyes. "No. He didn't because she was too emotional. But he was going to, which means he will when the time is right."

"Rose said Fisher and Angie are going to her cousin's wedding in Costa Rica."

Averting my gaze for a few seconds, I nodded. "He told me that too."

"And you're okay with the guy you supposedly love going to Costa Rica for a week with the woman he agreed to marry? You realize they'll be staying at a hotel in the same room, probably with one bed, right?"

"I don't know what the sleeping arrangements will be, but I trust Fisher."

She didn't have to tell me that. I hadn't let my brain go there yet. Now it was *there*.

He could sleep in the same bed as her without having sex. They'd done it before, except for that one time they did have sex.

She bounced out the door that day, skipping on clouds and sliding down rainbows. And he kissed her back. It wasn't a one-sided peck. He kissed her back.

Because he enjoyed the kiss.

Because he probably enjoyed the sex.

Of course he enjoyed the sex! It was sex!

My mind lurched into action, a malfunctioning amusement park ride, flinging riders into the air plummeting to their deaths.

"If you trust Fisher, why is he still engaged to Angie? Is he stringing her along? Stringing you along? Having his cake and eating it too?"

"I think if anyone is to blame for this situation, it's me and Angie. We know the details, even if we've chosen to not share all of them with him. We know he essentially met us for—in his mind—the first time just months ago.

So for either one of us to play the victim here, it's laughable. You and I cringe at what I'm doing because we see the big picture. I'm involved with an engaged man who's been 'in love' with his fiancée for nearly thirty years. That sounds terrible. And if or when Angie finds out, she'll play the devastated fiancée role, and everyone will feel sorry for her.

"But in Fisher's mind, it's not like that. In his mind, he met us both a few months ago, and he fell in love with me. And everyone told him he was in love with Angie. It would be like me grabbing some stranger off the street, bringing them here, and telling you that you love them ... now act accordingly. Is that all it takes? Would you just embrace that stranger? Love them? What if I said you love this person more than Rose? Would you fall in line? Would you trust me and just ... *love* this stranger? Commit to forever with this stranger because I said, 'Trust me. You love her.' No. You wouldn't because it sounds utterly preposterous because it *is* utterly preposterous! And the fact that Fisher has fallen in love with me *twice,* all on his own, without any recollection of our past or anyone telling him he should love me ... *that* means something. No—" I shook my head. "That means everything."

Rory nodded several times, lines of deep thought trenched into her forehead. "It's a good speech, Reese. Very persuasive. But it doesn't change reality. Fisher isn't with you. To ninety-nine percent of the world, he's with Angie. Engaged to Angie. Childhood sweethearts who are destined to be together. And he hasn't done anything to change that. Why is that? Is it because he hasn't really made his decision?"

"No. It's because he does remember his family. He does remember his friends Rory and Rose. And that *does* mean something to him. It means he trusts all of you. So when you tell him how much he loved Angie, it makes him question himself. It makes him fearful of what might come from his memories if he does get them back. And he's not a monster, despite what you might think now. Even if he doesn't remember his life with Angie, he accepts that it happened and that it meant a lot to a lot of people, maybe even him. Clearly him too since he agreed to marry her. So it's not about *stringing* anyone along. He's not having his cake and eating it too.

"This isn't some party or game for him. He's simply in love with me. He wants to be with me because that's what his heart tells him. But his brain won't let him be anything but beholden to his past until he gets his memory back or at least enough of his memories to properly explain to Angie and everyone else why he doesn't love her the way he loves me. And it's cruel for anyone to judge him for living in real time, for having feelings in real time.

"He could have been injured worse. He could have been confined to a wheelchair for the rest of his life, and nobody would have told him to just get his ass up out of the chair and pretend to walk simply because he used to be able to do it. It would make all of us feel better if he would just be the exact same person he used to be. We have to accept that his mind and his heart may never feel or love the same way as before the accident."

There. I drew my own sword and fought for Fisher the way he did for me. Only I had to use way more than three words, and I still wasn't sure Rory was ready to surrender.

"Why doesn't he tell Angie?"

"Because she will be devastated. He's getting pieces of his memory back. And if I were to take a guess, I think he wants to end it with her, having some true recollection of how he felt about her. I think he needs to feel a little emotional pain too." My voice broke and tears burned my eyes. *I* was living in real time, not only convincing Rory of everything, but also convincing myself. "I'd imagine it's like losing someone and having no body, not true proof of death, but having a funeral anyway. There's not the same kind of closure. I think Fisher doesn't merely want to end things; I think he wants closure."

"And if he doesn't get it? If he doesn't get his memory back ... his closure ... what's he going to do?"

I shrugged. "He's giving it until the end of the year. Six more weeks. And if he still doesn't have enough memories to remember why he fell in love with her..." I cringed because the analogy sounded terrible, but I'd already put it out there "...then he'll bury the empty casket."

That made Rory flinch. It started out as such a great analogy, but it ended rather morbidly.

CHAPTER TWENTY-FOUR

Rory wasn't happy. Not with me. Not with Fisher. Not with Rose.

It surprised me, and I think Rose too, that Rory struggled to accept the situation. After all, she went to prison and lost her marriage (and her daughter for five years) because she fell in love and that love caused a lot of damage. Rose speculated it wasn't what had happened as much as Rory felt like everyone knew but her. Everyone that mattered.

The following weekend, I got a phone call while cleaning the bathroom.

"Hello?"

"Hey. Just found your name in my contacts. Who knew I had your number?"

I grinned, flipping the toilet seat down and taking a seat. "Hi. Who knew?" I hadn't seen or talked to Fisher since Rory caught us in the hallway. We were trying to do things right, if there was such a thing as right. And it was clear that being together always led to situations like me half naked and tossing all intentions for human decency aside. All morals. Everything to make room for Fisher and only Fisher.

"Whatcha doing?"

"Cleaning the bathroom. What are you doing?"

"Thinking you should let me take you to lunch."

Biting my lip to hide my grin as if he could see me, I told my eager heart to chill. "I have to help clean the house. My grandparents are coming for Thanksgiving this week."

"Rory's parents?"

"Yeah. My dad's parents would not be caught dead having Thanksgiving here."

"Why?"

"Because their ex-daughter-in-law not only went to prison for growing marijuana, she also kissed a girl."

"And she liked it."

I giggled. "She did."

"Well, you need to eat. Give me an hour."

"I shouldn't."

"Fifty-nine minutes and not a second past."

I laughed. "Rory *just* started talking to me and Rose again. Not more than a few words, but it's something. I think lunch with you would take me back ten steps with her."

"Then don't tell her. Say you're running to Target for something."

It was a dumb idea. I needed to act a little more grown-up. I needed to actually *be* a little more grown-up.

"Fine." There was always tomorrow to be grown-up.

"Where do you want to meet?"

"McDonald's on the corner."

"Okay. Ten minutes?"

I nodded before answering, my grin ready to break my face. "Ten minutes." I quickly combed my hair, brushed my teeth, and reapplied deodorant. My ripped jeans and tee would just have to be good enough. "I need a couple things from Target. Do you need anything?" I yelled down the stairs.

"We're good," Rose replied.

They'd been downstairs for quite a while. I had a feeling they were doing more talking than cleaning. Talking about the big five-year deception.

Fisher was already at McDonald's when I pulled into the parking lot. I walked around to his driver's door and opened it.

"What are you doing? Get in." He eyed me with such a bright gleam in his eyes. It did all kinds of things to me.

"Thought we were having lunch."

"We are. But not here. I just thought we'd meet here so you could leave your car and ride with me."

I stepped onto his running board so I could lean into the cab and get my face up in his face. "Do you love me today?" I grinned, our mouths a breath apart.

He smiled. "I do."

I kissed him and his hand snaked around my waist as he kissed me back. "Then buy me a burger and fries and tell me about your Thanksgiving plans. Tell me how your week's been. Tell me anything." I bit his lip and tugged it.

Fisher grabbed my ass. "We could get it to go. Drive

back to my place. Eat and still have time to do other *things*."

I ran my hand along his extra scruffy beard then my thumb traced his bottom lip. "Things, huh? You and your things."

He bit at my thumb. "You like my things."

I giggled. "I do. Too much, really. So let's grab a table and a couple of Happy Meals and stay out of trouble for one day."

His gaze swept along my face once before he dropped a final quick kiss on my lips. "You win."

I hopped down and he followed me. Then he took my hand and led me inside. I wondered what he would do if he saw someone he knew ... saw someone who knew he was engaged. My hand in his hand.

"What are you getting?" he asked as we approached the next open register.

"Duh, we're getting Happy Meals."

He chuckled. "Um ... we are?"

"Yes. Hi. We'll take two hamburger Happy Meals with apples, one with juice and one with a chocolate milk."

"No fries?"

I glanced back at Fisher and his confusion over not having fries. Then I turned back to the guy at the register. "And a small order of fries."

He laid down a ten. I handed it back to him.

"My treat." I winked. Yup. Big spender for our under-seven-dollar meal.

We took our Happy Meals to a booth by the window. As I unpacked my stuff, including the

Avengers toy, I noticed Fisher was staring into his sack but not pulling anything out. A confused look stole his face.

"What's wrong?"

After a few slow blinks, he gazed at me. "You bought my work crew Happy Meals."

As I'm sure Angie did with the slow return of Fisher's memories, I waited for him to reveal just how much he knew before I rushed to fill in the blanks. Did he remember a piece? A chunk? Or everything?

"I did. Well, technically you did. I used a company credit card."

Fisher continued to stare into his bag. "Why? Did you do it to be funny? Did I tell you to do it? Was I cheap?"

I giggled while unwrapping my burger. "No. You weren't cheap. Had you been cheap, you wouldn't have taken food to your crews at all. You were very generous. And I wasn't trying to be funny. I was collecting toys for Rory. She used to collect Happy Meal toys before she went to prison. So I continued her hobby for her."

Fisher glanced up at me again. "Do you still collect them?"

"No." I grinned with a slight head shake.

"Then why are we eating Happy Meals?" He pulled out his sandwich and apples.

"Because I thought it might jog a memory. And it did."

It was possible the memory I was trying to jog involved his workshop and zip ties. I so badly wanted to just tell him, but the part of me that wanted him to remember on his own was stronger. Maybe I would mention zip ties another day.

"Huh ..." He relinquished a tiny grin. "Thank you."

Tapping a sliced apple on my bottom lip, I grinned. "You're welcome. So how was your week after Rory lost her head?"

He shrugged, shoving a wad of fries into his mouth. "Uneventful. Just work. I tried calling Rory several times, but she's not taking my calls."

Chewing my apple slowly, I nodded. "What about Angie. Am ..." My nose wrinkled. "Am I allowed to ask you if you saw her this past week?"

Fisher eyed me suspiciously for a few seconds before nodding. "You can ask me anything." He slid his leg forward so it rubbed against mine. "Yes. She came over Tuesday night. She brought pizza and cake samples."

My eyes widened. "Cake samples?"

"They were good. I didn't really have a favorite. She assumed I'd like the chocolate with peanut butter. But it was my least favorite."

"Cake samples for Thanksgiving? Christmas? New Years?"

He smirked, gulping half the bottle of chocolate milk. "Wedding," he said, wiping his mouth with the back of his hand.

I cleared my throat, unable to read him. The smirk. The casual mentioning of cake. Was he baiting me? "Whose wedding?" Two could play his game.

After an exaggerated pause, his expression swelled with amusement, a little pride for his worthy opponent.

"*Whose* indeed. She casually suggested she move back in with me, and I countered with calling off the wedding."

The hamburger dropped from my hand, an unexpected *thunk* on the tray like the unexpected *thunk* of my heart halting, paralyzed with disbelief.

My nose wrinkled. I felt Angie's pain. Fisher didn't need to say another word. I knew where the story was headed. At least, I thought I knew. But why ... *why* did I feel so bad for Angie? We were in love with the same man. On different teams, but at the same time, we were Team Fisher.

"What did she say?" I managed to say just above a whisper.

"She got a little emotional."

Annihilated. Fisher annihilated her heart. If Angie kept herself from telling him about the miscarriage until he remembered it on his own, she knew how to toss her heart into a bunker so he wouldn't see her true suffering. I knew this because it was what I would have done. It was what I *had* done with Fisher on more than one occasion.

"Then she asked me to think about waiting at least until after the holidays since I'm slowly getting pieces of my memory back."

"Well..." there was still a hoarseness to my voice, a crippling of emotions "...that's what you wanted too."

He leaned back and ran his hands down his face. "No. I mean ... yes. I did. But I don't anymore. I want *you*. And I can't for the life of me imagine what I might remember that would change how I feel about you. There's no way I had stronger feelings for her." He shook his head slowly. "A stronger feeling doesn't exist. It's just not possible."

After a pregnant pause, I compelled my reluctant gaze to meet his. Love never looked so tortured.

"I think about you a lot and touch myself."

Fisher's eyes flared as he eased his head to one side and then the other, checking for anyone who might have heard me. Speechless Fisher was such a rare sight.

"Where ..." He held his fist to his mouth and coughed. "Where did that come from?"

I shrugged. "What you said, I never expected it. So raw. So honest. And it reminded me of all the reasons I think about you ..." I grinned. "And touch myself."

"Fuck you," he whispered with a grin, "for giving me a hard-on in McDonald's, three feet from the PlayPlace."

I giggled. "I had to lighten the mood. It's hard to love you and yet feel sorry for another woman who loves you too."

He cringed, scratching his jaw. "Right? If Angie were a terrible person, this would be so much easier."

"It's not that long. And I don't blame her for not wanting you to call off the wedding right before the holidays. Her first Thanksgiving and Christmas without her mom. That would be pretty terrible of you. But then I think of what Rory walked in on last weekend, and that was pretty terrible of you too. It could have just as easily been Angie popping by. Then what? Can you imagine explaining that to your family? Nothing says happy holidays like a S-E-X scandal."

Fisher laughed, glancing around us again. "You

realize half of these kids can spell, right? And who doesn't love a good S-E-X scandal?"

"The person not getting any S-E-X."

The woman at the table next to us cleared her throat and scowled at us.

"Let's go." Fisher gathered our trash and we took our PG-13 conversation out of the G-rated play zone.

"Are you still going to the cousin's wedding?"

Fisher unlocked his truck and turned toward me as he leaned against the side of his truck, kicking his foot back onto the tire. "Afraid so." He fiddled with the key fob in his hand, chin tipped to his chest.

"When is it?"

"The weekend after Thanksgiving."

I nodded. "It's Costa Rica. You'll have fun."

Glancing up, he shot me the hairy eyeball. "Fun?"

"She's your friend. It would be sad for that to change since you've known her since you were six."

"I don't know her."

I frowned. "But I think you will. You made a baby with her." That came out sounding much different than it did in my head. "I'm just saying, that has to give you a second's pause. Right? If someone brought a stranger to me and said I didn't remember them, but I made a child with them, even if the child died, I'd need a moment to process what that meant."

"It was hardly a child. She was only two months pregnant."

"Well, I was raised to think of a child at any stage of life after creation as being alive ... a *life*. And maybe I've changed my views on a lot of things over the past five years, but that hasn't changed for me. So yeah, I know I've thought about the baby you made with her. And my mind has run in so many directions ... like what if she wouldn't have miscarried? Would you be married to her? Would you have other children with her? And then, had you been in the same accident and not remembered her, would you have fought harder to get back that life ... those feelings?"

Nobody ... not Rory or Rose ... not his family ... not Angie ... nobody was allowed to say I swooped in and stole Fisher. Even when it didn't benefit me and my interests, I went the extra mile to make Fisher really think about his decisions. Probably because he made me think about mine five years earlier. He made me consider more than our selfish desire to be together. And because of that, I left.

Did I want him to choose Angie? No. I wanted him to choose me with all his memories of her. I wanted him to find happiness with me without any fear or self-doubt.

"Are you in that scenario?" he asked.

"Does it matter?"

"Maybe. I think I would have still fallen in love with you. But I would have felt a greater responsibility to my wife and kids. The kids more than my wife. So you can spin this any way you want to spin it, but it doesn't change my current situation. And I'm not married. I don't have kids. She *did* miscarry the baby. *That's* my reality. Playing the what-if game is just stupid. I'm not going to do that. So stop trying to make me fall in love with her."

Collapsing into his chest, I lifted my head and kissed his neck. "Fall in love with *me*."

He grabbed my face and kissed me. "Done."

"And do it again tomorrow."

He grinned. "Tomorrow? Thought you only ever wanted today."

My hands slid behind him, worming their way under his jacket and shirt, caressing the warm skin along his back. "You make me greedy."

"Greedy? Is that the best word you've got?"

I grinned. "Delirious?"

"You can do better." He nipped at my lips as his hands covered my butt.

"Wanton?"

"Now we're getting there." He kissed my neck. "Keep going ..."

I giggled, sliding one hand just beneath his waistband, my nails pressing into the hard muscles of his glutes. "Brazen."

"Move your hand to the front of my jeans ... then you can be brazen."

"That would be more inappropriate."

"You think?"

I gasped as his hand made a swift transition from my butt to diving into the front of my jeans and panties.

In. McDonald's. Parking. Lot.

"Titillating. Salacious. And maybe a little indecent." He rubbed me in slow circles.

"Provocative?" he whispered in my ear.

"F-fisher ... s-stop."

"I did."

I felt the curl of his lips along my cheek, a triumphant

653

grin. He had stopped. It was me moving against his idle hand.

Yanking his hand from the inside of my jeans, I took a quick step backward, flushed and a little breathless.

After biting back his smile for a few seconds, he eyed the family climbing into their minivan parked on the other side of my car. "I think about you a lot, and then I touch myself." He slid his gaze to mine and added the most mischievous grin.

My cheeks flamed.

His lips twisted for a beat. "Not as good as you touch me, but it suffices."

Dirty talking in the parking lot of McDonald's. Who did that?

We did.

It wasn't something you could put on a dating app. The things that really made two people click were not something anyone would ever even think to put on a dating app.

"Twelve across. A bird's wishbone."

Fisher blinked once. *Once!* "Merrythought."

"I hate you." I turned and stomped my way to the driver's side of my car.

His soft chuckle followed me, and before I could shut my door, he planted his body in its way and ducked his head, putting his big, arrogant mug in my face. "Nine down. Extravagant boasting."

I didn't know, so remained silent so he'd think I didn't care.

"First letter is G, fourth letter is C."

I still didn't know.

"Gasconade." He kissed my mouth, but I didn't kiss him back. "I liked you. Five years ago ... I liked you."

My anger subsided, being replaced with curiosity. Why did he say that?

"You knew I liked crossword puzzles. That's why you mentioned it. You were trying to jog a memory. But I hadn't forgotten about my love of crossword puzzles. I also hadn't forgotten that I didn't tell people about it. But you knew. That's why you made them for me. That's why you tease me with twelve across. I liked you. That's the only reason I would have told you. I liked you a lot. I wouldn't have told you had I not liked you a lot. Because Angie knows I won spelling bees, but she's never mentioned the puzzles. She's oblivious to it, which means I never told her. So ... the question I have for you is ... did you know I liked you?"

I met his gaze that was just inches from mine. "I wasn't in Denver that long. And I knew Angie. We went on a triple date. Remember? I told you that. And I met Teagan. She was an orthodontist. Remember her?"

He shook his head, eyes narrowed.

"Well, you slept over at her place more than once."

"Then there was Tiffany the interior designer. Remember her? Rose fixed you up with her."

Another slow head shake.

"I met your harem. I knew you enjoyed your women. So what do you think? Do you think your friend's daughter, the eighteen-year-old virgin living in your basement, knew that you liked her? Do you think you took time out of your sex life to bond with her over crossword puzzles?"

"Yes." He nodded slowly.

He was *so* close to remembering. I just wanted him to do it. I wanted to be there when he remembered more about me than my Happy Meal deliveries. I wanted him to say "I loved you." I didn't want to tell him that he loved me. So I gave him the inch he was searching for, maybe the inch, the nudge he needed.

"I was having a rough day. You took me to your parents' house and showed me your boxes of crossword puzzles. Nerd status on full display. So if that meant you liked me ..." I shrugged. "Then I guess you liked me."

Fisher did that squinting thing, a painful expression. His brain tried so hard to remember, to repair the connections, to bring back the images and the emotions that went with them. "I liked you so much ... I hate that I can't remember that feeling. But it's the only explanation. I must have been scared out of my mind to tell you. Or maybe it was Rory. She would have killed me. We've seen that."

I bit the inside of my cheek while returning a single nod, trying to hide my disappointment.

He liked me a lot.

Was that emotionally a step above getting Angie pregnant? Puzzles over a baby?

"I'm going to go home and think about this."

"Okay." I drew in a breath and held it along with all my emotions.

"If I don't get to see you before Thanksgiving, have a good one."

"Yeah, thanks. You too."

"Love you."

I nodded as my heart ached.

Tell him!

It was such an agonizing predicament. Tell him and feel heartbroken when he didn't remember. Don't tell him and drown in the anxiety of *wanting* him to know. Angie told him everything or nearly everything and she received zero satisfaction in return.

"Love you." I slid my hand into his hair and leaned forward, pressing my lips to his.

CHAPTER TWENTY-FIVE

I HAD to make an actual trip to Target after McDonald's with Fisher so I didn't show up empty handed. It wouldn't have mattered. Rose and Rory had a much better distraction sitting at the kitchen with an open bottle of wine and three glasses.

"Hey," I said with fake enthusiasm after preparing myself when I saw her vehicle.

Three women in yoga pants, sweaters, and fuzzy socks. Three women with their hair in various ponytail positions. And not a speck of makeup.

"Join us. I'll grab you a glass. Angie just needed a little girl time." Rory's hard gaze was a little more intense at the moment. Angie's visit resurrected her anger. Rose nervously chewing her lips confirmed it.

"How have you been?" I took a seat, feeling over-dressed in jeans and damp panties from Fisher's hand down them. Yes. I absolutely thought about that while smiling at his fiancée. Ironically, I found it easier to feel sorry for her when I wasn't in the same room, except the wedding dress day. I fell victim to that trap like everyone else.

"I've been better." She rolled her eyes.

Maybe Rose and Rory thought I'd feel uncomfortable. Guilt-ridden. It wasn't my fault that Fisher loved me.

"Oh?" I curled my lips between my teeth and smiled at Rory when she set a wine glass on the table and slid the wine bottle toward me.

"Fisher wants to postpone the wedding. And I don't know what to say. I've done everything I can to help him remember me, remember us. And he is getting some memories back, but it's not enough to give him the bigger picture, to make him feel what he felt before the accident."

"I'm sorry to hear that." I felt Rory's judgmental gaze on me, but I didn't give her a single glance. My brain was caught on the word "postpone." Cancel and postpone were not the same thing. So who was telling the truth?

"He's just been really distant with me. I moved out. We agreed to 'date.' We were intimate. Things were back on track. Then it all came to a sudden stop. It's hard to fall in love with someone when you never see them."

They were intimate? Once? Right? Just once?

"Absence makes the heart grow fonder." I tried that on for size. It received three out of three frowns.

"I think I need to try a different tactic. I've requested a room with a king bed instead of two queens on our trip to Costa Rica. And I've scheduled a couple's massage the day before the wedding. Maybe the issue is I've been trying too hard to get him to remember how he used to love me and not enough time making him fall in love with me now. You know?"

Yes, I knew. That was my MO. Except I didn't try to make him love me. He just did. It was effortless and inevitable. Was that enough to thwart temptation on his horizon?

"I shopped for all new lingerie for the trip. Maybe spice things up a bit? He can't say no to lace and satin, right?"

Rose cleared her throat just as I opened my mouth to speak. I had a lot to say on the matter.

"Just don't set yourself up to be disappointed. I really don't think the issue has anything to do with physical attraction. You're beautiful. What man wouldn't be attracted to you?"

Rory slid her gaze to Rose, and I had to stifle my giggle. Rose was taking it too far, making Rory a little jealous.

What woman wouldn't find you attractive?

Angie nodded. Of course she knew she was attractive. No need to show even a little bit of modesty.

"Have you considered the possibility of there being someone else?"

I eyed Rory with caution. Where was she going with that? She didn't look at me like I was supposed to fall to my knees and confess. Maybe she was gently preparing Angie for what I'd hoped would be the inevitable. And I kinda loved my mom for that.

"Wow ..." Angie's eyes widened like two brown saucers.

Nope. She hadn't thought about that.

"No. I mean ..." She shook her head. "No. That's not Fisher. He wouldn't do that. Did he say something to you?"

Rory shook her head. "No. He's never said a word to me." I didn't miss the hint of bitterness in her tone. "But if he doesn't remember his past with you, he might not feel..." Rory pressed her lips together, searching for the right word "...committed."

"No." Angie didn't care for that possibility. "Not Fisher. We've been friends for too long. He knows this has been my dream. And before the accident it was *our* dream. Besides, who would it be? Nobody. He goes to work. Comes home. Hangs out with you guys. No."

"Maybe he's on a dating app. Just hooking up. Meeting his needs without the pressure of remembering his past or leading you on." I grunted and flinched when Rose kicked my shin.

"What?" Angie seemed to find that possibility even more appalling than the idea of him simply being with someone else.

I personally viewed a random hookup for sex much less threatening. That was just sex.

I, however, wasn't just sex to Fisher. Angie should have wished for that. Instead, she was going to lose Fisher to the adorable and cute girl she never saw coming. The way she never noticed our magnetism on the triple date to the concert or her complete unawareness that while she slept in Fisher's bed that night, he had the head of his cock pressed between my legs on the pool table.

They were destined to always be friends (if she was lucky) and we were destined to always be lovers, no matter how destructive and shameless our path to each other ended up being.

Man ... I sure hope that's our destiny.

"I don't think you know Fisher very well." She scoffed.

Rose wrinkled her nose. "Well, I don't know about now. But when you and Fisher weren't together, he was ..." She shot Rory a quick look as if she'd offer some backup.

"He was a ... *virile* young man with an active dating life." Rory for the win.

I was getting tired of Angie's string of shocked expressions. Even at eighteen, I hadn't been *that* naive. Whether I liked it or not, I had to acknowledge Fisher liked sex, and he wasn't the godly man who worried about love or marriage before sticking his dick into someone. Or part of his dick, in my case.

Angie drained the rest of the wine in her glass. "You know ..." She twisted the stem of her glass in one direction and then the other. "We weren't exactly being careful about birth control before the accident. Which was crazy. I had a wedding to plan. A dress purchased. But part of me ..." She shook her head and laughed. "I wanted to get pregnant. I was even late with my period and thought ... this is it." Her grin vanished. "But it wasn't. I got my period the week before his accident. And I know it's stupid, but had I been pregnant, I think, even with the accident, we would have been married by now. That's just Fisher. Maybe he's not the exact same person he was before the accident. But at his core, he's still the same good man. He would have done the right thing.

And I know ... I just know we would have eventually fallen in love again because it's us. It's always been us."

I had to hand it to Angie. She unknowingly brought her A-game. It wasn't the orphan standing in front of a full-length mirror, but it still packed a punch. My desire to keep my hands up, fisted in front of my face, dissipated. Maybe because it was easy to forget that Fisher didn't remember our love the way I did. His love for me spanned months, not years.

Was I getting too comfortable? Too confident? Could four days in Costa Rica derail us?

I finished my wine and pushed my chair back a few inches. "I'm going to finish cleaning my bathroom."

"Happy Thanksgiving if I don't see you before then." Angie smiled.

"You too. Do you have plans?"

"Fisher's parents' house, of course." She shrugged like, *duh*.

Duh indeed.

I should have known. I think I did know. But ignorance really was bliss when it came to my boyfriend and his fiancée.

"Tell them hi for me."

The woman they don't know they're supposed to love yet.

"Sure thing."

I sulked to the bathroom. Scrubbed the hell out of the shower and then the floor with Matt Maeson's "Hallucinogenics" blasting through my earbuds.

CHAPTER TWENTY-SIX

My grandparents were scheduled to arrive on Wednesday, a nice buffer between Rory and me. Things were better, but she wasn't completely giving up all her anger. I had let it slide, but if she didn't shake out of it by Thanksgiving, we were going to have a "You Went To Prison" talk. For the rest of my life, I reserved the right to play that card. She abandoned me during the most delicate and influential years of my life.

Basically, all my imperfections would be blamed on her temporary absence. Okay, not really. But I did have every intention of using that excuse when things got rough. And since the *incident*, things had been rough.

"Fisher's coming over," Rory announced Wednesday morning as I read a book on the sofa while Rose knitted something that resembled a scarf from the chair next to me.

"Okay," I said in a controlled tone, even if inside she'd lit a fire of anticipation with her news. "Why? Are you two back on speaking terms?"

"He's coming over to quickly install a rail by the toilet. My mom can't get on and off the toilet that well right now. Her knee is bad."

"Nothing like waiting until the last minute," I said.

"She wanted him to do it last week, but she stopped talking to him, so he had no way of knowing," Rose said, tossing my mom a wry grin.

"Anyway, I'm just letting you know. He's coming over to *work*."

With wide eyes, I nodded slowly. "Okay. Thanks for telling me. Otherwise, I might have thought he was coming over to have sex with me since you spoiled my last chance at it."

Rose snorted and quickly covered her mouth. Rory narrowed her eyes at me.

Biting my lips together, I kept a fairly straight face.

Seconds later, there was a knock at the door. My tummy flipped several times and my heart did its crazy thing where it liked to skip a few beats.

"Hey," Fisher said to Rory when she opened the door.

"Thanks for doing this," Rory said almost begrudgingly.

"Sure. I would have done it sooner had I known you needed it."

"Well, I've ... been busy." Rory led him to the bathroom.

But Fisher glanced back and saw me and Rose in the living room, and his face exploded into what I'd decided was his Reese Only smile.

I bit my lower lip, but it hid nothing.

"Fisher, are you coming?" Rory all but barked at him. Rose sniggered as did I.

"Yes, ma'am," Fisher said.

While he installed the bar, Rory made stuffing to be cooked the next day and Rose worked on pies. I had no cooking jobs yet, so I meandered down the hallway to the bathroom.

"Leave him alone so he can finish up," Rory instructed.

"Yeah, yeah," I pretty much ignored her. I was twenty-four not four. "Need help?" I asked, standing in the doorway as Fisher finished drilling holes in the wall.

"I'm good." He stayed focused on his task.

I loved watching focused Fisher. It was foreplay for me. The stern focus on his face. The bend and stretch of his arms and large capable hands. The way his tongue would make a lazy swipe along his lower lip when he was measuring something and marking it with the pencil he kept behind his ear. The fact that his jeans rode low but only showed the side waistband of his briefs instead of plumber's crack. Poor plumbers ... it wasn't like they all had big guts, poorly fitting jeans, and seemingly no underwear.

"Whatcha thinking about?" He caught me off guard when he shot me a quick glance over his shoulder.

I smirked. "You don't want to know."

Fisher's gaze made a quick, appreciative swipe along the full length of my body. "Don't be so sure."

"I was thinking about plumbers' cracks."

"I don't have a plumber's crack."

"I know."

"Because you're staring at my ass?"

"Yes."

He chuckled without turning toward me again. "How's it look?"

"No comment. Rory probably has the room bugged. I'd hate to be in timeout for Thanksgiving. Have you uh ... remembered anything new since I saw you on Sunday?"

"Yes."

"Oh? What's that?"

He screwed the plates onto the wall. "I remembered my senior prom."

"That's ... interesting. Did something prompt it?"

"Yes and no. I think there was a trigger, but the memory wasn't immediate. It came to me later while I was sleeping."

"What triggered it?"

"Angie stopped by and showed me something. And I think that did it." He attached the bar to the plates.

"That's vague. What did she show you?"

"The dress she bought for her cousin's wedding and the coordinating tie she bought for me to wear."

They were going to wear coordinating outfits to her cousin's wedding. How vomit-worthy. "And that triggered memories from prom?"

"Yes. The coordinating outfits."

"So you dreamed of what? Shopping for a bowtie, cummerbund, and pocket square to match her dress?"

"Not exactly." Fisher tested the rail, using it to help him stand, pushing down on it with his weight.

"Then what exactly?"

"You'll take it wrong."

"I doubt it," I said reflexively.

As he returned his tools to his tool bag, he blew out a slow breath. "We had a hotel room that night. A friend who graduated two years early, but also went to prom because his girlfriend was younger, got the room for us when he booked one for himself and his date. I remember staring at her light pink dress on the floor the next morning and yes ... my matching bowtie and cummerbund."

The next morning. I swallowed past the thick lump in my throat. He was two for two. Both of his memories thus far about Angie involved sex. It wasn't exactly how he presented them to me, but I could read between the lines.

They had sex ... she got pregnant.

They had sex ... the next morning he stared at their clothes on the hotel room floor.

He was remembering sex with Angie while remembering Happy Meals with me.

"See..." he derailed me from my train of thought "... you're taking it wrong." He brushed a little drywall dust off his shirt and jeans.

"I'm not taking anything wrong. You're remembering sex with Angie." I lifted a shoulder and dropped it like a ten-pound weight. "Was it good sex?"

Resting one hand on his hip, he dropped his chin to his chest and pushed another long sigh out his nose. "I don't want to have this conversation with you. You asked me a question. I wanted to be honest with you. But I don't want the strange cherry-picking of memories my brain seems to be doing to drive us apart. Just ... don't let it go there."

Go there. I wasn't supposed to let my brain go there, but his brain could go wherever it wanted to go. "I don't feel like that's an answer to my question." Self-destruction was a lit fuse.

You saw it.

You sensed its impending urgency, it's impending doom.

You felt panicked.

But you also felt helpless to do anything to stop it.

Fisher glanced up at me with a frown on his face. "If I say no, you won't believe me. If I say yes ... well, I don't know how you'll react. So why can't I just plead the Fifth here?"

I may have been ten years younger than him, but that didn't mean I was born yesterday. If it hadn't been memories of good sex, he would have said as much, and he would have gone to great lengths to make me believe the truth. That wishy-washy explanation was a yes. He remembered having good sex with Angie.

Fantastic ...

So a week before he was set to go with her to Costa Rica (her and her new lingerie and a king bed), he was having good sex dreams about her.

Forgive me, but I *was* still human with a tendency to have irrational feelings and an instinct for jealousy.

I drew in a long breath of courage, weak courage at best. Then I exhaled it. "Well, it's wonderful that you're slowly getting your memory back. And at least you're getting a sense of why you fell in love with her and agreed to marry her. The sex was good. But I think I already knew that because I came to your house that morning after the two of you had good sex that was apparently my doing because I questioned your ability to get and sustain an erection." With a fake smile, I averted my gaze to the floor. "I'll get the vacuum."

"Reese ..."

I didn't pause. My heart had already shifted into defense mode. Fight or flight.

"Did he finish the job?" Rory asked as I retrieved the handheld vacuum from the entry closet.

Yes. He finished crushing my heart.

"He did. Just needs to clean up the drywall dust." I held my breath or at least most of it while taking only tiny inhales and exhales like a woman in labor while I shouldered past him blocking the doorway.

"Reese ..."

I turned on the little vacuum which silenced him, and I took lots of time making sure I sucked up every speck of drywall dust. Before I got it shut off, he squatted behind me, his hand taking the vacuum from mine and shutting it off.

"I love you today," he whispered in my ear.

Nope. Wrong four words. I loved those words on any other day. They just fell flat when all I could think about was him having sex with Angie because it seemed like that was all *his* mind cared to remember about her. Rory's words replayed in my head.

A virile young man.

I highly doubted *virile* young men were immune to sex dreams, especially the lingering thoughts they provoked. Just because one didn't want to think about something didn't mean they had control over it. There was no way I wasn't going to be thinking about him and Angie having sex, and it *definitely* wasn't because I wanted to think about it.

"Thanks for putting up the bar. I'm sure my grandma will really appreciate it."

"Are you punishing me for my honesty?"

With pursed lips, I shook my head a half dozen times. "You asked me."

My head shake quickly transitioned into a series of nods. "I did. Stupid me. I think I'm done asking you about anything."

"Reese." He took a step forward and reached for my waist.

"No." I shifted to the side, wedged between the toilet and the vanity as I held my hands up to let him know I didn't want to be touched.

"It means nothing ... at least nothing that you're worried about."

I grunted a laugh. "You're going to Costa Rica with her. It might end up meaning something."

"Why don't you trust me?"

I rubbed my temples. "We've been over this. Even if I convinced myself it's safe to trust you, I don't trust your memories lurking at every turn. One trigger after another. I mean ... that's all it could take. One trigger to remember why you said yes to her. And what if that comes on the heels of a beautiful wedding where everyone is in the mood for love? Good friends. Food. *Alcohol.* Dancing. Coordinating outfits. A shared hotel room."

"You're being ridiculous."

"And you're being stupid!"

Fisher flinched. And the noise in the kitchen silenced. Everyone and everything was silent except the lingering echo of my outburst.

"If you're done, it might be time for you to leave." Rory appeared a few feet from the bathroom door. "What do I owe you, Fisher?"

Keeping his back to her, he stared at me, but I kept my attention focused on the floor between us.

"Nothing. You owe me nothing." He snagged his tool bag off the floor and headed straight to the front door.

Click.

It closed behind him.

"Want to talk about it?" Rory said.

"No." I still had lots of anger to unleash as my "no" came out a little harsher than intended. "I don't want to talk to you, not after more than a week of you not talking to me. I don't want your opinion, a lecture, a long string of I-told-you-so's. Just ..." I handed her the vacuum and made a sharp left into my bedroom, slamming and locking the door behind me.

CHAPTER TWENTY-SEVEN

Dear Lost Fisherman,

I'm really mad at you right now. And I don't care if it's rational thinking on my part or not. Sometimes a person just needs to be irrational. This front that I've been holding up is exhausting. One can only show bravery for so long. Even the strongest people break sometimes. I wish I was immune to insecurities, but I'm not. I wish your I-love-you's made me feel more confident in us, but they don't.

I know Angie's still dazed with disbelief that you can't remember the first girl you ever loved. The girl you met when you were six. I get it. Because I'm struggling with us. It's equally as hard for me to imagine us falling in love twice without you remembering the first time. And I can't even articulate how badly I

wish you would remember us. Not deduce the fact that you must have liked me a lot to show me your nerdy cruciverbalist heart, but actually feel what that really meant. I can't tell you how many times the eager words have sat on the end of my tongue, desperate to jump out and just tell you. Tell you that we were in love. Tell you that you were my first and forever love. And in my gullible, fairy-tale head, you magically remember everything and we live happily ever after.

Fuck fairy tales.

Seven across. Hint: Disloyal. Ungodly.

Faithless.

I was angry. Angry that it was Thanksgiving and she was with him.

Angry that I had to endure the long stares from Rose and Rory while my grandparents yapped about their aches and pains.

Angry that Fisher hadn't tried calling me to apologize for … I didn't even know. But *something*. Really, he needed to apologize for something.

And if I were being completely honest, I was angry that he got on his motorcycle that day. Angry that he lost his memory. Maybe that meant I wouldn't have moved back to Colorado. That might have meant we wouldn't have had the possibility of a second chance. But as I simmered like a pot of soup left on the stove too long, I started to think Michigan sounded pretty good.

"How's your job, Reese?" Grandma took a breather

from her winded explanation of ailments and their corresponding medications to finally show a little interest in her granddaughter.

"It's the best job. I love the midwives I work with. I'm so excited to start my master's program next year."

"She does love it. We get to see her come home with no sleep after a long birth but boundless energy because she loves it so much." Rory, for what felt like the first time in nearly two weeks, shared a genuine smile.

"That's amazing, dear. We're so proud of you. Is everything else good? Do you have a boyfriend? Or a girlfriend?"

I loved the way they accepted my mom for who she was. The way they loved Rose. If only my dad's parents could have been so loving. Like God. I believed God loved everyone. It was just what felt right to me ... when I started thinking for myself.

Thanks to Fisher.

"I have a boyfriend."

Rory and Rose visibly stiffened.

"And where is he today?" Grandpa asked.

"Having Thanksgiving dinner with his family."

And his fiancée.

"Will we get to meet him before we go home?" Grandma asked as she wiped her red painted lips with her napkin.

"I'm not sure." I used my fork to fiddle with the remaining food on my plate.

"What does he do?" Grandma kept coming with the questions.

"He works in construction."

"Oh," she replied quickly. "Rory, doesn't your old landlord do that too? What's his name?"

Rory grabbed another dinner roll and took a generous bite while nodding. "Fisher," she mumbled over the roll.

"Does your boyfriend happen to know Fisher?"

I grinned. "He does, actually. They're really close."

Rose cleared her throat and fisted her hand at her mouth to hide her unavoidable laughter. Rory didn't find it quite as funny.

"That's nice, dear. Is it serious? Will I be attending my granddaughter's wedding soon?"

"It's serious, but no wedding. I'd like to finish school first."

Rory ...

The epitome of a mother waiting for her daughter to get her heart broken. And she wasn't wrong. There had already been a lot of heartbreak with what felt like unavoidably more to come.

"Well, I do hope we get to meet him."

"Me too."

"Speaking of Fisher ..." Grandpa spoke up, and for a second I'd forgotten that Fisher's name was just mentioned. I thought my grandpa magically knew or figured out my secret. "How's he been since the accident?"

"Yes," Grandma jumped in. "Has he remembered his fiancée?"

"He's doing well." Rory plastered on a believable smile. "Getting back a few missing memories, but not enough to remember being engaged to Angie. So that's been a little rough. And I'm not sure if they'll stay together, to be honest."

"Why is that?" Grandma questioned.

"There might be someone else in the picture."

"What?" Grandma's hand pressed to her chest on a gasp.

"It's complicated at the moment, but we highly suspect he has found someone else."

"Well, someone needs to talk some sense into that young man. He can't just abandon his fiancée. And what kind of woman would even dream of swooping in and stealing another woman's man after a horrific accident?"

Rose eyed me like an older sister who just realized her younger sister was about to get in trouble.

"Well, Mom, in all fairness to Fisher and this other woman, *if* there is another woman, he doesn't remember Angie. She's basically been this stranger claiming to be his lifelong friend and the love of his life. We can't totally blame him for not feeling what he doesn't know he's supposed to feel and therefore finding it easy to ... get distracted by someone else."

"I'll give Fisher a pass, maybe." Grandma frowned. "But not the slut moving in on him."

Rory's mom was outspoken like my dad's mom, just in a different way. However, they probably would have both agreed that I was a slut.

Rory flinched and so did Rose. Me? Nope. I didn't flinch. I could see it from both sides. And because I could see it from both sides, I thought we all needed a little coming to Jesus moment.

"It's me," I said.

677

"Sorry. What, dear?" Grandma said, smiling at me ... the slut.

"I'm the slut."

"Reese," Rory whispered, closing her eyes and shaking her head.

"Excuse me?" Grandma squinted.

After taking a sip of my water, I calmly set it on the table and grinned. "*Fisher* is my boyfriend. And we fell in love over five years ago. And as wrong as that probably seems to everyone else, the only thing that was wrong was the timing. But we have an unexpected second chance. And we've fallen in love again. Well, I've never stopped loving him, but he ... he's fallen in love with me again. And he doesn't remember what we were before now. And that's heartbreaking and frustrating. But it's also beautiful and maybe even perfect. And I realize this is a really hard pill for everyone else to swallow, but our love has nothing to do with Angie. I don't think her ties to the man who doesn't remember her makes what *we* have wrong. So let's all take a timeout here and not call people sluts when we haven't walked in their shoes. I realize it's often the Christian way, but I think I can love God *and* love every single one of his children without judging anyone. And the last I checked, you're also sitting at the same table as my lesbian mother and her partner, whom we love so very much. And it's hard to imagine anything about their love is *wrong*. Wouldn't we all agree?"

Rose wiped a tear from her face, and Rory's emotions shined in her eyes too.

My grandparents held an even mix of shock and embarrassment in their expressions.

I stood, tossing my napkin onto the table. "I'm going to take a few minutes to myself. Call me when pie is served."

Nobody said a word. And I was grateful. I didn't want apologies or awkward attempts to explain away the previous conversation where I was labeled a slut. Had I not been the slut, it could have been somebody else's daughter or granddaughter.

Everyone means the world to someone. Or at least they should.

When I collapsed onto my bed, I called Fisher. After multiple rings, it went to voicemail. So I called again ... and again.

On the fourth call, he answered. "Hi," he said in a neutral tone. "I'm eating dinner. What's up?" He was eating dinner with his family. His whole family and Angie.

"I love you today," I said.

Silence.

More silence.

"Say it. Say it back to me, Fisher. Like you mean it. Like it matters."

"Can we chat about this later?"

"I said it. In front of my grandparents ... after they unknowingly called me a slut. I said it. I'm tired of not saying it. I'm tired of feeling guilty. Just ... say it and let everyone else *fucking* deal with it."

He cleared his throat. "So you clogged the garbage disposal?"

I pressed *End*.

Throwing my arm over my face, I grumbled and

growled, just like the old Fisher. I was angry with him and the rest of the world. And I know it wasn't fair for me to ambush him like that—after all, he stood up to Rory and unapologetically told her that he loved me.

But I wanted him to make the gesture without getting caught first. Was that too much to ask?

Maybe.

"Stupid ..." I whispered to myself. "Stupid. Stupid. Stupid." Just minutes earlier, I had given my family a long speech on being kind and not judging others. I just left the kitchen with the words *everybody means the world to somebody* in my head.

Was Angie someone's world since her parents died and Fisher lost his memories of her? It was such a kind thing of me to ask Fisher to destroy her in front of his entire family on Thanksgiving. I was ashamed of myself.

And tired.

Getting a call that a baby was ready to come into the world was exactly what I needed. But that call never came.

"Hey." Rory smiled at me when she opened my door a crack. "Pie is being served."

"Okay," I said, staring at the ceiling.

The door clicked shut, but it did so with Rory on my side of it. Then the bed dipped. She laid herself next to me, also staring at the ceiling, as she reached for my hand.

"I know he loves you," she said. "I just want you to have it easier than I had it. I don't want love to be this complicated and messy for you."

"Messy ..." I laughed a little. "That's how we know it's real."

"I adore Fisher ... or I did. And honestly, it's just all been *a lot*. I was hit pretty hard, completely out of the blue. It would have been a lot to handle five years ago, but add in the accident, his memory loss, and Angie ... well ... it's more than my heart and brain can reconcile at the moment. And I know ... I *know* I have no right to say this, but I'm going to say it anyway. Seeing you and Fisher that day in that situation was not what any mom wants to see."

I laughed and laughed some more. Rory started to giggle too. She definitely had *no* right to say anything to me. She saw Fisher enjoying my breasts. I saw Rose doing so much more to her.

Rolling toward her, I tucked my hands under my cheek. "I know it's not the way you imagined ... it's not the way I imagined ... but your little girl is in love. And it's big. And all-consuming. It's scary. It's exhilarating. And real. So if you want to be the mom you didn't get to be when I was going through my teenaged years, then I'm going to need a hand to hold and a shoulder to cry on as I fight like hell to get my prince."

"Your prince ..." She gave me a sad smile and rested her hand on my cheek.

"I need you to want my happiness more than Angie's. And I know that's hard because Angie is a good person. And her love story with Fisher is pretty amazing. But it's not forever. I just ... I know it."

Rory nodded slowly. "I've got you."

CHAPTER TWENTY-EIGHT

AFTER PIE.

After an apology from my grandparents.

After playing six games of Hearts.

Fisher called me.

"I'm calling it a night." I excused myself from the game when I saw his number on my phone's screen. It was close to ten-thirty at night. "Hi," I answered in a meek voice just as I reached my bedroom.

"I'm in your driveway."

My heart sucked at staying in chill mode or staying mad at him very long.

"Want to go for a drive?"

"I suppose." That was my version of chill, even though I was already grabbing a hoodie to wear over my leggings and heading down the hallway.

"Take your time."

"Okay." I ended the call while I pulled on my wool-lined boots.

"Going somewhere?" Rory asked as they picked up the cards and glasses from the table.

"I am." I grinned.

"Okay. See you in the morning."

Was she assuming I was coming home after they went to bed or not until morning? I was twenty-four. It didn't matter. But what did matter was I knew she knew who I was leaving with and she didn't give me anything but an honest smile.

"Goodnight."

Everyone else told me goodnight as I went out the front door. A few snowflakes swirled in the cold air, and my lost fisherman was in his truck waiting for me.

When I climbed in, he gave me a reserved smile. I felt certain that was all he dared to give me after my unexpected call to him during Thanksgiving dinner with his family.

Fisher drove us to his house, and I wasn't surprised. We didn't speak on the short ride. When we arrived, he climbed out, but I didn't. Stopping at the front of the truck, he looked at me expectantly for a few seconds before he made his way to my door and grabbed the handle. But he didn't open it right away. He paused and that look spread across his face. The concentration. The wrinkled brow and narrowed eyes.

Then he lifted his gaze and kept it on me as he slowly opened my door.

"I opened your door for you, but I acted like I didn't want to do it. I told you to pull the lever to make it open. I think I was an asshole to you."

I couldn't help but wonder if all his memory loss was

physical from the accident or if some of it was psychological. Did he have emotional reasons for not wanting to remember his love for me? His love for Angie?

"Sometimes." I nodded, but I grinned too. I had a love-hate relationship with Fisher's asshole side.

I turned to get out, but I wrapped my arms around his neck and my legs around his waist instead. "I'm sorry *I* was the asshole today when I called you. It was stupid. I don't know what got into me." I buried my face in his warm neck and kissed it.

Fisher shut the door and locked his truck before carrying me inside the house. "It's all going to be over, settled, done. Soon. It just ... has to be."

I released him, easing to my feet. We took off our boots and he slipped off his fleece jacket as I pulled off my sweatshirt.

"Drink?" He curled my hair behind my ears.

"No," I whispered, gazing up at him.

"Bed?" A hopeful grin stole his lips.

"No," I whispered.

"Then what can I do for my beautiful girl?"

"Dance with me."

Fisher's eyebrows lifted a bit. "Dance?"

I nodded.

"I'm not sure I'm a dancer."

I shrugged, retrieving my phone from my sweatshirt pocket. Taking his hand, I pulled him to the kitchen. "Dim the lights. I know you love ambient lighting."

"How do you know that?" He turned on some accent lights and dimmed them while I tapped a song on my phone. Judah & The Lion's "Only To Be With You."

"Because I know you."

"What if I want to know you like you know me?" He pulled me into his arms, and we swayed in a slow circle.

"You do, my lost fisherman ... you do."

"Did we dance? Are you trying to bring back more memories?"

"No." I kissed his neck as his hands slid from my lower back to my butt. "Just making new ones."

We danced and we kissed.

One song led to another song. It didn't matter that he wasn't a dancer and neither was I. Our bodies molded and moved, perfectly together and in sync with each other's own rhythm.

Fisher's hands stayed on the outside of my clothes, yet touched me intimately.

The graze of his hand over my breast, my butt ... the slide of his fingers up my inner thigh.

Open-mouthed kisses.

Soft moans.

More dancing.

We weren't sneaking around. We weren't rushed. It was just us, and we had the whole night.

I was exhausted with no desire to sleep.

I was turned on, but not wanting to take it any further yet.

I was perfectly content, but insanely eager.

We were messy and alive and living in the moment. Our love only mattered for a day.

A kiss.

A breath.

Eventually the songs ended, leaving us in silence

dotted with the soft sounds of our kisses. Yet we kept swaying like we made our own music, like we had our own rhythm. I couldn't help but imagine a life with Fisher. A real life where we'd enjoy dinner and talk about current events, work, or plan a trip.

After dinner we'd do the dishes and listen to music like tonight. It would lead to dancing and kissing, a seemingly unhurried passion, but we'd still leave our clothes in a trail down the hallway because we would forever be that couple. We'd make love in a frenzy before falling asleep in each other's arms, only to wake in the morning and do it all over again, only slower and with the soft glow of the morning sun on us. We'd look into each other's eyes the whole time, starting everyday perfectly connected.

Or ... and I liked this dream the best ... we'd eventually have to give up our morning sex because we'd wake to the pitter patter of tiny feet charging toward our bedroom to wake us up. And we'd steal long minutes every morning to tickle little bellies and kiss soft cheeks while a chorus of giggles and squeals filled the room.

And on mornings, if we were lucky, we'd distract them with a thirty-minute show on a television or a tablet while we jumped into the shower ... together.

"What's going through that beautiful head of yours?" Fisher asked before kissing the top of said beautiful head. My cheek had been resting on his chest, feeling his heartbeat, as we swayed in silence.

"I want this," I murmured.

"Want what? More dancing?"

Lifting my head, I gazed up at him and smiled. "More ... everything."

Fisher blinked several times as his knuckles brushed my cheeks. He knew. He knew what *more* and *everything* meant. "Me too." He kissed me while walking me backward out of the kitchen. And I begged for it to be like my dream.

It was.

He broke our kiss to remove my shirt. And we sneaked another kiss before we removed his shirt. More kisses.

My bra.

His back against the hallway wall while I kissed his chest and unbuttoned his jeans.

More kisses and more steps ensued as he inched my leggings south, but just barely past my butt. Fisher's strong hands slid inside the back of my panties, gripping me, pulling me close, rubbing me against him.

The brush of his bare chest along my nipples while his tongue teased mine ... it was intoxicating. Everything about us felt all-consuming. We were memories in the making, ignited by a past he couldn't remember and fueled by a desire for a future that seemed painfully just out of reach.

"You're so..." he kissed down my body, kneeling in front of me "...fucking beautiful." His tongue teased my navel as his hands worked my leggings and panties the rest of the way down my legs. "And sexy ... god you're so sexy." His mouth moved lower.

My hands found their place in his hair, and they curled into fists, forcing him to look up at me. "I had the biggest crush on you." More heat found its way to my cheeks, taking me back to that eighteen-year-old girl, out of my mind infatuated with him.

A slow smile worked its way up Fisher's face as his hands slid along the back of my legs, coming to a rest just below my butt. "Yeah?"

Why was I embarrassed? Why did my heart go wild in my chest making my tummy feel nervous? I wasn't retelling our past to him. I wasn't telling him how he felt about me. I wasn't telling him anything he had to reach for to truly understand. They were *my* feelings.

They shaped me as a woman in ways he'd never know even if he did remember everything. And I wanted him to see me. All of me.

"Yeah." I bit my lower lip for a second. "I had no idea sexy wore jeans, a faded tee, and work boots. I had no idea sexy drove a truck and mowed the lawn without a shirt. Well ..." I giggled. "I should've known sexy mowed the lawn without a shirt. On mornings we rode to work together, I was so giddy. I practically sprinted to your truck, slowing at the last minute to act cool and controlled. Then I prayed you had music playing so you didn't hear my heart so out of control. And I'd stare at your hands on the steering wheel, those veins up your arms, your full lips as you'd lick them after taking a sip of your coffee." I slowly shook my head. "I was in deep, feeling things I'd never experienced before. And it felt so wrong, but I couldn't stop. And you didn't help ... you and your effortless sex appeal just ... *every single day*."

He stood slowly, kissing my chest and neck on his way to my lips. And before he kissed me on the mouth, he paused, letting his gaze ghost along my face. "I didn't think I could love you more." He swept my hair away from my face before weaving his fingers through it. "I was so fucking wrong."

We kissed.

Clothes vanished along with the rest of the world. And I knew we were an unstoppable storm. But ... how much damage would we do in our pursuit to be together?

I died a little when he sank into me. It felt different. We felt different.

Fisher's heavy breaths washed over my cheek as his lips found my ear. "*You* are my favorite place in the world."

I gripped his backside as my legs wrapped around him.

That spoke to my soul, that *place* that defined us because we were everywhere our souls took us. And maybe that was Heaven. And maybe that was Hell. But in that moment, it was in a bed of messy sheets and tangled limbs.

It was a pretty *fucking* amazing place.

A LITTLE BEFORE four in the morning, I wormed my way out of his enveloped arms. I kinda loved that he held me so close, like he didn't want to ever let me go. After peeing, I stole a hoodie from his closet and pulled it over my head. Closing his bedroom door behind me, I tiptoed to the kitchen and opened the fridge.

"Score." I grinned at the plate of holiday leftovers he

must have brought home from his parents' house. Pulling off the plastic wrap, I swiped my finger through the cold mashed potatoes. "Oh my gosh, those are good." I skipped the fork and made a second swipe through the mashed potatoes with my finger. They had a buttermilk taste to them.

"Are you really eating my lunch?"

I jumped and turned toward Fisher, licking the potatoes from the corner of my mouth.

He sauntered toward me in nothing but his charcoal gray briefs that hugged him in *all* the right places. "Stop eyeing my cock while licking your lips."

My gaze snapped up to meet his as my tongue made a quick retreat back into my mouth. I grinned. "These are the best potatoes I've ever had. And if you tell Rory that, I'll kill you."

"Why are you eating cold potatoes?" He ducked and kissed me.

My hand pressed to his warm chest. "Because I love almost everything cold. After my dad died, I lived on leftovers. My grandma made huge batches of everything, and we'd essentially eat leftovers for a week. And I was either hanging out with friends or working, so I often grabbed cold leftovers and ate them on the go." My fingers made a return trip to the potatoes, and I held it up to him.

Fisher wrinkled his nose. "I'm not a fan of cold potatoes."

"No?" I tilted my head to the side before slowly sucking my finger.

An unhurried grin curled his lips. "Was I snoring?"

I shook my head. "I had to pee. Then I decided I was hungry."

"I like this on you." He tugged the strings to *his* hoodie. "Not as much as I like me on you, but it's nice."

Popping a piece of cold turkey into my mouth, I teased the waistband of his briefs with my other hand. "How was Thanksgiving with your family?"

Fisher watched my fingers at his waistband for a few seconds before lifting his chin along with one slightly raised eyebrow. "It was okay. Lots of kids. Lots of everything. My mom gave a sappy toast that was more like a speech about how grateful she was that my life had been spared. It started a cry fest. I'm glad to be alive, but can we stop talking about it?"

I giggled. "How dare your mom express such gratitude for her child on *Thanksgiving*."

"I'm just not a fan of being the center of attention. That's Arnie's thing. Not mine."

"Try being an only child. There's no escaping the center."

He nodded slowly. "So ... you told your grandparents about us?"

"I did." I smiled. "It felt amazing, like we were real." I covered the plate with the plastic wrap.

Fisher grabbed the plate and returned it to the fridge. "We are real."

I reached across the island to grab an apple from his big bowl of them. "You know what I mean. *Official*."

"I don't know what you mean."

"Oof ..." I sucked in a sharp breath when he pinned

me to the counter, my chest stretched over it with a shiny green apple in one hand.

"I don't know what you mean, because I heard nothing after you bent over my counter." His fingers teased my outer thighs. "And I discovered you're not wearing *anything* under my sweatshirt."

"Fisher ..." I gulped. It was a compromising position I hadn't been in before. He restrained me using his body and the counter instead of zip ties, but the effect was the same.

"You can't be in this position..." he hiked the hoodie up, completely exposing my bare butt "...with callipygian tattooed on your very sexy and shapely ass..." his knee nudged my legs apart a little wider "...and not expect me to fuck you."

Before I could respond, the head of his hot, wet cock slid between my legs, teasing my clit. I liked the new Fisher too much to spend much time missing the old Fisher, but when he talked dirty to me, letting me know I was going to get *fucked*, pinned against the countertop, I welcomed the glimpse of old Fisher and every ounce of the forbidden he brought with him.

"WANT TO COME IN?" I asked Fisher when he drove me home a little before nine Friday morning.

"I actually have a few jobs to check on."

I frowned. "You're making your crew work the day after Thanksgiving?"

"Deadlines, baby."

"One cup of coffee."

"Dinner tonight."

On a sigh, I gave him a reluctant nod. "Here. With my grandparents."

It was his turn to frown. "Is Rory ready to have me over for dinner? It killed her to ask me to install that bar by the toilet."

"She adores you."

"She has coffee and wine with Angie. And she does Angie's hair."

"She does?" I narrowed my eyes.

With a tight smile, he nodded a half dozen times.

"Huh. I didn't know that."

Fisher's gaze shifted to the front door as Rory and Rose came out in their sweatshirts, jogging pants, and tennis shoes.

"They must be escaping my grandparents for a walk. I bet it's a long walk."

They eyed us as they made a big production of stretching on the porch.

"Call me when you get home." I reached for the door handle.

"No kiss?"

I shot him a sideways glance. "I figured you didn't want to kiss me in front of them."

"I'm not the one getting grounded. What do I have to lose?"

Rolling my eyes, I leaned over the console. "I'm twenty-four. I think my grounding days are over."

He slid one hand behind my neck and grinned just

before kissing me with no urgency to stop, with lots of tongue, and a little moan on his part. "Bye, beautiful."

Fisher lit up my world in the most spectacular fashion.

"Have a good day." I climbed out of his truck and strutted my stuff to the front door as Rory and Rose gave Fisher a tiny wave.

"Good morning," Rose said.

"Mor ... ning ..." I singsonged, wearing a grin that was nearly too big for my face.

"Did you have a *fun* night?" Rory asked before smirking.

I reached for the door handle. "Fun night. Fun morning. Fun shower. Just so much fun."

Rose snorted a laugh.

"So help me ... if Fisher doesn't make this all okay in the end, he's not going to live to see his next birthday."

"Wow, babes. Prison really toughened you up," Rose said, grabbing my mom's hand and dragging her toward the sidewalk.

I didn't want Fisher to miss his next birthday, but I loved seeing my mom on my team. It meant everything to me.

CHAPTER TWENTY-NINE

For every step we took forward, it felt like we took two backward.

Fisher had to cancel dinner with us because his family (including Angie) were getting together when some of his extended family paid a surprise visit. That visit lasted the rest of the weekend.

Work on Monday and a mom of twins going into labor on Tuesday spilled over into Wednesday. I crashed when I finally got home. And by Thursday morning, Fisher was on his way to the airport with Angie for four days and three *nights* in Costa Rica.

I kept my chin up and feigned any confidence that tried to slip away when I had time to think about something other than pregnant mamas. On Friday morning, Fisher called me.

"Hey!" I answered my phone on my way to work.

"Good morning. You working?"

"On my way now."

"Well, I fucking hate that I didn't get to say goodbye in person."

"It's life." I meant it, but it still didn't ease my own disappointment. I want to say what a mature adult would've or should've said in that situation.

"Not the life I want."

I smiled.

"Yeah, in-person goodbyes should be mandatory. How is Costa Rica?"

"Green."

I laughed.

"What's on the agenda for today?"

"Apparently massages and rehearsal dinner."

"Massages, huh?" I pretended it was news to me. "Sounds relaxing. I could use a massage."

"I'll massage you when I get home."

"Mmm ... that would be amazing. How's your room?"

With the king-sized bed.

"It's nice."

Nice. That was what he gave me. And I didn't have the nerve to ask about the specific sleeping situation. It would have led to the "why don't you trust me" speech.

"Where are you?"

"Just finished jogging on the beach. I'm in the lobby. I need to go back to the room and shower."

Was he going to lock the door to the bathroom?

Jealousy, irrational or not, whacked away at my chest, making me hurt everywhere.

"Angie doesn't jog?"

"She was still asleep."

"Oh ... are you sharing a room?"

Ugh! I hated playing dumb. Fishing. Waiting to catch him in a lie. But I couldn't make myself stop. It was a terrible feeling.

"Uh ... yeah. The place is booked."

"So you tried to get your own room?"

He sighed. "Reese, don't do this. Nothing good will come of it. I'll be home Sunday night. It's just two more nights. I'm not happy about this situation, but we've discussed this ad nauseam. One month. It ends in one month. We've got this, right?"

I nodded. Of course he couldn't see my nod or my pouty face.

"I love you today."

I kept nodding.

"Reese?"

"Yeah."

"I love you. You. *Youuu*. Okay? Don't doubt that for one second. Go to my house. Crawl in my bed. And think of all the *things* I'm going to do to you when I get home on Sunday."

"Yeah."

"Jesus ... stop. Give me more than a 'yeah.' Tell me you love me. Or be honest and tell me you're pissed off that I agreed to come here. Give me something more than one emotionless word."

I pulled into the clinic's parking lot. "I love you. And I'm pissed off that you agreed to go to Costa Rica with your fiancée."

"Stop calling her my fiancée," he said with a defeated tone.

"Is she still wearing the diamond ring you gave her?

When she introduces you to everyone at the wedding as her fiancé, are you going to correct her? If not, then she's your fiancée. And I'm the slutty mistress."

"Reese Capshaw, knock that shit off."

I cringed, rubbing my hand over my face. Why couldn't I stop? Why was I in self-destruction mode? And why couldn't I get out of it?

The unfairest part for him was he had no way to make it right. Not while he was there with her. Fisher was helpless. And I was hell-bent on making him feel terrible. It wasn't one of my finer moments, but it was honest. It was human.

"I'm at work now. I have to go."

"This ends. When I get home this ends. I'm not doing this any longer. Fuck my memory. Fuck family loyalty. I can't do this another month. I want you. That's it. You. So go sulk. You have three days for your pity party. Then I'm going to tie you to ..."

Oh shit. SHIT.

I knew it happened the second it happened. And not only was I not with him, but I was not even in the same country. And it freaked me out. It scared me for a million reasons.

"Jesus ..." he whispered.

And me? I ended the call. The equivalent of turning and running away as fast as my feet could take me.

Running to hide from the truth.

Running to escape reality.

Running to slow down the inevitable catching me.

Fisher triggered a memory by himself. A big one. The one I wanted him to remember in McDonald's where I could do damage control. Help him make sense of it. Help him understand why ... why I did what I did.

"Oh god." I stared at my phone as Fisher tried calling me back. "No. God no. Shit. Shitshitshit! FUCK!" I tossed my vibrating phone into my bag and covered my face with my shaky hands.

I was late for work, and Fisher was in Costa Rica with the memory of him zip-tying me to the stool in his workshop.

"I'm so sorry I'm late," I said to Holly as I hustled to peel off my jacket and toss my bag into the cubby.

She laughed looking at her watch. "I'm not sure two minutes counts as late. Is everything okay?"

"Yes. No." I shook my head before taking a deep breath. "It's a crazy situation."

"Well..." Holly leaned back in her recliner and sipped her tea "...Isabella had to cancel her appointment this morning. So I have time."

I twisted my lips. "It's really messed-up. Promise not to judge me?"

She chuckled. "Oh, Reese, you have no idea how sordid my life was before I became a midwife." She smirked. "Grab your coffee. I'm all ears."

It only took a few more seconds for me to nod and grin. "Okay."

My story took up the full two hours we had free that morning, and Holly scowled at me when I left her with the Costa Rica cliffhanger. But I didn't have any more to give her because the story was still being written.

When I took a break that afternoon to grab a snack and check my phone, there were a string of twenty-five missed calls and a string of messages from Fisher. Messages with all caps and exclamation points. And a few screen shots.

"Oh no ..." I cringed, scrolling up through the messages. It was the first time Fisher had messaged me since five years earlier which meant when he brought up my name in his messenger, he saw those five-year-old texts.

Innocent texts telling me to drive myself to work or informing me of what time we'd be leaving. Then there were texts of him apologizing for telling his family that I had tummy issues.

Fisher: *I'm sorry.*
Fisher: *Are you going to stay mad at me forever?*
Fisher: *I'll call my family and tell them it was a lie. That I just wanted to be alone with you.*

That was one of the screen shots. Along with the message:

Why did I want to be alone with you?

Another screen shot.

Reese: *Hi. Rose isn't going to tell Rory or anyone.*

Tell Rory what?

Where are you?
Answer your phone.
I'm sorry.
Please pick up your phone.
Don't make me call Rory.
Or the police.

WHAT THE HELL?!!!!

Fisher: *If you're not dead, text Rory and tell her you made it safely to Houston. Don't be a total asshole about it.*
Reese: *Go fuck yourself!*

PICK UP YOUR GODDAMN PHONE!!!!!
MESSAGE ME THE FUCK BACK!
I ZIP-TIED YOU TO THE STOOL IN MY SHOP! WE WERE MORE THAN FRIENDS AND YOU GODDAMN KNOW IT!

The last text I received was five minutes before I checked my messages.

Who are you? Why did you do this to me?

My eyes filled with tears. I shouldn't have hung up on him. Not only were we not together, I left him with crazy pieces to what must have felt like an unsolvable puzzle.

I panicked.

I panicked because I was angry at the Costa Rica situation.

I panicked because I didn't have time to talk.

I panicked because I couldn't see his face and he couldn't see mine. I thought he would remember pieces of our intimacy when I could give him a look, and he could maybe see at least what I felt for him even if his feelings for me at the time were still missing. He wasn't supposed to be so far away.

With her.

And her lingerie.

And her sexy dress.

And her sleeping in the same bed with him.

It wasn't supposed to happen that way. Life seldom did.

I didn't have time to call him, but I needed to do something.

Don't be mad. PLEASE don't be mad. PLEASE let's talk about it when you get home. I love you.

After I sent off the text, I grabbed a glass of water and stared at my phone, waiting for him to read the text or text me back.

Nothing.

Maybe he was getting a massage. With her. But that at least meant he wasn't so mad he no longer cared to reply to me.

My short break ended, and I had to get back to work without a response from Fisher. Just ... a bunch of angry all caps messages from him.

How did I never think about our texts? How did he

not scour through all his messages right after his accident to piece together some missing memories?

I'd imagined so many scenarios. Memories lost forever. Retrieved memories. The possibility of him remembering something big about him and Angie. And that something taking him away from me. What if she would have been pregnant?

But never did I think *our* time together would be the pulled thread that threatened to unravel everything. And it ate at me the rest of the day. I couldn't think of a worse scenario than him being angry and confused because of me and Angie being the one there to comfort him.

On my way home, I called him, hoping he wasn't at rehearsal dinner yet.

"I can't talk now." That was how he answered his phone.

My heart clenched and a new round of tears stung my eyes. "I love you. I've loved you for *so* long."

"I can't talk now." His voice was so cold.

"When can we talk?"

"When I'm ready."

I swallowed my shaky emotions. "Are you with Angie?"

"She's still in the shower."

Still ... what did that mean? *They* were in the shower and she stayed after he got out? It made me feel nauseous.

"I couldn't talk earlier. I was late for work."

"Well, I can't talk now. I guess we'll talk if or when it works out."

"If? Don't do this. Don't cherry-pick pieces of your

past and try to piece them together by yourself. Making assumptions. Nothing about us was simple."

"No shit."

"Fisher," I said as my voice cracked.

"Angie put it all on the table. What the fuck did you do? Was it a game?"

"No! It wasn't a game. I wanted ..." I sighed. It sounded so good, so *right* in my head for the longest time. It made sense. It felt romantic even. So why did it feel all wrong when it mattered the most?

"I have to go."

"Fisher ..." I grasped for every last second, but all I could do was say his name. "I love you."

"I have to go." Fisher ended the call.

I batted away my tears and drew in a shaky breath. He needed space, but he wasn't getting space. He was getting Angie, and there wasn't anything I could do.

CHAPTER THIRTY

THAT NIGHT, it felt like all the bad things I had done in my life were being served back to me in the cruelest revenge. Like God was mad or Karma was having a nasty case of menstrual cramps.

"Do you uh ... happen to follow Angie on Instagram?" Rose asked after dinner, glancing at her phone while on the floor.

Rory was just above her on the sofa, stroking Rose's hair with one hand while holding an open novel in her other hand, readers low on her nose. "Me?"

"No," Rose said. "You, Reese?"

I'd reread the same page in my book for nearly an hour, thinking only of Fisher. "No. Why?"

"She has pictures from the rehearsal dinner with Fisher. And it's captioned 'Time to cut him off.'" Rose held up her phone.

I scooted to the edge of the recliner and leaned forward, squinting. Fisher was sitting at a table, laughing while holding a beer in one hand. The table space in front of him was filled with empty beer bottles.

"Looks like he's having a good time." Rose cringed. "Of course, he's going to feel like shit for the wedding tomorrow."

"Good." I frowned.

That got Rose's and Rory's attention.

"Trouble in paradise?" Rory asked, eyeing me over her readers.

"Kinda," I frowned. I wasn't going to say anything, but I couldn't keep my mouth shut any longer. Not with Fisher drunk in Costa Rica with Angie.

"This morning I talked to Fisher on the phone right before I had to be at work. He said something that triggered a memory of us. An intimate detail. And I freaked. Major panic. Completely lost my head and hung up on him when he started to question me. And by the time I got a break, I had a million messages and missed calls from him. He *just* found our texts from five years ago. They are confusing, and they did nothing but fuel his anger. So he knows we were more than friends, but only from a few vague texts and another cherry-picked memory." I stared off to the side, chasing away the emotions that threatened to make me cry. I didn't want to fall apart. Not yet.

"And now he thinks you lied to him. Or the omission of the truth which feels like a lie," Rory said.

Biting the inside of my cheek, I nodded.

"He'll be home Sunday. That's not that far away. You can talk it over then."

Another nervous nod.

"Reese?" Rory said my name slowly.

I forced my teary-eyed gaze to her.

"He won't do anything stupid." She read my mind.

But I wasn't so sure.

Did he like me more than a friend when he had sex with Teagan the orthodontist? Did he even think twice before having sex with Angie after his accident? I mean ... it wasn't that long after that he decided he liked me. What if sex wasn't a big deal to men like it was to women? Not that I could talk ... I gave away my virginity to Brendon when deep down I knew I was never going to marry him.

"What if he does?" I whispered.

"He won—" Rory started to reassure me.

But Rose cut her off. "What if he does?" she asked.

"Rose. Stop," Rory said, tossing her book aside and sitting up straight. "You're not helping."

"What if I am helping? What if preparing your heart for the worst is the best idea? So let's do it ... let's imagine the worst. Fisher has sex with Angie in Costa Rica. And maybe they fall back in love. Or maybe it brings back more memories and he remembers really loving her. Then what?"

I captured my tears with the arm of my sleeve before they fully escaped. "I don't know," I whispered.

"You do," Rose said. "You know. You know you'll be heartbroken. You know it will take time to get over him, and maybe you'll never get completely over him. But you'll go on to pursue your career. You'll go on to find new love. You'll survive. You'll live. So there you have it.

That's your worst-case scenario. Once you accept it, then every other scenario won't seem as bad."

"Rose ..." Rory frowned. "It's not that easy and you know it. And honestly, that's not necessarily the worst-case scenario. If Fisher has sex with Angie, but then comes home and tries to say it meant nothing, *that's* a pretty bad scenario. Because Reese won't be able to trust him. It would be easier to know that it's just over. Done. But trying to move on and rebuild trust would feel tortur-ous. I don't know how anyone truly gets past that. I mean ... Fisher fell in love with Reese and they ...well..." she grimaced "... had an affair or cheated or whatever you want to call it, but he didn't know or feel his love for Angie. I'm not sure that makes it right, but it at least makes it *different*. And even taking his memory into consideration, I don't know how Angie will ever be able to forgive and forget, even if he does decide he wants to be with her."

My tears were gone. All I could do was sit idle in the chair and slowly blink at them. "You two are the worst. I want to go on record saying you are *the worst*."

They shot me shocked expressions.

"I feel zero percent better and one hundred percent worse. I ... I ... I can't believe you just said all those terrible things. How am I supposed to sleep? How am I supposed to function or even breathe for the next two days with images of Fisher and Angie having sex?"

"Sweetie, we were just trying to ..." Rory shook her head frantically as if she could take it all back, as if there was a rewind button.

"Yeah, Reese, I wanted you to prepare yourself just

in case. I'm not saying I think that's what's going to happen," Rose said with a lot more concern in her words.

"I told you he would never do anything. And I mostly meant it. Is that what you want? Do you need us to sugarcoat it, to possibly lie to you? Do you want us to tell you that Fisher is above every other man and that no amount of anger, alcohol, or temptation would ever lead him to do something he shouldn't do?"

"Yes! That's exactly what I want you to tell me."

Their eyebrows shot up their foreheads, lips parted.

I sighed, dropping my head into my hands. "I should have told him everything. Me and my stupid fantasy about him falling in love with me a second time without remembering or *knowing* anything about the first time. I did this ... this one is on me." My head lifted to look at them. "He might have sex with her." A new round of tears burned my eyes, but I kept them at bay. "I'm not stupid. He's human. Even the best humans make mistakes. Maybe by not telling Angie, sneaking around, pretending that time would make things less painful for her and his family, we were really just setting ourselves up to implode."

After a few silent moments, Rory murmured, "Maybe he thinks about it, tells Angie everything, and comes home to the woman he loves."

That made me cry.

I WASN'T friends with Angie on Instagram, but her account wasn't private, so I had the opportunity to drive myself *fucking* insane for the next two days.

Rory and Reese attended some family fun event at the school. So on Saturday, I spent the day stalking Angie hard on Instagram. Looking at every picture she'd ever posted and reading every caption. Had I known about it or looked for her account earlier, I'm not sure things would have progressed as far between Fisher and me.

I mean ... I knew social media rarely portrayed the real stories of people's lives, but it was easy to get caught in the trap of believing it. A picture was worth a thousand words, right? Take that times another thousand because I swear Angie had nearly a thousand pictures on her page.

A lot before the accident.

Some since his accident.

All of them said she and Fisher were in love.

My Saturday would have been less destructive and less tragic had I spent it overdosing on pills or slitting my wrists. Seriously, Angie's Instagram page was a dark hole of death for me.

Kissing.

Laughing.

Big smiles.

Photos in the mountains.

A ton of photos of Fisher with his shirt off. *MY naked fisherman.*

His family.

Some outing on a boat.

Kiss. Kiss. Smile. Smile.

She even posted photos of them in bed! Not porn, but

definitely a little racy. Him sleeping with the sheets low, obviously naked beneath the sheets. A weird-angled photo of his arms around her waist and his legs scissored with hers. The sheets covered the right areas, and she captioned it: soul mates.

What was that acronym everyone used? Oh yeah, FML. Really ... *fuck my life*.

Recent photos included the shot that Rose showed me of Fisher getting his fill of alcohol, but also of their room in Costa Rica confirming that they only had one bed. An hour earlier, she'd posted a shot of her reflection in the mirror of the hotel room. She was in the bathroom with a towel wrapped around her body and another one wrapped around her head, and Fisher was already dressed in his suit for the wedding, looking out the window with his hands casually slid into the front pockets of his pants.

My heart cracked again and again, barely hanging on.

Her caption was: My Future Husband. With a heart emoji.

My level of obsession hit the most destructive low when I heard Rory and Rose pull into the garage. I grabbed a bottle of wine and an opener and ran to my room and closed the door. When one of them knocked and opened the door a crack, I remained perfectly still on my bed, with my back to the door, so they thought I was taking a nap. When the door softly clicked shut again, I sat up, pulled the hidden bottle of wine out from under the blanket, and opened it.

Over the next hour, Angie documented the wedding

in her Instagram story with a nice mix of still photos and short videos.

The venue on the beach.

Clips from the ceremony.

Her and Fisher holding hands, posing next to the bride and groom.

"We're going to dinner. Pizza? You coming?" Rory knocked on my door. I quickly set the bottle of wine on the floor where she couldn't see it, nearly falling out of bed onto my butt. Then I grabbed a book from my nightstand and buried my nose into it just as she opened my door.

"I'm uh ... good." I couldn't tell if my words were slurred, so I yawned to hide anything that might make her suspicious. It was incredibly hard to pretend you weren't drunk when you were.

"Sure you don't need a break? Or you can bring your book."

"Good." Another yawn. "Totally good."

"You sound exhausted. Might want to go to bed early and get more sleep, in case you get called for a delivery."

Oh my gosh ...

She was right. I was on call and drunk. Only Rory didn't know I was drunk.

"Okay," I managed.

Once I heard the back door to the garage close, I stumbled out of bed and drank a hundred gallons of water to flush out the alcohol ... give or take ninety-nine gallons. Then I spent the next hour on the toilet peeing out all the water, eating chips from the bag, and monitoring Angie's Instagram page.

Kill me now.

I'd always felt like saying "yes" to Brendon, and then losing my virginity with him when I knew I wasn't going to marry him, was my lowest of lows.

Wrong.

My self-destructive drunk ass on the toilet, stalking Fisher and Angie in Costa Rica was my new low. I should have deleted the app and gone to dinner with Rory and Rose. When my bladder gave me a break, I took my pathetic self to my bedroom, and I deleted the Instagram app. Then I prayed, on-my-knees-hands-folded prayed, for God to make it stop. I left it up to Him to determine what that meant. I just wanted something ... anything ... everything to stop.

While I waited for his answer, I grabbed my Bible from my bookshelf and plopped onto the bed. Suddenly I was inspired to read some 1 Corinthians about love and marriage inspiration.

It doesn't envy. Well ... too late.

It doesn't boast. It is not proud. Clearly Angie needed to spend a little more time in God's Word.

So many things love was not supposed to be.

Rude.

Self-seeking.

Easily angered.

Keeping no record of wrongs.

Never delighting in evil.

Demanding its own way.

Had I believed all that, then the only conclusion I would have come to was ... I couldn't love Fisher.

But for the record ... neither could Angie with her mega boasting and larger-than-life pride.

Thou shalt not judge.

It wasn't all restrictive. There were a few things love *was* supposed to be.

Patient.

Kind.

Rejoicing in truth.

Hopeful.

Enduring in every circumstance.

Wow! Was I incapable of loving Fisher the way God intended for humans to love one another?

Feeling a little nauseous and mentally broken, I slid my Bible onto my nightstand, pulled my blankets over me, and fell asleep.

CHAPTER THIRTY-ONE

SUNDAY MORNING WAS ROUGH. My head felt like it had been shaken with a 6.0 magnitude earthquake.

"Muffin?" Rory asked.

She and Rose eyed me from the kitchen table. They wore matching white robes and big smirks.

Squinting against the light from *all* the window shades drawn open, I shook my aching head.

"I knew something was up when I asked you about dinner last night. But the un-flushed toilet, empty bag of chips on the bathroom floor, and empty wine bottle next to your bed this morning confirmed it. Not to mention your Bible next to your bed. Wanna talk about it?" Rory slowly sipped her coffee.

I poured myself a cup of coffee and filled a tall glass with water before taking two pills for my head. "So you knew I wasn't right, but you went to dinner anyway?" I shuffled my feet to the table and plunked my butt onto the chair.

Rory shrugged. "What's that saying ... something

about the only way to get past something is to go through it? I noticed you were going through it. And I didn't want to stop your progress."

With a grunt, I sipped my coffee. "Yup. I'm making amazing progress. Here's what I now know. Angie posts *everything* on Instagram. Fisher loved her. Maybe does again. And I have no clue how to love. I'm an expert in anti-love. I should move back to Michigan. Finish my master's. And forget I ever met Fisher Mann."

"Ouch." Rose wrinkled her nose. "So much for clarity after a rough night."

Resting my elbows on the table, I rubbed my tired eyes. "Isn't life just a rocky road of mistakes? A journey to enlightenment or Heaven or wherever? I mean ... what do we really know when we die? What did we really learn?"

"What's the point?" Rory said.

"Exactly." I gave her a tight-lipped smile. "And what is wrong with the world? Why do we have to spend so much time recording our lives and sharing them with the world? Granted, I didn't get a cell phone until I was nearly a legal adult, and I do have social media accounts, but why does something that's so time-consuming make us feel so terrible most of the time? And why do we do it? Why do we voluntarily subject ourselves to it? What a waste of life."

Rory chuckled. "I spent five years in prison, so I agree with you. But let's talk about the real issue. How much time did you spend on Angie's Instagram account yesterday?"

I sighed, hanging my head. "All of it. Every single picture she's ever posted and every single caption she posted with them is burned into my brain. It was the most suicidal thing I have ever done." I took another sip of my coffee. "I'm not proud of it. And I deleted the app." I retrieved my phone from my hoodie pocket and brought up the screen. "But then I downloaded the app again this morning. And I officially hate Fisher Mann and his *fiancée* Angie." I showed them the post from late last night, after I'd already gone to bed. It was a photo of him sleeping on his stomach, arms next to his head, sheets *so* low on his back that it seemed unlikely if not impossible that he was wearing anything at all. Angie captioned it: My Whole World.

Rose and Rory blinked slowly at the phone screen, but Rose's gaze drifted away from it first. She had already seen it. They had nothing to say. And I had no tears left to cry. I told Fisher I was in it for as long as I felt like I was actually *in* it.

Well, I was no longer in it.

"Reese ..." Rory said softly as I pushed back in my chair and stood.

I shook my head. "It's fine. I actually feel sorry for her. The only way she can feel like he loves her is if he hates me. And I think this weekend ... he's hated me."

I THINK Elliott Trenton Davies decided to announce his impending arrival Sunday afternoon just so I could avoid dealing with my so-called life. Around four in the afternoon, I received the call from Holly with permission to "not rush" because she knew Elliott's mom's contractions were years apart. But she was a first-time mom who required some guidance in being patient. And Holly excelled at patience. Even though she knew the new mom would not be holding her baby anytime soon, Holly shared in her excitement and vowed to be with her every step of the way. That was code for Holly would sit in the corner of the room, reading a romance novel, while the mom and scared but eager dad worked through tiny contractions together. As long as the mom was still smiling, Holly knew no baby would be arriving soon.

So I took my time, taking a shower, eating dinner, and packing my bag with my own books, snacks, and lots of water.

"Hope it all goes well." Rory smiled as she unloaded groceries.

I hiked my bag onto my shoulder and tucked my feet into my shoes. "Me too. I don't know when I'll see you. This could be a *long* labor."

"Wouldn't that be a blessing."

I knew what she meant. And I felt it too. Fisher and Angie would be home later, and I needed to *not* be home. Not be available to him and his anger or pathetic excuses. Not put myself in the position to explode and say things that would make everything exponentially worse.

"Yes." I scrounged a smile for her. "It really would be." I shut the door behind me.

Elliott's mom did, in fact, labor for almost twenty-four hours, during which time, I received one text from Fisher.

I'm home if you want to talk.

If I *wanted* to talk. Not "I'm home, we need to talk."

I replied as soon as I had a quick chance.

I'm at a birth.

He didn't reply.

It was almost seven o'clock Monday night before I made it home.

Rose and Rory were decorating the house for Christmas.

"Hey, sweetie. How'd it go?"

On a sigh, I smiled—a tiny one. "Good. A boy. Seven pounds, nine ounces. Mom cried. Dad cried."

"Did you?" Rose asked.

I shrugged. "I might have got a little teary eyed because I just ..." On another sigh, I frowned.

"You're tired. Emotionally drained." Rory said.

I nodded. "So drained. I'm going to crash. I'll see you in a hundred years."

"Love you."

"You too," I mumbled, dragging my feet and slumped body to bed.

THE NEXT MORNING, I woke a little before five and couldn't get back to sleep. It also didn't help that it sounded like someone was mowing our lawn. I peeked out the window. It had snowed overnight. A lot. And Fisher was snow blowing our drive and sidewalk.

Of course he was ...

Rory and Rose's room was tucked in the back corner of the house, so they likely didn't hear him. Lucky them.

Ten hours of sleep was enough for me, so I showered and dried my hair. By then it was five-thirty, and I no longer heard the snowblower. When I peeked out the front window, Fisher was loading the snowblower and his shovel into the back of his truck.

Without a real goal in mind, I slipped on my jacket, hat, and boots and went out the back door, opening the garage door which turned on a light. Fisher glanced in my direction for a second before closing his tailgate. He made his way up the driveway as I stood in the garage between the two cars with my hands in the pockets of my jacket.

"Thanks for doing that," I said with reserved emotion. My heart hurt too much. There was so much to say. And I didn't know where to begin or if it was even the right time to have the conversation. Did he have other driveways to clear? Work to do?

"It's no big deal." He dusted snow off his jacket and coveralls. His scruffy face was wet from the snow.

"Do you have time to grab coffee?" He pulled up his coat sleeve to look at his watch. "Starbucks opens in fifteen minutes."

Starbucks. He could have invited me to his house for coffee so we'd have total privacy, but he invited me to Starbucks. I didn't know how to interpret it. But I also knew I needed something from him. And maybe that was his goal too. Maybe he needed something from me. Were we going to Starbucks to break up? Were we even still together? Were we *ever* really together?

I nodded once. "Okay. Let me grab my purse."

"Okay."

After I grabbed my purse, we headed down the driveway, Fisher's gloved hand held mine, but it wasn't an intimate gesture. It was a friendly gesture, just making sure I didn't slip and fall.

After we got in the truck, it only took a few minutes to get to Starbucks. Not a word was murmured on the way, and it only intensified the pain in my chest.

Again, Fisher held my hand as we made it through the parking lot that hadn't been plowed and into the empty Starbucks, save for two employees behind the counter.

"My treat. You plowed the driveway," I said like I would have said to a kind stranger. "Coffee. Black?"

He nodded and headed in the direction of a table while I ordered our drinks. And instead of taking a seat and waiting for my name to be called, I milled around the registers reading all the advertisements for their holiday drinks. Anything to put off the inevitable.

"Here you go." The guy at the register set the two drinks on the counter.

I took a deep breath and made my way to the table. Fisher had his gloves on the table and jacket off, but his beanie still on, and a sad look on his face. Once I got seated and unzipped my jacket, it took a few awkward seconds for our gazes to lock. But once they did, I knew there wasn't any more small talk to be said.

"We were more than friends," he said like it physically pained him to say it.

I thought it was a statement, but maybe it was a question. Maybe he needed confirmation that what he remembered was real.

"We were more than friends," I echoed, giving him confirmation.

"And you didn't tell me this why?"

With a tiny head shake, I rubbed my lips together. "For several reasons. At first, I didn't think it was beneficial information to share given the fact that you were engaged and we hadn't seen each other in five years anyway. And I didn't want to give you something you couldn't remember and make you feel like you owed me something in return. Some sort of emotional acknowledgment. And honestly, I didn't need it. I liked where we were going. I liked our present. And the closer we got, the less I cared if we shared the past."

I stopped. I had a truckload of other things to say, but I had to pace myself and get a feel for where his head was after recent revelations.

"So we ... what? We were just fucking around?"

"There was a physical attraction. And we messed around, yes."

"Messed around. But we weren't sleeping together because you already told me you gave that other guy your virginity. Correct?"

I nodded.

"Did I try to have sex with you?"

I took a sip of my coffee and then another sip, buying *all* the time before clearing my throat. "No."

He blinked several times, an unreadable expression pinned to his face. "Why not?"

"Because I was upfront with you that I wasn't going to have sex with you."

"But oral didn't count?"

My cheeks filled with embarrassment as I glanced toward the counter to see if anyone seemed to be listening to us. "Do we have to go into such detail? Does it matter?"

"I'm just trying to understand."

"Well..." I kept my gaze pointed to the counter "...you have amnesia, so you might not ever really understand."

"Maybe if you give me all the facts, all the details, then I can understand."

"Like Angie? She gave you everything. Do you understand your love for her? Or should I say, before you left for Costa Rica, did you understand your love for her?"

"What's that supposed to mean? Before I left for Costa Rica ..." He narrowed his eyes.

"Did you have a nice time? Was the couples' massage in the same room? And how does that work? If they do, in fact, think you're a couple, does that mean you undress for the massage in the same room? Did you take off all your clothes for her? Did she take hers off for you? What about the room where you stayed? Were there two beds? Because in the photo on Instagram, it looked like there was only one bed. And before you answer that, fair warning ... Angie told me, Rose, and Rory all about her plans for you two on the trip. She requested a room with one bed instead of two. The couples' massage. Oh, and we must not forget the sexy lingerie she bought to wear for you. How did you like that?

Did you try to have sex with *her*? Or did you settle for oral like you did with me? Was it all-night oral? Because the photo of you on Instagram sleeping in bed made you look thoroughly exhausted. Oh ... and it definitely looked like you were naked under the sheet resting so low on your torso."

I was so angry my hand shook as I gripped my coffee. My heart raced. And my jaw worked overtime grinding my teeth.

"Are you done?" he asked, looking completely unaffected by my long spiel.

I stood. "I think *we're* done."

Fisher's gaze fell from me to his coffee cup, and after a few seconds, he nodded, pulling on his jacket and sliding his gloves onto his fingers.

I didn't mean it. I was just *so* mad and so hurt. And tired. Rory was right. I was emotionally spent for the next hundred years. Why didn't he have a defense? One single comeback or explanation for his actions? Why couldn't he at least lie to me, show a little desperation like the idea of us ending affected him? Was it because everything I said was true? Did he not have a defense? Did he want things to end between us?

"I'll take you home." He took my hand to lead me to the door, and I yanked it away. Falling in the snowy parking lot would have been less painful than enduring another second of him touching me after touching her.

Fisher had the nerve to give me a little flinch, like he was scarred by my gesture. I brushed past him to the door and trekked through the snow to his truck.

When he pulled into my driveway and put the truck in *Park*, he turned toward me. "Am I him?"

I grabbed the door handle and gave him a slow glance. "Who?"

"Your first love? You told me he wasn't ready to be found. And you call me your lost fisherman. Am I him? Did you fall in love with me? Am *I* the schmuck who wouldn't take your virginity even after you offered it?"

That moment was the very reason I never told him about us. It was a terrible feeling to be so emotionally exposed without an ounce of recognition. I didn't want the "did you love me?" I wanted the "I loved you, and I remember it. Every feeling. Every moment. Every single emotion."

I opened the door and spoke the only truth I knew for certain at the moment. "I will never regret not giving you my virginity." I jumped down and shut the door, not looking back for a single second.

As soon as I opened the door, Rory and Rose were right there. They'd been watching out the window. And while they had no idea what had been said between us, the look on my face must have said everything.

"I'm sorry," Rory's brow wrinkled as she took a step forward with open arms.

I couldn't take any steps. All I could do was fall into hundreds of pieces and hope my mom could catch all of them.

I thought we were strong enough to make it through.

I thought it was finally our time.

I thought wrong.

CHAPTER THIRTY-TWO

Babies made everything better.

On the one hand, they reminded me of the life I wanted for myself, the life I'd imagined with Fisher. But they were also symbolic of transition, transformation, moving forward. A reminder that we are such tiny parts of something so much bigger.

How many babies were created from a love that died? Yet they moved forward. Love can live in small ways even after it dies. Fisher nudged me, he shifted my journey in life. And while we didn't have a tiny human to show for our love, I was a nurse and a midwife in training because I met Fisher Mann, and he was the reason I went with Brendon. Had *he* been the one to take my virginity, I wouldn't have had the strength to leave.

Fisher's love led me to a job I loved. A purpose that meant something to me. A feeling of accomplishment and unfathomable personal satisfaction. And I could hate him for a lot of things, but I couldn't regret us or all the reckless moments that sent us spinning in a whirlwind of passion and love.

Love. It *was* love.

I knew it always would be love. A tragic love, but nonetheless *love*.

"Are you married?" Abbie asked me as I weighed her four-week-old daughter in the clinic.

I smiled. "Not yet. I've been a little unlucky in that department." I handed Abbie her little peanut.

Abbie sat in the rocking chair with her and breastfed her while we waited for Holly to join us for the well-baby check.

"I feel ya." Abbie chuckled while gazing adoringly at her little girl. "Drew and I have actually been married twice."

I looked up from my table after recording the weight. "Seriously?"

She nodded. "We got married right out of high school against our parents' wishes. But we were in love. Neither one of us had any idea what we wanted out of life. We just knew we wanted to be together. But being together didn't pay well, neither did our minimum wage jobs. It got increasingly hard to squeeze happiness out of a love that nobody supported. And it led to fights and resentment. Then it led to divorce in less than a year. And we didn't see each other again for ten years. Crazy, right?

"He went to college. I went to college. Drew ended up in Maine, and I came back here for a job. We both had been in several serious relationships. And when Drew came home one Christmas, we ran into each other at an Avalanche game. And it was instant sparks. He was in a relationship at the time and so was I. But it didn't matter. I swear we both knew it too. I actually remember thinking, this is going to get messy."

Messy.

Of course she said messy.

"So hearts were broken and lives were disrupted again so you could have your second chance?"

Twisting her lips for a second, she nodded. "Pretty much. But look at this little princess. I have no regrets."

Before I could say any more, ask a single one of my twenty questions, Holly came into the room.

But Abbie's story haunted me for days.

SATURDAY MORNING, I woke to voices in the other room. After throwing on my robe, I opened the door a crack.

Angie.

WWJD?

WWJD?

Really, what would he do?

I wasn't okay. It had been two weeks since the Costa Rica trip. And I hadn't talked to Fisher since our morning at Starbucks, and neither had Rory or Rose to my knowledge.

Was Angie there to gloat? Should it have mattered?

Jesus needed to tell me what to do because I wanted to tell her everything. Woman to woman. If she was going to marry the man I loved, she needed to go into it with her eyes wide open. Jesus would've told her the truth, right?

As I opened the door a little farther, I could hear their conversation.

"Did he say who?" Rory asked.

"Nope."

"Did he say how long it's been going on?" Rose probed.

"He said it didn't matter. I asked him a ton of questions, but he said the answers didn't matter." She sounded so defeated, her voice weak and even a little shaky.

"Does his family know?"

"No. I asked him not to tell them until I leave." She sniffled. Yeah, she was crying.

"Leave?" Rory sounded surprised.

"I'm going back to California. And after I have time to make sense of this, to figure out what I did wrong, I'll either come back and face his family or I'll at least call them. They are my family too, but they're his real family. And I don't want there to be sides to take. That's not fair."

"It was unexpected. A tragedy in so many ways. He could have died. He could have been crippled for life," Rose said. "But he lived. And sometimes when we love people, we have to give them what they need even if it's not us. Life takes so many unexpected paths. Forever is rarely realistic."

"I miss him already," Angie said.

And dang it anyway, I teared up. I teared up because she had no idea that anything she had done was hurting me. I teared up because she was just a woman who fell in love with Fisher Mann. And it was nearly impossible to not fall in love with him.

"H-he lived ... but I still l-lost him."

I wiped my eyes as I leaned against the doorframe and listened to the *mess* I helped create.

"I'm so sorry for your pain," Rory said, and I imagined her hugging Angie. Someone needed to hug her.

I gently closed my door and sat on the edge of my bed. When did he break things off with her? Did that change things between us? Did he sleep with her in Costa Rica? A goodbye of sorts? How did I feel about him?

So many confusing and unanswered questions.

Did I feel her words? Did they ring true for me too? Did I lose Fisher, but he didn't die? Did I lose Fisher, but he didn't end up with Angie?

Was that the right choice all along? Did he need to start fresh? Walk away from the past he couldn't remember and find someone completely new?

I didn't know. And by that point the pain was rather numbing.

A while later, there was a knock at my door.

"Yeah?"

Rory opened the door. "Morning."

I smiled. "Morning."

"Were you listening?" She gave me a sad smile while taking a seat next to me on the bed.

"For a little while."

"He ended it."

I nodded. "When?"

"The night they got home from Costa Rica. Angie

had to go out of town for work the following week, probably for the best, and so this has been her first chance to tell us. She'll be okay."

I glanced over at Rory, eyes narrowed. "I heard enough of the conversation to know that she's not going to be okay anytime soon. Why would you say that?"

Her nose wrinkled. "I'm Team Reese and I don't want you to feel responsible because you really are not responsible. Had he not fallen in love with you, I don't think he was going to fall back in love with her."

"So two weeks ..." He'd broken up with her when we went to Starbucks, but he said nothing.

"Give him time, sweetie. I think he's dealing with his own loss. He's lost hope of getting his memory back, and that has to be hard to accept."

He lost faith too. Faith in me. Faith in us.

I knew from experience that losing faith sucked. And it was lonely. And you did reckless things. You made poor decisions.

Maybe we needed another five years apart like Abbie and Drew. Or maybe it was really *never* going to be our time.

"It sucks that she's losing her new job over a guy."

"She's not. She put in for a transfer, that's all."

I nodded. "That's good, I guess."

"So ... Christmas is next week. I think we should make cookies today. Pop popcorn to string on the tree. And maybe drive around and look at lights tonight. I think we could all use a little Christmas cheer."

"Yeah," I said, lacking all cheer.

"Rose and I are going to run errands. We have some

shopping to finish up. And then we'll grab groceries on the way home so we can make cookies."

I nodded. "Give me twenty minutes to shower and I'll go with you."

Her nose wrinkled. "We can't buy things for you when you're with us."

"Fine. I'll stay here and watch movies."

"Now, that's a great idea. You've been working a ton of hours. It's about time you just relax."

I handed her a fake smile and even faker enthusiasm. She rolled her eyes. "See you in a few hours."

After she left, I grabbed a shower, dried my hair, and dressed in my comfiest sweats and fitted long-sleeved tee.

Fuzzy socks.

Hot chocolate.

Netflix.

Halfway through the first movie, a sappy love story, and drunk on chocolate and spray whipped topping, I brought up my messages, specifically my texts with Fisher. And I typed a message.

It was you, my lost Fisher Mann. I loved you. And you loved me. Just wanted you to know that in case you never remember. It was messy, but we were real.

I stared at the message and thought of all the reasons to send it. Then I thought of all the reasons not to send it. Then I pressed send because my heart needed more closure than leaving his truck and telling him I would never regret not giving him my virginity.

After all, he most likely took Angie's years ago, and where did that get her? Them?

I felt like the note he wrote in his graduation card to me was his way of getting closure. Five years after the fact, but clearly it was something he needed to say to move on and marry Angie.

But I didn't want to be engaged to another man and suddenly feeling unsettled emotions for Fisher. I wanted closure before I moved on.

Fisher: I know.

I know? Really? That was his reply? It seemed ... well, a little arrogant. Like ... of course I loved him?

I started to send another message but I had no idea what it needed to say. What was the comeback to "I know?" If I was looking for closure, then I got it. I said what I needed to say, and it shouldn't have mattered whether he responded or not. Yet there I was with a frown on my face, feeling like it *did* matter.

Taking a deep breath, I let it go. That was all I could do. Just let it go. Accept the closure. After all, I clearly wanted him to know since I sent him the message. So what was the big deal with him replying with "I know?"

Maybe I should have replied with an "Okay. Great. Just making sure. So ... nice knowing ya. Have a good life."

I continued playing the movie for all of two, maybe three minutes, before I shot to my feet. Grabbed my keys, jacket, boots, and marched to my car. It took me less than two minutes to get to Fisher's house.

Knocking on his front door several times, I hugged my arms to my chest. The door opened. "What exactly does—" I bit my tongue and my face morphed into a constipated feeling smile. "Hi," I said to the stranger opening Fisher's door.

"Hey. Can I help you?"

"I ... um ... was looking for Fisher. But I'll come back later."

"He's downstairs. We're playing pool. I just happened to be up here grabbing more beer, so I answered the door. Come in."

I shook my head. "No. I'm fine. I'll come back." I started to back away from the blond dude with dimples and an overly friendly grin.

"Did someone knock at the door?" Fisher popped his head around the corner from the top of the stairs.

"You have company, I think. The more the merrier. But she's a little skittish." Blond dude chuckled, patting Fisher on the shoulder and disappearing to the kitchen and probably the basement.

"Speaking of company, I didn't know *you* had company. I'm leaving." I turned.

"Reese, you can come in."

"Nope. I'm good."

"Did you need something?"

"Nope." I got to my car but the door was locked. I didn't remember locking the door. And I also didn't remove my keys from the ignition.

It beeped. How did I not hear it beeping? Oh, that's right, I was on a mission until Dimples ruined it.

"Reese ..."

"Nope." I needed another word, but suddenly it hurt to be so close to him. Suddenly I wasn't okay with us being over no matter how much closure I tried to get from him.

I started down the sidewalk, heading home to get the spare set of keys to my car.

"Reese ..." Fisher was closing in on me, so I took off running. "Jesus ... what ... why are you always running from me?" He chased me down the sidewalk, but I wasn't that fast in my snow boots.

Before I could turn the corner, his hand grabbed the back of my jacket. I stopped and wriggled out of his hold, turning toward him, breathless and a little rabid.

"I'm always running from you because you are the worst, Fisher Mann. The. Worst. You make it impossible to love you and just as impossible to *not* love you. But the worst part is you make it impossible to be with you. And you just ... let me go. All the freaking time. And you go off to Costa Rica and screw around with Angie and sleep in the same bed and do god knows what else with her. Then you *again* let me get out of your truck that morning after coffee and you. Let. Me. Go.

"AND I had to find out from Angie that you broke things off with her. Why? Why did I hear it from her and not you? So you don't want to be with me. Fine. But have the decency to say *something*. Don't be an arrogant jerk who says 'I know' when I get the nerve to message you about how I loved you. So yeah ... I'm running from you because you are bad for me. And I should have known it years ago. But more than any of that..." I turned and tucked my cold hands into my pockets as I continued trekking toward my house "...I'm running away from you because I locked my *fucking* keys in the car."

"You kept the truth from me when it could have been the thing that gave me my memory back."

"Angie gave you the truth. It didn't give you your memory back."

"Why keep the truth from me? Why do it after you already knew I was in love with you?" Fisher stayed a few feet behind me.

"You wouldn't understand, and it doesn't matter now."

"Well you drove to my house because *something* must still matter now."

"It was a mistake. I shouldn't have texted you. I shouldn't have driven to your house." I picked up my pace again, but not to a run. "I thought I needed some sort of closure, but I was wrong. Being away from you is all the closure I need." I batted away the tears and made sure he didn't catch up to me, didn't see my tears.

"Say it. If you don't say it, you know you'll regret it."

Screw my tears.

I whipped around. "I didn't tell you because I wanted you to remember us and how you felt about me all on your own. And I wanted to be there when it happened. I wanted to see the look on your face. And I wanted it to convey the feelings I had when I realized you were falling in love with me for the second time without ever remembering the first time. I wanted to know if you felt this sense of awe and fate like it was impossible for us to not fall in love at every possible opportunity."

Fisher deflated. He couldn't even look at me.

So I turned and continued my journey home.

"We messed around on the pool table. In your bedroom. My closet. My bed. The downstairs kitchen. My workshop."

I halted at his words, but I couldn't turn around because I wasn't sure if I was really hearing what I thought I was hearing.

"And we slept on the screened-in porch one night after I went out with Rory and Rose. You tripped at one of my job sites and ended up with a nail in your hand. I carried you to the truck. And the whole way I smelled your hair. And I thought ... if I could spend the rest of my life smelling her hair, I'd die a happy man. Did *you* know that? Did you know how much I liked the smell of your hair and the floral scent of your skin, and whatever you put behind your ears and down your neck? Yeah, that shit drove me crazy insane."

I couldn't turn around. Or blink. I could barely breathe. But I could cry. And I did. So, so much.

He thought. If he thought. He knew. If he knew. He remembered ... everything.

"Five years ago, I loved you and you loved me. It was really fucking messy ... but we were real. It just wasn't the right time. Our timing seems to always suck. And I'm sorry about that. But you're here. And I'm here. And my best friend from high school is in town for the next two weeks, and you should come play pool with us."

I turned a degree every second, like a ticking clock, until I faced him—that gleam in his eyes.

"I love you today." He shrugged a shoulder. "And I'm going to wake up and do the same thing tomorrow."

I had so many questions. *Did* he have sex with Angie in Costa Rica? That was my biggest question, or so I thought. But as I inched my feet in his direction, I realized it didn't matter. If I wanted to cross that threshold back into his life, it couldn't matter. If I accepted his love and gave it freely back in return, there were Biblical rules about love I'd have to follow.

It was never jealous or demanded its own way.

It wasn't irritable.

It didn't keep record of being wronged.

Love never gave up.

Never lost faith.

Love was always hopeful.

And it endured through every circumstance.

However, before I could take that final step back to him, there was a question he had to answer.

"Were you ever going to come for me?"

Fisher smiled that glorious, unmatchable grin, and it instantly sent a new round of burning tears to my eyes. It blew my heart up like a balloon, and it rattled my stomach, sending those familiar, tiny wings aflutter. "I was thinking about it."

"I found my lost fisherman," I whispered as I took that final step and wrapped my arms around him, our lips reuniting after too long apart.

When we pulled back an inch and gazed at each other, he grinned again. "I told you, all you needed to do was go knock on his door." He wiped his thumbs along my cheeks. "Don't cry. I don't want Shane to think I made my girl sad."

"You remember."

He grinned. "I remember. I just had no idea the memories of us would be so ... NSFW. And when it happened, when I remembered the *feeling,* it felt indescribable, in some way like the universe was laughing at me. How could I have not known? Not like my brain forming the memory, more like my soul tapping on my heart and saying, 'Yo, dumb ass, remember her? We love her. 'We will always love her.'"

I rested my forehead against his chest and laughed. "Not safe for work ..."

"No joke." He took my hand and led me back toward his house. "You know, I can't play pool anymore without getting an erection. Do you have any idea how awkward that is when you're playing against a dude?"

I giggled.

When we reached the basement, Fisher released my hand and grabbed a beer. "Shane, this is Reese. Sorry we disappeared. She's a little skittish."

I narrowed my eyes at Fisher.

"Nice to finally meet you. This guy hasn't shut up about you in days. After two beers, everything turns into Reese-this and Reese-that." Shane sipped his beer in one hand while resting his other hand on the pool stick.

"That's not true." Fisher rolled his eyes while opening his beer bottle.

My scowl turned into a smirk. I felt ten feet tall, even if he was doing all this *thinking* and *talking* about me while I was miserable assuming he no longer wanted to be with me.

When I turned back toward Shane, Fisher stood behind me, snaking his hand possessively across the top of my chest as he ducked his head and whispered in my ear. "It only takes one beer for me to talk about you. But I think about you all the time. And sometimes..." his whisper got even softer "...I touch myself." He playfully teased my ear with his teeth eliciting another giggle from me.

"Who's playing?" Shane asked.

"Reese. She's freakishly good at whatever she does. She kicked Arnie's ass in ping-pong."

I glanced back at Fisher, and he winked at me.

Over the next two hours, we played pool. Shane told me all about Fisher's shenanigans in high school. And Fisher called Shane out on a few of his own. I had to resort to college stories, which were much more recent because I went to a Christian academy and therefore had no exciting stories during that time in my life. The most taboo thing I had ever done was pull Fisher's towel from his waist and give him head in his closet, but Fisher already knew that, and Shane *didn't* need to know it.

"I have to get home." I glanced at my phone screen. "Rory and Rose were shopping, but now they're home and looking for me. We're making cookies." I returned my pool stick to the rack. "Nice meeting you, Shane. I hope we get to hang out again before you leave."

"Yeah, that would be great." He plopped down onto the sectional and turned on the TV.

"I'll walk you upstairs." Fisher took my hand and led me to the front door. Always ... *always* me following Fisher off a cliff or to the ends of the earth.

"I have a million questions." I trapped my lower lip between my teeth and wrinkled my nose.

"And I'll give you a million answers. Just not until Shane leaves town."

Nodding slowly, I whispered, "In two weeks ..."

"But I'll answer one now. So pick the one that matters the most."

I rolled my eyes. "That's not fair."

"Ask me."

Did you have sex with Angie?

"When did you remember ... everything? And *do* you remember everything? Do you remember all your memories of Angie?"

"That's three questions."

"Fisher ..."

He kissed me once. "I remembered after I got drunk off my ass at the wedding ... because I was so pissed off at you."

I frowned.

Fisher didn't. He kept grinning and kissed me again. "And I remember all my memories of Angie."

Another kiss.

"I remember everything."

Another kiss, but slower.

When he released my face, I stood motionless for several seconds. "You *knew* that morning we had Starbucks? And you didn't tell me? Not only did you not tell me, you completely played dumb about it. You asked me questions you already knew the answers to."

He shrugged. It was an arrogant shrug, like he had every right to not tell me the truth that morning at Starbucks. As I started to protest his arrogance, my conscience got the best of me, halting my words. I slid into my jacket and pulled on my boots.

"Shane doesn't know I lost my memory."

I narrowed my eyes before returning a small nod. I wasn't sure why he didn't tell him, but I figured it didn't matter.

As I opened the door, he grabbed my wrist, and I turned back toward him. A slightly pained expression stole his beautiful smile. "You. I've told you about my memory. That's it. No one else."

"What do you mean?"

"I mean, I didn't tell Angie. And I didn't tell my family. Not Rory or Rose. Not anyone at work. Just you."

Still a little confused, I added another nod. He wanted to tell them, so he didn't want me saying anything.

"I'm not going to tell them. You know. And you're the only one who ever needs to know. Except my doctor. I'll tell my doctor."

"W-why?" I shook my head.

"I know I hurt Angie. And when I told my family, they were hurt too."

That answered another one of my questions. He told his family.

But did he tell them about me?

"But it would have been worse for everyone had they known I made the decision knowing how I felt about her before the accident. I think it's easier for them to believe that I can't marry her or that I've fallen in love with someone else because I simply can't recall my feelings. They are *all* so sure that I would marry Angie tomorrow if I only remembered. So that's the deal. I don't want them to know. I'm not going to tell them. And I don't want you telling anyone either. Not even Rory and Rose. Can you do that?"

I didn't know. That was a big ask on his part.

Fisher pressed his lips together and canted his head. "Need I remind you that you kept a big secret from me ... because you thought it was for the best?"

"And look how that turned out."

He grabbed the collar to my jacket and brought his lips to mine without touching them. "I *am* looking at how that turned out."

He won. Fisher always won.

"When will I see you again?" I changed the subject, realizing that I'd lost.

"Shane's on East Coast time, so he goes to bed by ten. What kind of cookies are you going to bring me? You know I have a thing for your cookies ... your muffins ... your whole damn bakery."

I matched his grin. He remembered that conversation.

"Now you're just flexing."

He barked a laugh and released my jacket. "Not yet. I'll do that for you later ... after I eat your cookie. Maybe bring extra frosting. I have an idea."

"So you have time to eat my cookie, but I can't ask you any more questions for two weeks?"

"Exactly."

Grumbling in the naked fisherman style, I headed out the door to walk home.

CHAPTER THIRTY-THREE

"Spill," Rory said the second I walked into the house.

"Spill what?" I unzipped my jacket.

"You were over at Fisher's. We drove by there."

"Oh that..." I hung my coat in the closet and padded my way into the kitchen to wash my hands and start helping with the cookies "...yeah, we're back together." I could not have been more coy.

"What? How? Who? WHAT?" Rory tossed me a hand towel as she and Rose cornered me.

My coyness quickly vanished. "Yes!" I fisted my hands at my chest and squealed. "I texted him, basically for closure. And he texted me back this weird, vague response that just ... ugh ... *ate* at me. So I drove over there. Some stranger answered his door. Turns out, it's his best friend from high school who's staying with him for the next two weeks. That was awkward, so I went to leave and Fisher ..." Then it hit me.

His speech. Our big moment. I couldn't share it with

them because it was all about him remembering us—remembering everything. And how he felt about me. Carrying me to the truck and smelling my hair. Sure it might have sounded weird to anyone else, but it was so romantic.

AND I COULDN'T TELL ANYONE!

"And Fisher what?" Rose asked. She and Rory had wide eyes and hung on my every word.

"Uh ... well ... Fisher felt really bad for not having called. But after breaking up with Angie and telling his family, he needed some time. And out of respect for both Angie and his family, he thought it was best to keep his distance from me. And he knew I was angry with him, so he thought we both needed to take some time and space. But..." my enthusiasm rebounded after that rambling version of the half-truth "...he was so excited to see me. And it was like nothing else mattered."

They seemed disappointed in my story. And it wasn't the most dramatic ending to a love story, but it was all I could give them.

"So you talked? Worked everything out? He told you everything that did or didn't happen in Costa Rica?" Rory eyed me suspiciously.

I nodded.

"And did he have sex with Angie? Because I can't see you being okay with that." Rose gave me the same untrusting look that Rory gave me.

I made my decision before I stepped into his house. I chose us, even if he had sex with Angie in Costa Rica. If I believed the giving of my body to another in that way was the most sacred part of a relationship, the defining characteristic of love, then I would not have given my virginity to Brendon without marrying him. I would not have been interested in Fisher, the furthest thing ever from a virgin, and I would not have been able to love him after he and Angie had sex the night before our Target trip.

"He didn't have sex with her." That was my answer. And maybe that was a lie. Another lie I would never confess to Rory and Rose. And maybe it was the truth. I didn't know. And it wasn't going to change my love for Fisher. The second I hung up on him and didn't return his calls or texts, that was the moment I could no longer call him mine.

I abandoned him when he needed me the most.

That worked. They smiled and hugged me. "So happy for you, sweetie. Both of you."

"Thanks. So ... let's make some cookies."

MARIAH CAREY BELTED out the lyrics to "All I Want For Christmas Is You" while we made cutout sugar cookies, chocolate crinkles, and peanut butter blossoms because Rory thought Fisher might like them. I didn't break her heart by telling her that Fisher wasn't the peanut butter fanatic he used to be.

Then we strung popcorn for the tree and used the rest of the popcorn to make a batch of caramel corn. After that, we nearly passed out from too much sugar while watching *Last Christmas* and *Elf*.

And finally, I grabbed my spare keys, packed up some cookies (and frosting), and headed to Fisher's house after Rory and Rose went to bed. Tapping lightly on his door, I shivered from the gusty cold wind that night that promised to bring more snow by morning.

"Hey." Fisher answered the door with a very pleased expression.

"Cookie delivery."

He chuckled. "We've been waiting for them."

We?

I stepped inside to a kitchen filled with guys. "You have ... more company," I said with a tight, fake grin.

"Yeah, Shane rounded up the whole crew for dinner and ... they're still here." Fisher took the container of cookies.

"Yo, Reese!" Shane said with a drunk man's boisterous enthusiasm. "Fisher said you were coming with cookies."

"Yo," I replied with a very bummed girlfriend's dismay as I removed my jacket and boots.

Fisher opened the container and set it on the counter for the pack of wolves to devour, but not before snagging one of each for himself and putting them on a paper towel. "Guys, this is Reese. These are the guys."

They laughed and I rolled my eyes. It was all too reminiscent of his pathetic introductions when I met his family.

"The game's on downstairs. Let's go." One of the guys said, and the rest of the pack followed with their beers and cookies.

"This isn't what I saw happening tonight," I murmured to Fisher as we brought up the rear.

"Me neither. But they're here, and I can't just abandon them."

I bit my tongue. Abandoning groups and sneaking off to be alone was our thing. Did he not remember that?

A few of the guys sat at the barstools, two other guys played pool, and the rest of the group sat on the sofa or floor in front of the sofa to watch the game.

I snagged a blanket from the back of the sofa and plopped down next to Fisher.

"I don't need a blanket, baby. It's plenty warm," Fisher said.

"It's not that warm yet." I covered him with the blanket, eliciting a frown from him. It lasted a full five seconds before his body went rigid and his lips parted with an audible inhale.

"Reese ..." he whispered.

"Huh?" I turned my attention to the television, wetting my lips while he grabbed my arm—the arm attached to the hand down the front of his jeans and briefs.

I wasn't sure what got into me, but I suspected it had something to do with repression. Fisher was finally mine, and I didn't have to hide it from the world anymore. We were no longer forbidden lovers. And while his friends knew nothing about our forbidden love, and therefore I had nothing to prove to them, I still felt the need to claim Fisher in a public way.

My guy.

My hand on his cock. (Now MY cock)
All the kisses belong to me.
All the nights out belong to me.
Me in his tub.
Me in his bed.
Me. Me. ME!

My unsettled possessiveness seemed to spur on my hand, and Fisher whispered, "Fuck," under his breath while yanking my hand from the inside of his jeans and then yanking me off the sofa.

"Be right back," he said to whoever was in earshot as he dragged me up the stairs. I didn't miss the few looks in our direction. They knew what we were going to do, and while that made my face flush a bit, I didn't care. In fact, it was really out of our way to go upstairs when there was a perfectly good pool table right there.

When we reached his bedroom, we heard someone in his bathroom.

Fisher growled and pulled me toward one of the spare bedrooms, but one of his friends was sitting on the bed, talking on his phone. He held up a finger like he would be just a minute.

Fisher growled and pulled me to the guest bathroom. The door was locked.

Another growl.

His grip on my hand tightened. Frantic Fisher was my new high. Anticipation zipped through my veins. I liked him out of control with his need for *me*.

"The pantry?" I laughed, a little in disbelief as he pulled me into the walk-in pantry.

"Really?" He turned me to face the wall with a few hooks on it and random things like bags, a broom, and some grilling tools hanging from them. "A hand job in front of my friends? Who are you?" Fisher pressed my hands to the wall and yanked my sweatpants down to my ankles followed by my panties.

"I hope ... I'm yours," I said in a shaky breath, rattled by what he was doing to me and how much it thrilled me.

He chuckled. "You're mine alright." I liked his fast hands. He was impatient boot-shopping Fisher with his cock out as he thrust into me in a matter of seconds.

"Fishe—" I wasn't prepared for that quick of an invasion.

He silenced me with his hand over my mouth and a harsh "shh" in my ear. Fisher moved with intention with one hand giving attention to my clit while his other hand snaked up my shirt and used my breast like a handle.

It was quick and dirty ... and I liked it.

And we finished, just minutes later, he fetched a new roll of paper towels and handed me several squares.

My hero. I laughed at the thought.

My hero also leaned against the corner of a shelf and opened a bag of popcorn, eating it while watching me pull up my panties and sweats. Then he grinned while I looked around for a place to put the wad of paper towels that had *his* mess in it.

I slipped it into my pocket.

He smirked. "Don't forget to take that out before you wash those. It's like Kleenex. It'll make a mess in the washer and dryer."

"You look a little too pleased with yourself." I

snatched the bag from him and grabbed a handful with my non-cleaning hand.

"You started it."

"You invite me over for bakery fun. I brought extra frosting! Then I get here only to discover it's a sausage fest."

"I want you to come to Christmas dinner with me. Rory and Rose too, of course."

"How did we go from sausage fest to Christmas dinner?"

"I want my family to know it's you." His hand dove into the bag of popcorn. Fisher discussed our relationship and the sheer gravity of telling his family like it was nothing more than an invitation to grill out with neighbors.

It was Christmas with his family! The family who just learned about the end of his engagement to the woman they loved like their own.

"Yeaaahhh ..." I grimaced. "But do *they* want to know quite so soon?"

"Yes. My mom's words were, 'Well, dear, if you're in love with another woman, she must be really special. So you need to bring her to Christmas dinner.'"

I fed my anxiety with another huge handful of popcorn, then I mumbled over it, "I think you should tell them ahead of time." I chewed a bit and swallowed. "There is no reason for a surprise. Unless you're a celebrity, nobody likes to be the mystery guest at a party."

He shook his head, stealing the bag back and closing it with a chip clip. "It will be fine."

"Let me rephrase it for you. If you don't tell them

ahead of time, I won't go with you. And I'm on call this week. When you dumped me after coffee at Starbucks, I volunteered to be on call over Christmas with one of the other midwives. So I can't make any guarantees, even if you do tell them ahead of time."

His head jerked backward. "I didn't dump you. I dropped you off at your house, but I didn't dump you. *You* were the one who left me with the parting words of 'I will never regret not giving you my virginity.'" Fisher used a feminine voice while mocking me.

"Well I don't." I tipped my chin up. Even with a pocketful of his cum, I had no regrets.

"You had me. Before I got my memory back, you had me. I thought this first love of yours was a total schmuck for not taking it if you offered it. But now I remember why I wasn't camping out all night to be first in line for the virgin lottery."

I bit my lips to keep from laughing. *Virgin lottery?*

"You carried that V-card like a bomb. I wanted *nothing* to do with it. The responsibility? Given the fact that you were eighteen and clueless as to where you were going in life? No thank you. You can 'not regret' not giving it to me all you want. But I 'not regret' not taking it from you even more."

I like riled-up Fisher. I'd always liked that version of him. It was hot. There was no other way to describe it.

Virgin lottery.

V-card bomb.

Double-downing on not regretting his decision.

The intensity in his jaw when he clenched his teeth,

showing a little animalistic anger. That was a "yes, please" from me.

"Wanna do it again?" I said, reaching for the button to his jeans.

"Fuck yeah, I wanna do it again." He grabbed my face and smashed his mouth to mine.

CHAPTER THIRTY-FOUR

I MAY HAVE JINXED Christmas that day in Fisher's pantry. While Rory, Rose, and I were enjoying potato leek soup and lots of cookies on Christmas Eve, I got called to a birth.

Twins!

Magnus Andrew Howard and Minnie Ann Howard.

Two little five-pound bundles of holiday joy born on Christmas, just after three in the afternoon.

Fisher's family had Christmas dinner scheduled for noon to accommodate his sisters' schedules with their in-laws. I texted him and told him to eat without me.

I finally arrived just before seven that night. Lights and wreaths adorned their house. I barely got a second knock on the door before Fisher opened it.

"Merry Christmas." I gave him a sad smile. It was an amazing day, but I was disappointed I missed Christmas dinner with his family.

As soon as I stepped inside, before I could get out of my coat or remove my boots, he framed my face gently

754

and kissed me. And I melted. It was exactly what I needed after a long twenty hours at a birth. "Merry Christmas." He looked up and nodded to the mistletoe.

I grinned, and that was when I noticed the onlookers in the living room. Just his parents, Arnie, Rose, and Rory. And that was the moment. Yes, Fisher had told them ahead of time that I was the other woman. But it did very little to ease my nerves in that moment. "Hi," I said a little sheepishly because I didn't see them there before Fisher kissed me. "So sorry I missed dinner."

Fisher took the bags of gifts in my hands and my coat while I toed off my boots and glanced down at myself. I did a quick change in the car before heading to his parents' house in the dark. It was possible I had my sweater on backward or some rogue sock from the laundry stuck to my jeans.

"You had more important things to do. Merry Christmas, honey." Laurie met me halfway and hugged me. It felt genuine. Not for one second did I feel like the less desirable replacement to Angie.

"Merry Christmas."

Pat stood and hugged me too with an equally generous embrace and sincere "Merry Christmas."

"Bro stole my girl. Not cool." Arnie winked before getting in on the hugfest.

"Hi, Arnie." I had to bite my tongue because I almost said, "He stole me before I was *your girl*."

I headed straight to Rose and Rory for hugs too since I hadn't seen them yet that day.

"How was the birth?" Rory asked.

"Pretty special. I don't know if anyone could be

having a better Christmas than them. Two perfect little peanuts."

"That *is* hard to beat." Rose nodded and smiled.

"Hungry?" Fisher asked when I turned around to look for a place to sit.

"Yeah, I'm kind of starving."

"Let's get you fed. Come on." Laurie took my hand, very Fisher-like of her, and led me to the kitchen.

Fisher stayed in the great room, leaving me with just his mother.

Laurie set out tray after tray of leftovers. "There's a plate in that cabinet to the left of the sink. I can heat it up in the oven or the microwave. Do you have a preference?"

"Cold," I said, eagerly dishing food onto my plate.

"No, honey. It's really no problem. You can't have cold Christmas dinner."

"She can." Fisher appeared in the kitchen after all. "She's an odd duck. Likes everything cold."

That wasn't totally true. I liked my fisherman hot.

And impatient.

And a little dirty.

He swiped his finger through my potatoes as I had done with his Thanksgiving leftovers. I grabbed his wrist before he got his hand to his mouth and I sucked it off his finger.

His eyebrows lifted a fraction as he made a quick glance at his mom. I think I may have made him blush. Typical guy ... a little finger sucking sent his mind reeling into inappropriate territory.

"She's been working, Fisher. I wouldn't blame her for

biting your finger off for attempting to steal her food."
Laurie returned everything to a nice PG rating.

"Mmm ... yes. My girl is ferocious." He playfully
kissed me, licking the side of my mouth.

My girl.

I liked being his girl, even if I was a woman. The
truth of time still remained unchangeable—I would
always be ten years younger than him.

Laurie rolled her eyes at Fisher's obnoxiousness.
"Make sure she gets anything she wants or needs, Fisher.
I'm going to sit down," Laurie said before leaving the
kitchen.

"Hear that?" I leaned against the counter and held
my plate with one hand while shoveling food down with
my other hand. "Anything I want or need. Wanna know
what I need?"

Fisher smirked, chest puffed out, chin up. "What?"
He waggled his eyebrows suggestively.

"A bed," I said with my mouth full. "I'm so tired it
hurts."

"Oh, baby ..." He took my plate from me and pulled
me into his body.

I could have fallen asleep right then and there. We
stayed another hour, everyone drinking wine, and some
crazy cocktail Arnie put together, and opened gifts.

Me?

I didn't drink a drop, and my gifts from his family sat
piled on the floor in front of me. The second I sat on the
sofa next to Fisher, I was out, nestled into his side. The
next thing I knew, he was gently waking me while
everyone stood by the door saying their goodbyes.

His parents gave me hugs goodbye while Fisher put on my coat and guided my feet into my boots like someone would do to a child. I was *so* tired.

"Keys?" Fisher felt around in my pockets and found my keys. "Who's driving her car?" he asked Rory and Rose.

"I can drive," I mumbled.

A chorus of nearly everyone chimed, "No you can't."

Rose grabbed my keys and Fisher wrapped his arm around me and helped me to his truck as Arnie followed with the gifts.

"You bringing her home?" Rory asked.

"What do you think?" Fisher replied while I climbed into his truck.

"I think you're stealing my daughter from me," she said.

"Then you think right," Fisher replied after helping me fasten my seat belt.

I didn't remember the ride home. I sort of remembered Fisher carrying me into his house, but that was a little fuzzy at the time. The next thing I remembered with any clarity was waking in his arms, naked save for my panties and his T-shirt. A warm ray of sun squeezed through a tiny gap in his blinds as I sat up slowly.

"Stay in bed," he mumbled.

I chuckled, hopping out of bed. "I have to pee."

"Fine," he said with a little grumble. "Then come back."

While I washed my hands, I noticed something different about his closet, but it was too dark to say for sure what it was, so I tiptoed to the entry and turned on the light.

One entire wall was exposed, open to the closet of the guest room.

"Thought you were coming back to bed?" Fisher slid his arm around my waist from behind me while kissing my shoulder.

"What are you doing to your closet?"

"I'm making an access door to the other room."

"Why?"

He kissed his way to my neck. "Because it's going to be a nursery."

I turned slowly, eyes narrowed.

"I'm pregnant," he said.

"Stop." I giggled.

"I think it's yours, but I'm not going to lie ... Shane and I had a few drunk nights."

More giggles as he bent down and picked me up, tossing me over his shoulder and swatting my butt.

"Fisher!"

"Bed. We are not getting out of this bed today. I took the day off just to be naked with you."

I laughed when he deposited me onto the bed. "Tell me. What are you really doing in your closet?"

He settled between my legs, kissing my neck again while inching my shirt (his shirt) up my torso. "I'm going to ask Nurse Capshaw to move in with me, and I know she has a lot of scrubs, so I'm giving her more space by stealing a few feet from the other closet."

I wriggled to the side to get out from under him,

scooting to the back of the bed like home base. "You're going to ask me to move in with you?"

Still on his stomach, he lifted onto his elbows. "I'm going to ask you a lot of things, but that's coming up soon on the list. Spoiler alert ... you say yes."

My lips did that twitching thing where I tried to hide my amusement or maybe it was just unfathomable happiness. "Wow. The man who couldn't remember the best hand job of his life is now predicting the future?"

"Absolutely." He army crawled toward me.

"Fisher ..." I opened my bent legs. He filled the space with his broad shoulders, and instead of doing what I thought he was going to do ... what I was offering him ... he rested his forehead against my stomach and slid his hands along my outer thighs. "Can I do it now?"

"Do what?" I asked with a soft voice, running my fingers through his messy hair.

"Can I love you *forever*?"

I swallowed a little emotion that had been building since I saw the closet. "Yes."

EPILOGUE

FISHER

SHE SAID YES ... and she never stopped saying yes.

Yes to moving in with me.

Yes to weekend trips to ski.

Yes to movie nights or Arnie's concerts.

Yes to helping me in my shop.

Yes to waffles for dinner and cold pizza for breakfast.

Yes to long baths and quickies in the shower.

Then I made her a crossword puzzle that was a treasure hunt.

"I'll see you soon, if you're as smart as you say you are." I kissed her head and handed her the puzzle and a pencil.

"Where are you going?" she asked when I got to the back door.

"You'll see." I left.

It took her just over an hour to solve the puzzle and follow the clues they spelled out which led her to me.

"Really?" She rolled her eyes as she walked toward my table at McDonald's. "All that for a Happy Meal?" She eyed the sack opposite me.

"It's probably cold since you took so long." I sipped my chocolate milk.

"The average person wouldn't have known half of those words. You're such a geek." She pulled out her hamburger and apples. "No fries?" She nodded to my empty burger wrapper.

I shook my empty sack. "I've had two orders waiting for you."

Another eye roll just before she took a bite of her sandwich. "I'm going to make you a puzzle that takes you to the grocery store. A list of the things we need."

"Sounds fun." I rested my face in my hands.

"Why are you acting so weird?"

I shrugged. "Am I?"

"Yes." She chuckled, setting her hamburger down after three bites. That was her ritual whether she realized it or not.

Three bites of her sandwich.

Half of her apple slices.

One big sip of her juice.

And then a fishing expedition for the toy in the bottom of the sack.

She pulled out the toy and frowned. "This is an old one. How on earth did they have this to offer?" She inspected the Sponge Bob treasure chest, cracking it open to reveal a diamond ring. After several blinks she glanced up at me.

I nodded to the small group of kids who volunteered

literally fifteen minutes earlier to help me. They yelled at the same time. "Will you marry the fisherman?"

Reese jumped and shot her gaze to them. Most of them fell into goofy fits of giggles with their hands covering their mouths. And the small gathering of parents at nearby tables all looked on with big grins, maybe even a few nervous grins. I mean ... what if she said no?

Reese turned back to me, and I was waiting on one knee because that's what you did when you wanted your girl to say yes more than anything.

"Are you going to say yes?" I asked after she blinked a thousand times.

Lifting one shoulder, she relinquished a grin. "I'm thinking about it."

"Thinking is overrated." I took the ring and placed it on her finger just before kissing her. "Say yes," I mumbled over her lips.

She kissed me while nodding, and when the kiss ended ... it was another glorious *yes*.

As I WAITED for my bride to make her way down the aisle in the church that would have made her dad proud and *did* please her dad's parents, I got a little emotional for reasons that had nothing to do with the stunning woman in white.

She never asked. Not once.

I promised a million answers after that Christmas, but Reese never asked. It was like Angie no longer existed in her mind.

She never asked if I had sex with Angie in Costa Rica. I didn't.

She never asked about my memories of Angie—our engagement, how I felt about her, or why I said yes when she proposed. And unless Angie told someone, the truth remained buried in the past.

I said yes because she was my friend. I said yes because my family adored her. I said yes because she had just lost her mother. I said yes because we were *good enough* together. And I said yes because I had already let *the one* go.

But the most revealing part of my memory returning involved the morning of the day of my accident. While the accident itself still remained a black hole in my mind, and for good reasons probably always would, I recalled the heated argument I had with Angie.

Irritation.

Pressure.

Regret.

She had been moving a hundred miles per hour with wedding plans, and it made it hard to breathe. What should have been a happy time in my life felt like impending doom. So after she showed me tux swatch number eight hundred and fifty and asked my opinion on ten different shades of fucking white for the linens at the reception, I cracked. I said some things I instantly regretted. As tears rolled down her cheeks, she muttered the words, "Do you even want to marry me?"

And I spoke my truth with a whispered, "No."

I wasn't engaged when the truck knocked me off my motorcycle. And Angie shared everything about our past that suited her narrative, her desperation to keep me. And given the short amount of time between breaking off our engagement and the accident that afternoon, nobody else knew the truth.

The funny part? I wasn't mad. People did desperate things for love. Angie didn't know about my relationship with Reese. She didn't think her slight omission hurting anyone. Her actions, although dishonest, were also out of love. She did love me. She did take care of me after my accident as I had taken care of her after her mom died. And maybe she thought I would fall in love with her again. My accident serving as a reset on our relationship.

So what?

It didn't stop me from falling in love with Reese for a second time.

It didn't stop her from giving me all the yeses.

And since I never told anyone but Reese and my doctor about my memory returning, it really didn't matter.

So as Rory and Rose walked Reese down the aisle, I fought the ache in my chest, the feeling that I was undeserving of such perfection. She was about to marry me without the answers to her million questions. Reese loved me like I had always imagined God (if He existed) loved us.

My heart pounded so violently; it was hard to hear past the whooshing sound in my ears. But the second Rory and Rose took their seats, and Reese placed her hand in mine, my heart found its normal rhythm again, and I could hear the final notes of the harp and her whispered, "Hey, handsome," as she grinned.

I swallowed so hard and fought to keep my shit together. There was no way I was going to cry when my girl showed such control, like marrying me was just the next simple step in her journey.

I made it to the end with dry eyes, but just barely. Reese gave away a tear or two when I said the words "I do." And my thumbs quickly caught them as the minister gave me permission to kiss my bride.

For a guy who was in no hurry to get married, I walked my wife out of that church with a puffed-out chest and the cheesiest grin.

***

"It's likely I won't be able to answer my phone, but I'll call you as soon as possible. If things get really sticky, you know my mom and Rose will happily come help. If it's an actual emergency—"

"Call 9-1-1. Got it," I said.

Reese frowned. "Of course, but I was going to say, call Holly. She's not on call, but she lives across the street from the birth center."

"You know ... this isn't my first rodeo." I rocked our little girl like the fucking pro I was while our three-year-old son played in his room. It was Reese's first full day back to work (her first birth) since maternity leave.

I knew how to warm milk and thaw more if needed.

Diapers? No problem.

Crying? I had the best football hold and most

soothing gait in the whole damn state, and my wife knew it.

It was the weekend, so there was a one hundred percent chance her family and mine would be popping in nonstop to get their baby fix or take Aiden to the park and to get ice cream.

"Fisher ..." She frowned before leaning over to kiss Claire's tiny cheek as she rested on my chest in the recliner.

"You've been spoiled. Most working moms don't get to wear their babies to work. You can't wear her to a birth. So just go before the baby arrives without you."

Reese had been so spoiled that way. She looked like a woman from Ghana wearing Aiden and now Claire to work ... magically tied to her with some long piece of material. And that worked for clinic days when no one was in labor.

After she kissed Claire, she hovered over my face, surrendering enough of her pouty demeanor to offer me a tiny grin because she knew I was right.

"She won't take a pacifier, so don't even try."

"I know." I smiled. "She's like her dad ... only the real deal will satisfy her."

I managed to squeeze a bigger smile from her as she rolled her eyes.

"Are you going to kiss me?"

She slowly rubbed her lips together, teasing me as usual. "I'm thinking about it."

The End

BOOK TWO BONUS CONTENT
SELECT CHAPTERS FROM FISHER'S POINT OF VIEW

FISHER
CHAPTER SIXTEEN

I CAVED.

After sufficient pestering from family, I made an appointment with a therapist. It wasn't overly thrilling, but at least I could say I went. As I entered the office, a younger man started to brush past me. Then he stopped.

"Oh, hi," he said.

"Hey," I replied and kept walking because I didn't recognize him.

"Fisher, right?"

I turned. "Yeah. Do I know you? Sorry ..." I shook my head. "I had an accident and my memory of certain things and people isn't great."

"Sorry to hear that. I'm Brendon, Reese's friend. Uh ... from church. I'm an attorney." He shook his head. "Not ... that that matters. I'm not her attorney. And maybe we're no longer friends. I'm not sure. I haven't seen her since she broke off our engagement."

What the fuck?

"Engagement?"

Brendon frowned. "Yeah," he whispered. "In less than twenty-four hours, I got engaged and my heartbroken. Shortest engagement ever."

Really ... what the actual fuck?

"That's ..." I had no idea how to respond. I was glad she didn't marry that Brendon guy, but he seemed like he wasn't okay. "That's rough. She's uh ... actually back here in Denver."

Brendon nodded, mouth corkscrewed. "Really?"

"Yeah. She's a nurse. Working to become a midwife. And she's living with her mom at the moment."

"A midwife ..." Something resembling a small grin replaced his forlorn expression. "She'll be a wonderful midwife. If you see her, tell her I said hi."

I continued to study his expression. It transformed into something like pride. "I will."

That night and most of the following day, since I still had so many things I couldn't remember, I focused on what I could remember.

Reese was engaged, not for long. But still ... engaged. I wondered if Rory knew? She never mentioned it. Or maybe she did. My memory wasn't exactly reliable.

When I returned home from an evening jog, Reese was standing at the end of my driveway, staring at my house. Maybe waiting to knock on my door? She was probably worried that Angie was there.

"She's out of town," I said, removing my earbuds. "She asked me to take her car to get the oil changed if I had time. Seemed like a nice thing to do."

She grinned at me like she wasn't listening to me talk about the woman everyone thought I was going to marry.

"One in eighty thousand babies are born en caul. That means it comes out of its mother's body still in the amniotic fluid sac. It's the most amazing sight. I ..." She shook her head.

She was the most amazing sight.

"I can't even describe it. But I saw it. I. Saw. It!"

Something that could only be described as the perfect feeling, the purest happiness, took over my entire body. "Do you need to kiss somebody?"

Again, she shook her head. "Not somebody. I need to kiss *you*."

"Then what are you waiting for?"

Her giggle did things to me (so many things) as she leaped into my arms and kissed me with her soft hands framing my face. I grabbed her butt. I wanted to grab every inch of her and never let go. At the same time, I thought about Brendon. Did she look at him the way she looked at me? Did she give him the same smile?

"You got your cast off. How does it feel?"

"Better on your ass." I pulled her closer. "Are you coming inside? Or did you just come here to stare at my house?"

Reese gave me her dramatic eye roll. "Nobody was home at my house. And I had to tell someone, so I ran over here."

"So I *am* just somebody?"

She clenched the neck of my hoodie. "I share you, so you have to share me and my enthusiasm. If you must know, I was looking for my mom and Rose first because occasionally I value self-preservation. And I was reminded of that when I got here and saw Angie's car."

Reese shared me with nobody. There was no competition. How could she not see that? I so badly wanted to say the words, but nothing in my life had been simple since the accident. I didn't feel like it was really even my life. I felt like I was trying to live the life everyone thought I was supposed to live, like everyone knew me better than I knew myself.

And maybe that was the case before Reese. She changed that. I knew one thing, the only thing that mattered—I liked me with her, and that was no accident.

"Come trim my beard before I get into the shower."

"Your cast is off."

I smiled, taking her hands and returning them to my face. "Come trim my beard before I get into the shower."

"I have to get home soon. I'm still on call for the next few days."

"Come trim my beard before I get in the shower."

Again, she rewarded me with that laugh that I felt in every cell of my body. "Remember what I said about self-preservation?"

Guiding her hand to my lips, I kissed her palm. "I would never hurt you. What do you want for your birthday?"

Stealing her hands from my face, she chuckled. "To not go camping with you and your fiancée. I realize you can't say you're sick because you never get sick, but you could make up some excuse."

"How do you know that I never get sick?"

"Because you told me." She shrugged.

Why couldn't I remember her? She was the most

unforgettable person I had ever met. "I don't remember that."

"I know you don't. Trust me ... I know."

That bothered me so much more than she knew. Taking her hand, I pulled her away from the front door.

"I'm going home." She tried to move away from me.

"Eventually," I said, keeping a tight hold on her hand.

"Fisher ..."

"Nurse Capshaw, queen of the veiled birth."

After I closed the door and tried to release her hand, she squeezed mine like I had just done to hers. "Veiled birth?"

"It's another term for en caul," I said.

"I'm aware. But how do you know that?"

With a shrug, I gazed down at my feet for a beat. "Probably a crossword puzzle or something."

"I haven't put that in my puzzles."

As I started to turn away, she tugged my hand again. "Fisher Mann ... you like crossword puzzles. You liked them before I made them for you."

I'd had this feeling for quite some time that Reese was always on the verge of saying more, like every time she spoke, she stopped just short of ... something.

"Are you genuinely asking me or are you testing me?"

"What do you mean?" She bit her lower lip.

"I know so much about Angie that there are some days I don't feel like I've lost memories of her. I start to wonder if the events in my head are my memories or things I've been told because I've been told *everything*. The only test I have with her is my feelings. I don't remember how I felt about her. But with you it's different."

"Different how?" She released my hand.

"I feel like you've given me bits and pieces, on a need-to-know basis. My story with Angie makes sense in my head. Childhood friends. On and off again relationship when we got older. Me doing my thing. Her doing her thing. Our families keeping us connected. She comes back to town for her mom. We rekindle our romance. Even if I don't *feel* it now, it makes sense to me."

With an uncomfortable grin, she widens her eyes and fiddles with the hem of her shirt. I noticed she did that a lot when she was nervous. "Well, that's good."

"From everything my family has told me about who I was, I don't think I would have taken a part-time employee to my workshop. I wouldn't have showed her how to sand anything. Yet that's your story."

She wouldn't look at me. "You thought a lot of Rory. I'm sure it was a favor to her. And I was relentless. You probably just did it to shut me up."

There was something … I couldn't put my finger on it … just something that she was hiding from me, but I had no clue why.

"Why were you so certain I'd like crossword puzzles?"

"I wasn't. Why are you being so weird? Have you remembered something? Memories can return slowly, and they can cause confusion as you try to piece them together and make sense of them."

"Do you know an attorney named Brendon?"

She swallowed so hard I thought she might choke on her tongue. It said everything.

"What? Why?"

"Because I saw him yesterday."

"Where?"

"At my therapist's office."

"You have a therapist?"

I nodded.

"Since when?" she asked.

"Since yesterday."

"Why?"

"We're not talking about me."

"We are. Why?"

"Because I was in an accident. I'm missing part of my memory, and I have a fiancée and maybe a girlfriend." That sounded so fucking insane. I hated it. "And it's not my point anyway."

"What's your point?"

"Brendon recognized me. He must be a patient at the same office. He was leaving when I arrived. He said hi. Of course, I had to apologize for not knowing him and give him my quick spiel about my accident."

Her nose wrinkled into a tiny cringe. "How is he?"

"Why do you ask?"

She shrugged. "No reason. I mean ... I haven't seen him in years. We used to go to the same church, not too far from here."

"So you were church friends?"

After a pause and a narrowed eyed inspection of me, she nodded.

"Just church friends?"

"Brendon was the one who convinced me to go to Thailand. He's actually the friend who went with me."

"He's the one, isn't he?" It bothered me ... so fucking much.

"Yes, I just said he's the one who went with me to—"

"No. That's not what I'm talking about. He's the one you loved. The one we talked about. You said he's with someone else, but not married. I told you to go knock on his door."

After several blinks, she pinched the bridge of her nose. "Why do you think it's him?"

"That's not an answer."

"It's not him."

"Fuck ..." I rubbed my temples. My head hurt. "I didn't see that coming."

"Why?

"Well, because he casually mentioned having not seen you since you agreed to *marry him* and broke off the engagement all within twenty-four hours."

She wet her lips and rubbed them together but offered no immediate response.

"I told him you were back in Denver. He said to tell you hi. So ..." I laughed, but it wasn't funny. "You were going to marry Brendon for two seconds, and he's not the guy you were talking about? The other guy must be quite something if he's the one you think about when you think of love instead of the guy you said yes to marrying."

She whispered, "He is."

"Is he the reason you broke up with Brendon?"

"No. I ... I only said yes to Brendon because he asked me in front of a group of people, and I didn't want to embarrass him. The reason I didn't marry him was because I still hadn't done anything for myself. And I wasn't ready for Wife and Mother to be my new titles and full-time profession, which was funny because I had been watching all these babies come into the world. And I was longing for a husband like the men holding their wives' hands. The love. The family. I wanted it, just not yet. And I didn't want it with Brendon. And that truly sucked because he was ... I'm sure still *is* an amazing, kind, smart, and loving man. Just not the one for me."

I had no chance.

"What if I can't live up to him? Will I be the next Brendon?"

"No. You won't be the next Brendon because he got a parting gift, I suppose."

"What was that?"

"My virginity."

What the fuck?

"You loved someone else, but Brendon from *church* took your virginity?"

"*Took* might be a strong word. I gave it to him. Persuaded him to take it." She sheepishly glanced up at me.

"Why didn't you give it to the guy you loved?"

Her lips twitched like she was holding back a grin. "He didn't want it."

"What?" Did I hear her right?

"He knew the timing wasn't right for us. And he knew, at the time, that I had mixed emotions about my V-card. After Rory going to prison, my dad dying, and attending a Christian academy while living with my ultra-conservative grandparents ... Jesus, God, and every chapter of the Bible haunted me."

"But you wanted to have sex with him?"

Again, she bit back a smirk. "Yes."

I hated the fucker. "I rescind what I told you about him. Don't go knock on his door. He doesn't deserve you. If he didn't have the balls to man the fuck up when you chose him, then he didn't deserve it or you. He choked, and that's pretty pathetic."

She laughed. "Yeah, well ... I didn't look at it like that. So let's not stone him for his decision. Besides, you have some things in common with him."

"Such as?" I widened my stance, crossing my hands over my chest.

"You weren't going to let me go past second base."

"Fuck. Stop. Just ... no. We are never talking about that again. It was a joke. I would have hit the damn home run and you know it."

Reese shouldered past me with some attitude. "Sure. Sure. That's what *he* said."

"He's an idiot."

A giggle left her lips. "Sometimes."

When I caught up to her in my bathroom, I shrugged off my shirt and sat on the vanity bench. She placed a towel on my legs to catch the hair. It fell to the floor when I spread my legs to pull her between them.

She giggled again and turned on the trimmers as I rested my face in her chest and inhaled slowly. God ... I loved every second I got to spend with her. "I missed you," I murmured.

"It's only been five days." She ran her free hand through my hair, and it sent shivers down my spine.

"And nights," I said, lifting my head. "Nights too. Don't forget nights."

"Because we've spent so many nights together?" She started trimming my beard.

We hadn't, and it was a crime. I needed to rectify that immediately.

"You're with me every night. In my dreams. You're naked, except for my tool belt. You're always wearing my tool belt."

She laughed. "Sounds interesting. Am I building something?"

"No. You're always just teasing me." Haunting me ... she haunted me every night.

"Funny. In my dreams, you're always a baby with an adult head, sucking a pacifier."

Smart ass ...

"Not funny." I gripped the back of her thighs, and she jumped.

"Careful. And it's actually quite funny."

She could laugh at me. I didn't care. All that mattered was her saying that I was in fact in her dreams. And she was in my bathroom, nestled between my legs with her tits in my face and her fingers tracing the lines of my face after every stroke with the trimmers.

"Perfect. As usual." She set the trimmers on the counter. "Well, my trim is perfect, considering what I had to work with."

I liked her goading me. I liked her ... everything. I just ... liked her so fucking much.

"I'll grab the vac hose to sweep up the mess."

"Leave it," I murmured, pulling her closer.

Again, she pressed her delicate hands to my face. "So handsome," she whispered.

It felt like heaven. Closing my eyes, I took a long breath.

"Did you tell your therapist about me? I know it's none of my business, but—"

"Yes." I opened my eyes. "I told her I'm engaged to a woman I've known nearly my whole life. But I'm in love with a woman I've known for a breath, maybe two."

She pulled in a shaky breath like I stole it from her. I wanted to take her breath away. It was the most stunning sight.

"You love me?" she whispered.

I shrugged. "I'm assuming that's what this annoying feeling is."

"Annoying feeling?" She narrowed her eyes.

"The increased heart rate I get just from thinking about you. The stupid smile that I can't seem to wipe off my face because I'm thinking about you *all the damn time*."

She grinned, and I wanted to capture it and the feeling in my chest, locking both in a safe place so I could have them on the days that weren't so amazing, the days I didn't get my Reese fix.

"The dreams," I continued. "The driving by your house just to see if your car is there. Lack of focus on anything or anyone but you. It's ... it's bad." I lifted my gaze to hers filled with tears. "What about you? Do you have any feelings toward me? Or do you just want into my pants? Be honest ... am I the girl in this relationship?"

"Fisher ..." she whispered.

I had her. All of her? I didn't know. Was there still some guy out there who held her heart even if he didn't take her virginity? Could I compete with her first real love?

She pressed her lips to mine, and I forgot about any other guy because in that moment I. Had. Her.

And I wanted all of her.

My fingers found the waist of her jeans, and she didn't stop me when I unbuttoned them and eased down the zipper. She was ineffable, taking my breath away. Not just one breath ... all of them.

As I kissed the skin next to her panties, she threaded her fingers through my hair and whispered, "I love you, my lost fisherman."

Her lost fisherman ...

Was I truly lost? Or was I found for possibly the first time in my life?

I guess it didn't matter what she said as long it started with the word "my." I'd be anything as long it involved being hers.

"This is so messy," she whispered as I gazed up at her.

"That's how we know it's real." I stood, removing her shirt while she lifted her arms, offering me everything.

When my lips found hers again, I eased her bra straps off her shoulders, wanting to feel the warmth of her skin next to mine.

She reached around and unhooked it, letting it fall to

the floor between us. Fuck the old memories ... I just wanted the ones I was making with her in that very moment.

The tickle of her fingertips along my abs.

The eruption of goose bumps along her skin as the pad of my thumb brushed her nipple, it hardening under my touch.

The growl in my own chest that I almost didn't recognize.

The slow dance to the bed.

My new memory took photos of her heavy gaze on me as she reclined onto the bed ... as I peeled off her jeans. "Not even death will take this memory away from me."

More emotion filled her eyes. And I kissed my way up her body, tasting her slowly while sliding off her panties.

Her hips lurched from the mattress. "Fisher ..."

I couldn't hide my grin, the high it gave me to unravel her slowly. As I made my way up her body, she opened her legs wider, teasing my chest with her fingers, my abs, and the muscles along my back. My impatience warred with my greater desire which was to make it last for as long as possible. Guiding her onto her stomach, I kissed the sexy curve of her backside, memorizing all of it. Then I saw something ... ink.

I grinned against her skin. "What ... do we have here?" I nudged her butt toward the window to get some light for a better look. "A tattoo? You have a tattoo?" I didn't see that coming, not in a million years.

She twisted to glance back at me.

"Callipygian," I read her tattoo slowly.

"I was drunk, hence the hidden tattoo on my butt. It means—"

"It means you have a shapely ass. Alcohol makes you confident and a little vain." I laughed just before biting it. For some reason, that hidden tattoo made me want her exponentially more. I had a feeling that she might never stop surprising me, and that made me ... possessive.

It made me resent everything Angie had supposedly been in my life. It made me resent my family's love for her. It made me want to strangle Brendon for proposing to her and do even worse things to the guy she first loved.

"Ouch!" She wriggled beneath my hold, rolling onto her back. "How do you know that word?"

I nudged my way between her knees. "Because I have the same word tattooed on my ass."

"You do not." She giggled, reaching for my hair as my mouth dipped between her spread legs, making her squirm, moan, and breath heavily. "Stop teasing me," she pleaded with a strained voice, her fingers gripping my hair harder.

I sucked her clit, and one of her hands released my hair and smacked the mattress, clawing at the sheet as she gasped.

I did that to her. Not Brendon. Not the pathetic guy who wouldn't take her virginity. Me. Only me. So fuck them. They had their chance and blew it. I had no intention of ever letting another guy have a chance with her.

"Don't hurry me." I kissed my way up her body before retrieving a condom from the unopened box I bought the day we went to Target. My ego gobbled up the expression on her face.

That's right, Reese. There was no way I could have sex with Angie again after that day in Target.

"Wipe that grin off your face." She rolled on top of me, pinning my arms next to my head, her hair falling around my face. I was done. All patience vanished as she lowered her mouth to mine.

As I guided her hips over me.

As she sat up, eyes heavy.

As I pushed inside of her.

My past? What past?

I sat up and kissed her so hard I thought I might bruise her lips as I fought to stay in control. My greedy hands explored every inch of her body. Being inside of her, the sweet taste of her tongue flicking against mine, the intense pressure of her fingers digging into my back, and her legs wrapped around me ... it stole every last bit of reason in my head.

When she came, I crashed my mouth to hers, swallowing every breath, every moan, just ... all of her.

"My therapist is going to be really pissed off with me," I laughed as she rolled toward me, nestling her body to mine, her face in my neck. One of my hands claimed her butt while I buried my nose in her hair, inhaling the floral scent.

"Why?"

"Because she told me to take a step back, to not get distracted by the physical part of my relationships."

"I'd get a second opinion. Because in my humble opinion, we should do this again ... maybe even a lot."

Again, I laughed. "I second that opinion." Giving her head a quick kiss, I rolled over and sat on the edge of the bed. "I'm going to take a shower. You should join me."

Reese sat up, hugging me, her perfect tits pressed to my back as she bit my earlobe. "I'm going home. You distracted me with sex, but I wasn't done telling the world about the birth I witnessed."

Twisting by torso, I glanced back at her. "Are you saying the birth was more memorable than the sex?"

Jumping out of bed, she threw on her clothes like the house was on fire. "I'm saying it's my constitutional right to not answer your question."

"You can't plead the Fifth on this." I snatched my shorts from the floor and headed to the bathroom.

"Did you hear me say that birth was one in *eighty thousand?*"

After donning sweatpants and a tee, I returned to the bedroom, leaning against the threshold, crossing my arms over my chest. "Tonight, you were one in a billion ... times infinity. But if I didn't live up to one in eighty thousand, then I think we're done here." Total bullshit. We were never done.

"You're right." She squeezed past me and retrieved her shirt from the bathroom floor. "Angie has been giving you everything. She wants you to remember how you felt about her. And if I were wearing a diamond ring you gave me, I'd probably be doing the same thing. Retelling our story to you a thousand different ways. But for me, it doesn't matter if you loved me then, it only matters if you love me now."

I turned toward her.

She gave me a sad smile. "Just ... love me today."

Done.

"I love you today," I whispered.

She smiled like I returned the right answer. "Thought you were going to shower."

"After I drive you home."

Her grin grew as she stepped toward me, taking my hand and guiding me to the front door. "You're one, Fisher."

"One in what?" I asked.

"Not *in* anything. Not one in eight thousand. Not one in a billion times infinity. You're just one. *The one.*"

She slayed me with one of my favorite things—words.

FISHER

CHAPTER TWENTY-NINE

Commitments I made with my family and with Angie kept me from Reese for days. Her work schedule robbed us of one last chance for a goodbye before I had to board a plane to Costa Rica with Angie.

The end wasn't coming soon enough for me. My altruism started to fade. It wasn't that I didn't love my family and understand their love for Angie. It wasn't that I didn't see it a little bit from Angie's perspective either. Our long friendship and the years we were more than friends meant something to her, and it probably meant something to the pre-accident version of myself. But time wouldn't change the outcome.

I loved Reese. Period.

On Friday morning, I stole a moment to call her, hoping she wasn't already working.

"Hey!" she answered with such enthusiasm my heart nearly busted from my chest. God ... I missed her.

"Good morning. You working?"

"On my way now."

"Well, I fucking hate that I didn't get to say goodbye in person."

"It's life."

"Not the life I want."

"Yeah, in-person goodbyes should be mandatory. How is Costa Rica?"

"Green."

She laughed, and it fed my starving soul.

"What's on the agenda for today?"

"Apparently massages and rehearsal dinner."

"Massages, huh?" There was a change in her voice. A little less jovial. "Sounds relaxing. I could use a massage."

"I'll massage you when I get home."

"Mmm ... that would be amazing. How's your room?"

"It's nice."

There was a pause. I didn't know what to say because the only words that ran through my mind were, *"I miss you so damn much."*

"Where are you?" she asked.

"Just finished jogging on the beach. I'm in the lobby. I need to go back to the room and shower."

"Angie doesn't jog?"

"She was still asleep."

"Oh ... are you sharing a room?"

I cringed. Total asshole for letting that slip. There was nothing to hide, but she didn't know that because I was too damn far away to make her look at me, to kiss her, to remind her in every way that she was it for me. Absolutely everything.

"Uh ... yeah. The place is booked." I played it cool,

not trying to sound guilty when I hadn't really done anything wrong.

"So you tried to get your own room?"

On a sigh, I pinched the bridge of my nose. "Reese, don't do this. Nothing good will come of it. I'll be home Sunday night. It's just two more nights. I'm not happy about this situation, but we've discussed this ad nauseam. One month. It ends in one month. We've got this, right?"

Another long pause.

"I love you today," I said.

Nothing from her.

"Reese?"

"Yeah?"

"I love you. You. *Youuu.* Okay? Don't doubt that for one second. Go to my house. Crawl in my bed. And think of all the *things* I'm going to do to you when I get home on Sunday."

"Yeah." Her voice broke.

"Jesus ... stop. Give me more than a 'yeah.' Tell me you love me. Or be honest and tell me you're pissed off that I agreed to come here. Give me something more than one emotionless word."

"I love you. And I'm pissed off that you agreed to go to Costa Rica with your fiancée."

"Stop calling her my fiancée." Again, I sighed. I was just so tired of waiting. It was so much harder than I imagined it would be. With Reese, I felt impatient. I wanted her in the moment. In every moment.

"Is she still wearing the diamond ring you gave her? When she introduces you to everyone at the wedding as her fiancé, are you going to correct her? If not, then she's your fiancée. And I'm the slutty mistress."

"Reese Capshaw, knock that shit off."

She blew out a slow breath. "I'm at work now. I have to go."

"This ends. When I get home this ends. I'm not doing this any longer. Fuck my memory. Fuck my family loyalty. I can't do this another month. I want you. That's it. You. So go sulk. You have three days for your pity party. Then I'm going to tie you to ..."

It was so vivid, too vivid to be the memory of a dream.

My workshop. Happy Meals.

And zip ties.

I tied her to the stool and did things to her that were *not* professional or any sort of favor to Rory.

"Jesus ..." I whispered.

We didn't *just* fall in love.

"What the fuck, Reese ..." I shook my head as everything in the lobby spun, as the chattering of people distorted into nothing more than distant echoes.

"Reese?" I held my phone out, blinking hard to see the screen because the disbelief ... the reality of it made me dizzy and nauseous. She ended the call.

I called her back.

It went to voicemail.

I called again and again, leaning against a large pillar next to the elevators. Closing my eyes, I fought for more. There had to be more.

When I first met her ...

All the moments that led to me tying her to a stool,

removing her pants, and burying my face between her spread legs ...

It wasn't okay for her to leave me with that. Nothing was okay.

Calling her another dozen times, I slowly started to lose my mind just as I thought I was getting it back.

Angie: Where are you?

As I stared at Angie's text, I brought up that window on my phone and scrolled down. Did I ever text Reese? She worked for me, so surely I did.

When I found her name, I scrolled through messages from years earlier.

Fisher: I'm sorry.
Fisher: Are you going to stay mad at me forever?
Fisher: I'll call my family and tell them it was a lie. That I just wanted to be alone with you.

I texted her a screenshot of those old texts with the message: **Why did I want to be alone with you?**

I knew, sort of. But I needed her to piece it all together. I needed everything. And something told me she was the only person who could fill all the empty holes.

Another old text:

Reese: Hi. Rose isn't going to tell Rory or anyone.

"Tell Rory what," I whispered to myself as I continued to shake my foggy head side to side.

I read more texts that didn't register yet. So again, I took a screen shot and sent it to her.

Fisher: *Where are you?*
Fisher: *Answer your phone.*
Fisher: *I'm sorry.*
Fisher: *Please pick up your phone.*
Fisher: *Don't make me call Rory*

My message after the screenshot was a little more impatient: **WHAT THE HELL?!!!**

The police? Why would I have threatened to call the police?

I continued reading the old texts from later dates.

Fisher: *If you're not dead, text Rory and tell her you made it safely to Houston. Don't be a total asshole about it.*
Reese: *Go fuck yourself.*

With every text I read, my anger grew. Why did she keep this from me? I called her again—over and over.

No answer.

So I texted her again.

PICK UP YOUR GODDAMN PHONE!!!!!
MESSAGE ME THE FUCK BACK!
I ZIP-TIED YOU TO THE STOOL IN MY SHOP! WE WERE MORE THAN FRIENDS AND YOU GODDAMN KNOW IT!

Angie texted me again, so I tried to pull myself together before heading back to the room to shower. She spent the next hour talking to me about the day's plans and the wedding. I heard nothing.

Just before our massage, I messaged Reese again: **Who are you? Why did you do this to me?**

After the massage, I turned my phone back on. There was a text from her.

Reese: Don't be mad. PLEASE don't be mad. PLEASE let's talk about it when you get home. I love you.

Love? I wasn't sure she knew what it meant to love someone.

When we returned to the hotel, Angie took a shower and I helped myself to the mini bar. There wasn't enough alcohol to make me forget that one memory, but I needed something to numb the pain.

As I downed my second bottle of vodka, my phone vibrated. I debated not answering it when Reese's name appeared on my screen, but I wasn't as cruel as her.

"I can't talk now." Okay, I was a little cruel.

"I love you. I've loved you for *so* long."

"I can't talk now."

She breathed out a defeated sigh. "When can we talk?"

"When I'm ready."

"Are you with Angie?"

I found it rich that she wanted so much information from me when she gave me nothing.

"She's still in the shower."

"I couldn't talk either. I was late for work."

I downed more alcohol and stared out the window.

"Well, I can't talk now. I guess we'll talk if or when it works out."

"If? Don't do this. Don't cherry-pick pieces of your past and try to piece them together by yourself. Making assumptions. Nothing about us was simple."

"No shit."

"Fisher ..." her shaky voice broke as she said my name. She was crying.

"Angie put it all on the table. What the fuck did you do? Was it a game?"

"No! It wasn't a game. I wanted ..." She paused.

When she didn't continue, I tossed the bottle in the trash. "I have to go."

"Fisher ... I love you."

I ended the call.

FISHER
CHAPTER THIRTY

"My fiancée is the most handsome man ever," Angie said, straightening my tie after I did a sloppy job of tying it. "Did you get into the minibar?" Her nose wrinkled before she glanced at the trash.

"We need to talk," I said, stepping back and ignoring her minibar comment.

"About?"

I slipped on my jacket. "Not now. I can't think, but soon."

She frowned. "You've been off all afternoon. And now you're raiding the minibar. What's going on, Fish?"

"Later." I headed toward the hotel room door as she checked her makeup one last time in the mirror.

We attended the beach wedding, but I couldn't wait for the reception. I needed more alcohol. I did what I was told to do.

Pose.

Smile.

Hold Angie's hand like we were a real couple.

Finally, I had a beer in my hand.

And then another.

And another.

It seemed like magic that I woke up in the hotel room, but I couldn't remember how I got there.

"We need to get this off you," Angie said.

"No." I shoved her hands away as she unbuttoned my pants. "It's not you."

"Fisher, stop." She fought with my hands, again trying to get my pants off. "You have vomit all over you."

"Stop," I repeated, losing the fight. "It's not you."

"It is me. Who do you think I am?"

Fisher ...

Reese's voice.

She's naked in my tub. Then she's backed against a wall saying something. "Are you going to kiss me?" I kiss her.

She trips going up a hill. There's a nail in her hand. I carry her to my truck.

Those eyes ... she's scared but trying to be brave.

So much guilt ... she's eighteen, and I can't stop thinking about her.

She's sketching crossword puzzles in my truck. A cruciverbalist. With a nervous glance at me, she bites her lower lip like she thinks I'm judging her for her hobby. I'm not. I'm fucking mesmerized by it ... by her.

Fisher ...

Her voice.

Her touch.

Her tears.

Arnie's concert.

JEWEL E. ANN

Her naked on my pool table.

So much guilt ... it's not our time. I have to be the adult, but I selfishly want her.

Her nervous hands removing her clothes. We're in the basement in her old bed.

We're in my bed and I'm rolling on a condom. Tears ... I'm making her cry. My chest hurts and I can't breathe. I love her, and I'm letting her go.

"Sorry, baby," Angie said as cold water washed over my naked body, erasing Reese's voice in my head, but the images remained.

Her.

Us.

It was all there. We are more than friends. We were lovers. Forbidden. And I let her go.

"What's going on, baby? Why did you drink so much? Are you trying to kill yourself again?"

"It's not you," I said again, the slur of my voice so foreign to my own ears as she washed me with pungent soap and a washcloth.

"It is me, baby. I've got you."

Everything moved in slow motion. Her helping me out of the shower, forcing me to drink water. Vomiting half the night. Waking up naked in bed as she sat next to me sipping coffee.

"Morning, baby. We have to check out soon."

My fucking head. I sat up slowly, realizing I was naked. "Jesus ... did we ..."

"Wow." She set her coffee aside and curled her hair behind her ears. "Seriously, Fish? Does the idea of having sex with your fiancée really repulse you that much?"

Tugging the sheet to wrap it around my waist, I eased my legs off the side of the bed and bowed my head while my other hand rubbed my temples. I drank more the previous night than I think I had ever drank in my life. And even then, it didn't stop me from remembering everything.

"I broke up with you ..." I whispered.

"What?"

"I broke up with you," I repeated a little louder. "Before my accident, I broke off the engagement."

Silence.

When she didn't respond, I lumbered to my feet and stopped when I reached the end of the bed, lifting my gaze and my throbbing head to look at her.

Tears filled her eyes. "You remember."

"Yeah," I continued toward the bathroom.

"How much do you remember?"

"Everything," I said, just before shutting the bathroom door.

Angie couldn't find a single word to share with me on the flights back to Denver. I had lots to say, just not on the plane.

"I love you," she said, climbing out at her friend's house before I could say anything.

I retrieved her suitcase from the back. "Angie ..."

Still, she wouldn't look at me. "Not yet. Just ... please. Not yet.

I nodded slowly.

THE NEXT DAY, I texted Reese: **I'm home if you want to talk.**

Reese: I'm at a birth.

It was for the best that I couldn't see her yet. I wasn't sure what I would say, and I needed to finish some things with Angie. Her roommate was working, so I met Angie at her house.

"Hey," she said with a reserved smile while motioning for me to come inside.

I toed off my boots and shrugged out of my coat.

"Can I get you something to drink? Coffee? Beer?"

I shook my head.

"Well, have a seat." She nodded to the sofa and sat at the opposite end.

After some awkward silence, she blew out a breath and stared out the front window. "I don't remember a day in my life where I didn't love you, Fisher. You've always been my best friend." And just like that ... she cracked, wiping a few tears. "That morning ... when you broke off the engagement, I felt like it was a knee-jerk reaction to other things going on in your life. I felt like you didn't want to discuss fabric swatches and cake flavors, so you overreacted and called off the wedding."

I thought about that morning and the days leading up to it. Honestly, I hadn't been quite right since Rory and Rose went to Michigan for Reese's graduation. Since I wrote her the note on the card. Since I told my heart it was time to really let her go. Every day after that started to feel like a second-choice life. And Angie felt like a consolation prize. I deserved more. Angie deserved more too. I knew it then, even if I did a terrible job of articulating it.

"Angie," I pressed my lips together and gazed at the floor for a few seconds, "I ... I love you too. We've been through too much for me to not love you. I just don't love you like a man should love his wife. Maybe..." I shook my head "...I don't know, maybe I did at one point. Somewhere along the way, the love I felt started to feel like an extension of the love my family has felt for you. Not being with you felt like a disappointment to not only you, but to my family. And that's no excuse; it just is."

She sniffled, wiping more tears.

It wasn't easy breaking her heart. I did love her.

"That morning, I did have a knee-jerk reaction, but it wasn't breaking off the engagement. It was how I did it. And had I not been in an accident, I know I would have apologized for how I ended things. I just didn't get the chance."

"Was..." she drew in a shaky breath "...was there someone else? *Is* there someone else?"

It was time. I had the memories. I couldn't hide behind the things I didn't know, didn't remember. She deserved the truth, even if she didn't give the whole truth to me. Was I supposed to hate her for loving me too much? For holding on too hard?

"Yes," I whispered.

She choked on another sob, trying to keep from falling apart as she silently shook. I reached over and rested my hand on hers, giving it a tight squeeze.

"Y-you love her m-more?"

Swallowing past my own emotion, I nodded.

"Who?"

"H-how long?"

Panic overtook her. Maybe it wasn't panic; maybe it was pain.

"Does she know about m-me?"

"Angie ..." I said softly. "Don't do this. It doesn't matter. I'm sorry ... it just doesn't."

She pressed her other hand to her chest and cried.

I kneeled in front of her and pulled her into my chest, wanting to take away the pain that I'd caused but knowing it had to happen. We had to say the words and feel the pain. I knew my inability to love her the same way had to hurt the most, but I wasn't immune to my own pain. Part of me felt like a failure. Hurting her also hurt me.

OVERNIGHT IT SNOWED, and I woke early to start clearing driveways, including Rory's and Rose's. I was grateful for the distraction. I was grateful to feel close to her.

After I finished, I loaded up the snowblower and glanced back at the house and the open garage door. Reese stood inside in a jacket, hat, and boots. It took everything I had to not run to her and tell her I remembered everything. My mind harnessed my heart, telling it to be patient. It still had some things to work out, questions that needed answers.

As I trekked back up the driveway, Reese gave me a half smile. "Thanks for doing that."

"It's no big deal." I brushed snow off my coat. "Do you have time to grab coffee?" I glanced at my watch. "Starbucks opens in fifteen minutes."

Her lips twisted for several seconds before she nodded once. "Okay. Let me grab my purse."

"Okay."

When she returned with her purse, I took her hand and helped her down the slick driveway. We made the silent trip to Starbucks. The silence killed me. Again, taking her hand, I guided her into Starbucks.

"My treat," she said as we approached the counter. "You plowed the driveway. Coffee. Black?"

I nodded.

As she ordered our drinks, I grabbed a table, pulling off my gloves and shrugging out of my jacket. After she brought our drinks to the table, she slipped off her jacket, only giving me a quick, shy glance.

"We were more than friends," I said, feeling unexpected pain from the words. I thought I had it under control, but being so close to her messed with my emotions.

"We were more than friends," she murmured before sipping her coffee.

"And you didn't tell me this why?"

Slowly shaking her head, she pressed her lips together for a moment. "For several reasons. At first, I didn't think it was beneficial information to share given the fact that you were engaged, and we hadn't seen each other in five years anyway. And I didn't want to give you something you couldn't remember and make you feel like you owed me something in return. Some sort of emotional acknowledgment. And honestly, I didn't need it. I liked where we were going. I liked our present. And the closer we got, the less I cared if we shared the past."

"So we ... what? We were just fucking around?"

I wasn't asking anything I didn't already know the answer to. Maybe it was shitty of me not to tell her that I remembered everything, but I felt like I deserved to have that moment. To ask questions. Maybe I felt like I deserved to lie a little too. I so badly needed to know why. And I needed to know if she was done lying.

"There was a physical attraction. And we messed around, yes."

"Messed around. But we weren't sleeping together because you already told me you gave that other guy your virginity. Correct?"

She returned a careful nod.

"Did I try to have sex with you?"

Her forehead wrinkled as she stared at her coffee before taking another sip. "No."

No. Why did she say that? It wasn't the truth. Did she know the truth? Did she think the last time we were together before she left with Brendon that I was bluffing? Did she think I rolled on a condom only to test her? It wasn't a test. I was done "doing the right thing." I was done pushing her away. And I knew she'd leave me to find the life she had yet to live. Still, I wanted her.

It wasn't about being her first, despite what I said, despite what she read into that night. I wanted her to feel my love in the rawest, most intimate way possible. It was just that simple.

"Why not?" I asked.

"Because I was upfront with you that I wasn't going to have sex with you."

"But oral didn't count?"

She blushed and glanced away from me. "Do we have to go into such detail? Does it matter?"

"I'm just trying to understand."

"Well, you have amnesia, so you might not ever really understand."

"Maybe if you give me all of the facts, all the details, then I can understand."

"Like Angie? She gave you everything. Do you understand your love for her? Or should I say, before you left for Costa Rica, did you understand your love for her?"

"What's that supposed to mean? Before I left for Costa Rica ..." It bothered me that she didn't trust me. It hurt.

"Did you have a nice time? Was the couples' massage in the same room? And how does that work? If they do, in fact, think you're a couple, does that mean you take off all your clothes for her? Did she take hers off for you? What about the room where you stayed? Were there two beds? Because in the photo on Instagram, it looked like there was only one bed. And before you answer that, fair warning ... Angie told me, Rose, and Rory all about her plans for you two on the trip. She requested a room with one bed instead of two. The couples' massage. Oh, and we must not forget the sexy lingerie she bought to wear for you. How did you like that? Did you try to have sex with *her*? Or did you settle for oral like you did with me? Was it all-night oral? Because the photo of you on Instagram sleeping in bed made you look thoroughly exhausted. Oh ... and it definitely looked like you were naked under the sheet resting so low on your torso."

Okay. I wasn't the only one who felt hurt. I could have pled my case and told her the truth, but the truth wasn't pretty either. She was right about somethings and wrong about other things. I was sure Angie had lingerie to wear for me, but I got drunk off my ass so she didn't get the chance to wear it. However, she saw me naked because she had to bathe me after I vomited all over myself and probably her too. As I pondered the right answer, I decided there wasn't a right one. I chose silence, even if I knew Reese might drown in my silence.

I loved her. And she loved me. We would get past this, but it would take time. It would take a rebuilding of trust. And it would take forgiveness.

But at that moment, things were too painful. And that pain was blinding.

"Are you done?" I asked.

She stood. "I think *we're* done."

Oh my beautiful word girl ... we're just getting started.

I dropped my gaze, biting my tongue before nodding and pulling on my jacket. "I'll take you home." With her hand in mine, I started toward the door, but she yanked it away.

That stung.

We made another silent trip back to her house. After

I put my truck into *Park*, I glanced over at her. "Am I him?"

She gripped the door handle. "Who?"

"Your first love? You told me he wasn't ready to be found. And you call me your lost fisherman. Am I him? Did you fall in love with me? Am *I* the schmuck who wouldn't take your virginity even after you offered it?"

She opened the door. "I will never regret not giving you my virginity."

Before I could respond, the door slammed shut and she didn't look back once.

Of course I wanted to chase her. When she walked away, my heart was stuck to her hand, ripping into pieces with every step she took. But we needed time. I needed to let Angie make an exit from my life that wasn't demeaning. If she knew it was Reese, she'd feel betrayed by Rory and Rose. I didn't want that. Not yet. So I tried to do the right thing and offer everyone a little more time.

Every fiber of my being knew we were meant to be together.

Five days.

Five months.

Five years.

It didn't matter.

We would be okay. Our love was that strong. *She* was that strong.

ACKNOWLEDGMENTS

I have to thank my amazing readers first and foremost. As I experimented with different ways to publish this story, you stood by me, eagerly awaiting my words in whatever form I decided to share them.

Thank you, Jenn, for dealing with the chaotic summer version of me—juggling a million projects and constantly changing publishing schedules.

Thank you, Nina and the hardworking team with Valentine PR for all the Zoom calls and sheer love of this story. It's an honor to work with people who believe in me.

My editing team! These souls have a very special place in the afterlife for making sense of my gibberish and polishing it into something worth sharing with the world. Max, I can't wait to take this new journey with you as not only my editor, but also my agent. Leslie, Kambra, Sian, Monique, and Amy, thank you for sacrificing your enjoyment of my stories to make me look like a competent author. I feel like my success belongs to you as well.

As always, a big thank you to my family for supporting me during moody times, frantic schedules, a million frustrations, and everything in between. You inspire me.

ALSO BY JEWEL E. ANN

Standalone Novels

Idle Bloom

Undeniably You

Naked Love

Only Trick

Perfectly Adequate

Look The Part

When Life Happened

A Place Without You

Jersey Six

Scarlet Stone

Not What I Expected

For Lucy

The Fisherman Series

The Naked Fisherman

The Lost Fisherman

Jack & Jill Series

End of Day

Middle of Knight

Dawn of Forever

One (*standalone*)

Out of Love (*standalone*)

Holding You Series

Holding You

Releasing Me

Transcend Series

Transcend

Epoch

Fortuity (*standalone*)

The Life Series

The Life That Mattered

The Life You Stole

Receive a FREE book and stay informed of new releases, sales, and exclusive stories:

Mailing List

https://www.jeweleann.com/free-booksubscribe

ABOUT THE AUTHOR

Jewel is a free-spirited romance junkie with a quirky sense of humor.

With 10 years of flossing lectures under her belt, she took early retirement from her dental hygiene career to stay home with her three awesome boys and manage the family business.

After her best friend of nearly 30 years suggested a few books from the Contemporary Romance genre, Jewel was hooked. Devouring two and three books a week but still craving more, she decided to practice sustainable reading, AKA writing.

When she's not donning her cape and saving the planet one tree at a time, she enjoys yoga with friends, good food with family, rock climbing with her kids, watching How I Met Your Mother reruns, and of course...heart-wrenching, tear-jerking, panty-scorching novels.

www.jeweleann.com

Made in the USA
Columbia, SC
04 December 2024

48424287R00450